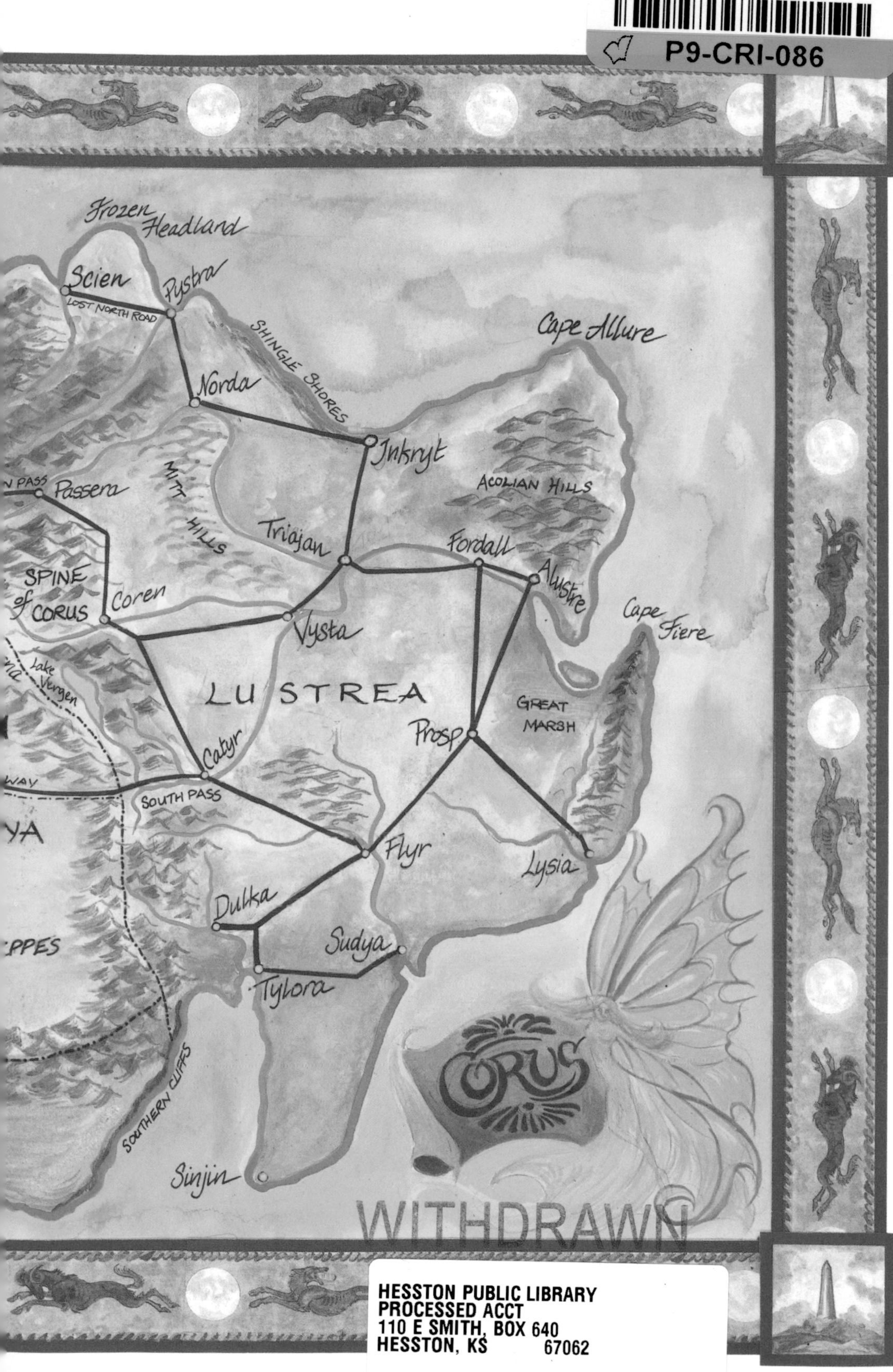
Frozen Headland
Scien
Pystra
LOST NORTH ROAD
SHINGLE SHORES
Cape Allure
Norda
Inkryt
MITT HILLS
ACOLIAN HILLS
Passera
Triajan
Fordall
Alustre
SPINE of CORUS
Coren
Vysta
Cape Fiere
Lake Vergen
LUSTREA
GREAT MARSH
Prosp
Catyr
SOUTH PASS
Flyr
Lysia
Dulka
Sudya
Tylora
SOUTHERN CLIFFS
CORUS
Sinjin

ALECTOR'S CHOICE

Tor Books by L. E. Modesitt, Jr.

The Corean Chronicles

Legacies
Darknesses
Scepters
Alector's Choice

The Spellsong Cycle

The Soprano Sorceress
The Spellsong War
Darksong Rising
The Shadow Sorceress
Shadowsinger

The Saga of Recluce

The Magic of Recluce
The Towers of the Sunset
The Magic Engineer
The Order War
The Death of Chaos
Fall of Angels
The Chaos Balance
The White Order
Colors of Chaos
Magi'i of Cyador
Scion of Cyador
Wellspring of Chaos
Ordermaster

Ghosts of Columbia

Of Tangible Ghosts
The Ghost of the Revelator
Ghost of the White Nights

The Ecolitan Matter

Empire & Ecolitan
(comprising *The Ecolitan Operation* and *The Ecologic Secession*)

Ecolitan Prime
(comprising *The Ecologic Envoy* and *The Ecolitan Enigma*)

The Forever Hero
(comprising *Dawn for a Distant Earth, The Silent Warrior,* and *In Endless Twilight*)

Timegods' World
(comprising *The Timegod* and *Timediver's Dawn*)

The Green Progression
The Parafaith War
The Ethos Effect
The Hammer of Darkness
Adiamante
Gravity Dreams
The Octagonal Raven
Archform: Beauty
Flash
*The Eternity Artifact**

*Forthcoming from Tor Books

L. E. MODESITT, JR.

ALECTOR'S CHOICE

The Fourth Book of the Corean Chronicles

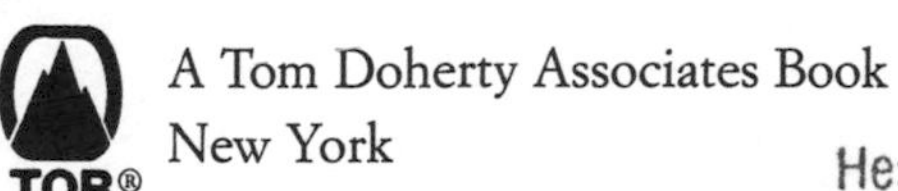
A Tom Doherty Associates Book
New York

ALECTOR'S CHOICE: THE FOURTH BOOK OF THE COREAN CHRONICLES

This book is printed on acid-free paper.

Edited by David G. Hartwell

A Tor Book
Published by Tom Doherty Associates, LLC
175 Fifth Avenue
New York, NY 10010

www.tor.com

Tor® is a registered trademark of Tom Doherty Associates, LLC.

Library of Congress Cataloging-in-Publication Data

Modesitt, L. E.
Alector's choice: the fourth book of the Corean Chronicles / L. E. Modesitt, Jr.
p. cm. — (Corean chronicles ; 4th.)
"A Tom Doherty Associates book."
ISBN 0-765-31387-1
EAN 978-0765-31387-4
I. Title.

PS3563.O264A79 2005
813'.54—dc22

2004063757

First Edition: June 2005

Printed in the United States of America

0 9 8 7 6 5 4 3 2 1

For Ree and Renn Zaphiropoulos

Proud towers rise to challenge sea and sky,
Green needles that capture the dullest eye,
and palaces and halls with columns strong and true
with glory, song, and pleasures for the few.

So seemly are those soaring spires
That few remember the fierce desires
and fewer still the price Acorus pays
for each alector's unending days.

Yet towers unseen in the higher chill,
hold ancients with a different will,
who also ask a price, more long delayed,
but still upon your living spirits laid.

Landers, which fate and bargain will you take?
Which deadly compromise is left to make?

ALECTOR'S CHOICE

1

Colonel Dainyl looked down at the stack of reports on his desk. He was almost afraid to take his eyes off them. The moment he looked away, more reports appeared. He knew that wasn't so, but it was the way things *felt.* Although he was the number four Myrmidon officer on Acorus, when he studied all the reports, he felt more like a glorified lander clerk.

He pushed the resentment aside. He'd had his years as a flying officer, more than most Myrmidons, and he'd been rewarded for long and faithful service. He could have easily been one of the rankers who spent decades or longer in service, yet who never became more than a squad leader or an undercaptain—if that.

He brushed back a lock of shimmering black hair, hair that needed to be trimmed, he reminded himself, and glanced toward the window that looked out on the headquarters courtyard. There, on the raised stage, a pteridon had just landed, folding back its long blue leathery wings. The Myrmidon rider vaulted from the saddle and handed the dispatch case to the headquarters duty squad leader. So early in the morning, it had to be the incoming daily message run from Ludar.

For a moment, Dainyl just watched the ranker and pteridon. Then he looked down at the report he had been reading—the quintal operations report from the Seventh Myrmidon Company at Dulka.

At the sound of boots on marble, he looked up once more, this time toward the open study door that allowed him a view, such as it was, of the main corridor of Myrmidon headquarters. Submarshal Tyanylt walked quickly past Dainyl's open door toward the one remaining study on the corridor—that of Marshal Shastylt.

Dainyl could sense . . . something, and Tyanylt looked determined—or worried. That was unusual for any alector, and especially for Tyanylt, who never showed emotion other than a calm pleasantness—even when Dainyl used Talent-senses, although Dainyl had always been careful only to use those senses to receive.

Not that there was anything that Dainyl could have done to alleviate

Tyanylt's worries. The submarshal was his direct superior and had always maintained a certain reserve, more so than the usual for an alector. Tyanylt was well respected, and well connected to both the Duarch of Elcien and the Duarch of Ludar—and to the high alectors who surrounded both Duarchs.

The colonel forced his attention back to the report, noting that Majer Faerylt had cited the loss of a skylance and the receipt of a replacement from Lyterna. Dainyl paused, then reread the section. How could a Myrmidon have lost a skylance without losing both rider and pteridon? That had not happened in centuries. He jotted down a note to ask for a fuller explanation.

As he turned to the section summarizing Seventh Company's flights for the last two-month quint, the slightest flash of purpleness—something sensed by his Talent, not seen by his eyes—flared before Dainyl.

Almost without thought, he was on his feet and out of his study, nearly running toward the marshal's closed doorway. He came to a halt outside the door, but he could sense nothing through the heavy wood. Usually, he could sense *something*.

"Sir?" he called. "Are you all right?"

There was no answer.

"Sir?"

With still no answer, Dainyl opened the study door, his hand ready to grab his holstered sidearm as he stepped into the chamber, closing the door behind him. Marshal Shastylt lay half-sprawled on the floor beside his wide desk. Several papers lay strewn on the green marble floor, as if the marshal's hand had knocked them from the desk as he had fallen.

Once inside the study, Dainyl could sense the marshal's lifeforce—weak, but steady—and that he was breathing. Submarshal Tyanylt was not breathing. As Dainyl watched, his lifeforce and aura finished fading, then vanished. Within moments, all that remained on the smooth green marble floor of the study were Tyanylt's uniform, sidearm, and boots.

Dainyl swallowed. While he'd seen more than a few Cadmians, and other landers and indigens, die over the years, he had only seen a handful of Myrmidons die, their bodies vanishing into dust nearly instantly—in accidents and once after a death sentence for gross negligence—but he'd never seen a high-ranking Myrmidon or alector die. That just didn't happen, and certainly not in the Myrmidon marshal's study.

The marshal groaned, faintly, and Dainyl immediately knelt. He could sense no broken bones or severe internal injuries. So he gently turned the marshal onto his back and waited.

Within several moments, the marshal's lifeforce had purpled into greater strength, and his breathing was steadier. Shortly, his eyes opened.

Dainyl helped him to his feet. With his shimmering black hair, unaging alabaster face, and violet eyes, the marshal looked no different from any of the other most senior alectors, save that he was a span or so taller than Dainyl's two and a half yards. Shastylt's eyes flickered to the clothing and boots on the floor. His lips tightened slightly, but he said nothing as Dainyl helped him into the chair.

Dainyl waited while the marshal caught his breath.

"Has anyone else been in here?" Shastylt finally asked.

"No, sir. I sensed something, and when no one answered, I came in and closed the door behind me."

The marshal nodded slowly, his deep violet eyes fixing on Dainyl.

Neither alector spoke.

Dainyl waited, holding his Talent shields, not certain how the marshal might react.

"You *do* understand, Dainyl?"

"Yes, sir." Dainyl understood all too well. In whatever had transpired before he entered, Tyanylt had crossed the marshal—and paid the price.

"You have always been cautiously decisive. That is a good characteristic." He swallowed, then coughed, straightening in the chair. "You may not know this, but the submarshal was several decades older than I."

There was no reason Dainyl would have known. Alectors never showed their age, holding the same appearance from early adulthood until death, until that time when they could no longer hold their lifeforce.

"He was deeply concerned about some trends he was seeing all across Corus, and he could see that his lifeforce was failing."

Dainyl knew that the marshal was lying, and that Shastylt knew that Dainyl recognized that. The colonel nodded. "I just felt something and knew something had happened."

Shastylt cleared his throat. "Tyanylt and I have both known that Acorus faces a transition in the next few years, one that will change everything."

Every alector knew that. Ifryn was failing, as its lifeforce was drained away, and in the next decade the Archon of Ifryn—based on the recommendation of the Highest Fieldmaster—would have choose where to transfer the master scepter, either to Acorus of Efra. That choice would decide the fate of two worlds. "That choice does not have to be made that soon, does it, sir?"

"Preparations must be made, one way or another, and how those preparations are handled may also affect the choice." Shastylt reached out and lifted the goblet of water on the corner of the desk, taking a small swallow. "Submarshal Tyanylt felt most strongly about the decisions made by our High Alector of Justice. Tyanylt reported his concerns to the Highest, and was told that, while he had identified some valid problems, plans would have to go forth as outlined, especially since Submarshal Alcyna in Alustre had no such concerns. Not many are allowed to question the Highest. None are allowed to refuse the Highest."

Since the Myrmidons' prime function was to ensure and enforce justice, the High Alector of Justice on Acorus was effectively the director of all Myrmidon activities. For a submarshal to refuse his duties . . . Dainyl shook his head. He could understand a submarshal's resigning. It had not happened often, but there were precedents. But to refuse without resigning?

"I see you understand."

"Enough, sir." It was all too clear that, in the contest of wills and lifeforce between the marshal and the submarshal, the marshal had prevailed. Dainyl also understood that it would be foolhardy to oppose both the Highest and the marshal.

"A most cautious response. That is fitting for these times." Shastylt glanced to the uniform on the floor. "There will be a week of mourning for the death of the submarshal. He served Ifryn, the Archon, and the Duarches long and well, but lifeforce fails even the most powerful in time. I will have to meet with the Highest to determine how he wishes to proceed."

"Yes, sir."

"For the moment, you will remain as director of operations and maintenance, as before." Shastylt smiled, an expression not so much of triumph as one that showed the relief of someone who had successfully passed a great trial. "That will be all, Colonel."

Dainyl nodded respectfully.

"If you would summon the duty officer on your way out?"

"Yes, sir." Dainyl half bowed once more, then turned and departed, closing the door most carefully behind him, as he headed back down the corridor to the desk of the day's duty officer—Undercaptain Ghanyr. His steps were firm on the green marble floor.

2

Mykel ambled over to the edge of the grape arbor that he could just touch without stepping out from under the roof of the warm-weather dining porch. The golden red grapes were perfect, ripe, but still firm, glowing in the orange-tinged light before sunset. He eased one from the rear of a bunch, shaded enough so that it was cooler, and taken from where its absence wouldn't be noticed until his parents harvested that section of the vine.

"I saw that." His father laughed, stepping through the rear archway with a bronze tray holding six heavy goblets. "A captain in the mounted rifles, nearly twenty-six years old, and you're still snitching grapes."

Mykel turned and grinned. "Just one. They're best right off the vine." He popped the grape in his mouth—slightly tart, but still sweet, and cool. He was careful not to let any of the juice escape. The pale blue dress tunic was one of the few he had that wasn't a uniform, and he'd inherited it from his grandfather two years earlier.

"Don't let your mother catch you. She wants those as ripe as possible for the holiday wine." Olent set the tray down in the center of the long table, then straightened.

"Has he been pulling grapes off the vine again?" asked Viencet, following his father through the archway, carrying a large pitcher of wine drawn from the cask in the cellar.

"Some things don't change," replied Olent.

Viencet, who was barely seventeen, shook his head. His flowing blond hair—darker than Mykel's—momentarily flipped away from his head. Mykel didn't much care for his youngest brother's hairstyle, but had never said anything. Once Viencet joined a guild, or became a Cadmian, the long locks would go. In Faitel, only day laborers, small farm holders, peasants—all usually indigens—or students—generally landers from the skilled crafting or larger landholding families—had long hair.

"The fowl will be ready in just a bit." Aelya announced from the archway, smiling at her husband, and their sons. "Try to leave the grapes alone, Mykel."

"I'm trying."

"You always were." His mother smiled broadly before disappearing into the house.

Mykel blotted his forehead with the back of his hand. Early harvest was hot in Faitel and even warmer in Elcien, unless the westerlies blew hard off the ocean for several days straight.

"You have to go back on Londi, don't you?" asked Olent.

"I have to be back before midnight on Decdi. I'll leave on the early coach." That wasn't quite true, because Mykel really had until muster on Londi morning, but he wasn't about to wait until the very last moment.

All the same, Mykel found it hard to believe that sixteen days of his two-week leave were already over, and that he just had three more nights—and two full days—before he had to head back on his return to duty. He was fortunate that he was stationed outside Elcien, just seventy vingts from home.

"Will you get more leave when you become an overcaptain?" asked Viencet.

"*If* I ever make overcaptain. No. All officers get four weeks leave in a year, and that's only when we're in quarters. There's no leave when we're deployed."

"I can't see being a Cadmian, or even a city patroller," offered Viencet. "I wasn't very good in the basic physical training. Not like you."

"It's not just physical." Mykel replied, trying to keep his voice even. Why did so many people, even his brother, think that Cadmians were all muscle?

"No. You also have to believe in things, like why you can't cut too many trees, or plant too many of the same crops, or use wood when stone or steel will do—"

"Viencet . . ." Olent drew out his younger son's name. "There are good reasons for those."

"Oh, yes, I'm sure—"

"Viencet!" barked Olent, turning his broad and muscular frame.

Viencet lowered his eyes. "I'm sorry, Father."

His voice wasn't that sorry, Mykel reflected, but, as the old saying went, Viencet listened to the windsongs of the ancients. Not that anyone even knew if the ancients had even sung. After an awkward silence, he asked, "What are you thinking of doing when you finish your studies next Quintem?"

"I don't know. I don't want to work for any of the artisans' or engineers' guilds. If you're a lander, you do the hard work that takes brains, and if you're indigen, or if the alectors think you're stupid, you end up in the coal mines or as a laborer and die young."

"You're anything but stupid." Viencet was bright—but lazy and stubborn, not that Mykel was about to say that, although his grandfather had—often and loudly—before his sudden death.

"Besides, in most of the respected guilds, you can't ever say a word about what you do."

Mykel understood that. He'd never liked the guilds' silence rules, either. "There are still the building crafts and trade, even factoring."

Viencet shrugged. "I'll never be a master tiler like Grandfather or Father. When I see the mosaics Father does . . . The head of the Structural Engineers had his last one turned into eternastone."

Mykel pursed his lips. His father had never mentioned that. Supposedly, the transformation process—kept to the recorders of deeds and the highest of alectors—cost hundreds of golds and was used for great works of art, or for the most important buildings, and, of course, the high roads of the Duarchy. He turned to his father. "You never told me that."

"It was good. It wasn't that good," replied Olent. "They wanted it eternal because it's in the receiving hall of the artisans and displays their seal."

"Does that make it eternal?" asked Sesalia, Mykel's older sister, who had stepped through the archway carrying a large covered casserole on an enameled bronze tray.

"The Hall of Justice in Elcien has been standing for more than three centuries, and it looks like it was finished yesterday. I won't be sticking around long enough to find out if my poor mosaic will last that long." Olent laughed. "Like my own da said, you have to take pleasure in what you do, not in what people might think about it years from now."

Sesalia set the casserole in the middle of the table. "Everyone should sit down. Mother and Bortal are bringing the fowl and the bread."

Olent took the chair at the head of the table. Mykel slipped onto the chair to his father's right, across from Sesalia. Aelya appeared and set the serving platter in front of her husband before taking her seat at the other end of the table. The squarish Bortal hurried after her, setting a basket of bread on each end of the table, then settling between his wife and Aelya. The last one to the table was Viencet, who seated himself to Mykel's right.

Olent looked at Aelya, then cleared his throat. "In the name of the One Who Was, Is, and Will Be, may our food be blessed, and our lives as well, in the times of prosperity and peace, and those which are neither. Blessed be the lives of both the deserving and the undeserving that both may strive to do good in the world and beyond, and may we always recall that we do not judge our worthiness, but leave that judgment to the One Who Is . . ." After a moment of silence, he lifted his head and looked to Aelya. "You prepared it, dear."

"Thank you, but it's in front of you."

Mykel's father took three slices of the fowl, then nodded to Mykel. Mykel took two, before lifting the platter and handing it to Viencet, who, in turn, held it while Aelya served herself. Next came the lace potatoes, the steamed sprouts, and the bread. Aelya had cooked and served the fowl the way Mykel liked it best—roasted and basted with sesame oil, then served with a sauce of powdered groundnuts and mint. The lace potatoes were crisp on the outside, but hot and moist inside.

"Excellent," he said, looking to his mother. "Thank you."

"You're welcome, dear." Aelya glanced at Sesalia. "I miss the children."

"We don't," replied Bortal, glancing sideways at his wife. "I might get to eat my entire supper."

"Oh . . . they're always sweet," replied Aelya.

"They are, indeed," suggested Olent, "but with four of them, I can see how Sesalia and Bortal might enjoy a meal or two without them."

Aelya sniffed.

"I'll bring them by tomorrow," Sesalia promised. "You can feed them midday dinner and see how sweet they are then."

Mykel grinned. He'd helped Sesalia the day before.

"Ah . . . how are things going with you?" asked Bortal quickly, looking at Mykel. "You won't have to go off and fight anytime soon, will you, like with those raiders in the north?"

"The Reillies?" Mykel shook his head. "Not for a while. They've been pushed back practically to Blackstear. The land's not bad there—it's the northern part of the Vales of Prosperity—and the Duarches have granted them the rights to use it, except for timbering. If they raid anyone, they lose that right."

"Raiding, that's in the blood," suggested Olent.

"That's why I said it would be a while," replied Mykel. "They'll try to settle down. Can't do that much anyway now. We killed half the men who could carry weapons."

"I'd always thought you'd become an engineer," interjected Sesalia.

"Landers can only be apprentice engineers. The *real* engineers are alectors," volunteered Viencet. "Even the head mining engineers are alectors. The ones at the mines just do whatever the alectors in Ludar say."

"Farlak is a real engineer," suggested Aelya.

"He's Father's age," countered Viencet. "He does twice the work of all the alectors, and has for years. They made him an assistant engineer last year. That's where they start the most junior alectors."

"It's always been that way," Mykel pointed out.

Olent cleared his throat, loudly.

"You think that Mykel should be a colonel?" Aelya arched her eyebrows at Viencet. "Or a Myrmidon captain commanding pteridons? Or that you should start as a master tiler?"

Viencet winced.

Mykel offered an easy smile. "I'm just a Cadmian captain of mounted rifles. That's good enough for now."

"Not that many become officers," Sesalia said.

"All my brothers tried," added Bortal. "Corylt was the only one they took. He's only a squad leader, and he's two years older than Mykel." The blocky tile-setter frowned. "He's in Zalt. That's where they've just finished the high road between Tempre and Southgate. His last letter said that they might see some action, but he couldn't say where. You heard anything?"

"Someone's always unhappy somewhere," Mykel said. "Could be the Reillies in the north Westerhills, or the nomads in the hills east of the Dry Coast . . ."

"What about the ancient ones?" asked Viencet.

"There aren't any left. Just a few ruins here and there."

"How do they know? The Ancienteers say they're biding their time."

Mykel laughed dryly. "If the Myrmidons on their pteridons and the recorders of deeds with their Tables can't find any trace of them, there aren't any."

"Do the Tables really exist?" asked Sesalia. "Have you seen one?"

"No," Mykel admitted, "but I've been ordered places where we've found exactly what the recorders said we'd find, and there hadn't been any alectors or pteridons anywhere near."

"Maybe the Tables don't really exist," suggested Sesalia. "Maybe the alectors just claim that they do so that they don't have to explain how they know things."

Mykel shrugged. "That could be; but however they know, they do know. I wouldn't want to try to keep anything hidden from them."

"Who are the alectors?" asked Viencet. "I mean . . . where did they come from?"

"Where did we come from?" asked Olent. "We both came from the Great Beyond in the time before time, and the alectors have been our guides and mentors."

"You really believe that?" Viencet gave a laugh that was almost a snort.

Olent gave an embarrassed smile. "That's what we're taught, and I don't have a better answer. Do you?"

"They're not that much smarter."

"Even a little brains means a lot, Viencet," countered Olent. "They're also much, much stronger, and I've heard that arrows bounce off them. If you have a better idea, what is it?"

"I don't know. I just don't think all that's true."

"Then where did we all come from?" asked Olent. "We've never found any ruins used by people or alectors, and only a few things that were used by the ancients."

Mykel tended to believe Viencet was right, but he'd already seen enough of Corus to know that what his father had just said was also correct. But unless or until he learned more, he wasn't about to step into the argument. Besides, what good would it do? Viencet would just argue more, and his father would get his back up. From what Mykel had seen, the Duarches ruled Corus, and they didn't do it that badly. In dealing with the Reillies, Mykel had seen what a mess both indigens and landers made of things.

After a moment of silence, Sesalia spoke. "Bortal laid the foundations for another bedroom."

"Another bedroom?" Mykel blurted.

"Congratulations!" Olent beamed.

"Five mouths . . ." Mykel bit off the words and forced a smile.

His older sister turned. "With the Duarches' stipend for a fifth child, we can build the new room and still have silvers left over." She smiled.

"I'm glad it will work out," Mykel offered as gracefully as he could. Five children? Even five well-behaved children? He reached for the fowl platter and took another slice, followed by a healthy dollop of potatoes. He did like the way his mother cooked.

3

Dainyl stepped out of the steaming shower, wishing that he didn't have to, but there was only so much hot water, even for an alector, even for a Myrmidon colonel, if one married to an assistant to the High Alector of Finance. He quickly wrapped himself in a heavy towel and dried before he got too chilled. After all the generations that had passed since the coming of the alectors to Acorus, he would have thought that they would have adjusted to the chill of the world, but it hadn't happened. Not yet, although the Duarches kept assuring all the alectors that the place was markedly warmer than it had been in the centuries after the first seedings.

Hurriedly, Dainyl finished drying and pulled on his undergarments. Straightening, he glanced at the full-length mirror that showed a muscular figure of average height for an alector, roughly two and a half yards, with the shimmering black hair and alabaster complexion. His midsection remained trim. While alectors might not age, they could certainly get fat if they overindulged, and Dainyl had a fear of that, rare as it was. He slipped into the dressing area off the bedchamber, where he donned trousers, undertunic, and boots.

"The girls have your breakfast ready. We'll eat in the sunroom," called Lystrana from the base of the stairs. "It's brighter there, but it's a cool day for so early in harvest."

"Thank you. I'll be right there." With that warning from his wife, Dainyl decided to put on an old tunic. He'd change to his uniform tunic after he ate. On warm days, the hottest of mid- and late summer, he ate breakfast in his undertunic.

He hurried down the stone steps to the main level and out toward the sunroom, with the wide glass windows overlooking the courtyard garden. As he passed the archway to the kitchen, Dainyl nodded to Sentya and Zistele. "Good morning."

"Good morning, Colonel." The two serving girls—blonde landers, of course—wore sleeveless tunics. Dainyl could see a trace of perspiration at the hairline of Zistele, the younger.

Lystrana was almost glowing as Dainyl stepped into the sunroom, and her smile was dazzling as she rose from the circular table and stepped around it toward him.

"You look happy," he said.

"I am. We've waited so long."

"Just ten years. Some of the lower alectors never receive permission, and I'm not exactly the highest of the high. It's more because of you than me."

"It could be because you'll be the next submarshal."

"That's far from certain, and even a submarshal is less than a high assistant." Dainyl and Lystrana had talked over Tyanylt's death—quietly and when no one else was around—but neither could think of a reason for his death except for what the marshal had suggested. Going against superiors was always dangerous, regardless of whether one was correct.

"Why doesn't matter." Lystrana threw her arms around him and hugged him tightly. She was almost as tall as he was, and her body melded with his. "You don't care, do you?"

"Of course, I care. I've been as impatient as you've been. I may not show it—"

"Oh, no. That's not what I meant." She whispered in his ear. "A boy or a girl. That's what I meant." She leaned back slightly in his arms, her violet eyes intent on his face.

Dainyl grinned, ruffling her shimmering black hair with one hand. "Whatever will be."

"You always know the right things to say, and you mean them."

He hoped that he did.

"You need to eat." She stepped out of his arms. "Your day starts earlier than mine."

They seated themselves across the table from each other. The early-morning sun was not yet above the courtyard walls, but at least there was no chill from the full-length glass panels between the pillars that showed the fountain and the garden beyond.

Zistele appeared with a pot of steaming cider, pouring it into the crystal mug set on the table beside his place.

"Thank you." He liked the taste of ale better, but the heat of the cider was also welcome.

Zistele nodded, refilled Lystrana's mug, and stepped away. Sentya slipped a platter in front of him, one with egg toast perfectly golden and three slices of lean ham. Beside the platter on the left, she placed a small bowl of freshly sliced peaches. Then she withdrew to leave the couple alone.

Lystrana had finished but half of her breakfast while waiting for him, and she took a sip of the hot cider.

Dainyl ate several bites, then sipped his own cider before asking, "What does your day look like?"

"Long." Lystrana offered a rueful smile. "I was working on the accounts for the new coal mines north of Faitel, but now the bursar in Tempre has misplaced something like three thousand golds from the Lanachronan main administrative account."

"Misplaced . . . or stolen?"

"Misplaced, most likely. He reported it long before anyone might have suspected, and the regional Alector of Justice has already determined he isn't lying."

"Landers." Dainyl snorted. "You're lucky he's not an indigen. They're even less perceptive."

"That's not always true, and we're not supposed to call them that," Lystrana reminded him.

"It's better than calling them steers, the way some do, just because they feed the lifeforce that we need."

"Careful, dearest. Even in the *Views of the Highest,* they're both called steers. Kylana has pointed that out more than once."

"Even some alectors are steers in the way they think. The *Views of the Highest* suggests that, too," Dainyl pointed out.

"Kylana—and your marshal—would rather avoid thinking about that. She says that if it looks like a steer, acts like a steer, and talks like a steer, it is a steer."

"Alectors look the same, but we have varying levels of Talent, and that's a big difference. Landers and indigens even look different, most of the time. Most landers are blond, and some even exhibit Talent. No indigen ever has."

"I think you've made your point. Again."

Dainyl laughed softly. "I should never forget that my wife is a brighter and more important personage than is this poor colonel."

"Poor Dainyl," teased Lystrana. "You command hundreds, and you think yourself less than a wife who has but a small study adjoining the High Alector of Finance."

"A wife who knows where every gold in Corus lies," he retorted humorously, "and probably every alector who collects interest on each. And I don't command anyone directly."

"Most of the usury is by landers. You know that. They're far more interested in golds than in power."

He did, but found it hard to believe, even if his eyes reminded him every day. The dwellings in the merchants' quarters were far more opulent than those of most alectors. Even the Duarch's Palace in Elcien and the various mansions of the Highests were comparatively modest, and they comprised but a fraction of the alectors' quarter. Dainyl and Lystrana's dwelling was modest, with but four bedchambers, one of which was a seldom-used guest chamber, plus, of course, the lower-level servants' quarters. They only had the two girls, while most successful merchanters had staffs of a half score or more.

"You'll have to go to Tempre, then? By Table?" he asked. "It's important enough that you can miss the sentence of justice this afternoon?"

"I was at the last one, in the spring, and the one before that," Lystrana replied. "I don't need to be reminded of what happens if we abuse power. You'll be there for me."

"We provide the guard—and the pteridons. I'm not looking forward to it." Dainyl had come to dread those times justice was laid down upon an alector, infrequent as they were.

"I know."

"You're fortunate you can use the Table," he said, trying to change the subject.

"Nothing else is practical. By sandoxes, it's almost a week each way. Even if there were a Myrmidon courier headed there, it's a day and a half each way by pteridon." Lystrana smiled ruefully. "Besides, it's occasionally useful to have an alector from Elcien appear immediately in response to a problem."

"You will be back tonight?"

"You had plans for end day?"

"I had thought we could hear the concert at the Palace on Novdi evening. Colonels and above, and their spouses, were invited. I'd thought you would have gotten your own—"

"I did." Lystrana smiled warmly. "I didn't know if you wanted to go . . . and I didn't want to say anything in case you didn't."

Dainyl again marveled at his wife. "You could stay in Tempre tonight and come back midday tomorrow if you need more time. I didn't mean . . ."

"I know. But if I can't find the missing golds in a day, it will take all the records and a week." She sighed. "Even local translations are tiring, but I am glad for the Tables."

"Will that be a problem . . . later?"

Lystrana shook her head. "Not while I'm pregnant. Afterward . . . I wouldn't want to carry a child to most of the provincial centers—except Alustre . . . or Soupat, because it's actually warm enough."

"Your Highest needs you too much. No one else has a better feel for the Duarchy's accounts."

Lystrana smiled. "You'd best be going."

Dainyl swallowed the last of the cider and rose. "You'll be late this evening?"

"I wouldn't think so." Lystrana also stood. "Sentya! We're finished here."

"Yes, alectress." Sentya appeared with a tray before Dainyl and Lystrana had left the sunroom.

"She's good, I have to say," said Dainyl, following his wife upstairs to their chambers.

"We pay her to be good."

Unspoken was the thought that, without the alectors of Ifryn, Sentya and all the landers and indigens would still be living in mud huts and scraping out a bare existence from a cold and barren land.

Back upstairs in the dressing chamber, while Lystrana bathed, Dainyl hung the old and warm black tunic on the rack on his side of the chamber and donned his uniform trousers, dark gray, and his shimmercloth tunic, brilliant blue with dark gray piping. He adjusted the collar and fastened the gray officer's belt in place. Next, he checked the crystal charge level in his sidearm—the standard light-cutter for a Myrmidon officer—then slipped it into the holster on the left side of the belt.

Last came the gray gloves. Depending on how cool it was outside, he might actually wear them. The ride to Myrmidon headquarters would warm him some, especially if the hacker stayed on the sunnier streets.

4

Many worlds have life, but on most, life remains little more than pond scum, lichens upon the side of a rock facing a cold sun, or tiny animalcules darting through stagnant waters, too unaware to comprehend danger, however dimly, and too limited for their offspring or their offspring's offspring ever to rise from those waters to awareness and thence to aspirations and dreams to place a stamp upon an uncaring and indifferent universe.

Upon that mere handful of worlds hosting life-forms that rise above a thin grasp of rock and water, two kinds of life exist—that which is aimless and that which is directed, either self-directed or directed from without. Long have there been those who claim that higher life is always directed from without, and that such guidance proceeds from a supreme being, a deity who shapes a world until intelligence emerges, then reveals the divine will to selected individuals.

This is a most comforting belief, yet, like most unthinking beliefs that offer comfort, there is little in the universe to support it. The multiplicity of barren worlds, as well as the demonstrated failures of such "divine guidance" in our own long history, should disabuse all but the most misguided of the illusion of the involvement of a supreme being in the affairs of life and living beings.

In fact, as the chronicles of hundreds of centuries demonstrate, life arises by chance and as it will. All too often higher life upon a world will arise, then vanish, at times leaving no record of its passing, at others, leaving ruins that suggest either poverty of spirit and aspiration or little of either, save procreation. Is then life a game of chance, a set of bone-dice rolling itself against the odds?

Views of the Highest
Illustra
W.T. 1513

5

At a quarter past the second glass of the afternoon, Dainyl began his preparations for the administration of justice scheduled to begin at the third glass, preparations he had expected to make, but not oversee completely. When he had arrived that morning, he had learned that the marshal had left for Iron Stem, leaving Dainyl fully in command of a proceeding that was exceedingly distasteful. All Dainyl knew was that the Cadmian officer in charge there had sent an urgent dispatch. The marshal had left no instructions.

First, the colonel took out the crimson armband that signified alector misconduct or blood wrongly shed, or both, and fastened it into place on his upper left sleeve below the shoulder. Then he checked his sidearm and straightened his tunic.

After leaving his study, he went to find Undercaptain Zernylta, third squad leader and acting commander of First Myrmidon Company in the absence of Captain Ghasylt, who had left with the marshal early that morning to fly to Iron Stem.

Zernylta was standing by the duty desk, talking with the duty officer, Undercaptain Yuasylt.

"Zernylta?"

"Yes, Colonel?" Zernylta was a slender alectress, but tall and wiry. Like Dainyl, she had blue eyes, rather than the violet usual for most alectors. Her crimson armband was already in place.

"Third squad will be escorting the prisoner. Are they prepared?"

"I just checked. They all have their armbands and sidearms, and the crystals are fully charged. The prisoner was brought in a glass ago, and he is in the holding cell. The duty coach is already standing by at the Hall of Justice." She paused. "What was he actually convicted of, Colonel?"

"According to the briefing sheet," Dainyl replied, "he abused his house servants, physically and sexually, and he used Talent contrary to the Code of the Duarches."

"Stupid," murmured the black-haired woman. "Abusing steers is bad enough, but to force sex, and then use Talent to cover it up—he deserves more than he'll get."

While that wasn't possible—the sentence was death—Dainyl understood what she meant. Being an alector granted one power, but also entailed great responsibility, and the Archon and the Duarches punished abuse of that power severely. There wasn't any option, not with so few alectors compared to the millions of indigens and landers.

He nodded and walked down toward the north end of the building to check the holding cell and third squad. After inspecting and checking all that was necessary, finally, at a quarter before the third glass, Dainyl stepped out into the courtyard behind the headquarters building. The two remaining squads of First Company—first and second squads—and their pteridons were forming up to the south of the flight stage. Third squad would be escorting the prisoner, and half of fourth squad had gone with the marshal, while the other half was out flying dispatch runs.

Dainyl turned and surveyed the circular graystone platform that stood in the center of the courtyard behind the Myrmidon headquarters—the flight stage for the pteridons. The stone stage stood a yard and a half above the paved courtyard and also doubled, if infrequently, as it did now, as the site for the administration of justice to alectors. The raised stones were empty, with only the justice stand—a crossbar affixed atop a single post—set in place for what was to come.

After several moments, Dainyl turned back to the south and walked toward Undercaptain Ghanyr. Behind the undercaptain were four Myrmidon rankers and, set as closely as they could be, which still took a square a good thirty yards on a side, five pteridons, blue wings folded back, blue crystalline eyes looking forward.

Did the pteridons anticipate what would come? Dainyl had never known, even with his own, back when he'd been a ranker, then a junior officer.

"We're ready, sir." Ghanyr glanced down at his arm and the crimson armband. "Hate wearing it."

"We all do. That's why it's required."

"Yes, sir."

Dainyl moved toward Undercaptain Yuasylt, who had left the headquarters building just before the colonel, and second squad and its pteridons. The pteridons of third squad were ranked just behind those of first and second squad, but without their riders, since third squad was providing prisoner escort.

"Almost ready, Colonel," announced Yuasylt.

"Good." Dainyl wasn't certain he was ready, necessary as what was about to happen might be. As he had surveyed the courtyard and the squads of First Company, alectors from all around Elcien had begun to arrive, coming in by themselves, in groups of two or three, and standing on the north side of the landing stage. He could see several assistants of the Duarch, quietly noting who had appeared.

Finally, Dainyl turned. "Myrmidons, ready!"

"First squad, present and ready!"

"Second squad, present and ready!"

With that, Dainyl turned and waited, standing at attention.

As Dainyl and the Myrmidons continued to wait, more alectors slipped into the courtyard. With just a few moments before the third glass of the afternoon, more than a hundred alectors—besides the Myrmidons—stood waiting. Although the day was not that hot, Dainyl could feel perspiration oozing down the inside of his uniform, more a result of his own discomfort than of any real heat, pleasant as the cloudless harvest afternoon was.

From the headquarters building came three deep chimes. All conversation and whispers died away.

The High Alector of Justice stepped from the headquarters building. He wore a tunic and trousers of purple, trimmed with black. Upon his upper left sleeve was a crimson armband identical to the ones worn by all the Myrmidons. Across his chest was a black sash. Behind him were his two assistants, attired in a similar fashion, except without the sash. One carried the lash, with its black tendrils, tipped with razor-sharp barbs. The other carried the mace of justice.

The High Alector climbed the steps to the landing stage and walked to the center, placing himself three yards back of the empty justice stand.

"Bring forth the malefactor!" The High Alector's deep voice boomed across the courtyard.

The doors of the headquarters building opened, and Undercaptain

Zernylta stepped out, followed by two rankers. Behind them stumbled an alector in nearly shapeless dark red trousers and shirt, barefooted, with his hands manacled behind his back. Two more Myrmidons walked behind the malefactor.

The courtyard remained quiet as the Myrmidons escorted the alector in red to the steps onto the stage, then to the justice form.

The High Alector stiffened slightly as the Myrmidons unshackled the prisoner. Dainyl could sense the immense well of Talent marshaled to strike, if necessary, but the malefactor did not move as his wrists were clamped to the frame and a red hood was slipped over his head. The Myrmidons stepped back, re-forming behind the alector and his two assistants, one male and one female.

In the silence, the High Alector stepped forward. "We are here to do justice. You are here to see justice done. So be it." He turned toward the alector strapped to the frame "You, Bealtyr of Elcien, have abused those who trusted you. You have betrayed the trust placed in you by the Archon and the Duarches. You have deceived, and you have cheated all who live upon Acorus by your acts. For your crimes, you have been sentenced to die."

The High Alector paused, then turned to accept the lash from the taller assistant, who then stepped back. The other assistant stepped forward, holding the Mace of Justice in her hands.

"Justice will be done." The High Alector of Justice raised the lash, and struck.

The barbs on the lash were sharp enough to shred normal cloth and flesh with but a single blow, but the lash was as much symbolic as physical because, as the lash struck, the High Alector used his Talent and the crystals concealed within the Mace to rip chunks of the very lifeforce from the malefactor. Rather than waste that energy, it was funneled to the pteridons formed up behind first and second squads, who drew it and stored it for when they would next fly.

The High Alector needed but five strikes from the lash barbs before the figure in the tee-frame slumped forward, unconscious, blood splattered across his back and oozing over the red garments.

Brief as those five strokes had been, even so, Dainyl had to brace himself against the agony radiated from the malefactor and Talent-spread across the watching alectors. He watched as several alectors swayed. One young man pitched forward, and those beside him barely caught him before he would have struck the paving stones of the courtyard.

Two more strikes of the lash followed before Dainyl could sense the emptiness that signified death. He managed to keep his lips tight together.

"Justice has been done." The High Alector nodded to the assistant with the Mace.

She turned the Mace on the figure in the frame. A pinkish purple haze flared over the dead alector, then vanished. Only the empty frame remained.

Actually, the Mace was attuned only to the specially treated red clothing. With death, the alector's body would have turned to dust and less in moments, but the use of the Mace provided absolute visual closure.

Had justice been done? Dainyl wasn't sure of that. He was more than certain that, without the visual and emotional reminders provided by the spectacle—and the required regular attendance by all alectors—that far more abuse of position and Talent would have occurred. Great power required even greater checks, as pointed out so clearly in the *Views of the Highest,* and by there being two Duarches sharing the administrative powers delegated by the Archon on Ifryn.

But did such checks provide true justice? That was another question, one that Dainyl could not answer, not honestly.

6

On Novdi afternoon, two glasses before sunset, Dainyl and Lystrana stepped through the center archway and into the concert hall of the Palace of the Duarch of Elcien. Dainyl wore the blue-trimmed gray formal uniform of a Myrmidon colonel while Lystrana wore brilliant blue trousers and a matching shimmersilk shirt, with a short vest of paler blue. The vest was short enough that the wider, silver-gray belt that matched her boots was fully visible.

Dainyl surveyed those already seated, without seeming to do so.

"Seventy-five," murmured Lystrana so softly that only he could have heard her, even with Talent-boosted hearing. "We're late."

He repressed a faint smile, as they moved forward. "Not too late. The Duarch isn't here."

Twenty-five tables were arrayed in an arc on the polished marble floor. Five chairs were set around one side of each circular table, positioned so that all five could view the dais on which four empty chairs awaited the performers. The center two tables—reserved for the Duarch and his wife and guests—provided an unobstructed view of the dais.

The octagonal floor tiles of green marble were linked by smaller diamond tiles of gold marble, and each tile was outlined in brilliant bronze. The center of the floor just below the performing dais was inset with an eight-pointed star of golden marble a yard across, also outlined in a thin line of a brilliant bronze. The hangings on the side walls were green velvet, trimmed in gold, and set at precise intervals to damp echoes without muting the quality of the sound.

"We can sit with Kylana and Zestafyn," suggested Lystrana.

"Of course." Dainyl understood that his wife's mild words were anything but a suggestion. Kylana was the assistant to the High Alector of Transport, and her husband was officially the Duarch's liaison to the regional alectors. Effectively, he was the head of intelligence for the Duarch of Elcien.

"Your mother is at the next table," murmured Lystrana.

"I wouldn't have expected her. She usually avoids chamber concerts."

"Exactly."

Dainyl continued to the table ahead, then stopped and bent, smiling at the black-haired woman—not that any alector had hair other than shimmering black—who looked no older than her son. "I hadn't expected you here."

Alyra returned her son's smile. "Every so often I do come to a concert." Her smile widened slightly as her eyes moved to Lystrana. "Congratulations, dear."

"Thank you. Might I call upon you in the future?"

"Always . . . you've done so much for Dainyl."

Dainyl kept smiling. Lystrana *had* done much for him. She'd advised him and guided him for nearly thirty years, long before they were married, from when he'd been an undercaptain with few prospects—and he'd listened and learned, especially about enhancing his Talent. He'd never been able to learn much from his mother, not with her arrogance.

"He's done it all himself, Alyra. I'm just good at listening." Lystrana smiled warmly, projecting warmth in a way that Dainyl had great difficulty emulating. "We must talk later. I see Kylana beckoning."

Dainyl kept his smile in place until they were well away.

Lystrana squeezed his hand gently, then spoke to the woman at the table they approached. "Kylana . . . if we could join you?"

"We'd be delighted." Kylana gestured to the seats to her husband's right. She was extremely short and slender for an alector, not even quite two yards tall, with a narrow face and deep-set golden eyes—a throwback to a bad translation by her grandmother, she'd claimed. Dainyl suspected it was the result of her own translation from Ifryn to Acorus, not that he would ever have said so.

Lystrana eased into the chair beside Zestafyn, and Dainyl took the one to Lystrana's right.

"The word is that you had an interesting day in Tempre on Octdi," offered Zestafyn, turning to Lystrana.

"The missing golds, you mean? They weren't missing at all, it turned out. Just misrecorded." Lystrana paused as a lander serving girl appeared. "The Vyan Amber Crown."

"The same," added Dainyl.

The server girl nodded politely and slipped away.

"Victyn was most relieved," continued Zestafyn. "He is a good sort, especially for a lander, and he does try very hard."

"Sometimes, those are the worst," observed Kylana. "They wish to follow every rule and procedure. They forget who gave them those procedures. I wish that we were allowed to tell them of Ifryn and the power that resides there. Then, they wouldn't forget."

Dainyl had his doubts about that. Even alectors tended to forget about powers that were distant and not exercised. That had been one of the points of the public execution—public only to alectors.

"Dearest," replied Zestafyn, "that may be, but it's a waste of time to blame a tool for operating the way it was designed."

"Zestafyn is so philosophical," said Kylana.

"Just practical." The liaison's deep voice was matter-of-fact.

Dainyl nodded as politely as he could, hoping that it wouldn't be too long before the Duarch appeared and the concert could begin. Unlike many, he'd actually come for the music. At times, he had to wonder what a concert might be like in Illustra, with a full orchestra and thousands of compositions from which to select. Then, if Acorus were to be chosen to host the master scepter, there would be more music, and plays, and a greater flowering of art and innovation.

A single high chime interrupted his thoughts—and the conversations around him. All the alectors stood as the Duarch entered the concert hall. At three yards in height, he was an impressive figure even among alectors, with his brilliant white face, flashing purple eyes, and hair so deep and black that, paradoxically, it seemed to radiate light. His smile and the Talent behind it warmed the room.

"Please. I apologize for being late. Let us enjoy the music."

Beside the Duarch was his wife, who also functioned as a regional auditor, and her smile was almost as warm. One hundred and seven alectors now sat at the tables in the concert hall. Roughly two thirds of the alectors assigned to Elcien, reflected Dainyl, a trifle low for a concert, but then all had heard the quartet before. The novelty was not in the players, but in the latest compositions sent through the great translation tube from Ifryn with the infrequent translations of Myrmidon rankers or other lower-level alectors.

Dainyl was in fact a rarity, a senior Myrmidon officer born on Acorus who had worked his way up from being a ranker into the officer corps. That he had not tested well as a youth so many years before had always put off his mother and doubtless had retarded his progress. Then, too, it had not helped that he had been thought to have limited Talent and had no ties to the Duarches and no close personal links to any of the high alectors, and had not had any until he had met Lystrana—and those were but indirect. Under the circumstances, he'd done extraordinary well. Myrmidon officers with limited Talent and no connections seldom rose above majer, and never above colonel.

He glanced up as the four performers, all in the black and green of music, walked onto the dais and bowed to the Duarch before seating themselves, the hand-harpist on the far left, beside the five-string violist, and both across from the side-flautist and knee-bassist.

"They've been practicing this recital for a month," Lystrana said mildly.

That such practice took place after the musicians' normal duties was understood.

Three notes from the hand-harp, slow and deliberately struck, filled the hall. Then, the slow deep tones of the bass followed, joined by the viola.

Dainyl let the music wash over him, pushing aside the worries of the week.

7

Standing easy in his maroon-and-gray uniform, Mykel waited on the platform to the west of the river towers for the coach from Faitel to Elcien. South of the platform was the River Vedra itself, channeled between eternastone walls. Each river-wall held a causeway wide enough for four transport coaches abreast.

"Think it'll be late?" asked a Cadmian ranker several paces away.

"Never seen one late yet," replied his companion. "Alectors want the coaches to run when they're supposed to."

With an amused smile, Mykel shifted his weight from one boot to the other, then glanced to the western end of the platform, where a handful of alectors waited beyond the stone railing separating the two sections. While the alectors never showed age, not any that he had seen, Mykel knew that the ones waiting were younger. Senior alectors traveled by pteridon, or through the mysteries of the Halls.

The captain snorted. Mysteries, indeed. For all their greater height and strength, the alectors were still mortals, although they had their secrets and guarded them zealously.

Low in the western sky, he could barely make out the half disc of the larger moon, Selena, more golden near the horizon. The green moon—Asterta, the one some called the warrior moon or the moon of misery—had set glasses earlier, well before dawn.

He turned, his eyes taking in the nearer of the two green towers, a cylinder with a pointed tip that soared more than a hundred yards into the silver-green sky. Between the two towers were the major piers for the boats and barges that traveled the river carrying everything—the steel pigs and dreamdust from Iron Stem, the wines from the Vyan Hills, and the grains and livestock from the fertile rolling plains between Krost and Borlan. All of it came down the Vedra to Faitel, where the iron was off-loaded for the artisans and engineers, and what was not off-loaded went first to Elcien, then south through the Bay of Ludel to Ludar.

Downstream and to the west of Faitel were the shipyards, and upstream and east of the center of the city were the ironworks and the golden-walled compounds of the engineers' and artisans' guilds. If Ludar could be called the artistic heart of Corus, and Elcien the spirit and intelligence, then Faitel was where art and spirit were forged and almost everything of great value was fabricated—from the bronzed coaches pulled by the sandoxes to the great ships that had conquered the oceans.

Mykel's reveries were brought to a halt by the double chime of the bell that announced that the coach to Elcien was coming. He looked eastward as the sandoxes turned into the concourse on the north side of the platform. There were two—each more than four times the size of a draft horse—with even more massive shoulders, and scales that shimmered purplish blue. The deep-set eyes were golden brown ovals, with pupils blacker than a starless night. In the middle of the broad forehead was a single triangular scale a good ten times the size of the less distinct purplish scales that covered every span of the sandox. The sandoxes were harnessed to a modified cross-rig with wide black straps and leather-sheathed chains.

Behind the pair were the bronze-sheathed transport coaches, each nine yards long. The forward coach was split into two sections, the front compartment for alectors, with wider and well-cushioned seats, and a rear section with far less luxurious seating. The second coach contained a single compartment, all standard seating. The drivers' seat high on the front of the first coach had ample space for the two alectors who controlled the sandoxes and the coach, and was provided cover from sunlight and weather by curved bronzelike metallic roof sheet.

Just as the sandoxes and coaches slowed to a halt, there was a shout from the river side of the concourse platform. Mykel turned, as did the two women to his left, and the pair of Cadmian rankers to his right.

A man jumped onto the top of the stone railing of the western platform and leveled a weapon—an ancient crossbow—at the nearest alector. Before Mykel had taken more than a single step, the bearded figure had fired, and the quarrel slammed into the shoulder of the alector, spinning him half around. Before Mykel took a third step, the alector on the forward coach had lifted his light-knife. A bluish beam struck the bearded man, and his entire figure flared into blue-yellow flame. Within instants, a blackened body pitched off the railing.

Mykel's mouth opened as he realized the crossbow quarrel had bounced off the alector's shoulder. He had the feeling that the alector was in a fair amount of pain, but he couldn't have said why. Still, from such close range, the bolt should have gone through the alector. Absently, he recalled what his father had said. Arrows bouncing off alectors didn't seem so far-fetched, after what he had just seen. But how did they do that? Was their skin that tough? Or were those shiny clothes special? Or both?

His lips quirked. He wasn't likely to find out. Not anytime soon.

The concourse bell rang rapidly, and Cadmians in the uniforms of the road patrols appeared from the station west of the concourse. Within moments, the charred figure had been lifted into a handcart and pushed away. The injured alector had vanished.

"Never seen anything like that," muttered one of the rankers beside Mykel.

"Maybe one of those Ancienteers," replied the other.

"Thought they just hid away in the peaks and stuff."

"Crazy folk, never know what they'll do."

Mykel agreed with that, especially about some of the strange cults that had appeared in the outlying lands of some regions, like the Iron Valleys, North Lustrea, Deforya, and the higher mountains in the southern part of the Coast Range. He'd hadn't heard much about the Ancienteers, except as a group that worshipped the vanished ancients. His grandfather had once said that the true ancients were beautiful women with wings who were colder than ice. They didn't sound like anything Mykel wanted to worship.

The boarding bell rang, a quick triplet, and Mykel eased a silver from one of the slots on the inside of his belt before moving toward the steps down to the embarking area.

The two Cadmian road patrollers on the mounting steps scarcely looked at Mykel as he handed his silver to the attendant and stepped through the open door and into the coach. He settled into a window seat three rows back. As in all of the coach compartments, save the forward section for alectors, there were four narrow oak seats, two on each side of a center aisle. With the thin seat cushion, they were almost comfortable on a long journey. Almost.

Mykel noted an attractive woman in dark blue, hoping she would take the seat beside him. Before he could offer, a squarish man wearing a brown tunic and matching boots eased into the seat. "Sorry, Captain, but there's not that much room."

"There never is," replied Mykel politely, guessing that the man was some sort of factor.

A single long chime sounded, and the attendant closed the coach door. Mykel glanced around the coach. Most of the thirty-two seats were taken, although the attractive brunette was sitting alone. With the slightest jolt, the coach began to move. Before long, the sandoxes had the coach up to speed and coolish air flowed through the louvers forward and overhead.

With nearly three hours ahead of him for the seventy-odd-vingt journey, Mykel surveyed the river, taking in the barges being towed upstream by the steam tugs on the inner causeway. An ocean freighter—he could tell that because it did not have the sails of a coaster nor the narrower beam and shallower draft of a river craft—forged downstream. Above the bridge flew the pennant of the Duarchy, two crossed scepters, both metallic blue, not quite identical, set in a sharp eight-pointed, brilliant green star.

"Strange business there on the platform," offered the man seated beside Mykel. "You ever see anything like that before?"

The captain turned from the window. "No. I suppose there's a first time for everything."

"I meant the arrow bouncing off the alector. I've seen crazies before." He paused. "Makes you think. Maybe there are reasons we don't know why they're alectors . . . besides they're being big and tall." After another pause, he smiled. "I'm Floriset, crop factor."

"Mykel, captain, Fifteenth Cadmian."

"Wouldn't want your job these days. Everywhere you look, there's another bunch that thinks they can do things better than the Duarchs." Floriset shook his head. "You seen much action against them?"

"In the north Westerhills against the Reillies last year."

"Tough, they said."

"Not that tough. We didn't need to call in the Myrmidons, the way they did in Soupat." Mykel laughed, quickly asking, "How is your business?"

"Some days are good. Some aren't. Had a mild spring, with rain in most places, and a bit more rain through the summer. Good hot late summer and a dry early harvest. Makes it hard."

"That sounds good," offered Mykel, "not bad."

"Too good. Bumper crops all over the place, especially in wheat corn. That'll drive the prices down. Be hard on the farmers way to the east. Might speculate in some land there." The factor laughed. "Just have to buy as much as I can and hope next year's weather's worse."

"Did the Reillies make things hard last year?"

"Hard on folks to the north, but I'd laid in more stocks, and when the prices went up after they burned the granaries in Harmony, I made a few extra silvers."

"More like a few hundred, I'd wager," suggested Mykel.

"A few." The factor grinned, but for a moment. "Works the other way at times, too. Couple years back, I'd figured that the short drought would last another year. Was wrong about that, and had to unload stocks as I could. Storage charges woulda eaten me alive, otherwise. Took a loss of more than a half copper a bushel." He shook his head. "Like to have done that one over again."

"Life's like that," Mykel replied.

"It is indeed, but you can't help wishing."

Mykel nodded, then leaned back and closed his eyes. It would be a long ride, and he could use the rest.

8

When Mykel finished the two-vingt walk from concourse platform at the river station to the gates of Cadmian headquarters, he was perspiring, and glad he'd taken no gear home with him. He could have taken a carriage for hire from the station, but he'd seen no point in spending a silver, not on a pleasant day when he did not have to report until muster on the next morning.

The last quarter vingt—five hundred yards—before the open stone gates at the end of the stone-paved avenue was clear of dwellings, just an open hillside between the northern edge of the less than attractive town of Northa and the walls of the Cadmian headquarters. The compound was set at the base of the hills that rose northeast of the river and footed the Coast Range itself, with walls that ran almost a vingt on each side.

In contrast, the Myrmidon headquarters compound was far smaller than the Cadmian headquarters and was situated on the west end of the isle of Elcien itself, facing into the generally prevailing winds. That made it easier for the pteridons to lift off, or so Mykel had been told, although he'd never seen one of the blue-winged fliers up close, but only from below as they soared in and out of Elcien, often casting shadows across those below.

The two rankers on guard duty stiffened as Mykel walked toward them.

"Captain Mykel . . ."

"Always back early . . ."

"Good day," he said warmly. "Anything unusual, Cheant?"

"No, sir."

"Good." Mykel smiled, a cheerful expression that also indicated that he knew none of the rankers would have told him anything—not out in the open. Cheant's guilty look suggested that more than a few things had occurred during Mykel's furlough, none likely to be good.

As he crossed the paved courtyard on the west side of the compound, striding toward the junior officers' quarters, he caught sight of another captain hurrying toward him. "Kuertyl!"

"Back early, I see." The younger captain's eyes did not quite meet Mykel's level gaze.

"Always."

"You never carry anything, either."

"Not when I visit my parents. No point in it. I wear the uniform traveling, and old clothes while I'm there." His eyes fixed on the younger officer. "Cheant was on gate duty. He had that look. What's in the wind?"

"No one's said anything."

Mykel cleared his throat and waited.

"Word is that something happened in Dramur. No one's saying anything, but a Myrmidon officer came in on Novdi, landed his pteridon right beside the headquarters. Swerkyl had to go find the colonel and Majer Vaclyn. The alector spent a good glass with the two of them, then another glass or more with the majer. Then he flew off. Swerkyl says he heard the words 'Dramur' and 'Dramuria,' and 'Third Battalion.' Then the majer went to his target range and practiced with those throwing knives of his."

"That means he wants to kill someone," reflected Mykel. "You sure it's Third Battalion?"

"Swerkyl wasn't sure, but it's got to be us. We're next on the deployment schedule. Our companies are the only ones at full strength and ready to deploy."

"Figures . . . Anything else about Dramur?"

"No. Not yet." Kuertyl added quickly, "Did you hear about Scien? They're closing the post. No one knows why. The companies there are being reassigned."

"Should have been closed years ago. It's at the end of nowhere.

Colder there than at Blackstear in full winter." Mykel grinned at the younger captain. "You should be glad. They can't send you there when you foul up your next assignment."

"Or you," riposted Kuertyl.

"I never foul up." Mykel laughed.

"I have to meet with Majer Vaclyn in half a glass—"

"On end day? Is this about Dramur?"

"Wish it were. We didn't do so well in squad-on-squad training last week. You'd better watch out when he comes to you." Kuertyl turned and hurried toward the headquarters building.

Mykel frowned. He wasn't surprised that Kuertyl hadn't done that well, but it worried him that Vaclyn was meeting with officers on end day, especially after practicing with the throwing knives. That was never a good sign, and it suggested that the colonel was not only pushing to get the companies ready to leave, but less than happy with readiness. Dramur? That was all too hot, almost as bad as places like Sinjin and Soupat.

Mykel walked more deliberately toward the officers' quarters.

9

One of Dainyl's few luxuries was taking a carriage from the house to the Myrmidon headquarters on the west end of Elcien. Lystrana had calculated it, and paying the three coppers each way was far cheaper than having a personal carriage. A hacker named Barodyn had taken advantage of Dainyl's modest self-indulgence and waited outside every working morning.

When Dainyl stepped out of through the gates of the front courtyard, Barodyn leaned back in his seat and swung the coach door open. "Good morning, Colonel, sir."

"Good morning." Dainyl offered a smile as he climbed into the coach and closed the door. He didn't say another word as the hacker eased the coach away from the mounting block.

Nor did Barodyn.

After two turns, and an arc around the public gardens of the Duarch, the coach was headed west on the Boulevard. There was only one, down the middle of the isle from the bridge in the east to the gates at the Myrmidon compound at the west end of the isle.

Dainyl looked back at the gardens, with their precisely trimmed hedges and stone paths, with the fountains, and the topiary of all manner of creatures, including a lifelike pteridon and a long hedge sculpted into the likeness of two sandoxes and a set of transport coaches.

A woman—an alector—and a child walked through the gates of the garden. Dainyl frowned. He should know them. There weren't that many children allowed, only a handful every year, depending on the reports from Lyterna. Still, the woman didn't look familiar.

His eyes moved to the Palace of the Duarch ahead to his left, south of the boulevard, opposite the Hall of Justice. The golden eternastone glowed in the morning light, and the two towers were green-pointed cylinders that almost melded with the silver-green sky to the west.

Dainyl smiled. Built on an island of solid stone, Elcien was indeed a marvel—from the perfectly paved boulevard and streets, the stone dwellings and their tile roofs, the shops and market squares that held everything produced on Acorus, the docks and warehouses where vessels from across the world disgorged their goods, and, of course, the Palace of the Duarch. Even the air smelled fresh, coming from the south, and pleasantly moist.

Past the center of Elcien, to the west of the palace, were the trade quarter—on the southwest—and the residence quarter for those merchants who could afford it. Beyond them was Dainyl's destination. The low bluff on the west end of the isle of Elcien that held the Myrmidon compound was separated from the rest of the city by a graystone wall four yards high, with but a single set of gates. The gates were open and unguarded, as were those at all Myrmidon compounds. Because all alectors had some degree of Talent—if minimal in the case of many rankers, couriers, and low staff—anyone not belonging would be sensed instantly, and few indigens or landers wished to take twenty lashes for being in the wrong place.

The hacker reined up outside the gates. "Colonel Alector, sir?"

As he stepped out, Dainyl handed over the two coppers, plus an extra copper.

"Thank you, sir."

As Barodyn turned the coach for hire back toward the trade quarter, Dainyl walked quickly through the gates and toward the headquarters building, a square structure no more than twenty yards on a side and but a single story in height. The sole Myrmidon in the receiving area was the staff senior squad leader, Zorcylt.

"Good morning, Colonel."

"Good morning, Zorcylt. Is the marshal in yet?"

"No, sir. He and Captain Ghasylt are on their way back to Iron Stem."

"Iron Stem? Again?"

"Yes, sir. He left two messages on your desk. There's been more trouble there, but he didn't say what."

Dainyl wasn't looking forward to the messages. He offered a grin. "You have any ideas?"

"Well, sir . . . I did hear something about the coal mines there. That was all."

"What squad has the duty?"

"Second, sir. Undercaptain Yuasylt. All five have reported and stand ready, sir."

"Are we expecting any dispatches from the palace for the morning flight?"

"No, sir. The message banner is white."

"Do we have a report on inbound shipping?"

"No, sir. Vorosylt lifted off almost half a glass ago, but it's a quartering wind, and maybe a headwind beyond the straits."

Dainyl nodded. That left three fliers—Yuasylt and two others—from the duty squad for any other dispatches or surveillance work. In many ways, he missed flying, but he didn't miss the glass upon glass that he would have been away from Lystrana. "I'll be in my study."

The colonel walked down the corridor to the doorway just short of the one to the marshal's spaces. Once inside his own study, he closed the door. Rather than settle behind his desk, he picked up the top envelope. The light dusting of Talent across the seal had not been tampered with. A faint smile crossed his thin lips as he released the Talent-seal and opened the envelope. He began to read.

After a time, he set the short document on the top of the desk and walked to the window. The flight stage was empty, but the dispatch rider and pteridon would be there shortly.

He'd expected to read about Iron Stem and coal mines, but the first message was brief, warning him that the Duarch's intelligence sources had reported unrest in Dramur, and the possibility of an actual insurgency.

Because the terrain was not optimal for the Myrmidons and with the unsettled situation in Iron Stem, the marshal had ordered a Cadmian battalion to begin preparations for deployment to Dramuria.

Dainyl didn't care for that—not when the marshal had stated that the unsettled situation in Iron Stem might be worse. Worse than an insurgency? Worse than the loss of higher-level lifeforce that could entail, directly and indirectly? What was missing from the message worried him. Did it have to do with the concerns that had cost Tyanylt his life?

He turned back to the desk, opened the second envelope, and began to read.

The engineers in Faitel had gone to Iron Stem in early spring and opened a second coal mine. The High Alector of Trade in Ludar had arranged for additional malcontents to be trained as miners and transported to Iron Stem. Somehow—and the marshal did not explain how it had happened—the local trade director, a lander, of course, had failed to make adequate preparations for housing the additional miners. Rather than admit his failure in obtaining the necessary cut stones or brick required for the barracks, in late summer he had decided to overcut the oaks in the area. The local garrison commander, a Cadmian overcaptain, had been forced to use two companies of mounted rifle to stop the timber harvesting. Then, someone had placed explosives in the main shaft of the coal mine and detonated them, shutting down the mine completely, and killing nineteen miners. The device used showed some considerable knowledge, the kind that could result in crude cannon.

Dainyl winced. Cannon and artillery were on the banned lists, not to be mentioned, and an immediate death sentence for any lander or indigen caught attempting to fabricate them. The recorders who used the Tables for surveillance continually scanned for evidence of such efforts, and so far there had been none in years, so far as Dainyl knew.

The existing stocks of coal for coking the ironworks at Iron Stem were sufficient only for a month—one of the reasons why the additional mine was being developed. An engineering team was being sent from Faitel with the equipment to reopen the mine, but it was likely to be at least another month before production could resume.

The overcaptain had rounded up the miners and requested an Alector of Justice. The High Alector of Justice had said that a marshal was all they deserved and had dispatched the marshal, with a guard of four pteridons.

Four pteridons? Dainyl frowned. Why would anyone do that? Every day the malcontents who were sentenced to the mines didn't work added a day to their term. Stone-and-brick housing was warmer and more comfortable than timber—and the winters in Iron Stem were *cold,* if not so cold as those in places like Blackstear and Scien. Then, mature oaks provided better lumber, especially when they were harvested according to plan, and not just hacked down for a momentary need. Mature forests provided far more additional lifeforce than cutting and replanting with young trees and seedlings.

Didn't the landers and indigens understand? Every tree, every additional stock animal, each one added to the lifeforce and supplied the strength to improve life all across Corus. He snorted. Perhaps some landers did, but most didn't, and even fewer truly cared.

A marshal was probably more than whoever had blown the shaft deserved.

Still . . . that a lander or an indigen had used explosives in such a fashion was disturbing. Equally disturbing was the marshal's judgment that Iron Stem was potentially worse than an insurrection in Dramur.

After several moments, Dainyl turned back toward the door. He had to check the dispatches before the duty flier could depart.

10

Londi morning had come all too early, Mykel decided, as he stepped into the officers' mess, yawning. Although the mess held just a half score of small wooden tables, he was the only officer there.

"The same as always, Captain?" asked the steward.

"Yes, please, but water the hot cider just a touch." That was so he didn't burn his throat.

"Yes, sir."

Mykel took a corner table, and, shortly, the steward brought him a mug of cider and a platter with three slices of egg toast, drizzled with molasses syrup, along with two slices of ham, and an overripe golden apple. On the side was a quarter of a lime. "Apple's best I can do, sir."

"That's fine. Thank you." Mykel cradled the mug in his hands under his chin and let the warm cidery air rising from the mug wreath his face for a moment. After several sips, he picked up the apple and took a bite. It was mushy. It shouldn't have been. Apples were in season.

With a grimace, he picked up the lime section, squeezed what he could over a section of the apple where he had taken a bite, then ate apple and lime juice. Then he forced himself to eat the lime. He took another sip of the cider, and, with relief, a bite of the egg toast.

Dohark had entered the mess and was headed in his direction, platter in hand. The blocky older captain slid into the chair across the table from Mykel. "Kuertyl tell you about Dramur?" He took a bite of egg toast.

"He said something about it. You think he's right?"

Dohark, his mouth full, shrugged, then swallowed before speaking. "He's not so good in the field, but he always knows what's going on in headquarters."

"What do you know about Dramur?" asked Mykel.

"Big island, maybe five hundred vingts long, Got sharp-assed mountains smack down the middle, and it's hot and dry, except for a wet part on the west side. Hotter than Soupat. Only place with lots of people is Dramuria, and it's a port. Oh . . . and it's got bats, some of 'em bigger than kids. That's why there's a port. They send mals there to mine the bat shit and ship it to Southgate. Put it on a field, thin-like, and it'll make anything grow."

"So why do the Myrmidons want us there?"

"Because they don't want to go and deal with a bunch of unhappy mal miners. That's why." Dohark took a long swallow of ale.

Much as Mykel liked ale, he couldn't stand the taste of it in the morning. "What is it about Dramur? Bat shit isn't that valuable, is it?"

"Maybe the alectors think it is. They get pretty tight when folks cut down trees they shouldn't, things like that. My cousin, he had a swamp on the corner of his place, outside of Salcer. Decided that he could grow gladbeans there, make a bunch more silvers. He started to drain and fill, and before you knew it, there was an alector on his doorstep, telling him to put the swamp back the way it was. He was lucky—only got five lashes in the square."

"Five lashes for draining a swamp? And he had to put cropland back to a swamp?"

"Don't you remember your school lessons, Mykel? Swamps and

forests are good for the land. Make it more productive. Don't see how, but who's going to argue with an alector?"

Mykel fingered his chin. What sort of sense did it make to leave a swamp, a place where there were bugs and snakes, and stagnant water, when you could turn it into a productive field? Still, Dohark was right. You didn't argue with an alector.

"First glass after noon, we're doing drills against Fifteenth," Dohark said. "Your boys best do better than last time."

"We'll show you a thing or two." Mykel grinned.

"Like your backsides clearing the drill field?" Dohark rose from the mess table.

Mykel laughed, letting the older captain depart. Then he finished the last of the ham and made his way from the mess to his study in the headquarters building.

Once there, he looked at the stack of paper waiting on one side of the wall desk. He could only hope that it would hold routine seasonal reports. Mykel riffled through the papers, suppressing a groan. He'd forgotten about the training reports, and with the afternoon drills, he'd be writing late into the night for the days ahead.

At that moment, there was a knock on the door. A squad leader, wearing the white braid of the headquarters' staff, stood in the doorway.

"Captain Mykel, sir, Majer Vaclyn requests your presence in his study. At your soonest convenience, sir."

"I'll be right there."

Mykel only waited until the squad leader was away from his door before following him back to the south end of the building. The majer's study door was open.

"Have a seat, Captain." Majer Vaclyn gestured to the chairs in front of the desk. "Please close the door behind you." He was a typical Cadmian officer from pure lander stock, tall and muscular, blond, with fair skin and light green eyes. From appearances, except for the too-ruddy cheeks, he could have been Mykel's cousin. He wasn't.

"What have you heard?" Vaclyn leaned back in his chair. On the corner of the desk were an oily rag and a sharpening stone—recently used on one of the majer's throwing knives.

"Sir?"

"There are rumors all over the compound. I'd like to know which ones you've heard so that I can set you straight."

"The whole battalion's being sent to Dramur." Mykel offered an easy-going smile. "No one seems to know why."

"That's because no one has been told why, except the colonel. Your story has the basic parts right. Then, you always do get that right." Vaclyn gave Mykel a broad smile that the captain trusted not at all. The majer cleared his throat. "On Septi, Third Battalion will embark on the *Duarchs' Valor*. Full field kit, just like any deployment. The Myrmidons expect that our mission will take from two seasons to a full year."

Mykel waited to see if Vaclyn would actually tell him the mission.

"A significant number of malcontents who have been serving terms as bat-dung miners have managed to escape. There are only two companies of Cadmian foot stationed at the garrison there, and they provide security for the mine . . ."

Prison guards, in effect, reflected Mykel.

". . . Our task is twofold. First, we are to provide protection against the raids, both for the dutiful miners and for the local inhabitants. Second, we are to bring the fugitives to justice." Vaclyn paused, then asked, "Do you have any questions, Captain?"

While Vaclyn's tone was perfunctory, as if he didn't want questions, Mykel replied. "Yes, sir. What sort of weapons do these fugitives have? Do they have mounts? Are any of the locals supplying them?"

"We have not been given such details. Doubtless, we will be briefed in the next few days. Any shortages in your company's supplies, mounts, or authorized gear should be authenticated and reported by noon tomorrow."

"Yes, sir." Mykel offered a curious and open smile. "Sir . . . if I might ask, what is it like, talking to a Myrmidon colonel?"

"He was very direct, and very brief. They always have been when they've talked to me. And, Captain," added Vaclyn, rising as he spoke, "this afternoon's drills will be the last before we embark. I trust I'll see some improvement." After the briefest pause, he added, "Did you have a good furlough?"

"Yes, sir. It was good to see my family." Rising from the chair, Mykel offered a pleasant smile. Vaclyn's question had been little more than perfunctory, but he had asked.

Mykel nodded in respect, then left the majer's study, closing the door behind him. The majer's response to his question about the alector puzzled him. Kuertyl had suggested several long meetings, and the majer had said the meeting was short. Vaclyn had lied to Mykel before, but this time he had felt like he was telling the truth—and so had Kuertyl. Mykel had to wonder whom he was misreading. He hurried toward his study.

He kept walking, quickly, thinking. He and the squad leaders would have to audit all the equipment again, just to make sure nothing had disappeared in his absence. And then he'd have to finish all the reports after that.

11

On Duadi, Dainyl had made a point to be at Myrmidon headquarters for morning muster, since he would be the only senior officer there. Just before the glass, he stepped out of headquarters and strode into the courtyard.

"Company! Ready!"

The rankers and the undercaptains commanding each of the four squads stiffened. The pteridons did not move, but they seldom did at muster. The compound was more than a vingt square, not because of the number of Myrmidons but because each pteridon required its own quarters—and each pteridon square was thirty yards on a side with a massive perch across the roof. The muster of a Myrmidon company was impressive, for all that there were only twenty-one pteridons in a company, since a single company's pteridons in ground formation took up an oblong a good hundred fifty yards by a hundred.

Dainyl's eyes took in the nearest pteridon, the one behind Undercaptain Ghanyr. The blue leathery wings, when folded back against their bodies, were more than ten yards long. Extended, each wing was nearly twice that. The blue crystal eyes glittered like gemstones, but gemstones the size of platters. Beneath those eyes that held an inner darkness and seemed to take in everything and nothing was the long blue crystalline beak, hard enough to shatter iron. Dainyl's pteridon—when he had been an undercaptain—had used its beak to shear an iron bar as thick as his wrist with one quick snap.

The shimmering gray saddle was strapped in place at the thickest part of the neck, above the shoulders that anchored the wings. In the holder attached to each saddle was a blue metal skylance that, when fully charged with the combination of light and lifeforce, could spew forth a line of blue fire capable of incinerating a squad of men in an instant.

Each of the two comparatively short legs ended in three crystal claws—two opposed by one, so that a pteridon could grasp whatever it wanted, or perch in the most unlikely of locales, since the claws were as hard as the beak.

Three undercaptains reported their squads ready to fly, with most of third squad absent and accompanying the marshal.

"Stand easy," Dainyl replied.

Only the slightest easing of posture followed his words.

"The marshal and the captain are still in Iron Stem. They're likely to be there a while. I'll let you know more as soon as I do. Dismissed to duties."

As he turned, Dainyl thought he caught a sense of amusement from one of the pteridons. He'd often wondered what—and how—they thought. When a rider was injured or killed, the pteridon returned with the rider. It would not fly again without another rider—and transferring allegiance to another rider was an elaborate procedure unless the first rider was dead.

Pteridons were Talent-created creatures that tapped the forces of life and nature, and for that reason, there were only eight Myrmidon companies in all of Acorus. Still, eight companies had always been more than enough when a single pteridon and rider could take out an entire company of mounted rifles in a fraction of a glass. The number of pteridons was dictated more by the size of Corus and by the need for rapid communications that did not rely on the fourteen Tables than by any armed opposition—since there had seldom been any arms raised against the Duarchy except by infrequent and ill-organized lander and indigen uprisings over trifles.

Dainyl was headed back to his study when Zorcylt called out, "Colonel? There's a message here."

The senior squad leader held an envelope sealed in purple. The colonel recognized the seal of the High Alector of Justice. "It must be for the marshal."

"No, sir. It has your name on it."

Dainyl took the envelope. "When did this come in?"

"While you were inspecting the company, sir."

"Thank you." Dainyl headed back to his study. Anything from the

Highest—or his assistant—he intended to read in private. After closing the door, he checked the Talent-seal—unbroken—and then opened the envelope. The message inside was brief: "Your presence is requested at the Hall of Justice at the eighth glass today."

The seal was that of the Highest.

Dainyl left his study, heading back to the duty desk.

"I've already summoned the duty coach, sir," Zorcylt said.

Less than half a glass later, Dainyl was striding up the wide golden marble steps of the Hall of Justice, the morning sun of harvest falling on his back.

Above the topmost step rose the goldenstone pillars of the receiving rotunda, pillars rising thirty yards to the base of the frieze that extended exactly eighty-one yards from corner to corner. Above the frieze that depicted the aspects of justice conveyed by the Duarchy, the mansard roof of man-sized tiles glittered a hard metallic green.

The colonel stepped into the receiving rotunda, where under a glass hence petitioners would assemble. Overhead, twenty-seven yards above, arched a ceiling of pink marble, so precisely fitted that even an alector with full Talent could have detected no sign of a joint, or of mortar. Octagonal sections of polished gold and green marble, joined by the smaller diamond tiles, composed the floor of the receiving rotunda, each octagonal section of green marble inset with an eight-pointed star of golden marble.

Another set of goldenstone pillars separated the receiving rotunda from the main Hall, where the empty dais on the south wall held the podium of judgment. Dainyl's boots glided over the marble in the Hall empty except for him, as he turned left and continued to a pillar on the south side, behind and to the left of the dais. There, he paused, then vanished to the sight of those without Talent before reaching up and turning the light-torch bracket. While that very minimal use of Talent to conceal himself would not have misled any of the higher alectors, it was most useful—and required—to keep things hidden in plain view from the landers and indigens. As the seemingly solid stone moved to reveal an entry three yards high and one wide, only a Talented alector would have seen anything but a solid stone pillar. Beyond the entry was a set of steps lit by light-torches.

He stepped through the entry into the warmer air, and the stone closed behind him. For all his height and heavy muscle, his boots barely whispered on the stone steps. At the bottom of the long staircase, he turned right along a stone-walled corridor until he reached the next to last doorway on the north side. There he stopped. He had only gone any farther a handful of times, and only with the marshal.

"You may enter, Colonel." The alector who stood in the chamber was a tall figure with flawless alabaster skin, even paler than that of the colonel, with the same shimmering black hair, and deep violet eyes, unlike the deep blue of the colonel's. The older alector did not wear a uniform, or the garb used for administration of justice, but a tunic of brilliant green, trimmed in a deep purple, with matching trousers.

Dainyl inclined his head, murmuring politely, "Highest, I am here to serve."

"As are we all." After a moment, the High Alector of Justice continued. "How long has it been since the first translations to Acorus?"

"The very first? Slightly more than five hundred years." Dainyl contained his puzzlement at the question, one he had certainly not expected.

The High Alector shook his head. "That is what we have said, although nowhere is that written. The first fieldmaster struggled onto this soil more than twice that long ago . . ."

Dainyl kept a pleasant smile on his face, although he could sense that there was something wrong with what the High Alector said.

". . . Where we stand was covered with snow for half the year, and the Bay of Ludel was frozen over for most of that time. He was a lifemaster as well, and made changes to some of the animals who lived here." A wry smile crossed his lips. "You do not need to know all the details now. Suffice it to say that we have labored long and hard to bring warmth and prosperity and the benefits of Ifryn to this chill world."

"As we are doing on Efra, are we not?"

"That is true, although the task is easier there, because it is naturally warmer." The High Alector lifted his hand in a gesture that froze Dainyl's words. "That is not for us to discuss now. Your Talents do not lie in translation or life-forming, but in ensuring the peace here on Acorus."

"There is a particular problem, Highest?"

"All problems are particular, Dainyl. Those who talk of problems in general either fail to understand or wish to avoid or obscure the issues at hand."

Dainyl tried not to stiffen. His words had been spoken as courtesy, not in condescension or in arrogance. He waited for the High Alector to continue.

"Some of the steers have grown restless. With all the libraries and schools, some of them have learned nothing. Left to themselves, they would squabble like spoiled children. All around them are marvels, and yet they do not see."

Where? What do you wish of the Myrmidons or the Cadmians? Those were the questions Dainyl wanted to ask. Instead, he inclined his head politely. The High Alector would say what he wanted in his own time and in great detail.

"A group of steers, and perhaps even some from the older lander lines, are plotting a revolt in Dramuria. Marshal Shastylt has indicated such to you." The older ifrit looked to the younger officer.

"He left a brief message, sir. I have not seen any reports."

"The report from Majer Herryf went to the marshal and the submarshal. This majer would have two companies of Myrmidons patrolling the skies of Dramur. The marshal and I decided that you should evaluate the situation without reference to the report. That way you can confirm or modify the majer's views independently. It seems unlikely that a few unhappy steers could suddenly generate a revolt with any local support. What do you think of that possibility?"

"I would share that feeling, but if there is to be an insurrection, Dramur would seem a likely locale. The city garrison is small, and the harbor more easily defended. They are isolated from the high roads and Tables and thus cannot see all the benefits that accrue to them. There's been no recent history of hardship there, and they do not know how well off they are. Also, if the uprising fails, the rebels could flee to the Murian Mountains. The cliffs there would be difficult for the Cadmians to attack without taking significant casualties. The canyons are narrow enough that we could not use the pteridons to the fullest advantage."

"You speak as though you knew about this."

Dainyl felt the lifeforce pressure of the High Alector, but his own shields were more than adequate. "I have heard nothing. I'm not a liaison to the recorders of deeds, Highest, and neither the marshal nor Alector Zestafyn has passed any intelligence to me. I merely speculate on the basis of what I know about Dramur." He'd certainly flown over it enough in years past, and it could not have changed that much in the five or so years since he had last been there.

The High Alector nodded brusquely, his deep-set purple eyes remaining cold. "As you know, lifeforce conditions upon Ifryn will reach the point of accelerated diminishing returns within the next thirty years." He snorted once. "That may be too optimistic, but the High Fieldmaster would prefer not to risk a full-body translation anytime soon. Any resistance by the local steers must be quelled, and with as little knowledge passing among the steers as possible, particularly among the more educated and trained landers."

"I understand." Dainyl comprehended all too well. Both worlds—Acorus and Efra—were competing to see which would hold the Master Scepter of Life, and thus succeed Ifryn as the Ifrit capital under the Archon who ruled all alectors. Whichever did would receive the more Talented alectors from Ifryn and would become the better world upon which to live. By their nature, the more intelligent steers had always caused trouble. There was no help for it, not when intelligence was linked to strength of lifeforce. The High Fieldmasters would excuse minor uprisings and incidents as to be expected, but a large organized revolt in Dramuria could easily prejudice him against making Acorus the successor to Ifryn. "The High Fieldmasters . . ."

The ifrit in green laughed, long, melodiously. "Drecorat wants matters as uneventful as possible. All high fieldmasters have felt the same way. They care little about what is right or just. He once told me that there is no such thing as inherent 'right' or justice among all the worlds of the universe. The universe does not care. Its rules reward survival—and power. If you would have what you call justice, you must have the strength and the will to create it and to enforce it." The High Alector looked hard at Dainyl. "We must show that strength and will."

"As always." Dainyl would have liked a hint of what the Highest wanted in more concrete terms.

The older alector smiled, a hard and condescending expression. "We have already established grandeur and beauty and grace here. We have created peerless art, where there was none before. Out of mud and squalor we have built such, and it must not be undermined."

Left unspoken was the understanding of the price a world paid for such grandeur and beauty. "What would you have the Myrmidons do, Highest?"

"The Myrmidons? Nothing. I would have sent Submarshal Tyanylt, but . . . he felt otherwise. You are the acting submarshal, and the task falls to you. This appears to be a matter involving steers, and it should be handled by steers—except for you and two Myrmidons of your choice. They will take you to Dramuria. You will be there as my representative and to observe how the Cadmian battalion handles the situation."

"And the two pteridons at my disposal?"

"You may use them for dispatches and for reconnaissance. I would prefer that, unless matters take an unforeseen turn, the Cadmians deal with the matter."

Dainyl was getting a very chill feeling about his assignment.

"You may well understand what is not said, Colonel. I would appreciate that understanding remaining unspoken, even to your wife."

"Yes, Highest."

"Good. As Marshal Shastylt may have told you, the Cadmians will be traveling on the *Duarches' Valor*. They will leave Elcien on Septi and arrive in Dramuria no later than the following Tridi. You will leave on Septi. That should give you enough time to meet with the local Cadmian majer in Dramuria, the guild heads, and the council chief in Dramuria—and the director of the mining operation."

Dainyl nodded.

"If there is anything else, you'll know. As always, you must behave and act as if the highest of all alectors are the Duarches."

Why was the Highest mentioning that now? It was an unspoken code, and breaking that code had led to more than a few alectors' deaths in the early years. Had someone let the secret slip? Was that the source of the revolt?

"Enjoy your time away from Elcien." The Highest nodded to dismiss Dainyl.

The colonel half bowed, took a pace backward, and gave a last bow before turning and making his way back to the stairs.

As he climbed the steps and crossed the halls, more than a few thoughts swirled through Dainyl's mind. From what had been said, and not said, conditions on Ifryn were becoming even less favorable far earlier than anticipated. Dainyl suspected that the lifeforce mass there was declining precipitously. That, in turn, meant that the Duarches of Acorus were being pressed to build lifeforce more quickly. More coal would have helped, as would more of the fertile bat dung from Dramur. Instead, there was less of each, and using the pteridons would only draw more heavily on the world's reserves. The Highest was planning to use Cadmian lives, if necessary, to reduce such a drawdown.

Dainyl would have preferred to talk over his suspicions with Lystrana, but the Highest might well learn if he did—and that was not something Dainyl was about to chance, not after all the tens of years it had taken him to become a colonel of Myrmidons on Corus—and certainly not after what had befallen the submarshal.

He was also aware that his assignment was a cross between a test and an opportunity and that the Highest did not wish him to have the advantage of Lystrana's knowledge and wisdom.

He walked down the stone steps from the Hall of Justice to the waiting duty coach.

12

After muster on Duadi, Mykel conducted a gear inspection before returning to his study in the headquarters building. There, he took out the folders he had found earlier—those of the two rankers in his company from Dramur—Polynt from third squad and Chelosyr from fifth squad. After taking a last look through the folders, he wrote up three more of the individual training reports as he waited for Bhoral and the two rankers.

Then there was a knock on the door. "Sir?"

"Come on in." Mykel stacked his papers, stood, and watched as the senior squad leader ushered the two rankers into the study, closing the door after them.

Polynt was tall, angular, blond—and looked even younger than Mykel's brother Viencet. Chelosyr wasn't that much shorter than Polynt, but he was brown-haired, square-faced, stocky, and muscular, and seemed almost squat in comparison.

"You both know that we're headed to Dramur." Mykel studied the two.

Polynt moistened his lips, while the slightest hint of a smile hid in Chelosyr's eyes.

"Your records show that you're both from there. Is that right?"

"Yes, sir." The responses were almost simultaneous.

"Tell me about the mines there."

Polynt looked at Chelosyr.

The older and more muscular ranker shrugged, then looked at Mykel. "That's one reason why I signed up with the Cadmians, sir. Maybe, it just mighta been me, but always seemed to me that when they got short of miners, lots of fellows all of a sudden got caught doing things they said they hadn't and ended up serving terms in the mines. Fellows like me, younger sons of smallholders, folks who don't have a craft or much coin. Figured that I'd get a better deal in the Cadmians, and couldn't get much worse than staying in the shambles outside Dramuria. 'Sides, don't care what they say, that bat dung really stinks."

"How did they get short of miners?"

"Miners die. Knew of a couple got buried. Others got sick. Some couldn't take it and ran for the high mountains and the jungles. Guards got most of them—killed 'em—but some always got away. Not much of a life there, either, always looking over your shoulder."

"The ones who got away—did any of them get hold of rifles or weapons?"

"Don't know, sir. Never knew any, just heard stories."

Chelosyr knew more than that, but Mykel looked to Polynt. "What can you add?"

Polynt glanced from Chelosyr to Bhoral, then to the captain. Finally, he began, his voice low. "Heard tell . . . just heard, sir . . . could be that there's someplace worse than the mines. Couldn't think what it'd be. Dust . . . there's dust everywhere. Stinks, worse'n you can imagine. Takes years for the smell to leave anyone lucky enough to live through a term there. Guards there, they got whips with iron tips, leave a man's back wide open with one lash. Then the nightwasps get in the wounds. Hurts and itches so bad men'll throw themselves downshaft . . ."

Mykel had suspected something of the sort, but suspecting and hearing were not the same. He waited until Polynt finished before asking, "What's Dramuria like?"

Again, Polynt deferred to Chelosyr.

"Sort of like a cleaner version of Northa, except it's got some big houses on the hills, and it's a port . . . ships that carry out the bat dung, they bring back iron stuff, and tin and stuff that won't hold the stink. Other ships, they bring in cloth and regular cheese, wines . . ."

"Cheese?" asked Mykel.

"No milk cows on Dramuria, sir. Nightwasps bite 'em, and they waste away. That's what they say. Some half-tame aurochs for meat."

". . . won't let folks burn out the nightwasps, either," added Polynt. "That's 'cause they got a real sweet honey the factors make into a special drink, some kind of honey-brandy."

Mykel kept asking questions. In the end, he didn't learn that much more.

Once the two rankers had left, Mykel turned to the senior squad leader. "Anything else I should know?"

"I'm having Fessyt keep a close eye on Kalosyr until we're embarked."

"Woman trouble?"

"The idiot married a former pleasure girl from Northa. He says she's a former pleasure girl. I think she still is. She's betting he'll get it in Dramuria, and she'll get his back pay."

"How many others has she married?" asked Mykel dryly.

"Who knows? If he comes back, she'll have the marriage canceled on some pretext. If he doesn't . . ." Bhoral shook his head. "At least, he's not a squad leader with more than ten years in. This way, if it comes to that, there's no widow's settlement."

"What else?"

"We're short two mounts for replacements, but we should have them by Quinti . . ."

After Bhoral left another half glass later, Mykel stood, then left his study. He walked down the corridor, pausing outside the last doorway on the north end. He pressed down on the lever, opened the door, and stepped inside. The headquarters library wasn't that large, a room three yards by five with shelves against all the walls and a set of back-to-back bookcases in the middle of the room.

After searching through the shelves, he finally found a thin volume with a lacquered cover, entitled *Geography of Acorus*.

It took him a quarter of a glass to find the section on Dramur, and less than half that to read through it. There were no maps of the isle, and only a paragraph or so describing it.

> . . . the isle runs close to five hundred vingts from the northern tip to the southern cape, but is no more than a hundred and fifty vingts at its widest. The Murian Mountains run down the center of the isle, extending from the northern headlands to Mount Dramanat, a volcano located some fifty vingts north of the southern cape. The mountains

are rugged, their rock unstable, and have never been fully explored. The principal products of Dramur are guano and dyestuffs from shellfish, which come from the eastern side of the isle. Although the lands to the west of the mountains are fertile and suited to a number of crops, the main product is shimmersilk, from the golden spinning spider. The only sizable town or city is Dramuria, located on a natural harbor on the southeast side of the isle some seventy vingts north of the southern cape . . . less than half a score of other towns and no more than a score of villages and hamlets . . .

Mykel blinked. That was it. There was more about mere towns elsewhere, such as Hyalt in Lanachrona, than about an entire isle.

He shook his head. As usual, the books hadn't been much help.

13

In the dim light of the sitting room on the main floor of the house, Dainyl took a last sip of the brandy, then set the small goblet on the side table. "It's not bad." He stretched, lifting his long legs just off the green carpet, then let himself settle back into the armchair whose legs would have been too long for all but the tallest landers. "The landers do make good brandy."

"In addition to boosting the lifeforce of Acorus, you mean?" asked Lystrana.

"Someone has to. Although we need it, we certainly can't generate enough to sustain us."

"That's what the landers and indigens are for."

"And for making Acorus a better place for us." Dainyl picked up the goblet and took another sip. "It is good."

"Better than good, actually," replied Lystrana, "although Kylana is always claiming that everything here is second-rate compared to Ifryn."

"She might know. We were born here. She's one of the few recent translations who supposedly held a position of import in Illustra."

"Supposedly?" Lystrana laughed. "You mean that you have your doubts about Kylana?"

"No more than about her husband. He knows far more than he ever lets on. I wish I dared ask him about Tyanylt, but that wouldn't be wise."

"No, dearest, it would not be. Unlike the Duarchs, he does not have a loyalty imprint, but he would still report that."

Dainyl wouldn't have minded Zestafyn or the Duarch knowing some of the details of what had happened, but not his involuntary involvement. "Kylana bothers me. She's like all the others who've translated here recently. If it's not from Ifryn or if it hasn't been praised as the best in Illustra, then it must not be very good. Against that, how can we compare?"

"We can't, but there aren't more than a few translations every year."

"No. Ifryn's comfortable, and no one wants to take the risks—not until they don't have any choices."

"Of course. That's why the fieldmasters developed shadow matches. So they could imprint knowledge without the risks of leaving Ifryn and its comforts."

"They don't always take. Even when they do . . . I don't think I'd want to be either of the Duarchs," mused Dainyl. "Why would anyone want to have to have a partial shadow match?"

"You don't want power enough, dearest. They are those with great Talent who wish to be duarch, and who aspire to being Archon one day if the master scepter comes to Acorus, and they must have some check imposed on them to ensure their loyalty."

Dainyl snorted. "Shadow matches, loyalty imprints . . . all that misses the point."

Lystrana laughed. "What point? I don't think you made it."

"My point was going to be"—Dainyl paused and raised his eyebrows dramatically—"comparisons are dangerous. We know that translation changes appearance. Does it affect taste? Smell? How would we know? If things smell the same, is that because they do, or because a translated body senses smells relative to the new world?"

Lystrana held her glass, sniffing the brandy. "There isn't a good answer to that. It's subjective, and I'd subjectively say that this brandy is better than any we've had before. That shows improvement. Besides, we're still Ifryn, even if we're here. Until we have the master scepter here, we're still linked to Ifryn and the Tables."

Dainyl stretched again, stifling a yawn. "I suppose we'd better get some sleep . . ."

Lystrana straightened in her chair, but made no move to rise. "You're leaving tomorrow, and you haven't said much about your assignment. Are you fretting about it? It's not like you to be so quiet." Her eyes did not leave Dainyl's.

"There isn't much to say. I've told you what I know." He shrugged. "The Cadmian Third Battalion is being posted to Dramur. I'm being assigned to observe and report. That's one of the occasional assignments that fall to colonels, especially those acting as submarshals."

Lystrana laughed. "And the marshal wants to see just what you can do without him or me looking over your shoulder."

Dainyl grinned. "Marshal Shastylt never *said* anything like that." The Highest had, but he didn't have to tell Lystrana that. "What I don't understand is why, if they want to observe what I do, they're sending me to Dramur. The Highest can use a Table to look anywhere, but the Tables don't show alectors or anyone using Talent. So how can they observe what I'm doing, unless they have another alector there?"

"You're not *known* to have much Talent, not beyond strong shields and flying," Lystrana said. "Usually, when alectors are given observation assignments, they choose those known to be Talented."

Dainyl had thought about that. "That suggests that they don't think I could detect another observer? Or does the marshal wish to see if common sense can replace Talent?"

Lystrana raised a single eyebrow, and Dainyl raised both. He couldn't do just one, the way she could. They understood each other perfectly.

After a moment of silence, Lystrana asked, "Did you know that payments for the guano have dropped off in the last weeks, but those for the purple dyes haven't?"

"No, I didn't." He could have guessed about the guano, with what he did know, but he hadn't thought about the comparison between guano and dyestuffs. "Who pays for the guano?"

"Generally, the agricultural factors in Southgate, Tempre, and Borlan. They resell it to the lander growers. By using mals to mine it, the Duarches are effectively subsidizing the final prices." Lystrana did not quite look at her husband. "That's another way of subsidizing the growth of lifeforce mass. The more crops that are grown, the more they warm the world. It's not that simple, but it does work that way."

Dainyl knew he had to be careful, but he didn't see that talking about lifeforce mass would violate the Highest's orders. "Is there any relation between the amount of guano used and the increase in higher lifeforce generated?"

"There has to be, but I don't know what it is. Those at Lyterna would know. That's what they study, or part of it. Everything ties together. That's why we've pushed things like coal mining. Burning the coal helps warm the air, and in time those vapors and particulates help stimulate plant growth. Using coal also means that fewer trees are cut, and the older growth trees also boost lifemass more than newer growth. The landers still don't understand that replanting isn't the same, not for centuries. The same is true for iron and steel, and stone and brick. The more structures that are built of those, the less wood that is used, and that is more important over time, because stone structures last longer." She laughed apologetically. "I wouldn't even try to estimate how guano production and lifeforce mass growth might relate, except that lifeforce is like a pyramid. It takes a broad base of lower lifeforce to support a narrower base of a higher level, and that supports a narrower base above that . . ."

"And we're at the top of the pyramid, siphoning off the lifeforce that helps support us."

"So far as we know," Lystrana replied. "How would we recognize something higher?"

That was a good question, one for which Dainyl didn't have an answer. "Would we want to recognize something superior? Or would we be like Kylana, always insisting that whatever it was that was labeled good in Illustra was the best?"

"Be careful. Her husband does have the Duarch's car."

"And I have yours, which is even better." Dainyl rose from the chair, smiling and moving toward his wife, then extending a hand.

Lystrana took it, although she did not need it.

14

The greatest struggle that faces any people, especially a people who that would be great and leave an imprint upon a universe that offers neither reward nor punishment, is to see the universe as it is, not as they would have it be. Because all life begins with the irrational and evolves away from it, all beings capable of even the most basic of thoughts begin with an attachment to the irrational. Feelings precede thought, and all who have borne and loved an offspring understand the strength of such emotion. Yet that strength of feeling should serve a true perception of what is, and that perception must be grounded in what is observed, what can be proved, and what can be replicated, without fault, without deviation, time after time.

In any society, even in a higher civilization such as ours, only a comparative handful of individuals ever escape from the tyranny of the irrational. Nor should it be expected that any greater number should so advance themselves in that manner of thought and outlook. That is so because true perception requires one to turn his or her back upon the comfortable and the familiar and to question not only what others see as the acceptable and proper way of life, but one's own predilections and observations. Few have the strength and insight to do so; fewer still the will.

Of the insects, there are millions upon millions upon millions. Of the rodents and lizards and the fish in the streams and the oceans, there are millions upon millions. Of the cattle in the fields and the sheep in the meadows, there are many millions. Of those of our shape who toil in the fields and in the manufactories, there are millions. Yet, of those who lead and guide them, who see each world as it is, there are but scant thousands. That is the way of life and the universe. To see it otherwise is but an illusion of the irrational.

Views of the Highest
Illustra
W.T. 1513

15

As Dainyl had known from his own past experience, the flight to Dramur was long. While Quelyt and Falyna were more than courteous, Dainyl would rather not have ridden a pteridon as a passenger, in the second silvery saddle behind Quelyt, when he had once been a command flier. There was no help for that. Still, once he was airborne, with the wind in his face, and the land—or water—spread out below him, he felt much of the same marveling pleasure that he had in years past.

Pteridons were too rare to be spared for officers who did not fly regularly, not when the creatures were linked to one Myrmidon and could not be flown by anyone else. For all that, no pteridon had a name. None was necessary, because no pteridon answered except to his rider—or one of the highests who used special crystals in the rare cases when a rider could no longer ride—or was promoted out of that status, as Dainyl had been. Neither event happened often. Dainyl had been a rider for nearly eighty years, but then, so had many of the Myrmidons. Some had been riding for close to a hundred, but the average was closer to sixty. His time as a Myrmidon didn't count the more than ten years he'd toiled as a sandoxes second driver on the transport run from Hafin to Krost. Most younger alectors spent some time as drivers; it was both necessary and expected. Dainyl's term as a driver had been longer than most.

The first night, Dainyl and his escorts stopped at the Cadmian compound in Southgate, the usual resting point for Myrmidon couriers headed to Dramuria. While the tireless pteridons could have flown straight through, a full day of flying was more than enough even for seasoned Myrmidons. Dainyl was slightly sore on Octdi morning, although he would not have been stiff at all years before.

They were airborne again just before dawn and followed the coastline southeast, passing above the Dry Coast, so named because there were almost no sources of water—not rain, not streams, and not even wells or springs. The Dry Coast ran from twenty vingts below Southgate all the way around the southwest coast of Corus to the Southern Cliffs—nearly eighteen hundred vingts in all, with but a single town. The section to the west of the Southern Cliffs was the Empty Quint, although where the Dry Coast ended and the Empty Quint began was far from clear. Not that it mattered, since little lived there, and the high alectors in Lyterna had determined early on that attempting to increase lifeforce mass in that area would have been futile.

The one town along the Dry Coast was Ascar, some three hundred vingts from Southgate and slightly more than that from the northern cape of Dramur. A single small stream ran from the southern part of the Coast Range to Ascar, and there was a small natural harbor, used mainly because the fishing off the Dry Coast was among the best in the west of Corus.

The second day's journey consisted of several brief stops, a quick early midday meal at Ascar, a few more stops, then a longer leg over the channel and on to Dramuria.

As they flew southward over the water, every so often Dainyl looked back, more up and to his right, to find Falyna and the other pteridon. Because of the vortices created by the wings, all Myrmidon formations—or single trailing fliers like Falyna—always flew higher than those in front, a V formation that extended aft and upward as much as necessary.

When they reached Dramuria, late in the afternoon on Octdi, the two Myrmidon riders circled their pteridons twice around the Cadmian compound on the bluff on the northeast edge of Dramuria, directly above the harbor and the main portion of the town—set north of the small river that drained out of the Murian Mountains to the west and north. The town itself was built of local graystone, and all the roofs appeared to be of a reddish tile. Dainyl could not see any marked changes in either the town or its environs since he had last been there. Slightly more ground might have been cleared in the lowlands west of Dramuria, and the road that arrowed northwest to the mountains—and to the mine—seemed to have little traffic upon it.

The Cadmian compound was the same as any other in layout, except smaller, a stone-walled square half a vingt on a side, with the headquarters buildings directly behind the west-facing gates, and the barracks and officers' quarters on the north side, the stables and shops on the south, all separated by the central courtyard.

Falyna swept in first, the pteridon coming to a graceful flaring halt, wings wide, then settling onto the greenish gray stone of the central courtyard. Quelyt followed.

After dismounting, Dainyl had to admit to himself that he was glad enough to put his legs on the ground and stretch. Then he turned to Quelyt. "Thank you. A very good flight. I know it's not the same with a passenger, but I appreciate it."

"Thank you, sir." Quelyt nodded. "That last leg always seems so long." He grinned ruefully. "That's because it is, and there's no place to take a break."

They both turned at the approach of a Cadmian senior squad leader, who stepped up to them, stiffened to attention, and half bowed.

"Sir?" The squad leader looked up at Dainyl.

The Myrmidon colonel could sense the concern that bordered on fear.

"Colonel Dainyl. I'm here to see Majer Herryf."

"Yes, sir. Yes, sir. I'll send word to him."

The squad leader's words told Dainyl that either Herryf had not been told of his imminent arrival or he was not expected as soon as he had arrived. Dainyl hoped it was the latter.

"He's not here, in the compound, at the moment?"

"No, sir."

"Then we'll just get settled. Officers' quarters for three Myrmidons, and"—Dainyl gestured toward the square stone buildings with massive perches above them—"the squares for the pteridons."

"Yes, sir. The squares are always ready, and the senior officers' quarters are always ready, sir, and there are others. . . ."

"Good. I think I can find my way to the quarters. If you would take care of the fliers and their pteridons."

"Ah, yes, sir."

While Dainyl had been talking to the squad leader, Quelyt had unfastened the colonel's duffel. He handed it to Dainyl.

"Thank you," Dainyl said. "I'll check with you both after I talk to the major. We'll probably need to do some recon flights in the next few days."

"Yes, sir."

Dainyl turned, leaving the senior squad leader with the two Myrmidons and moving quickly toward the quarters on the north side of the compound. It felt good to stretch his legs. As he walked, he studied the almost-empty compound, far more vacant than it should have on an Octdi evening, even after duty hours. Did the Cadmians in Dramur take all of both end days off?

Another squad leader hurried toward Dainyl as he walked across the courtyard. "Colonel, sir . . . if you would allow me to help you?"

Dainyl smiled. "I can carry my gear, but guidance to my quarters might help."

"Yes, sir. This way, sir."

The officers' quarters were in the most northwestern of the structures along the north wall, directly north of the headquarters building. The visiting senior officers' quarters—effectively only for majers and above—were on the upper level of the two-story structure.

Dainyl found himself escorted to the quarters on the northwest corner.

There, the squad leader opened the door and gestured. "Sir, these are the best. Even the Myrmidon marshal found them most comfortable."

"Thank you. If someone would let me know when the majer arrives?"

"Yes, sir, Colonel."

Dainyl closed the door and stepped farther into the quarters, effectively a large room with an attached second chamber holding a bath and facilities. The bed was long enough, a full three yards. The writing desk was wide enough and set before one of the windows, with a light-torch in a wall bracket directly above.

He sniffed. The room smelled relatively clean, and he didn't sense any obvious vermin. He decided against bathing, but used the facilities and washed up before unpacking his duffel and hanging up his second uniform. It didn't need it, not when it never wrinkled. He left the light-cutter in its holster.

After walking around the room for a time, stretching his legs more, Dainyl seated himself at the desk. The desk chair and desk were almost too low to use, but he angled his legs to the side, considering what he'd seen on the flight in, and jotted down his thoughts.

He'd have to ask the council director about mine and the dyeworks. Lystrana wouldn't have mentioned them without a reason beyond the comparative note that the decline in guano receipts had not been accompanied by a corresponding decrease in other trade revenues.

He wrote down ideas as they came to him, for more than half a glass.

Thrap—the knock on the quarters' door was almost tentative.

Dainyl could sense that it was a Cadmian. "Yes?"

"Colonel, sir, the majer is here, and awaits your instructions and orders. He would like to know if you would you like him to come to your quarters, or to meet in the headquarters?"

"I'll meet him in the headquarters immediately." Dainyl stood.

"Yes, sir." The Cadmian turned and left.

Even though he had not met the majer, the man's attitude already bothered Dainyl. Dainyl was his superior officer, in more ways than one, and the man was sending a subordinate to inquire. When his own superiors wanted something, Dainyl didn't send undercaptains or squad leaders to find out. He just went. Sending subordinates was the mark of someone officious and all too willing to spend others' time.

The Cadmian trooper was waiting in the courtyard below the steps from the upper level, and Dainyl followed him across a courtyard darkened by the long shadows of the compound's western wall.

They entered headquarters through the front arched entrance, past a duty squad leader, who straightened, and stated, "Colonel, sir, welcome to Dramuria, sir."

"Carry on."

Dainyl continued toward the end of the corridor, but he could sense that, outside of his guide and the duty squad leader, and the majer, the headquarters building was deserted.

"That's the majer's study, there, sir," offered the guide.

"Thank you." Dainyl walked to the open doorway.

Majer Herryf stood just inside. "Colonel, welcome to Dramur." Herryf was short and dark, with short-cut stringy black hair and eyes that protruded slightly—clearly a Cadmian who'd worked his way up from an indigen background—or whose parents or grandparents had.

Dainyl nodded. "Thank you." He waited to see what the majer had to say.

"Colonel . . . I hadn't been informed that we would be receiving a senior Myrmidon officer, or I would have been here to greet you personally."

"Sometimes, messages don't always arrive in a timely fashion." Dainyl studied the chairs set before the majer's desk and decided to remain standing. "Since you haven't been notified, I'll make it very simple. Next week, probably on Duadi, a battalion of Cadmian mounted rifles will arrive here on the *Duarchs' Valor*. They are being deployed here to deal with the mining situation." He paused for but a moment. "Tomorrow, I'll need to meet with the director of the mines and the head of the governing council of Dramuria. I expect that you can set those meetings up after we finish here."

"Colonel . . . it is getting late in the day."

"I know, but you notified the marshal of a problem you felt required Myrmidon attention. I've flown two straight days to get here. This appears to be a matter of some concern. If it is, we should not worry about such . . . customs . . . as end-day relaxation. Should we?"

"Ah . . . not when you put it that way, Colonel. I'll do what I can."

"I expect to meet with them both tomorrow." Dainyl smiled coolly. "Now . . . what has happened here in the last week? Will we need to put the Cadmians into the field immediately?"

"Cadmians, sir? I had thought that perhaps a company of Myrmidons . . ." offered Herryf.

"When it does not appear urgent enough to discuss immediately? For a handful of disgruntled miners hiding in the hills?" Dainyl lifted his eyebrows.

"They are most resourceful, Colonel."

Dainyl could sense the impatience restrained behind the cultivated politeness. The majer was definitely a man who expected that people see things his way and no other. "Resourceful or not, a battalion of Cadmian mounted rifles should be more than enough." Dainyl paused. "That is, unless there is something that you did not convey in your reports."

"No, sir. I wrote out everything in my report to the marshal."

"Your report suggested the possibility of an insurrection, but I do not recall any detailed information on the weapons available to these would-be rebels."

"There's blasting powder missing. That's what the director of the mine reported. As I told the marshal."

"That is not terribly useful," Dainyl pointed out, "unless they have some way to turn it into munitions. Do you know if they do?"

"If I'd waited until they did, the marshal would not have been pleased."

"He is not displeased with you. He took your report seriously. That is why a full battalion of mounted rifles is arriving. You'll need to arrange to billet and feed them."

"Five companies of a hundred, sir?"

Dainyl nodded. "Now . . . what didn't you put in the report? The things you couldn't prove that worried you?"

Herryf smiled politely, but, again, Dainyl could sense the arrogance and calculation.

"The volume of guano shipments is down, and at this time of year, it generally starts to rise with the cooler weather. The mine director has been talking with the local justicer, and it appears that more young men are being sentenced to the mines."

"If they're troublemakers . . . ?" suggested Dainyl, trying to draw the majer out.

"Some are, but most are just careless. That's not good because their families are supporting the rebels. I can't prove that, but . . ."

"What else?"

"We had almost twenty rifles stolen," admitted Herryf. "They were listed as being in the armory. I *know* they were there in the spring, but they're not there now. Until this past year, we've lost less than one rifle per year."

"How did that happen?"

"I don't know, sir. That's one of the reasons . . ."

After a moment, Dainyl spoke. "You have two companies here, and they keep the compound, and serve as guards at the mine. Are all their rifles accounted for?"

"Yes, sir."

"By number?"

"Sir?"

"I suggest you check the maker numbers against the inventory. Or have you?"

Herryf looked down, his arrogance vanishing.

"Let me know the next time a rifle vanishes. Immediately."

"Yes, sir." With Herryf's ready assent came a sense of puzzlement.

Dainyl didn't bother to explain. He was beginning to see why the Highest had not wanted to send a company of Myrmidons. He also needed to find out a great deal more from Herryf, and some of that would have to wait until he knew what questions to ask.

Still . . . he could learn some things now. "How many men are assigned to the guard detail each day?"

"How many prisoners have been shot trying to escape . . ."

"How many of your Cadmians are from Dramur . . ."

Dainyl had more than a few questions. He also knew that he didn't know enough to ask some of the more important ones because he didn't know what they were.

16

Despite two long and tiring days of flying, on Novdi, Dainyl woke early—with the sky a dark greenish gray. He washed and dressed and made his way down to the mess, barely after dawn, where a sleepy-eyed cook fixed him egg toast and ham, with biscuits, and poured him a pitcher of ale. Like most alectors, he found that the ale helped in digesting the Corean food.

Only as he was leaving did he see a captain walking toward the officers' mess.

"Captain?"

The young-faced Cadmian captain stopped and stiffened. "Yes, sir, Colonel?" Like Herryf, he was dark-haired, and his skin was darker. Unlike the majer, he projected neither arrogance nor fear, just a sense of concern and puzzlement.

"I take it you have some sort of duty today?"

"Yes, sir. Two of my squads have mine duty."

"Do you go with them?"

"Usually, I let the senior squad leader take the morning, sir, and I relieve him at midday. The other squads are on standby here at the compound."

"Do the companies that aren't on duty have off all of Novdi and Decdi?"

"Yes, sir. The other company does. It's always been that way."

"Have you seen any signs of trouble with the miners?"

"There's always someone making trouble, sir. Complaining about the work-gang bosses or the food or something. They do it when they're in a group, and you can't see who's yelling."

"Anything besides complaining?"

The captain cocked his head, clearly wondering whether to say more. After a moment, he replied. "Some . . . we've had more of the mals trying to escape in the last season."

"Have any actually escaped?"

"I'd guess so, sir."

"You'd guess? You don't know?"

"It's like this, sir. The mine road crosses the Muralto River, and it's a good ten–twelve yards wide and more than five deep where the bridge is. The bridge crosses a gorge. Some of them have jumped from the bridge." The captain shrugged. "It's a good twenty yards, and it's pretty steep. Some of them hit the rocks and die right there. We've found bodies downstream, but the ones we don't find, there's no way to tell whether they made it or the sleuers got them."

"Where else do they try to escape?"

"Some try to climb the crags above the mine. The mals'll stage a fight, and when things settle down, someone's missing."

"You don't use your weapons to break up these fights?"

"Sir, begging your pardon. We try not to. If we did, we'd have a lot fewer miners."

"I'm sorry," Dainyl replied. "I should have seen that." He had seen it, but he wanted to hear what the captain said. "How many have tried to escape in the last season?"

"I'd have to check the records, sir. We keep track of that. I'd say . . . maybe ten, could be fifteen. Usually we find six or seven bodies, one way or another, out of every ten who try."

The colonel nodded. "Thank you, Captain. I'm sorry to have kept you from breakfast."

"I'll manage, sir." The young captain smiled.

Dainyl was ready to leave the man, but couldn't resist asking a last question. "What do you see as the problem with the miners?"

"A lot of them are scared, sir. They claim funny things are going on in the mine. We've never seen anything, but . . . the miners say there are things up there, and deep in the mine."

"I see." Dainyl paused. "Thank you."

"Yes, sir."

The captain headed toward the mess and Dainyl toward his quarters.

Once back in his room, the colonel considered what the captain had said, especially compared to what Majer Herryf had said. The captain had been telling the truth. So had Herryf. Yet one saw the mals doing the mining as frightened, perhaps terrified, enough to jump into rivers in gorges, and the other saw the mals as part of a rebellion.

He hadn't been in his quarters more than a quarter glass when there was a knock on the door. "Colonel Dainyl, sir?"

Dainyl moved to the door and opened it.

The Cadmian squad leader who stood outside his quarters door was short, broad-shouldered, with black eyes and a swarthy cast to his face. Despite the light brown hair, his antecedents were mainly indigen. "Squad leader Rhasyr, Colonel. Majer Herryf has detailed me to escort you." He smiled. "Majer Herryf arranged for an early meeting with Director Donasyr. The Council Director will be available after that at your convenience. I had one of the larger mounts saddled for you."

Dainyl could sense the general good nature of the squad leader, and that helped lift his irritation at the majer. At the very least, if Dainyl had been expecting a senior officer, he would have escorted the officer, and if he'd been unable for other reasons, he would have made sure the escort was an officer of appropriate rank. Then, there weren't that many officers. The one captain had duty, and there was only one other. "I'll be with you in just a moment."

"Yes, sir. I'll wait below for you."

After closing the door, Dainyl walked to the desk and folded the sheets of paper with some of his questions, slipping them inside his tunic. He checked his sidearm, then made his way outside and down the steps.

Rhasyr not only had two mounts, but two other Cadmian troopers as well. "An officer such as you, sir, you must have at least a small honor guard." He inclined his head.

"Thank you." Dainyl turned to the two rankers. "I appreciate your being here so early."

The younger of the two looked almost frozen; the older inclined his head, and said, "Thank you, sir."

Dainyl mounted, and the four rode across the courtyard to the open gates, where a pair of guards watched them leave.

Beyond the compound walls, the graystone road was less than four yards wide, and there was no shoulder, just reddish clay with scattered clumps of grass that was half-tan and half-green. As with all Cadmian compounds, the first half vingt away from the walls was level and clear, with the only vegetation being grass. Beyond that were low trees that were scarcely taller than Dainyl's head as he rode beside Rhasyr.

"What are the trees?"

"Casaran nuts. They are very bitter." Rhasyr grimaced. "They soak them in salt water and dry them. Then they crush them. They make good fodder for horses and livestock. We need it because there is not enough grass here for proper grazing, and the good grass only grows on the plains south of the big mountain."

"What other crops grow here?"

"Not much, sir. Everything except the wheat in the south comes from the west. The biggest crops are maize and the apple bananas. They have plantations for the bananas in the west, across the mountains. They're very tasty."

Dainyl hadn't heard of apple bananas. "Where are the dyeworks?"

"Those are at Santazl. That's on the bay south of Dramuria. Most of the young ones learn to dive early, and they bring up the purple clams. The black comes from the squiddocs. They must use nets for those, and heavy gloves. Poisonous things, and nasty. Some of the dyeworkers get killed every year. I don't know that being a dyeworker is much better than being a miner, except the dyeworkers can go home at night."

The road curved southward through a hillside cut, descending toward a stone bridge over a stream. Beyond the bridge, the fields and nut orchards ended, and the graystone houses began.

"How far?" asked Dainyl.

"The mining building is just across the bridge, and a couple hundred yards up the road that turns into the mine road farther out."

As they crossed the bridge, Dainyl glanced at the water, then upstream. So far as he could tell, no one was fouling the water. Clean rivers were important in growing lifeforce mass.

About fifty yards beyond the bridge, the four turned right at a stone-paved boulevard. They rode for but a fraction of a glass, before Rhasyr said, "There. That is the mining building."

The building before which Rhasyr reined up was a square one-story stone structure no more than twenty yards on a side. The red tile roof was highest at the rear and sloped forward, with eaves overhanging the front wall by a good three yards to form a covered porch.

As Dainyl dismounted and handed the reins of the bay to Rhasyr, a man stepped onto the smoothed stones of the porch.

"You must be the colonel. I'm Director Donasyr. Do come in." Like Herryf, Donasyr was short, squarish, and dark, but unlike the majer, his eyes did not bulge. They were a dark gray and deep-set under bushy black eyebrows. He wore a short-sleeved brown tunic and matching trousers, with dark brown boots.

"We will wait for you here, sir," Rhasyr said.

"Thank you." Dainyl stepped up onto the porch, then had to duck his head to go through the doorway into the narrow foyer, following Donasyr into a conference room holding a circular table and five chairs. The single window looked out on the empty boulevard.

"My study's filled with reports and papers." The mine director smiled, but only with his mouth. Behind Donasyr's pleasant and well-modulated voice, Dainyl sensed irritation and anger. "Take any seat, please."

Dainyl sat in the armless wooden chair that faced the window across the table. Donasyr either had to sit close to the colonel, or with his back to the window. The mine director sat down across from Dainyl.

"Tell me about what's happening at the mines that's different," Dainyl said.

"We're losing workers. Some are getting killed trying to escape, and some are escaping. Worst of all, none of them are working as hard as they used to. I've checked the food rations. I've even increased them some. That didn't help. For a time, I got Majer Herryf to send more guards, but that didn't help either. I switched the overseers around. That didn't help. I returned them to their original duties. That didn't help."

"Do you have any ideas why this is happening?"

"If I *knew,* I could do something about it." Frustration spilled into Donasyr's words.

"When did you notice this?"

"Midsummer. After the . . . incident. Two miners died. Found 'em at the end of a tunnel. Not a mark on them. None of the others could say how it happened. I even had one or two flogged, but that didn't change anything." Donasyr shrugged and gave the nervous headshake again. "After that, production dropped off, and the number that tried to escape went up. We've got more bodies than we did last summer, and production is down by almost two fifths."

Those were facts that no one had mentioned to Dainyl. "I'm a little surprised that you direct the mines from here," offered the colonel.

"You couldn't get anything done up there," replied Donasyr. "There's the smell, and the bugs. Also, I need to be down here to take care of the shipping and financial arrangements, and to keep track of the payments as they get transferred to our account in the Duarches' Bank."

"Who gets the payments?"

"They're split. The crafters and the guilds put up some of the money. So did the council, and a few of the eastern seltyrs. The return isn't that great after expenses, but it's created jobs and kept Dramuria independent of the seltyrs."

Dainyl talked to Donasyr for almost another full glass, but he wasn't certain that he learned much more than he had in the first few moments. More details, certainly, but nothing that shed any additional light on what was happening at the mine.

In time, he thanked Donasyr and left the building. Outside, Rhasyr and the other two Cadmians were waiting on the shaded front porch, although the midmorning sun had turned the day pleasantly warm for Dainyl.

The colonel gestured toward the docks. "The council building's still off the square?"

"They have talked about building a new one for years," replied Rhasyr, "but no one has."

The four mounted and began to ride into Dramuria. From all the carts and peddlers, Novdi was a market day. As they rode slowly down the middle of the main street, avoiding carts and wagons, Dainyl was aware that more than a few eyes focused on him. He listened to those murmurs he could pick up.

"Myrmidon officer . . ."

". . . means trouble when you see one of 'em . . ."

"Don't stare at him, Georgyt! They can kill you with a look . . ."

Dainyl was tempted to turn and smile at the woman and her small son, out of perversity. He refrained.

Like the mining building, the council building was a small graystone building with a red tile roof, but the tiles were far older, and many were cracked. The building was oblong, rather than square, and the front eaves only overhung the stone porch by little more than a yard.

Dainyl dismounted, again handing the bay's reins to Rhasyr, and walked toward the main entrance, a door painted a bright blue. Before he got there, it opened.

"Colonel Dainyl, do come in!" The voice out of the shadowed foyer behind the door was hearty, and Dainyl half expected a burly man, but the speaker was slight and rail-thin. "Might as well use my study. One place is as cluttered as another. Oh . . . I'm Sturwart, the current head of the council. For another season, that is."

"I'm happy to meet you, Sturwart."

"I figured it would be better for you to talk to Donasyr first. He likes to spend end days at his place out west in Cyalt. The later you talked to him, the less he'd tell you." Sturwart scurried ahead of Dainyl down a corridor and through another doorway. He gestured at the study, more spacious than the conference room at the mining building, with a desk stacked with papers, a small square table with three chairs, half-filled with papers, and two bookcases overflowing with volumes. The two windows were high and narrow, and open.

Dainyl settled into one of the chairs at the table, gingerly.

Sturwart dropped into the chair across from the alector. "Anyway, you probably know as much about the mine as Donasyr does. He's never out there, just collects the coins, writes the reports, and leaves the running to the overseers and the guards. Today, he'd tell you less than he would most days because he'd already have been in Cyalt if he hadn't had to talk to you."

"His family is there?"

"Hardly! His wife likes the big place on the hill here in Dramuria better. He's got a girl in Cyalt, more like his daughter's age. Everyone knows it. Then, with a wife like his—she's a beauty all right, but got a tongue like a sabre—I'm not sure I wouldn't be tempted that way."

"You say that the overseers run the mine?"

"Every way that counts, every way that counts . . . and most of them are good men. Do the best they can. Sad business when people get sent there."

"Some have said that justicer sentences to the mine are more frequent when Donasyr needs more miners," suggested Dainyl.

"I've heard that for years. Heard it about Haldynt—he was the one the guilds picked to run the mines before Donasyr. I can't say it might not happen now and again, but mostly it's the other way around. When there are too many young men without places to go—apprenticeships, or the Cadmians, or family lands—they get in trouble, drink too much, fight too much, and they get sent to the mine. The families complain that the justicer was told to get more miners. The justicer denies it, and that just makes people think that he's lying."

Dainyl got the impression that Sturwart was telling the truth. "That's always a problem."

"Always been a problem, and always will be. What else can I tell you?"

"Who gets the golds after the merchanters in Southport or wherever pay for the guano?"

"They come to the council, most of them. The mine belongs to Dramuria, the town itself, the crafters and guilds and partly to a few of the big growers. They have a fifth. Been that way forever. The council approves Donasyr's requests for what he's spending. He has a good year, and he gets a bit extra. Not a lot extra, though. Don't want him holding back on food to the miners, or tools. That'd be a bad business. We also pay for one of the Cadmian companies."

Dainyl had not known that. "What can you tell me about the troubles at the mine?"

Sturwart tilted his head and paused for a time, the longest he'd been silent since Dainyl had been in the council building. Finally, he spoke, more slowly. "You know . . . I wish I knew. Production's down, but the miners aren't getting fed any less. Went up there a bunch of times to check. Even went when no one knew I was coming. I've been talking to the ones whose terms were over, too. They won't talk. Scared-like, but they're not scared of the guards or the overseers. Something's going on in the mine, I'd say, and it's happening when the overseers aren't watching." Sturwart looked straight at Dainyl. "Couldn't prove it any way that I know."

"We received a report about disgruntled miners starting a revolt . . ."

Sturwart laughed, shaking his head. "Donasyr keeps track of that, and so do we. Always be folks who won't learn that life has rules. You work, or you go hungry. You don't want to work at what's here, you join the Cadmians, or go someplace else, or you get stuck in the dyeworks or the mine. Some won't learn, and they end up in the mines, and the rules there are tougher. Some can't take it, and they try to escape. There were fewer than twenty who weren't accounted for in the last year. Don't know about this year. Even if they all made it, twenty of that kind wouldn't begin to start a revolt."

Dainyl nodded, sensing once more that the council head believed his own words totally. "Why do the growers own a fifth of the mine?"

"Years back, town needed golds to finish the road paving and the buildings up there. The growers around here put up the coin, and they get a fifth of the proceeds after expenses. Or they can get more of the guano at a reduced price, or some combination."

"Do any of them take the guano?"

"Some, like Ubarjyr, use it on their casaran plantations."

"Where could I find the heads of the guilds?" Dainyl had strong doubts he'd learn anything from the guild directors, but the Highest had suggested he talk to them.

"You won't find Bleamyr or Tulcuyt today or tomorrow. I can arrange for you to meet them here on Londi, say around the ninth glass, in the morning."

"I'll be here," replied Dainyl, rising.

"That's for certain. One can always count on the Myrmidons. Always can." Sturwart rose and headed toward the doorway and the corridor beyond. "Any other questions you have, I'll be here, too, on Londi."

"I'm sure there will be some. I appreciate your patience and willingness to be here."

"Glad to be of help. Without you, we wouldn't have a whole lot, now, would we?"

Dainyl smiled again as he left the building, glad to be out in the warmth of the white sun, under the cloudless silver-green sky. He mounted, then nodded to Sturwart, before looking at Rhasyr. "Back to the compound."

"Yes, sir."

Dainyl could tell that the stalwart Rhasyr was relieved to be heading back to the compound, both from his feelings and from the fact that he and the others kept blotting their brows. Dainyl was enjoying the day, one of the most comfortable he'd experienced in almost a season, but it was unseasonably hot, even for the local Cadmians.

After they crossed the bridge and headed up the wide and curving incline toward the compound, ahead to his left, Dainyl sensed someone radiating fear. He could not quite locate the source, and as the bay carried him onto the flat of the bluff, with the compound little more than two vingts ahead, his eyes and Talent scanned the area to his left, amid the nut trees.

Crack, crack.

He was rocked back in the saddle, his right shoulder twisted violently. He hadn't even been able to locate the sniper. Even so, the light-cutter was in his left hand almost instantly, and his eyes jerked to his right, his Talent probing for the source. He could sense a single man on the low rise in the middle of the trees less than a hundred yards away, and another sprinting away.

Drawing on the lifeweb, he raised a deflection shield around his head and neck as he turned the bay off the road.

"Sir!" called Rhasyr from behind him.

The man remaining raised his rifle once more, but this time the shot went wide, as did the third and fourth shots.

Dainyl was less than thirty yards away when, abruptly, the man dropped the rifle, next to another weapon lying on the clay. One hand went to his belt, then to his mouth. He swallowed and smiled as Dainyl reined up. He was not wearing anything like a uniform, just a shapeless gray short-sleeved shirt, and gray trousers—and sandals, rather than boots. His beard was unkempt and his brown hair greasy and long.

Dainyl glanced to the north, but trying to find the other shooter would have been difficult, and he needed to find out what he could from the one at hand. "Why did you fire at me?" Dainyl kept the light-cutter aimed at the man, even as he tried to sense if there were others around besides the man who had fled. He found no one. Behind him, he could hear the three Cadmians.

"To kill you. You are a monster. All of you are monsters."

"All of who?"

"You alectors. You do not belong here."

"Who told you that?" probed Dainyl.

"Those who know, even better than you." The man swallowed convulsively, again. "You . . . will . . . see."

Dainyl could see his lifeforce fading. Then the man pitched forward, dead.

"Sir?" called Rhasyr. "What happened?"

"He shot at me," explained Dainyl. "He swallowed something—poison."

A look of surprise and horror passed between the Cadmians.

Dainyl did not show the surprise he felt. It had been years since anyone had fired at him. The bullet had flattened against the lifeforce-reinforced uniform tunic. While it had not penetrated the tunic, the fabric had spread the impact across the front of his upper chest and shoulder, and he would have an enormous bruise across his chest and shoulder in the days to come, even after drawing on the lifeforce web.

"Get his body and carry it back to the compound. His rifle, and the other one there, too."

"Ah . . . sir . . . ?"

"Whatever he swallowed won't hurt you." Dainyl waited as one of the junior Cadmians dismounted, recovered the rifles and handed them to Rhasyr, then hoisted the body of the man across the front of his own saddle.

When the Cadmian had remounted, Dainyl turned his mount back toward the road . . . and the compound. While he hated to draw lifeforce, he left the physical shield in place.

Lystrana had warned him, and he never underestimated her abilities. He just hadn't expected an attack from such a quarter and so soon.

The most puzzling aspect of the day had been the man who had shot at him, then killed himself. There were always some who disliked alectors. That was to be expected. What had been so unusual had been the man's words. He clearly had been indoctrinated somehow, and whoever had done the indoctrination had told him only part of the truth. Alectors certainly were not native to Acorus, but neither were the indigens nor the landers. So who was behind the attempt? Did they really think that they could kill more than a handful of alectors? What good would that do—for anyone?

Dainyl couldn't say he understood, but he knew he needed to, and quickly.

17

Immediately after breakfast on Decdi, Quelyt and Dainyl were airborne under high and hazy white clouds, soaring northwest from the Cadmian compound toward the jagged peaks and spires of the Murian Mountains, where lush greenery alternated with black and red rock.

Dainyl leaned slightly left to get a better view of the road to the mine. His right shoulder sent a jolt all the way across his body. He could only hope that the soreness and stiffness would subside within a few days. Majer Herryf and the Cadmians were trying to identify the dead man, and to see if the rifle—which was clearly Cadmian issue—had come from the garrison at Dramuria. Dainyl doubted that it could have come from anywhere else, but if it had, he was facing a much bigger problem.

He studied the road that led to the guano mine, empty except for two wagons rumbling downhill toward Dramuria. Once below the switchbacks just southeast of the mine, the road traveled straight along a ridgeline leading southeast to Dramuria, through the town, and to the high-walled covered bins at the southeastern section of the docks, where the guano was stored waiting for shipment to Southgate or the river ports of the Vedra.

Even from the air, the mining compound looked secure. The compound was set on a triangular bluff with the Muralto River below. The western end of the bluff was blocked by a stone wall with a single gate. A second wall with another gate crossed the bluff about a third of a vingt to the west of the first. The space between the two was bare red clay. There were no walls on the top of the bluff, just the cliffs to the river below.

The cliffs that dropped to the river from the bluff were sheer, and at their base was a rocky shingle that sloped into the river. The stone at the base was wide enough that diving into the water from the bluff would have been impossible, and the height of the bluff, a good hundred yards, would have made climbing down extraordinarily difficult.

"Toward the mine, now!"

The pteridon's wings lifted it into a climb as it headed to the northwest.

The mine was even less to look at—a single cavelike opening, around which was a circular area of flattened rock and clay. From that apron a narrow road wound down from a single guarded gate through four switchbacks. Carts were pulled out of the mine by teams of miners in harnesses, then dumped from a ramp into the guano wagons.

Three wooden guard towers ringed the apron, and a stockade fence joined the towers and ran from the innermost towers to clifflike sections of the mountain. The only exit was through the gate to the road beside the southern guard tower. If the guards were distracted, an extremely agile miner might get over the fence, but the sides of the rock apron were totally exposed, and it seemed highly improbable that large numbers of miners could have escaped.

The colonel looked back and studied the road. Between the mine itself and the miners' compound below, the road was enclosed by a stone wall on both sides, and beyond the wall were steep slopes and open rock faces. As the Cadmian captain had told Dainyl, there was one bridge, over the gorge to the northwest of the compound.

"Quelyt? Can you circle up around some of the lower peaks here?"

"Yes, sir."

The pteridon climbed once more, circling up and toward a rocky spire several vingts due west of the guano mine. Dainyl could see another cave, higher and to the west, and could sense a concentration of lifeforce—more bats, and another source of guano in the future.

The Murian Mountains were not that high, rising between two and three thousand yards above the sea. Flying above the higher summits, with several hundred yards to spare, was close to the highest point a pteridon could fly. Above four thousand yards, and less over desert areas or ice and snow, the pteridons could not draw enough lifeforce to hold altitude—or sometimes, as the earliest Myrmidons had unfortunately discovered, to exist at all.

Dainyl tried to gather in a sense of the lifeforces. There was certainly life there, but, with the exceptions of another two bat caves and several bird rookeries, not the concentrations that would have marked small settlements or a rebel camp.

Then . . . after several circles of the rocky spire, for an instant, just an instant, Dainyl sensed two flashes of lifeforce—traces he had never sensed before. One was a faint red-violet, and the other, nearly a mist somewhere beneath him, was golden green.

"Can you come down a little?" he called to Quelyt.

"Not much, sir. Could hit a downdraft here."

"As much as you can, then."

Quelyt was being more cautious than Dainyl would have been, but then, the pteridon was carrying double, and Quelyt wasn't that familiar with the terrain.

After another lower circle, during which Dainyl could sense nothing, he called to the ranker, "You can head back to the compound now."

"Yes, sir."

As the blue-winged flyer soared down and to the southeast, Dainyl wondered what creature—or creatures—could have a red-violet and golden green lifeforce. Red-violet wasn't that different from pteridons, but it had not been the same. Dainyl knew pteridons. And he'd never sensed anything golden green. Ifryns all were purplish, if in different shades, and landers and indigens ran from black to yellowish brown. Yet the contact had been so brief that he wasn't certain what he had sensed. He couldn't report that to the marshal, not when he'd been so careful to hide the extent to which Lystrana had been able to help him develop his Talent.

By the time the pteridon settled onto the stones of the Cadmian courtyard, it was close to midday, and pleasantly warm despite the high hazy clouds.

Dainyl dismounted, then turned to Quelyt. "Thank you. I may need your help later."

"Any time, sir. Not as though we're doing dispatch flying here."

"One of you may have to do that, when I have to send a report to the marshal."

"We figured that, Colonel." Quelyt grinned. "The marshal always wants reports."

"We'll see." After a smile and a nod, Dainyl turned and walked swiftly across the sun-warmed stones of the courtyard to the headquarters building. The compound remained almost empty, except for the end-day duty squads and officer. He doubted that he would find Majer Herryf in his study, even though he had asked the majer to make sure that the dead man and the rifle were investigated immediately.

Before Dainyl had gotten three steps into the building, the duty squad leader rose from his desk in the foyer. "Colonel, sir, Captain Meryst is standing by for you, sir. His study is the second one on the left."

"Thank you." Dainyl wasn't at all surprised. Herryf was the type to delegate anything that infringed on his time.

Even before the colonel reached the study door, the captain was on his feet, half-bowing in respect. "Colonel, sir." Captain Meryst was not the one Dainyl had met before. Unlike Herryf and the other young captain, Meryst was fair-skinned, if not white like an alector, with small freckles across his face. He was tall for a lander, close to two yards, and painfully thin.

"Captain. You had the duty today?"

"No, sir. That's Captain Benjyr. He's at the mine. Majer Herryf said you wanted anything we could find about the man who shot at you as soon as we could."

Dainyl gestured to the desk. "You can sit down." He took the single chair across from the captain. It was low, and his knees felt cramped enough that he wished he'd remained standing. "What have you found out?"

"The man had been a miner. That was easy. The miners are tattooed.

There's a number on their left ankle. The man who shot at you escaped over a year ago. Devoryn was his name."

"Was there any record of how he escaped?"

"Yes, sir." Meryst frowned. "Most of them jump or dive off the bridge. Devoryn didn't. Somehow he was one of the handful that no one saw escape. He just wasn't there when they mustered them to go back. I did check the records for the last two years. Until this year, there were only four like that. About eighteen, if I counted right, that went off the bridge that we never found any traces of."

"How many went off the bridge and didn't make it?"

"Thirty-three, sir."

That surprised Dainyl. "How many miners are there? Some two hundred?"

"Right now, the roster lists two hundred and seventeen."

"How many have died while serving in the mine?"

"Not that many, sir. Eight over the past year, and most were in accidents."

"But a fifth of them have tried to escape in ways that kill more than half of them?"

"More like a tenth, sir. You see, maybe half the miners in a year are there for five to seven months—for the minor offenses."

"Do you know if this . . . the one who shot at me . . . if he had been there more than once?"

"I'd have to check more for sure, sir, but I don't think so. The number on his ankle is one of those used about a year ago, and he escaped in the late winter."

"What about the rifles?"

"They were from here, sir."

Dainyl looked at the captain, raising his eyebrows.

"Ah . . . it looks like . . . I mean . . ."

"Are you trying to say that one of the rankers either lost or gave his rifle away, then took one from the armory? And that the one that the escaped miner had was that ranker's rifle?"

"Ah, not exactly, sir. The missing rifle belonged to a squad leader named Hirosyt. He finished his term a month ago, and no one knows where he went."

"So . . . he lost or gave the rifle to one of the rebels, and used his position as a squad leader to lift another rifle from the armory?"

"It looks that way, sir."

"I would strongly suggest, Captain, that every rifle in both companies be checked against the records."

"We've already started, sir. We'll know by tomorrow."

"What about the other one?"

"It's a standard Cadmian rifle, and it was never issued to anyone. Someone took it directly from the armory."

Dainyl asked another round of questions, and a full glass passed before he stood to leave. "Thank you, Captain. I look forward to hearing what you have to tell me tomorrow."

"Yes, sir."

As he walked back toward the mess, Dainyl considered what he'd learned. First, there was a way to escape the mines that wasn't suicidal. Second, conditions had to be even worse in the mines than anyone believed. When that many miners tried escapes with such a high fatality rate, something was driving them. His thin lips curled. Ifryn was dying, and even Talented alectors were hesitating in trying translations to Acorus and Efra—and death was certain in time if they didn't. Yet death was far from certain as a miner, but people were dying to get away.

Dainyl had already suspected that the so-called rebellion had to have been helped by someone in the Cadmian compound. The question was just how many rifles the rebels had. There weren't any other sources of weapons, not in any large numbers. While smuggling was possible, he would have thought it highly unlikely, if not impossible, given that rifles were only produced in Faitel and Alustre, and only for Cadmian units.

The other troubling thing had been the escaped miner's words. Dainyl had no idea who would have known what the man had said—except another alector—and that was a frightening thought indeed. It just wasn't something that an alector would do, and Dainyl doubted that there had even been any alectors in Dramur during the time the prisoner had been in the compound or afterward. The more he learned, though, the less he liked what he was finding out.

18

At the ninth glass on Londi morning, Dainyl walked into the council building. Sturwart and an angular blond man waited in the director's study. Both stood as Dainyl entered.

"Colonel, this is Bleamyr," offered Sturwart. "He's the head of the crafters' guild. Tulcuyt will be here shortly, but he was out on his boat this morning, and had some trouble with his nets. Can't see as I'd be adding much. So I'll leave you two and let you know when Tulcuyt comes in." With a smile and a nod, the council director departed, closing the door behind him.

"Colonel, we don't see Myrmidons often," said Bleamyr, a puzzled tone to his words.

Dainyl sat down on Sturwart's desk, then gestured to the chairs. "Please sit down. The chairs are a bit small for me."

"I can see that." Bleamyr smiled. "Sturwart said you might have some questions."

"I have a few, because of the mine. Have any alectors been here recently, besides me?"

"Not for a few years, leastwise," replied Bleamyr. "I don't think we've seen an alector here since, well . . . after the big storm that bashed up the harbor, and that was a good six years ago. We send our reports every quint, and that's been it."

Dainyl nodded, catching the feel of truth in the crafter's words. "What is your craft?"

"Me? I'm an ironworker. In the old days, I'd have been called a smith, but things like nails, bolts, all that, they come out of Faitel and arrive here in boxes and crates. Most of what I do is decorative ironwork, grillwork, or locks and bars for strong rooms, that sort of thing."

"Do you do work for the mining compound?"

"Just when something needs repairing. Probably been a half year since I've been there."

"I'd heard that more young men were being sentenced to the mines. What do you think?"

Bleamyr squinted, although the chamber was dark, with the light-torches off, and the sole light that coming through the two high windows. Finally, he answered, "Every few years, someone says that. We started keeping track of the ones who were in the guild. Year in, year out, it doesn't change. It's mostly those who drink too much, or those who think they're fitted for better tasks."

"Did you ever know someone named Devoryn?"

Bleamyr snorted. "He's in the mines now, unless something fell on him. He was one of the troublemakers. Used to be a laborer for Asadahl, the plumber. Must have smelled too much lead. Kept telling everyone that Asadahl stole the plumbery from his uncle. Asadahl gave him the job out of charity. Devoryn was always wandering off. Said he needed time to himself, up in the hills. People would ask him why, but he never said. That was one thing he'd close his mouth about, and it was always open. Anyway, it must have been two years ago, Devoryn went out of his head and tried to brain Asadahl with a lead ingot. Busted his arm. Justicer then, that was Goeryt, sent him to the mine." Bleamyr paused. "Why did you want to know, Colonel?"

"He was one of the miners who escaped who we know survived."

"Well . . . he spent enough time in the hills and in the rugged places south of the mine. I suppose he could have made it, if anyone did. How did you know he survived?"

"He tried to shoot someone, and the Cadmians caught him. He took poison."

"Sounds like Devoryn. Never did have much sense. Him and his wild ideas."

"What were those ideas?"

"You know, I don't know. Never paid any attention. No one with any sense did."

They might not have, reflected Dainyl, but he wished they had. "There's been talk of the escaped miners trying to take over the town, even all of Dramuria."

"That's Majer Herryf again. Not that I have anything against the majer, but he's talked to us at least three times in the past season about that. Says there could be a hundred miners up there, and if they got the shamblers and the plantation workers together, they'd outnumber his Cadmians." Bleamyr shook his head. "That'd never work. Even if they did overrun the Cadmian compound, one company of your Myrmidons would fry them in moments."

"That's what's puzzling about the talk," Dainyl replied.

"The only thing I can figure is that there have been more miners getting away than the majer realized, and he figures he's got to do something. There's nothing to live on up in the higher hills, not for more than a handful of men. They're already raiding and stealing stuff from the outlying plantations. The majer told the growers that guarding the fields wasn't the Cadmians' task. I've heard that some of the plantations have been using dogs at night. That's here in the east. The big western growers, they don't have to worry."

"Have you heard anything else? Do these men have weapons?"

"Some say they do. Some say they don't. I don't know . . ."

Dainyl kept asking questions, but learned nothing significantly new, either about the mines, the so-called rebels, the guilds, or about Bleamyr.

The door opened. "Colonel . . ." Sturwart's voice was apologetic. "Tulcuyt's here."

"I'll be with him in just a moment." Dainyl stood and looked at Bleamyr. "Thank you very much. You've given me a much better idea of what we're facing."

"I don't know that it changes things much, but anything you want, I'll try to help with."

Bleamyr left, and Tulcuyt—a man with a weathered and leathery face—walked in and half bowed to the colonel.

In the next glass, Dainyl learned almost nothing new or different from Tulcuyt, except that the boatmen had seen a number of fast schooners—the kind used by smugglers—off-loading in a sheltered cove some thirty vingts north of Dramuria several times over the summer. What they were off-loading, Tulcuyt didn't know, because no fisherman would tangle with armed smugglers, except there were crates being passed to the flatboats receiving the smuggled goods.

In the end, Dainyl thanked the head of the fishers' guild, as well as Sturwart, and left the council building. Rhasyr and the two Cadmians were waiting outside, patiently.

"Back to the compound. I don't think I'll be leaving it again today."

"You would not mind, Colonel, sir," asked Rhasyr cautiously, "if we did not tell Captain Benjyr that, not until after the midday meal, sir?"

Dainyl laughed. "Right after the midday meal."

"Yes, sir."

Back at the compound, after getting something to eat and retrieving his flying jacket and gloves, Dainyl searched out his Myrmidon rankers. He found them in the sunlight next to the squares where their pteridons were sunning themselves.

"Colonel?" Quelyt and Falyna straightened.

"Who wants to take me flying?"

"Might be better if I did, sir," replied Falyna. "Trading off works better. Where to, sir?"

"There's a cove on the coast, maybe twenty-five vingts north of here. I'd like to go there, then head west to the mountains. Smugglers have been landing things there. I'd like to see if there are trails or paths to somewhere north of the mine."

"North, it is." Falyna grinned. "I'd rather fly than sit around, sir."

Dainyl understood that all too well. In the past, when he'd been a lowly ranker, he'd spent far too much time waiting to fly, rather than flying.

Within moments, Falyna had donned her jacket and gloves, and the pteridon was carrying the two Myrmidons northward along the coast. For the first ten vingts there was an outer bank, mostly of sand, if with some grass and bushes, but the bank vanished when the coastline swung more to the northeast. Dainyl only saw three fishing craft, all in the protected waters between the inner shore and the outer bank.

The cove was as Dainyl had envisioned from Tulcuyt's description, a half circle less than a vingt across cut out of a low bluff, with an entrance no more than a few hundred yards wide.

"Lower, if you can, above the beach, when you head west!"

"Yes, sir."

Dainyl thought he could make out a narrow footpath threading between the man-high, greenish gray, brush olives, the kind with long and sharp thorns. There was a natural depression or narrow valley that led upward toward the hills, and the mountains beyond, almost between two plantations that held the nut trees. Dainyl could make out the path—or a path—in places, but he didn't Talent-sense anyone on or near it. Still, he wanted to see where the trails from the cove might lead. As Falyna neared the higher hills, the valley ended, and so did any trace of the path.

"Take us up, in the higher ranges right ahead," Dainyl called.

With the plantations so close to the hidden trail, if the escaped prisoners were anywhere, they had to be higher in the hills, perhaps even in the mountains beyond.

Circling to gain altitude, several times, the pteridon lurched in the turbulent air, but finally rose above the lower peaks.

A glimmer—or a reflection from something to Dainyl's left—caught his eyes.

Dainyl concentrated. On the edge of the short bluff below a peak, still several hundred yards above them, there was something . . . something that drew both his eye and his Talent. Was it a faded golden green? He wasn't sure.

"Can you get over that bluff?" Dainyl called. "The one just to the left above us?"

"We can try, sir. It's getting rougher."

The pteridon strained, and the blue wings lifted them higher, until they were almost level with the edge of the bluff. For a moment, Dainyl could make out a golden archway—hidden back inside a natural cave, but they swept past, and the rock blocked his view.

Then the pteridon's left wing was buffeted upward, and they slid sideways through the air, losing hundreds of yards, before Falyna and the pteridon recovered, all too close to another jagged ridge that had been well below them moments before.

"Better head back, Colonel." Falyna gestured to her left, where the clouds had moved closer and gotten darker.

"Go ahead." If Dainyl had been flying solo, he would have made another pass, but the pteridon was carrying double. That reduced maneuverability and the altitude the pteridon could reach.

Dainyl looked back once more, but he could see nothing of the mysterious cave.

After they had landed in the courtyard and dismounted, Falyna turned to Dainyl. "A little touchy there, Colonel. I'm sorry we couldn't get any closer, but the wind was picking up, and there was a good chance of another downdraft—"

"In better weather, could you set me down on that bluff?"

Falyna frowned. "If we went at dawn. The air would be colder, and calmer. That'd be worth another couple hundred yards in altitude." She paused. "Might I ask why, Colonel, sir?"

"There's a building inside that cave. We didn't build it. I don't think the locals did, either."

"You think it's the rebel miners?"

"I don't think they built it, but they might be using it."

"Maybe both Quelyt and me should come. We can circle there if we're not carrying you. Flame anyone if you get into trouble."

Dainyl smiled. "Maybe you should."

"Glass before dawn, sir?"

"A glass before dawn." As he left Falyna, Dainyl had another idea. Rather than head for his quarters, he made his way to the headquarters building, where he found Captain Benjyr in his study.

"Colonel, sir . . . ?" Benjyr jumped to his feet.

"I have a favor to ask, Captain. I'd like to talk to a handful of your rankers about their duties at the mine."

"Ah . . . yes, sir. Third and fifth squads are on standby."

"Good. If you would escort me there?"

Dainyl followed the captain across the courtyard to the barracks. He had loosened his jacket, but not taken it off.

Benjyr stepped into the second doorway and called out, "Stenslaz?"

A squad leader jumped up from where he had been sitting on a foot chest. "Yes, sir?"

"The colonel here wants to ask the men a few questions about their duties."

"Yes, sir." The squad leader looked around. "There's no study here, sir."

Dainyl smiled. "It's nothing that has to be too private, and it won't take much time for each man. We can just talk outside in the courtyard."

Dainyl walked out into the sunlight with the captain. After the chill of flying, the warmer air and sun in the courtyard felt good. "You can stay if you want, Captain."

"If it's all the same, Colonel . . . there are a few reports . . ."

Dainyl grinned. He understood about reports. "Go take care of them."

"Thank you, sir." Benjyr nodded, turned, and walked quickly back across the courtyard.

Through the open doorway, Dainyl could hear the Cadmian rankers.

"What's he want with us?"

"Wearing a jacket, and he looks cold . . ."

". . . say they like it hotter 'n we do . . ."

"Daclyt, you go first," called the squad leader.

A few moments later, a ranker appeared. He looked barely old enough to carry a rifle. "Colonel, sir?"

"Yes. I have a few questions for you. You can tell anyone you like about what I'm asking." Dainyl offered a smile.

It didn't seem to help. Daclyt still looked frightened as he stared up at the colonel.

"What are the prisoners—the miners—like?" asked Dainyl.

The Cadmian ranker moistened his lips. "I'd guess they don't want to be there. They don't work any harder than they have to. The complain about the smell. They complain about the food. They shouldn't. We eat the same stuff for the midday meal."

"Exactly the same?"

"Pretty much. It's the same chow line. We just get to eat first . . . well, half of us do."

"Have you ever shot a prisoner?"

"Shot at a couple. Captain told us not to shoot to hit 'em on the first shot, not unless one of us might get hurt. Never hit one. Solisyr's the only one in the squad ever hit one. Fellow had a big stone . . . was trying to brain another prisoner . . ."

After a glass and a half and talks with almost twenty of the Cadmians, Dainyl thanked the squad leader and walked slowly back toward his quarters. He had a better feel of how the rankers felt and acted, and that just made matters more puzzling.

Dainyl was certain that everyone he had talked to was telling the truth as they saw it. It would have been much simpler if he had discovered an ill-managed mine with brutal guards—except for four things. First, the kind of men sent to the mines weren't the type to throw themselves off of bridges or cliffs or try to scramble over stockade fences with armed guards watching them. Second, the Cadmians he had seen and the ones he'd talked to weren't brutal. Third, Devoryn had known far too much about alectors. Fourth, the marshal and the Highest had sent a battalion of Cadmians—and Dainyl—and neither the marshal nor the Highest had been in Dramur. Nor was there any record of any other alector having been there recently.

And then there was the matter of the submarshal's death. That was hardly a coincidence, Dainyl felt, although he could not have offered a shred of proof as to why he felt that way.

19

The *Duarchs' Valor* docked in Dramuria a good two glasses before dawn on Duadi, at the one pier large enough for deep-sea vessels, but it was well past dawn before Mykel and Bhoral led the troopers and mounts of Fifteenth Company down the ramp to the stone pier. Even so, the half-disc of Selena was still bright overhead, although Asterta had long since set.

There on the pier, Fifteenth Company formed up behind Seventeenth and Sixteenth Companies, closer together than Mykel would have preferred. As the last mounts of Thirteenth Company formed up on the pier, Mykel looked back toward the ramp. Above and behind the ramp, cranes were swinging into place, preparing to off-load supplies, including ammunition, spare rifles, and fodder for the battalion's mounts.

Mykel was ready enough to head out. The vessel itself bothered him. The ship had no sails, and, unlike the lander river craft or the river tugs on the Vedra, it didn't use coal or steam. There weren't any stacks, and the vessel *hummed* its way through the ocean. Yet almost all the equipment abovedecks was powered by the crew, from the winches and the capstan to the water pumps. The engine compartments were sealed, according to what several crew members had told Mykel, and only the chief engineer or the captain and the exec ever entered them. One of the deckhands said it was the same on all of the Duarchs' ships.

"Another mystery," he murmured. He'd never liked mysteries, especially ones that suggested great power being hoarded. While the ship itself had disturbed him, that unease was as much a symptom of the situation in which he was finding himself as the ship itself. The alectors had built a ship that could travel faster than a mount over all but the shortest of distances. They had pteridons and skylances, and weapons that could turn a man to ashes—and yet they needed a battalion of mounted rifles to deal with a few handfuls of rebel miners?

Finally, Majer Vaclyn gave the order to the battalion. "Mount up!"

Mykel waited before he relayed the order. He and his company still had to wait almost a quarter glass before the rear ranks of Sixteenth Company began to move out.

From the saddle, riding off the pier at the head of Fifteenth Company, Mykel took in what he could of Dramuria. He hadn't been all that impressed with the view he'd gotten from the deck of the ship. There were but two piers in the harbor, and the *Duarchs' Valor* had barely fit at the larger one, while the vessels at the smaller inshore pier had all been fishing vessels, most of which had cast off before dawn. His eyes took in the handful of warehouses, all of graystone, and looking ancient, just beyond the piers.

A light wind blew out of the south, barely enough to keep the morning from being unpleasantly warm. Even so, he occasionally had to blot his forehead. There was also an acrid and unpleasant smell carried on the wind, something between manure, offal, and rotten meat.

Mykel surveyed all that he could, taking in the stone gutters that separated the sidewalks from the street, deep enough to suggest that at least some of the time rain was heavy, and lingering on the signboards over the shops—with neat images and lettering, yet with faded paint.

Early as it was, there were already a few people on the stone sidewalks bordering the wider street up which the battalion rode. Some looked at the riders, and some didn't, but most of those who looked were children or younger adults, usually men. The young women might have looked, Mykel felt, but did so more discreetly.

Very few of the buildings along the main street were of more than one story, but whatever their height, all had roofs of dull red tile, and most of the dwellings and structures lacked shutters. Even the main road itself was of the same graystone, with hollows worn by years of iron-tired wagons.

"Place seems worn-out," said Bhoral quietly.

"It's hot here. It's late in harvest, and nearly as hot as midsummer in Faitel or Elcien. I'd be worn-out working here, too." Mykel offered a low and rueful laugh. He wasn't looking forward to serving even two seasons in Dramur, although the winter might prove pleasant. He hoped it would, if it came to that.

The sound of hoofs on stone echoed through the morning, loud enough that Mykel couldn't hear if the people along their way were saying much of anything. The main street was straight as a quarrel, aimed northwest at the mountains, and Mykel wondered if the Cadmian compound happened to be in the hills below the jagged peaks. As his eyes traversed the higher peaks, a mix of red and black rocks, with intermittent greenery, he sensed something. What he couldn't say, but he looked northward more intently.

Two huge birds were circling a peak to the northwest. He looked again. "Those are pteridons."

"Does look like pteridons, sir."

There was no doubt in Mykel's mind, none at all.

Seventeenth Company turned onto a narrower but still stone-paved road that crossed over a stream, certainly not the main river, then headed uphill, presumably toward the Cadmian compound. Sixteenth Company followed, and so did Mykel and Fifteenth Company.

He glanced back over his shoulder. He could only see one pteridon in the sky over the peaks, but there had been two. Why was Third Battalion being deployed to Dramur if the Myrmidons had already sent in pteridons?

"You're not liking the pteridons, sir?" asked Bhoral.

"I have to wonder what we're getting into," Mykel replied cautiously. "No one mentioned pteridons."

"It's always that way. They never tell us everything." Bhoral laughed. "Me, I'm happier that they're here."

Mykel wasn't, but he smiled anyway, because he couldn't have explained his feelings except in a general way. Any place that had problems requiring both Cadmians and pteridons was not someplace where the duty at hand was going to be easy.

20

A glass before dawn on Duadi found Dainyl standing with Quelyt and Falyna, between their pteridons in the courtyard of the Cadmian compound.

"You want down on that little bluff below the peak, sir?" asked Quelyt. "I'll land with you, and Falyna will circle. That way, I can cover you, and she can make sure nothing else comes up or down the peak." He smiled ruefully. "She's a better shot, too."

Dainyl had been about to suggest that, but, instead, he just nodded. "Good plan." Although he was wearing his uniform tunic and padded flying jacket, another shot to his injured shoulder, and he'd be facing a good three weeks before he could move it without pain, if not longer. It was still sore and bruised from the single shot he'd taken.

There was also the unspoken credo of the alectors, which applied especially to the Myrmidons: Alectors were invulnerable. There were so few that the steers could never be allowed to consider them vulnerable like other mortals. Too many shots, and Dainyl would find that image hard to maintain. If he showed vulnerability, he might well find himself removed from the Myrmidons and relegated to necessary menial work within the Duarch's Palace, or at the Vault of the Ages in Lyterna—if not worse.

He looked to Quelyt. "We'd better get flying."

"Yes, sir. It's still cool and calm. No sign of clouds around those peaks."

Dainyl waited until Quelyt had mounted, then climbed into the second silver saddle. The pteridon's wings extended, and, with the sharp burst of Talent, they were airborne, moving eastward into the wind off the ocean.

Dainyl looked to the south, where he could see a large vessel moored at the ocean pier. That had to be the *Duarchs' Valor,* with the Cadmian battalion. What the Cadmian mounted rifles could do, Dainyl had no idea, but his orders were very clear. He was to observe, not to interfere . . . unless something went terribly wrong. If it did, he would have to act quickly; and then, if the situation got worse, all blame would fall on him.

He forced his concentration back to flying and their destination. As the pteridon's wings moved, and they gained speed and altitude, Quelyt guided them back around to the northwest, setting a course toward the higher peaks opposite the smugglers' cove. Unlike the afternoon before, the air was far calmer, and much colder. Despite his jacket and gloves, and the insulating properties of his boots and uniform, Dainyl could feel the chill seeping into his feet and fingers. Acorus was a beautiful world, but it was a cold one.

Quelyt had clearly decided to gain altitude before they neared the peaks, climbing through the more stable air away from the mountains.

"That one?" called Quelyt.

"No! Farther north. The summit's angled."

Quelyt had to circle several of the peaks with various outcroppings just below their summits before Dainyl located the one for which they were searching.

"That one there! With the angle, and the flat space below."

"Be tight to land there, sir. Hang on."

The pteridon managed to make it onto the space, although its left wing tip seemed to graze the rugged stone escarpment above the cave.

Quelyt sighed, then smiled. "Don't want to do that often, sir."

"Let's hope not."

After dismounting, Dainyl drew on lifeforce to hold deflection shields, then unholstered the light-cutter before stepping toward the irregular opening of the cave, which looked to be about three and a half yards tall at the highest point. Behind him, Quelyt had the skylance ready.

Dainyl stopped well short of the entrance. Even from where he stood, as he had glimpsed the day before, a good five yards back into the darkness, there was indeed an archway—like no archway he had ever seen or heard described. The material looked to be stone, like the eternal goldenstone of the Hall of Justice, but the shade of gold was different, wrong, amberlike, but somehow holding green within it. The stone extended seamlessly from the blackish lava of the sides of the cave. There were no joints, no marks of tools. The base was narrower than the midsection, and the top rose into a graceful point level with Dainyl's eyes.

After a moment, he could sense there was no living creature nearby, except for some rodents and small birds. He glanced upward toward the summit, another fifty yards above. There was no sign of any other opening, and no sense of anything living nearby other than the Myrmidons and small creatures.

"It's all right," he called back. "There's no one here. I think this was one of the places of the ancients."

"Didn't know they lived this far south."

"It's old. Very old." That he could also sense. He took another step forward and studied the entrance to the cave. The stone was lava, the hard black kind. Although the cave looked irregular, it wasn't natural. He took another step, this time into the dimness of the cave, still holding the light-cutter at the ready. His boots left the only prints on the reddish sand.

Abruptly, he paused and studied the floor of the cave. It was uneven where he stood, but just a yard ahead, it was smooth, far too smooth to have been created by any steer, even a lander. His eyes followed the floor to the archway. Beyond it, there was no sand, just the finest layer of reddish dust covering green tiles. Tiles, not smoothed rock, not the amber green stone, yet those tiles contained the same energy as the archway. Beyond the archway, a corridor extended farther into the mountain, with walls also of the featureless amber green. The small corridor, less than a yard and a half wide, and only two yards in height, ended abruptly only another four yards or so beyond the archway, not in the black lava that framed the archway, but in a smooth wall of the amber green stone.

Dainyl stopped just before the archway and extended his Talent-senses. He could feel residual lifeforces, so faint as to be close to nonexistent, red-violet and golden green.

He let his gloved fingers slide over the stonework of the archway, so smooth that the gloves could find no rough edges. Knowing he was being foolhardy, he still stepped through the archway, carefully lowering his head. Nothing happened.

He bent down and studied the green floor tiles. They were not actually tiles, but a pattern impressed on greenstone, with indentations that formed simple squares. His eyes traveled to the end of the short corridor. Near the end, the floor changed so that there was a large square, almost, but not quite, the width of the corridor, a yard by a yard, roughly. The square was just a shade lower than the surrounding tiles.

He took several careful steps forward until he was standing just short of the dust-covered square. His mouth opened. There on the floor was a perfect silver mirror, inset and made of some sort of stone. In the dimness and through the dust, Dainyl could see his own image looking down at the mirror. He closed his mouth, and so did the image.

He probed it with his Talent, but, for all that he could tell, it was a mirror, nothing more. Except it was on the floor. An empty tunnel, exquisitely if simply constructed, near the top of a peak in the middle of nowhere, with a mirror set into the floor, one fashioned out of stone.

He stepped back and studied the short corridor and the wall. He extracted his belt knife and tapped the walls with the butt, gently, listening. He even leaned down and tapped the mirror.

Yet, for all his scrutiny, the walls seemed and felt solid. So did the mirror. The corridor tunnel appeared to be what he saw and sensed, and he had the feeling that he could have stood there for years and learned nothing more.

Finally, he turned and walked out of the tunnel and the natural-looking, but artificial, cave. Once outside, he turned and studied it again. After several moments, he turned once more and made his way back to Quelyt and the waiting pteridon. He sheathed the knife, but not the light-cutter, and kept his eyes trained on the cave entrance.

"What is it, sir?"

"I don't know. I wish I did. It's a perfect tunnel that goes back four or five yards, and ends. The workmanship and artistry are superb, and yet it's all hidden away up here on a mountain peak where no one's been in years, maybe in centuries. It just ends, as if it were meant to be that way. There's even a mirror in there, but it's on the floor. But why . . ." Dainyl shook his head. "They must have been able to fly, or had creatures like pteridons, because I can't see or sense any other way in of out."

"You think, maybe it was some sort of observation post?"

"It must have been something like that, and they weren't too concerned about anyone else flying. It's not that well hidden from a flier, but you couldn't see it at all from above or below, and it's located where climbing to get here would be almost impossible."

"Well . . . the ancients did leave things here. That's what I always heard."

"I don't think we'll ever know why it's here. It's not as though there are any ancients around to ask." Dainyl smiled ruefully. "We'd better get back. I imagine the Cadmians will be arriving at the compound before long, and I'll need to meet with their majer." He climbed into the second saddle, asking himself how he was going to report what he had found—and if he should until he knew more.

21

Dainyl wasn't looking forward to meeting with the Cadmian battalion commander, not in dealing with such an unsettled situation. How he handled the situation would be evaluated by both the marshal and the High Alector of Justice, and his own future in the Myrmidons was under consideration. It had to be. Otherwise, after the submarshal's untimely death, he should have been promoted or moved out, but neither had occurred.

He also didn't feel it was wise to avoid the majer.

At the eighth glass on Tridi morning he went to find Majer Vaclyn. It would have been simpler for Dainyl to have taken over Majer Herryf's study. Certainly, as the senior officer present, and as a Myrmidon, he had that authority, but doing so would have tacitly stated he was in command of all operations in Dramur, effectively undermining his status as an observer. That would be all too obvious to the marshal and the Highest. Dainyl had to remain an observer—unless and until matters deteriorated badly. Despite the lack of evidence of such an incipient deterioration, Dainyl had few doubts that it would happen. He just didn't know the particular path catastrophe would take, but, according to the *Views of the Highest,* it would occur, since both majers were steers seeking power beyond their ability. That was true of alectors as well.

He found Majer Vaclyn in a small study at one end of the barracks on the east end of the compound, a space barely three yards by four with little more than a desk and several chairs. Foot chests were stacked against one wall.

The ruddy-faced majer stood immediately as he caught sight of the Myrmidon uniform and the colonel's stars.

"Majer Vaclyn." Dainyl smiled politely.

"Colonel." Vaclyn's voice was measured. "What brings you to Dramuria? I understood that the operation here was a Cadmian effort, and one not involving the Myrmidons."

Dainyl could sense a combination of anger and consternation, but he continued to maintain a pleasant expression as he replied, "You are absolutely correct. It is a Cadmian operation. Because the marshal had to rely upon reports, he did decide to send an observer, to make sure that there were not events and situations that had not been misrepresented."

"Misrepresented? The matter seems simple enough. The battalion has been deployed here to deal with a possible rebellion, or some other form of uprising."

"That is true," replied Dainyl. "Yet Majer Herryf cannot explain who these rebels are and where they might be, only that an excessive number of prisoners at the mine are escaping."

"If that is the case, Colonel, why are we here? Escaping prisoners do not make a rebellion."

"You may well be right, Majer. That is why we are both here. If there is no rebellion, you and your men will be able to spend the fall and winter in a warmer locale, and I will be able to report to the marshal that Majer Herryf was excessively worried." There was *something* about the majer, something . . . almost Talent-connected, yet the majer had no Talent. Dainyl would have to observe that as well.

"You're suggesting that there is a problem?" asked Vaclyn.

"I am suggesting nothing," Dainyl pointed out. "I have been here only a few days longer than you have. Majer Herryf has been here much longer."

Vaclyn frowned, then spoke. "Colonel . . . you are a Myrmidon, and some of your fliers were seen overflying the hills north of the mines. Is there any information that you can share with us?" Vaclyn's voice was polite, but there was still anger behind it, if more subdued.

"So far, Majer, information has been hard to come by. What we have discovered is that an unknown number of Cadmian issue rifles have reached the rebel miners, and that other goods have been smuggled into Dramur. The smugglers have used the cove on the eastern shore some twenty-five vingts north of here, and whatever those goods happened to be, they were transported westward along a narrow path that leads toward the area north of the mine where there may be a number of escaped miners who are armed. So far, they have not attacked any Cadmian units. The plantation growers to the north have been raided, but apparently for food, and not in large numbers."

"Sounds more like Majer Herryf wants us to nip something in the bud," speculated Vaclyn. "Might not be so bad as if we'd been later." He looked directly at Dainyl again. "Is there anything you need from us?"

"Not at the moment. I just stopped to pay my respects and to let you know why I was here." Dainyl offered a polite smile. "I will let you know of anything else that might prove helpful."

As Dainyl left the study, he caught a few fragments of the words exchanged by the rankers in the outer corridor.

". . . that's a Myrmidon colonel . . ."

". . . trouble for the majer . . ."

". . . makes enough for himself . . ."

Dainyl concealed an internal wince at the last words. The last thing anyone needed in Dramur was a Cadmian officer prone to mistakes—and what he had overheard suggested he was saddled with two. He just hoped that the ranker was more disgruntled than accurate.

22

On Quattri, just after dawn, Mykel was holding a mug of ale, knowing he had to drink something. He'd had the choice of wine, boiled water, or ale. He had taken the ale, and wondered if he shouldn't have chosen water, or even the cheap wine. Before him was a platter of fried fish and fried apple bananas. He wasn't certain either qualified as breakfast.

"There he is! Always early to eat!" Dohark's voice carried through the small stone-walled mess.

Mykel looked up. Dohark and Kuertyl were headed for the table he'd staked out in the corner, both with platters and mugs in their hands. They sat down across from him.

"You're just looking at the food?" asked Dohark.

"I'm not sure it is food," replied Mykel dryly. "Not for breakfast."

"Don't want to go hungry now," said the older captain.

"I'll eat it." Mykel would eat what was available. He just didn't have to like it.

"What's your schedule?" asked Dohark.

"Fifteenth is moving north tomorrow, a good day's ride. Could be longer. We get to look at a trail that the rebels are using. What about you?"

"Like you, tomorrow. We're going to squat around some cove, hope that some smugglers show up with contraband. At least, it ought to be cool, right off the ocean." Dohark turned to the fresh-faced Kuertyl. "What about Thirteenth?"

"We're supposed to patrol the road from the plantations in the west." Kuertyl shrugged, then took a sip of the ale. "It's not bad. The ale, I mean."

Mykel had already taken a swallow. He'd had worse, but not for breakfast.

"You hear that a Myrmidon colonel came to see the majer yesterday?" asked Kuertyl.

"Any idea why?" asked Dohark.

"Word is that the colonel is just here watching," replied the young captain.

"Vaclyn needs watching. Always has." Dohark laughed and turned to Mykel. "You remember that business east of Klamat—"

"That's over," Mykel said easily. He didn't want to remember it. Vaclyn had wanted a frontal charge by Mykel's whole company on a handful of Reillies dug in behind a timber barricade. Mykel had pretended not to have heard the order and taken a squad over a rise and started firing from the side. The Reillies had surrendered within moments. Even after that, the colonel had left the majer in command of the battalion, but Mykel had figured that was because the majer had managed to hide the fact that he'd given a stupid order. What Mykel didn't understand was how the majer kept getting away with less than brilliant decisions—or was it just that his captains and senior squad leaders bailed him out? And no one really cared how the task got done, just so long as it did without too many casualties?

"True enough, and it's not like we can do anything . . ."

Mykel looked hard at Dohark, and the older captain stopped.

"Get carried away sometimes," Dohark said.

"You were saying?" prompted Kuertyl, who hadn't known about the incident because he'd been an undercaptain with the Second Battalion at the time.

"Old history," said Mykel. "Very old—"

"All history's old," interrupted Heransyr, the captain in command of Seventeenth Company, a smallish officer, with deep-set hazel eyes, whose uniforms never seemed to show a crease. "That's why it's history. Mind if I join you?"

"Please do," suggested Mykel, before looking back at Kuertyl. "What else can you tell us about the colonel?"

"Colonel?" asked Heransyr.

"The Myrmidon colonel who's here," explained Mykel. "What about him, Kuertyl?"

Kuertyl glanced at Dohark, who ignored the look, then finally spoke. "He's big, like all the alectors. One of the locals told me he'd been out flying all around the mountains, even in the storms a couple days back. They said one of the rebels took a shot at him when he was out riding, and the bullet bounced off him, and he rode out and caught the rebel without even using a weapon. He just looked at the fellow, and he dropped over dead."

"I'm sure he did," replied Dohark. "Just dropped over dead because someone looked at him. They got lances that turn people into torches, but I never heard of someone dropping dead without a weapon being used."

"With alectors, you never know," suggested Heransyr. "They are alectors."

Dohark looked at Mykel. Mykel smothered a smile at Heransyr's knowing tone.

Kuertyl finished taking a long pull of ale before answering. "Anyway . . . that's what one of the squad leaders said. He was there. The colonel's been meeting with the mine director, and with that Majer Herryf, and with important folks in the town."

"Frig . . ." muttered Dohark.

Kuertyl turned to the older captain.

"Look, Kuertyl," Dohark said slowly. "He's a Myrmidon colonel. That's means he outranks every Cadmian officer. There probably aren't five Myrmidons that outrank him. He's down here talking to everyone? Dramur's a nothing place, except for bat shit. So why are we here? Why is he here? Something stinks, and it's not just bat shit."

"Something they don't want a lot of people to know about," suggested Mykel. "We're here in the normal rotation, and we don't have any Myrmidons around." He gave a crooked grin. "Not officially. Just a couple to ferry the colonel around. Except that they're checking out the mountains and the mine from the air?"

"Oh," said Kuertyl.

Even Heransyr's knowing smile faded.

"So don't think this is just a set of routine patrols," added Dohark. "You could get real familiar with unfamiliar dirt here, and that merchant's daughter in Faitel'd have to find another handsome captain."

Kuertyl flushed, ever so slightly.

"It might not be that bad," said Mykel, "but until we know that, better be really careful."

Dohark rose. "I think it's time for an unannounced gear inspection."

Mykel smiled. "Not a bad idea. I'll let you start." The word would get around, and then he'd follow up with Fifteenth Company.

23

Beginning on Sexdi, Mykel and Fifteenth Company spent four days under a bright sun that was more like summer than fall, riding westward along the stream valley that held a trail supposedly used by smugglers. The only way to see what was on the trail was to ride it, and Majer Vaclyn had chosen Fifteenth Company for that duty. After battling the thorny brush olives, the heat, and the damp, they found no recent traces of smugglers.

Then, after they completed a last sweep of the valley on Decdi, the majer ordered them back to the Cadmian compound, where they had Londi for some recuperation. On Duadi, they rode north thirty vingts to patrol a twenty-vingt section of road—ten vingts on each side of a small town scarcely larger than a hamlet called Enstyla. The road, in a winding fashion, eventually made its way south to Dramuria.

The company was housed in an empty barn that had once been used for cattle—until the losses from the nightwasps had made it far too unprofitable for the grower to continue. Now he was getting a few silvers for the use of the barn and well.

"This town is the one where the growers around it have been complaining about raids," Majer Vaclyn had told Mykel. "See what you can do, either to find out if they've really been raided, or to stop the raids. If you can't capture the raiders, shoot them. But make sure that they're raiders and not locals."

On Tridi, just before midmorning, Mykel rode northward at the head of fifth squad, along a part of the road that ran through grassland that showed as much clay as grass. As on the previous days, the sky was mostly clear, with a hint of clouds building over the peaks to the west. No animals were grazing in the nearby fields, and probably had not in a while, since the scattered tufts and clumps of grass were nearly calf high. The fields were not fenced, and it had been a good vingt since the squad had passed a cot.

Mykel alternated riding with the squads, since each squad was handling a different section of the road. As he shifted his weight in the saddle, he had to wonder how patrolling roads would stop raids. The raiders weren't exactly going to ride up and down the roads announcing their intentions, and those who did use the roads would look like anyone else who belonged there.

Still . . . Mykel was a Cadmian officer, and there were times when he just had to follow orders and try not to make a stupid mistake doing so.

Ahead, coming up a long gentle rise from lowlands that held trees, there was a wagon creaking toward fifth squad, an old wagon that seemed to sag in the middle, pulled by a single swaybacked horse.

Mykel moved the chestnut to the head of the squad and eased out in front of the squad, just slightly, moving toward the wagon and the two men on the bench seat. The driver flicked the reins, pulled them back, and the wagon slowed to a crawl, then a stop.

Both men looked at Mykel, and the squad behind him, but neither spoke.

Mykel concentrated on the teamster, after a quick study of the younger man seated beside the bearded driver. "Have you seen any folks up here that don't belong here?"

The teamster kept the reins in his right hand, but tilted back the tattered and wide-brimmed woven frond hat with his left. Then he spat to the side of the wagon away from Mykel. "You're the first folks we've seen since we set out."

"Not just this morning. Over the past few days."

"You Cadmians are looking in the wrong place. All those escaped prisoners are in the hills north of the mine." The man's words were even, with a touch of anger behind them, but they didn't feel right to the captain.

"I don't recall mentioning escaped prisoners," Mykel said politely. "We also know that someone has been smuggling as well. You might have seen them."

"Told you. We haven't seen anyone."

"We'd heard reports that some of the escapees might have moved eastward . . . might be lifting a little food here and there." Mykel looked squarely at the teamster.

"Well . . . Captain. Now, I can't say that there might not have been a few things missing here and there, but how could anyone tell whether it's from shamblers sneaking up here or a loose prisoner or two?"

"I imagine you couldn't," replied Mykel with an easy smile. "If you do find out, we'd like to know. Either way, you'd be able to keep more of what you grow if we could catch them."

"On the roads?" The teamster laughed. "Not sow-eared likely!"

Mykel eased the chestnut back and gestured for the squad to let the wagon pass. As the wagon rolled southward, Mykel strained to hear what the younger man was saying.

". . . not like that banty rooster yesterday . . ."

". . . got to watch 'em all . . . just 'cause he talks nice, don't mean nothing . . ."

Mykel had to wonder whom the teamster had run into the day before. Dohark certainly wasn't banty. It could have been Kuertyl—or maybe Heransyr, with his elevated notion of his own importance.

What was certain was that the patrols were going to be long, and hot, and that they were going to upset some people. Yet, if he didn't patrol, Majer Vaclyn and the Myrmidon colonel would be unhappy with a certain captain.

Mykel turned the chestnut back northward.

24

On Quattri and Quinti, the squads of Fifteenth Company had patrolled the road north and south of Enstyla. Each morning, Mykel made sure to tell his squad leaders to emphasize courtesy and politeness if they did stop anyone. On Sexdi, his morning briefing was no different.

"Everyone is sir or madam, and you are terribly sorry to stop them. You are checking for contraband weapons and asking if they have seen anyone who looks out of place," he had told each squad leader. "Treat them like they were your aunts or uncles, with politeness, but with firmness."

Mykel had chosen to patrol with third squad, on the northernmost section of the road assigned to Fifteenth Company, and he rode northward beside Chyndylt, the third squad leader. Sexdi was cooler than the previous days. Even in late morning, a wind blew from the northwest, making the day pleasantly breezy—the first such since they had arrived in Dramur.

"Glad you're with us today," said Chyndylt. "Hope we get this kind of weather every time you're patrolling with us."

"It should get cooler as we get farther into fall and winter," replied Mykel.

"We could use some cold. Never thought I'd say that after the winter up in Blackstear." Chyndylt laughed.

Both Cadmians stopped talking as a one-horse cart turned from a side lane on the west side of the road half a vingt north of Mykel and headed down the rutted clay toward third squad.

"Couple of women," observed Chyndylt as the cart neared.

Mykel scanned the road to the left, but could see nothing through the widely spaced casaran nut trees. "We might as well say good day to them."

"The younger one does look sort of pretty, sir."

Not only did she look attractive, Mykel realized, but there was *something* about her that went beyond the physical. He forced himself back to the duty at hand, smiling ruefully. "I don't think she'll be looking on us with any favor, Chyndylt." He kept riding until he was within thirty yards of the cart.

The younger woman—dark-haired and wearing a pale green long-sleeved shirt, dark gray trousers, and a darker gray vest—was driving. She showed no sign of wanting to stop as the cart continued down the middle of the road.

"Just when are you going to clear the road?" she called out, her voice conveying irritation, yet without being shrill.

"After you stop, madam, and we exchange a few words," replied Mykel politely.

With a sigh visible from a good twenty yards away, the driver jerked the cart to a halt. The horse snorted. The gray-haired woman sitting to the left of the driver said not a word.

Mykel reined up beside the cart horse, in a position where he could grab the leads, if necessary. "I am sorry to ask you to stop, madam, but we've been assigned here to patrol the road. Have you seen anyone who doesn't belong here, someone who might have escaped from the mine?" He smiled politely at the woman, who looked to be younger than he was.

"There aren't people like that around here. Not around our estate." The driver's green eyes hardened. "Now . . . will you let us pass, trooper?"

"Captain, madam, Captain Mykel, Fifteenth Company." Mykel eased his mount forward toward the cart and the driver. Outwardly, she showed no sign of nervousness, but he could sense it all the same. That could be just because she'd been stopped by twenty-two men. That would make any woman nervous. But it didn't feel like that to Mykel. "We're also looking for contraband weapons."

"Weapons, Captain? What would two women be doing with weapons?" The driver eased herself, almost imperceptibly, toward the side of the cart closest to Mykel.

"Madam, anyone could be carrying weapons." He reined up beside the cart, his eyes dropping to the space under the driver's seat. "Like that rifle you're trying to hide."

"Rifle?"

"The one you moved your trouser leg to cover," Mykel said dryly. "Chyndylt, please cover these ladies while I look at their weapon." He looked to the driver. "I'd appreciate it if you would move over. I'd rather leave you alone."

"Scarcely a manly sentiment, Captain." The words were cold, cutting, despite the slight huskiness in her voice, but the driver moved away from Mykel.

As she moved, he quickly leaned forward in the saddle and lifted the rifle away, careful to keep the barrel down and away from anyone. Then he straightened and checked the weapon, clearly Cadmian-issue. He looked to the plate under the stock. It was blank, and so was the flattened space on the underside of the barrel. Both should have held numbers, identical numbers.

"I'm afraid we'll have to keep this, ladies," Mykel said politely.

"Keep it? Just who do you think you are, riding up and taking things from two women going about their own business? How are two women supposed to protect themselves out here? You couldn't find one of those so-called raiders if you had ten times the men you do. Riding up and down roads . . ."

Mykel kept smiling, wondering how long she would rail at him.

"You call yourself a captain, but you're more of a thief than those poor prisoners you're looking for. They didn't take hard-earned goods . . . they were just stupid, and drank too much . . ."

"Madam," Mykel began . . .

"I am not a madam, and don't call me that, and you may not have my name, either. I know your kind."

"All right!" the captain snapped. "Enough."

The tone of his voice stopped the woman's tirade. She looked at him as if he had suddenly become an alector or grown an arm from the middle of his chest. Yet there was strength, not fear, and he had to admit he admired that.

Mykel spoke into the sudden silence. "You are carrying a Cadmian rifle. That is against the Code. I could have you both charged and flogged, at the very least. I doubt that you are the guilty party, but possession is a flogging offense as well."

The younger woman's eyes widened, and Mykel felt that she had had no idea that carrying a Cadmian rifle was indeed a crime.

"It is most clear that you did not intend to commit a crime, and I doubt that anyone even told you that possessing a military weapon was a crime. I will have your names and the rifle, and you may go on your way."

"You'd leave us unprotected?" asked the older woman, speaking for the first time.

"Madam," Mykel replied, trying to keep his tone polite. "For the entire past week, everyone has been telling us that there was no need for us to patrol the roads. They have told us that there are no rebels, no escaped prisoners, and no danger. If there is no danger, then there is no need for a rifle."

The older woman looked down.

"Your names and your home, if you would," Mykel asked.

"Kamrita."

The sense of falseness was so great that Mykel snapped back. "That's not your name."

"Rytora."

"Neither is that."

"Rachyla of Stylan Estate," the driver replied, in a lower voice, for the first time showing a trace of tentativeness.

The captain looked to the older woman.

"I'm her aunt, Astylara."

"Astylara and Rachyla of Stylan Estate," repeated Mykel. He looked to Chyndylt. "Have your men check the cart, and underneath. Carefully, and just for weapons."

"You . . ." murmured Rachyla. "My father will . . ."

"I am doing the duty I was assigned, madam. I am certain he will understand that." Mykel forced another smile, waiting as the two rankers pulled back the tarp covering the tear of the cart and revealing a half score of baskets filled with shelled nuts.

"There's nothing underneath, sir. Nothing but the nuts in the baskets."

"Cover their load, and step back." Mykel turned to Rachyla. "You ladies may proceed, but I would suggest that carrying contraband rifles is not a wise form of protection at present." He eased his mount back and watched as the woman flicked the leads, and the cart began to roll southward, away from Mykel and third squad.

"You think you should have let her go?" asked Chyndylt. "You know what the majer said."

"We have the rifle." Mykel paused. "It doesn't have any numbers or markings."

"It doesn't? How could it not . . . it has to be smuggled, then."

"I'd judge so," replied the captain.

"And you let her go?"

"I don't think that it would have been a good idea to turn a major landholder's wife or daughter over to a justicer to be flogged for carrying a rifle she said she needed for protection." Mykel's voice was dry. "Besides, we know who she is, and we have the rifle. If the majer—or the colonel—wants her flogged, he can get her."

And, sometime during the patrol, Mykel would have to write a report on the incident, to turn over to the majer along with the rifle. He'd bent the rules, but going by them blindly would have been worse—far, far worse. Either way, he'd pay, but that was often what happened to junior officers. Using judgment was a danger, but so was not exercising it.

He took a deep breath and squared himself in the saddle, looking down at the contraband Cadmian rifle that he held. A week of chasing smugglers and escaped prisoners that no one had ever seen, and he had exactly one rifle to show for it—taken from a woman connected to some wealthy lander.

25

Sexdi morning dawned bright, but breezy, cooler than it had been on the two previous days. As he crossed the courtyard in the blue shimmersilk jacket he wore over his uniform when flying, heavy gloves in hand, Dainyl wished he had decided to take the inspection flight earlier, when it had been warmer, but he had not, and there wasn't much point in remonstrating with himself over the decision. What he did know was that he couldn't afford to put it off longer. There was too much he did not know about Dramur.

Quelyt was waiting by the square set aside for his pteridon. Behind him, the pteridon crouched, blue crystal beak slightly parted.

"Where are we headed now, sir?"

"West, over the mountains. There are some large plantations over there, or so I've been told. We need to look at them."

"We can do that." Quelyt paused. "Can't say I've ever been there."

"Neither have I," replied the colonel, a wry tone to his words.

It had taken Dainyl more than a week to realize what he was missing—or one of the things he was missing. There were had been a number of references to the "big growers" or the seltyrs in the west, but always in passing. He'd finally decided that, before asking more about the west, an inspection flight would be in order. That way, he hoped, any answers that he got would make more sense. Certainly, according to the maps, there were but a handful of hamlets to the west of the Murian Mountains, and two small natural harbors.

When he had been a ranker, or even a flying officer, and had been dispatched to Dramur, he'd never flown west of the mountains. All the dispatches and transport had always dealt with Dramuria and the Cadmian compound. He was acutely conscious of that lack of knowledge about the west side of Dramur.

"I'd wager it's a good two glasses to the west shore."

"If it takes all day, we still need to do it."

"Yes, sir." Quelyt checked the harnesses, and then mounted and strapped himself in.

Dainyl followed him, and in less than a quarter glass, they were airborne, climbing westward away from the Cadmian compound.

To the immediate west of Dramuria, the dryness of the winter was all too obvious. Dust swirled up in the light winds, and the vegetation, from what grass there was to the leaves on the casaran trees, was tinged with brown or tan. Even on the stone road that eventually led to the guano mine, the few carts threw up fine dust that Dainyl could see from almost a vingt in the air.

A winding dirt or clay road branched off the mine road north of the town, less than half a vingt beyond the point where the road to the compound separated from the mine road and curved uphill and eastward. Given the narrowness of the road west as it headed toward the mountains,

Dainyl could certainly understand why the larger growers preferred to send their produce by boat.

The wide blue wings beat evenly, and the air was calm enough that Dainyl was able to get a steady view of the hills to the east of the mountains. Like the area to the north, around the mine, the slopes were a mixture of open ground, sandy and rocky, with scattered bushes and trees. The trees were scraggly pines of some sort, and the leaves on the bushes a faded green that suggested very little moisture had fallen recently.

For a time, as the pteridon carried the two Myrmidons westward, over the dry foothills, the peaks of the mountains seemed as far away as when they had first lifted off from the compound. Then, after they had flown almost a glass, the hills began to steepen into low peaks, far lower than those around the mines to the north of Dramuria. The tops were rocky, expanses of gray and black stone.

Within another quarter glass, the ancient lava on the peaks had given way to sandstone alone, and more evergreens were evident. Several times, Dainyl lost sight of the narrow road winding its way through the hills, then the low mountains, but just when he thought it had vanished for good, he caught sight of yet another section of road.

Then they were over the mountains, and heading lower.

The hills to the west of the mountains were far greener than those on the east side, and also looked less rugged, with rounded crests and wider and shallower valleys. The trees were evergreens, mostly, from what Dainyl could see, and there were few patches where nothing grew. While the hillsides were not lush, they were well vegetated.

Quelyt turned and called back. "Looks greener over here."

"Quite a bit."

In places, Dainyl thought he saw evidence of timbering, but whoever had been cutting had been doing so selectively, so that there was mixed old and new growth. He smiled wryly. While timbering was frowned upon, he doubted that any of the high alectors would bother with a lander grower who was cautious enough to cut so carefully.

Ahead, just to the left of the winding road, was a long ridge. At one end was a villa, with grounds surrounded by a stone wall.

"Take us over that villa!"

The pteridon banked slightly, then straightened.

The estate grounds enclosed by the stone wall were easily a vingt square, with several gardens, and fountains. Gracefully curved stone lanes ran from the main gate to the outbuildings, the stables, then to a separate lodge set before an oval pool surrounded by a stone terrace. The main villa was a rectangle with a courtyard within, and four separate gardens. One of the gardens held a hedge maze with white gravel or stone paths. Another held an array of flowers—winter or not—whose blooms were clear from above.

The pteridon swept past the villa before Dainyl could note everything.

"Do you want another look, sir?" called Quelyt.

"No. Just keep heading for the coast."

Dainyl kept scanning the rolling hills, with meadows, long lines of trees, perhaps some of which were the local apple bananas, and recently tilled fields.

He could see other estates, certainly of comparable size to the first, if not larger, and the winding road that they had followed had become straighter—and wider—and headed for the coast, and what looked to be a harbor.

Every so often, he could make a out a clump of houses, more like hamlets than villages, but there weren't many more of those than villas from what he was seeing.

They passed over another estate, except there were two villas within the walls, and each was larger than the first villa that Dainyl had seen. The outbuildings were numerous, including several across from stables that could have passed for barracks, except for the laundry hung on lines behind the structures. He didn't see a pool, but there was an open riding arena, although he could make out neither riders nor horses at the moment.

The growers in the west were definitely far better off than those in the east.

"That looks like a harbor ahead," he called to Quelyt. "Let's see what it looks like."

"Heading there, sir!"

The gently rolling hills actually rose as they neared the coastline. The harbor was small, but well protected by rock bluffs, almost as if a volcanic caldera had once stood there, and the ocean had broken through on the west, leaving a circular green bay. Dainyl saw two stone piers and a schooner tied to one. Several buildings, warehouses, stood at the shoreward end of the piers.

Small harbor or not, the warehouses looked to be almost as extensive as those at the port in Dramuria. Given what Dainyl had seen, that didn't surprise him. What did surprise him was that there were no large villages.

Most of the people seemed to be gathered into the buildings on the villa grounds. What also surprised him was that no one had mentioned the apparent wealth of the western growers.

"Now what, sir?" asked Quelyt.

"North along the coast for a while. Then we'll swing back east."

"Yes, sir."

Dainyl doubted that he would see anything much different from what they had already observed, but he wanted to make sure. He had the feeling that he might not have the time to make another trip for a while.

26

After a long day's patrol on Sexdi, Mykel had done two things. First, he had made inquiries in Enstyla about Rachyla and Stylan Estate and obtained directions to the estate. Then he had written up his report for the day and dispatched it with a scout to Majer Vaclyn, who had set up a makeshift headquarters in the nearby hamlet of Eltorana. The report had included a summary of all the patrols, although the single rifle taken from the well-attired woman was the only direct evidence of any illegal or rebellious activities among all those riders and wagons observed or stopped.

Early Septi morning, more than a glass before dawn, the scout returned with written orders to Captain Mykel that Fifteenth Company was to suspend patrols for the day and await the majer's arrival "for further orders." Mykel passed the order to Bhoral to have the company ready to ride when the majer arrived.

Majer Vaclyn did not arrive until the ninth glass of the day, when he summoned Mykel to meet him outside the barn used by Fifteenth Company. The majer stood in the shade afforded by the northeast corner of the structure, well away from the squad from Thirteenth Company that had accompanied him.

Mykel approached on foot and nodded. "Good morning, Majer."

"It is morning, Captain. I am not convinced that it is good." Vaclyn's right hand dropped to his belt, his fingers briefly touching the hilt of the throwing dagger sheathed there in place of the standard Cadmian belt knife. There was a second dagger on the other side of his belt. Neither was regulation, but, so far as Mykel knew, no one had ever said anything about the weapons.

Mykel waited, sensing the majer's anger.

"You have not even set up a proper study—or a command position, I see, Captain."

"I've been riding with the various squads, Majer."

"And how could they reach you in the event you were needed?"

"Each squad leader knew where to find me, sir."

"I'm sure." Vaclyn extracted several folded papers from his riding jacket. "I have your report here, Captain. I cannot say that I understand it. You found a woman with a contraband rifle. You took the rifle, but you did not take her into custody."

"We confiscated the rifle and warned her of the offense, Majer."

"We have been searching for contraband. She had a contraband rifle. Yet you saw fit not to bring her in, Captain? On what authority and on what basis did you decide to ignore both your orders and the Code?" Vaclyn's voice was cutting.

"I believe I wrote that out in my report, sir—"

"What you wrote has no basis in regulations or in the Code. Could you explain to me, again, this time in terms I might understand, why you didn't?"

"Yes, sir." Mykel nodded, politely. "The woman was dressed very well, in the kind of clothes that showed she had golds. She was accompanied by an older woman, also well dressed, and she was driving a horse cart, the kind that was almost new and well kept. She was shocked that I would ever dare to stop her. The single rifle was the only piece of contraband."

"And that was why you didn't punish a violation of the Code?"

"No, sir. The rifle had no numbers, and that indicated that it was not stolen from a Cadmian unit. Either it was an unauthorized gift, or it is an indication of a much greater degree of smuggling. Because of those possibilities, seizing and punishing the woman did not seem to justify the risks. She seemed very well placed in Dramur. We are already being seen as more of a danger to people than are the rebels and smugglers. I did not see how punishing her would help matters. I had thought that a visit to her estate, and a quiet explanation to either her father or husband, might well gain more information and results than punishing her immediately. I did obtain her name and location and verified them."

"And I suppose you intended to make that visit?" Vaclyn's tone was cutting.

"No, sir. I will, if you think it best, but I had thought that someone with greater position and authority, such as you, might make a better impression and gain more."

"We're here to uphold the Code, Captain."

"Yes, sir." Mykel managed to keep a polite expression on his face.

"Explain to me again how letting this woman go upholds the Code."

"I could not have proved that she even knew the rifle was there." That was stretching things, but not by a great amount, because the woman was the kind who could easily claim that before a justicer. "It was under the bench seat of the cart. She was not holding it, and she never looked at it. There was no other contraband in the cart, even hidden on the underside. Since she was obviously well connected, possibly to someone of great wealth, and since the rifle had no numbers, I felt that prudence was called for. Had she brandished the weapon, or used it in any fashion, then there would have been no question about applying the Code."

Vaclyn frowned. "But you had a squad there who observed the weapon."

"She had an aunt, also well attired, and most proper. We are foreign Cadmians. I may have misjudged the situation, sir, but I felt it wiser to err on the side of caution, rather than excess. If there are rebellious activities taking place on her estate, they could not be concealed that quickly. If there are not, then taking someone respected into custody might easily push the landowners into supporting the rebels."

"I can see your concerns, Captain, but people must learn that the Code is the Code, and that the laws are the laws, and position does not excuse breaking those laws."

"Yes, sir. Do you wish me to take Fifteenth Company to her estate and convey a warning to her?"

"Do you even know where this estate is, Captain?"

"Yes, sir. As I told you, I verified its location and her name. She is the eldest daughter of the landholder, a man named Ubarjyr. The estate is some thirteen vingts north of the center of Enstyla, and two vingts west."

"Then perhaps we should make a call on this Ubarjyr, although it well may be too late, given the fashion in which it has been handled."

Mykel merely nodded, although he had few doubts that handling it in the manner suggested by Majer Vaclyn would have been worse than the way in which he had handled it.

In less than a quarter glass, the troopers of Fifteenth Company—and those in the squad from Thirteenth Company that had accompanied the majer—were riding northward through a cool and breezy morning.

The majer did not offer any information or conversation for the first five vingts.

"Could you tell me how matters are faring with the other companies?" asked Mykel, after the long silence.

"Seventeenth Company is patrolling the area on each side of the road to the mine. They have apprehended two escaped prisoners."

"And the others . . . ?" prompted Mykel politely.

"Sixteenth Company has been patrolling the east–west road to the south of here. They have so far been unable to apprehend anyone or anything. Thirteenth Company has been providing security at Eltorana. Fourteenth Company has been patrolling the highlands to the north and west of the mine. They have encountered resistance and have taken some fire. They have killed several of the insurgents, but have not yet taken any prisoners to obtain information."

"Would you judge that the majority of the insurgents are in the area being covered by Fourteenth Company?"

"That remains to be seen, Captain. It is clear that Fourteenth Company has been most successful so far."

If getting shot at was a measure of success, Mykel wasn't so certain he wanted that kind of success. The majer was not about to offer more information, not without Mykel's prodding, and that prodding would just upset Vaclyn more. So he rode quietly beside the majer.

They continued northward to the lane to the estate and westward on it until they came to a pair of elaborately carved wooden gates blocking the lane. There were two small raised guardhouses, set on heavy timbered bases in back of and overlooking the closed gates. A timber stockade extended roughly fifty yards on each side of the gates. The one on the right side ended at a pile of boulders that filled the gap between the stockade and a rocky hillside rising thirty some yards above the lane. On the left the stockade ended partway down a gully filled with brush olives.

"You!" the majer snapped at the man in the left guardhouse. "Open those gates!"

"Sir, these are the lands of Seltyr Ubarjyr. We do not admit anyone he has not invited."

"We are here on the orders of the High Alector of Justice. Open the gates."

"I do not know this High Alector of Justice. I know that you have not been invited."

"Ready rifles!" ordered Vaclyn.

"Ready rifles!" Mykel repeated.

More than one hundred rifles appeared in the hands of the troopers.

"We are not *anyone*!" snapped the majer. "I am Majer Vaclyn, and we are here under the express orders of the Marshal of Myrmidons and the High Alector of Justice. If you don't open those gates by the time I finish speaking, you three will be very dead guards."

The three guards at the closed gates looked at the line of mounted riflemen.

One of them murmured, ". . . dead men, either way."

"Open the gates!" ordered the taller guard.

After several moments, the gates creaked open, revealing a stone-paved if narrow lane heading due south beyond the gates. Some fifty yards beyond the gates, the lane was bordered by trees, which provided an arching cover of foliage. In the distance, upon a low hill, Mykel saw an extensive villa, with brilliant blue tile roofing.

"Third squad, Thirteenth Company!" ordered the majer, "hold here and keep the gates open!"

"Yes, sir! Holding here."

"Forward!" called Vaclyn.

Fifteenth Company, forward!" Mykel repeated.

As they neared the house, they passed a long and low stable. Mykel noted that several stableboys who scurried back into the stable had been oiling the wood of a horse cart—the one used by Rachyla or an exact duplicate.

Ahead was the villa, surrounded by a sandstone wall slightly more than two yards high, with the only entrance an opening marked by two sandstone pillars, on which were hung a set of decorative iron gates, drawn open. Beyond the gates was a paved entry courtyard, with a circular fountain set directly between the gates and the roofed portico that stood at the top of the wide stone steps. Behind the portico was a covered walkway leading to the villa itself.

A darker-skinned man in washed-out blue trousers and shirt appeared at the top of the sandstone steps. His eyes darted from side to side as he looked at the two officers and the company drawn up in the outer part of the courtyard.

"You can announce us, Captain."

"Majer Vaclyn, Captain Mykel, here to see Ubarjyr and Rachyla," Mykel told the man.

"Ah . . . they are not here."

Mykel smiled politely, and directed his rifle—one-handed—in the general direction of the man. "That's not true. I happened to see Rachyla's cart outside the stable, and it was being cleaned and oiled."

"I meant that Seltyr Ubarjyr was not here, sir."

"Then we will begin by seeing Rachyla until the good seltyr returns," replied Mykel.

"I cannot . . . make her appear . . . officers . . ."

"She has a choice," Mykel said reasonably. "She can invite us in, or we can invite ourselves in with our rifles."

Suddenly, the dark-haired Rachyla appeared under the portico. Although she stood in the shade, to Mykel, she seemed almost luminous. "What are you officers doing here?"

"We came to see you and the seltyr," Mykel replied. "To talk over a few things."

"I cannot imagine what such matters might be," the woman replied. "We have nothing of interest to you."

Mykel could sense the untruth, yet she did not exactly reek of duplicity. She had stated something that was not true, yet projected her words with utter conviction. He wanted to smile at her effrontery. "You have a great deal of interest to us, especially after your trip south on the road to Enstyla yesterday."

"You must be mistaken, officers," Rachyla replied. "I never left the estate yesterday." Her smile was guileless.

Mykel sensed her satisfaction in confronting them. She was up to something. What?

Abruptly, he turned in the saddle. "Bhoral! Take fourth and fifth squads! Surround the stables. Rifles ready! Return any fire you receive!"

"Fourth squad!"

"Fifth squad . . ."

"What—" began the majer.

"She's stalling us," Mykel said in a low voice. "The only reason for that is to allow her sire to escape or to bring in reinforcements." He rode forward, practically to the base of the steps, his eyes surveying the pillars and the wall behind them.

For the first time, Rachyla looked uncertain.

Mykel vaulted out of the saddle, rifle in hand, and went up the stone steps two at a time.

Crack! Crack!

He was less than a yard from Rachyla when the first shots echoed from beyond the courtyard wall.

"All squads, fire at will!" he ordered.

The next shot went past his ear, just as he grabbed the woman's forearm and pulled her behind one of the pillars—away from the line of fire from the eastern side of the portico.

"Shoot to kill!" yelled the majer.

"Let me go!" demanded Rachyla, aiming a kick at his groin.

Mykel took her boot on his outer thigh, then grabbed the boot and yanked, dropping her on the stone—hard. For the moment that she was stunned, he brought the rifle up and turned, firing instinctively in the direction from which he had been attacked, willing his shots to strike.

Men in green, carrying Cadmian rifles, appeared at the top of the walls and began to fire at the troopers. Only a handful flattened themselves against the stone, most remaining standing.

Within moment, most of them were down, one way or another.

Rachyla shook her head, as if trying to clear her senses, and started to scramble away. Mykel grabbed her arm and dragged her back down the steps toward the first squad. "Hendyl! Tie her up, and don't let her get away."

After thrusting Rachyla at the ranker, Mykel scrambled back into the saddle, but by the time he was mounted, the attackers had vanished. "First squad! Hold position. Take out anyone who fires! Second and third squads, follow me!"

Mykel turned the chestnut and headed back out through the entry, two squads following him. As he had thought, some of the seltyr's men were fleeing toward an orchard. "Rifles away. Sabres out!"

Mykel was adequate with a sabre. Riding down men who ran from him, he didn't have to be better than that.

When the two squads re-formed just short of the orchard a quarter glass later, only a handful of those who had fled had escaped. Another half score had been wounded or captured.

"Back to the villa. Get the prisoners moving."

Another quarter glass had passed by the time Mykel and the two squads and the prisoners were back inside the walls. Only half of first squad remained in the courtyard, with the mounts of the other half score. The bodies of two troopers had been strapped across their saddles, and two others were having their wounds bound.

"The majer took a half squad into the place, sir," Hendyl reported.

Mykel nodded. "Just hold here, rifles ready." He raised his voice. "Second squad. Hold here for backup! With the prisoners. Third squad, we're headed for the stables." The whole situation was a mess, but he could only do what he thought best.

By the time he reached the stables, fourth and fifth squads had already re-formed, with fewer than ten prisoners that the squads were herding back past the outbuildings to the main house. Mykel saw a good score of bodies sprawled on the open space around the stables.

"Sir! There were a good two squads worth out here," announced Bhoral. "Not any good with the basics. They couldn't shoot that well."

"Cadmian rifles, too?"

"Yes, sir. We got those collected."

"How about casualties?"

"One dead, maybe three wounded. We've got everything secured here, sir."

"Good. Thank you, Bhoral. Stand by here. I'll take third squad back to the villa."

"Yes, sir."

As he turned the chestnut back toward the villa, Mykel surveyed the road to the gates and the surrounding areas. He saw no one moving, except for Cadmians. It had been a mess, but it could have been worse, much worse. All the information he had been given had been about smugglers and escaped prisoners, but no one had even hinted that the rebels—or those who had broken the Code and obtained smuggled Cadmian rifles—were the wealthy seltyrs of Dramur. That worried him more than the attack itself had.

When he returned to the villa courtyard, Majer Vaclyn and the half of first squad he had commandeered were returning from within the villa, ushering three servants, who carried a dead man dressed in ornate green—the seltyr Ubarjyr, no doubt. On the steps, her hands bound behind her, Rachyla stood, her eyes hard and cold. She did not look in Mykel's direction, but at the majer. Had her eyes been a rifle or a crossbow, the majer would have been dead.

Vaclyn turned to Mykel. "Your report, Captain."

"We captured or killed almost a company's worth of retainers. We've lost three men—so far—and about that many wounded. They were using Cadmian rifles. Squads four and five are holding the stables and outbuildings."

Vaclyn nodded grudgingly, then said, "We need a complete search of the buildings and grounds, Captain." He paused but for a moment, "Just one contraband rifle, now?"

Mykel thought about pointing out that he had never felt that there had been just one, only that he had not seen the wisdom in taking Rachyla into custody at that point. He decided against correcting the majer. "Quite a few, sir. Would you mind if we used two squads to search, one to guard the prisoners, and two to make sure that we don't get attacked by any more of this seltyr's retainers?"

"That sounds most prudent, Captain. I will be accompanying you personally. I would suggest that you observe the seltyr's study."

Mykel turned to Gendsyr. "Send a scout to Bhoral at the stables. He's to use one squad to search the buildings for contraband and one to stand guard. Have first squad stand guard here."

"Scout to the senior squad leader, yes, sir."

The captain caught Chyndylt's eye. "Third squad will search the villa for contraband. No looting, and no souvenirs!"

"Yes, sir."

Mykel dismounted and let the majer lead the way along the covered walkway from the portico to the main entrance to the single-level villa. The roof of the walkway was supported by columns of ivory marble, and between the columns were raised planters containing a profusion of small purple-and-gold flowers. The walkway itself was of plain ivory marble.

Double doors, of solid golden oak and carved with half reliefs of vines and grapes, stood ajar at the villa's entrance. Just inside was an oblong foyer, only four yards deep but a good eight from side to side. On the walls were hung tapestries with interlocking designs of purple and gold, woven with threads that seemingly matched the colors of the flowers bordering the walkway.

Majer Vaclyn walked through the archway opposite the entrance and down another marble-floored corridor, the sound of his boots muffled by the heavy green-and-gold carpet runner that covered the middle of the corridor floor. The right side of the corridor was composed of a waist-high half wall, with regularly spaced structural marble pillars, that separated the corridor from the covered section of the central courtyard. Inward from the covered area was an open area holding five fountains, and four herb gardens, one in each corner.

"The next door is the study," announced the majer.

Just outside the study, Mykel saw a body that had been pulled to the side of the corridor, leaving a series of blood smears on the polished white marble. He bent down. The dead woman was the one who had accompanied Rachyla. "Sir? Did Fifteenth Company shoot this woman?"

"No . . . not that I saw, Captain. She was dead when we got here."

Vaclyn thought he was telling the truth. So who had shot Astylara? Why?

The seltyr's study measured a ten yards by fifteen, with bookshelves on all the walls. Less than a quarter of the shelves held books. Most of the spaces were filled with decorative objects—golden vases, small statues of horses, one of a pteridon with spread wings, the bust of a beautiful woman wearing an elaborate golden choker adorned with emeralds and diamonds.

The single desk was of black oak, and completely bare except for an open ledger.

At one end of the study—in a weapons rack—were three Cadmian rifles, all polished and shimmering. Suspecting that the magazines were full, Mykel checked. They were, as was the magazine of the rifle lying on the far end of the heavy Indyoran carpet that covered most of the marble-floored study. The splotches of blood on the top of the barrel had dried.

Just beyond the rifle, a bookcase was swung away from the wall, revealing a chamber beyond. Several books lay on the marble floor. Two were open, pages loose from where bullets had hit them. Blood was splattered on the floor as well.

"Seltyr Ubarjyr was coming out of that chamber there when we came through the door. He didn't get his rifle up in time."

Mykel could tell the majer was lying. Ubarjyr had been holding the rifle, but he'd never raised it. He would have tried to make a deal, and

Vaclyn wasn't interested in deals. He wanted the dead body of a rebel landowner. A dead body with contraband rifles around was much more convenient. Mykel did wonder why the majer had used a rifle, rather than his beloved knives.

"You should look in the chamber, Captain."

Mykel did, although, from Vaclyn's tone, he knew what he would find.

Four cases of Cadmian rifles were stacked on one side of the long and narrow room. On the other were close to forty smaller cases of ammunition.

"Quite a bit of ammunition here," Mykel observed, knowing that the majer would need an acknowledgment.

"There is, isn't there?" Vaclyn looked hard at Mykel. "What have you learned today, Captain?" The majer's voice was low and hard.

"There's more rebel activity here than meets the eye, and it's not just escaped prisoners."

"That is brilliantly obvious." Vaclyn snorted. "You could have lost your entire company! The only reason that you didn't is that these rebels hadn't learned to use their weapons well. There is a reason for following the Code directly. From now on, Captain, you take anyone with any contraband into custody. I don't care if it's the local justicer or the wealthiest grower in Dramur. Do you understand me?"

"Yes, sir."

"One more incident like this, and I will recommend that you stand court-martial for insubordination and recommend your dismissal in disgrace."

"Yes, sir." Mykel managed to keep his face immobile, furious as he was.

"Your talents obviously lie more in direct action, Captain. Tomorrow, Fifteenth Company will ride to relieve Fourteenth Company, and you will patrol the area north of the mine, and you *will* capture or kill, as necessary, the escaped miners."

"Yes, sir."

"We will search the rest of the villa. With a room like this, we probably won't find any more, but we need to look. We'll take whatever wagons the estate has to transport contraband back to Dramuria."

Mykel searched the hidden room, but found nothing more than the rifles, the ammunition, and five locked chests, doubtless containing golds, although he did not break the locks. By shifting them, he could hear and feel the coins move.

Then, once Majer Vaclyn had left, he went back to the desk and looked at the open ledger, studying the entries. He saw nothing about rifles or ammunition, but the number of golds spent on various things, from bolts of cloth to horses and even iron rods, was staggering. One entry alone for bolts of cotton was two hundred golds—four times more than the cost of a factor's great house in Faitel.

For Mykel, the question remained—why had Ubarjyr risked everything to smuggle in so many rifles and so much ammunition? It didn't make sense, not with what Mykel knew.

He shook his head. He needed to get back to overseeing his men. Although he had assigned squad leaders whom he trusted not to loot, it would be better if he were supervising what the men were doing.

27

As both the majer and Mykel had suspected, a search of the estate buildings revealed no contraband besides that already found in the secret chamber off the study. It did reveal a hidden storeroom filled with recently sewn uniforms in green with gold trim and with several score cartridge belts, along with the leather cut for several score more.

Once Fifteenth Company had gathered the wagons filled with rifles, ammunition, uniforms, and cartridge belts, Majer Vaclyn had returned the estate to the care of the steward—with severe warnings about supporting smuggling and handling contraband weapons. Then the majer had accompanied Fifteenth Company, the prisoners—fifteen of the men in the green uniforms and Rachyla—and the wagons for several vingts southward. Mykel had really wanted to talk to Rachyla, but he wasn't about to try that with the majer around, not when Vaclyn already thought he'd initially let her go because she was attractive.

She was, Mykel admitted to himself, but that had not been his reasoning, not that he'd ever convince the majer. So he kept riding, and listening to Vaclyn.

"Some of these growers . . . they've been a law unto themselves, and they have to learn that the Code applies to them just like everyone else . . . and it applies to us as well, Captain. I don't want you forgetting that."

"No, sir." Mykel wasn't about to forget how Vaclyn thought about that.

After another quarter glass, the majer turned in the saddle once more, his eyes on Mykel. "Here is where I leave you, Captain. I'll be heading directly to Dramuria to report on this to the Myrmidon colonel. I expect you to ride straight through with the prisoners and the evidence. Be alert! Someone might try to ambush you to get the weapons."

"Yes, sir." Mykel had thought of that already. He had two lines of scouts out.

"Good day, Captain." With that, the majer had nodded and ridden ahead with the squad from Thirteenth Company.

Mykel and Bhoral rode silently until the majer and his squad were well out of sight.

"What do you make of all this, sir?" asked the senior squad leader.

"It seems clear that someone among the alectors had a good idea that something was about to happen here."

"If they knew that, why did they send us?"

"Maybe they didn't know who had the guns and where they were, just that they'd been smuggled to Dramur. Pteridons aren't very effective if you don't know where to point those lancers. You could burn up a lot of villas and destroy a lot of estates and not get anything."

"So we're doing the grunt work, sort of moving targets to flush these rebels out?"

Mykel offered a rueful laugh. "It's beginning to look that way."

"I still don't see why the seltyr just didn't open up the villa and invite you and the majer in. We couldn't have found those hidden rooms, not without bashing holes in the walls, and even the majer wouldn't have done that."

Mykel wasn't sure about that.

"If we came back, ready to do that, we wouldn't have found anything," Bhoral concluded. "Or they would have set up a real ambush."

Thoughts along those lines had occurred to Mykel. "I think I'll see if the young woman might answer some questions."

"Good luck, Captain. She looked like she'd be happy to see us all flogged and flamed."

Mykel turned his mount back along the road until he reached the wagons and the string of mounts that carried the uninjured prisoners. Although Rachyla still had her hands tied behind her, she rode more easily than did Mykel as he eased his mount around and up beside her.

She kept her eyes straight ahead, ignoring the captain.

"Good afternoon, Rachyla."

Rachyla did not look at Mykel, nor did she answer.

"Since you're not responding to pleasantries, perhaps you'd like to tell me why your father gathered all those rifles. He had to have known it was against the Code."

Rachyla said nothing, and she continued looking at the troopers before her and the road.

"Did you think I could just let you go on breaking the Code? Or that the majer would allow me to?"

She still said nothing.

"How could you—or he—believe you could stockpile all those Cadmian rifles without someone finding out?"

There was no response.

"He was building his own army. There were uniforms and cartridge belts. How could he possibly have thought he could get away with it?"

She turned in the saddle and stared directly at Mykel. "You are an idiot, Captain. He was betrayed by those he trusted, just as you will be." Then she turned away, looking directly ahead of her at the long and gently winding road that led back to Dramuria.

Mykel tried another long string of questions, but the one response was all that he got from her. After riding beside her for more than three vingts, he finally rode back to the head of the column, where he eased his mount up beside that of Gendsyr.

"Captain?"

"I just had a few questions, Gendsyr, about what first squad was doing with the majer. I'll have to write a report on it, and I wasn't there." Mykel offered an embarrassed smile.

"Wasn't really all that much. After you took care of the ones firing at us, he ordered half the first squad to follow him. Didn't take all that long before he was back, and so were you."

Mykel should have realized that Gendsyr would have been left holding the courtyard. "Who went with the majer who could tell me what happened?"

The squad leader turned in the saddle. "Halomer! Ride up here!"

"Coming, sir." Halomer was an older ranker, probably older than Mykel, who rode well and slipped his mount between those of the captain and the squad leader.

"Captain here wants to know what you did in the villa with the majer."

"We just followed him. Everyone pretty much got out of the way until we got to that study. Some servant tried to stop us, and the majer clubbed him aside and charged inside. That was the first time there were any shots."

"Did anyone from first squad fire their weapons in the study?" asked Mykel.

"No, sir. The majer went in first, and he had his rifle out."

"So he killed the seltyr?"

"I didn't see that, sir. I was behind the majer. He fired, and when we got in there, the seltyr was down. He was dead."

"You searched the rest of the villa after that?"

"No, sir. The majer looked around the study. Then we went back to the front under those pillars. That was when you came back. We didn't do any searching until you ordered it."

Mykel nodded. "Thank you. That's all."

"Yes, sir."

As Halomer let his mount drop back, Mykel turned to Gendsyr. "Is there anything else I missed that I should know?"

The squad leader frowned. "Don't think so, sir."

With a faint smile, Mykel nodded. "Thank you." He eased the chestnut forward to rejoin Bhoral in the van.

Why had the majer killed the seltyr? Was it because he knew that the man would somehow escape, because of his connections and wealth? Vaclyn had certainly seen enough to be that cynical, and he was zealous enough to want to see the Code upheld, almost at any cost. That he had certainly made clear to Mykel.

Ubarjyr had been betrayed by those he had trusted. That Rachyla had believed. But how could anyone trust smugglers or whoever dealt in contraband weapons?

Had the Cadmians in Dramuria been involved? Was that why Majer Herryf had been unable to supply any detailed information? That was certainly a possibility. But he had no proof, although that sort of conspiracy would certainly explain many of the strange aspects of the Third Battalion's deployment to Dramur, including why Majer Vaclyn had made sure that the seltyr had been killed.

All Mykel could do was keep his eyes and ears open—and try not to trust anyone. He shifted his weight in the saddle and took a deep breath.

28

Darkness had long since fallen over the Cadmian compound north of Dramuria by the time Mykel and Fifteenth Company arrived on Septi night. While Bhoral settled the rest of the company, Mykel and second squad escorted the captives to the confinement barracks. There, the senior squad leader in charge of the confinement barracks told Mykel that Rachyla would be confined in the officer's cell on the ground floor of the adjoining building.

Mykel walked beside Rachyla, her hands still bound behind her. Four troopers followed them. In the dimness away from the wall lamps, she stumbled on an uneven stone, and Mykel steadied her with a hand on her shoulder.

"If you don't mind, Captain . . ."

"Just making sure you don't try to escape," he answered lightly.

"You think that a mere woman could escape from here? With so many brave Cadmians around?" Her voice was openly scornful.

"If anyone could, you could," Mykel replied quietly.

Her only response was a disdainful laugh.

There were two guards already posted outside the officer's cell. An iron grate covered the closed shutters.

"Sir?" asked the guards.

"This is Lady Rachyla. She will be confined here. I'd like to check the quarters."

The two guards exchanged glances.

"One of you can come in, or not, as you please. My men will guard outside until I leave."

"As you wish, sir. So long as she stays safe inside."

"She'll stay." Mykel had his doubts about her safety anywhere, but there was little that he could do.

The shorter guard opened the heavy wooden door. Mykel stepped inside and glanced around the spartan room, dimly lit only by the wall lamps outside on each side of the door. All the cell held were a bed, a desk, and a stool, plus pegs on the wall. A chamber pot stood in one corner. He walked around for a moment, then turned. "Bring the lady inside."

"I can walk in myself." She did.

"You can close the door. I need to ask her some questions."

"Yes, sir."

Mykel had no doubts they thought he had other ideas, but he also didn't want any rankers hanging over his shoulder. He waited until the door *clunked* shut. The cell was dark, but the faint light seeping through the shutters was enough. His night vision had always been good.

"Turn around," he said.

"Why?"

"So I can untie your wrists."

Rachyla turned.

"Don't move. I may have to cut these."

He didn't, but he did have to use the point of the knife to loosen the outer knot. Before he finished loosening her bonds, he sheathed the knife. Then, leaving her to work free the last of the rope, he stepped back.

She turned to face him in the dimness. "Such an honorable man you are, Captain. I never would have guessed."

"Sit down. I need some answers." He raised his voice, facing the door.

"I am *not* sitting on the bed, Captain."

"Then sit on the stool or stand," Mykel replied. "As you please."

"What would please me would be to depart here." Rachyla continued to stand.

"That is unlikely, although if anyone could manage it, you probably could."

"I am the captive, and you seek to flatter me? Are you so deprived that you would seek pleasure from a prisoner? Do you think I would sell myself so cheaply?"

Once more Mykel could sense that her words were not bravado, but more like a statement of fact. "No. You might find yourself forced, but you would never sell yourself."

"You know me so well?"

"No. I don't know you at all. I can tell some things about you, and that's one that was obvious from the time I saw you driving that cart. Why were you carrying that rifle? Had someone just left it there, and you didn't want to be bothered by taking it back?"

The moment of silence was enough for Mykel to judge that he was close to the truth. He laughed, ruefully. "And you wouldn't give anyone the satisfaction of knowing that. I should have guessed."

As he looked at her, he thought he saw, despite the darkness, a trace of brightness in and around her eyes. "I'm sorry. I wish it had been otherwise. I imagine you do as well."

"I don't need pity, Captain. Or false sympathy. Or anything else."

"Did you know your father was stockpiling so many weapons?" Mykel really didn't want to ask the question, but he needed to ask some, just in case Vaclyn inquired.

Rachyla didn't answer.

"You said he was betrayed? Who betrayed him? The smugglers who brought the weapons?"

"Do you think my father would ever have trusted a smuggler to keep his word, Captain?" Rachyla laughed, a full but bitter sound.

"Then who was it? The local council?"

"The council is nothing. Neither are your alectors. The true and rightful rulers of Dramur are its seltyrs."

"The true and rightful rulers? You deny the Duarches?"

Rachyla looked straight at Mykel, but said nothing, offering what might have been a faint and sad smile.

"You truly believe that?"

She remained mute.

"If you did escape, what would you do?"

There was no answer.

Mykel laughed, gently and stepped back. "Good night, Lady Rachyla." Then he rapped on the door. "I'm finished here."

When the door opened, all six Cadmians had rifles trained on the doorway.

Rachyla's brief laughter filled the courtyard, cut off as one of the local Cadmian rankers closed the door, shoved both the heavy iron bolts into place, then snapped the lock shut.

"Thank you." Mykel inclined his head to the guards.

"You find out anything, sir?"

"A little. Not as much as I'd like, but she wasn't about to say more now."

"She will in time. They all do. Every one."

That might have been, but Mykel was convinced that Rachyla was anything but everyone.

He looked at his own rankers. "Let's go."

As he crossed the courtyard, he thought about his brief interaction with the seltyr's daughter. Rachyla didn't care for him, and she shouldn't have, given what he had been forced to do, but she had also been giving him a message, and that message was most clear. Someone in the Cadmians, or in the government of the Duarchy, had been involved. Who or why—those were questions whose answers were the merest speculation.

If what she had intimated happened to be true, Mykel and Fifteenth Company, indeed, the entire Third Battalion, faced a much more complicated situation than anyone could have known—and there was nothing Mykel could say about it. The majer wouldn't listen, and there was no one above him, not within hundreds of vingts, to whom Mykel dared entrust such information. Not until he knew more.

He did wish that he'd met Rachyla under other circumstances, but that wouldn't have made any difference. She was wealthy—and he was a crafter's son and a city boy, and now she was likely to spend years in confinement, or even be executed, and it was largely Mykel's doing. All he'd had to do would have been to ignore the rifle.

He laughed, ironically. That was the one thing he couldn't have done unless he wanted to be responsible for scores of Cadmian deaths.

29

After a short early-morning flight on Octdi with Falyna—a flight that revealed nothing, including in the area around the ancient tunnel—Dainyl was walking across the Cadmian courtyard when Captain Meryst hurried up to him.

"Colonel, sir . . . Majer Herryf would beg your indulgence to join him in his study at your earliest convenience."

"Thank you, Captain." Dainyl smiled politely. "Did he say what might be so urgent?"

"He said that a large cache of contraband weapons had been discovered in an unanticipated location, sir. That is all he said, except that I was to tell no one that, save you."

"I will be there shortly, then." Dainyl debated making the arrogant majer wait, but such tactics would be lost on the majer and only make his own day longer. He turned and followed the captain, shortening his stride to match steps with the much smaller Cadmian officer.

Two Cadmian officers bolted upright as Dainyl strode into Majer Herryf 's study. Behind Dainyl, Captain Meryst closed the door, taking care to remain outside and leave the three more senior officers alone. Dainyl repressed a smile of amusement at Meryst's quiet tact, so at odds with Herryf 's manner.

"I am sorry to bother you, Colonel." Herryf nodded to the other officer, standing beside him. "Majer Vaclyn has arrived with a . . . startling report."

Dainyl disliked Herryf 's fawning and apologetic tone even more than the majer's arrogance, which remained beneath the subservience. "What might that be?" He turned to the Third Battalion majer, the older of the two Cadmian officers.

"Colonel, you might recall that the Third Battalion has been patrolling the roads north of where the smugglers were detected. On Sexdi, the captain of Fifteenth Company discovered a single rifle in the horse cart of the daughter of a local seltyr. The rifle was Cadmian-issue, but without the usual maker's stamped numbers. Because the woman seemed unaware of the rifle, and because the captain decided to proceed cautiously, despite the requirements of the Code, of which he has since been made well aware, I took command of Fifteenth Company yesterday morning, and we proceeded to Stylan Estate, the dwelling of the woman, who turned out to be the daughter of Seltyr Ubarjyr . . ."

At the seltyr's name, Dainyl noted a certain uneasiness in Majer Herryf, but he merely nodded for the long-winded Vaclyn to continue.

"Fifteenth Company found a closed and locked outer gate, and when we reached the seltyr's villa, we were attacked by more than fivescore uniformed retainers using rifles. The rifles turned out to be Cadmian weapons. Fifteenth Company subdued the insurgents with minimal casualties. There were over fourscore of them killed, including the seltyr, and fifteen captured, while Fifteenth Company, under my direction, lost but four rankers and had five wounded. After the skirmish, we inspected the villa and found another five cases of rifles, more than forty cases of ammunition, as well as uniforms and cartridge belts."

"You say that the seltyr was behind this?" asked Dainyl.

"Yes, sir," replied Vaclyn. "The last cases of rifles and ammunition were discovered in a hidden room that opened only into his private study."

"You seem to have been most effective, Majer. You may recall that I am here only as an observer, however."

"Yes, sir," replied Herryf smoothly, "but as an observer, we thought you should be the first to know about this. If you wish, and, of course, only if you wish, you could interrogate the captives. One of them is the seltyr's daughter."

"You brought her here?"

"How could we not, Colonel?" Vaclyn seemed to expand with indignation. "She was the one who had the first contraband rifle, and the one who was trying to delay us while the insurgents tried to get into position to attack."

"Under those circumstances, I imagine you could see no other alternative." Dainyl paused. "I suppose it could not hurt to talk to some of them." He didn't like the idea, but if there was information that had not been uncovered, and the marshal found out later . . . that would not be at all in Dainyl's favor. He smiled at Herryf. "Is there anything else?"

"Ah . . . no, sir."

"Then, if you would have someone escort me to the captives." He looked to Vaclyn. "My congratulations, Majer."

"Thank you, sir."

Herryf followed Dainyl out of the study, and beckoned to Captain Meryst. "Please take the colonel to the captives."

Meryst half bowed, then turned to Dainyl. "The woman is in a room set aside for officers. It is in a separate building. Would you prefer to see her first or after the others?"

"First, I would think."

Meryst led the way to a building in the middle of those set close to the compound's south wall. The ground-level door at the east end was guarded by a pair of Cadmian rankers.

"Her name is Rachyla. She is the eldest daughter of Seltyr Ubarjyr." Meryst stopped before the pair of guards outside the door. "The colonel will be interrogating the prisoner."

One of the guards took out a large, tarnished, brass key and inserted it into a lock. With a heavy click, the lock opened. Then he retracted both iron bolts. Dainyl had to lower his head to enter the room, and once inside, the top of his head almost touched the low ceiling.

The door closed behind him, although he did not hear the click of a lock again.

The woman, her hair as dark and shimmering as that of an alector, was seated on a tall stool at a small desk, writing. She turned to the door as he entered. Her face froze, and she turned away.

"Your name is Rachyla. How did you end up here?"

The woman did not look at Dainyl, but he could sense anger. Not fear, but anger.

"You're fortunate that you're a woman," he said mildly.

Rachyla did not answer.

"You were involved in a revolt," said Dainyl quietly. "That was not exactly wise."

"I have nothing to say to you."

"You are angry. Yet we have never met."

"I have nothing to say."

Behind the anger was also a sense of dread and despair, a strange combination.

Although he tried a number of questions and approaches, even with a hint of Talent-projection and -persuasion, she said nothing more. While she did not seem to be Talented, she was resistant to mild Talent-persuasion, and Dainyl decided against using greater Talent, since there was no certainty that it would work and the effects could be detected by a Talented alector, such as the marshal or the Highest. After close to half a glass, he left.

From there, Meryst escorted him to the holding cells in a squat and square building set against the southeast corner of the compound.

The guards brought the first prisoner to the interrogation room, where Dainyl sat in a too-small chair. The man was young. His left arm was bandaged heavily, and he slumped onto the stool. His eyes avoided Dainyl.

"Why did you fire on the Cadmians?"

The rebel did not answer.

Dainyl tried to Talent-project compulsion on the slightest level. After a moment, he asked again, "Why did you fire?"

The young man shivered, then replied, "Squad leader said to fire on them, sir."

"Did you hit any of them?"

"I don't know. They shot back so quickly. They killed so many of us. So quickly. Their captain, he shot three or four himself."

"Who commanded you?"

The rebel looked at the colonel blankly.

"Who was in charge of the squad leaders, and who was in charge of that person?"

"Oh, Nurqueyt, he was the captain. His orders came from Seltyr Ubarjyr."

"Who gave orders to the seltyr?"

"No one, sir. No one gives orders to a seltyr." The young man looked appalled, then added quickly, "Except an alector, sir."

"How long had you been training?"

"A season or so, sir. But we only got the rifles three weeks ago, maybe four . . . it was after Pabolar's birthday."

"Are there other companies training?"

"I don't know, sir."

"What do you think?"

"There might be a few others, but there aren't many. Captain Nurqueyt said that we were fortunate. The rifles were hard to come by . . ."

Dainyl talked to the young man for another quarter glass. After that, he talked to all the others, and it was well into the afternoon before he returned to his quarters. All of the captives had said variations of the same things.

Two things had stood out. The first was the anger of the lander woman. She had not only immediately recognized Dainyl as an alector, but his presence had angered her—not frightened her. That alone suggested that she had seen alectors or known of their actions. Then there were the rifles—and the timing of their arrival in Dramur. The High Alector of Justice—or Marshal Shastylt—had to have learned about the incipient rebellion early, perhaps even while the rifles were on their way to Dramur. That was likely to be the explanation he received—if he could find a way to ask that question in a fashion that didn't threaten his own future. If he even bothered with the question . . . because it seemed clear enough to him that somehow the marshal and the Highest had arranged for the rifles to be shipped to the seltyr. Why was another question, and one he needed to be more careful in investigating, far more careful, he suspected, than had been Submarshal Tyanylt.

30

Mykel and Fifteenth Company rode northwest over yet another narrow road, toward the town of Jyoha. Both sides of the road were without shoulders and bordered by brush olives and other growth, but all of it was just high enough and thick enough so that seeing more than a few yards into the growth was difficult. At the same time, he was following a map about which he had more than a few doubts with orders that he trusted even less. How exactly was he supposed to "capture and subdue rebel forces opposed to the Code of the Duarches" with almost no information on how large such forces might be or where they were.

As he rode and studied the road, rising slowly before him to cross between two low hills more than a vingt ahead, Mykel tried to figure out where he had erred in the mess at Stylan Estate. Should he just have followed the Code blindly, as the majer had demanded? Mykel still thought that his instincts had been right. If he taken Rachyla into custody immediately, Seltyr Ubarjyr would have protested. His daughter would have been returned, either flogged or merely admonished, and at some time in the future, armed attacks would have occurred, either against one of the battalion's companies or against other growers. Certainly, the seltyr had to have been making plans to arm his forces for some time. But why? And for what purpose?

Why had Majer Vaclyn gone out of his way, even put himself in danger, to make certain that the seltyr was dead? Was that because he feared that the seltyr's capture would create a rallying point? If matters were so desperate, why hadn't a company of Myrmidons been sent in? Or was Vaclyn covering up something?

Who in the Duarchy had betrayed the seltyr? It had to be someone high enough—a regional bursar? Someone even higher? But why would anyone higher, an alector, even bother with a local grower? Why would anyone want to arm locals, when the alectors went out of their way to keep rifles out of the hands of landers and indigens? Mykel took a deep breath. For all his questions, he neither had answers nor any way to find them, and worrying over them would just distract him from the tasks at hand.

He looked at the rise in the road ahead, where it passed between the low hills. Although he couldn't say why, something bothered him. That was another problem. His feelings were often right, but he'd been raised as a city boy, and he couldn't always explain—either to squad leaders or to his superiors—why he had done something or not done it.

One of the scouts reined up short, more than a half vingt ahead of the vanguard. Mykel watched as the trooper pulled out his rifle and fired at the ground in front of him. A plume of dust rose, more than should have. The trooper nodded and started to turn his mount.

Crack! At the sound of the rifle, both scouts completed the turn and spurred their mounts back toward the van of Fifteenth Company.

"Company halt! Rifles ready!" snapped Mykel. "Road oblique! Both sides!"

First squad swung out to the left, and second to the right, as much as they could, in a staggered formation that allowed more rifles to be aimed at an enemy ahead.

Another short volley of shots chased the returning scouts, all coming from the brush-covered hillside to the right of the road. None appeared to strike the two Cadmians.

"Take cover on the right!" Mykel ordered.

As the scouts neared, Mykel gestured them to him. "What did you find?"

"Pits . . . holes in the road," explained Gerant, reining up and bringing his mount as close to the brush olive as he could. "Looked like sharpened stakes in them. Not all that deep, maybe a third to a half yard, but deep enough to mess up a mount. If you were riding hard . . ."

Mykel understood—a broken leg or worse for the mount and a broken neck for the rider.

Over the next quarter glass, there where were no more shots, and no sounds from ahead. In the end, Mykel chose slowness and cover, using the first two squads to advance on foot, using poles to probe any suspicious ground and keeping close to the brush olives. Fifteenth Company took no other shots, but more than two glasses passed before the company held the rise. They also discovered more than a score of pits, most a yard wide and a third of a yard deep. A darkish substance had been smeared on the stakes. Pickets had been posted in all directions, but Mykel doubted they would see or hear anyone.

"Have them use something to break them and fill the holes," Mykel told Bhoral. "If we leave those . . . how many riders will get hurt, including some of our own dispatch riders? Can you imagine what the majer will have to say, especially after the mess in Enstyla?"

Bhoral nodded slowly. "Sorry time when mounted rifles have to fill holes in a road."

"There's no help for it."

Mykel looked at the descending road that was barely more than a lane. It circled around the base of the western hill until it headed almost due west, but only for another vingt. Then it turned back north and climbed between two more hills.

He had to wonder how many more traps and ambushes lay ahead before they reached Jyoha—where they were supposed to establish a base from which to attack the escaped prisoners who were part of the rebel forces. According to the map, Jyoha lay less than ten vingts away.

Ten long vingts.

31

By Londi morning, the more Dainyl considered the implications of what he had observed, the less comfortable he felt, especially as a mere observer in Dramur. Yet he had very little proof that he could bring to the High Alector of Justice, or for that matter, even indirectly through Lystrana to the Duarch of Elcien himself. Not only that, but bringing forward his suspicions looked to be most unwise. The only hard evidence was something like a hundred and fifty Cadmian rifles without maker's marks or stamps to indicate whether they had been made in Faitel or in Alustre. While some landers might have been able to manufacture their own weapons, crafting on the captured rifles was both high and standardized—and any facility that could provide that would be hard-pressed to remain concealed. More important, the rifles looked and felt as though they had come from an artisan facility.

There had been a skirmish at Stylan Estate, where the contraband had been found, but nothing to indicate what had prompted the revolt, or the breaking of the Code on the use of Cadmian weapons—and none of those who survived could explain why any of it had occurred. Dainyl had no doubt that it all involved some objective of the Highest and the marshal, but he had no idea whether that purpose advanced the goals of the Duarchy or was a plot against the Duarches—or against other high alectors.

All the other events were not matters that he could safely report, not in full, or events without enough behind them for any meaningful conclusions to be drawn. He could report the attack on himself, but not what the attacker had said. He could report that the lander woman would not talk to him, but he could not point out that she was resistant to the use of Talent. He could point out that someone was smuggling the rifles into Dramur, but not who or why. He could report the ancient tunnel, although he wanted to wait on doing that.

And behind all that was one other constraint, one that faced all Myrmidons, indeed, all alectors. Compared to the total lander and indigen population of Acorus, the Myrmidons were few. Even the total number of Cadmians was small, particularly the battalions from Elcien and Alustre or Dereka, rather than locally recruited and trained Cadmians, such as those under Majer Herryf.

For all that, he needed to do something. At the very least, he needed to find out what Herryf was doing and saying, and to do so, he needed to risk revealing what he had kept hidden for years, but then, he and Lystrana had kept those abilities hidden just for a situation such as he now faced.

With a wry smile, he left his quarters and made his way down to the courtyard and toward the headquarters building. He walked toward the north side of the structure and into the deep early-morning shadows. There he paused, until he was certain no one was looking in his direction before he raised a full Talent-shield. With the shield in place, he planned to take advantage of common misperceptions.

Because alectors were so much bigger than landers, most landers and indigens had no idea how quietly an alector could move—or that an alector's Talent could provide a concealment from the eyes of all without Talent, and that was from all indigens and almost all landers.

He moved silently through the shadows until he reached the main entrance, where he slipped past the duty desk and the unseeing squad leader who sat there. Concealed by Talent or not, Dainyl kept to the side of the corridor. Talent-hiding wouldn't keep someone from walking into him.

Captain Benjyr and Majer Herryf were alone in the majer's study.

Dainyl used his Talent, hoping that the illusion would hold, to project an image of a closed door, while he opened the door and eased into the study. He made his way to the corner out of the direct sunlight coming through the window.

Neither man looked up.

". . . have they done?" asked Herryf. "Besides kill one of the most respected seltyrs in Dramur, imprison his daughter, and slaughter a hundred of his retainers? They hold the roads. They ride through the plantations and upset the remaining growers. They search wagons looking for rifles that aren't there. Miners are still escaping, or disappearing, which is worse, and the guano output continues to drop. The council, the factors, and the growers have fewer and fewer golds, and prices for food are rising rapidly. All this, and I have heard nothing from these outland Cadmians. I have heard nothing from the Myrmidon colonel. He just watches as Dramur is unraveling."

"I had thought Majer Vaclyn might have kept you informed, sir. He and his captains haven't said much at all, except for Captain Kuertyl. He is the kind who trades information the way the factors trade goods."

"What has he said?"

"The officers and rankers are less than pleased with you. They feel that you should have handled the problems with the miners with our forces."

"How? We've been trying for over a year. I was forbidden to create another company. I was told I could not work with the council to create a local militia. What choices did I have?"

Dainyl had not been aware of what Herryf had suggested, but he wasn't surprised that the marshal would have limited the forces under the majer's direct or indirect control.

"Sir?" ventured Benjyr. "I was asked to tell you something."

"By whom?"

"I don't know. It was dark, and they approached me outside my brother's house."

He was lying about that, Dainyl knew.

Herryf paused, then asked, "What was this message of great import?"

"Some of the growers to the north think that the Cadmians are there to take their lands."

"How would they do that?" Herryf shook his head. "Some people will believe anything."

"Sir, they say that the Cadmians will keep searching until they find weapons and rebels. Then whatever growers where they're found will be accused of supporting the rebels and sent to the mines, and their lands put up for sale, or maybe just turned over to the council. The colonel spent a lot of time with the guilds and the director . . ."

Herryf frowned. "That doesn't make sense. Alectors don't care that much about lands or trade. Why would they . . . ?"

"Sir, I didn't say it made sense. That's what some of them feel."

About that, Dainyl could sense, Benjyr was absolutely convinced.

"I'll have to talk to Majer Vaclyn. He won't listen, but I'll have to talk to him."

"What about the colonel, sir?"

"There's no point in that, except to alert him. He'd deny anything. If the alectors aren't involved, he would say that they weren't. If they are, he'll say the same."

"Two more miners escaped yesterday," Benjyr said quietly.

"How? There's an extra company of Cadmians guarding the mine road."

"No one knows. They were missing when they were mustered to march back to quarters. Every span of the mine was searched."

"They must have been hiding somewhere, and then they escaped the stockade after dark." Herryf glared at the captain. "This sort of thing makes us look incompetent, and it adds to the illusion that there is some sort of overwhelming force against us."

"But . . . sir . . . you reported . . ."

"I reported we needed an additional company of Cadmians to deal with the escapees, and that, in time, unless we got a permanent addition to the compound, the escaped miners would present a problem. I wish I'd never made the report. I was told—told, mind you, Captain—that I was reporting an insurrection and to expect a full Cadmian battalion and a Myrmidon observer."

Behind his Talent-shield, Dainyl frowned. That was what he had been told by the Highest, and he had conveyed that to Herryf in one fashion or another, but Herryf seemed to be telling Benjyr the truth about what he had reported to the marshal—or the submarshal.

Herryf stood. "I need to walk around the compound, to be seen. You might as well accompany me."

"Yes, sir," replied the captain.

Dainyl waited until they had left before slipping out of the study and the headquarters building.

32

From the saddle of the chestnut, as the company headed westward, Mykel glanced across the ramshackle sheds and run-down holder's dwelling that served as a base for the Fifteenth Company. They had spent almost a week patrolling in and around Jyoha, without ever seeing a rebel or an escaped mine prisoner. That might have been because Fourteenth Company and Dohark had captured the few that were careless or less adept at avoiding the Cadmians.

Fifteenth Company had seen plenty of hoofprints, but neither the horses that made them nor the men who rode those mounts. In following tracks and patrolling the roads, they had lost two mounts to the poisoned stakes in the concealed pits in various lanes and roads, and two troopers had been injured when the mounts went down. Four others had been stung by nightwasps and had turned up with fevers and welts the size of a man's hand.

"I'll keep fourth and fifth squads with me," Mykel said to Bhoral, confirming what he had told the senior squad leader earlier. "After I talk with some of the crafters in the village, we'll look at that lane that winds up toward the ruins of the old sawmill."

"Still don't understand that," replied Bhoral. "They built the sawmill, and the Myrmidons burned it down? Why would they do that?"

"That's one of the things I'm going to try to find out."

He'd already tried talking to some of the crafters and found out next to nothing, but he'd kept looking and listening, and now he was ready to try again.

Short of the town, Bhoral and the first three squads split away, and Mykel and his smaller contingent continued westward. The fields on each side of the lane into Jyoha were filled with plants, supposedly all sunbeans. The beans were actually oilseeds that, when pressed, provided a golden oil that was used for lamps across Dramur. Some was shipped to Southgate as well, according to the grower who had leased the rundown and near-abandoned holding to Third Battalion. Mykel had seldom seen any workers in the fields, but the sunbeans didn't seem to require much care, and that might have been why they had displaced other crops.

The houses on the east side of Jyoha were one story and of mud brick, unlike the cut-stone dwellings in Dramuria. The roofs were of faded red tiles. Some houses had been plastered with stucco, then washed with pastel colors, mostly blues and greens; but that had been sometime ago, for the wash had faded, and the red showed through, giving the walls a pinkish tinge.

The three women doing wash by a well looked away as the Cadmians neared, and another mother scurried out from a small one-room dwelling and scooped up a bare-bottomed toddler and carted her back into the mud-brick hut, closing the warped plank door firmly.

Several men stood on the dusty porch of the one tavern in Jyoha, whose doors were closed. Two stared at Mykel. He looked back until they dropped their eyes.

Mykel reined up outside the chandlery, then turned to Dravadyl and Vhanyr, the fourth and fifth squad leaders. "Ride around the village and see if you can spot anything interesting. Swing back here in half a glass."

"Yes, sir."

"Try not to shoot anyone." Mykel offered a wry grin. "We don't need any more pits dug in the roads."

"We won't—not unless they shoot first," replied Dravadyl.

The captain dismounted and tied the chestnut to the hitching post, two squat pillars built of mud bricks connected by a rusty iron bar. He crossed the narrow porch and stepped into the chandlery, letting his eyes adjust to the dimness. For the last few days, he'd stopped there every day and bought something, usually some item of provisions that he turned over to one squad leader or another. After dismounting and tying the chestnut to the rail, he made his way inside.

A man not that much older than he was stood in one corner, rearranging some cotton shirts folded on a corner table. In a village as small and as isolated as Jyoha, the chandlery carried far more items than it would in Dramuria, but fewer of each. Mykel didn't recall there even being a chandlery in Faitel, not that he'd ever seen.

"Good morning, Harnyck," Mykel offered.

"Morning, Captain." The man's voice was even, neither friendly nor unfriendly.

Mykel walked to the case that served, after a fashion, as a cooler, where he selected a small round of hard yellow cheese. Holding it up, he asked, "How much?"

"For that one, seeing as it's you, Captain, two silvers."

"Since I don't want special treatment, Harnyck," Mykel bantered back, "how about one."

"You're not talking like a good Cadmian officer, Captain. That's the kind of bargain a smuggler would force on a father needing milk for a starving bairn."

"I'm glad you think so highly of me. A silver and two."

"You give me one and three, and it's yours."

Mykel threw up his hands. "What can I do? One and three." He fumbled in his wallet, then extracted the coins.

Harnyck took them.

"I was wondering if you could help me."

"What are you looking for?"

"Information. Not about people. About the town."

"Might be able to help." The man refolded a shirt, brushing off a small cobweb and setting it back on the table. "Might not."

"What did people grow out east before the sunbeans?"

"They tried the casaran trees, but the soil's not right. What nuts they got were too bitter. Not even the oldest nag would eat fodder with them in it. Then they tried wheat corn, but the rust got it. The growers like the sunbeans because they don't take much work until harvest, and you get two crops a year here."

"You know what happened to the old sawmill?"

"The Myrmidons burned it. No secret about that. Old man Baholyn decided the pines in the hills would make good cheap timber, and he bought out the lands to the west. Didn't pay more than a few coppers a stead square. Once he had the land, he built the mill. He'd been running it a quint less than a year, sending timber to Dramuria, and coins were flowing in here for the first time ever. Then two pteridons dropped right out of the sky. One of those big alectors walked up to him and told him to close the sawmill and to stop cutting the timber." The chandler laughed. "Baholyn bowed and said he would. You don't argue with them."

"No, you don't," Mykel agreed. "But why did they burn it?"

"He closed down for a week, maybe two, and then he started running it at night. He did everything at night, even carted the cut timbers and planks down to another barn on the edge of town. I guess he figured that nothing would happen if the place looked closed during the day. He got away with it for another quint. Then the pteridons came back and turned their lances on the mill. The Cadmians from Dramuria were here, too, and they surrounded the town. Baholyn hid somewhere. The big alector had the troopers gather everyone in the square, and he made it real clear. The town turned over Baholyn, or there wouldn't be any town. Gave everyone a glass. Said that every quarter glass that passed after that, they'd torch another house, and they'd start with the biggest." The man shrugged. "Took a glass and a half before Baholyn's daughter told 'em where he was. Her place was next. They flogged him in the square till he was dead, and then they burned his body to ashes."

"How long ago was that?"

"Not quite ten years."

"What do people here think about the guano mine?"

"It doesn't do us much good. The soil here isn't that good, and we could use the bat shit here, but folks can't pay what they will in Southgate or wherever they ship it."

"What about the miners?"

"They say some of them escaped. That's why you're here, isn't it?"

"Has anyone seen any?"

"No. Don't know anyone who has. Leastwise, no one who's talked to me about it."

"We keep finding tracks of horsemen around Jyoha, but I can't say that I've seen more than one or two people riding. Most use carts or wagons—or walk. Who are the riders?"

"Don't know as I could say, Captain."

"I don't mean names," Mykel said with a laugh. "I meant . . . Are they young bloods, the younger sons of growers, riding around because they've golds and little else to do? Or are they raiders? Or these rebel miners that everyone talks about and no one seems ever to have seen?"

"Can't say as I know."

Mykel laughed. "I know. No one *knows,* but you've probably got a better idea than most. How about a guess, Harnyck?"

"Don't have enough growers around here for bloods. Land's too piss-poor for even one seltyr. Same's true for raiders. Same'd seem to be true for rebels, as well."

"So . . . who are we talking about?"

"Seems to me, Captain, that you're doing the talking."

"You've got me again." Mykel waited.

"Lots of smallholders don't have coin, can't pay their land rents. Can't stay there, neither, or the growers'd catch 'em and send 'em to Dramuria for a judgment. They'd have to work it off in the mines. Even if they paid off one, there'd be another waiting. Law says you can't take their land if they spend at least one night a week there. Doesn't say how long on that night." Harnyck smiled, brittlely. "What else are they going to do?"

Mykel had the feeling that the chandler was telling the truth, but only because he'd chosen his words carefully. The captain wasn't sure that he'd learned much of anything when he left the shop. Outside, he only waited a few moments before the two squads returned.

"What did you see?" Mykel asked after he mounted and joined Dravadyl. Followed by the two squads, they rode away from the square and toward the stone bridge over the small creek on the west side of Jyoha.

"Nothing we haven't seen before. We get the looks that tell us to go away. People keep away, and it's like any other small town, far as I can figure. Did you have any luck, sir?"

"Not really. The chandler said the Myrmidons burned the sawmill. They also flogged the owner and burned him in the square back there. They told him to close it. He ran it at night."

"Stupid. You don't mess with alectors."

Mykel nodded.

The arched bridge was barely wide enough for two mounts abreast, and the sound of hoofs echoed dully on the stones. Once past the bridge, Mykel ordered, "Scouts out! We'll take the lane to the left."

"Scouts out, sir!"

The narrow lane showed few signs of travel, except by livestock, probably the small sheep that were among the few domestic animals besides horses resistant to the nightwasps. Less than five hundred yards up the lane, the meadows ended, replaced by low trees, the tallest no more than head high, and all set amid a forest of large stumps.

After rising gently for another hundred yards, the lane leveled and brought them out onto a flatter area, one without trees. It had been the sawmill site. The ground still held depressions that once might have been wagon tracks, and on the left were the ruins of the old sawmill.

Mykel let his eyes rove over the ruins. All that was left were the stone sides of the dried-up millrace and the mud-brick walls of the foundation, both blackened from the flame of the skylances. The sunlight glinted off glassy parts of the ruined brickwork. Nothing grew around the foundations. The nearest clumps of grass were ten yards from the blackened foundation.

"Ten years ago? Just ten?" asked Dravadyl. "Looks like it happened a lot longer ago."

Mykel thought so, too, but he knew that the chandler had not been lying.

"Hoofprints here, sir!" called one of the scouts at the south end of the open space. "Squad-sized. Some group as before, looks to be."

Mykel rode forward to where the scout waited. "How old?"

"Not today. Hasn't rained since we been here. Could be a week. I'd say more like three–four days."

"We'll follow them and see what we can find."

For a glass and a half, Mykel and the two squads followed the tracks—carefully—with the pace slower and slower as the lane became a path that turned into a trail through more of the low trees, growing between the stumps of old-growth pines and firs.

"This must have been where they were cutting the trees," mused Mykel.

"Pretty large ones, sir," replied Vhanyr, who had moved up to ride with Mykel and Dravadyl. "Like those over there."

Mykel looked more closely. The shorter trees and seedlings ended less than half a vingt ahead. Beyond that, the taller old-growth pines rose like a brown-and-green wall. The smallest of those giants was thirty yards high.

"Look sharp!" he called to the scouts.

The trail ended in a clearing beside the creek short of the forest to the south. Whoever they had been tracking had used the clearing as a campsite, with cookfires, long since cold.

"They forded the creek and headed into the forest," reported Dhozynt, the fifth squad scout. "Do you want us to follow them?"

"Not today," Mykel said. "We'll head back."

He wasn't about to take just two squads into a massive forest he didn't know, not when they'd had more than enough problems on relatively clear roads and trails. If Majer Vaclyn wanted that, the majer would have to show up and lead the company into the woods.

Just looking at the giant pines gave Mykel an uneasy feeling, as if there were something beyond. He laughed, softly. There was—a group of rebels with mounts and hostile intentions toward him and his men.

He forced himself not to look over his shoulder as they started the ride back to Jyoha. He would send a report to the majer about what the chandler had said—that the riders were poor men who were trying to keep their lands in bad times.

33

The morning was chill, not so bad as the time Dainyl had been in Blackstear and his breath had been frozen fog—that had been during what the locals had called late spring—but the day promised to be clear. In the early light, the peaks of the Murian Mountains stood out against the silver-green sky when Dainyl crossed the courtyard, wearing his blue flying jacket as he made his way to the officers' mess.

As always, the pair of local Cadmian officers avoided even looking at him as he seated himself. The steward brought him an ale immediately. He sipped it slowly, thinking about what he had overheard and the patterns revealed by Majer Herryf's latest reports. Most important of all, while escape attempts had continued, the pattern of those escapes had changed. Far fewer mals were diving off the bridge or trying to climb the stockade. Despite the use of more Cadmians as guards, a greater fraction of the escapees was vanishing without a trace. Both Sturwart and Donasyr had tried to conceal that the escapes had risen significantly in the past few months. Was that because they didn't want more Myrmidons coming to Dramur? Or because they didn't want to lose control of the mine to the growers? From his observations, it was also clear that neither the local Cadmians nor the landowners had anything to do with the escapes.

The steward returned with a platter and a basket of bread, slipping them onto the table silently. Dainyl took another swallow of the ale before trying the heavily fried egg toast.

Using Talent to boost his hearing, he listened as he began to eat.

". . . still wonder why he's here . . .

". . . hear that they sent the captain who found those rifles out to chase the escaped prisoners . . . Jyoha's the ass end of the east . . ."

"Their majer makes what we got look good. The one officer that finds something, and they give him shit duty . . ."

Dainyl mentally marked that comment and kept listening, but neither Benjyr nor Meryst said anything more of immediate interest to him. After he finished with his breakfast, lacking, as usual, any sensibilities of finer taste, he left the mess and stepped back out into the light but chill breeze that swept across the courtyard.

As he looked to the northwest, he sensed *something*, a use of Talent that wasn't normal. He hurried toward the squares where the pteridons were hosted, hoping either Quelyt or Falyna was there.

Falyna stepped forward as she saw the colonel approaching. "Sir? Something wrong?"

"I don't know. Are you ready to fly? With a passenger?"

"Yes, sir. We're the duty, such as it is—"

"Good. Let's go. Head for where we found that ancient tunnel."

"Yes, sir."

Dainyl didn't feel like explaining. How could he? He couldn't afford to reveal that he was following a Talent-trace, not when he'd been careful to hide that he had any significant Talent besides shielding. While that had been true many years before . . . it wasn't now, and he didn't want to lose the advantage of being underestimated in that fashion, especially not after Tyanylt's death and what he had discovered so far in Dramur. *Nothing* known to more than two people, and sometimes not even that, remained secret from the High Alector of Justice.

After Falyna mounted the pteridon, Dainyl followed, settling himself into the silver saddle behind her.

With a spring and a burst of Talent, the pteridon spread its wings and leapt into the sky, headed eastward into the prevailing wind. Within moments, taking advantage of the thermals over the warmer water off the coast, Falyna and the pteridon were high enough that Dramuria looked like a toy village below. Then the Myrmidon turned the pteridon to the northwest and continued climbing as they headed toward the peak of the ancients.

With the air so chill, the pteridon could climb higher, but the cold seeped through the insulating fabric of Dainyl's uniform and even through the flying jacket.

Falyna looked back at the colonel. "Straight to the peak, sir? You want me to set down there, like before?"

"Circle it, first. I'll let you know. Keep your lance ready when we get near."

"Yes, sir."

Abruptly, the pteridon dropped a good fifty yards, then began to climb again.

Dainyl looked down to his left as they drew abreast of the mining complex, but he could feel no Talent being used there, although he could make out a column of miners entering the mining compound. *How many more would vanish today? And how?*

He forced his attention to the terrain ahead.

As they drew nearer to the angled peak, Dainyl could still sense, faintly but clearly, the use of Talent, almost two lines of Talent, one red-violet and the other greenish gold, although the two seemed interlinked.

"That peak there?" called back Falyna.

"The one that angles, just to the left."

"Got it, sir. Don't see anything, not any more than last time."

"Can you circle a bit higher?"

"We can try."

As the pteridon swept past the cave, Dainyl caught a glimpse of the golden green arch—and of two figures, one stocky and one far smaller. The stockier figure seemed to be of red-violet, the slighter one of golden green.

"Don't see anything there, sir!" called out Falyna.

"Make another circle!"

"Yes, sir."

The red-violet vanished from Dainyl's Talent-perception. One instant, it was there; the next it was not.

As Falyna brought the pteridon around for another pass, Dainyl studied the foliage and the rocky slope below the cave/tunnel and the bluff. He thought he could sense several landers or indigens several hundred yards below.

"Skylance ready!" he called.

"Lance ready!" returned the Myrmidon ranker.

The pteridon swept past the opening to the short tunnel again.

Dainyl could make out, literally suspended in midair, a hazy sphere of golden green. In that instant, as he watched, the sphere—at least he thought it was a sphere—vanished. It didn't move; it just wasn't there.

"Nothing there, sir."

There wasn't, not any longer, but Falyna hadn't seen either presence, and that meant some sort of strong Talent-shielding, although Dainyl hadn't sensed it.

Crack!

As Dainyl was rocked back in the pteridon's second saddle, pain lanced through his right shoulder, the one that had barely healed from the last set of bruises. Dainyl raised shields around his neck and head, all too aware of the drain his action would place on the pteridon.

"Sir!"

"I'm fine. Use the lance!" snapped the colonel. "Straight below the bluff." The lifeforce-imbued uniform and jacket had kept the bullet from breaking through his jacket and tunic, but he would feel the impact for days.

"Coming round, sir. Hang tight!"

The pteridon began to lose altitude, if slowly.

"Can't stay up here, sir!"

"Go right over that grove of trees ahead. Flame the center."

Crack! Crack!

Dainyl could feel the force of one of the bullets against his shields, and, the corresponding loss of height by the pteridon.

A line of bluish flame arrowed from Falyna's skylance toward the stand of evergreens that clung to the slope ahead and below. Yellow-and-blue fires flared, flame fountains that almost reached up to the pteridon as it passed overhead, a good hundred yards above where the trees had stood, amid the steeper rocky slopes and cliffs.

With those fires, Dainyl could sense the deaths of the men who had hidden in the trees.

"Another pass, sir?"

"No. None of them could have escaped that." At least, the fire had killed all that were nearby, and it would have been far too wasteful of lifeforce to flame more of the forest and the living things within it. "Just head back to the compound."

"Yes, sir."

Once they were well away from the mountains and ridges, Dainyl released his shields. His entire body was trembling from the effort it had taken to hold them that long, because he had been forced to share the draw on the lifeforce around with the pteridon—or they would have crashed into the mountains themselves.

As they headed back down to a warmer altitude and toward the Cadmian compound just north of Dramuria, questions swirled through his thoughts.

The golden green lifeforce had to have been one of the ancients. It had matched the aura residue in the short tunnel. Where had the ancient come from? How could it have vanished so quickly? Why hadn't he felt it before? What creature had created the red-violet lifeforce? Was the tunnel site some place of worship for the indigens or the landers? Where they worshipped or sacrificed themselves to the ancients? Had they fired at him to protect the ancient? And why now? That last question bothered him more than the others.

According to what little he had been able to read on the previous inhabitants of Acorus, they had retreated to the north and to the colder and higher places as the planet had warmed as a result of the seedings. But they were supposed to have died off centuries before. Dainyl certainly had seen no reports of them anywhere.

Was the cold the reason why it had appeared when it did? Or had alectors simply not been around when the ancients appeared because the ancients preferred extreme cold while alectors shunned it?

Dainyl shifted his weight in the saddle and harness, wincing as the straps pressured his injured shoulder. As a mere observer, he'd taken more injuries in a few weeks than he had in years as a Myrmidon ranker.

Falyna brought the pteridon in smoothly, but Dainyl was, for once, more than glad to put his boots on the stones of the compound courtyard. He just stood there for a moment.

"Hit you, didn't they, sir?" asked Falyna.

"It didn't break through, but I'll have trouble with the shoulder for a while."

"Were they the rebels?"

"It doesn't matter now." Dainyl looked to the northwest, where a pillar of smoke rose. As an alector, he was supposed to be encouraging the growth of lifeforce, not destroying it.

34

Another week had passed, and, even in Dramur, the nights were chill, especially for troopers in the sheds converted to rough barracks, and in the small house Mykel used as well. They had not lost a mount to the pit traps for days, although they had been fired upon from a distance on several occasions, but no one had been wounded.

On Duadi morning, a still day with low clouds that promised rain that had yet to arrive, Mykel looked at the dispatch he had received from Majer Vaclyn, his eyes centering on the section that he'd read over and over.

> . . . Your task under the Code is to bring these lawbreakers to justice. It matters not whether they are breaking the law by refusing to pay their debts or by actual revolt. If they will not surrender to lawful authority, you are to use whatever force is necessary under the regulations governing the Cadmian Peacekeeping Authority . . . Once the lawbreakers are bought to justice, you are to report the results to higher authority as expeditiously as possible.

Whatever force was necessary. Mykel didn't like the orders, and he'd hoped that his report to the majer would have suggested that his mission was unwise. The majer clearly didn't see it that way, and Mykel had one of two choices. He could refuse and be flogged for failure to obey orders, then imprisoned for the remainder of his term at hard labor, probably in the very mine that seemed to be part of the problem. Or he could carry out his orders, but, hopefully, in some way that did not make the situation worse.

He wasn't sure how to carry out the orders without making things even worse, and he didn't feel like ruining his life. He snorted. How many officers ended up doing what he was going to do, knowing that the orders were idiotic, but not wanting to be punished for saying so?

He folded the dispatch and slipped it into the pouch that he put in the chestnut's saddlebags. Then he turned to Bhoral, who had been waiting quietly in the long morning shadow of the sagging barn.

"Majer didn't read your report, did he, sir?"

"He read it. He disagrees. Breaking the Code is breaking the Code. Those who break it must be punished, even if they didn't have a choice. People don't choose to have crops fail. They don't choose where their parents settled, and not everyone has brains to escape their fate."

"Those that don't, they get punished for their lack of brains," Bhoral replied. "We all get punished one way or another. That's life. You do the best you can."

Mykel laughed, harshly. "I'm going to talk to the chandler. Have the scouts meet me in half a glass. You know where." He mounted the chestnut and rode westward, past the bedraggled sunbean fields. Some of the villagers actually looked at him as he rode past, although none addressed him.

He reined up outside the chandlery and dismounted, tying the chestnut to the rail. He'd continued to stop every day to buy something, although often it was only a for a copper or two. Captains didn't have that many free coins.

The chandler watched as Mykel hurriedly crossed the front porch, but said nothing as the captain stepped inside and studied the tables and shelves, many of which had far fewer provisions than on the previous day.

Mykel walked to a shelf on the side wall. There in an open, carved box, which looked as though Harnyck had been dusting or polishing it, was a miniature knife in a sheath. He slowly picked it up, noting that it was not even as long as his palm was wide. The leather of the sheath was old, blackened, and cracked. The knife was all one piece, with evenly rough-patterned black stone, almost like onyx, inlaid on each side of the hilt, forming a grip. The metal was silvery, with a hint of copper or bronze. Unlike most knives, it was double-bladed, and the blade was narrow. It looked exceedingly sharp.

"What's this?"

"A knife, looks like to me." Harnyck's voice was even.

"Is it for sale?" Mykel eased the knife back into the sheath, which, old as it looked, was doubtless far less ancient than the blade.

"I wouldn't sell that to my worst enemy."

"Then you ought to be able to sell it to me." Mykel knew he *had* to have the knife, but not why. That was a frightening feeling, because he'd never had to have anything.

"Bad luck to sell it. Worse luck to keep it," Harnyck said slowly.

"Do you know someone poor, who needs coins?" asked Mykel.

"These days, who doesn't?"

Mykel extended five silvers he couldn't really afford. "You give these to them, and the knife to me."

Harnyck looked at Mykel. "I can't refuse that, Captain, but you'll be wishing I had."

"I won't back out." Mykel laid the coins on the shelf. "Tell me why."

"A bargain's a bargain." Harnyck smiled and picked up the coins. He handed the knife to Mykel. "I give you this, of my own free will, and you have offered to take it of yours."

"I have," Mykel agreed.

"It's a knife of the ancients. You knew that when you saw it. For that artistry, it's worth a score of golds. You know that, too, I'd wager."

"I know it's valuable. That's not why I wanted it."

For the first time, Harnyck smiled. "I could tell that, too. My father told me only to give it to a good-hearted enemy in a time of great trials. He also said that it would either destroy or make the man who received it."

"I'm glad you think so highly of me." Mykel's humor was forced, and he realized that he'd probably said the same exact words to the chandler before.

"You will do terrible deeds, Captain. All who have held that knife have." Harnyck smiled again. "Leastwise, that was what my da told me."

Mykel wasn't cheered by the chandler's smile. Slowly, he slipped the knife inside his tunic. "I already have. I probably will again. Most Cadmians do."

"At least, you know it." Harnyck stepped back. "The silvers will help some bairns . . . and not mine. I'd not stoop to that." He paused. "Good day, Captain."

"Good day, Harnyck."

Mykel's mouth was dry as he left the chandlery. What in the world had he done? Five silvers? Why? What did the knife mean?

He untied the chestnut slowly, then mounted, turning the horse back eastward to meet with the men he had assigned to watch the comings and goings around Jyoha. Again, on the way from the town, some looked at him. None said a word, and none smiled.

35

Tridi had passed without a word from the observers he had stationed, but early on Quattri, well before dawn, one of the messengers from the scouts had awakened Mykel with word that a number of women were leaving the village along the lane that led to the sawmill.

Mykel had Bhoral roust out the entire company and quickly readied himself. Before pulling on his riding jacket, he took out the knife of the vanished ancients, easing it from its sheath and looking at it once again. The blade was smooth and shiny enough that it should have shown a reflection, but it did not. There was not a mark of corrosion or rust on it, and the metal was at least as hard as steel, if not harder, but not nearly so heavy. The facings on the grip were of a stone that looked like onyx, but was far harder. The blade was sharp enough to shave with, too sharp, if that were possible—Mykel knew, he'd tried and cut himself—and double-edged, unlike most knives, but like a dagger. Yet the blade was too short for a single killing thrust, for all its strength and sharpness. There were no markings and no inscriptions.

After a moment, he replaced it in the sheath and tucked into the inside pocket of his riding jacket. When he had time, he would make a special slot on the inside of his belt for it. It couldn't hurt to have another knife, one that wasn't obvious, small as it might be. He picked up his rifle and headed for the makeshift stables.

Mykel finished saddling the chestnut, then rode out into the open space before the sheds that served as barracks. He glanced up at the dark sky. Through the thin night haze he could see Asterta, the warrior moon, almost at the zenith. Warrior moon, but for which warriors did the moon bode victory? As he dropped his eyes to the dimness around him, Bhoral rode up.

"Company's almost ready, sir."

"Good. We'll take the back lane south. I'll take first and second squads up through the fields and through the second growth. You take the others on the sawmill road."

"Yes, sir. Scouts out! Company forward!"

While every sound seemed amplified in the predawn grayness, no one seemed to look out of the handful of cots set off the south lane, although smoke rose from most of the chimneys. Near the end of the lane, the company turned westward onto the cart path that crossed the main road south. After another quarter glass Mykel could see the lane he sought to his right.

"Bhoral?"

"Sir?"

"Time for you to take squads three, four, and five."

"Yes, sir." The senior squad leader turned his mount and pulled off to the side.

Mykel kept looking over his shoulder until he was sure that Bhoral and the three squads were clear.

Shortly, a scout appeared out of the trees on the west side of the path. "Captain?" The scout rode forward and swung his mount alongside that of Mykel. "Look to be about two squads, near that first campsite we found. Couldn't get too close. They've got pickets, but they're only fifty yards out and on the lane side. Not all that careful."

"Good. Are you ready to ride ahead and take over point?"

"Yes, sir."

Once Jasakyt had joined the other scouts at the front of the squads, Mykel turned. "Squad leaders forward," he said quietly. "Pass it back."

Gendsyr and Alendyr appeared within moments, one riding on each side of Mykel.

"We'll be crossing the fields, then following the edge of the older forest. We'll ride up until we're thirty yards away and form into a firing line, rifles ready for immediate fire. If they hear us, we'll quick time into position. First squad to my left, second to my right. I'll give them a chance to throw down their weapons. If there's any resistance, I'll order immediate fire. Quiet riding from here on."

"Yes, sir."

Close to a hundred yards farther south, the scouts turned westward, heading up the long and gently sloping field alongside a fence whose weathered rails lay on the ground in as many places as they sagged between posts. Just before the hillcrest, the scouts rode across a downed section of the fence, through the low second growth bordering the field, and toward the older forest a quarter of a vingt away.

Mykel kept listening, but the only sounds were those of mounts breathing, the swishing of branches pushed aside, and the intermittent cracking of broken branches under hoofs. When they reached the edge of the older growth, the scouts fell back closer to the main body, and the squads followed the more recent tracks toward the older campsite.

He and the two squads were still a good hundred yards away from the clearing when a woman's scream pierced the comparative stillness.

"After me!" Mykel urged the chestnut forward as fast as he dared through irregular second-growth forest. "Rifles ready!"

The screams and yells seemed to go on and on, and a handful of rifle shots echoed through the gray morning.

When Mykel rode through the last low trees and reined up, he found riders in gray, some in shapeless rags, all facing toward the lane from the sawmill, around two handcarts.

Among the yells, and shouts, he could hear several clearly.

". . . Cadmians are coming!"

"Flee! Ride away!"

Mykel glanced around him. Out of the ragtag array of riders, only a handful had even seen Mykel's two squads. "Firing line! Ready!"

Mykel never had a chance to offer surrender. The riders broke into two groups, clearly bent on escape.

Crack! One of the troopers in the second squad slumped in his saddle.

"Fire!" Mykel snapped, bringing his own weapon up and firing as he did.

Crack! Crack! Crack! Fifteenth Company fired the first volley almost simultaneously.

Something flew by Mykel's head, but he sighted and fired again, watching but momentarily as an angular man in brown toppled from his saddle.

Three of the riders, two of them with long spears, or makeshift lances, turned their mounts and charged toward Mykel, and the slight gap between the two squads. The captain kept firing, and one of those with a lance went down as his mount collapsed under him.

Mykel finished the magazine. There was no time to reload as the second lancer bore down on him. Urging the chestnut forward, Mykel rode toward the rebel.

At the last moment, he ducked under the lance, then swung the rifle across the man's neck and jaw. There was a sickening crunch, and the rider swayed in the saddle, his eyes rolling back. The third rider had gone down as several of the rankers in squad two had concentrated their fire on the group.

Mykel reined up and glanced down at his rifle. The barrel assembly was bent away from the stock behind the bolt. Rifles weren't meant for use as swords or lances.

He swung the mount back toward his squads, as much as to get out of the line of fire as to see if he could pick up a rifle.

By the time he turned the chestnut and reined up, the skirmish was effectively over. There were two rebels still in the saddle. One was slumped over, holding the mane of the swaybacked mare he rode, and the other was trying to hold a shattered right arm in place with his left.

Somewhere, he could hear a woman sobbing, and another cursing.

"Cease fire!" The order was unnecessary, since there was no one left to fire at.

"Reload!" he ordered as he rode toward the mount of the downed trooper. Vyschyl's right eye was wide-open. A crossbow quarrel had gone through his left. Mykel's lips tightened, as he eased the rifle from where it was wedged. "Re-form by squad!" He wiped the rifle clean and reloaded, although the magazine needed but two cartridges.

"Gendsyr!"

"One man injured, sir."

"Alendyr?"

"One and one."

"Squad one, check for wounded, but be careful. Squad two, hold and stand ready."

Mykel rode slowly forward across the former campsite, letting the chestnut pick his way around the fallen raiders or rebels. His eyes surveyed those who had fallen. He saw two iron-tipped wooden lances, several old swords and sabres—and only a single rifle, Cadmian, of course. Mykel's quick estimate of the dead raiders was around thirty.

Bhoral waited for him on the lane side of the clearing.

"There must have been women hiding here, sir. They were the ones who gave the alarm."

"I don't know that it did them that much good."

"I did a quick count. I think we lost three on my squads, sir."

"One dead, two wounded, on mine," replied Mykel.

Four troopers dead. With only a handful of rifles among the rebels, there shouldn't have been that many casualties, but he hadn't thought that they wouldn't even consider surrender.

He took a deep breath. Nothing was going as anyone had planned or thought.

"Let's check their weapons and anything we can. Take care of our wounded. Let their women take any of their wounded."

"Sir?"

"They got away while we were checking weapons," Mykel said evenly. There wasn't any way that the poor ragtag fugitives were part of an organized rebellion, not the way the retainers of Seltyr Ubarjyr had been. What was he going to do? Drag them back to Dramuria for flogging and death—for being poor? He'd already done enough.

"Yes, sir."

Bhoral didn't approve. He and Majer Vaclyn would have agreed. Mykel turned his mount back toward first and second squads. He'd need to have the men gather enough in the way of useless weapons to support his decision, although he had his doubts that such evidence would count for much.

Midmorning came and went before Fifteenth Company had gathered its own dead and wounded and searched the rebels' bodies—discovering but a few coppers, no silvers, and nothing of value. There were four rifles among the weapons used by the dead men. Two were older models of Cadmian rifles, dating back at least twenty years, if not longer, and two were more recent. All were numbered. There were only half a score of cartridges. The remainder of the armaments were bows, ancient blades, and two crossbows with cables so frayed that Mykel would have been unwilling to wind and use them. The handful of raider rifles had taken three other troopers and wounded four more. Mykel doubted that one of the wounded Cadmians would live through the morning, not with the sucking wound in his chest.

The tracks around the site suggested that perhaps two or three men had escaped on horseback, and possibly one or two on foot. The women who had brought provisions had left as silently as they had come, with their handcarts—and with the three survivors of what had been a massacre. Mykel had seen no reason to stop them. He hadn't wanted to kill their husbands, brothers, and fathers—except that between his orders and their reactions, he and Fifteenth Company had been left with little choice.

Bhoral rode up to where Mykel surveyed the skirmish site a last time. "We're ready to go, sir. Chyndylt got a wagon for our wounded."

"We'll go back the way you came, not through the town."

"Better that way," the senior squad leader said.

Neither way was better. One wasn't as bad.

36

Mykel rode alone as Fifteenth Company started back to the makeshift base. He'd ordered the slaughter of men and boys—some hadn't been as old as Viencet—because the majer had ordered him to capture them or kill them, and because none of them had wanted to be taken—probably to the mines. He wondered more about the conditions there, if no one would surrender.

More important, what was he supposed to do now? He smiled wryly. According to his orders from the majer, he'd accomplished the job. He'd killed the poor rebels, almost every one. Of course, he didn't see any of Third Battalion being used to search every seltyr's and large grower's estate, and that was where the largest number of rebels and weapons had been found so far. But then, doing that would definitely have provoked a rebellion—if it were even feasible, given only five companies and more than a score of possible estates.

He glanced to the north. The dawn haze had turned into thin clouds, with darker gray massing behind them. After another quarter glass of solitary riding, he turned in the saddle. "Bhoral? I'm going to take second squad into Jyoha when we reach the north end of the lane."

The senior squad leader's brows wrinkled. "If you think so, sir."

"I'm worried, too," Mykel said. "That's why we'll go there now. The longer we wait, the more likely someone will try more things like stakes in the road."

"Why do you want to go in at all, sir?"

"So that I can report to Majer Vaclyn that we destroyed the rebels and that everything was quiet when we departed."

"Departed, sir?"

"That's right. You get the men ready. We're riding out as soon as we can, back to Dramuria."

Bhoral cocked his head to the side, then nodded slowly. "Might be better that way, sir. For the men."

What the senior squad leader wasn't saying directly, Mykel knew, was that it might not be better for one Captain Mykel. "I'm thinking about them, senior squad leader."

"Yes, sir. I'll take care of it."

"Thank you." Mykel raised his voice. "Second squad! Forward, along the left! Form on me!" He urged the chestnut forward, to open up distance between himself and first squad. Before long, Alendyr rode forward, at the head of his squad, and eased his mount up beside Mykel's.

"Sir?"

"We'll need to take a quick ride through Jyoha. Rifles ready the whole time. I may make a stop or two."

Unlike Bhoral, Alendyr nodded immediately. "Yes, sir. I can see that, sir."

No one spoke on the ride north to the turn, and the loudest sounds were those of hoofs on the road and the creaking of the wheels of the wagon carrying the wounded troopers.

As Mykel had suspected, once they headed westward for Jyoha, all the dwellings bordering the road were shuttered, long before Alendyr ordered, "Rifles ready!"

Not a soul was in sight. Even the main street of the village was empty.

Mykel reined up in front of the chandlery. Instead of tying the chestnut, he handed the reins to the ranker in formation behind Alendyr. Then, rifle in hand, he crossed the porch, eyes searching, ears alert. He opened the door. From the counter at the rear of the shop, Harnyck looked up at the captain, then turned and walked out the door in the rear.

Mykel nodded to himself. He could take anything, but Harnyck would not sell it. He slowly surveyed the chandlery, then turned and left—without touching anything. Outside, he remounted the chestnut silently and turned his mount to continue farther into the village.

His next stop was at the cooperage, not because he needed any barrels, but because it was the nearest shop that was not closed and shuttered. Once again, he handed the reins to a ranker and made his way to the doorway, his rifle ready. Even before he stepped inside, he heard the rear door open. The cooper's shave lay on the bench, rocking back and forth.

Mykel turned and remounted. Then he nodded to Alendyr. "Back to camp."

Usually, when there were unseen eyes on him, particularly in unfriendly places, Mykel was aware that he was being watched. On the ride back to the temporary base east of Jyoha, he did not sense anyone looking at him and second squad, and the lack of that feeling bothered him more than if he had felt hatred poured out at him, as had so often been the case with the Reillies in the north, when Third Battalion had driven them out of the Vales of Prosperity because of their raids on more productive holders.

Bhoral was waiting, still mounted, in the open ground north of the barracks sheds. He held something.

"You didn't ride into any trouble?" asked Mykel.

"No. Too quiet, if anything. What about you?"

"No one in Jyoha will have anything to do with us. Chandler walked out of his shop when I came in. So did the cooper."

"We could take what we need," pointed out the senior squad leader.

"I don't think so," replied Mykel. "It's better to return to Dramuria. What do you have there?"

"Boy ran up and handed this to me," Bhoral said. "Then he ran off." He leaned forward in the saddle and extended the folded paper to the captain.

Mykel took it and opened it. He read slowly.

> Captain—
>
> You can do whatever you wish in Jyoha. No one will lift a hand to stop you and your men. No one will talk to you. You can take goods, but no one will sell them. You may remain as long as you wish. I cannot accept golds or silvers or coppers. Nor can anyone so long as you and your company remain. . . .

Mykel snorted. He could have slaughtered the entire town for rebellion, he supposed, and Vaclyn might well have executed the leading crafters, but what good would that have done?

He folded the missive and slipped it into his tunic. "Our landowner thinks our job is done and that we might best be chasing rebels elsewhere."

"Yes, sir." Bhoral's tone was level, with the lack of emotion that revealed great doubt about the veracity of his captain's summary.

"Let's get on the road, Bhoral." Mykel did his best to keep the resignation out of his voice. The majer wouldn't understand, and Mykel wasn't sure he could explain, but Jyoha needed to be left alone—for a long time, he thought.

And they needed to get as far from Jyoha as they could before the rain started to fall.

37

Yet another two weeks had passed in Dramuria, and Dainyl knew little more than he had earlier. His shoulder had healed, and a week before, he had sent off a dispatch to the marshal noting Fifteenth Company's successful destruction of one rebel force and the capture of smuggled Cadmian rifles, as well as reporting that he and Falyna had been fired on and that the attackers had been destroyed. He had sent a copy to the High Alector of Justice, and kept one for his own personal records. He had not mentioned the ancient tunnel, since that would only have confused matters even more.

From what Dainyl had seen, there was no real revolt in progress, just the normal dissatisfactions of landers and indigens who thought that they should have more than the land and their labors had produced. According to the two Cadmian majers, there had been scant progress in rounding up rebels. The captain in Jyoha had earlier reported finding traces of raiders, but had not yet been successful in running them down—unless he had done so in the last few days. Yet neither majer had blundered enough for Dainyl to step in. He couldn't very well overrule them and take over because he *thought* they were in the process of creating a mess.

That the marshal and the Highest were involved in some sort of machination was all too clear, but Dainyl had yet to figure out why and for what purpose, because neither would have hazarded their positions for anything trivial, and it made no sense for either to scheme to become Duarch, because the Duarch had to be loyalty-imprinted, and neither the marshal nor the Highest would want to lose that much personal freedom. It almost argued that they were acting on behalf of the Duarch, but Dainyl certainly couldn't assume that. Nor could he assume otherwise.

Then there was Lystrana. Alectors were not supposed to hold the romantic notions of the landers, but Dainyl had to admit he missed her, and not just for her intellect and judgment.

He couldn't do much about the plots in Elcien, but perhaps he could do better with the ancients. Although he'd sensed them—or one of them, the one with the feel of golden green Talent—almost daily for a time, on the three occasions he had flown out there they had vanished, with no traces, before he had arrived.

On Quinti morning, well before dawn on a day that would be cold and clear—at least in the morning—Dainyl dressed carefully, with skintight undergarments he had not worn in years, designed for the times when he had flown dispatches to Blackstear and Northport, and with heavier gloves and a cold weather flying cap. He fastened a waist pouch to his belt and an empty water bottle. He also checked the crystal storage of his sidearm. It was full.

After an early and hearty breakfast in the officers' mess, where he filled the bottle with ale, he made his way out to the courtyard to meet Quelyt. Falyna had yet to return from delivering Dainyl's dispatch to the marshal in Elcien.

"Good morning," Dainyl said cheerfully. "Good time and weather for flying."

"This early . . . does that mean that you want to go back to that tunnel up on the peak?"

"More than that," replied Dainyl, with a rueful smile. "I want you to drop me off there and come back and get me up just before sunset. The air should be still by then, shouldn't it?"

"Usually, sir. But you can never tell."

"If it's not, you'll have to come back first thing tomorrow morning."

"Hope we can get back this evening. Otherwise, it'll be a long and cold night up there." Quelyt laughed.

"I've seen colder, but you're right."

Quelyt adjusted the second saddle, then turned to the colonel. "Anytime, sir."

The pteridon lowered its shoulders and neck. The ranker eased into his harness and saddle, and Dainyl followed. There was almost no wind, and Dainyl could sense the extra Talent-draw it took the pteridon to get airborne. Still, before long, Dramuria lay beneath and behind them. In the chill gray air, with the glow of the sun barely touching the eastern horizon—the waters of the gulf between Dramur and Corus—the flight was smooth.

Less than ten vingts from their destination, the sun burst into the morning sky, and the Murian Mountains stood etched against the darker silver-green sky to the west. Despite the chill on his face, Dainyl couldn't help but smile at the beauty of the vista before him.

As they circled in to land at the end of the short bluff, Dainyl extended his Talent as much as he could, but did not sense either of the ancients. The landing was far smoother than the earlier one, but Quelyt had still air and was more familiar with the site. Dainyl eased himself out of the harness and dismounted, stepping away from the pteridon.

"A half glass before sunset, sir? You sure about that?"

"I'm sure." Dainyl gestured at the steep slope below. "If the indigens could climb up that, I could always climb down."

"I'll be here, sir." Quelyt's tone showed that he didn't like the idea of the colonel climbing down a mountain. "Half a glass before sunset."

Dainyl nodded and stepped as far back as he could and crouched. There wasn't that much extra space for the pteridon's wings.

Once Quelyt was airborne, he made a circle, waved, and headed back to Dramuria.

Dainyl could sense that there was no one in the short tunnel, either in the cavelike outer section or in the short tunnel beyond. Because he did not know just how much the ancient creatures might perceive, he did not enter the cave or tunnel, but explored the area around the small bluff. After a quarter glass, he found a hollow space between two boulders only a few yards downslope, if on the colder north side. Others had rested there, it appeared, from the flattened and smoothed appearance of the reddish sandy surface, but not recently.

He hoped that he was not on an idiot's quest, sitting near the top of a peak, in winter no less, if a far warmer winter than in Blackstear or Scien. Yet it was clear that the ancients were shy and skittish—or cautious—and he could not escape the feeling that they were somehow involved with some of the strange and unsettling conditions in Dramur.

Or did he feel that because he needed some other cause for the strangeness than the sense that the marshal and the Highest were gaming on some deeper level than he could imagine? Or that he needed to rule out the ancients in order to deal with the marshal—if he even could?

The sun climbed higher, and Dainyl waited, but there was no sign of the ancients—or of anything else. To pass the time and to get some warmth from the sun, he eased into the light, but only far enough that he could not be seen from the unnatural cave above. From there, sitting on an outcropping, he could just see the charred trunks of the pines from where the locals had shot him. Why had they done that? Except for the Reillies in the north, and a few other isolated groups, most landers and indigens knew that attacking a Myrmidon or an alector would result in the destruction of the attacker. Alectors could never show vulnerability, and the response was always immediate and absolute.

How many times would he have to wait on a peak to see if an ancient would appear? Did he have that much time? What else could he do?

The sun climbed higher. Dainyl doubted that the Highest or the marshal had meant for him to undertake exactly this kind of observation.

Noon came and went, and Dainyl drank some of the ale from the water bottle at his belt. He should have felt that he was wasting his time, but the sun on the rocks and the insulated clothing kept him from feeling too chill, and the view of the east side of Dramur was indeed stunning in the full sunlight. He could almost forget, for a few moments, why he was there and what lay waiting for him back in Dramuria.

Abruptly, he could sense the red-violet of Talent, and more than one being. He glanced around, but he could see nothing, although the feel of the red-violet grew increasingly stronger.

He turned to see two squat figures, almost caricatures of indigens, with rough and rocky tannish skin into which crystals were embedded, appear to ooze out of the very rocks to his right, taking shape less than three yards away.

Dainyl moved quickly, and the light-cutter was in his left hand, aimed at the creatures. They had no necks to speak of, flat noses that barely protruded, slit mouths, and eyes almost flush with their flat faces. Although they wore no clothes, they had no obvious external organs.

Were these the ancients?

They did not move forward, and neither did he.

Then, golden green Talent-aura cascaded across the bluff.

Dainyl looked up to see the golden green sphere hovering less than five yards away, slightly above his eye height, and within it, a miniature figure, resembling a lander female, but no more than half the size of a large lander. The soaring small woman was winged, and an iridescence shrouded her figure, enough that it served as well as clothing.

As you are, you do not belong here. Although the soaring creature did not speak aloud, the words were clear within Dainyl's mind.

"As I am? What else would I be?"

That is for you to decide. If you do not change, you will die. You have been warned.

Then, she was gone. Or rather, she had vanished to sight, although his Talent showed that she had risen and headed toward the tunnel. In just moments, she had vanished to both sight and Talent.

Dainyl blinked. In the time that he had spoken to the soarer, as good a term as any, the two squat creatures had vanished back into the rocks. There was no trace of aura or Talent.

He shook his head. Had they really been there?

Slowly, he climbed back up to the bluff. There was no reason not to enter the tunnel, not now. He examined every span of the tunnel, but there were no tracks on the dust and sand except those of his own boots, from the last time he had been in the tunnel. He studied the square mirror on the floor, testing it, tapping it gently, probing as he could with his Talent. No matter what he did, it seemed to be but a mirror, but why was it on the floor and not upon the wall?

He straightened. He could sense the Talent-residue of the soarer, but not of the squat creatures. What were they? Creatures who served, like pteridons? Who traversed the earth and stone in the fashion that pteridons traveled the sky?

How could he possibly tell either the marshal or the Highest what had happened? Or Quelyt or Falyna? He couldn't—especially about the warning, a cryptic statement made without words and received through Talent, he surmised. Received by a Myrmidon colonel known not to have that degree of Talent, tracking a creature that had supposedly died centuries before.

His laugh was soft and sardonic. He'd wanted to find the ancients, and they had found him, and his discovery seemed almost as useless as not having made it.

If you do not change, you will die. What had she meant? How could he find out? And what had she meant by "you"—Dainyl or all alectors?

He still had a long afternoon ahead of him. He looked to the north and west, but outside of a slight haze, the sky was clear. He might get back to Dramuria by sunset, for all the good it would do him.

38

Fifteenth Company did not reach the Cadmian compound in Dramuria until late afternoon on Sexdi in a light rain. Mykel had not pushed his men; he'd seen no reason to do so. Although he'd come up with a rationale for leaving Jyoha, he wasn't looking forward to facing Majer Vaclyn. He had unsaddled the chestnut, carted his gear back to the officers' quarters, and was finishing drying and oiling his rifle—the rifle he had taken from the dead Vyschyl—when someone was knocking on the doorway.

"Yes?" Mykel set the rifle in the weapons rack and walked to the door, opening it.

Jiosyr, Vaclyn's senior squad leader, stood there. "Majer Vaclyn would like to see you immediately, sir. In the headquarters building. He said that anything else could wait."

"I'll be right there, Jiosyr."

"I'll wait out here for you, sir."

Mykel shut the quarters door. He debated changing out of his damp uniform, but decided against it. He did hang up his soaked riding jacket to dry before turning and leaving the quarters. He had the copy of the letter from the grower in his tunic, but his guts told him that it was better not to show it to the majer. He would wait and see.

Jiosyr followed him all the way to the compound headquarters.

Mykel found the small study where the majer waited, his door open. "Sir, you requested my presence immediately."

"You do understand the meaning of that word, unlike many others. Please come in and close the door, Captain." Vaclyn did not rise from behind the desk where he was seated.

Mykel stepped inside, closing the door. He remained standing, respectfully.

"Did you receive orders to return to Dramuria, Captain?" Vaclyn's voice was mild, but Mykel sensed the anger beneath. But then, the majer seemed to be angry most of the time.

"Your last orders to me, sir, were to report to you as expeditiously as possible once I had dealt with the rebels. With the possible exception of one man, we wiped out all those riders I had reported. Since one man is not a rebel force, I believe that we accomplished the goals you set forth, and I am here reporting to you."

"You . . . wiped them out?"

"Yes, sir. This group, as I had reported earlier, was not well armed. They had but four rifles, some crossbows, along with spears and blades. I did bring those back for your inspection, sir. They refused to surrender. They attacked before I could even offer terms. We had no choice but to fight."

The majer stared for a time at Mykel. Finally, he shook his head. "Captain, you are a difficult officer. You complain about your orders, but always so politely and courteously that few would even consider your reports a complaint, yet you find rebels where no one else can, and you dispatch them . . . expeditiously." He frowned. "What were your losses?"

"Three in the skirmish, sir, and one from a chest wound later."

"You have lost almost ten men, Captain. No one else has lost any."

"That is true, sir. We have also fought more, and we have killed close to a hundred and fifty rebels and raiders." Mykel did not point out that no one else had discovered any rebels.

"Ten for one is barely adequate for a Cadmian force."

"Yes, sir." Mykel kept his voice level, even pleasant. "We'll do better in the future."

"I expect no less. Colonel Herolt expects no less."

"Yes, sir."

"What is the state of matters in Jyoha?"

"It was quiet when we left. I don't think they believed that we could find the raiders, or that the raiders would fight to the death. The people didn't want to look in our direction."

"Good. They need to show a little respect." Vaclyn frowned. "Still . . . we cannot abandon Jyoha for long, or there will be more raiders and rebels. After your efforts, it might be wiser to send another company, rather than send Fifteenth Company back." He smiled.

Mykel didn't care for the smile. He waited.

"Since you seem able to find things that no one else can, Captain, I am reassigning Fifteenth Company to patrolling the mine road and providing support to the local Cadmians. Prisoners are disappearing, and no one can find them. It appears to be the sort of mission at which you excel. Your men may have tomorrow off. Your new duties will begin on Octdi."

"Yes, sir."

"And Captain?"

"Yes, sir."

"You are riding on the cliff edge of insubordination."

"Yes, sir. I will endeavor to be more tactful in the future, sir." Mykel wasn't about to protest, not when things could have been much worse.

"That would be a good beginning, Captain."

"Yes, sir. By your leave, sir?"

"You may go. We'll go over your new duties tomorrow, at the second glass of the afternoon."

Mykel bowed, then left. He needed to know more about what was going on with the mine. Prisoners disappearing? He wasn't certain whether he liked that or the majer's smile less.

Rather than return to his quarters, he headed for the officers' mess. He hoped to find one of the Cadmian captains—before he talked to Kuertyl or had to talk to the majer again about Fifteenth Company's new assignment. When he entered the mess, he saw Kuertyl and Heransyr engaged in a conversation, one that Mykel didn't wish to join, not yet, but Meryst was sitting by himself, looking as though he might be almost ready to leave.

Mykel hurried over. Meryst had seemed slightly more approachable than Benjyr. "Could I join you for a moment?"

Meryst looked up, surprised. "Certainly. I had thought you were up north in Jyoha."

"We just returned a glass ago." Mykel eased into the chair across from Meryst.

"How did Jyoha go?"

"Not well," Mykel admitted. "We tracked down a group of raiders. They attacked us rather than surrender. They killed one trooper with a crossbow right off, and . . ." He shrugged. "When it was all over, most of them were dead."

"You don't sound pleased about that."

"They were hungry men forced off their lands, most of them, anyway. I was ordered to capture or kill them—or face court-martial. It wasn't put quite that way."

Meryst's ironic laugh was sympathetic. "It never is."

"So . . . now we've been assigned to the mine road and supporting you. I hoped you could tell me what you know, what we shouldn't do—that sort of thing. Majer Vaclyn was telling me that prisoners are disappearing. We're supposed to help so that doesn't happen." Mykel gave a crooked smile. "I have a feeling that it's not that simple."

Meryst laughed. "You have that right. The prisoners are disappearing in the mine. They're counted when they enter, and they're counted when they leave. If anyone is missing, that crew is cordoned off, and the tunnels they were working are searched. So are all the other tunnels. We've lost ten miners in the last two weeks. No bodies, and no one saw them go."

"Is this something new?"

Meryst gnawed his lower lip with his upper teeth. "There have been disappearances before, in the mines, not with prisoners climbing the stockade or jumping from the bridge. But only one or two a season, if that. These numbers . . . there's no record of anything like this."

The mess steward arrived with a mug of ale. "There is only flatfish tonight, sir."

"Whatever there is, thank you."

The steward bowed and hurried away.

Mykel took a swallow of the ale. His throat *was* dry, and while fish was better than bread and cheese and dried meat, it wasn't that much better. "Do you have any idea why or how?"

Meryst shook his head.

Mykel could tell that the other man had an idea, but wasn't about to share it. He'd either been ordered not to say, or didn't feel comfortable saying what he felt. Mykel would have wagered on the second. "Have you been taking fire from rebels in the hills around the mines?"

"Once in a while, but no one's been hit. Not yet."

"You think that they're shooting more than they used to?"

"Until a season ago, or less, no one ever shot at us," Meryst replied.

"What's going on, do you think?"

"I wish I knew. The first thing was the prisoners disappearing. That started at the end of summer. Maybe sooner. I was on furlough for two weeks. Then some of the prisoners wouldn't go into the mines. They said it wasn't safe, but no one had been hurt. We had to flog a bunch." Meryst's face tightened as he spoke. "Then more of them started trying to escape."

"Why would the seltyrs get involved?"

"The seltyrs? What do they have to do with the mines?"

"Seltyr Ubarjyr was outfitting an entire company of mounted rifles . . ." Mykel went on to explain what had happened in Enstyla. He was surprised that Meryst didn't know.

"I'd heard that you'd had trouble up in Enstyla," replied Meryst. "When I asked Majer Herryf, he just said that you'd taken care of the problem. He didn't want to talk about it."

Mykel paused. Since Enstyla, Fifteenth Company had spent almost no time in Dramuria. It was possible word hadn't gotten out. "Why would the seltyrs care about escaped prisoners?"

Meryst laughed. "How many do you think they put there? Ubarjyr was the worst."

"What do you mean?"

"Not all the bat shit goes to Southgate and the Vedra river ports. The bigger growers get some of it. The soil isn't great here, you know. There's an unspoken agreement. It's not written anywhere. The more miners that come from a seltyr's holdings and retainers, the more they get. It's a good way to get rid of anyone who complains and to get more of the bat shit for worked-out lands. The council director and the director of the mine just look the other way. They always need more miners. They've found another one of the caves, but they don't have enough miners or golds to open it yet. That's what the word around Dramuria is, anyway."

"Doesn't the justicer have to find them guilty of something?"

"The justicer belongs to the growers. Always has."

"You think Ubarjyr was building a private force to protect himself?"

Meryst shrugged. "I don't know. It's possible."

The longer Mykel was in Dramur, the less he liked what he was discovering. But it had often been that way on deployments. That was why Cadmians were deployed. Still . . .

"There's not much I can tell you about the seltyrs. They keep things to themselves," added Meryst.

"Is Rachyla—the seltyr's daughter—still in confinement?"

"You interested in her?" Meryst grinned.

"She's good-looking," Mykel admitted, "but I think she knows more than she's saying. I'd like to talk to her, but . . . if I go through Majer Vaclyn . . ." He shrugged.

Meryst nodded. "I can see that. How about the first glass after muster tomorrow? We take over the guard then."

"I wouldn't want to cause you trouble." Much as he wanted to see Rachyla, he did not want to put Meryst on his majer's bad side.

"There won't be. Your majer will be talking to Herryf that early. I'll let the guards know you're trying to find out something to help us all from getting shot. That's true, isn't it?"

"I hope so. I think she knows where the rifles came from. If we could find that out . . ."

Meryst smiled. "It would help."

"It would. Thank you." Mykel decided to change the subject. "If I could ask one other thing. How have you been handling road patrols on the mine road?"

"We send a patrol up front, first, or we did. Thirteenth Company has been doing that lately, gives us more men to watch the prisoners . . ."

As Meryst talked, Mykel listened.

39

Septi morning dawned chill, cloudy, and windy, and the air was raw and damp. As he crossed the compound courtyard, Mykel decided that it was the coldest day he'd experienced so far in Dramur, and the damp chill made it feel colder than it was. Almost to the moment, at one glass past the morning muster, he approached the officer's cell. To his relief, he found Meryst standing by the locked door, talking to the guards.

"Good morning, Captain," offered Meryst, turning to face Mykel.

"Good morning."

"We wish you the best of luck in finding out something." Meryst laughed. "Neither the Myrmidon colonel nor either majer has had much success."

"Then I can't do any worse," replied Mykel.

Both the sentries and Meryst smiled broadly. One of the two Cadmian rankers produced the heavy brass key, unlocked the lock, slid back the pair of iron bolts.

"You won't need more than a glass, will you?" asked Meryst.

Mykel understood perfectly. Vaclyn and Herryf always spent a glass discussing things in the morning. "That's if I can persuade her to talk. Much less if I can't."

"Let's hope you can."

Mykel hoped so as well, but he wasn't counting on it.

The sentries held their weapons ready as Mykel opened and door and stepped inside.

"You could announce yourself." Rachyla sat on the side of the bed. She wore gray trousers and a heavy green shirt, with slippers, rather than boots. Mykel noted the dark circles under her eyes, but those piercing green eyes looked anything but defeated or beaten.

"I'm sorry. I thought you'd be up."

"I am up. It's just a matter of manners, Captain. What do you want?"

"To talk to you."

"So that you can get more information from me?"

"I've gotten very little." Mykel laughed easily. He remained standing, a good two yards back from the narrow bed. "You might consider what you could tell me without betraying anyone. That way, I might understand what is happening."

"I'm not aware that Cadmians considered understanding of great import."

"Some don't. Some do."

"Don't pretend. I don't like it."

"How about this, then? Forty men died earlier this week, because they attacked my company. They'd been driven off their lands, not by Cadmians, but by growers, because they couldn't pay their debts. It doesn't make sense, and I really would like it to make sense."

"So that you could find a better way to kill more people?"

"Rachyla . . . for what it's worth, I'd like to remind you that I didn't take you into confinement when I found that first rifle. My men didn't start shooting at your father's men until they fired at us first. Hard as it may be for you to understand, I would rather not kill people."

"For that, to make you feel better, I'm supposed to betray people?" Her eyes never left his face.

Mykel snorted. "I asked you to explain what you could without betraying anyone."

"Anything I say will betray someone."

"Why did your father need rifles? I don't see how explaining that would betray anyone."

"An unarmed seltyr is without honor. A seltyr who has no rifles when others do is unarmed."

That didn't make sense, unless . . . "Who else has rifles?"

"Did I say that others have rifles, Captain?"

Mykel waited. Sometimes, saying nothing worked better than saying anything. He just looked at Rachyla, taking in the black hair swept up onto the back of her head, the clear skin, and the deep green eyes. She had a nose that was strong, but not overlarge, and long fingers. Her cheekbones were high.

A good quarter glass passed.

"You're more patient than the majers," she finally said. "Or the Myrmidon."

"I have more at stake. So do you."

More time passed.

"You know that there are two types of growers, the larger ones, like my father, who are called seltyrs, and those who are just growers . . ."

Mykel nodded, waiting.

"There are also the growers of the east, and those to the west. Those in the west are more prosperous. They do not need the guano. They do not need irrigation ditches. They have always believed that the growers of the east have hidden their coins. We grow casaran nuts, but they grow apple bananas and use their spiders to create shimmersilk. Those bring far more in golds. With enough golds, one can buy anything, even Cadmian rifles. What else could my father do?"

"The western growers are planning to take over the east of the isle?"

Rachyla shrugged. "Now . . . with your Cadmians here, who can tell?"

Mykel considered. She could well be lying, but . . . it didn't feel that way, and he usually had a good sense about that. Then, did he want to believe what she said? "Do you have any idea why they would risk it?"

"No. I would judge that they felt that the Duarch would not care so long as the guano and dyes and shimmersilk kept coming. Would you say I was wrong?" The corners of her mouth lifted into a sardonic smile.

"No," Mykel admitted. "Did your father ever speak to Majer Herryf?"

"How could he, without revealing what he knew and becoming a target?" Her face hardened again. "You and your men did a great favor for the western growers."

"It wasn't meant as such," Mykel pointed out.

"No. I can see that you did not mean it that way. Does it matter what you meant? My father is dead, and I am here, and one day, I will be found dead—or put before a justicer and quickly found guilty of something I did not do and executed. Or I will just vanish, and no one will be able to explain how it happened."

Mykel could see how she could believe that. She was probably right, too, and that bothered him.

"No one talks to me, except you and the majers. Even the evil one only came once."

"The evil one?"

"The Myrmidon colonel. All of them are evil, deep inside. They do not belong here."

"Where? Here on Dramuria?"

"They do not belong on our world. They are different. They even smell different. We will be here when they are long gone." Abruptly, she closed her mouth.

Smell different? Mykel frowned. "How could they smell different?"

"They do."

"Just how will they depart when they have the Myrmidons and the flame lances?"

"I have said all that I will say."

"And more than you would have," Mykel said gently.

"You are not so evil as the others, Captain. For that, you will pay dearly."

"When did the western growers plan to attack?"

Rachyla shook her head.

"Do you know who was the one the other western growers looked to?"

The only response was an enigmatic smile.

She had said all that she would say. He bowed. "Thank you. I'll see what can be done."

"You are as confined as I, Captain. Your cell is merely larger. You can do nothing." The green eyes focused on Mykel, just taking him in, neither judging nor dismissing.

After a moment, he bowed once more, then turned, and rapped on the door.

Again, the Cadmian guards had their rifles trained as Mykel left the officer's cell. The angular guard quickly threw the bolts and snapped the lock closed.

"Did you learn anything?" asked Meryst.

"More than I expected, less than I hoped. I'll have to look into some things. Then I'll know. I don't want to say much until then. She just might be telling me things that aren't true."

"Seltyrs and their families haven't been known for their directness," replied Meryst. "I learned that a long time back."

"I've gathered that." Mykel bowed. "I thank you and hope that this will lead to something that will help us both."

"So do we."

Mykel nodded, then turned, walking northward across the courtyard. What could he say to either majer? He wasn't supposed to have talked to Rachyla, although he hadn't officially been prohibited from doing so. He had no real proof that the western growers had gotten rifles, and he wouldn't until or unless those growers revolted or attacked—or unless the Third Battalion raided the western seltyrs. Majer Vaclyn would have no compunctions about conducting such a raid, and the results would certainly trigger a revolt, whether the seltyrs were innocent or guilty.

So what was he to do? He couldn't risk telling the majer, and yet . . . what if the western growers were planning a surprise attack?

If pressed, if the majer did find out he had visited the woman, Mykel could say that she had told him that there were more rifles in Dramur, and that included the western growers, but that he had not been able to discover either names or locations.

He didn't want to say even that. Majer Vaclyn wasn't above using stronger methods to get Rachyla to talk, but Mykel doubted those would work—except to injure or disfigure her—and what was the point of that?

Sometimes, he wondered what the point of anything was.

40

The weather had held, and Dainyl had returned to the compound late on Quinti. He had not discussed what had happened on the mountain, except to tell Quelyt that he had had a brief glimpse of something that might have been an ancient. That was more than shading the truth, but what else could he say? That a creature that was supposed to have died centuries before had told him to change or die? Without explaining what she meant?

How had she even known his tongue? That alone would have been troubling enough, not to mention her ability to vanish without a trace, and that of the blocky creatures with her to melt into the very stones of the mountains. Yet . . . if she were such a threat, why had there been no sign of her and her people for centuries? All of Corus teamed with indigens and landers and more than a few alectors, and there had been no reports of the ancients in generations.

He paused. That was not quite true. He had heard of no reports. That did not mean that there were none.

Add to that reports of an insurrection that was not, or not much of one, and the entire situation in Dramur was troubling, perhaps troubling enough for him to act, except that he had no better idea than the Cadmian majers did about what was really going on. If he were to take command immediately, he reminded himself, how could he improve the situation? Far better to continue to observe and reflect, until he either knew enough to act well—or until he had to act because the majers had blundered so badly that he had no choice.

In the time he was reflecting, he noted the return of Fifteenth Company. Since he had had not received any report about that return from either majer, after breakfast on Septi he made his way to the small study in headquarters that Majer Vaclyn had taken over.

The majer jumped to his feet as Dainyl entered. "Colonel, I hadn't expected you."

Dainyl gestured for Vaclyn to take his seat. Then he sat on the edge of the chair across from the majer and looked down and across the desk at the Cadmian officer. "I would appreciate a short report on what Third Battalion has done in the past week."

"I can write something up, sir."

"Just tell me."

"Yes, sir." Vaclyn squared himself and looked at Dainyl. "Fifteenth Company has just returned from Jyoha. The company was successful in tracking down and encircling forty armed raiders. Regretfully, the raiders chose not to surrender to custody and attacked. Virtually all of them were killed or died shortly thereafter of wounds received in the battle. Fifteenth Company suffered four losses and several wounded."

"Who is the captain?"

"Captain Mykel. He was the one under my command when we took out the seltyr's force in Enstyla."

"He seems to have learned well from you." Dainyl's tone was bland, much as he disliked Vaclyn, and the majer's exaggeration of his own efforts. He also could sense a residue of Talent.

"He and his men use weapons well, sir. Since they have returned here, I will be rotating Thirteenth Company north to the Jyoha area shortly. I've assigned Fifteenth Company to handle the patrols on the mine road and in the surrounding area."

"What of the other companies?"

"Fourteenth Company is patrolling the valley trails used by the smugglers. They captured a small boat of smugglers last Londi, with several cases of ammunition, but the three men handling the boat have not so far been helpful or informative. They remain in custody. Sixteenth Company has been on station north of the valley trails, but has seen no sign of other rebel forces, either from the growers or from escaped prisoners. Seventeenth Company has been patrolling the roads through the mountains from the western plantations. The company's presence has been effective in discouraging brigandry. That had been a problem, according to Majer Herryf."

"With the exception of the places where Fifteenth Company has been, everything seems settled, then."

"Yes, sir."

"Might you happen to have a report from this Captain Mykel on his activities."

"He briefed me when he arrived here last night, sir. I have not yet written up a formal report."

About that, the majer was clearly lying, and not a little upset behind the pleasant façade. Dainyl decided to press slightly. "When you've finished it, I would like to see it." He smiled. "Matters are so quiet that it would be useful to read about what action has taken place. Is there anything else I should know?"

"Not that I can think of, Colonel," replied Vaclyn, "but if anything should come up, you will be the first to know."

Dainyl extended a Talent-compulsion. "Have you met with any other alectors besides me?"

"Ah . . . just the marshal when he briefed Colonel Herolt and me before we embarked for Dramuria."

That was true enough—but why was there a residue of Talent after so long?

"Did you spend much time with the marshal? Just you?"

"Only a few moments. He cautioned me to be wary of the seltyrs' machinations."

Vaclyn believed that to be true as well.

Dainyl stood. "Thank you."

"Yes, sir."

Dainyl made his way out into the courtyard, where a chill and raw wind blew from the northeast. He missed the warmth of even the winter sun, although it was not truly a winter sun, not so far south.

Should he go talk to Captain Mykel? Dainyl shook his head. There were times when it was better to let matters take their course, as Lystrana had so often told him. This was one of those times. He did wonder why the marshal had impressed the matter of seltyr machinations upon the majer. What part did that play in whatever the marshal and the Highest were doing? They were clearly setting the Cadmians against the seltyrs, but Dainyl had not the slightest shred of real proof that he could show—or anyone to whom he could tell what he had discovered.

All he could do was wait for an opportunity. As a former Myrmidon ranker, though, he hated to wait. He'd always felt that acting earlier worked better than waiting; but at the moment, he had no real choice—not after what had happened to Tyanylt. He'd also learned that he had to pick his battles carefully, and picking one now would be fatal.

41

Octdi morning was every bit as blustery and chill as Septi had been when Mykel turned in the saddle of the chestnut gelding to look back down the road at the sagging barracks behind the two stone walls across the high bluff. To the east of the walls were the sheds where the prisoners slept. Then he looked ahead again. The road from Dramuria to the guano mine was paved with rough-cut graystone, soft enough that over the years the iron-rimmed wheels of the wagons carrying the guano to the port had worn wide tracks into the very stone.

The first ten vingts from Dramuria were used by holders, by traders, all manner of people, but that was not the part of the road assigned to Fifteenth Company. Fifteenth Company was responsible only for the two-vingt stretch that ran a vingt southeast from the bluff prison compound southeast toward Dramuria and a vingt northwest over the river bridge and up to the mine—as well as an arc five vingts deep around that road, with all the side roads and lanes.

There were stone walls two yards high on both sides of the road from the prison camp gates to the mine itself. A stockade surrounded the mining area. Even the sides of the bridge over the Muralto River were two yards high, but they were of timber, rather than stone.

In his briefing on Septi, Majer Vaclyn had been very clear that Mykel was to be out with his troopers all the time, and that he was not to follow the lax example of the local Cadmian officers. So, early on Octdi morning, Mykel was leading fifth squad on the sweep of the road before the local Cadmians marched the prisoners to the mine.

"Sure wouldn't want to be them," observed Vhanyr, the oldest of the squad leaders in the company. "Can smell that shit from here, and we're a vingt away with the wind at our back."

"We'll be smelling it more than we'd like." Mykel couldn't see anyone on the road, or in the rocks above and beyond the stone wall. At two yards high, the wall was really only good for slowing most prisoners down, but since the prisoners were shackled in pairs, two yards of stone should have been enough.

On each side of the road, a trooper rode beside the wall, close enough to be able to look ahead and over it, to make sure that no one was on the other side.

"Glad we're out of Jyoha," said Vhanyr. "Those folks were scary."

That was true enough, reflected Mykel, but Fourteenth Company had been there earlier, and Majer Vaclyn had doubtless given Dohark the same kinds of orders he'd impressed upon Mykel. He'd probably be giving the same orders to Kuertyl for Thirteenth Company.

Crack! . . . thwingg! A bullet ricocheted off the surface of the road, and powdered stone puffed up momentarily ten yards in front of Mykel.

Mykel jerked his head to the left, and had his rife aimed. He didn't see anyone, but the shot had come from the rocks above the road ahead of them and to his left. It had been aimed at Dhozynt, the lead scout.

"Eyes open to the left!" he ordered. "Keep moving!"

He had a feeling, just a feeling, about where the shooter had to be, and he kept the rifle ready, his eyes darting back to that spot from each other part of the rocky slope.

He'd ridden another fifty yards when he saw a flicker.

Crack! . . . crack! His two shots were measured, and he had willed each of them to strike, a habit he'd formed soon after he'd learned how to handle the Cadmian rifle. It worked, for whatever reason, because he always hit what he aimed for. Shooting was the sole Cadmian skill at which he could say that he truly excelled.

Abruptly, a gray-clad form sprawled across a rock, fifty yards upslope, and a rifle clattered against stone as it skidded downslope.

"You want us to get the body, sir?"

"I think we'd better. Without evidence, Majer Vaclyn doesn't like to believe us," replied Mykel. He realized that he shouldn't have put it that way, but he was getting tired of the majer's arrogance. "I'll cover them."

"Palam, Voeret! Head up there and bring down that body. The rifle, too, and anything that he left. Captain and scouts are covering you!"

Mykel didn't feel as though anyone else happened to be up in the rocks, not right above them or nearby, but he wasn't about to relax his guard, not when he was the one who'd ordered the men up after the dead rebel.

He was not reassured when the two troopers struggled back with the body and the rifle, even when he looked down at the gaunt bearded form lying on the graystone road. The dead rebel wore a dark gray tunic and trousers that blended in with the rocks above the mine road. On his feet were heavy crude sandals, not boots, and his belt was a length of rope tied at one side.

"The belt pouch has cartridges, sir," offered Voeret. "Not many. The rifle is one of ours. It's got a number, not like the ones in Enstyla."

"Put the body over the back of a mount. We need to sweep the road ahead." As he reloaded, so that he would have a full magazine again, Mykel glanced back toward the prison compound. The local Cadmians were forming up the prisoners for the march up to the mineworks. The sniper had delayed the road sweep, and fifth squad needed to get moving.

Was that the point of the sniping? To distract them?

When everyone in fifth squad was ready once more, he nodded at Vhanyr.

Mykel had ridden another half vingt when he began to feel someone, something in the rocks ahead. He felt foolish, but he aimed where he sensed *something* and loosed one round, then a second, and finally a third. There was silence on the road as the echoes of the shots died away—but only for a moment.

A volley of shots ripped out of the hillside.

"Take cover behind the wall!" snapped Mykel, following his own advice, if belatedly, and easing the chestnut up beside the wall. He flattened himself against his mount's neck and studied the slope.

"Fire at will!" he ordered, then he aimed and fired, concentrating hard on a patch of gray that was not quite right in color.

The rebel slumped, and Mykel began to search for another target.

For a time after the initial flurry of fire, the shots on both sides were intermittent.

After perhaps a quarter glass, there was no more fire from the hillside, and—seemingly—no one remaining up above them.

Mykel waited . . . and waited.

In the end, they found five bodies—all with numbered and marked Cadmian rifles. All had been dressed in dark gray, with sandals, instead of real boots, and all had miners' tattoos on their ankles.

The local Cadmians barely looked at the bodies as they marched the prisoners up past fifth squad, stationed in two ranks of nine on each side of the gate into the mineworks.

Mykel kept swallowing, trying to escape the smell of the guano, but he listened to the murmurs of the squad as they watched the last of the prisoners enter the mineworks.

"What is it . . . about the Captain?"

That was one of the newer Cadmians. Mykel had to concentrate to remember the man's name—Herast.

". . . always been like this . . ."

". . . ever get wounded?"

Someone laughed.

Mykel doubted he'd ever live that down. In his first skirmish as an officer, he'd stood in the stirrups and half turned to give an order, and one of the Reillies had fired and hit him in the side of the buttocks, more like the back of his upper thigh, but the word among the rankers for more than a year was that the undercaptain finally understood being a pain in the ass.

Finally, the heavy wooden gates closed behind the last Cadmian guard.

"Let's head back." Mykel nodded at Vhanyr.

"Double column! Forward! Look lively!"

Mykel had been bothered by the local Cadmians' indifference to the six bodies, but then, everything about Dramur was beginning to disturb him—and he still worried about what to say about what Rachyla had revealed. His fingers dropped toward the ancient's knife, but he did not touch it.

42

Falyna arrived back from Elcien late in the afternoon on Octdi, bearing a series of dispatches. Only one was for Dainyl. Along with that dispatch came a sealed letter. Dainyl slipped the letter from Lystrana into his jacket, to read later.

Falyna had begun to unsaddle the pteridon, after handing the two other dispatches to Quelyt. In turn, Quelyt set off on foot to deliver the dispatches for Majer Herryf and Majer Vaclyn to their senior squad leaders.

"What did you hear in Elcien? asked Dainyl.

"No one's saying much, but there's a mess out east in Iron Stem," replied Falyna, undoing the girths. "Marshal Shastylt was only in Elcien for two days the whole time we were there. Zorclyt said that he'd come back to talk to the High Alector of Justice—more like he was ordered back—and then showed up at headquarters and dashed off the dispatches and headed back to Iron Stem again."

"What else?"

"They sent Yuasylt and his squad to Hyalt, something about brigands in the hills that the local Cadmian garrison couldn't handle. Undercaptain Chelysta was complaining that the duty rosters were too thin, with two squads in Iron Stem, and one in Hyalt, and us here."

"They've been thinner than that many times." Dainyl could recall times when he'd been an undercaptain, and his one squad had done all the dispatch flying for weeks at a stretch.

"Not for a while, though. Folks forget."

That was true enough. "Anything more?"

"Not much. One of the assistants to the High Alector of Justice was taking one of those Tables to Dereka and got caught in the middle of a wild translation. The Highest will have to find another assistant." Falyna looked at the colonel. "If you took over as his assistant, you could stay in Elcien. I'd wager they'd consider it."

Dainyl suppressed a frown behind a laugh. "I've met the Highest on one or two occasions. He's most formidable. I'll stay in the Myrmidons so long as they'll have me."

Falyna snickered. "Colonel, I have to admire how you can suggest that another alector would translate his own mother twice and smile."

"I didn't say that."

The flier just grinned.

"I'd better find a quiet spot and read what the marshal has in store for us," Dainyl said.

"I should have kept you talking longer, sir."

Dainyl waved Falyna off, but with a smile, and headed back to his quarters.

Once he was alone, he settled himself on the end of the bed and looked at the envelope. It was addressed to Colonel Dainyl, with no other titles. The Talent-seal had not been tampered with, and Dainyl opened the envelope, extracted the sheets of the dispatch, and began to read.

Colonel—

Both the High Alector of Justice and I have read your single dispatch about the situation in Dramur. It would appear that the unrest there has been fueled by differing causes, and your prudence in remaining an observer is to be commended.

The matter of the unmarked Cadmian rifles has been referred to the High Alector of Engineering in Ludar, with a request that the manufactory inventory and shipping processes be reviewed. While a few hundred rifles should not in themselves present an insurmountable problem to the Cadmians, you are requested to keep a close eye on these matters in the event that the situation should deteriorate further.

What is most disturbing is that the local steers would even think to fire upon an alector. Your immediate action in destroying the would-be attackers is also to be commended. Such acts cannot be countenanced, particularly now . . .

Particularly now? Why was now any different from the generations before? Because the time was nearing to transfer the master scepter? And because disruptions would count against Acorus in deciding which world would succeed Ifryn in power and glory?

. . . You must be especially alert against anything that might lead to a full-scale insurrection. At the same time, as has been emphasized, you must not intrude unless and until it is clear that the Cadmian battalion cannot handle the situation.

Those words were an indication that Dainyl had read the situation correctly.

I would suggest weekly dispatches, but that must be dictated by circumstances. Both the Highest and I count upon your discretion and judgment in these matters.

The signature was that of Marshal Shastylt.

Dainyl read the entire dispatch, really a letter of instructions, again. He would indeed have to be most careful as events unfolded.

Finally, he opened the letter from Lystrana. Unlike the marshal's dispatch, the Talent-seal on hers had been tampered with, but Dainyl had expected that, since Lystrana would have had to have left the missive with the marshal. He smiled as he read the salutation.

My dearest,
Although the house is not large, it feels quite so, and more than a little empty without your presence. When I wake in the morning, I still look to your side of the bed, and at night, I often reach out, but find only cool covers. I also miss your warm smile and enthusiasm for the day . . .

Thankfully, although I would rather have you here, as always, I have been much occupied with reconciling bursars' and other accounts and financial details occasioned by the reductions in coal production and the ramifications for all sorts of crafting and artisan work over the next two or three quints . . .

Had the disruptions at Iron Stem been that severe?

. . . Fortunately, Zestafyn has provided a great deal of assistance, without which projections for the Highest would have been most difficult.

Zestafyn? If the head of the Duarch's intelligence operations were supplying information to Lystrana, matters were far worse than the tone of her letter suggested; but then, the reference might have been for the benefit of the marshal or whoever had tampered with the seal and read the letter.

. . Your mother stopped by on Tridi. It was most kind of her. She was quite solicitous and hoped it would not be too long before you returned. She said that your direct and practical approach to solving difficult problems usually meant that you were never away for that long, but that meant you spent much more time afterward polishing and smoothing displaced scales, and that someday there would be scales that could not be smoothed back into shape. I said that you always had to be practical, and that you would choose the best time to act. We laughed about that, especially when I told her about the calculations over your morning carriage ride. She was also most complimentary about the improvements to the house, and quite warm and gracious in talking about you.

I almost forgot to tell you that I have officially been named as the chief assistant to the High Alector of Finance. It doesn't change what I'm doing, but it is recognition. I look forward to seeing you, whenever that may be.

Above her signature, she had written, "With all my love."

Dainyl smiled at those words. Then he nodded slowly as he considered the entire letter. What Lystrana was telling him was that what he was involved in was extraordinarily delicate, so delicate that even his mother was worried, and she seldom had expressed worry. He doubted that his mother had said any such thing, or even visited the house, but it was Lystrana's way of making a point in a letter she had known would be read.

The two letters emphasized what he had feared all along—that far more was going on than anyone not involved knew or even than those involved could or would explain and that if he took his usual and more direct approach, his troubles would compound themselves. Yet Lystrana had also suggested, indirectly, that he would have to act that way . . . at the right time.

He just hoped he could recognize that decision point, or points.

43

Duadi was a cloudy day, although the clouds were high, and a cold wind, chill for Dramur, whistled through the fields and scattered woodlands. Mykel rode beside Chyndylt, as he had for the past week, after the efforts on the mining road had quieted that area. With that success, Mykel had hoped that he would hear little from the majer. He had been mistaken.

Majer Vaclyn had not been totally pleased. He'd sent a short dispatch that asked Mykel if it had been necessary to tie up the road for over a glass and keep the miners from working when the mine was already suffering from lowered production. He also suggested that Mykel should have recaptured at least some of the attackers.

Mykel had sent back a polite reply, in which he noted that it was difficult to allow the prisoners to travel a road under fire from rebels hidden above the road in the rocks, but that he would attempt to do better, should the situation occur again. He'd had to stay up late in the tiny cubicle in the run-down auxiliary barracks near the mine to write up his response, as well as a more detailed account of both the action. He had also written a second copy for his own records.

Because matters had continued to remain quiet on the mining road, Mykel had been accompanying Chyndylt and third squad on patrols of the lanes in the lower hills east of the mining camp. Chyndylt had earlier reported that the squad had been taking sporadic fire every day, but that they had never been able to get close to the snipers. Whoever had been firing always chose places where they couldn't be seen.

By the end of another week's patrols, with Mykel accompanying the squad, matters had improved somewhat. While two of third squad's rankers had been wounded, enough to send them back to Dramuria, the squad had killed three snipers. Mykel had killed two, although it was only clear to third squad that he had taken out one of them, and that was fine with him. He would have been happy if he hadn't been credited with any.

He had sent back a brief report with the wounded troopers in which he noted that one rebel had lived for a few moments after being shot, but all that questioning could get from the dying man was that more rifles would come "from the west" to add to those stolen from the Cadmian compound. That was as much as any rank-and-file rebel would know, Mykel surmised.

Earlier, just past midmorning, someone had fired at the squad, but from a more distant rise, without hitting anyone, and had used the lane to escape. Mykel had seen no sense in pursuing, not when it might have led into a trap. The rest of the morning had been quiet, except for an occasional jibe from holders.

One had stood behind a tree and called, "Found any real rebels yet?"

The murmurs from the squad as they had ridden past the holder's cot had been worrying to Mykel.

". . . mouthy bastard . . ."

". . . like to shoot him . . ."

". . . not the one being shot at . . ."

Mykel could see both sides. He didn't see any real rebellion. The shooting at troopers hadn't happened until after Third Battalion had arrived. The Cadmians hadn't shot anyone who hadn't shot at them first, and they were getting tired of being targets. So was Mykel, but he wasn't the one who could change the orders. If he protested or ignored them totally, he'd end up court-martialed and flogged, with someone else succeeding him and carrying out the same orders.

"There's another cot up there," said Chyndylt. "Three men working on a trestle, looks like they're doing something to a chimney."

"I don't see anything like rifles." Mykel continued to survey the road and the surroundings, as did the scouts, but nothing appeared out of the ordinary.

As the squad neared the square stone house, with faded yellow shutters, the two bearded stoneworkers turned, watching the squad. Neither said anything.

From one of the windows came another voice. "There go the brave Cadmians. They shoot because they can't speak. Brave, brave, Cadmians."

"Hush . . ." That was a woman's voice.

"I won't. They don't do any good, just kill good men who were sent to the mines because they were poor. Or because they angered the seltyrs. Ride on! Ride on, brave Cadmians."

Mykel winced. At least, the idiot had enough sense to stay out of sight.

The unseen woman said something, and the man did not taunt the passing squad again.

The last of third squad was a good hundred yards past the cot before Chyndylt spoke. "I'd wager he wouldn't dare to say that face-to-face."

"That's not a wager I'd take," replied Mykel.

"Why are they so angry?"

"They don't want us here. They think that we're tools of the seltyrs and the growers."

"But . . . the majer *killed* one of the seltyrs, and Fifteenth Company destroyed his private arms force. If the seltyrs had their way, we wouldn't be here."

"Things like facts and truth don't change people's feelings," replied Mykel.

Another glass passed, and, as noon approached, ahead Mykel saw a gray-haired man carrying stones, apparently to extend a low stone wall that paralleled the lane. The man fitted each stone, then turned to a pile behind him for another. As the squad neared, the man stopped and watched.

His eyes avoided Mykel's as the captain rode past.

"Brave, brave Cadmians . . ."

The words were just loud enough to be heard. Mykel hoped no one else did. But hoping probably wasn't enough. For a moment, he debated, then eased the chestnut aside and started to turn to head back toward the rear of the squad.

Crack! Crack!

"Third squad! Turn and hold!" Mykel snapped.

He finished wheeling the chestnut. When he looked back, less than ten yards away, a figure lay slumped over the knee-high stone wall. It was the gray-haired man.

The last four Cadmians had halted on the lane just forward of the fallen man. As Mykel rode toward them, past the rest of the squad, he had no doubts that the holder was dead.

"What happened here?" demanded Mykel, reining up. "Who shot him?"

There was no answer. Mykel's eyes hardened, and he began to look over the last four Cadmians—Rykyt, Jonasyr, Polynt, and Mergeyt.

Polynt looked at the captain with some concern, but not at all nervously. Jonasyr didn't look at Mykel at all.

The squat and dark-haired Mergeyt swallowed.

"Yes, Mergeyt? Did you shoot him?"

"No, sir. Polynt did. The fellow said we had to be brave to kill honest folk. Told us to go back where we came from. Then, he looked at Polynt. Maybe he said something. Maybe he didn't, but Polynt plugged him."

For all the nervousness Mergeyt displayed, Mykel knew the ranker was telling the truth.

"What happened, Polynt?" Mykel asked.

"Mergeyt shot him," replied the tall blond ranker. "The old fellow called him useless as a teats on a boar, and worse-smelling than bat dung." Polynt looked directly at Mykel without any nervousness at all.

"I didn't!" Mergeyt's voice rose almost to a squeak.

Mykel turned to Jonasyr. "What happened?"

"I don't know, sir. I was looking up front. I just heard the shots. Polynt and Mergeyt were riding back of us."

The captain knew what Rykyt was going to say before the angular and weathered lander ever did.

"I heard 'em talking, sir, but not who said what. Then there were shots."

Mykel wondered . . . if they just buried the body? No. With his luck, someone would find the man, and then he'd be facing a flogging to the death. How . . . ?

He almost hit his own head as he realized he had the answer. Before he said a word, his own rifle was out. "Polynt! Mergeyt! Hand your rifles to Rykyt. Both of you. Butt first. Now!"

"Yes, sir." Polynt handed over his rifle easily, almost casually.

Mergeyt's hands were shaking as he did.

"Rykyt, check the magazines."

"Polynt's weapon's warm, sir. Two shells missing."

That was as he suspected. "What about Mergeyt's rifle?"

"Cold, and fully loaded, sir." Rykyt's eyes narrowed as he looked at Polynt.

"There's a mistake, sir. Mergeyt switched weapons on me." Polynt projected complete sincerity.

"We'll see about that. We'll have a hearing. I think the Myrmidon colonel's still in Dramuria. They're pretty good at finding things out." One way or another, Mykel needed to get some other officer besides Majer Vaclyn involved. He looked at the other older ranker. "Jonasyr. See if there's anyone in the cot over there."

There was no one else in the cot, and the signs were that no one else lived there.

So the dead holder's body went with them, and Mykel dreaded making the reports, but there was no safe way to hide what had been done, and no way to justify it—not that didn't leave him open to even greater risk and punishment.

44

Slightly past midafternoon on Duadi afternoon, after returning to the mining barracks briefly, Mykel rode south to Dramuria with third squad. He left Fifteenth Company under Bhoral, with instructions to continue the same patrols, except for the area that third squad had been covering. No one was to patrol there.

The ride to the Cadmian compound in Dramuria took more than two glasses, and Mykel brought the squad in the smaller east gate, where they would not visible from the headquarters building. Since Majer Vaclyn seldom inspected or visited the stables or the troopers' barracks, Mykel had a good chance of working matters out as he planned. It was worth the attempt.

Before he left the barracks area where third squad was quartered, Mykel gave specific orders to Chyndylt. "Keep third squad together. Keep Polynt under guard, and don't let anyone talk to anyone until I return, or until you get direct orders from someone senior."

"That bad, sir?"

It was probably worse, but Mykel wasn't about to say so. "Not if we handle it right."

When he reached the headquarters building, he eased inside and looked along the main corridor. He didn't see Majer Vaclyn. He made his way to the duty desk.

"Is Majer Vaclyn in?"

"No, sir," replied the squad leader. "He left a few moment ago. He said he wouldn't be that long."

"Thank you."

Mykel couldn't find Captain Meryst, but Captain Benjyr was in his study in the headquarters building.

"What can I do for you, Captain?" asked Benjyr.

"I need a moment with Majer Herryf. Is he around?"

"He might be . . ."

"It's important that he and Majer Vaclyn know something, but if Majer Herryf doesn't know about it, and I report to Majer Vaclyn . . ."

"I think he's still in his study."

Mykel followed the other captain down the corridor.

"Sir," said Benjyr, opening the study door slightly, "Captain Mykel of Fifteenth Company would like a few words with you."

"Have him come in."

Benjyr smiled at Mykel. "Good luck." His voice was low.

Mykel stepped into the majer's study. The door clicked shut behind him.

"This is rather unusual," began Herryf. "You report to Majer Vaclyn. For whatever it is, I should send you to him."

"Yes, sir. I'm not asking you to do anything. Something happened that I thought both you and Majer Vaclyn should know. He stepped out, and the duty desk didn't know when he'd be back. I thought that you might be able to counsel the majer if you knew."

Herryf frowned.

"Let me explain, sir. Fifteenth Company has been taking a lot of sniping. I've sent two men back here wounded in the last week . . ." Mykel quickly summarized what had happened, then went on. ". . . we're being called outland Cadmians, and everyone thinks you've been pushed aside. We won't be here forever. We never are on deployments, and it seemed to me that you'd have to deal with the results of what we do."

"That is most considerate of you, Captain, but it would have been less trouble for all of us if your man hadn't shot a Dramuran."

"There's one other problem, sir. The Cadmian who did the shooting is a Dramuran. He's one of two in my company."

"I'm not sure how that changes matters, Captain."

"It may not. If Polynt is executed, that's two Dramurans dead, and Third Battalion killed them both. It is a difficult situation. I even have to ask if the man who shot the holder might have fled Dramur and might have had a grudge against the holder."

Herryf frowned. "Why would you think that?"

"There were words exchanged, and it seems strange that, just from nowhere, a ranker would shoot someone. Polynt denies it all, of course. The thing is, if it is a grudge shooting, then that's one thing, and it ought to be handled as a case of murder. If it's not, then you and Majer Vaclyn both need to know that all of this taunting on patrols is having an effect."

"Are you sure that it doesn't reflect lack of supervision, Captain?"

"Every company in Third Battalion has been sniped at, sir, but Fifteenth Company has taken more attacks than anyone."

"Are you hoping that this is something local?"

"I don't think it is, sir, but I don't know. There's no real way for either me or Majer Vaclyn to find out. You could, and that would make sure this is handled in the proper fashion."

"I can see your concerns. You also don't want to be blamed for a failure that's not in your control, either, I imagine."

"I'm responsible, one way or another, sir. I'd just like to limit the damage." Mykel tried to convey both sincerity and concern. "I had thought, with a Myrmidon colonel here, there might be something he could do . . . but that decision rests with you and Majer Vaclyn."

There was a knock on the study door. "Captain Benjyr, sir. Majer Vaclyn has returned. I told him you might need a few words with him. He said that he'd await your pleasure."

Herryf smiled faintly and stood. "Lead the way, Captain."

"Yes, sir." Mykel offered a half bow and turned, stepping out of the study. He could only hope that he could present matters in a way that restricted Majer Vaclyn's actions, but much of that depended on Herryf. He knew he could not trust either majer to act fairly unless it was in each's interest to do so, and he had to set matters so that they saw matters in a similar light.

Majer Vaclyn's mouth almost dropped open as he saw Mykel, but he merely nodded as Majer Herryf followed Mykel into the small study.

"Majer," Mykel began, "I was looking for you, but you were out, and, since the matter I was seeking you for also involved Majer Herryf, I sought him out while I was waiting for your return. As you know, Fifteenth Company has been patrolling the mine road and the surrounding area in an effort to capture rebels. We have taken sporadic fire for weeks now . . ." Mykel went on to explain exactly what had happened with the third squad patrol. "Because this matter will affect both of you, and because—"

"Who knows about this?" snapped Vaclyn.

"The people in this room, sir, and third squad. No one else. The holder lived alone. That was another reason why I returned immediately with third squad. Polynt is under restraint in the barracks at this point, and the squad is under orders not to talk to anyone about the matter."

For several moments, there was silence.

Then Vaclyn turned to Herryf. "Majer . . . you have had more time to consider this, and you're more familiar with the local situation. What do you think?"

Herryf smiled politely. "I think your captain was very wise in considering what the local implications might be, particularly with a Myrmidon colonel observing us. His immediate referral to us speaks well of your example and oversight, Majer."

Mykel managed to keep his face impassive. Herryf saw a definite advantage in not having Mykel made an example, but where was the local Cadmian majer headed?

"As you may not know," Herryf continued, "I had raised the matter of the rebels with the Marshal of Myrmidons and Cadmians sometime ago. I had requested the authority and golds to establish another company. That request was . . . deferred. Then, your battalion was deployed here. For these reasons, for either one of us to hold a court-martial over the officers and men involved could be seen as less than impartial."

"You are suggesting that we request the colonel act as justicer, then?" asked Vaclyn.

"He has that authority, and as an observer, he has even more impartiality."

"That does have merit," reflected Vaclyn.

"Since the incident did occur with Third Battalion, of course," Herryf added, "I could not make such a request, but I would be pleased to concur and add my strong recommendation. My very strong recommendation."

"The recommendation will be ready in the morning, Majer," Vaclyn replied. "I appreciate your counsel and support."

"If we do not act together," replied Herryf, "we may well suffer separately. If there is nothing more?"

"Not at the moment. Captain Mykel and I will need to discuss the details."

Herryf nodded. "Thank you, Majer . . . Captain."

Once the study door closed, Vaclyn looked hard at Mykel. "Why did you even bring this here?" The majer's voice was low and did not conceal both anger and displeasure. "You could have handled it there."

"No, sir. The holder was an older man, with lands. People know him. You can't keep eighteen troopers quiet. Not when the guilty one is trying to blame his riding mate. I'd just as soon have shot Polynt myself, but then every trooper in the company would be asking who I'd shoot next."

"You think you were so smart, in making sure Majer Herryf knew."

"Sir, the whole compound would know within a day if I tried to keep it quiet. He was here when I came looking for you. He had to know that I'd been on patrol. He's not stupid."

Vaclyn's hand blurred toward his belt.

Mykel knew what was coming, and he also knew that Vaclyn wasn't aiming to kill or injure—unless Mykel moved.

Thunk! The throwing knife vibrated from where it had embedded itself in the doorframe behind and to the left of Mykel's ear.

"Captain . . ." Vaclyn's voice oozed menace. "I do not like games. I do not like schemes. What does it take to make that point to you?"

"Sir . . . I am trying to do the best I know how. It is hard on the men, being shot at from cover day after day, and having the locals make cracks and comments all the time. We're protecting these locals from escaped prisoners and brigands, and they think we're the enemy. Majer Herryf pointed out that all the Cadmians are considered as less than impartial, and with Polynt being from Dramur, if you or the majer find him guilty, lots of people here would say that he was a scapegoat, that we picked the one of the few Cadmians from Dramur to blame. By referring it to the colonel, you avoid that. No one questions an alector—"

"It's still a game." Majer Vaclyn smiled coldly. "This time . . . this time . . . you just might be right. Unlike the last time. Since this was your idea, you write the first draft of the request. I'll expect it here in my study in less than two glasses. Is that clear?"

"Yes, sir."

"Oh . . . one other matter. I've let things cool off in Jyoha, but I'll be sending Thirteenth Company off on Quattri to make sure things don't go back to the way they were."

"Yes, sir."

"Write up that draft. Make it good, Captain, very good. After that, you will also draft a report, just the way you told it to us. Tonight. Majer Herryf and I will see Colonel Dainyl in the morning. You and your squad are to remain within the compound until this is resolved. You may go, Captain."

Mykel left. He did not look at the knife in the doorframe. He'd heard about the majer and his knives, but this was the first time he'd been a target—even as a warning. Matters were definitely not good, but they could have been far worse. Still . . . he had a long night ahead of him. He also wondered how long it would be before the majer found some way to bring him before a court-martial—and why the majer was out after him.

45

Over the days since he had received his latest instructions from Marshal Shastylt, Dainyl had flown twice to the peak of the ancients, after sensing something, but the soarer and her creatures had vanished long before he arrived. Could she sense him as well as he could her? Most probably. He wanted to learn more, but since he had not, he started the weekly report the marshal had hinted would be appropriate, including a few words stating that he had discovered a tunnel of the ancients venerated by at least some of the indigens near where he had been shot.

He had received no reports from either majer since Vaclyn had briefed him on Fifteenth Company's elimination—or massacre—of the rebels in Jyoha. By occasionally talking with Benjyr or Meryst, he had discovered that while attacks on the mine road had decreased, other attacks had not, and mine production continued to decline. His patience with the majers and the situation was more than wearing thin.

On Tridi morning, as he was leaving the officers' mess after his early breakfast, he saw Majer Vaclyn and Majer Herryf headed toward him. He had no doubts that something had gone wrong, but he stopped and waited, smiling patiently.

"If we could have a moment of your time, Colonel?" asked Vaclyn.

"I presume you would prefer a less public place," replied Dainyl. "If so, I would suggest Majer Herryf's study. There is more space there."

"Thank you, Colonel," replied Vaclyn.

As he followed the two majers back to the headquarters building, Dainyl wondered what had gone wrong. Once they were inside Majer Herryf's office, Dainyl faced the two. He did not seat himself, partly to make them uncomfortable and partly because he didn't feel like cramping himself into too small a chair.

"We have a problem, Colonel," offered Vaclyn.

Both majers had more than one, but Dainyl just nodded.

"One of the Cadmian rankers from Fifteenth Company shot a cot holder out on the north road. The man wasn't doing anything. The company captain happened to be with the squad. His report, and it's supported, states that his ranker just shot the man in cold blood. The evidence seems straightforward. The situation is not. The ranker claims that he's being blamed and that a comrade did the shooting. He is also one of the few rankers from Dramur . . ."

Dainyl listened as Vaclyn described the situation and concluded, ". . . if I hold a court-martial and find him innocent, the locals will find it unacceptable. If I find him guilty, after all the snipings and insults, the battalion will think that matters will just get worse, and they'll be tempted to shoot at anything that looks dangerous. If Majer Herryf holds the court-martial, much the same thing will happen, except worse."

Dainyl could see both sides of the problem.

Vaclyn handed Dainyl a thick envelope. "In there is our request that you act as justicer in this matter. The captain's full report is also enclosed. As an observer and a representative of the Duarches, you will be seen as impartial in a way that neither of us would be."

Much as he disliked the situation, Dainyl had to admire the manner in which the two had acted. By presenting the matter to him, they could portray themselves as acting in the highest and best manner, while avoiding the worst of the repercussions. Dainyl had the duty to represent the Duarches as impartial and just. If he turned his back on the matter, he would only convey that the Duarches did not care about justice or about the Cadmians' discipline.

Dainyl laughed.

The two majers managed to maintain their façades, but Dainyl could sense the worry. He waited a moment before speaking, letting the silence draw out.

"You have both managed to avoid dealing with this, and you have created a situation where it is in the best interests of the Duarches for me to act as justicer." He smiled again. "You have both been most clever, and I will serve as justicer in a court-martial, but . . . the local Dramurian justicer will sit close at hand so that I may consult with him about local matters." He could sense the relief of both majers.

"The court-martial will begin the day after tomorrow," Dainyl added. "This is not a matter that should be delayed. I will need a list of all who witnessed the event, especially the captain and the squad leader. The relatives of the dead man should also be informed. They will be present at the court-martial." He turned to Herryf. "You will arrange for the local justicer to be here. You will not tell him why, except that I desire his presence."

"Yes, sir."

After he left the two majers, Dainyl walked back to his quarters, pondering. He could not imagine how the two majers had put aside their differences, but perhaps necessity and ambition did occasionally surmount personal feelings.

46

On Quinti morning, Dainyl was in the small hall being used for the trial well before the eighth glass of the morning. He had a folder containing his notes, some questions, the request from Majer Vaclyn, and the report from Captain Mykel.

Cadmian troopers were lining up benches. One table and two chairs had been set on a dais, and a narrower table with three chairs placed to the left of the dais. One of the chairs on the dais actually had been made to seat alectors. As he glanced around the hall, Dainyl was surprised to find Sturwart there, at one side of the hall, talking to a darker-skinned man with iron gray hair. Behind them were four locals—a gray-haired woman, a younger blonde woman, and two men slightly past youth. They had to be relatives of the slain cot holder.

Sturwart turned. "Colonel! I'd like you to meet Justicer Alveryt."

Dainyl crossed the hall, then stopped a yard or so from the pair.

"You had asked for me to be present, sir," said the older man.

"I'm pleased to see you. As you may have heard, it is a court-martial for murder."

"Serious as that is, an alector and a senior Myrmidon officer does not require a mere local justicer." Alveryt smiled politely.

"Need is not the same as wisdom," Dainyl replied, smiling and projecting a sense of friendliness. "As a justicer, you can explain to others and why matters were the way they were. Also, I have some questions about the trooper accused of the murder, and I may need you to interrogate him in matters about which I do not have any knowledge. Finally, were I not here, it is possible that this might have come before you, and I thought you should be here."

Alveryt bowed. "You are most considerate." He smiled. "It also serves your purposes."

"Of course," Dainyl admitted.

"There will be a record of the trial?"

"I have arranged for that." Dainyl might have a few sections removed from what was given to the justicer, but that would probably be unnecessary.

"That will prove most useful," suggested Sturwart. "Many people are upset about the patrols by the Cadmians."

"The Cadmians are upset that people are shooting at them."

"Is that not just talk? Except for Seltyr Ubarjyr, that is?"

"I have not seen the latest numbers on casualties, but I know that there are ten or twelve dead Cadmians and as many who have been wounded in the past few weeks."

"That many?" Sturwart was honestly surprised.

"I am most certain that the numbers are higher now." At the sound of boots on the stone, Dainyl turned. A Cadmian captain—doubtless Captain Mykel—and a squad of Cadmians had appeared and were taking places on the benches. A single trooper sat in the chair for the accused, with two armed Cadmians behind and flanking him.

"If you will excuse me," Dainyl said politely to Sturwart. Turning to Alveryt, he added, "I would appreciate it if you would take the other chair at the table."

Alveryt laughed softly. "I can see which chair is mine."

Dainyl couldn't help but like the justicer. Dainyl's Talent showed that Alveryt was honest and direct, but, as Dainyl had learned many years before, that might not be enough.

As he and Alveryt took their places at the table on the dais, three Cadmian rankers settled at the narrow table to the left, with pens and stacks of paper, ready to record the proceedings. Within a few moments, Majer Vaclyn appeared, followed by Herryf. Both majers settled into the pair of chairs to the right of the dais.

Dainyl looked to Vaclyn. "Is everyone present?"

"Yes, sir."

Dainyl waited a moment for the murmurs among the Cadmians to die away. "This is a Cadmian court-martial. All procedures of justicing will be followed. Cadmian trooper Polynt, of the third squad of the Fifteenth Company of the Third Cadmian Battalion, has been charged with the murder of holder Casimyl of Lecorya. Trooper Polynt, stand and step forward."

Polynt did so, his eyes meeting those of the colonel.

"You have been charged with murder. How do you declare?"

"I did no murder, sir. I declare that I am innocent."

"The man charged has declared his innocence. Let it be so noted." Dainyl nodded to Polynt. "You may be seated until called again."

Polynt sat without speaking.

"A moment, if you would, Colonel?" murmured Alveryt.

Dainyl turned and leaned toward the justicer. "Yes?"

"I did not recognize the name of the trooper," said Alveryt in a voice that barely carried to the colonel, "but he is indeed from Dramur. He was a laborer in the dyeworks at Santazl. His name then was Apolynt. He was called Pol. He murdered his uncle and took his golds and fled Dramur. An abandoned boat was found, and everyone thought he had drowned."

"How did you know him?"

"He was sent to the mines before that for lifting coins from a potter. I heard the case."

"Thank you. We'll get to that later." Dainyl turned back toward the Cadmians. "Captain Mykel, commanding officer, Fifteenth Company, step forward."

The blond and lanky lander captain stepped forward, stiffened, and offered a slight bow.

"You were with third squad when the shooting took place, Captain?"

"Yes, sir. I was riding at the front of the patrol."

"Did you see the holder before he was killed?"

"Yes, sir. He was working on a stone wall, but he stopped as we neared. He looked at us. He wasn't pleased to see us, and he murmured something like, 'Brave, brave, Cadmians.' I watched him for a moment, but he just stood there."

"How did you know he had been shot?"

"I didn't know who had been shot, but there were two reports from a rifle at the rear of the squad, and I told Chyndylt to hold the front of the squad, and I rode toward the rear to see what had happened . . ."

Dainyl watched the captain closely, Talent-sensing as well as listening while the captain explained his actions, and how he had determined who had fired the shots. Two things were obvious. First, the captain was telling the truth and had acted relatively quickly and decisively, for which Dainyl was grateful. Second, the captain might well be a latent Talent himself, although he was clearly unaware of that ability. In that respect, he would have to be watched, another headache for Dainyl.

". . . then Polynt said Mergeyt had switched rifles. I checked the numbers on each rifle immediately and had trooper Rykyt verify the numbers. When we got back to our temporary base, I cross-checked those numbers. The rifle that killed the holder was the one issued to Polynt. It was the one he was holding when I rode up." The captain stood waiting.

"Did you see anything to suggest that the rifles were switched before you got there?"

"No, sir. There was more than a yard between their mounts."

Dainyl paused, then asked, "In the past, did Polynt ever use his rifle on bystanders—or men who had surrendered? Or behave more violently or less predictably than other troopers?"

"No, sir. If anything, he was cooler and more levelheaded than many."

"Thank you, Captain, that will be all for now. You may be seated."

Mykel bowed, and returned to his seat.

Dainyl looked to the accused. "Trooper Polynt, would you please step forward?"

Polynt rose and took two steps forward. His eyes met Dainyl's easily.

"Tell us what happened on the lane when the holder was killed."

Polynt shifted his weight from one boot to the other, ever so slightly, but continued looking directly at Dainyl. "It was like this, sir. We were riding patrol. We'd been riding patrols all over Dramur. Every place we rode, people would yell at us or say things in low voices. They'd tell us to go home, or to leave honest folk alone. I've heard that before. You get used to it, but I was riding with Mergeyt, and we were in the last rank that day. Been a long day, sir, and we'd been shot at twice. Luck would have it, no one got hurt that day, but we'd already lost maybe ten men in the company, and another ten or so been wounded trying to track down the rebels and troublemakers. We saw this old fellow working on a stone wall. He stopped working, just watched us as we rode up. Sort of sneered, he did; then he said something to the troopers a couple of ranks up. I didn't hear what he said, but they sort of got stiff. One of 'em, I think it was Sofolt, put his hand on his rifle, but he didn't do anything. We got close, and the old fellow looked at me and Mergeyt, and he said something like, 'You're such brave Cadmians. You think you're so brave, but you're as useless as teats on a boar. Go on, brave, brave Cadmians.' Well, before I could even think to say anything, Mergeyt took out his rifle and plugged the fellow. Took two quick shots. That was all. I looked at him, and then he threw the rifle at my chest. 'Course, I caught it, and quick as I couldn't believe, he'd grabbed mine. Then, the captain rode back, and I was sitting there in the saddle with a hot rifle." Polynt paused, then added. "That's what happened, sir." His eyes had never left Dainyl's.

The most frightening thing about Polynt's statement was his belief in his own words.

"Did trooper Mergeyt say anything?" asked Dainyl.

"He might have, sir. I don't rightly recall."

"Captain Mykel wrote a report, which will be included as part of the record. In that report, he noted that the rifle that you held, the one that had been fired, was your rifle, that the maker's numbers matched those of the rifle issued to you. If trooper Mergeyt had used his weapon, that rifle should have borne his numbers, not yours. How do you explain that, trooper?"

"Sir, I can't explain that. I just know what happened, just like I said."

"I will have further questions for you later, trooper. Please take your seat."

"Yes, sir."

"Trooper Mergeyt. Please step forward."

Unlike Polynt, Mergeyt was nervous, shaking slightly as he stepped forward. "Yes, sir?"

"Please tell me what you saw."

"Yes, sir. Wasn't like Polynt said, sir. Not exactly. I mean, well, there was the old fellow. He was laying stone, and he said stuff, but I wasn't paying no attention. Not until he looked at Polynt, and he said something like, 'Worthless pup, come back to foul your own den?' Hiding behind a Cadmian uniform, now. Such a brave, brave Cadmian.' Polynt didn't say nothing, just took out his rifle and shot him. Had to turn in the saddle, sideways. After that, the captain came riding back, and he had his rifle out, made both us give our rifles to Rykyt . . ."

As Mergeyt finished talking, Dainyl managed to keep from nodding.

Nervous as the trooper was, he was telling the truth, even if he had kept looking away from Dainyl. "Thank you. You may sit down."

Dainyl looked at Polynt. "Step forward."

Polynt did. "Trooper Mergeyt has said that the holder said that you'd come back to foul your own den? Why would the holder have said that?"

"He didn't say that, sir. He just talked to Mergeyt."

"Is there any reason why he would have said something like that?"

"He didn't say that, sir."

"Aren't you from Dramur, trooper?"

"Yes, sir."

"Did you know the holder?"

"No, sir."

"Please take a seat and remove your left boot, trooper."

"Sir?"

"You heard me. Remove your left boot."

Polynt stiffened ever so slightly, and just momentarily, before sitting down. Slowly, he removed the left boot.

"Lift your trouser and show us your ankle."

Polynt did.

"Would you please explain the number on your ankle?" From the corner of his eye, Dainyl saw Sturwart's mouth open, but the colonel kept his concentration on the trooper.

"I can't, sir. I just can't."

Dainyl could sense both the truth and the frustration in Polynt.

"Do you see a number there?"

"Yes, sir."

"Has it always been there?"

"I . . . don't know, sir."

"Do you know how it got there?"

"No, sir."

"You may put your boot back on." Dainyl turned. "I would like Justicer Alveryt to explain the tattoo on the trooper's ankle, and how it came to be there."

Alveryt nodded slightly and cleared his throat. "Until I saw the trooper this morning, I did not realize who he was. His name is Apolynt, and he is from Santazl. He was convicted of theft from a potter here six years ago. After his term in the mines, he was suspected of having committed a murder, but he ran into the night. When an overturned boat was found in the gulf, several days later, he was believed dead."

"Trooper Polynt, is your name Apolynt?"

"That's what my father called me. I never used the name."

"Are you from Santazl?"

"Yes, sir."

"Were you sentenced to the mines?"

"Yes, sir."

"Were you not asked if you had been convicted of a major crime when you joined the Cadmians?"

"I don't rightly recall, sir."

"Are you not aware that concealing a crime to join the Cadmians is a flogging offense?"

"No, sir. I never heard that."

Once more, Dainyl could sense the internal confusion in the trooper, a confusion that bore a sense of Talent-manipulation.

"You may be seated."

Polynt reseated himself.

"Trooper Rykyt, step forward."

The trooper who stepped before the dais was older.

"Please describe what you saw concerning the killing of the holder."

Dainyl listened carefully to Rykyt and the other troopers he called, but nothing any of them said cast the slightest shadow of doubt on what Captain Mykel had reported. After all the witnesses had been heard, slightly before noon, Dainyl let the silence draw out for a time as he studied Polynt.

The ranker had killed the cot holder. There was no doubt about that, and there was little doubt that Justicer Alveryt thought so as well. The fact that he had fled Dramuria after committing one murder—and could not say where he had been—and that someone had used Talent on the man's thoughts to block those memories—that was far more disturbing, because it meant either one of the highest of alectors was involved, or that there was a highly Talented lander loose. Dainyl liked neither of the possibilities. Still, he had to make a judgment on the facts before him and to pass sentence.

"Polynt, please rise and face your judgment."

The trooper did. For the first time, there was uncertainty and fear in his eyes.

Dainyl stood and looked down at the trooper. "By the authority vested in me by the High Alector of Justice, under the Code of the Duarches, and the regulations governing all Cadmians, I hereby confirm that the accused has had the right to state his case, and that all parties to the offense have been heard. The holder Casimyl of Lecorya was shot and murdered on his own holding. This proceeding has established beyond any doubt that you, Apolynt of Santazl, committed that murder. For that murder, you will be flogged until dead. Your sentence will be carried out one glass before sunset tonight." Dainyl paused just briefly, then added the ritual phrase. "Justice has been done; justice will be done. This court-martial is hereby concluded."

"No! I didn't!"

Polynt started to move, but before he took half a step, the Cadmian guards seized him. In moments, his hands were bound, and a gag was across his mouth.

Dainyl noted that Captain Mykel had been right there. He and his men had anticipated what Polynt would do, and they had been ready. That was the mark of a good officer, but a good lander officer who might discover his Talent was something else again. Yet good officers were always hard to come by, and many who were potentially Talented never did discover their Talent.

That meant that Dainyl would be the one to watch Captain Mykel. There were no other alectors near, and, equally important, after what he was discovering, whom else could he trust?

47

Mykel stood facing north in the Cadmian compound, third squad before him. The entire squad, including Mykel, wore red armbands—the sign of blood shed wrongfully.

Chyndylt took one step forward, then stiffened, and snapped, "Third squad, ready, sir!"

"Thank you, squad leader. Stand fast." Mykel about-faced, so that he looked directly at the T-shaped flogging stand directly before him.

On the right of the flogging stand was Majer Vaclyn. Beside it on the left waited a thick-thewed figure in black wearing a black mask and cowl, and holding the execution whip, with its razor-sharp barbs.

"Third squad stands ready, sir," Mykel reported.

Majer Vaclyn barely looked at the captain before raising his voice. "Bring forth the prisoner."

As he waited, although his head did not move, Mykel's eyes flicked to the west, where the white sun hung just above the walls of the compound, then back to the flogging stand, a reminder not only of what awaited Polynt, but what could await any Cadmian who failed badly—including Mykel.

Hands bound behind him, Polynt was escorted to the T-shaped form in the middle of the south side of the courtyard. The four Cadmians who led him also wore red armbands, although they were from the local Cadmians stationed permanently in Dramuria. They positioned him so that his chest was against the cross member of the stand. Then, his feet were tied loosely to the stand before his arms were unbound, and his wrists strapped to the stand.

Once the condemned trooper was secured to the stand, and gagged, the four Cadmian escorts turned as one and marched southward beyond the stand. There, they about-faced and came to attention.

Majer Vaclyn stepped forward, clearing his throat and speaking. "You have taken life, and life will be taken from you. You have created pain and suffering, and with pain and suffering will you die. May each lash remind you of your deeds. With each lash may you regret the evils that you have brought into this world." He stepped back and nodded to the whipmaster.

Mykel could sense that, for the majer, the words were merely a procedure. They should not have been. There should have been meaning behind them. Then, for Polynt, perhaps that was fitting, for the trooper had never had any appreciation of any life besides his own, and the final words before the lash meant as little to him as they had to the majer.

Mykel should have guessed that Polynt had served time as a prisoner. The trooper's description of the guano mine had been too graphic—and too out of the character that Polynt had presented as a trooper. The captain's lips tightened—another failure on his part, and he was probably most fortunate that the Myrmidon colonel hadn't picked up on that.

The whipmaster stepped forward, raising the whip. The first lash ripped away fabric from the back of a tunic from which all insignia had been removed. Polynt convulsed, but the heavy gag muffled any exclamation or moan he might have uttered.

As the whipmaster continued to strike, Mykel watched, outwardly stolid, despite the blood and agony before him. At moments, a faint line of pain seemed to fall across his own back, but that had to be his own imagination. Then, as Polynt began to sag in the T-brace, Mykel heard a muffled impact behind him as someone from third squad collapsed, most likely one of the newer rankers.

Someone condemned was seldom actually lashed to death, but whipped until insensible. Then the whipmaster and executioner put a dagger through the heart. When that finally happened, all too close to sunset, Mykel felt a vague sense of relief, along with an emptiness and a sadness. Polynt's death wouldn't bring back those he had killed. It would ensure he killed no one else, and it *might* deter some trooper from following Polynt's example.

Vaclyn stepped forward once more. "Justice has been done. He stepped back.

Four members of the death squad stepped forward and cut the body from the whipping frame, laying it on a flat handcart that two others had rolled into position.

"Dismissed to officers," Vaclyn stated flatly.

Mykel turned to face third squad. Many rankers were pale. Mykel suspected he might be as well. "Squad leader, you have the squad. Restricted to quarters until morning muster."

"Yes, sir." Chyndylt turned. "About-face! Forward!"

Mykel stood silently for a moment.

"Captain!"

At the words from the majer, Mykel turned. "Yes, sir?"

"I need a word with you."

"Yes, sir." Mykel walked to the majer, stopping short a yard away and waiting.

"This has been a most distasteful situation. Cadmians should never be on trial for murder. This whole incident suggests that your leadership has been less than superb. In fact, your leadership has been barely adequate at times."

Mykel waited, his face calm. Saying anything would just make matters worse, and Mykel was partly to blame, if not for any reason that the majer knew.

"You'll be returning to the mine patrols first thing in the morning with third squad," declared Vaclyn. "You will report to me every Octdi afternoon, here at the headquarters building, no later than two glasses past midday. You will bring one squad, a different squad, each Octdi. You will begin this Octdi. Is that clear?"

"Yes, sir."

"Good." Vaclyn's smile was cold. "You may go, Captain."

Mykel offered a slight bow, the least he dared, before turning and walking back toward the barracks. He'd need to talk to Chyndylt, and he might as well get that over with first.

No matter what he did, matters between him and Majer Vaclyn could only get worse. He would have to continue to document everything he could, however he could, in between riding and supervising patrols.

Why did Vaclyn dislike him so much? Because the majer was afraid that Mykel would reveal how incompetent he was?

Mykel shook his head. Vaclyn was too incompetent to recognize his own shortcomings, and too self-centered even to consider whether he had shortcomings. What Mykel didn't understand was why the majer remained in command of the battalion. Sooner or later, Vaclyn would make a mistake that his captains couldn't rectify and that Colonel Herolt couldn't cover up. Then what?

Mykel snorted softly. What would happen was that some captain would be blamed—most likely Mykel—and flogged or executed, or both.

The court-martial had bothered Mykel, not because of the outcome, but because he had sensed that something had not been right about the entire situation. What that might have been, Mykel had not been able to determine, only that he felt that way. Polynt had deserved death, probably for two murders, if not more.

Even so, the execution itself had been hard for Mykel, because flogging to death was painful. At times, he'd felt like he'd suffered some of the strokes, even though he'd only had to stand in front of third squad and watch. That had to have been an overactive imagination. What else could it have been?

Quietly, he headed for the barracks as the last long light of the winter sun faded in the west.

48

As the long shadows that preceded twilight stretched across the compound, Dainyl watched from the corner of the headquarters building as Majer Vaclyn exchanged words with Captain Mykel. The captain's posture remained formal, neither relaxed nor stiff with anger, but Dainyl could sense a core of feeling—hot rage encased in cold control.

After the captain turned, Dainyl moved toward the majer.

Vaclyn looked up, surprised at the alector's appearance. "Colonel."

"Majer." Dainyl projected a faint sense of curiosity. "I saw you talking to Captain Mykel, and you seemed concerned."

For several moments, Vaclyn said nothing. Dainyl could sense that he was irritated at what he felt was an intrusion, but the colonel held a pleasant expression on his face and waited, using his Talent, as well as his eyes and ears, to study the majer.

"I am, Colonel. Any time a ranker behaves the way Polynt did is a matter of concern."

"I can see that, but Captain Mykel reacted well under the circumstances."

"He reacted. That was the problem. He never should have let it happen, Colonel. Good officers anticipate matters like that."

Dainyl had trouble seeing how the captain could have foreseen an unpremeditated murder by a man who had successfully hidden his background from a number of Cadmian officers. Polynt had obviously changed his name enough so that he would not have been linked to a murder in Dramuria. He'd also enlisted in the Cadmians in a place remote enough from Dramur that no one would have thought to have checked his ankle for a prisoner's tattoo.

"I can see your concerns," returned Dainyl. "Still . . . Captain Mykel should not be judged too harshly. He wasn't the first one who failed to discover that Polynt was an escaped prisoner."

"If you will pardon my directness, Colonel . . . Captain Mykel's difficulties cannot be excused by the failures of others."

"That is true," Dainyl replied smoothly. "A commander's shortcomings should not be blamed on those above or beneath him. Your point is well-taken, and all officers in the Myrmidons and Cadmians should be held to that standard."

Once more, Dainyl sensed the faint and distant feel of Talent about Vaclyn, yet he could sense nothing beyond that—and he knew he should, but not what or how. Not for the first time, he wished he had been given greater training in Talent, but because he had not manifested Talent when young, he had never been afforded that opportunity.

"Thank you, Colonel."

Dainyl doubted Vaclyn would be thanking him, not if the majer truly understood the meaning behind his words. "Thank you very much, Majer. I wish you and Third Battalion well in your efforts to deal with the rebels."

"Thank you, sir. We'll make sure that there isn't a real rebellion, choke off this unrest before it gets out of hand."

With a last smile, Dainyl turned and walked briskly toward the officers' mess, where the food was barely edible, but the ale not too bad.

49

There are those who claim life is sacred in and of itself, or on behalf of some deity, yet they do not refer to all life, but that of their own kind. If they do claim that of all life, then they are either ignorant, or hypocrites, or both. To live, every being steals from another, for to live one must consume food. Consuming food is taking the life of another, or eating what another might have consumed to live, if not both. All cannot be equally sacred if one is prey to the other, and thus less than the other.

One who truly believes that the end purpose of life is but to create more life—for whatever purpose—is not a thinking being, but a steer as fit for slaughter as any in a livestock pen. The smallest of creatures strive to reproduce to the limits of the food at hand. If beings capable of thought and reflection only strive to eat, pleasure themselves as they can, and reproduce to the limits of their world, what makes such beings any different from those millions of so-called lower creatures who live but to eat and reproduce? Can such beings be truly said to reflect any higher purpose than that of all other animals?

Such beings will claim that they are indeed different, for they have tools, and they have developed weapons and cities. Yet the jackdaws and ravens use tools, and a weapon is but one form of tool. The ants and termites have cities. To say that one's own form of life is special, or sacred, does not make it so. Nor does the assertion that some unknown and unproved deity has declared a people or a faith special make either a faith or a people special. Again, that is but an assertion based on a faith that has no root in what is, except a desire for it to be so.

The actions and the purposes of a species are what determine its worth. Those actions must be more than the assertion of privilege and blind reproduction. Those actions must challenge the worlds and the stars. They must create beauty, art, and devices that none have seen before.

Life is not sacred or exceptional merely because it exists, or because one asserts that it is, but by what it attempts, and by what it achieves. That is what has always distinguished us. We have not striven merely to reproduce, or to comfort ourselves with toys, pleasures, and food. We have changed whole worlds, and we have created art and beauty where there was none before.

What we have done is what has given us the right to claim that we are above the steers . . .

Views of the Highest
Illustra
1513 W.T.

50

A good two glasses before dawn on Sexdi morning, Dainyl walked across the courtyard from the temporary quarters that had become less and less transient, and more and more cramped. The night before, he'd been up late writing the report on the court-martial, included in the weekly dispatch to the marshal that Quelyt would be taking back to Elcien in a glass. Ahead of Dainyl, beside one of the squares, waited Falyna and her pteridon.

The colonel adjusted the shimmersilk flying jacket and heavy gloves.

While they weren't necessary in the light east wind blowing across the compound, they would be in the chill heights above and around the Murian Mountains.

Falyna inclined her head to the colonel. "Good morning, sir."

"Good morning, Falyna. You ready to fly me up there?"

"Yes, sir." The Myrmidon ranker paused, then added, "If you'll pardon my asking, Colonel, and I wouldn't ask anyone, but you were a flier for a long time—"

"You'd like to know why I keep asking you to fly me out to where that ancient tunnel is? There's something that keeps coming back there. Sooner or later," Dainyl shrugged, "I hope that I'll be there when it is. I want to get there earlier today. We've been too late before. I can't help but think it has something to do with this so-called rebellion."

Falyna frowned, then nodded. "Those locals fired at us from right below there."

"It doesn't seem like coincidence."

"No, sir. You want me to set down and wait?"

"No. You could set down somewhere else, but not close. Give me a glass alone."

"We can do that."

Falyna felt that her colonel was wasting time, and perhaps Dainyl was, but he'd talked and questioned lander after lander over the weeks, read reports, and followed what the Cadmians were doing—and he knew very little beyond what he'd discovered in the first week.

He nodded to Falyna. "Let's go."

In moments, Dainyl was in the rear saddle and harness, and the pteridon sprang skyward, wings propelling it seaward into the wind. Once they were well clear of trees and buildings, Falyna eased the pteridon into a climbing turn toward the northwest over an ocean that was a dark, dark green, with scattered whitecaps. Then they were back over land, climbing above the casaran nut plantations to the north of the compound, headed for the Murian Mountains. The skies were clear, and promised to remain so.

Dainyl could not sense either the soarer or her creatures, but she visited the tunnel every second or third day early in the morning. He hoped that he had guessed correctly. His eyes moved to his left, down at the road to the guano mine, then to the mine itself.

Mines—the iron and coal mines in Iron Stem, the guano mine in

Dramur—all were having troubles. Iron Stem was close to the towering Aerlal Plateau, and the guano mine was in the lower reaches of the Murian Mountains. Was that because the ancients were involved, and because they preferred heights? Or just coincidence?

He could sense the greater use of Talent by the pteridon as it climbed until it was above the peak that held the tunnel, then began to make an approach into the light wind.

As soon as the pteridon touched down and half folded its wings, Dainyl unfastened the harness and slipped out of the saddle. "A glass from now!"

"Yes, sir." The ranker nodded.

Dainyl hurried back to the western edge of the bluff or ledge to get clear of the pteridon's wings. There he turned eastward and watched the wide-winged pteridon launch itself, then glide away, dropping lower as it left the higher peaks behind.

After a moment, Dainyl entered the ancient tunnel, lowering his head.

As so many times before, the only tracks on the fine sand were those of his own boots. There were no scratch tracks of birds, no swirled displacement created by snakes, or even fine lines drawn by insects—just the heavy indentations of an alector's boots.

From the outer metallic archway of the tunnel, he studied the mirror on the floor, a mirror that still puzzled him. Again, he probed it with his Talent. For the slightest of instants, the golden green that surrounded it seemed to stretch endlessly . . . somewhere.

A flash of golden green light flared before him, and the soarer hovered above the floor mirror. Dainyl's hand went to the grip of the lightcutter in his belt.

Do not touch that if you wish to live.

Faced with that cold green authority, Dainyl decided against trying to use the sidearm.

You have sought us. Why?

"Because the indigens seem to worship this place—or you—and because they attacked me. Because miners are disappearing. I thought there might be a link."

You have raised your steers upon our world. Should those among us not also feed?

Feed? What did that have to do with a revolt? Feed? Who was feeding on what?

You see, but you do not see. Go out and look at the world below.

"Why?"

So that you may see. So that you will be warned.

Warned? Dainyl didn't like those words at all. Still, he moved back from the soarer, one step backward after another, never taking his eyes off her. His Talent revealed nothing about her except the golden green nimbus of Talent-energy surrounding her. The soarer followed him, keeping the same separation.

Once outside the tunnel and the outer unnatural cave, Dainyl stepped sideways. The soarer glided past him, a miniature and perfectly formed winged woman perhaps half his size.

"Now what?" he asked, his eyes and Talent scanning her and the area around them. There was no sense or sign of the violet-red stonelike creatures . . . but there hadn't been any sign of the soarer until the moment she had appeared.

Behold the world. Look out across the lands.

Warily, Dainyl shifted his glance to the southeast, back toward Dramuria.

Abruptly, he was surrounded by a greenish light or mist. He blinked, forcing himself not to draw the light-cutter. Through the green he still saw the lands below, stretching toward the distant ocean, but in addition to what he had always seen, a weave of color assaulted him, lines and webs of brown, and black, and amber—thin lines, thicker lines, all intertwined. His second sense was that he saw a subtle weave that filled the entire silver-green skies, the warp and weft of lifewebs that seemed to intertwine, and yet never touch.

Under the sensory assault, he took a single stumbling step sideways before catching himself. What was he seeing? Was she trying to control him, use her Talent to destroy him? Or worse, enslave him?

We do kill, but only as we must. We do not bind. That weakens the lifewebs more than death. You see the webs of life, all life.

She might have been lying. Dainyl doubted that he could tell if she were, not with the power she projected, but he did not think so. Somehow, he did not doubt that the ancients could see the ties that bound the lifemass of Acorus. Why couldn't Talented alectors? Why hadn't he?

Look at yourself, alector. Look at yourself.

Almost unwillingly, he looked down at himself. Purplish pink threads sprang from him, merging into an ugly purple thread that arched away from him toward the northeast. Compared to the soft and warm colors of the web stretching out below the peak, the purplish pink that surrounded him was *wrong,* not subtly wrong, but oppressively so, a color and shade that did not belong on Acorus, that conflicted and fought with the tapestry formed by the softer lifewebs.

Yet he was an alector, and that purplish pink was him. Could he do anything about that purpleness? Should he? Why him? If he had seen the web and the clash of lifeforces, surely, others had also perceived it. He couldn't have been the first one, the first alector to sense that. Or could he?

You see? You are not of the world.

He repressed a shiver.

You must become one with the world—and of the world—or you will perish.

"That sounds like a threat."

As suddenly as it had come, the greenish mist had vanished—and so had the soarer. Dainyl stood alone outside the cave, looking down on the land. The warp and weft of the lifewebs had also vanished. Once more, he blinked. Had it all been illusion? He shook his head No, the soarer had been real, and so had what she had shown him.

He tried to call up what he had seen, but the only aspect he could sense was the purpled skein that was his own lifethread. He had always been able to sense a slight purplish aura around other alectors, and the faint silver-black-green around the few landers who had Talent, but he'd never seen himself that way.

What had he seen? Had it really been a web that linked all the lifeforces of Acorus? Or that of the higher life-forms? He knew that he had seen those interweaving and converging threads, yet he could not call up what he had seen, not by himself, anyway. That he could sense his own aura, and that it was similar to those of other alectors, was enough itself to suggest that what she had shown him was real, but why couldn't he sense beyond himself? Was his Talent that weak, compared to that of the soarer?

He took a long and slow deep breath, then turned and walked back to the amber-green-gold archway that framed the tunnel. His eyes lighted on the mirrorlike device in the floor of the tunnel. It had to be a transport device, something like a Table.

Slowly, he walked into the tunnel, his head low, until he stood on the mirror. He'd never used a Table, but according to Lystrana, the key was to visualize where you wanted to go. He concentrated, thinking of the one Table he had seen, in the Hall of Justice in Elcien.

Nothing happened.

He tried reaching out with his Talent, into the depths that had to be within or behind the mirror, but he could find nothing there.

After a good half glass of trying everything he could think of, Dainyl finally walked out of the tunnel to wait for Falyna to return. The mirror was a transport device, but how it worked . . . he couldn't determine, and he doubted that either he—or any alector—would ever understand or be able to use it.

The other phrase that the soarer had used . . . that those among them . . . *fed.* That suggested strongly that the other creatures, the ugly ones, had fed on the missing miners. Dainyl had no proof, but it all fit. It would explain why some of the miners vanished—and why the miners would do anything to escape.

Dainyl walked to the eastern end of the blufflike ledge, thinking. That might explain the disappearances—and the reason why those miners who had escaped were trying to create a revolt, but they were merely a handful. The soarer's revelations might explain the missing miners, but they didn't make anything any clearer as far as the Highest and the marshal were concerned.

What had become all too clear was that far more was happening than any of those involved knew or understood. Yet, if he reported what he had seen, he would reveal his own Talent and possibly threaten the marshal and the Highest—and, considering the fate of Submarshal Tyanylt, risk his own destruction. If he did not report on the ancient soarer, he might well betray his duty as a Myrmidon.

As the white sun rose out of the dark green ocean to the east, he stood and waited for Falyna to return.

51

On Septi, Mykel was back patrolling the mining road with fifth squad. The morning sweep had gone without incident, and the local Cadmians had escorted the prisoners to the mine and taken up their guard positions in the towers and along the perimeter. Mykel and fifth squad had continued to patrol the access road, but had seen nothing.

The cool winds around and below the mountains felt refreshing after the days spent in the Cadmian compound in Dramuria. There, Mykel had felt as though the walls were closing in around him. He'd never experienced that feeling of constriction in any other Cadmian compound. It had to be the situation facing him, where he could see no way out, no matter how hard he tried to avoid the traps set for him by Majer Vaclyn. Mykel knew all too well that people, even senior officers, often disliked others for no good reason, but much as he told himself that, he still kept trying to puzzle out why the majer had suddenly targeted him.

Now, in the late afternoon, he and fifth squad rode back to the mine, sweeping the road once more before the local Cadmians escorted the prisoners back to their camp. As the chestnut carried Mykel toward the mine, less than half a vingt away, the captain surveyed the road to the north. In the late afternoon the slope was shadowed, making hiding easier. While he could not see anyone, he had a feeling that somewhere in the rocky slopes to the west of the road were more of the escaped miners, waiting to take more shots at them. His lips curled. Based on what he had experienced so far, he would have been a naive optimist to feel otherwise.

"Eyes sharp, now!" Mykel rode another hundred yards or so, more and more on edge, but still not seeing or sensing any figures in the shadows above the road.

Crack! Crack!

The sounds of the shots were so faint that, for a moment, Mykel did not recognize them, thinking that he was hearing a hammer on stone or some other mining operation. He straightened in the saddle. "Rifles ready!"

"Fifth squad! Rifles ready!"

Continuing to ride, he eased his mount to the left, alongside the stone wall. From there he studied the rocky slope, but he saw no one and had no sense that they were being fired upon.

Another report echoed from the north. Was it from the mine itself? Were the prisoners trying to escape?

"Fifth squad, loose formation, quick trot! Forward!"

As they neared the mine, Mykel could hear more shots, definitely coming from the rocky slope above the mine to the north.

As he watched, one of the Cadmians in the guard tower staggered, then dropped his rifle and collapsed over the wooden railing. Mykel still couldn't see who was shooting, and exactly from where, but there were at least several snipers. When fifth squad reached the heavy wooden gates to the mine area, as suddenly as the shots had begun, they ended. Mykel had not seen a single rifleman, but at least one Cadmian guard was dead.

The gates creaked open.

Captain Benjyr was mounted on a roan, just inside. He looked at Mykel. "Too bad you didn't get here earlier."

"Did you send anyone up the slopes?"

"To get picked off? No."

Mykel turned in the saddle. "Vhanyr, I need your two best shots to cover me. I'm going up after the snipers. Put them in the north tower."

"Yes, sir."

"Going to be a hero?" murmured Benjyr.

Mykel looked back at the other captain. "No. I'm going because I'm the best shot and the least likely to get hit—and because you don't keep asking your men to take shots without taking them yourself." He eased his mount over toward Vhanyr. "I'll have to climb from this side. I'd be a plucked fowl if I went over the stockade on the north side."

After reining up back outside the gates, Mykel handed the chestnut's reins to Lasent, an older ranker.

"Take care, sir."

"Thank you. I'll try."

Rifle in hand, Mykel moved upslope steadily, using the shadows and the rocks for cover, keeping low. Riding boots were not made for climbing, and he slipped several times on the sloping sandy spaces between boulders.

A quarter glass passed before he was above the top of the mineworks and could begin to move northward. He felt—but didn't know—that there were rebels somewhere farther north.

Crack!

Mykel dropped behind an irregular chunk of old black lava. That single shot had been too close, but it also gave him an idea where the shooter hid, only slightly higher than he was. Mykel resumed his climb, more deliberately, and more directly uphill, rather than slanting to the north.

He had only climbed another ten yards or so when another shot ricocheted off the lava to his left. Flattening himself against the slope, beside an outcropping, he considered. He'd been right. There were at least two shooters, and one was to his left and one to his right. He decided to go after the one to the left first. If he went after the one to the right, the one to the left would be free to rake the mine road.

He peered around the sandstone, then crawled to the next outcropping . . . and the next.

After another thirty yards, he felt he was closer, much closer.

He heard a slipping, scraping sound, feet sliding on sandy soil. Turning slightly, he fired, hardly aiming at the patch of gray that looked different, but *willing* the bullet to strike.

"Oooh!"

The clatter of a dropped weapon followed the exclamation.

Mykel moved quickly, but not carelessly, keeping low and threading his way uphill and through the lava and sandstone. Before that long he was looking down at a man in gray, bearded and dying, sprawled and wedged amid the black lava.

"Who sent you after us?" Mykel demanded.

". . . couldn't say no . . ." The rebel half coughed, and his face contorted in agony. ". . . cold here . . . so . . . cold . . ."

He was dead.

Mykel noted the location and began to move northward through the rocks and infrequent scrub bushes. He thought he was higher than the other shooter, but the man easily could have moved to another position.

Crack! Crack! Both shots were high and wide of Mykel and suggested that the rebel had moved farther north but no higher on the slope.

Mykel peered from the side of another lava boulder, one smoother than most, looking northward. He had a good idea where the rebel was, but the man was keeping his head down as well. The captain darted to another boulder, then another, dropping down just before another pair of shots passed overhead.

Despite the cool air and the chill breeze, Mykel was sweating heavily. He definitely wasn't used to scrambling around on mountainsides. He took several long and deep breaths before resuming his crawling-and-crouching progress across the slope.

He traveled another hundred yards when he heard the clatter of rocks. He glanced around a taller irregular rock in time to see a patch dark gray against the darker lava downhill.

Mykel snapped off two shots, and the off-color gray vanished.

He keep moving, carefully and cautiously, toward where he thought the rebel had been. There were no more shots.

After another twenty yards, he paused. There was heavy breathing, and a low groan, not too far ahead. Could it be a ruse?

Anything was possible. He looked around, and finally found a fist-sized chunk of rock, then lofted it over the sandstone outcropping behind which he crouched.

The breathing subsided, then continued.

Mykel held his rifle ready, easing around the top of the sandstone ledge.

He needn't have bothered.

Below him, in a depression, lay a rebel. The man's rifle was less than a yard from Mykel, twice that from the wounded sniper, who looked blankly at the captain.

A golden green radiance washed over Mykel. He whirled.

In midair hung a winged woman, certainly no more than two-thirds his own height. A gauzy iridescence cloaked her figure, leaving only her head, shoulders, lower arms, and legs open to view.

For a moment, Mykel just gaped, holding his rifle.

Had the soaring woman—certainly an ancient, if the old tales were correct—anything to do with the rebels?

"What do you want? Are you with the rebels?"

They serve a purpose.

The wounded rebel looked up at the soarer, and whimpered . . . *whimpered.* "No . . . no!"

A blocky figure—smaller than Mykel, but larger than the soarer—seemed to ooze upward out of the rocks beside the gray-clad man. Mykel turned the rifle on the creature.

Do not use the weapon. He will die soon anyway.

"Who?"

The injured one.

Mykel's eyes darted from the rock-creature to the winged woman, then back to the rough-skinned creature that bent over the dying man. The creature barely touched the rebel, and the man shuddered. He was dead.

"How did you know?" demanded Mykel.

Fading lifeforce is obvious. Fading or not, it should not be wasted.

Not wasted? The creature had *fed* somehow on the dying man. Mykel repressed a shudder. "What do you want with me? Are you Death?"

Mykel received a wordless impression of mirth.

No more so than you are.

"What do you want with me?"

Nothing . . . now. You must find your talent to see the world beyond your eyes. You must understand what you feel . . . or you will perish. With those words, the green radiance vanished, and so did the soarer, leaving Mykel alone with a dead rebel and another stolen Cadmian rifle.

Mykel had no doubts there were no more rebels. Still, he was careful as he dragged the second rebel and carried the two rifles—both with numbers—downhill, his thoughts on what he had seen. The soarer had to have been an ancient, beautiful, but with a deadliness that made the Myrmidon colonel look clumsy and brutish. He had no idea what the other sand-skinned creature had been, save that it had somehow *fed* on the lifeforce of the dying rebel.

But how could he tell anyone what he had seen?

He also had no idea what the soarer had meant by finding his talent to see beyond his eyes. He doubted that he had any particular talent, except for shooting well enough to kill people. Or was that *how* he could shoot so well?

Abruptly, he realized that the soarer had not spoken to him, that her words had been in his mind. At the time, it had seemed normal, and unremarkable. Why had he felt that way? Could all the ancients do that? The miniature dagger set in the slots in his belt seemed to pulse green. He knew it hadn't. Daggers, even daggers of the ancients, didn't pulse. He had to have been imagining that. But why had he felt that way?

He pushed aside the questions until he had the time to think about them later.

Once he was within hailing distance of the gates, he called down. "I took out both of them. Vhanyr! Escort the prisoners back. Leave Lasent and Doytal to help me."

"You sure, sir?"

"I'm sure."

By the time Lasent, Doytal, and Mykel had finished recovering the other body, the road back down to the mine compound was empty, and the sun had set. As Mykel had expected, both dead men had tattoos on their ankles.

Mykel heaved himself into the saddle, then reloaded his rifle, glancing up as Captain Benjyr reined up beside him.

"You a mountain type?" asked Benjyr.

"I've learned." Mykel felt that admitting he was a city boy would only make things worse.

"They say you've killed nearly a score of rebels like that."

"Not that many," Mykel protested. "I would have liked to have gotten these two earlier, but you can't see them until they start shooting."

Benjyr nodded.

Mykel realized that the other captain was offering a silent apology, and that made him uneasy. "You've never had the men to go after them."

"We never had any real problems until a year ago. Then it just got worse and worse."

"There can't be too many left. I mean, escaped miners with rifles," added Mykel quickly. He had no idea where he'd gotten that idea, but he felt he was right about that. There could be hundreds of rebels in the lowlands, people forced off their lands, and unhappy growers, but they couldn't be all that many rebel miners left.

"You think the shootings will slow down?" Benjyr's tone was skeptical.

"Up along the mine road, but not elsewhere."

"I'm afraid you're right. Good evening, Captain." With a faint smile, Benjyr nodded and urged his mount down the road.

Before starting back down the graystone road himself, Mykel took a last look over his shoulder at the mineworks. He felt sorry for the local Cadmian ranker killed by the rebels, but he also felt sorry for the dead rebels—and for the families of all three men.

He also worried about what Majer Vaclyn would say the following afternoon about Fifteenth Company's failure to protect the guards at the mine. It didn't matter that such protection wasn't the company's primary task, or that there was no way to keep an entire mountain clear with less than a hundred men. The majer would still blame him for all the problems.

Not for the first time, Mykel had to wonder exactly what he and his company had gotten into. They were dealing with alectors and ancients, escaped prisoners seemingly bent on revenge, and rebellious seltyrs, and no one seemed to know why.

52

Under high and hazy clouds, roughly one glass after noon on Octdi, Mykel entered the west gate of the Cadmian compound at Dramuria. He carried little in his saddlebags except the copies of his letters and reports, including a brief summary of Septi's attack by the two escaped miners, but without any mention of the soarer. Those he was not about to leave in the mine quarters, not when he was reporting to the majer. Beside him rode Alendyr, the second squad leader, with the rest of the squad following.

"It'll be good to have a solid meal," Alendyr said in a low voice. "Too bad we can't stay for the night and sleep in a decent bunk."

"If we stay, Majer Vaclyn might find us something else to do," Mykel pointed out.

"That could be, sir. Patrolling the area around the mine hasn't been that bad. The growers and those folk in Jyoha were a lot worse."

Mykel reined up outside the stable and turned to Alendyr once more. "After the men deal with their mounts, any who need replacement equipment should take care of that. They can have the freedom of the compound until half a glass after the evening meal. That's when we ride out, back to the mine compound."

Alendyr laughed. "One good meal, anyway."

"It's the best we can do." Mykel shrugged and dismounted.

After he'd seen to the chestnut and arranged for some additional fodder for all the mounts in the squad, Mykel walked toward the officers' quarters, wondering what other captains were in Dramuria, or whether he was the only one reporting weekly to the majer. Carrying a soft leather case that held his reports, Mykel was still a good ten yards from the quarters when Dohark stepped out of the shadows cast by the building. The older captain glanced in the direction of the headquarters building, then gestured to Mykel.

"You look like there's trouble," Mykel observed as he neared the other captain.

"I don't know what you did, Mykel," Dohark began, "but the majer's looking for you. You're supposed to see him as soon as you get here. He's fingering those frigging knives of his, and he's got that look in his eye, like when you bailed him out with the Reillies by disobeying his stupid orders. He's so upset that he didn't even ream me out for getting here early."

"Did he say why?"

"No. He's got some of Kuertyl's squads locked away, under quarantine, but I haven't seen Kuertyl himself. I didn't want to ask."

Mykel frowned. He could understand Dohark's reluctance to probe when the majer was in one of his moods. Kuertyl and Thirteenth Company were supposed to be in Jyoha. Had something happened there? Or had some other seltyr attacked? Or had Rachyla escaped?

"Are all of us captains supposed to report here on Octdi afternoon?" asked Mykel, still trying to figure out what he'd done to upset the majer.

"I'd thought so, but I haven't seen Rhystan yet. Heransyr came in just a bit ago." Dohark shook his head. "Bad idea, having us all report on the same day."

Vaclyn was having more and more bad ideas, far more than in dealing with the Reillies on the last deployment, and Mykel and the other captains had been concerned then. "I suppose I should go see him."

"Don't get him any madder than he is."

Mykel laughed harshly. "Just seeing me upsets him."

"What did you do to him?"

The younger captain shook his head. "I haven't done anything different. If anything, I've tried to avoid upsetting him."

"Agree to everything."

Mykel nodded. He wasn't about to argue with Dohark, but he had been agreeing with the majer—except when it was going to get his men killed for no reason at all, and even then, he hadn't disobeyed any direct orders. Case in hand, he walked swiftly to the headquarters building.

Jiosyr was sitting at a small table outside the major's study. "Majer said you were to wait here, sir. He's with Captain Heransyr, sir."

Mykel nodded.

He tried not to pace, but still found himself walking back and forth, back and forth. A good glass passed before the study door opened, and Heransyr stepped out.

The dapper captain's eyes slid away from Mykel, and the smile he offered was weak, almost sickly. "Good day, Mykel."

"Good day, Heransyr. I hope things are going well for you and Seventeenth Company."

"That they are." Heransyr nodded and hurried away.

Behind him, Mykel heard Jiosyr close the door, leaving him alone in the corridor outside the study. The door remained closed only for a fraction of a glass before Jiosyr emerged.

"You can go in now, sir." The senior squad leader stepped aside, holding the study door. He avoided looking at Mykel. After Mykel entered the study, Jiosyr closed the door behind him.

Vaclyn had been pacing, but he turned at Mykel's entrance. His face flushed.

"You asked for me as soon as we arrived, sir." Mykel waited.

Vaclyn did not speak. He glared silently at Mykel.

Mykel could do nothing but remain silent.

"I'd like to know what you did up in Jyoha, Captain."

"I did exactly what you ordered me to do, sir, and I reported what I did. You told me to round up the Codebreakers. I surrounded them, and they refused to surrender. They said that they'd rather die than go to the mines or go back. They attacked us. We wiped most of them out. We lost two men, had several wounded. We returned here, as you had suggested. I reported what happened, and you ordered us to mine duty."

"Do you know what happened?" Vaclyn's right hand dropped to the hilt of the throwing knife at his belt, his fingers touching it lightly.

"What happened where, sir?"

"In Jyoha, of course. Are you deliberately trying to seem stupid, Captain?"

"No, sir."

"Then why are you asking such inane questions?

"Majer, sir . . . I don't understand. When I reported the roaming riders in Jyoha, I had deep concerns about trying to capture them. I wrote you those concerns. You sent back a dispatch ordering me to capture them or kill them if they resisted. Fifteenth Company followed your orders. The results were devastating. That was why I chose to withdraw, as you may recall."

"Captain . . . you were close to insubordinate."

Mykel waited.

"Before Thirteenth Company reached Jyoha, they were ambushed. Even children attacked them. They used arrows and crossbows and makeshift catapults. They dug huge hidden pits across the road. They threw gourds filled with flaming oil. This was your doing, Captain. You abandoned Jyoha and let this occur, and you misled me."

"How badly was Thirteenth Company—"

"Captain Kuertyl was killed almost immediately. Less than two full squads remain. They returned to Dramuria last night."

Vaclyn pulled his hand away from the throwing dagger, as if he had wanted to draw it and fling it at Mykel. "Beyond that, I also learned that you have been visiting the seltyr's daughter—and that you did not request my permission."

"I was attempting to find out more about the rifles—"

"You cannot be trusted, Captain. You have consistently ignored my orders and put your company into danger. You seem to consider yourself above the commands of your superiors."

"Sir . . ."

"Consider yourself confined to the compound, Captain. I will be recommending your court-martial for insubordination and for incompetence. I had warned you." Vaclyn's left hand dropped back to the hilt of one of his pair of throwing daggers.

Mykel studied the majer. "I would like to request that you reconsider that, sir."

"Reconsider? Who are you to tell me? You are an insolent junior captain who has consistently refused to follow orders. Your men are unruly and don't follow your orders. When you do follow orders, you change them to suit yourself. Get out of here! If you aren't in quarters within moments, you'll face additional charges."

"Yes, sir." Mykel bowed and stepped back.

Then he opened the door and departed, not looking back as he left the headquarters building. Anger welled up inside him. Vaclyn was not only being unreasonable. His decisions were bound to lead to some sort of disaster within months, if not days. Mykel didn't have that long. He had no doubts about how his actions would be written up in the report to

Colonel Herolt in Elcien—or to Colonel Dainyl, if the Myrmidon colonel even saw the report. Still, a Myrmidon colonel outranked a Cadmian colonel, and Mykel doubted that he had anything to lose, not the way matters were turning out.

He swallowed, then crossed the courtyard to the senior officers' quarters, where he climbed the steps to the second level and the open balcony fronting the four doors for the senior officers' quarters. Mykel knocked on the first door. There was no answer. He moved to the second door and knocked again.

"Yes?" The Myrmidon colonel's voice was deep, resonant.

"Captain Mykel of the Cadmians to see you, sir."

There was a pause. Then the door opened.

Tall as he was compared to most Cadmian officers, Mykel found himself looking up at the colonel. He swallowed and spoke, "This is highly irregular, Colonel, but I don't know how else to keep matters from getting worse."

"Could you explain, Captain? You might as well come in." The alector stepped back.

Mykel closed the door and stood waiting, but the colonel neither seated himself nor asked Mykel to do so, but merely looked at the Cadmian officer.

Mykel moistened his lips, then began. "This is a difficult situation, sir. I was ordered to report to Majer Vaclyn this afternoon, every Octdi afternoon . . ." He went on to explain the series of events, beginning with the discovery of the rifle and continuing through the majer's reaction to the trial of Polynt and the latest happenings in Jyoha—and the majer's reaction and the threat of a court-martial. ". . . because I worried about the situation in Jyoha, I had made copies of my report and the majer's orders." Mykel extended the sheets of paper.

The colonel took them without speaking and read through them slowly.

Mykel stood there, shifting his weight from one booted foot to the other, unable to read or sense any feeling from the Myrmidon officer.

Finally, the colonel looked up. "I appreciate your diligence, Captain, and your concerns. You will remain here in the compound while I look more into these matters. So will the squad you brought with you."

"Yes, sir." Mykel bowed, then stepped back toward the door, letting himself out.

From the senior officers' quarters he headed to the quartermaster's building, hoping to find Alendyr. The squad leader was there, talking with a squad leader from Seventeenth Company. Both men broke off their conversation abruptly as they saw Mykel.

"We may be staying here tonight, Alendyr. I will be, and the squad will be as well. I'll be in the officers' quarters, and, if you'll check with me tomorrow, we should know more."

"Yes, sir."

As Mykel walked away, he caught a few words.

". . . too bad . . . sticks up for you . . ."

". . . good time to be a squad leader, not a captain . . ."

Mykel had his doubts about it being a good time for either. When he reached the junior officer's quarters, he found two rooms on the ground floor empty. He took the one least dusty. There he put the leather case on the desk and sat down in the single chair. He hadn't brought much gear, as he had expected to ride back to the mine camp before dark.

Now what was he going to do?

The majer had been so upset that he hadn't even asked about recent events, but Mykel hadn't wanted to bring those up because Vaclyn would have just turned them against him. And, in fact, Mykel *had* ignored or evaded the intent of the majer's orders. According to discipline and the Code, it didn't seem to matter that the orders were generally unwise, or worse.

Mykel stood and walked around the small room, then seated himself again.

Would the Myrmidon colonel do anything? Or would he just support Majer Vaclyn. For all of Colonel Dainyl's calm words, Mykel had no idea what the senior officer would do.

Thrap. At the knock on the door, Mykel got up. "Yes?"

"Sir?"

"Who is it?"

"Jiosyr, sir."

What did the majer's senior squad leader want with him? Mykel walked tiredly to the door. He eased it open, little more than barely ajar. "Yes, Jiosyr?"

"Alendyr's been hurt, sir. One of your rankers took a knife to him.

I thought you ought to know. He's over in the infirmary. He's hurt pretty badly."

"Frig!" That was all Mykel needed. How had something like that happened? Alendyr was a good squad leader.

He hurried out of the quarters and around the corner into the long shadow on the east end of the building. He halted abruptly, realizing that Jiosyr had not followed him and that another figure waited in the shadows—Majer Vaclyn.

Vaclyn was smiling coldly. "I believe you were ordered immediately to quarters, Captain, and to remain within them."

"My squad leader's been hurt—" Mykel doubted that, but it was a better excuse than outright disobedience.

"A likely tale—like all your others." Vaclyn's smile widened. "Captain, you have been most insubordinate. You even tried to go around the chain of command. Now, you seem to be trying to escape. We can't have that."

Mykel waited until the last moment, then tried to jump to one side, but Vaclyn had anticipated that, and the throwing dagger knifed into his left shoulder.

Mykel tried to regain his balance.

"You're quick, Captain, but not quick enough."

"No!" snapped a deep voice, seemingly out of nowhere.

Colonel Dainyl appeared between Mykel and the majer, but the dagger was already in the air. With the pain stabbing through his shoulder, Mykel watched the silvery weapon bounce off the alector's tunic. The colonel's hand blurred to his belt, and a pistol-like sidearm appeared.

"He was trying to escape, Colonel!" The majer's voice rose. "He was."

A flare of blinding blue light enveloped Vaclyn. The captain blinked. When he could see again, a charred figure lay on the stones of the courtyard.

"Captain . . ."

Mykel leaned against the wall, trying to clamp the flow of blood from his shoulder with his good hand.

"Captain . . . you'll need some attention." The colonel stood empty-handed. "Can you walk to the infirmary?"

"If I don't wait too long," Mykel managed.

He took one step and then another. A strong arm steadied him. Now . . . if he didn't bleed to death on the way to the infirmary. Mykel kept walking, past the smoldering remains of the majer.

He supposed he should have felt some regret, but all he felt was relief—and another kind of apprehension. Why hadn't he seen the colonel? What did the Myrmidon have in mind?

He kept walking.

53

After Dainyl settled Captain Mykel in the infirmary, making sure that the wound was clean and well bound, the colonel hastened back toward headquarters. Whether he liked it or not, whether he had any effective strategies, with Majer Vaclyn dead, he had no choices. Majer Herryf had no idea how to command his own two companies, much less an entire battalion.

The sun was almost touching the top of the western wall of the compound when Dainyl walked into Majer Herryf's study in the headquarters building.

Herryf bolted upright. "Oh, Colonel . . . I hadn't realized you were here."

Dainyl closed the door. "Sit down."

Herryf sat.

"Majer Vaclyn just attempted to kill one of his captains, then me," Dainyl said coldly. "Did you have anything to do with it?"

The color drained out of Herryf's face. "No, sir. No, sir."

About that, the majer was telling the truth.

"I'm very glad to hear that. Majer Vaclyn is dead. I'm using my authority as acting submarshal to take over command of all Cadmian activities and forces in Dramur."

"Yes, sir." Herryf was so shocked that he lacked, momentarily, his natural arrogance.

"Majer Vaclyn's body is rather badly charred. It's in the courtyard at the east end of the senior officers' quarters."

"I had a report about a body, but no one knew—"

"It's the majer. You will dispose of the carcass." Dainyl looked sternly at the majer. "You will remain at the compound until I have had a chance to talk to all officers. Find me the majer's senior squad leader. Jiosyr, I think, is his name. I want to speak to him first."

"Yes, sir."

"Since I have to take command, I'll be needing this study. Until I leave, I imagine you can make do with the one Majer Vaclyn was using."

Herryf nodded.

"Now . . . find me that senior squad leader."

"Yes, sir." The Cadmian majer rose and hurried out.

As he waited for Herryf either to find the man or to report that he had fled, Dainyl considered what he knew in light of Vaclyn's attempted murder of Captain Mykel.

Dainyl had already noted that Vaclyn had been exposed to Talent-manipulation, but he had not had the ability to determine what had been done. In retrospect, there was no question that the marshal had used Talent to force a compulsion on the majer. Such compulsions were almost always worse than useless for anything but the simplest prohibitions, because they restricted both thought patterns and actions, and left the one who had been Talent-compelled in situations where he inevitably acted unwisely. The marshal knew that. Why had he wanted a comparatively low-ranking Cadmian officer to behave unwisely? It made no sense, but the marshal was anything besides stupid. He had wanted Vaclyn to act unwisely.

After hearing what the captain had said when he had come to Dainyl, Dainyl had used Talent to follow the captain unseen. The one surprise had been seeing Vaclyn's squad leader go to the quarters and lure Mykel from his room, but that suggested that the majer had feared what would come out in a court-martial.

"Sir?"

Dainyl looked up. Herryf stood in the doorway with a short senior squad leader.

"This is Jiosyr. The one you wanted to see."

"Come in, Jiosyr. Sit down." Dainyl pointed to one of the armless wooden chairs. He did not take a seat. Even without using Talent, he could sense the fear in the squad leader, who barely looked even in the general direction of the colonel, especially after Herryf had closed the door on the two.

"You must know that Majer Vaclyn tried to kill both Captain Mykel and me—and that he is dead. I've taken over command of Third Battalion."

"Yes, sir." Jiosyr looked at the stone tiles of the floor.

"Why was the majer so angry at the captain?"

"Sir?"

"I heard the majer's last words to the captain. He was angry. Why?"

Jiosyr was silent, and Dainyl contemplated using Talent to persuade him to speak. He decided to wait, his eyes on the slumped figure of the squad leader.

"He thought that the captain—Captain Mykel—was always trying to get around his orders. He said that he needed to be taught a lesson. Then . . . he told me we'd need to set up a court-martial, that the captain had gone too far."

"How had the captain gone too far?"

"He didn't say, sir. He just said that."

"What did you say to Captain Mykel to get him to leave his quarters?"

Jiosyr turned paler than milk and swayed in the chair. "Sir?"

"You're not going to be stupid enough to deny it, are you?"

The squad leader shuddered. "No, sir. Majer Vaclyn . . . he told me to tell the captain that his squad leader Alendyr had been knifed by a ranker and was in the infirmary."

Dainyl nodded. The captain had worried more about his men than orders or himself. He'd scarcely talked to the captain, but the more he heard and saw, the more he approved of the man—and the less sense Vaclyn's acts made. A good commander praised effective subordinates, both to their faces and in reports to superiors—then took a small share of the credit for their initiative and accomplishments. "Why did you do that?"

"The majer said he needed to get the captain to disobey orders one more time, that Captain Mykel was always so careful not to disobey when anyone was watching."

"Did you think this was the right thing to do?"

"No, sir . . . but what was I to do? I only need another two years for a stipend. The majer could have dismissed me without anyone stopping him. Eighteen years . . . gone for nothing."

"Your stipend was worth the lives of two men?"

Jiosyr stiffened. "Sir. I've killed Reillies and bandits and brigands. I did it because I was a Cadmian. I did it to protect people. There wasn't anyone protecting me. I'd let it be known, as I could, that the majer shouldn't be in the field. I even made copies of reports Colonel Herolt never would have seen, and I got them on the colonel's desk. No one did anything."

The sudden stiffening and the aura of truth were both almost overpowering, even to Dainyl.

"No one did anything," Jiosyr repeated. "That's the truth, sir."

Dainyl paused. "That will be all for now, Jiosyr. I'd appreciate it if you'd remain within the compound."

"Yes, sir." The squad leader paused. "What will you . . . do with me?"

"That depends on what else I discover."

After Jiosyr left, Dainyl considered what else was necessary. He needed to question Captain Mykel—in far greater depth—once the captain was feeling better. He still had to talk to all of the other officers. None of them would know anything about why Majer Vaclyn had acted as he had. Of that, Dainyl was most certain, but he had to go through the motions.

He stepped out of the study, looking for Herryf.

Nearly three glasses later, after Captain Rhystan of Sixteenth Company had left the study that had been Herryf's, Dainyl knew little more than when he started—except that Majer Vaclyn had barely been marginally competent before the Third Battalion had been deployed to Dramur. Even more puzzling was that all of the battalion's surviving captains would have done better if they had been in command.

Was the marshal out to discredit the Cadmians? Why? What purpose would that serve?

In the dimness of the study, Dainyl looked at the stone outer wall and then at the darkness beyond the single window. He still had no more answers—only more questions.

54

For Mykel, Octdi night was long—and restless. It was well past dark when the local healer finally allowed Alendyr and two troopers to escort him back to the officers' quarters. He slept, but not for very long at a time, and pain ran down his entire arm most of the time.

When he was awake, trying to lie still so that he didn't turn and send more jolts of pain up and down his arm and shoulder, his thoughts alternated mostly between the soarer and the alector. Majer Vaclyn's knife had gone through Mykel's tunic and undertunic like a hot blade through butter, yet his second knife had bounced off the Myrmidon's tunic. After having seen that once before when the crossbow bolt had struck the alector in Faitel, Mykel shouldn't have been surprised. In both cases, there had been a reaction—guards in Faitel, and the colonel's light-cutting sidearm. That argued that the alectors weren't invulnerable, but that there was something about the shimmering cloth that they all wore, an armor that didn't look like armor.

The soarer had been different, totally unafraid of the rifle he had held, yet she had known exactly what it was. She'd also told him not to use it on the other creature, and that suggested that, while she might not be vulnerable, the creatures were. A faint smile creased his lips in the darkness of the quarters. Just how likely was it that he would ever see either again?

For a few moments, he thought about Kuertyl. Had he caused the younger captain's death by following Vaclyn's orders? Was there any way he could have avoided it? His lips tightened. He could have stopped it only by massacring the entire town of Jyoha—or all the men and most of the women. Once you started killing people who weren't troopers or didn't think of themselves as such, where did it stop? By following the majer's orders, he'd turned an entire town into deadly enemies—and that had led to the death of Kuertyl and half of Thirteenth Company. How could a captain deal with stupid orders without getting killed, one way or the other, either by carrying them out or through discipline for insubordination?

In time, he did drift back into sleep.

The next morning, with his arm bound, Mykel took his time pulling himself together and washing up before making his way to the officers' mess. Minding what the healer had said, he was using the harness sling to reduce the weight on his shoulder.

Heransyr, Dohark, and Rhystan were seated around a square table in one corner of the mess. Dohark stood and waved. "Over here!"

Mykel gave an off-center smile and walked carefully toward the table.

Dohark had pulled out a chair, and Mykel took it.

"You look like shit," said Dohark. "Bat shit." He grinned sympathetically. "You know, Mykel, you don't get wounded like anyone else. Shot in the ass by Reillies and knifed by your own commander."

"The Myrmidon colonel really burned old Vaclyn to a cinder?" asked

Rhystan, pushing back a lock of lank brown hair off his narrow forehead.

Mykel nodded. "Used that light-cutter thing. Blue light—majer went up in flames."

A server looked at the latest arrival at the table.

"Ale, if you don't have cider," Mykel said.

"No cider, sir. Ale, water, or wine."

"Ale . . . and whatever you have for breakfast."

The server slipped away.

"Why did the colonel do that?" Heransyr frowned.

"The majer had already put one knife in me," Mykel explained. "Then the colonel appeared and told him to stop. Majer threw the knife at him instead of me. That probably saved my neck."

"Or your ass," added Dohark.

Rhystan shook his head. "Stupid. Don't attack Myrmidons. Everyone knows that."

"He was stupid, and about more than that," countered Dohark. "Remember when he wanted you to take a squad through that flooded field."

Rhystan started to say something, then closed his mouth.

"He was really angry," Mykel admitted. "He said I was to blame for Kuertyl's death." He took the mug of ale that the server set on the table, looking at it, but not drinking.

"He was. Didn't he order you to attack all those rebels in Jyoha?" asked Dohark.

"They were poor debtors, not rebels, and they didn't have many weapons, but he insisted that I bring them in. They didn't want to go to the mines." Mykel sipped the ale, wishing it were hot cider. "We had to kill them or let a lot of troopers get killed or wounded."

"Kuertyl's dead?" asked Rhystan.

"Jyoha—the whole town went up in arms. They made jars of flaming oil, and dug pits in the roads," Heransyr explained. "With poisoned stakes."

The orderly slipped a platter in front of Mykel. Breakfast was fried fish and greasy potatoes, with stale bread. He took a mouthful and corrected himself—soggy and greasy potatoes. He broke the bread one-handed, and crumbs sprayed across the table.

Heransyr turned back to Mykel. "Why do you think everyone's mad at us?"

Mykel took another swallow of ale before replying. "In Corus, the mainland part, most people want to do things the way the Duarches want. Here, nobody wants to do that. So there's no one who likes why we're here, and everyone's against us. When we were in Jyoha, we saw the ruins of a sawmill . . ." He went on to explain what he had learned.

"Sawmill seems harmless enough," said Rhystan. "Folks need planks and timbers."

"The Duarches don't do things without a reason," Heransyr said.

"Majer Vaclyn didn't, either." Dohark laughed, then stood. "I need to check my squad. Hope we can head back today, not that I'm all that happy looking for smugglers who won't show up so long as we're there."

Within moments, Heransyr and Rhystan rose as well, leaving Mykel to finish the last of his breakfast by himself.

Later, as Mykel walked out of the mess, he wondered about what Heransyr had said. The Duarches hadn't wanted a sawmill, and they did want the guano mine working. He'd also recalled someone talking about a swamp that had been drained. Dohark—he'd mentioned a cousin and something about the alectors not liking growing plants being cut down.

Was that why most buildings were of brick and stone? Was the guano so important that an entire battalion had been sent to Dramur—with a Myrmidon colonel to watch? But why?

"Captain Mykel! Sir?"

Mykel turned his head quickly, then tried not to wince at the jolt that went down his arm.

A Cadmian ranker was hurrying toward him. "Sir, Colonel Dainyl is looking for you."

"Lead the way." Mykel was not looking forward to seeing the colonel.

The duty squad leader in the foyer took a long look as Mykel and his escort passed, but said nothing.

The door to the study that had been Majer Herryf's was open. Mykel stepped in, and the ranker closed it. Colonel Dainyl sat on the desk, his long legs almost touching the stone floor.

"Sir?"

"How is your shoulder this morning?" Dainyl's deep voice seemed hoarse, and there was a redness around his eyes.

Mykel sensed that the alector was less than pleased to be in the study. But then, the word was that he was the acting submarshal for all the

Myrmidons, and he was now handling a position that should have been held by a much more junior officer—a Cadmian officer at that.

"It stings a bit," Mykel replied.

"You were lucky. Please have a seat. The chairs here are somewhat too cramped for me." Dainyl offered a grin. "From what I saw, the majer was very good with his knives."

"Yes, sir. I was lucky you were nearby."

"You still won't be going anywhere for another day or so. It could be longer. I sent a messenger to your senior squad leader saying that you would be here for several days and for him to continue the patrols you had set up."

"Thank you, sir." Mykel should have thought of that himself. He would have, he told himself, if he'd been thinking, and that meant that he'd been hurt worse than he was admitting.

"Why was Majer Vaclyn so angry with you?"

How was he supposed to answer that? Mykel refrained from taking a deep breath or sighing. "Majer Vaclyn thought anyone who disagreed with him was his enemy, even the captains under him. Most of us preferred to find ways to get the task done without sacrificing men unnecessarily. He got upset with me when I used a flank attack against a fortified Reillie redoubt rather than a frontal charge. I suggested that it wasn't wise to try to capture the forty fugitives in Jyoha. He sent me written orders insisting that I do so—" Mykel broke off. "I'm sorry. I told you that yesterday. He wanted us to stop the sniping at our patrols, but when we killed the snipers, he complained that we should have captured them."

"Did you know that Fifteenth Company has been the most effective company in Third Battalion?" asked the colonel.

"We've killed more people," Mykel admitted. "I'm not sure that's always effective. The majer didn't give me any choice. It seems to me that the more people you kill, the more there are that want to kill you. It's different when you're fighting other armed forces all in a body." He gave the faintest headshake. "Don't know why that should be, but people see it that way."

"They do," agreed Dainyl. "You didn't want to bring in the woman, did you?"

"That's not quite true," Mykel said. "When I found the rifle in her cart, I realized that she hadn't known it was there, but she didn't want to let me know that. I didn't see any point in taking her in then. That would have just alerted her father, and made everyone mad. The majer was very displeased. He told me that a Codebreaker was a Codebreaker."

The colonel merely nodded.

What was the alector after? Mykel couldn't tell, and that bothered him, because he usually had some idea what people wanted, whether he agreed with them or not.

"Was Majer Vaclyn always so indifferent to the opinions of his captains?"

That was another possible trap. Mykel considered the implications before answering. "He didn't get so angry in the past campaigns if a captain found another way to get the task done. He'd tell us we were lucky that it worked out, or he wouldn't say anything at all."

"The majer was less flexible here in Dramur?"

"That might be one way of putting it, sir."

"Why was he so angry with you in particular, Captain?"

"I really don't think he was, sir. I mean, he was angry at me, but it could have been any of the captains. Fifteenth Company just happened to be in places where things happened. If it had been Fourteenth Company, he would have been mad at Captain Dohark."

Again, the colonel nodded. "I understand that Captain Dohark is the most senior of the captains. Is that correct?"

"Yes, sir. Dohark, Rhystan, then Heransyr and me. Heransyr and I made captain at the same time. He might be senior, or I might."

"Have you seen any officers among the rebels?"

Mykel frowned. "No, sir, not that I know. That's the miners, the ones in gray. The rebels who were formed by the seltyr, they had squad leaders and captains."

"You've captured a number of rifles. Did the ones that the escaped miners had all have numbers? Did you notice?"

"I'd have to check my reports, sir, to be certain, but I'm pretty sure that all of the rifles the miners had were numbered."

"How many snipers were there at any one time . . ."

"Why have you often been the point man in chasing down rebels . . ."

"Have you heard any captives talking about either the Cadmians or the Myrmidons . . ."

The questions went on and on.

Then, the colonel stood, towering over Mykel and the desk where he had been sitting. "Thank you, Captain. You've been most helpful. I think you and your squad should remain here until Londi. If your shoulder is healing well, you could return to your company." He smiled. "You will have to let others do the scrambling through the rocks, if it proves necessary."

"Yes, sir." Mykel rose, carefully. "Thank you, sir."

As he walked back toward the barracks to convey the news to Alendyr—second squad would certainly like a few nights on decent beds and solid food—Mykel had to admit to himself that the colonel was no one's fool. He'd as much as told Mykel that there were two different revolts going on and that the majer had changed his behavior since coming to Dramur.

Mykel should have picked those up himself, and he hadn't.

55

Mykel slept better on Novdi night, but when the pain subsided and he inadvertently moved or tried to turn over, the resurgence of agony jolted him awake. Even though Decdi was a full end day, he woke with the sun. A cold and raw wind—chill for Dramur—seeped through windows and shutters designed for a climate that seldom saw real chill. After swinging his feet onto the cold stone floor, Mykel finally eased himself erect. He dressed and washed awkwardly, trying to avoid moving the arm below the injured shoulder.

The courtyard outside the officers' quarters was empty, and so silent that all he heard was the low moan of the wind and the echo of his boots on the paving stones as he walked toward the officers' mess. He hoped he wasn't too early to get something, but he could always come back if the cooks weren't ready.

When he walked into the mess, the only one there, besides one cook and the orderly server, was Colonel Dainyl. The Myrmidon looked to have finished the last of his breakfast.

"Good morning, Captain," offered the alector, standing as he spoke.

"Good morning, sir."

"Are you feeling better this morning?"

"Some," Mykel admitted.

"You need another day of rest. See me first thing after breakfast tomorrow."

"Yes, sir."

With a polite smile, the colonel departed.

Mykel eased into a chair at one of the tables, very gingerly.

"Is he always this early?" Mykel asked the orderly who appeared with a mug of ale.

"Earlier most days, sir."

Mykel wondered if alectors even slept.

Breakfast was egg toast, fried apple bananas, and some sort of fried fish that, thankfully, was white beneath the thick batter—and tasteless. Then, the egg toast was tasteless as well. The bananas were the most edible part of the meal. Mykel ate slowly. There was no reason to hurry. Even so, no other officers had appeared by the time he left.

His next stop was the barracks, where he found Alendyr.

A good glass later, after going over the supplies the company could use and tasking the squad leader with trying to obtain them, Mykel made his way to the officer's cell where Rachyla was confined.

"You need to talk to her?" asked the shorter guard of the two. "I don't know . . ."

Mykel's eyes hardened. "Do you want to take it up with Colonel Dainyl?"

"Ah . . . you've spoken to the colonel?"

"This morning, in fact." That was true enough, even if it hadn't been about Rachyla.

"He's here?"

"He was at the mess before dawn," Mykel said. "I'll be meeting with him again later."

"I suppose it's all right."

Mykel stood back as one guard unlocked the door, and the other held his rifle ready. After the bolts were slid back, Mykel stepped inside.

Rachyla looked up from the stool before the desk, on which sat a tray with a half-eaten breakfast—the same egg toast and fried fish Mykel had eaten, with the smallest morsel of fried apple banana at one side. Like Mykel, she had apparently found the apple bananas the best part.

"You. I'd thought they might be coming to reclaim what passes for breakfast." Her eyes narrowed as she took in the sling and harness.

"It's filling." Mykel stood well back from Rachyla, who wore the same trousers and shirt he had seen before. But then, from what hung from the pegs on the wall, she appeared to have but three changes of clothing. That was more than he had at the moment.

"I see you had some difficulty. I'd like to say I'm sorry, but that would be less truthful."

"You were right," Mykel said.

Rachyla looked puzzled. Her eyes centered on the bulkiness of his tunic over the wound dressings, the sling, and doubtless the paleness of his face. "What was I right about, Captain?"

"About being betrayed. Majer Vaclyn tried to kill me."

"He did not succeed, I see."

"Colonel Dainyl—I think you called him the evil one—he stopped him. The majer used his second throwing knife on the colonel. It bounced off his tunic, and the colonel turned him into cinders with his light-cutter."

"The knife . . . it went through your shoulder?"

"It didn't do too much damage." Mykel offered a rueful smile.

"It did more than you admit. Why are you here?"

"Because you said I would be betrayed. How did you know?"

Rachyla did not answer, although she did not lower her eyes and continued to look at him directly. Finally, she spoke. "It is always that way. Those who think are always prepared for evil from those they do not trust, and those they do not know."

"That is true, but you meant more than that."

"I meant what I meant."

Mykel took in her face, the intent green eyes, the smooth skin, and the alertness that suffused all her being. "You meant something that was more than a general observation."

"And if I did, Captain? Why should I share that with you?"

"It might do me some good, and that might do you some good."

"Goodwill? I think not. I am the daughter of the first seltyr who rebelled."

"The *first* seltyr who rebelled?"

"Did I say that? I meant the only seltyr who rebelled."

Mykel laughed. "You don't make mistakes like that, Lady Rachyla."

"Rachyla will do. One way or another, I will not be a lady much longer."

"Which seltyrs are likely to rebel next?"

"If any are, Captain, how would I know? I am quite isolated in my confinement here. You are the only one who actually speaks to me."

"Majer Vaclyn never talked to you?"

"I would not know your Majer Vaclyn if he stood beside you."

"He won't. He's the one that the colonel killed to save my neck."

"He has some use for you. The alectors only save those who are useful."

"How many of them have you met to be able to say that?"

"Me? I am a woman, and a young one, by their standards. Even lander women mean little, except for bearing children. There are no alectors in Dramur, save for your colonel and his retainers. How would I ever have come to meet one of them?"

Rachyla wasn't telling the truth, but then, she hadn't really lied, either. She hadn't answered his question. "Do you always avoid answering the question?"

"Captain . . . how could you think that? I have replied to everything you have said."

Mykel wanted to laugh. Another thought struck him. "What about your mother?"

Rachyla's face stiffened. "She vanished years ago. No one knows where she went."

"I see." Mykel had a very good idea what she meant. "You must be very much like her."

"What a strange thing to say, Captain."

"I think not."

"If you could understand what you feel, Captain, you could be a very dangerous man."

"*That* is a strange thing to say."

"You do not have to take my observations, Captain. I am just a woman and a prisoner."

Mykel doubted that Rachyla would ever be *just* anything.

"Who are the most powerful seltyrs—in both the east and the west?"

"How would I possibly know that?"

"The most powerful ones nearest to Stylan Estate?" prompted Mykel.

"No one ever shared such thoughts with me, and women do not visit armories, Captain."

He almost missed that reference. "Are there any growers who don't have armories?"

"I would not know. I have not visited more than a handful of other estates, only those close to Stylan. I could not imagine much difference."

In short, they were all armed to the teeth, and probably with contraband Cadmian rifles.

"Do the western seltyrs have more horses?"

Rachyla just shrugged.

From that point on, her answers were either shrugs or flat denials of knowledge.

As before, she had told him all she would tell him—just enough so that he would come back—a slight hint or two, doubtless true, but nothing that could be truly traced to her. A bargaining tool to keep him interested and to keep her from losing her mind in a confinement that probably was beginning to seem endless.

"Perhaps you will feel like talking more later."

"Perhaps, Captain. You must come back and see."

Mykel laughed softly.

The faintest hint of an ironic smile creased her lips and vanished.

Mykel rapped on the door. He did not look back as he left.

From the officer's cell and Rachyla, he walked to the stables to check on the chestnut. His mount had been groomed, and was eating grain from the manger in the stall.

Feeling tired, Mykel returned to his quarters and stretched out.

It was still before noon when he woke, but without much to do except recover, Mykel made his way across the courtyard to the mess. It was early enough that he was alone there. He sat down to puzzle out what he knew, sipping on the ale that the Cadmian server had brought him.

He had to admit that Rachyla fascinated him. She was intelligent, and she knew it, but not in the arrogant manner Mykel associated with alectors. She was attractive, but not beautiful. She was direct to the point of being sharp-tongued, but didn't seem vicious with her words. She was the heir to wealth, yet might be sentenced to death or years in the women's workhouse. He was a crafter's son, who would be lucky to survive and be stipended off as an overcaptain—a majer if he happened to get lucky. He took another swallow of ale.

In time, Dohark stepped into the mess.

Mykel saw the shining—and new—bars of an overcaptain on the older officer's collar. "Congratulations!" He paused, then added, "Sir."

"Might better be condolences," Dohark said gruffly, if warmly, settling down across the table from Mykel.

"You're in command of Third Battalion now?"

"And Fourteenth Company." The new overcaptain shook his head. "You know me, Mykel. I'm a savvy ranker who took years to learn enough to get by as a captain. What do I know about running a battalion?"

"You know all the things that a battalion commander shouldn't do," Mykel suggested. "That's more than Vaclyn knew."

"We're down to about four companies, in real strength," Dohark said. "Outside of that one seltyr and a few handfuls of rebels, we've found nothing. We've pissed off most of the people. You and I both know that patrolling doesn't work. We're not finding anyone except escaped miners and poor bastards thrown off their lands. It just gets people angry."

"Tell the colonel that."

"I did."

"What did he say?"

"He said we could cut down on patrols—except around the mine and along the road through the mountains to the west. We can't stop the patrols in the other places, but we can reduce them, put them on odd and different routes and schedules."

"That might help." Mykel paused. "There's something else. Do we know what's going on over on the west side of the mountains? They're supposed to have better plantations and more growers, and we haven't heard anything, except the business about guarding the road."

"What have you heard?" Dohark looked hard at Mykel.

"Not much . . . except a few words by the seltyr's daughter that I overheard when we went through that estate. Something about the western growers being better armed. I told Vaclyn, but he never did anything, and I didn't really want to say anything more. I've talked to her a couple of times, and she denies having said anything or knowing anything about the western growers." Mykel couldn't think of any other way to present what he'd learned, not without revealing how much guesswork was involved. By referring to Vaclyn, Mykel could make some use of the dead majer. He hadn't been useful while alive.

"You think we could . . . persuade . . . her to say more?"

"You might, but . . . you torture people, and they tell you want you want to hear. We need good information, not what we want to hear."

Dohark nodded slowly. "You got that right."

"I'd also wager that every big grower around has a hidden armory."

"I won't take that wager." Dohark laughed.

"So what do we do?"

"Tread real lightly, and plan for the worst." Dohark looked at the mug of ale that the orderly had set before him. "What else can we do?"

Dohark understood more than Vaclyn ever had. Mykel hoped it would be enough.

56

Because Dainyl had his doubts about the necessarily promoted Overcaptain Dohark, he had spent almost three glasses with Dohark over the end days. Dohark was respected by the other captains, and the man had a wealth of experience and common sense. He wasn't without insight, since he had already asked one basic question. If the western growers of Dramur were the most prosperous, why was all the attention of the Cadmians being focused on the eastern growers? Still, whether Dohark had the degree of insight and foresight a battalion commander needed was another question.

At that thought, Dainyl stopped. Since when had anyone asked that of a Cadmian battalion commander? The question had always been how effective a commander was in accomplishing what the Highest and the marshal needed done. The Reillies had been disrupting agriculture in the Vales of Prosperity and reducing lifeforce mass growth. The marshal had sent out the Cadmians to remove the Reillies and relocate them where their activities resulted in a net increase in lifeforce. The last thing either of the senior alectors wanted was a commander who might question *why* something had been ordered. Was that the reason why Dainyl was now acting submarshal? Because he had kept his questions to himself—and Lystrana?

He was also troubled that Quelyt had not returned from Elcien. With a two-day flight each way, and a day off in between, Quelyt should have been back on Decdi evening.

The next Cadmian to enter the study was Majer Herryf, greatly subdued from when Dainyl had first met him. The colonel waited for Herryf to settle himself before he half leaned, half sat on the edge of the desk and addressed the Cadmian officer.

"I've been thinking, Majer. You expressed worry about the escaped miners turning into a rebel force long before they became a problem. What led you to that conclusion?"

Herryf only met Dainyl's eyes for a moment before looking down.

"I'll let you think about that," Dainyl said. "There's another question that's never been really answered. Where do the western growers fit in? Their houses and plantations are far larger than those of the eastern growers, and the lands are more fertile. Yet, from what I can tell, Dramuria tends to be ruled by those in the east. I'd like your thoughts on that."

"Sir, the western growers are more prosperous, and they can grow a wider range of crops. They need less in the way of trade than the eastern growers."

"Why don't they trade with the eastern growers, then? Wouldn't it benefit both?"

"They don't like each other. They don't trust each other."

Dainyl cleared his throat. "Was this ever reported?"

Herryf looked up, his eyes wide. "Of course. I wrote a dispatch on the problem two years ago. Marshal Shastylt sent instructions back. He told me to stay on good terms with both and to avoid getting involved with the western growers whenever possible. I've done what I could, but that was part of the problem with the escaped miners. Some of them were heading west and becoming brigands. I wanted to create a local militia to deal with that, but the marshal said that two companies were enough to deal with brigands." Herryf gestured vaguely westward. "There's no way that two companies can cover all of Dramur and also handle the prisoners and guarding the mine and the guano shipments."

"Do you think that the western seltyrs smuggled in weapons to deal with brigands?"

"I don't know, sir."

Dainyl read that as an affirmative. "Do the western growers get any of the guano or the revenues from the mine?"

"Not that I've heard. None of the growers talk about that when we're around."

"When are you around the growers?"

"Not often. I sometimes see them when I check with Sturwart. Once in a while, one will come here to complain about brigands."

From Herryf 's demeanor, Dainyl was certain he wasn't getting the entire story.

"You're from Dramur, then?"

"Most of the local Cadmians here are, Colonel. My older brother inherited the family lands. He's one of the smaller growers still able to make ends meet."

"Here in the east?"

"There aren't any small growers in the west."

That was more than a little interesting, reflected Dainyl. "How many of the growers have stocks of weapons?"

"That, I would have no way of knowing. My brother and I seldom talk, less every year. Even if I did meet a grower, that's not something any of them would share with me. I'm sure you can see that, Colonel."

"Oh, I do." Dainyl stood. "I'd like you to think about how we might change what we're doing with the western growers. We'll talk tomorrow."

Herryf stood. "Yes, sir."

After the majer left, Dainyl stretched. The majer had been less than totally forthcoming, but it was obvious there was a disagreement between Herryf and his brother. It was also clear that the western growers worried Herryf.

It was time for another aerial survey of the west.

Dainyl donned his shimmersilk jacket and gloves. On the way out, he turned to the squad leader at the table outside. "Sheafyr, I'm going flying. I won't be back until later. If there are any problems, either Overcaptain Dohark or the majer will have to deal with them."

"Yes, sir."

Outside the air seemed less chill. With spring but a few weeks away, Dainyl hoped that the weather would continue to warm. Still, it was far warmer than late winter was in Elcien, or in places like Iron Stem or Scien.

Falyna was the duty flier, the only one, actually, on Dramur, and she scrambled to her feet as she saw Dainyl marching toward her. "Where to, Colonel? Up to that peak?"

"Not today. We're headed west, over the mountains, to take a look at some growers' lands there. I want to see what's changed since the last flight out there."

"That'll take a while."

"The rest of the day, I'd judge." It would take far longer than that to determine what else he didn't know about what had been happening in Dramur.

57

In the early morning, Mykel and Alendyr rode side by side up the stone road toward the mining camp and the mine. Behind them followed second squad. The late-winter air was almost warm, and there was no wind. Selena was low in the western sky, so low that it would not rise in the east until close to midnight. Asterta was low in the east, behind Mykel and to his right.

"Sir?" asked Alendyr. "What does the colonel want us to do about the patrols?"

"Keep patrolling, but with more care. I got the feeling that he wasn't happy about having to take over."

"In his boots, I wouldn't be, either," replied the squad leader. "Majer Vaclyn, begging your pardon, sir, he didn't do any of us any favors. Bhoral said that you near-on begged him to leave those folk in Jyoha alone. Was that right?"

"I don't know that I begged. I did tell him that I didn't see the use of it, and that it would just make matters worse. He insisted that a Codebreaker was a Codebreaker."

"When the Code says that a man who steals for his family, cause they're starving, has to be treated the same as a fellow like Polynt, who just robbed and killed when he felt like it—there's something wrong there."

Mykel thought for a moment. "Theft is theft. If you treat it differently, then everyone will have an excuse, and there won't be any justice. What's wrong is when a man who is able to work is driven off his lands and turned into a thief because he has no choices left. That's what happened in Jyoha."

"Happens more than there, sir."

Mykel took a deep breath. He didn't have a good answer for what Alendyr had said, and they were headed back to deal with prisoners and escaped prisoners, and some of them were probably no different from the men Mykel and Fifteenth Company had killed in Jyoha. "I'm sure it does. I'm sure it does."

The two rode another half vingt before Alendyr spoke. "You're being quiet, sir. Something we need to do?"

"No. I was just thinking." Actually, he'd been thinking about several things, including Rachyla. There was something about her that drew him, and he couldn't pinpoint it. He couldn't even come close. She was attractive, but he'd met more attractive women. She was intelligent, but he'd met other women who were. She came from wealth, but from Mykel's point of view, that was a disadvantage, because he'd never have wealth, and probably wouldn't know what to do even if someone settled a pile of golds on him.

"About what, sir?"

"More than a few things." Mykel grinned widely. "Women. Golds. I was also thinking about the road."

Alendyr said nothing.

"There are eternastone roads everywhere—except here. Why would that be?"

"Because we don't need them? You get here by ship, and ships don't need high roads."

"That's true enough, but Dramur is a big island. It's farther from one end to the other than it is from Elcien to Ludar or from Tempre to Hyalt, or lots of places that have high roads. Maybe they wouldn't fight so much here, if they had better roads. The only decent road is this one, from the port to Dramuria—" Mykel laughed abruptly. "Of course."

Alendyr looked at Mykel questioningly.

"I'm just a Cadmian captain. It's trade and people. The roads are links for trade to places where there are either goods or the people to buy them."

"But . . . sir, there's the road from Iron Stem to Eastice. It's more than five hundred vingts, and there aren't as many folks on that road once you leave Iron Stem as there are here in Dramuria. Same's true for the road to Soupat, or the one from Dereka to Aelta."

Mykel cocked his head. "I thought I had an answer, but you're right. There must be some reason, but I can't see it. Turning road paving into eternastone takes golds and some special equipment that the alectors use."

"Maybe they're planning for where there will be more people," suggested Alendyr.

"That makes as much sense as anything," Mykel agreed, although he wasn't certain about that, either.

After another hundred yards, he shifted his weight in the saddle, but gingerly, and looked blankly at the road for several moments. He was headed back to the mine, and he'd never even been inside the stockade, and those were where the prisoners were escaping—or vanishing.

He took a deep breath. He really needed to see the mineworks, much as he dreaded doing so. Maybe . . . just maybe, that would tell him something. If it didn't, he wouldn't feel guilty or as though he'd overlooked something.

58

Almost a glass passed from liftoff at the Cadmian compound before the pteridon cleared the highest points in the Murian Mountains west of Dramuria. From there the pteridon glided westward on wide blue wings, slowly descending across the more densely vegetated western hills. Falyna had followed, as Quelyt had earlier, the road that ran through the lower section of the mountains south of the mine.

After they had crossed the mountains and started downward, Dainyl could see the differences between the east and the west sides of Dramur, differences far more pronounced at the end of winter than they had been when he had earlier surveyed the area. In the west, the trees were even greener, and the fields that had just been tilled earlier were showing a green fuzz.

As before, Dainyl saw no carts or wagons on the higher reaches of the road, but scattered riders and wagons appeared on the road once they flew over the cultivated lands in the high, rolling hills.

"A little more to the south here, toward that estate with the two villas," Dainyl called forward, remembering a large riding area, one suitable for training horse troopers.

"Yes, sir."

The pteridon banked, then straightened, heading toward the villas of the estate.

Dainyl watched closely as they neared the large estate, then smiled coolly as he saw dust rising from the flat riding area to the north and east of the villas.

"Someone's riding hard there," shouted Falyna.

The pteridon blanked slightly right, then leveled out on a course directly toward the riders, about five hundred yards above the ground as the pteridon swept over the eastern stone wall. Some of the dust had begun to settle, since most of the riders had reined up to watch as the pteridon flew overhead.

All the riders were scattered in squad-sized groups across what Dainyl had earlier thought to be an outdoor riding arena. They all wore deep blue tunics—exactly the same color—and all had scabbards attached to their saddles. Dainyl couldn't see what weapons were in them.

"You see what I see, sir?" Falyna called back.

"Horse troopers, I'd say. You up for a low pass back over them?"

"We can do that, sir."

"Better have your lance ready, just in case."

The blue-metaled lance was in Falyna's hand even before Dainyl had finished speaking. For his own part, the colonel reached out with his Talent to draw lifeforce for shields.

The pteridon banked steeply southward into a tight turn, losing altitude swiftly, until they were headed back over the exercise yard at little more than a hundred yards above the ground. Dainyl leaned slightly to his left for a better view.

All of the riders had reined up and watched as the pteridon swept toward them. Several riders had pulled out rifles, but someone yelled something, and the troopers lowered the weapons. At the lower altitude, Dainyl could see that the riders also wore sabres. That suggested that the troopers might also have been trained with the blades before obtaining the rifles—or that the seltyr had other uses for the force.

"Another pass, sir?" called Falyna, as the eastern stone wall passed under the pteridon.

"No. That was enough. Climb back up and head west again."

The pteridon's wings beat more strongly as the Talent-creature began a climbing left turn.

The seltyr—or his captain—had been smart enough not to fire on the two Myrmidons, and that indicated that someone was well aware of what a skylance could do.

"They had rifles out," Falyna said over her shoulder. "Good thing for them they didn't try to use them."

"Yes, it was," Dainyl called back. "We need to look at some more estates."

"There's one to the north."

"Head over there."

The pteridon straightened on a northwest course. Dainyl shifted his weight in the second saddle and readjusted his harness. He still wasn't flying enough not to get uncomfortable—and they had at least two more glasses before they would return to Dramuria.

The next estate—one that Dainyl had not overflown before—had a square field that had been heavily ridden—but no horses or men were out or visible. Still, the field suggested that someone had been training or exercising sizable numbers of troopers.

"Sir!" called Falyna. "To the north!"

Dainyl glanced northward, where he saw a line of thunderheads rising on the horizon. "Let's start back!"

"On our way, sir."

Dainyl continued to study the ground beneath the pteridon's wings as the Talent-creature slowly climbed eastward. Clearly, more than a few of the western seltyrs had their own private horse companies—and at least one was armed with rifles—Cadmian-style rifles in all probability.

He found it impossible to believe that the marshal and the Highest did not know that, not with their access to the Table in the Hall of Justice. The real questions were whether all the high alectors and the Duarches knew, whether the marshal and the High Alector of Justice were keeping the information for their own purposes, and whether the High Alector of Justice and the marshal had done even more than withhold information.

The other question was more personal. Why had he not had Falyna flame down the horse troopers? He'd had that right. Because, he told himself, the troopers were following orders, and killing one set of troopers wouldn't have solved anything—and even the seltyr who had armed them would likely have escaped. That raised another set of questions, as well.

Dainyl didn't like thinking about any of those questions, especially about their implications. The only fact in his favor was that a Table did not reveal alectors and Talent-creatures, so that no one with a Table would have been able to determine where Dainyl had been and what he had observed. That was slight consolation.

59

Despite the aches in his back and shoulder, and a headache that had pounded at him half the night, Mykel struggled awake well before dawn on Duadi. The afternoon before, when thunderstorms had just pelted the area and he had felt even worse from a long day—even if there hadn't been any snipers on the road—he'd finally arranged to meet one of Meryst's squad leaders at the guano mine a half glass before dawn so that he could inspect the mine before any miners arrived. There clearly weren't enough miners or Cadmian guards to work at night.

Khelsyt—the squad leader—hadn't been that pleased with Mykel's request.

Mykel had insisted. "Miners are disappearing. You want me to tell this Myrmidon colonel that I don't even know where it's happening? He already took care of Majer Vaclyn with that light-cutter torch of his."

"Yes, sir. Half glass before dawn," Khelsyt had agreed, tiredly. "I'll have an overseer there to show you around."

As Mykel struggled into his uniform and made his way to the stable in the dim light of a morning that had come too early, Mykel half wished that, bad as he'd felt the night before, he'd just insisted on seeing the mine then. At the time, he'd thought he'd feel better after another night's sleep. He did, but not that much better, and he had no idea why he had a headache.

Two scouts—Sendyl and Jasakyt—were saddling their mounts when Mykel arrived at the ramshackle shed serving as a stable. Mykel's breath puffed white in morning air that was far colder than it had been recently, doubtless because of the icy rain and hail of the evening before.

"Good morning," Mykel said.

"Sir . . . we figured that lifting a saddle with that arm . . ." offered Sendyl.

Mykel glanced into the stall. His chestnut was saddled. "Thank you. I am a bit stiff in the mornings." When he stepped into the stall, he checked the girths, but the two had done a good job, for which he was definitely thankful. He slipped his rifle into the scabbard and led the gelding out of the shed. He mounted easily, but carefully. Even so, a jolt of pain went through his shoulder. The two scouts joined him immediately, and the three rode toward the mine road.

"We're going *into* the mine, sir?" asked Sendyl.

"Just for a little while. After talking to the colonel, it came out that none of us has ever been in it, and I couldn't explain why no one had." All that was true, if totally misleading, but Mykel doubted the colonel would object to his seeing how the mine was laid out and operated.

Sendyl and Jasakyt exchanged knowing glances. Mykel let them think that the colonel had picked on Fifteenth Company and its captain.

As they neared the outer gates of the prison compound, the sentries looked at the three riders. The gates opened, then closed once they were past. The gray paving stones were damp from the intermittent rain of the night before, but the sky was clear. A chill wind blew out of the northwest. The road was wide enough for three abreast. Mykel rode in the middle.

"Did either of you see anything interesting or different while I was in Dramuria?" he asked after they had ridden several hundred yards.

"No, sir. Pretty quiet for once," replied Jasakyt.

"Out on the road, that is," added Sendyl. "One of the squad leaders from the locals told me that another two miners just disappeared. One moment, they were loading a cart, and the next they were gone."

"Like that?"

"Overseers said that the miners hid before going down into the mine, and then the others told the story," Sendyl said.

"No one saw them or discovered tracks or anything?" asked Mykel.

"No, sir. But how would anyone get out of a cave in the rock?"

Mykel had a very good idea, but he wasn't about to offer it. "That's a good question."

"Strange place, if you ask me," murmured Jasakyt.

Mykel looked from the graystone paving blocks of the road to the still–grayish green sky, and then to the rocky hillside above the road and its walls. He should have inspected the mine right after Fifteenth Company had been assigned to patrol the mine and mine road. Then again, there were so many things he should have done—going to spread formations immediately, sending copies of his reports to Colonel Dainyl, talking to Rachyla more, perhaps even going to Colonel Dainyl earlier about the majer. Was he always going to learn things later than he should—and perhaps pay for it the next time with his life rather than a wounded shoulder?

The three rode another half vingt before Sendyl cleared his throat. "Sir, how long are we going to be here?"

"I don't know, and I don't think the colonel does, either."

The mine gates opened as the three rode toward them and creaked shut as the three passed into the stockade that surrounded the bluff holding the mine and the crude loading docks.

Khelsyt waited beside one of the empty wagons. "You can tie your mounts there." He pointed to the loading dock. "You'll be out of here before we bring the prisoners in for the day."

Mykel dismounted and walked his mount to the dock. Already, his nose was beginning to twitch. The odor, more like a stench that combined the worst features of sewage and manure, hung heavily in the air.

Standing by the timbered mine entrance was another figure, a man clad in what once might have been green, but was now a shapeless gray-brown coverall. His expression was stern, just short of grim.

"Nophyt, this is Captain Mykel. The Myrmidon colonel sent him for a quick tour."

Mykel inclined his head slightly. "I'm sorry to bother you, but . . ."

"When an alector wants something, the rest of us don't get much of a choice," replied Nophyt.

"Nophyt is the head overseer, really more of a mining engineer," explained Khelsyt.

"Much as anyone needs an engineer here," replied Nophyt. "Bats took an old lava tube, and the branches off it, just kept hanging there and dumping their droppings into it, until it got all filled up, or mostly so. Now they use the caves farther north. I figure that someday, we'll be mining those. Asked Director Donasyr why we weren't already, and he said that there were only so many folks with the golds to pay for the guano, and, besides, it'd last longer if we only mined one cave at a time. Anyway, I make sure that they dig out the shit evenly so that we don't get a wall of it falling on someone. Check the rock walls, too, every night and every morning, just to make sure nothing's developed a crack."

"Do the prisoners have to chop away rock in places to get to the guano?" Mykel asked.

"Sometimes. Either floors or the places bats get into where people can't. In another month, looks like we'll be opening up a gallery to get to a lower cave where they did that." The overseer gestured toward the weathered timbers that framed the entrance. "Better get moving."

From the bracing and the irregularities, Mykel could see that the mine entrance had once been a cave mouth.

At the entrance, Nophyt picked up a metal-and-glass oil lamp, already lit. "This is the main gallery. It was blasted out and enlarged a long time back." He walked back through the gallery to the rear, where a sloping tunnel led downward. In the middle of the tunnel floor were ruts worn into the stone. A heavy rope lay between the ruts. Mykel's eyes traced the rope to a windlass. Iron supports for the windlass had been set in holes in the lava.

"Once a cart's full they jerk the cable, and the windlass crew cranks it up."

Nophyt walked down the tunnel on the left, and Mykel followed, with the scouts behind. Khelsyt did not accompany them on the long walk down to the next level.

"Lower gallery here," announced Nophyt. "The cave branches off here. We use smaller carts down here. Some places, we just have pits, and they hoist the shit up in baskets."

Mykel tried not to swallow or breathe deeply, but he almost felt dizzy from the stench as he followed the overseer along one of the cave branches. Absently, he noted the irregular sides of the tunnel or cave, but the smooth floor. In some places, but far from all, the overhead was timbered and supported, although most of the timbers looked old and cracked.

They passed a wooden barrier on the right side of the cave tunnel.

"What's that?" asked Mykel.

"Drop tube. Goes straight down. So far as we can tell, not much guano on the sides, and the bottom's a good two hundred yards, maybe more."

The overseer headed down another long and gently sloping tunnel, walking and explaining, until he stopped in an open space surrounded by darkness. Without the oil lamp held by Nophyt, which cast but a circular glow, and not a terribly strong one, the cave would have been pitch-black.

Mykel thought that the air wasn't that good, although the odor seemed less. Then, it might have been that he was getting used to the stench.

"This is the deepest part we've found so far, not so much deep as far back," Nophyt said. "We have to rotate the crews working here. They don't like it here. Say it's dangerous."

Mykel looked around, but could see nothing beyond the circle of dim light. He closed his eyes and tried to imagine what it might be like in the dark. Despite his closed eyes, or perhaps because of them, he could see a faint red-purple glow from somewhere, almost seeping in at the edges of his vision, if he had had vision with his eyes open. Where had he seen that color?

His eyes flew open, and the color vanished. The rock-creatures with the ancient soarer! Was that why the miners feared the depths here? "Is this one of the places where miners have disappeared?"

"Don't know. No one ever sees 'em vanish. Some have disappeared from crews working here, but we could never tell if the crew hid that they'd escaped or if they disappeared."

"If the prisoners said they disappeared . . . ?" asked Mykel.

"Can't trust what they say." Nophyt snorted. "They'd say anything to get out of here."

"Could you close sections like this for a while? Until people forgot?"

"Not here. Director Donasyr wouldn't let us. This is where the guano is oldest, most concentrated, and effective." The overseer laughed. "It also smells less and gets the best price."

"You have different types of guano?" Mykel hadn't known that.

"More like different grades. The real old stuff is almost white, powders when you hit it with a hammer. It doesn't smell much." Nophyt gestured with the lamp. "Better start back up. Won't be long before they open the gates, and it takes longer walking back. Doesn't seem bad going down. Another thing heading back."

As he followed the overseer out of the works, Mykel knew where at least some of the missing miners had gone. There was really no way he was about to tell Dohark—or the colonel—what he thought. He certainly couldn't prove it, but if the prisoners thought that they'd be dragged into the depths and die at the hands of the rock-creatures, he could certainly see why some of them would do anything to escape.

60

Dainyl looked out the window of the commander's study, taking in the shadows of a late-winter afternoon in Dramuria as they stretched across the Cadmian compound. Londi had come and gone, and Duadi had almost done the same. Quelyt had not yet flown back from Elcien, and his delayed return suggested that all was not well in Elcien. Overcaptain Dohark had reported by messenger that most of the patrols undertaken by the companies of Third Battalion had been uneventful, except that Seventeenth Company had been attacked by several squads of horsemen with longbows and arrows and was pursuing them to the north of the western road.

Dainyl had immediately sent a messenger back to Dohark, suggesting that pursuit to the west was unwise, except in cases where the horsemen could be clearly cut off. He hoped that would be sufficient, since so far there had been no sign of any of the western seltyrs' horse troopers moving east. Dainyl thought it would likely be only days, weeks at the most, before that happened. For that reason, he had also alerted Dohark that the western seltyrs had armed horse troopers who could be used against the Cadmians.

He still fretted somewhat about the troopers he and Falyna had overflown. Marshal Shastylt would have destroyed them. Yet Dainyl didn't see what good that would have done. It would only destroy higher-level lifeforce mass, and lead to greater destruction, while not getting at the basic problem. He laughed softly. If . . . *if* he could ever discover the basic problem.

Then, there was the problem of the ancients. Much as he had tried, with his own Talent, he had been unable to re-create—or find, see, or sense—the vision of the world lifemass web that the soarer had shown him, for that was all that it could have been. The best he could do was sense, if he concentrated, the purple-pinkness of his own lifethread for less than a yard from him. Still, that was an improvement. The prediction that he would perish unless he changed still lurked in the back of his mind as well. Change? How? And why?

"Sir?"

Dainyl looked up to see Quelyt standing in the open doorway to the study. He stood. "I'm glad to see you. I worried that they might have pressed you into courier duty somewhere."

The Myrmidon laughed as he stepped into the study. "We did do a message run or two to Ludar, more as a favor, while we waited." He extended an envelope. "From the marshal."

"Any other dispatches?"

"No, sir." Then the ranker grinned. "There is a letter."

Dainyl shook his head. "Sometimes, you're a brigand, Quelyt."

"Only sometimes, sir."

"What's happening in Elcien?"

"It's hard to say, sir. The other fliers think that the mess in Iron Stem is finally settled, but there are rumors that someone killed five alectors on the regional staff in Dereka. They're missing, anyway, and that's not good."

"What else?"

"It was a frigging cold winter in Elcien, and it's still cold. Good to get down here."

"For winter, it's been pleasant here."

"Oh . . . one other thing, I almost forgot. A bunch of new alectors showed up in Elcien. Zorclyt said they'd been translated from Ifryn. Most of them will be sent to Alustre, he said."

Why Alustre? Dainyl wondered. "I believe you mentioned a letter?"

"Yes, sir. The lady delivered it to me herself, just before we lifted off." Quelyt handed the colonel a smaller and thicker envelope.

"Thank you."

"Do you have any flying you need done?"

"Nothing immediate." Dainyl lifted the dispatch from the marshal. "Unless I have instructions from the marshal. Falyna took me out on a survey of the west. The seltyrs there are raising private forces."

"Trouble everywhere."

"It looks that way."

Quelyt nodded. "We'll be ready."

After the Myrmidon ranker left, Dainyl closed the study door, and, as he walked toward the desk, opened the dispatch, again addressed to Colonel Dainyl. The Talent-seal was untouched. After reading through the third line, he blinked and reread the words, more slowly.

As submarshal you can no longer be spared just to observe what is occurring in Dramur. The High Alector of Justice has requested that you return to Elcien immediately, with both pteridons, so that you may be briefed on other matters of vital importance to the Myrmidons, as well as to all alectors of Acorus. This is a critical time, and the Highest and I will be calling upon your experience.

In addition, we need to consult on how best to handle the future of Dramur. Our scattered observations suggest that matters are not as you were led to believe and that a more unified long-term strategy is necessary. . . .

So far as Dainyl could tell, there had never been *any* strategy, just a vague set of orders to Third Battalion to do what was necessary to get rid of a few rebels. He kept reading.

Delegate responsibilities and duties as you must, and plan for a minimum absence of two full weeks.

Just as he was beginning to get some idea of the scope of the problems in Dramur, he was being recalled for consultations and strategy development? Why hadn't anyone developed a strategy before? Or had they, and it hadn't worked? Or was it working, and was Dainyl being recalled to make sure that he didn't upset what the marshal and the Highest had in mind? Yet the tone of the dispatch was neither derogatory nor threatening, and it did convey urgency, and it referred to him as the submarshal.

Dainyl set down the dispatch on the desk and opened the envelope from Lystrana. The Talent-seal was unbroken.

Dearest,
The seasons do stretch out, and with spring not too far away, I wish that you were here in Elcien with me. The days have been long, and especially on the many nights that I have worked late, it would have been so comforting to come home and to see you . . .

Late nights mean troubles, and the kinds of troubles Lystrana dared not put into a letter, even one she had handed directly to Quelyt.

> Almost a score of alectors have arrived from Ifryn in recent weeks, and a number are Table engineers who were sent to the High Alector of Engineering in Ludar. I overheard talk about the need for greater grid stability, and you know what that may portend . . .

Dainyl understood all too well. The Archon had determined that translations to Acorus and Efra had to increase significantly. Such a decision meant either the lifeforce mass on Ifryn was decreasing more rapidly than planned, or the Archon's control was once more threatened.

> . . . Now that iron and coal production in Iron Stem have resumed . . .

Resumed? They had stopped entirely? No wonder the marshal had always been out in Iron Stem.

> . . . and the manufactories in Faitel have been able to move toward reestablishing full production, I have had to recalculate so many figures in the Duarches' accounts, and that has taken many long hours. I fear that too late a spring will also affect the year's crops, and that will change the revenue projections and the scope of major engineering projects possible . . .

Major engineering projects? *What* was going on in Elcien?

> As always, I hope that it will not be too long before you can return, if only briefly, for my heart is empty when you are gone.

While the last words might have sounded flowery, Dainyl knew that they were anything but vacant phases. Without each other, life had less meaning for both of them.

Despite the warmth and affection wrapped around the veiled warnings, her letter disturbed him far more than did the marshal's dispatch. Together, they suggested that matters in Elcien were anything but favorable.

He refolded her letter and slipped it inside his tunic, then headed out of the study to tell the two Myrmidons that they would leave at dawn. After that, he would need to brief Majer Herryf and write a letter of instructions to Overcaptain Dohark.

61

The two days of flying north to Elcien were long and cold, including the stopover in Southgate. For the last hundred vingts, the air was turbulent, with a bitter headwind, and among the more unpleasant flights Dainyl had made, but part of the discomfort might have been that being a passenger was always worse than being the flier.

As Falyna turned her pteridon due east for the final ten vingts over the Bay of Ludel toward Elcien, Dainyl glanced down at the waters below, choppy and cold gray, with whitecaps clearly visible from five hundred yards up. Above, high gray clouds obscured the late-afternoon sun. To the north, dark gray clouds were building into a wall advancing inexorably on the capital isle, and to the northeast the higher peaks of the Coast Range were solidly coated with white. Even the lower hills to the west of those peaks were heavily splotched with snow.

As they neared Elcien, Dainyl saw that a miasma of fog and smoke had settled over the isle. Only the outlines of the walls and buildings of the Myrmidon compound were visible as Falyna's pteridon spread its wings into a flare and settled onto the landing stage.

With a certain amount of relief, Dainyl set his boots on the graystones of the courtyard outside Myrmidon headquarters. The wind—icy in comparison to Dramuria—gusted around him as he unfastened his gear from behind the second saddle and slung it over his shoulder.

As Quelyt and his pteridon landed, Dainyl turned to Falyna. "Thank you. Good landing, especially in these conditions."

"Comes with the task, sir."

They both smiled.

"You and Quelyt will have to check on when we head back, but it won't be for a week at the very earliest."

"Yes, sir."

Then Dainyl turned and walked swiftly across the courtyard and into the headquarters building. Zorclyt was waiting for him.

"Is the marshal around?" asked Dainyl.

"The marshal is with the Highest, sir," replied the senior squad leader.

"He left word that, if you arrived this afternoon or this evening, you were free to do what you wished and that he would see you here in the morning a glass after muster." Zorclyt grinned. "Oh . . . you can use the duty coach to take you home."

"I appreciate that." Dainyl lifted his gear, light, since he'd left much in Dramuria, and headed for the main entrance and the coach waiting outside. He did not need another invitation.

By the time the coach reached the entrance to his house, fat and wet flakes of snow had begun to drift down out of the wall of clouds just to the north of the city.

"Thank you!" he called to Convyl, one of the youngest Myrmidons without a pteridon assignment, and thus one of those saddled with coach duties.

"You're more than welcome, sir."

Dainyl opened the door and stepped inside, closing it behind him against the snow that was beginning to intensify. One of the housegirls—Zistele—jumped back from where she had been sweeping—desultorily—the tiles in the entry foyer. "Colonel, sir!"

"I'm back for a time. Is Lystrana here?"

"No, sir. She said she might be home earlier today, but she's not here yet."

Dainyl set his gear on the bottom step of the stairs to the upper level. "Is there—"

He broke off as the door opened behind him, and he turned.

Lystrana smiled broadly as she looked at Dainyl standing there in his shimmering blue riding jacket. She took two quick steps.

The embrace was long and warm.

"I had heard that you might be recalled for consultations," she said, finally breaking away from him.

For a long moment, he just looked at her, taking in her violet eyes, her clear alabaster skin, and the black hair that seemed to hold an energy all its own.

"I'm happy to see you, but I'm not pleased at the recall," he replied.

She raised a single eyebrow.

He laughed.

"We both need to eat. Even bread and cheese," she said. "You're looking tired."

"You look wonderful."

"I might, but I'm famished." Lystrana turned her head. "Sentya?"

"Yes, alectress?"

"If you would set out some bread and cheese on the table in the kitchen? And some of the red wine? The Vyan Grande?" Lystrana turned back to her husband. "It's warmer there."

"It's almost ready, alectress," answered Zistele.

Arm in arm, the two walked into the kitchen, where Sentya had set out a basket of bread still warm enough from the oven that Dainyl could feel the heat. Zistele had placed a tray on the smaller kitchen table. On it were three different wedges of cheese. After pouring the wine, Sentya slipped out of the kitchen, following the younger serving girl.

"Another long day?" asked Dainyl as he seated himself, glad to be where chairs were of proper height and breadth.

"They've all been long. I'll tell you later . . ." She inclined her head toward the front of the house.

Dainyl nodded. He broke off a chunk of the still-warm bread and took a mouthful, following it with a small wedge of cheese, then a sip from the purple-tinged crystal goblet.

"How are things going for you?" Lystrana asked.

"Not all that well," he admitted. "I can't help but feel that there wouldn't have been all this unrest in Dramur if the Cadmians hadn't been sent there." He sipped the wine slowly, enjoying the taste, as well as the warmth of the kitchen, boosted by the still-heated stove.

"That makes sense," Lystrana replied. "It has often been a technique used by the High Alector of Justice. They look at places where there is some unrest and likely to be more. Then they provoke violence before the perpetrators can become well organized."

"What am I doing there, then?"

"You are there to make sure that matters don't get out of hand. The technique is proved, from what I've been able to discover, but it is also dangerous."

"Did you know this before I left?"

Lystrana shook her head. "After your letter, I went into the archives. I also made some suggestions to Zestafyn, and his reactions confirmed my suspicions. It's nothing we could prove, dearest, but I'm convinced that is what is planned for Dramur."

"But why?"

She shrugged. "I don't know. I was hoping that what you could tell me might help in finding out why."

"I can tell you more than you want to know . . . about many things."

"Later." A broad smile crossed her face. "Later."

62

Despite the long flights to Elcien, on Quinti, Dainyl woke at dawn to the wind wailing outside the windows. When he opened his eyes, Lystrana was awake and looking at him.

"You still sleep like a child at times," she said.

"That's when I'm so tired I forget to worry," he replied, slowly struggling into a half-sitting position. "The older I get, the more tired I have to be."

"Breakfast won't be ready for a while, and you were going to tell me what the problems were in Dramuria." Lystrana propped herself up in the wide bed and looked directly at him.

He understood why she wanted to talk in their bedroom. "I was . . . except someone had other ideas." Dainyl grinned mischievously.

"Oh . . . I didn't see much protesting from a certain colonel." Her eyes smiled.

They both laughed, but only for a moment.

"What's happening in Dramur follows what you suggested last night, but there are things that don't fit. I'm certain that the marshal used Talent on the majer in charge of the Third Battalion of Cadmians, so that he would issue foolish orders and keep his captains from using their initiative . . ." Dainyl gave a summary of the events, including the unmarked Cadmian rifles, the smugglers, the uniformed horse troopers of the west, and the trooper who had been Talent-manipulated and committed two murders.

"Is that all?" asked Lystrana dryly.

"I wish it were. I've also run into an ancient and her creatures—"

"A real ancient?" interrupted Lystrana. "You're sure? Of course you are. But . . ." She shook her head. "There aren't any mentions, even in the archives, and I've read most of them."

"A very real ancient . . ." He went on to describe both his encounters with the soarer and her words. "There's a power there that's frightening. It's not just their power to transport themselves places, either. I can see that. Their mirror seems equivalent to a Table."

"You said that the creatures disappeared into the rock. I'd wager the soarer could do that as well."

Dainyl thought about that. "I wouldn't be surprised, but if they're so powerful, why haven't they shown themselves?"

"There can't be that many, not compared to all the landers and indigens. The only ruins we've found are in high and cold places. Even this tunnel is in the mountains, you said. We don't like either, and we're the ones most likely to sense them."

"Except for the landers with Talent," he said.

"They aren't many of them, and you know what the *Views of the Highest* says about that. There wouldn't be any if we could find them early enough."

"That's true." Dainyl paused, thinking about Captain Mykel for a moment.

"You think they're dangerous, even if there can't be very many?"

"I do. I couldn't say why, though." He paused. "I still can't figure out what she meant by changing or perishing, and not being a part of the world."

"The second part is true, dearest. We're not really a part of Acorus, not totally. We're linked through the Tables back to Ifryn. Even if the Archon decides to bring the master scepter here, our link to this world will be through it."

"But they don't regard the landers and indigens that way."

"No." Lystrana laughed sardonically. "They feed on some of them, though, it sounds like. It could be that they can't do that to us."

"Why not?"

"Because we're from Ifryn, even if we're born here. We're different. The landers and the indigens are partly Ifryn, but mostly adapted to and part of Acorus."

That made sense to Dainyl, but it left another question. "Why are they showing up now?"

"Maybe they aren't," suggested Lystrana. "There have always been disappearances. Maybe this is one of those times when an alector with strong shields encountered them."

"Neither Falyna nor Quelyt sensed them."

"I'd wager that they've always been around."

"You think that the Highest and the Duarches have hushed up reports about them?"

"It's almost certain," Lystrana concluded. "There would be pressure to find them, and that would divert resources and a great amount of lifeforce."

"And that would not please the Archon."

"No. And, if it's as it appears, trying to root them out of high places would be most costly. When there are so few of them, the Duarches are most likely just watching and waiting for them to finish dying off. There can't be that many left."

"I'm not so certain. The soarers are somehow behind the miners' escapes and attacks."

"I don't think a handful of escaped miners presents that real a threat to the Duarchy," she said.

"No, they don't. But why are the marshal and the Highest behind the contraband arms? I just wish I knew why."

"They could be using the miners as cover for their strategy to preempt trouble, couldn't they?" asked Lystrana.

"They might be, but there's more there. I just don't know what it could be." He shook his head. "As soon as I take over and get rid of the officer who's creating more trouble than he's solving, I get recalled here for consultations. They want things to get worse in Dramur. And I'm not in a position where I can do anything. I have to think that Tyanylt discovered something and didn't like it."

"You're probably right." Lystrana frowned. "There's no proof, except for the contraband rifles, and the High Alector of Justice can claim they were part of a strategy to preempt later trouble because, if the seltyrs were allowed to gather forces and arms more slowly, they would have a broader base of support. They also might start developing artillery."

Dainyl winced. Life-reinforced garments and Talent-shields didn't work against artillery. "So there's no way you can go to your Highest or to the Duarch?"

"Not unless we find out more," Lystrana replied. "When do you meet with the marshal?"

"In about two glasses, and I suppose I'd better start getting washed up and dressed."

Left unsaid as they climbed out of bed and into the chill air was the understanding that the meeting with the marshal would not be likely to produce anything resembling evidence.

In the end, Dainyl had to hurry through dressing and eating, and because he couldn't count on getting a coach to the Myrmidon compound, he left early, and walked, trying to think out what he could ask the marshal that was in character with what he was supposed to know.

The snow of the previous night had mostly melted, although the skies were still gray, and a wind blew out of the northwest. Dainyl was more than happy to step out of the raw morning and into the comparative warmth of the headquarters building, and glad that he was early enough to warm up before his scheduled meeting with Marshal Shastylt.

Before he headed to his study, he stopped at the duty desk, where Undercaptain Zernylta looked up, waiting. "Is the marshal in yet?"

"No, sir," she replied.

"I'll be in my study." Dainyl nodded politely and walked down the corridor past the still-vacant study of the submarshal. The door to his own study was closed. He opened it and stepped inside. The room was slightly musty, and there were stacks of reports piled on his desk. The colonel frowned. Certainly, the reports could have been sent with Quelyt or Falyna.

With a deep breath he sat down and began to read. After less than half a glass, he almost wished he had not.

Three of the reports were actually reports he'd sent to the marshal, and someone had read them, but there were no replies and no notations. The rest of the reports were the standard quintal reports from the various Myrmidon companies across Corus. Majer Dhenyr, the commander of the Fifth Company in Dereka, had reported the theft of two more skylances and requested replacements. How could anyone steal a skylance? They were either in their holders on a pteridon or stored in the pteridon's square, never more than a few yards from one of the Talent-creatures. *No one* stole anything from a pteridon. They didn't sleep, and their claws and beaks were lethal. They were virtually invulnerable to anything short of cannon—and there weren't any cannon on Acorus, not that the alectors of the Tables had been able to find. Besides, it would have been obvious if anyone had used cannon.

Third Company in Alustre had sent two squads north for reconnaissance around the North Road between Scien and Pystra, as requested by the marshal. Dainyl couldn't help frowning at that. Two squads for recon? Why? Dainyl knew that the two local Cadmian companies there had been scheduled for rebasing at Norda, but that should have been completed a season earlier.

"Sir?"

Dainyl set the report down and looked up at Zorclyt, who stood in the doorway.

"The marshal would like to see you now."

"Thank you." Dainyl stood and walked swiftly from his study to the door of the marshal's spaces.

"Come in, Colonel."

Dainyl closed the study door behind him, then followed the marshal's gesture and settled into one of the chairs across the desk from the head of the Myrmidons.

As Shastylt looked directly at Dainyl, the marshal's violet eyes were intent, the thin-lipped and wide mouth set in an expression of concern. The colonel had seen the marshal use that look before, and rather than respond, he merely waited. At some point, the marshal would speak, certain that his words would carry more weight after the silence.

"You have handled the situation in Dramur with care and with tact"—Shastylt paused, leaving his words hanging before going on—"when many would have been tempted to act precipitously. At times, it is best to let an infection come to a head, where it is concentrated, rather than treat it with palliatives that will only prolong the treatment and recovery."

Dainyl nodded politely. "I have watched closely over the years and attempted to learn how to distinguish such differences." What he wasn't about to say was that he didn't believe a word that Shastylt said, and that the analogy was misapplied to the situation in Dramur.

"Even when you have some doubts about the wisdom of a policy suggested by the Highest, you seem able to understand that you may not see all that there is to see."

"The higher I have been promoted," Dainyl replied easily, "the more obvious that has become."

Shastylt was the one who nodded. "For such reasons, the Highest and I have decided that you are indeed suited to be Submarshal of Myrmidons, particularly at this time. All Myrmidons are well aware you have held every position from being the newest ranker all the way up to being submarshal, and that will instill even greater confidence in them." Shastylt smiled, more professionally than with personal warmth as he extended an enameled box, setting it on the edge of the desk before Dainyl. "Here are your stars, Submarshal."

"Thank you." Dainyl bowed his head slightly. "I will do my best to live up to all the expectations and requirements of being your deputy."

"I am most certain you will. Tomorrow morning, you will be meeting with the Highest, one glass before noon, and he will be briefing you on certain critical aspects of your duties. These are matters of which only a few below the station of high alector are aware. We also will be promoting Majer Dhenyr to colonel to take over your previous position here at headquarters. As you may recall, he's been in charge of Fifth Company in Dereka."

"I've read more than a few of his reports," Dainyl admitted. "I must admit that the last one I read worried me greatly."

"About the missing skylances?" Shastylt nodded. "That has worried all of us. The lances are essentially worthless without a pteridon, but how they were taken is more than a little vexing. The majer and the senior regional alector have questioned everyone who could possibly have been near the pteridon squares there, but so far have turned up nothing. There have been more than a few matters like that recently, and once this business in Dramuria is wound up, you may have to undertake a more thorough investigation of some of them."

"I have heard that five alectors vanished in Dereka. Is that so, and part of the problem there?"

"It is, but I cannot say more until after you meet with the Highest." The marshal looked directly and intently at Dainyl. "I would be curious to know what happened to Majer Vaclyn to cause him to lose such control. If you can explain, that is."

"Yes, sir. No one can look into the mind of a dead man, but there were subtle indications of his . . . growing instability. He was an officer who did not have the ability to be promoted beyond majer. He was a competent company commander, but his grasp of greater tactics was limited. His captains have, over the years, quietly remedied his deficiencies. This is something far more easily done in operations against raiders than in the situation in Dramur—"

"How so?"

"In Dramur," Dainyl replied, "there is not one group of insurgents, but several. There are smugglers, who wish to avoid Duarchial tariffs. There are the escaped miners who, for superstitious reasons associated with the vanished ancients, will often resort to near-suicidal tactics to escape the mines and attack the Cadmian guards. There are former smallholders, forced off their lands by the seltyrs and the larger growers. There was at least one seltyr who was so alarmed by these combined factors that he had assembled his own company armed with the contraband Cadmian rifles." Dainyl paused. "Did you ever receive any reply, sir, to your inquiries about the source of those weapons?"

"A reply, yes. One that was helpful . . . not really. The High Alector of Engineering sent an inquiry to Faitel and one to Alustre. More than a thousand rifles are missing from the reserve storeroom in Faitel, but no one seems to know how and when it happened."

Dainyl winced visibly, even though the number was really no surprise to him after his inspection flight over the west of Dramur. "That many?"

Shastylt shook his head. "It could be more. There's been no response from Alustre."

No response? When the contraband weapons had been reported weeks before, when the high alectors had access to Tables and Myrmidon couriers?

"You look surprised, Submarshal."

"I'm less surprised by the numbers of weapons missing than I am by the lack of response and knowledge." Dainyl was walking on the edge of a steep chasm. To charge a high alector with incompetence or worse was unwise, but not to show some concern and even indignation would raise the marshal's suspicions.

"Some of the high alectors do not grasp the severity of the challenges we face in the next few years, and we must tread lightly until they or their successors understand fully those challenges."

Dainyl nodded. "It is clear that you are dealing with a most delicate situation, sir."

"As are you, Dainyl." Shastylt smiled. "I would that I could have you delegate you oversight of the Dramur situation to someone else, but, at the moment, there is no one else. Majer Dhenyr will have his hands full taking over your duties, especially now, and it would not be feasible to bring either of the senior majers from Alustre. The Myrmidons have always had to cope with fewer officers than we might wish otherwise." The marshal rose from behind the desk. "We will have to continue this discussion later. This afternoon, the Highest and I will be briefing the High Alector of Finance and the Duarch, but I did want to let you know of your promotion. It is effectively immediately. So you can put on the stars as soon as you have a moment. The Highest will be briefing you tomorrow; and then on Septi, we'll talk again."

As the marshal had stood, so had Dainyl. He did reach out and take the black-enameled box that held the eight-pointed silver stars of a submarshal. The marshal's stars were gold and green-edged, of course. "I look forward to that, sir."

He managed a pleased smile before turning and leaving the marshal's study.

Once back in his own study, a space that he supposed he would be leaving before long for the larger study that had been Tyanylt's, Dainyl sat down behind his desk, heavily. He was both surprised and alarmed by his promotion. Shastylt had as much as stated that some of the high alectors did not understand the coming crisis and would have to be replaced, and that the marshal and the Highest would be briefing the Duarch on something of great import. Dainyl was supposed to connect the two—but he doubted that such a connection was accurate.

More than anything, he felt that his position was more precarious, rather than less—and he had yet to meet with the High Alector of Justice.

63

Dainyl walked up to the duty coach outside Myrmidon headquarters roughly a glass and a half before noon on Sexdi. The sky had cleared the night before, leaving the heavens a brilliant silver-green. The white sun shone brightly, but the air remained chill.

"The Hall of Justice, sir?" asked the duty driver.

"That's right." Dainyl offered a smile and then stepped into the coach.

As the coach pulled away from the headquarters building, Dainyl sat back, thinking about what awaited him. The night before, he and

Lystrana had discussed, quietly and in their bedchamber, what the marshal had told him. She had not been able to add any more understanding or information. What was obvious, so obvious that neither had to speak it, was that times were getting even more dangerous, especially since Dainyl was thought to have limited Talent and no ties to the Duarches, and no links to any of the High Alectors—except indirectly through Lystrana.

Dainyl glanced out the coach window, his eyes taking in the Duarch's palace to the right, the stone glowing in the sunlight, and then the gardens, gray and winter brown. Did the Duarch of Elcien know what the Highest and the marshal were doing? Dainyl and Lystrana doubted it, yet neither dared bring matters before the Duarch without some real proof—and they had none—not given the Talent-strength of the marshal and the High Alector of Justice.

In less than a quarter glass, the coach pulled up outside up of the Hall of Justice.

"I'll be waiting over at the concourse, sir," said the driver.

"I don't imagine I'll be that long." With a nod, Dainyl turned and started up the steps.

Coming down the wide golden marble steps were two lander women, followed by a graying man and woman. The thinner of the two younger women was punctuating her words with sobs and tears.

". . . he didn't do anything wrong, he didn't. What difference did it make, adding a pinch of white lead to the wine here and there? . . . kept it from spoiling and tasted sweeter . . . the Highest wouldn't change anything . . . what will we do? Gil's dead, and they took the shop . . ."

Dainyl concealed a wince as he passed the four. Not only did lead poison those who had too much, but it also decreased fertility among the indigens and landers, and that meant slower growth of high-level lifemass.

No matter how often the schools taught that certain practices were not good for life, some landers and indigens would do them anyway if it brought a few extra silvers, or even coppers. And then they complained when justice fell on them, even when they had been warned.

At the top of the outside steps, without looking back, he stepped between two of the goldenstone pillars and into the receiving rotunda, crossing the octagonal tiles of polished gold and green marble, with their inset eight-pointed stars, stars exactly the same shape as those he now wore on his tunic collar. He could hear the petitioners in the main Hall, even before he passed through the goldenstone pillars between the receiving rotunda and the Hall.

The High Alector of Justice was not seated behind the podium of judgment, set directly before the Needle of the Duarches that soared upward through the high pink marble ceiling and well above the green exterior tiles of the roof. Rather, one of his assistants was, although Dainyl doubted that most of the petitioners would have noted the difference.

Dainyl slipped to the left toward the pillar on the south side that held the hidden entrance to the chambers below. While the entrance was on the side away from the podium and petitioners, as always, Dainyl used his Talent to conceal his opening the concealed entry.

After stepping through the square stone archway, and making sure it closed behind him, he released the Talent-illusion and made his way down the light-torch-illuminated stairway to the lower level and warmer air. He followed the stone-walled hallway to the Highest's chambers.

Even before he reached the door, a deep voice boomed out, "Please come in, Submarshal."

This time the Highest wore a tunic of deep purple, trimmed in brilliant green. The purple created a greater impression of gravity. Did the High Alector wear the purple when meeting with either of the Duarches?

Dainyl inclined his head, murmuring the ritual phrase, "Highest, I am here to serve."

"That you are." The High Alector of Justice motioned for Dainyl to follow him. Without saying more, the senior alector turned and walked through an open archway.

Dainyl followed and found himself in a smaller sitting room, also windowless, but lit by enough crystal light-torches that the chamber was more than comfortable.

The Highest seated himself in a curved oak chair without upholstery. Dainyl took the matching chair on the other side of the small ebony table. Despite the hardness of the wood, the chair's graceful curves were far more comfortable than many padded chairs in which Dainyl had found himself. He waited for the Highest to speak.

Several moments passed, and Dainyl could sense the use of Talent to scan him. As he had practiced with Lystrana, he did not react, but merely maintained his shields.

"Your shields improve every year, Dainyl."

"I keep practicing, Highest."

" 'Sir' will do, Dainyl." A half-humorous smile followed the words, then a pause, before the High Alector continued. "I must admit that the timing of events, even of your promotion, is less than optimal."

"I certainly didn't plan things that way, Highest," Dainyl said politely.

"I doubt anyone could have been that farsighted, even your lovely wife."

"She is quite farsighted, but neither she nor I anticipated a promotion at this time." Earlier, or not at all, had been Dainyl's own judgment.

"As Marshal Shastylt doubtless revealed, matters on Acorus are not as we would wish."

"He did suggest that, sir."

"Knowing him, he was circumspect. They may be worse than that. None of these difficulties would be especially troublesome by itself. The problems with the iron and coal mines in Iron Stem would be workable. A wild lander Talent in the rugged hills west of Hyalt would require no more than a battalion of Cadmians and a squad of Myrmidons. Grassland nomads have decided to raid merchant convoys on the upper steppe highway between Ongelya, and they hide in the high grasses so that pteridons are of little use—unless we were to burn the grass, and that just would make the lifemass situation less favorable. So another battalion must go there. There is your problem of what appear to be dual revolts in Dramur. There are unforeseen difficulties in Dereka—but I will not burden you with all of those. The marshal is dealing with Iron Stem and Hyalt, and, once you finish what you must here and in Lyterna, you will handle the difficulties in Dramur."

In Lyterna? What was he supposed to do in Lyterna? Dainyl decided against asking, for the moment. He was also concerned, because the Highest had not been quite truthful about the difficulties, but exactly how, Dainyl could not have said, only that the Talent-sense surrounding those words of the Highest had left him feeling most uneasy.

"Before we deal with Lyterna," the Highest went on, "there are some basic matters of knowledge that are not widely known. I will go through these quickly. Some you may have deduced, but I would be surprised if you know them all." He paused.

Dainyl nodded, waiting.

"For all practical purposes, the pteridons are nearly indestructible, as you may know. What you may not know is that their numbers are fixed.

Once the Dual Scepters have been placed on a world, pteridons as you know them can no longer be created . . ."

Dual Scepters? What Dual Scepters? Should he ask? Would Lystrana know?

". . . Upon occasion, wild translations may manifest themselves as feral and near-brainless pteridons or as other wild Talent-creatures, but they are short-lived and unusable. In the history of all Ifrit worlds, only a handful of pteridons have been destroyed, that is, until the lifeforce of the world on which they have been created itself fails. This does not mean that a pteridon cannot be destroyed, only that no one in recent eras has done so. It is possible. I will not tell you how. It is sufficient for you to know that such destruction is both possible and unlikely . . ."

Dainyl had not known what the Highest had just told him, but after his years as a Myrmidon, he could not have said that he was surprised.

"Second is the matter of Talented landers. As you should know, no lander who has displayed the ability to employ Talent can be allowed to live. What you likely do not know is that landers were designed and bred as more, shall we say, creative versions of indigens when it became apparent that the indigens were not multiplying world lifeforce mass quickly enough. What the designers did not realize until far later was that the creativity traits also allow the possibility of Talent, and that certain landers have demonstrated the potential to be highly Talented. Thus, they must be destroyed, and quickly, once discovered. This policy is never to be revealed or discussed with anyone besides a high alector, or the marshal. Is that clear?"

"Yes, sir."

"That is a matter of survival. Landers breed more rapidly and in far greater numbers, and they would exhaust the world's lifeforce all too quickly."

"What about crossbreeds between landers and indigens?"

"The offspring could carry those traits," the Highest replied. "We do not wish those traits to be spread. Talent may never surface in someone with the traits, and thus cannot be detected, Its emergence in landers cannot be predicted—except in those cases where both parents are Talented landers—and such an instance must never be allowed to occur."

"Yes, sir."

"Another related fact is that the so-called ancients are not all dead."

"Sir?" Dainyl hoped he counterfeited enough surprise.

"They are a dying race, among the last remnants of the life-forms fully native to Acorus. They are seldom encountered or seen, but they have a form of Talent, and they can be dangerous, according to the reports in the sealed archives. I have never seen one, but most of my predecessors have . . ."

Dainyl had the sense and feeling that the highest was skirting the truth about the ancients, if not outright dissembling.

"They prefer high and chill locations, and we believe that a small community lives somewhere on the Aerlal Plateau."

"That's too high for pteridons." It would be uncomfortable, reflected Dainyl, if not close to impossible, for an alector to function well or for long in that cold and altitude.

"Exactly. Should the ancients become a problem, we do have a contingency plan for dealing with them. It would be extraordinarily wasteful of world lifeforce, but such a plan has been developed. If you encounter such an ancient, it is to be reported immediately."

"Sir . . . I don't know if Marshal Shastylt told you, but I have found a tunnel with an ancient archway on one of the peaks in Dramur. There were no tracks there . . ."

"The marshal did report that." The High Alector smiled. "Their artifacts, like our eternastone and other preserved works, do not age. I have seen two of those tunnels with the amberstone arches myself, one in Deforya and one in the Spine of Corus near Passera." He cleared his throat. "The ancients can be most dangerous. Several alectors were killed in the early years after the seedings."

"Do we know how they are dangerous?"

"According to the records, they are accompanied by creatures that can suck the lifeforce from any living thing. They are supposed to be able to draw lifeforce themselves, but this has never been observed. Artifacts found in several places suggest that they are quite skilled. As a matter of fact, our light-torches are based on one of their designs . . ."

That was something else that Dainyl had not known.

"Now . . . there are other matters you will need instruction in, including the use of the Tables. For these, you will be flying to Lyterna on Octdi . . ."

"This Octdi?" Dainyl asked.

"I did say the timing was most inconvenient." The High Alector's voice contained a trace of irritation.

"I apologize, Highest. I was just thinking about the situation in Dramur."

"That seems to have stabilized for the moment, and what you learn in Lyterna may also prove helpful when you return to Dramur."

"Could you tell me what else I might be learning in Lyterna."

The High Alector laughed, warmly and humorously. "If I could explain all that, you wouldn't need to go. I won't say more because I want you to learn from the senior alectors who have studied Acorus far longer than anyone else. You'll find it both interesting and intriguing. That, I can assure you."

After years of experience in the Myrmidons, Dainyl had come to distrust anything a superior described as interesting. That usually meant dangerous, difficult—or both.

The Highest rose. "Congratulations, and my best wishes go with you."

Dainyl stood and bowed slightly in response. "Thank you." What puzzled him more than slightly was that the Highest had sincerely meant his best wishes, unlike some of the other statements he had made, which had been tinged with the feeling of incompleteness, or outright dissembling. The combination suggested Dainyl was being set up to be used as a tool—again.

As he left the chambers of the High Alector of Justice, he just wished he had a better idea of what sort of tool he was and for what purpose he was being shaped and honed.

64

Mykel looked at the bread and cheese in front of him. The cheese was white, hard, and not quite rancid. The bread was stale enough that each bite sprayed crust crumbs. Beside them was a green apple banana. Nothing looked appetizing in the dawn of a Septi morning that was the last in winter, but very little food had looked appealing in recent days.

Mykel was worried. Not because anything had happened, but because nothing had. From the moment Fifteenth Company had started patrolling in Dramur, they had run into problems of one sort or another.

Now, while the locals were no more friendly, no one seemed to pay any attention to the Cadmians, and no one had fired a shot at any of the squads in more than a week. People who had been shooting at Cadmians for months just didn't stop for no reason. Mykel hadn't gotten any answers from Captain Meryst, either, on his question about the crimes committed by prisoners who were missing. He doubted he would. Still, it had been worth a try.

His thoughts drifted back to Rachyla, as they often did. Was it just that he hadn't seen an attractive woman in months? He shook his head. She was striking, but not a raving beauty. There was too much understanding, and too much confidence in those green eyes, for most men to be comfortable with her. Was that why he was drawn to her? He frowned. No. As he'd noted to himself before, there was something else, something that he still couldn't identify, that worried at him even as it attracted him.

His lips curled into a faint smile. Maybe it was just that she was dangerous.

He looked down at his food. With a grimace, he peeled back the banana and took a bite. It was green, and edible, if barely. Out of the corner of his eye he saw Captain Meryst enter the dining shed, look around, and head toward him. Out of courtesy, Mykel stood.

"I'd hoped to find you before you left on patrol. I put in the inquiry along the lines you asked about." Meryst inclined his head. "How did you know?"

Although Mykel had asked about the crimes committed by missing prisoners, he had no idea what the other captain meant. "How did I know what?"

"Almost all of the miners who disappeared in the mine, something like twenty-seven out of the thirty where the justicer had records, were the violent types."

"Sentenced for murder or beating someone up?" asked Mykel.

"Yes. How did you know?" asked Meryst.

"I didn't. I wanted to know if there were any patterns as to why they vanished."

"Almost looks like the other miners just took care of them," suggested the local Cadmian captain. "They would have known."

"It could be," Mykel admitted. "Or it could be that the dangerous ones were the ones most likely to try anything to escape."

"Either way"—Meryst offered a faint smile—"I'd be interested in your thoughts on it sometime."

"I'll have to give it some thought." Mykel could sense that Meryst didn't accept his explanations, but the other captain wasn't going to press, not in the mess shed with rankers and squad leaders passing and listening.

After Meryst departed, Mykel reseated himself and looked at the remains of breakfast.

"It doesn't get any better, sir," called Dravadyl from an adjoining table.

"I could always hope," Mykel retorted.

Several rankers—and Dravadyl—laughed.

When he finished stolidly slogging through the cheese and bread, Mykel rose and made his way to the stable shed, where he saddled the chestnut. He'd planned to ride the mine road patrol with Chyndylt and third squad. He walked the chestnut out into the cool sunlight, looking around for the third squad leader.

"Captain!" called Bhoral. "The overcaptain sent us near-on a full wagon of ammunition. There's a dispatch for you with it." The senior squad leader hurried across the dusty stable yard.

"A wagonful of ammunition?" Mykel took the dispatch from Bhoral's extended hand.

"Must think we'll need it up here."

Mykel was afraid of that. He opened the dispatch envelope and began to read.

Captain Mykel—

Since you left Dramuria, a number of events that bear watching have occurred. Some of the seltyrs west of the Murian Mountains have been training armed horse troopers. In addition, we have just learned that a number of smugglers' craft were sighted sailing around the south cape almost a week ago. The vessels appeared to be heavy-laden. Those vessels may be carrying more rifles and ammunition.

On several occasions, Seventeenth Company has reported heavy fire from the hills on both sides of the road to the west and, at my request, is repositioning closer to Dramuria. Because Fifteenth Company has often been involved in heavy action, I have dispatched an additional ammunition wagon for you. Use the utmost caution in any pursuit actions. Report by messenger if you encounter and observe any large bodies of foot or mounted troopers.

Mykel read through the short missive once again, nodding as he did before handing the dispatch to the senior squad leader. He waited for Bhoral to read it.

After several moments, the older Cadmian looked up. "Overcaptain's worried, and he doesn't worry easy-like."

"Have all the men carry extra rounds on patrol, and find somewhere to put the wagon where it can be guarded. Pull some men from each squad for guards."

"Six men, I'd think, sir. One from each squad, and two from third squad."

Mykel grinned. "Because I'm riding with third?"

"It keeps the numbers equal, sir." The hint of a smile appeared at the corners of the senior squad leader's mouth.

As he rode toward the ammunition wagon, Mykel glanced at the peaks to the west of the camp. Would there be an attack from the west? Was water wet? Did nightwasps sting?

Even after he drew the chestnut beside Chyndylt and waited for the remainder of third squad to form up, Mykel continued to fret, both about Dohark's dispatch and about Meryst's information.

Why would the rock creatures—or even the soarers—have wanted to feed on the most violent prisoners? He couldn't escape the feeling the soarers had a way of knowing which men were dangerous, even if he had no idea how. The soarer's words also echoed in his thoughts—*You must find your talent to see beyond the world . . .* He had no idea how to turn his talent for shooting better into a broader talent, or even where to start—as if he even had the time to do so.

His fingers moved to his belt, and the slit and hidden sheath that held the ancient knife. Had she found him in the rocks above the mine because he carried the knife, or had it been a coincidence? Did it matter?

"Third squad, ready, sir!" Chyndylt announced.

"Head out!" Mykel glanced back at the squad, then at the road ahead.

65

While he waited for the marshal on Septi, Dainyl moved his papers and gear to the study that had been Tyanylt's. That took less than a glass, because Dainyl had never had many personal effects in his study and because everything that had been the former submarshal's had long since been removed. Then he went through the remainder of the reports that had piled up in his absence. For all the pages from the Myrmidon and Cadmian companies across Corus, there was surprisingly little new or detailed information.

An older report addressed one question. The closure of the Cadmian compound in Scien had been postponed until the coming spring when the snows ceased and the weather would be more suited to riding horses along the North Road to Pystra and south to Norda, where the existing compound was being enlarged to take another two companies. There still wasn't any information on why the Scien compound was being closed or the companies relocated to Norda—or about the need for the earlier Myrmidon winter recon flights.

The Twenty-third Cadmian Mounted Rifles from Alustre was being permanently relocated to Lysia. There was no explanation, except that the High Alector of Justice had ordered the move. Why Lysia? Although it was a seaport, it was another compound more than a little out of the way, well southeast of Prosp, and more than eight hundred vingts from Alustre by road.

At the request of the High Alector of Engineering, Seventh Company had sent a squad of Myrmidons to Coren for aerial reconnaissance of the town and forest fires. A battalion of Cadmians was en route from Alustre to deal with the revolt and unrest.

Another revolt? In yet another isolated locale? All Dainyl knew about Coren was that it was one of the few areas authorized for logging and lumbering and that the raw timber was sent down the river to Alustre. Why Seventh Company? The Myrmidons in Lyterna were far closer. Dainyl shook his head. It was winter. Between the storms, the cold, and the height of the mountains in the Spine of Corus, a direct flight was difficult, if not impossible, until late spring, and there were neither Myrmidon nor Cadmian outposts or compounds anywhere close to Coren.

Dainyl kept reading, trying to catch up on everything that he had missed.

Even though he had started right after morning muster, by two glasses past noon, he still had not read half of the reports he had dug up from the files and stacked on his new desk.

The door opened, and the marshal stood there.

Dainyl jumped to his feet. "Sir."

"Sit down, Dainyl." Shastylt closed the study door and settled into the chair across the desk from the submarshal. "I can see you've been busy."

"I was trying to catch up on what had happened." Dainyl reseated himself.

"You never will." The marshal laughed, once, harshly. "I never have, not on everything. I apologize for being late. Matters with the Highest took longer than I had thought. We have to make a quintal presentation to both Duarches next week." Shastylt offered a rueful smile. "Matters are not what we would like, and there are certain to be questions." He gestured toward the stack of reports. "You've found some of them, I'm sure."

"Has anyone discovered anything more about the problems in Hyalt and Dereka?"

"We've isolated the wild Talent in Hyalt, and our Myrmidon squads are closing in. That's likely to be finished in a matter of weeks, if not days. As for Dereka . . . nothing else has vanished, and no one can explain how the skylances vanished."

"What about the missing alectors?"

"They're still missing, with no signs of where they went. They left everything behind." Shastylt shrugged. "They were all on the Table contingent there, but they were off duty."

"First the skylances, and now alectors," mused Dainyl.

"We're leaving that problem to the senior alectors at Lyterna."

Dainyl got the unspoken message. "I was reading the reports. What can you tell me about what happened in Coren?"

The older alector offered a disgusted snort. "It's another instance where the regional alectors haven't paid any attention. So long as the timber came downriver, they thought everything was fine. The locals didn't like the rules on how and when and where to log, and some of them started forest fires . . ."

"So that they'd have even fewer trees to log? And more restrictions?"

"Sometimes, steers don't think. The local indigens killed the patrollers, or most of them, three weeks ago. We finally heard about it last week. The first time there was any sign of trouble, either the Myrmidons or the Cadmians should have been called in. In the end, we'll lose forests and lifeforce mass, a bunch of indigens, and some Cadmian troopers. Much better to see things in advance, the way you're handling Dramur."

Dainyl wasn't so sure he was seeing anything that much in advance in Dramur, or that the marshal and Highest wanted him to do so. "It doesn't always work out that way."

"No, it doesn't. I wish I didn't have to send you to Lyterna right now, but some rules we just can't break, even for convenience. You know, that's one thing that gets people into trouble. They bend the rules because they're pressed or because it's inconvenient, and then the next time it's easier, and before long there aren't any rules, and matters are worse than they would have been if they'd just put up with a little inconvenience." Shastylt smiled.

Dainyl easily sensed the lie. The marshal wanted him in Lyterna. Dainyl doubted that Shastylt was that enthusiastic about Dainyl learning more. Was that because Dainyl had gotten a grasp on what was happening in Dramur? Or because he had been about to, and neither the marshal nor the Highest wanted that to happen? "The rules become easier and easier to ignore."

"Exactly. Principles do matter, and which principles you act on and which you don't are equally important." The marshal stood.

Dainyl rose to his feet as well, waiting.

"Now . . . tomorrow, you'll take your two Myrmidon escorts with you. Fly the southern route, and stop in the way station at Syan. Be sure to enjoy some of the good wine while you're there. Asulet is expecting you in Lyterna, and he'll be the one training you on the use of the Table for travel and providing you with the submarshal's briefing and background. After they've had a day's rest, two if it's been a hard flight, you can dispatch the pteridons back here. You'll be able to return by Table, of course, right to the Hall of Justice. You'll find that to be a great convenience at times." Shastylt smiled wryly. "Only at times. We still have to deal with problems in places like Dramur and Iron Stem. Now . . . if you'll excuse me, I need to prepare some calculations."

"Yes, sir."

After the study door closed, Dainyl stood behind his desk, motionless, thinking.

66

"Warm afternoon, sir," said Chyndylt, from where he rode beside Mykel.

"Like summer in Faitel," replied Mykel. "Hate to think what summer here will be like."

The captain and third squad rode downhill, a half vingt ahead of the prisoners returning to the mine compound. The troopers had their rifles ready, if casually.

"Maybe they'll be sending us back by then."

"Not a chance."

"Haven't seen anything here today."

"No." Mykel doubted they would see many more of the escaped miners who had been sniping. They couldn't have been that numerous to begin with, and Fifteenth Company had killed close to a score. He was far more worried by armed horse companies from the west. While Fifteenth Company was more than a match for any single company raised in Dramur, Third Battalion was down to four companies, all understrength. He'd taken third squad back out earlier than usual for the afternoon road sweep, and had them ride down toward Dramuria for half a vingt before heading back past the camp to the mine. He hadn't seen any signs of riders, but that only meant that no one was riding at that moment—or not riding swiftly.

Mykel cocked his head. He'd heard something ahead, from near the mining camp. It might have been horses, or the report of a rifle. Yet it was early for the other squads to be returning from their various patrols.

"Eyes sharp!" he called out.

They rode another two hundred yards southward along the graystone road. Mykel could sense something was not as it should have been. He studied the walls of the prisoners' camp. The outer gates, which should have been open for the returning captives, were closed.

Then, as he watched, a line of riders in blue uniforms rode toward the walls, firing at the guard towers. The Cadmian guards fired back. Several of the blue-clad riders twisted in their saddles, and one slowly pitched back over the rear of his mount.

Mykel turned in the saddle. "Third squad! Close up on me!" As he spoke, he could see the attackers re-forming. It wouldn't be long before they started up the road toward third squad.

"We'll keep riding," he told Chyndylt. If third squad attempted to retreat, they'd end up pinned against the stockade at the mine. He doubted they could get through the prisoners, in any case. "Send back a scout to get as many of the local Cadmians up here as you can. We'll take the west side. Let them have the east."

"Yes, sir!"

"Third squad! Quick trot to the level flat ahead!"

Mykel kept watching the riders below, swirling under the camp walls, with an occasional rider being picked off by the tower Cadmians.

A horn sounded a triplet, then a second.

The swirling mass of blue coalesced into a rough formation.

"Third squad! Halt!" Mykel reined up on the flatter section of the mine road, below which was a slight incline down to the mining camp. The attackers would have to climb the rise, such as it was, but it was the best that he could manage.

The attackers began a charge, at close to a full gallop.

"Firing line! On the oblique!" Mykel barked out. "Bring down the lead mounts!"

His own rifle was up even before he had finished shouting out the commands. He forced himself to sight on the mount of one of the first riders in blue, squeezing the trigger with an even pressure, and willing the shot home.

Crack!

The lead mount lurched, then went down, at enough of an angle that the mount to the left also fell.

Mykel targeted another mount, more to one side, and fired, twice, before that horse stumbled and collapsed.

The continuing fire of the Cadmian rifles began to take a toll, and the blue-clad riders slowed behind a mass of fallen mounts and men caught in the space between the road walls.

To his left, Mykel saw Meryst and his rankers also laying down a curtain of fire. The attackers tried to bring their rifles to bear, but seemed hampered by their numbers and a lack of a clear formation and leadership.

As he reloaded, Mykel glanced back over his shoulder. A good ten prisoners, five pairs, each pair linked by chains, were running down the center of the road, between third squad and the local Cadmians, taking advantage of the local Cadmian troopers' concentration on repelling the attack of blue-clad riders.

"Save us! Save us!" The prisoners raced toward where the attacking horsemen had broken into groups behind all the fallen men and mounts.

A squad leader wheeled his mount toward the prisoners, then reined up and aimed his rifle over the fallen men and mounts. The first shot took the leading prisoner through the chest, and he sprawled onto the road dragging down the man chained to him.

More shots filled the space between the road walls. Several more prisoners went down.

A horn sounded twin doublets, twice.

The blue mass of riders seemed to swirl, then turn and retreat downhill.

Mykel fired the last shots in his rifle, watching as another trooper in blue sagged in the saddle, and as the rider beside the wounded man grabbed the reins and guided the disabled man's mount down the road toward Dramuria.

A scattering of shots continued, chasing the attackers downhill toward and past the walls of the mining prison camp. Two of the trailing riders were hit, one slumping over his mount's neck, the other flying backward and sideways off his horse, his body being jerked along for a good ten yards by the single boot caught in the stirrups before he struck the stones, unmoving.

The attackers had close to two companies, although it had been hard to tell exactly because they had not kept in much of a formation or in any real order.

"Cease fire!" he ordered, although most of the firing had died away. "Reload and hold!"

From the other side of the road, Meryst echoed the command.

Mykel glanced downhill at the wounded and dead prisoners sprawled across the graystones of the road. He looked sideways across a space of four yards at the other captain, catching Meryst's eyes. "The prisoners? Why did they shoot them?"

"The western seltyrs don't believe that a man can change," replied Meryst. "Once he has become tainted with evil, he can only be a slave or dead."

"So they shot the prisoners?"

"Slaves and prisoners cannot be allowed to escape."

Mykel winced. He looked at the dead mounts, and dead and wounded attackers strewn on the road. Then he glanced back around him. There were at least three empty saddles from those among third squad. Only three? That was in itself amazing, or a testament to the poor shooting of the attackers.

Where had the blue riders come from? Had they merely evaded Seventeenth Company? Or had they overwhelmed it?

67

After a late supper, and well after Sentya and Zistele had gone to bed—and to sleep—Lystrana and Dainyl sat in the darkened sitting room, each in an upholstered chair with a square table set in the corner between them. Lystrana had turned off the light-torches earlier. With their Talent, they needed little light to see. Each held a goblet of golden brandy.

"Neither the marshal nor the Highest want me back in Dramur anytime soon. That's clear." Dainyl fingered his chin, too square compared to that of most alectors.

"They're afraid that you'll put a stop to whatever they have in mind."

"They don't want me crossing them, the way Tyanylt did? Have you ever found out any more about that?"

"No. It's as though he never existed." She raised her eyebrow. "That's the way they have always dealt with those who will not follow their plans. Would you expect otherwise?"

"No. One could hope . . . but no."

"Some matters do not change." Lystrana lifted her goblet and sniffed the brandy. "This is good."

"Better than what Kylana remembers of Ifryn," replied Dainyl sardonically. "I wish that I could figure out what they have in mind. They want an armed revolt. What I don't understand is why. It's not merely preempting trouble. Things wouldn't have gotten this far for decades. Do you believe they're thinking that much ahead?"

Lystrana laughed. "They might be, but that doesn't explain why they don't tell you. There's something else." Her husky voice died away before she spoke again. "All of these revolts, these problems, are all in out-of-the-way places—Dramur, Hyalt, Iron Stem . . . Coren . . ."

"Coren? I asked the marshal. He said that the locals were protesting the logging rules and setting fires, and that it was weeks before word got to Elcien. What happened?"

"Someone started setting fires in the forests there last fall. Local patrollers began tracing the arsonists. Last month, there was another fire. They tracked the arsonists through the snow. The patrollers never came back. Another set of patrollers found blood on the snow, but no bodies. Three of them were shot and killed. One escaped. When he got back to Coren, he found that patroller headquarters had been blown up. The whole town revolted. It took weeks to get word back because the patroller had to hide until he could flag down a sandoxen coach."

"Why did the locals revolt?"

"What the marshal said was essentially right. The lifeforce alectors in Lyterna calculate how much should be logged on what schedule. There's some room for local needs and such, but some loggers always want more coins. Late last harvest they started logging more trees and sending them downriver in rafts. Somewhere west of Vysta, in the south part of the Mitt Hills, on the north side of the river, a trader opened a mill and began selling timber and planks to locals there. He wasn't paying his tariffs, and he was dumping all the wastes into the stream that drained into the river. He was caught and executed in Novem. That was when the fires started."

Dainyl shook his head. "Always the golds." He sipped his brandy.

"We all have our weaknesses, dearest."

"Maybe whatever this Asulet tells me when I get to Lyterna will make things clear." Dainyl had his doubts that any alector suggested by Shastylt would be of much help in figuring out what was behind the mess in Dramur.

"I checked the records. Asulet has been a senior alector in lifeforce management for more than a hundred years. It could be longer, but I'd have to get a seal-warrant to open the archives."

"Lifeforce management? What does that have to do with the Myrmidons?" Dainyl thought for a moment. "The Highest seemed to think it was important. He was dissembling about the ancient ones—the soarers—but not about that."

"They're keeping something about the ancient ones hidden. I checked again. There aren't any records anywhere about them. There's not a single real fact or a single specific location where one was sighted, or where any ruins or artifacts have been found."

"That's because they're more powerful than anyone wants to admit."

"I'd say it's because they're intelligent, and what we're doing is causing them to die out."

"There's no question they're intelligent," replied Dainyl. "You think that our management of lifeforce mass is causing them to die out?"

"They were already dying out. There were ruins when the first alectors arrived. If we'd had any conflicts with them, there would have been records of fights, legends, that sort of thing."

"But we're making Acorus warmer. If they need the cold . . ."

"Then we're causing them to die out," Lystrana said. "But if we don't, then what do we do when the lifeforce on Ifryn is gone?"

They sat in silence for several moments.

"Do you think the marshal and your Highest know you have more Talent than you've shown?" Lystrana finally broke the silence.

"I don't think so. What do you think?"

"I think that, if they knew, you'd still be a colonel—or requested to resign."

"Or dead?"

She nodded, her face somber.

"I'll have to be most careful." He paused, then added, "Tell me about the Dual Scepters."

Lystrana looked up, both concerned and surprised. "Who—"

"The Highest. He said that pteridons were created here, but more couldn't be once the Dual Scepters were placed."

"I didn't know that. I know that the Dual Scepters are somewhere in Corus in different places, that they have something to do with why the Tables work, and that without them we couldn't live here, because they're key to the link to Ifryn. Every time I've asked or hinted to know more . . . no one will say anything."

Dainyl nodded, slowly. "What about Table travel? How does it work?"

Lystrana raised an eyebrow.

"That's one reason why they're sending me to Lyterna. I'm supposed to be briefed on things that only the submarshal and the marshal—and I suppose the Highest—know, and I'm to be taught how to use the Table to travel."

"It's not that hard. They make it seem—" Lystrana stopped. "I shouldn't say that. If you can concentrate on the location vectors, it's very easy. If you can't, you'll die in the translation tubes or turn into a wild translation—and die very quickly thereafter."

"What are location vectors?"

"When you step onto a Table, you drop into darkness, and you see with Talent, not with your eyes. Your mind and Talent are what guide you; but wherever there's a Table, there's a location vector. To me, they look like long triangles, arrowheads. The one for Tempre is blue. The one for Elcien is white, edged with purple. Dereka is golden red."

"Is there any reason for the colors?"

"If there is, I don't know what it is," replied Lystrana. "Beyond identifying the location of the Table, that is."

"How do you use your mind and Talent?"

"It's something that you have to feel. I don't think you'll have to worry."

Dainyl could tell she was concerned. "Then why are you worried?"

"You've learned too much. You couldn't have Talent-read that when we were married."

"Why are you worried?" Dainyl asked again.

"Because . . . because you *should* do well with the Tables . . . but you never know. When I first tried it, I almost froze in the blackness. It was days before I felt warm. Clanysta was far more Talented than I was, but she stepped into a Table and never reappeared."

"Why do I have to learn in Lyterna?"

"You could learn anywhere there's a Table. I'd wager your Highest has several reasons." She took another sip of brandy and shifted in the chair so that she was facing Dainyl directly.

"He wants me out of the way. It gives him a way to keep me there longer. Someone else can teach me, and if I fail, it's not on his head."

"That covers it, I'd say."

"A revolt in Dramur . . ." mused Dainyl once more. "But why?"

"We won't solve that mystery tonight, dearest." Lystrana set down the goblet and rose, stretching sensually. "It's not too late, and you are leaving tomorrow."

Dainyl left his goblet on the table and stood, taking her outstretched hand.

68

Octdi morning dawned cloudy, with a cold drizzle sifting out of low-lying clouds, a day more reminiscent of midwinter than of the spring beginning on the coming Londi. The night before had been long. Mykel had fretted about Fifteenth Company's other squads, but all returned safely, and none but third squad had taken fire. The raiders had killed four troopers from third squad and wounded two others. Both of the wounded men looked to recover, for which Mykel was thankful.

According to Meryst, there had been thirty-three dead rebel troopers on the road, which was amazing given that the deaths had been caused by one squad and the Cadmian tower guards. Still, counting the dead and wounded, Fifteenth Company was less than four-fifths of authorized strength. It had been whittled away, man by man.

After the quick and fierce battle the night before, the night had been quiet, but Mykel still had a slight headache when he woke. Even before he had eaten, he'd sent out scouts. Then he went to the mess shack. The fried bananas and salted fried fish presented for breakfast didn't help either the headache or his mood. As he sat at the plank table in the mess shed, he forced himself to eat. Just as Mykel was finishing the final chunk of banana—he wanted the last taste to be other than fish, Meryst slipped onto the bench opposite him.

"What do you plan, Captain?"

"We'll be scouting and protecting the approaches to the camp. Fifteenth Company will not be doing any more patrols on the road to the mine. Have you seen riders in that blue before?"

"Not riders, but the blue is the color of the west."

Rachyla had been right, Mykel reflected, hoping she was still safe and healthy. He forced his thoughts back to the problem at hand. "That means there will be more attacks and troopers."

"Why do you say that?"

"You didn't tell me that it was the color of a particular seltyr or house or grower, but of the west. I'd wager that all the western seltyrs have adopted the blue. Probably all the ones in the east have their men in the green."

"That is the eastern color," Meryst admitted.

"That's all we need, a war between the east and the west, with Myrmidons flying everywhere."

"You had not heard? The Myrmidon colonel and his fliers left almost a week ago. They have not returned."

"That's even worse." Mykel could imagine the seltyrs deciding to attack the Cadmians—and each other—in the absence of the Myrmidons' flame lances. "Why would he leave now?"

"He did not look happy, I understand. He had received a dispatch from one of his fliers, and he left the next morning."

"That sounds like trouble somewhere else. Worse trouble." Mykel eased his way off the bench. "I need to see what my scouts have found out. I'd rather not be caught by surprise."

"You think they will attack here again?"

Mykel suspected that the attack had been to keep Fifteenth Company pinned down so that the attackers could move more freely. "I don't know. That's why I sent out scouts."

"You think they will stay that close?" Meryst's tone conveyed disbelief.

"We'll have to see." Mykel offered a smile before heading for the stable sheds.

Bhoral was waiting, lines of worry creasing his forehead. "No one's back yet, sir,"

"I didn't think they'd be. We need to go over some maps."

"You have something in mind, sir?"

"I do, but I want to see what the scouts find out." Mykel lifted his hand to push back too-long hair from his forehead, and thought the better of it as his shoulder began to twinge. Using his rifle the day before hadn't helped with the healing. He unrolled the crude map and pointed. "Here we are, and here's the road from the west. It's a good five vingts toward Dramuria from here. That's the only quick way that they can bring horse troopers in—or out. The road south from here is open for about half a vingt, to where the lanes split off . . ."

Bhoral listened as Mykel explained.

Then they waited another glass before the first scouts returned. Mykel had Bhoral gather the squad leaders in the stable shed—the only real space away from the Cadmian rankers.

Once scouts and squad leaders were assembled, Mykel turned to Sendyl, the first squad scout. "What did you find?"

"There's a squad, and they're about a vingt and a half toward Dramuria, almost a vingt past the crossroads on the east side of the road," reported Sendyl. "Small hill there, and they were hiding in a woodlot."

"Did they see you?"

"Afraid they did, sir. Took a couple of shots afore I got under the trees where they couldn't see me. That's when I sneaked through one of those nut plantations. I got close enough to get a better look. They were mostly just back of the first lines of trees. I circled to the south side of the hill. No one over there, and the ground's real open there, just poor grazing land. I had to come back the way I came so as they wouldn't see me leaving."

Mykel nodded, then looked to the second squad scout. "Gerant?"

"Went back over the side roads where the smaller growers are, along where Polynt . . . you know, sir. Anyway, there was a little rain there last night. Not a sign of riders, or even carts."

"Dhozynt?"

"Nothing to the north of the mine, sir."

Neither of the other two scouts had seen any other signs of large bodies of riders.

Mykel cleared his throat. "That squad to the south seems to be the only one nearby. They're there to keep us here and to report if we move." Mykel smiled. "We don't want them letting anyone know, now, do we?"

Several of the scouts grinned back at the captain.

Mykel looked to the five squad leaders. "I've got some maps here, and we need to be going over what we'll be doing this afternoon." He spread the map on an old plank wedged into a space between two wall boards, scarcely the best of map tables, but it would do to outline what he had in mind. The first step would be easy. After that, it got harder . . . much harder.

A glass past midmorning, Fifteenth Company formed up just inside the outer walls of the mining camp. Mykel rode back along the column to fifth squad, reining up opposite Vhanyr.

"Sir?" asked the fifth squad leader.

"Any last questions?"

"No, sir. Once we split at the crossroads, we're to start inspecting each side of the road, as if we're searching for something. We're to stay out of range until we hear you attack. Then we're to move up and keep any of the rebels from escaping."

"Good. I meant it about staying out of rifle range." Mykel didn't need to lose any more men when he didn't have to.

"Yes, sir." Vhanyr couldn't quite keep the trace of a smile from the corners of his mouth.

As he rode back to the front of the company, Mykel almost laughed. He still occasionally made statements that were overobvious. Any good squad leader—and Vhanyr was good—wasn't about to disobey orders to stay away from sniper fire.

"Company's ready, sir!" announced Bhoral.

Mykel nodded. "Let's go."

"Fifteenth Company! Forward!"

Mykel rode alongside Gendsyr at the head of Fifteenth Company. Bhoral dropped back to ride with third squad. Not for the first time, Mykel just hoped that he'd judged what lay before them correctly. Almost absently, the fingers of his free hand dropped to his belt and the slot that held the soarers' dagger. Matters had indeed gotten steadily worse since he'd been given the ancient weapon.

Should he discard it? A tight smile crossed his lips. Somehow, that would be worse. Either the weapon meant nothing, in which case it was stupid to get rid of it, or what the chandler had said was right. In the second instance, it was likely that discarding the weapon would cause him even worse problems.

Then . . . he could just be justifying keeping it. He shook his head. Arguing with himself over something like that was courting madness. He put the miniature dagger out of this mind and looked down the stone-paved road, clear of any riders or wagons.

By the time the two scouts reached the crossroads, where lanes led off to both the east and west, Mykel could sense eyes on the company. He forced himself not to look in the direction of the hill. Not too often, anyway.

"Fifteenth Company! Left turn! At the crossroads!" he called out just before he and Gendsyr neared the two clay lanes.

The lane to the west almost immediately turned southwest and followed a dry streambed. The one to the east ran straight for several hundred yards between a field of sunbeans on the left and an overgrown area on the south side, which might once have been a field but now sported scattered bushes and occasional trees, none higher than a horse's ears. After about a quarter vingt, the lane turned back to the northeast, slowly descending through various scattered holdings, with which Mykel and Fifteenth Company had become all too familiar.

They weren't going to follow the lane that far, but ride back south, and circle through a woodlot back toward the hill on which the seltyr's squad had been posted. The trees would keep them from sight until they were almost at the base of the hill.

Once he reached the woodlot, Mykel eased his mount to the side of the lane and looked back over his shoulder. Vhanyr and fifth squad had reined up and were beginning to study the shoulders of the main road, as well as the first ten yards of the west lane.

Mykel urged the chestnut forward until he was riding with the scouts. After another three hundred yards or so, he turned his mount onto a rutted track to the right side of the road, just between a tumbledown stone wall and the woodlot. On the east side was an orchard of casurans, perhaps the sorriest-looking nut trees Mykel had seen. Brown-splotched yellowing leaves drooped from sagging branches, and a bitter odor seeped from the neglected orchard.

". . . smells like shit . . ."

". . . worse . . ."

"Quiet riding," hissed Gendsyr.

Almost a quarter glass passed before the track petered out into a grassy oval perhaps two hundred yards by a hundred and fifty. Mykel looked to the southwest, where a wooded hill offered a gentle rise, with little undergrowth. From what the scouts had observed, anyone stationed on the northwest side of the hill in a position to observe the road would have trouble seeing the eastern and southeastern sides of the hill. A squad couldn't afford to post too many sentries in the rear, and one or two couldn't stop an attack.

"First squad, on me," he ordered in a low voice.

First squad was to ride up the northeast side of the slope, as quietly as possible until the blue troopers reacted. Second squad was to take the clearer southeast side, and third squad was to take the southwest side, holding back halfway up the slope. Bhoral and fourth squad were to hang back at the base of the slope, somewhere on the south side, to plug any gaps or reinforce as necessary. The plan of attack was simple.

Mykel recalled all too vividly a statement his father had made. Olent had finally finished the last stones of a mosaic in the entry foyer of the family dwelling. Mykel had only been twelve, and he'd suggested that the design was nice, but simple.

"Simple doesn't mean easy," Olent had said quietly.

The words had stayed with Mykel. This time, he just hoped that his simple plan wasn't too difficult to carry out.

The woodlot trees were mostly older short-needled pines, and the branches didn't really begin until they were head high. The trees were thick enough that it was hard to see more than ten yards ahead. That worked for and against Fifteenth Company.

Halfway up, he turned in the saddle. "Rifles ready. Pass it back! Spread to the left!"

The trailing troopers swung to the left, moving more quickly, while Mykel slowed, until he had a line abreast moving through the trees. He judged that they were less than a hundred yards from the top of the rise when he heard the first shout.

"Riders! Coming up the back of the hill! Riders!"

Mykel would have liked to move more quickly, but the trees were close enough together that the best he could do was a fast walk. Even so, he had ridden at least another fifty yards before he heard the first shot from the west. He kept riding, his rifle out.

Ahead, Mykel saw a blue uniform and fired, trying to *will* the bullet to its target. Then, to his right, he glimpsed another rebel—on foot. He immediately fired two shots, concentrating on the second one. He thought the man went down. Several bullets flew through the branches above his head, and short gray-green needles fell around him. He rode around a fallen pine, one that someone had started to trim, and caught sight of another rebel rider a good twenty yards ahead. He fired, and the man slumped. Mykel had the feeling that someone else had shot him.

From that moment, Mykel lost track. The only thing keeping the attack from turning into a melee where Cadmians accidentally shot Cadmians was the bright blue tunics of the rebels.

Mykel finally reined up in a small clearing where the rebels had apparently been waiting. There were still two mounts tied to pine trees. Four bodies in blue were crumpled in various places around the trees at the edge of the clearing. Alendyr and several of his men were herding two prisoners toward Mykel. Bhoral and several rankers from third squad appeared out of the trees to the left of the prisoners.

"Sir!" called Alendyr. "Caught these two trying to sneak down the hillside."

Mykel rode toward them and reined up. "What company are you? Who's in charge?"

"That was Alawart. You killed him."

"He was the squad leader?"

"Yes."

"Yes, sir!" snapped Bhoral, raising his rifle and pointing it at the captive's midsection.

"Yes, sir!" squeaked the young man, barely more than a youth.

"Who was over him?"

"That was the captain. Captain Mahwalt. He is Seltyr Ghondjyr's nephew." The youthful captive looked at Bhoral, and added quickly, "Sir."

"Does the seltyr have another company besides yours?"

"No, sir. Each seltyr has one company, except Seltyr Anatoljyr. He has two."

"How many seltyrs are there west of the mountains."

"I don't know . . . sir. Ten, fifteen."

Mykel guessed those numbers were high, but he had no way to tell. "Did Captain Mahwalt say when he'd be back?"

"He said we were to stay for two days, then ride south to the road to the west."

"Tonight, then, that was when you were to meet them there?"

The youthful trooper shrugged helplessly.

Mykel turned to the second ranker, with scratches across his face and cheek and blood running along his jawline. The slight wounds looked to have come from contact with pine trees, rather than weapons. "You. How many companies came over the mountains?"

"I don't know, sir. We rode with Seltyr Hamadjyr's men. There weren't any others."

"Did you attack or fight any other Cadmians?"

"No, sir. We heard shots to the north, but the captain said we weren't going there . . . sir."

"How many other companies are there in the west?"

"I don't know, sir."

Mykel kept questioning, but got no better answers. Abruptly, he glanced around the small clearing on the northwest side of the low hill. He could only see a score of his troopers. While he didn't sense anything nearby, nor could he see any troopers on the mine road, his men shouldn't be spread through the trees longer than necessary. He turned to Bhoral. "Get everyone re-formed back on the road. We're spread all over the place here."

"Yes, sir." Bhoral turned his mount. "Re-form on the road! By squads! Pass it on!"

Mykel picked his way through the trees, occasionally seeing a sprawled body in the brilliant blue tunic of the western seltyrs. Once they were back on the road, and waiting for third and fourth squads to rejoin them, Mykel looked up at the hill, then southeast.

"What do you think, sir?" asked Bhoral. "About what we should do next?"

"We ought to give this Captain Mahwalt a taste of his own tactics. They still don't shoot that well. It might be best to make sure that they don't get much more practice. First, we need to see what our own losses were and how many extra mounts and prisoners we have."

"Best I could figure, we killed maybe fifteen of theirs, could have been eighteen." Bhoral paused. "Looks like they got the prisoners over there. I'll be right back, sir."

With the midday sun beating down on him, Mykel felt almost uncomfortably warm as he surveyed the road from a high point on the shoulder. The only figures he saw were the Cadmians and their prisoners.

The squads were almost re-formed when Bhoral rode back and reined up beside Mykel. "Six prisoners, sir, and eleven mounts. Some of them look pretty fair."

"We'll keep the best ones for spares. You choose." Mykel knew that Bhoral was a far better judge of horses than he was.

"Yes, sir."

Mykel turned the chestnut, then raised his voice. "Squad leaders! Forward and report!"

Within moments, the five squad leaders reined up opposite Mykel and Bhoral.

"Report, by squads," Mykel ordered.

"First squad, two wounded."

"Second squad, one wounded."

Third, fourth, and fifth squads had no casualties, and Mykel looked across the faces of his squad leaders. "We'll ride back to the camp. We'll leave the wounded and the prisoners. The local Cadmians can handle them. They've had practice. Have the men eat—quickly—and water their mounts and pack their gear. Whatever happens this afternoon, we'll be heading back to the compound in Dramuria afterward. When we leave, we'll ride south to see if we can set up an ambush for the rebels where the western road turns off the mine road. From what I remember, there's high ground to the southwest, but we'll see what looks best after the scouts report." He paused. "That's all. Dismissed to your squads."

"Yes, sir," came the response.

Mykel waited until the squad leaders rejoined their men, then nodded to Bhoral.

"Company! Forward!"

Mykel kept glancing back over his shoulder as he rode back up the gentle incline of the road toward the mining camp. He saw nothing but his own company and the faint dust raised by its mounts.

69

Hazy high clouds, silvery against the silver-green sky, were drifting in from the west by the time Fifteenth Company headed south, but the air was so still that the early afternoon seemed more like late spring than late winter. As Mykel rode down the mine highway toward Dramuria, he glanced to his left, at the low, wooded hill that had been the site of the morning's skirmish.

He shifted his weight in the saddle, conscious of the lingering soreness in his shoulder, soreness that hadn't been helped by using a rifle. The attack on the seltyr's squad had left a bad taste in his mouth. Mykel certainly didn't want his men killed, but it bothered him that the rebels were sending out troopers so poorly trained and led. It was a waste of men because nothing would change, except that the Cadmians would lose some troopers, and, if all the rebels were so inept, they'd lose most of theirs.

He had more than a few questions. Who had picked out uniforms of such a bright blue that they stood out in any terrain? The maroon and gray of the Cadmians might not have blended in all settings, but the Cadmian colors didn't turn every man into a target. Why were the seltyr's men so poorly trained? Even the worst of the Reillies had fought far better—and they had only had crossbows and handmade single-shot long rifles. The seltyrs had more men and golds—and good contraband weapons. So why were their troopers so ineffective?

Mykel had drafted a brief report on what had happened in the past two days and given it to Captain Benjyr for dispatch back to Dohark with Benjyr's messengers. He'd also made arrangements for the wounded men—since none of the wounds appeared life-threatening—to accompany the local Cadmians returning to the compound in Dramuria. With his own company being whittled away man by man, Mykel wasn't about to spare even a single trooper for a message run when he could have someone else deliver it.

The five-vingt ride to the junction took more than a glass, without pushing, and three of the four scouts joined Mykel a good two hundred yards north of where the packed dirt road to the west branched off from the paved mine road.

"Jasakyt's still investigating that low bluff over to the west, there," offered Dhozynt. "Can't ride up it from this side, but he thought there might be a way up from behind."

Mykel's eyes followed the gesture of the fifth squad's scout. The bluff wasn't high, no more than two and a half yards, but it was almost vertical, and the red dirt and sand section facing the road extended more than a hundred yards from east to west. The eastern end dropped into a small area of wooded and marshy ground, not quite a small swamp, fed by the rivulet that ran between the road and the bluff. The western end merged with a hillside covered with patches of brush olives. On the south side of the western road, right at the junction, was a wooded area that rose slowly to the southwest, behind and to the east of the marshy ground. Low bushes and heavier undergrowth began within a few yards of the road.

The captain nodded and looked to his right, at the area on the north side of the western road, gently rolling fields that had been recently tilled. There was no cover there.

Jasakyt appeared, riding onto the road from behind a second hill, farther to the west.

"Company, halt!" Mykel ordered. He wanted no additional hoofprints on the western road until he'd heard from Jasakyt. While he waited for the last scout to reach him, he might as well assemble those he needed. "Squad leaders! Scouts!"

Vhanyr had just joined the group when Jasakyt rode up and reined in his mount. The scout had a broad smile.

"I take it that bluff is a good ambush point," Mykel said dryly.

"Yes, sir. You can get there two ways, and neither leaves much in the way of tracks. Could put the whole company up there, and no one could see 'em from here on the road."

"Do you know of a better place?" Mykel addressed the other three scouts.

"The orchard there'd be better for mounts," said Sendyl, "but you'd be downhill and riding up. Wouldn't want that."

Dhozynt shook his head. So did Gerant.

Mykel surveyed the squad leaders. "We'll set up here, and wait to see what happens. Squads two, three, and four will take positions on foot—at the top of that bluff. Squad one will be out of sight in the woods to protect our east flank." Mykel looked at Gendsyr. "Your men are not to move out or open fire until after their companies turn westward, and not before the squads on the bluff fire. If the rebels head north, we'll follow them until the right time to attack. If they turn west, keep your men under cover when you open fire."

"Yes, sir."

"Vhanyr, fifth squad will cover the west flank. You'll need to keep to the high ground. Don't open fire unless you're attacked, or until you get specific orders from me. Scouts—Sendyl, you head south along the mine road toward Dramuria. When you see the rebels coming, I want you to head back here early enough that they can't see you."

Mykel turned to the second squad scout. "Gerant, you'll have to ride east. I don't want to be surprised if they decide to head for the western road though those orchards over there. Watch the lanes and trails there. Jasakyt, you head west, say two vingts, just in case there might be more rebels riding this way. Dhozynt, you get to go back the way we came . . ." As he outlined his plan, Mykel could only hope that what he learned from the captives was accurate.

In less than half a glass, Fifteenth Company was in position. The stillness of the early afternoon was replaced by a light wind out of the northwest. From where he waited, hidden behind the low ridge of the bluff, Mykel looked northward. The clouds were slowly thickening.

His strategy was simple enough—use the bluff as a point from which his men could rake the rebels. The hill slope facing the road was steep enough that riders would find it difficult to climb, especially in the face of heavy fire. If necessary, Mykel's men could withdraw directly down the more gentle slope to the south.

Mykel kept looking at the clouds, listening for scouts or horses, but the afternoon was still, except for the low murmurs of the troopers, and the occasional *chuff* of a mount tethered downhill in the trees.

"You think the western seltyrs have ten companies over here?" Bhoral asked after a time.

"Who really knows?" Mykel had no doubts they had that many . . . somewhere.

One glass passed, then another. During that time, Mykel made several inspections, walking down through the wooded area to see Gendsyr and first squad, and back to the west to check with Vhanyr. The sun was touching the peaks of the Murian Mountains, and Mykel was wondering when he should call off the ambush and start the ride southward. At that moment, Sendyl rode up out of the woods from below and east toward Mykel. The captain eased out of his sitting position and hurried downhill to where the scout waited. Bhoral was close behind.

"There's two companies coming," Sendyl announced. "Riding up the road from Dramuria plain as you please."

"Coming up from Dramuria? There's no pursuit?"

"No, sir. But there's smoke down south. Not so far as Dramuria, but this side of the bridge on the north of the town."

"Do they have scouts out ahead?"

"No, sir. Outriders maybe two hundred yards forward of the van."

"How long before they get here?"

"A little more than half a glass, I'd judge."

"We'll be ready. You take a position as far south as you can and still stay under cover."

"Yes, sir."

As Sendyl headed back downhill, Bhoral cleared his throat.

Mykel turned to the senior squad leader. "What do you think?"

"I don't like it, sir. No scouts, no supply wagons, and they're riding around shooting and burning things?"

"You think they're a diversion? Some sort of setup?"

Bhoral shook his head. "Don't know, sir. Suppose they could be that stupid, but . . . ?"

"That's one reason why we're trying it this way. Even if there are more rebels coming from somewhere, we've got a good position. We've also got scouts out in other directions."

"Good thing, sir."

"If you'd go tell fifth squad, now."

"Yes, sir."

Mykel walked toward Alendyr. The squad leader looked up.

"Rebels headed this way. Half a glass. Keep it quiet."

By the time Mykel had passed the word to Chyndylt and Dravadyl, made a last quick inspection of the three squads, and returned to the position he'd chosen for himself roughly in the middle of the bluff, a quarter glass had passed.

Shortly, Bhoral reappeared. "Sir?"

"Why don't you take the west end, so that you can send out fifth squad, if necessary?" Mykel left unsaid that they wouldn't be in the same place.

"Let me know if things change." Bhoral hurried back to the west.

Mykel had picked a spot on the bluff behind a low scrubby pine, where he could look through the branches and survey the road without being seen by the riders. He stretched out on the ground, behind and under the pine, and began to watch and wait.

No riders appeared, and a rock dug into the front of his thigh. Carefully, quietly, he eased himself slightly to the side. The wind began to moan, picking up in intensity, into a brisk breeze. Mykel kept watching and, finally, two outriders in the brilliant blue of the rebels turned off the mining road and rode westward. Just when the outriders were almost below Mykel, the first riders of the main body turned. They had ridden no more than thirty yards, when someone called an order, and the outriders and the rest of the riders halted—scarcely in the best position for Fifteenth Company to attack.

Mykel hoped that none of his men would fire, not until the rebels moved farther into firing range. Several riders galloped northward along the mining road, but the rebel force did not move. Mykel had no way of knowing how far to the south it stretched, since all he could see was perhaps thirty riders.

At least a quarter glass more passed . . . and another. The day darkened, if without shadows, as the clouds to the north and west obscured the sun. Finally, a set of horn signals echoed through the afternoon, and the outriders urged their mounts forward.

"Ready," he murmured . . . "pass it along . . . quietly."

"Ready . . ."

As the riders in the van neared, Mykel watched closely, trying to pick out the captain of the first company. Finally, he could see a taller man with insignia on his tunic collar, and a silver shoulder braid—the kind Cadmians only wore on ceremonial occasions or in staff capacities at headquarters. He sighted, waiting, until the middle of the company was opposite him.

"Fire!" Mykel concentrated on the captain, aiming and willing the bullet toward the target. His shot was true, and the officer sagged, then slumped out of the saddle.

The shots of the first volley were nearly simultaneous, and deadly. Bluecoats were falling and flailing everywhere.

Mykel looked for a squad leader, but couldn't find one. So he just kept seeking clear shots. By the time he reloaded, a good third of the leading rebel company was down, either wounded or dead, and the remaining riders were still half-milling around. Only one or two of the riders on the road even seemed to know from where the shots were coming.

After reloading, Mykel fired one more shot.

Thump! Needles cascaded around him. A sharp pain shot along the side of his neck just behind his ear, then subsided.

Mykel flattened himself and touched his neck. He couldn't feel anything, except a fragment of wood—a long splinter. He pulled it out, and raised his rifle again, running through another magazine, then reloading.

Horns sounded, the handful of riders still in their saddles turned their mounts and dashed toward the mining road. There, the riders of the second bluecoat company were galloping northward, toward the mine. He frowned as he saw them slow, close to a vingt farther north, and turn westward, moving through the fields at a quick walk, well out of range.

Should he have his men mount up and follow? Mykel shook his head. He had no idea what might be waiting to the west, and it wouldn't be that long before it was dark.

"Cease fire! Cease fire!" He stood and stepped away from the pine to get a better view. Blue tunics lay strewn everywhere. Some men moaned. A horse was screaming somewhere.

"Bhoral! Get a quick count of the bodies, and get someone to round up all their weapons and ammunition. Send one of the scouts west, a half vingt or so, to make sure no one's headed back toward us. Get all the mounts clear of the woods and ready to ride."

"The bodies, sir?"

The last thing Mykel wanted to do was to deal with scores of bodies. He didn't have the manpower or the time—and there was at least one company of rebels on the road west of them. "Lay them out on the side of the road for now." Mykel turned to get the chestnut, but a ranker was leading his mount toward him.

"Squad leader said you'd be needing him, sir."

"Thank you, Rykyt." Mykel mounted and rode west, coming up on Vhanyr and fifth squad. "Take the road, and set up, just in case someone turns and comes back from the west. Second, third, and fourth squads are gathering weapons and ammunition"

"Yes, sir."

"Any casualties?"

"No, sir. Not a one."

"Good." When Mykel reached the western road, the surviving bluecoats were out of sight, somewhere to the west, and a clouded twilight had fallen.

After letting his mount pick his way back along the packed-dirt surface, he reined up just where the western road turned off the mine road, so that he could see both roads. There were but a handful of bluecoats lying on the graystones of the mine road.

He watched as his men stripped weapons and ammunition and dragged bodies to the side of the road. He said nothing about the quick searches of wallets. He doubted if many of the dead had jewelry of value.

Bhoral rode slowly toward Mykel, reining up.

"Do you know how many we lost?"

"Just one, sir. Trooper from first squad—Onstyt. Three wounded, two from first squad, and one from third. What about their wounded?"

"Put them on mounts. We'll take them back to Dramuria with us."

"Some are hurt pretty bad."

"Do what you can." Mykel stopped. A single rider was headed toward them from the west. After a moment, he recognized the scout, and raised his hand. "Jasakyt! Here!"

The third squad scout reined up short of Mykel. "Sir!"

"Is someone coming after us?"

"Not right yet, sir, but the riders that circled round Fifteenth Company, they got back on the road a vingt or so west of here. Thought I'd follow and watch for a time." The scout paused, then went on. "They joined a bunch more rebels, maybe close to half a battalion's worth. They're all heading west. Not in a hurry, I'd say."

"You think they have a camp somewhere here?"

"Hard to say, but if I had to guess, sir . . ."

"You'd wager that way, and so would I," Mykel concluded, turning to Bhoral. "Have them finish up as quickly as they can. We need to get back to Dramuria. The overcaptain needs to know. The men and their mounts need quarters and decent food and beds."

Most of all, Mykel needed to talk to Dohark—if he even happened to be there.

For all Mykel's urging, twilight was giving way to night before Fifteenth Company finally began to ride southward. The captives rode at the rear, with captured mounts carrying all the captured rifles and ammunition behind them.

"Getting to be a bloody mess," Bhoral said quietly from where he rode beside Mykel.

"Likely to get bloodier," Mykel replied. "I worry about Seventeenth Company. They were supposed to be patrolling that road."

"Maybe the westerners just avoided them."

"With half a battalion? Be pretty hard to do that on such a narrow road."

"Could have lured them north. Wasn't there a message about that?"

"That was days ago." It could have happened, but that was another reason why Fifteenth Company was riding back to the compound. The local Cadmians at the mine compound had walls and plenty of ammunition. Third Battalion's companies were scattered across all of eastern Dramur, without that much ammunition, little warning, and no walls.

Less than a vingt south of the battle site, Mykel began to smell the smoke—thick and acrid. Through the growing dusk that was almost night, he could see reddish embers ahead. Only because the wind was at his back had they not smelled the odors of burning cots and huts.

He turned. "Bhoral! Get those prisoners and their guards up front here. Right now!"

Even before he had finished the order, Mykel could feel the unasked question and answered, "They burned people's huts and stables. I want whoever's around to know that they didn't all get away. Bring them up right behind the outriders and me—with the rankers guarding them."

"Yes, sir." Bhoral turned his mount and rode toward the rear of the column. "Prisoners forward! Captain's orders! Quick as you can."

Before that long, the eight surviving captives lurched along in their saddles behind Mykel and the outriders. Even under the cloud cover, the night didn't seem all that dark to Mykel as they neared the rows of burning cots and barns ahead. He could see figures trying to salvage goods, struggling to tie up animals that had escaped.

"Riders!" called someone.

"Cadmians! Headed back with captives!" Mykel called back.

The first person he saw was a graying woman. She knelt by an open gate between two stone pillars, then looked up from an animal—a dog that had been shot—toward the oncoming riders. Then her eyes took in the captives in blue, and she sprang to her feet. She took one step forward before a wiry man appeared and laid a hand on her arm. Both watched silently as Mykel rode past. He listened as he rode past them and the smoldering remains of the cots and huts.

". . . Cadmians . . . didn't stop them . . ."

". . . killed a lot of 'em . . . captured some . . . you saw . . ."

". . . won't rebuild my cot and barn . . ."

The raiders had fired close to a score of dwellings and outbuildings, but they hadn't fired anything else along the road. Mykel had to wonder what they had done in two days.

When he finally turned his mount off the mine road and onto the spur road leading to the compound, through a break in the clouds he could see the small green disc of Asterta. "Warrior goddess," he murmured under his breath, "we did you proud today. Lots of bodies." Not that he believed that the smaller moon was a goddess, but it helped to vent some of his frustration.

The compound gates were open, but there was a full squad of local Cadmians stationed in the towers and just outside.

"Fifteenth Company!" Mykel called. "Returning with captives for resupply."

"Hold there!"

"Send someone out and check, and make it quick!" snapped Mykel. "We've got wounded men and captives, and it's been a long ride."

A squad leader and two rankers advanced gingerly, holding rifles.

Mykel snorted. "If we'd meant trouble, you'd all be dead, and we'd already be inside the gates. If you'd stand aside . . ."

The squad leader looked up at Mykel. He swallowed. "Yes, sir."

Mykel heard more low comments as he rode through the gates.

". . . captives . . . westerners . . ."

". . . knew they were up to no good . . ."

If everyone knew that, Mykel reflected, why hadn't anyone told them? Then, Rachyla had, in a way. He wondered if she were still all right.

The sound of hoofs on stone echoed through the night. There were few words between the Cadmians, a sign that most were exhausted.

As they neared the stables, Mykel turned to Bhoral. "Have Alendyr and second squad take the captives over to the prisoner's barracks. We'll let the locals sort that out."

"Good idea, sir."

Mykel hadn't even dismounted when a ranker hurried through the darkness toward Fifteenth Company, stopping short of the column. "Captain Mykel, sir? Are you there?"

Mykel could see the ranker plainly. Why couldn't the man see him? "Right here."

The ranker turned. "Sir. The overcaptain would like to see you right now."

Mykel glanced toward Bhoral. "More calls of duty. I'll check back with you. Make sure that all the men get their weapons cleaned and they get washed up before they sack out."

Bhoral chuckled. "They'll love that."

"Tell them I'm meeting with the overcaptain, and that I'll be in a piss-poor mood by the time he gets through with me. Tell them whatever you have to . . ." Mykel dismounted, handing the chestnut's reins to Fioryt, the closest Cadmian.

He followed the messenger through the darkness of the courtyard to headquarters. One thing was certain—his night vision hadn't suffered. Everything else had, though.

Dohark sat behind the desk in the study that had been Majer Herryf's. Before him was a large map. He looked up tiredly as Mykel stepped through the doorway, then gestured. "Close the door. Might as well use this study. Colonel's gone, and Herryf 's not real helpful."

Mykel shut the door, then stepped toward the desk and slumped into a chair across from the battalion commander. Dohark looked more tired than Mykel felt.

"You look like shit, Mykel," offered the overcaptain.

"So do you, sir."

"Tell me why you're here, when your station is at the mine."

"Two rebel companies attacked the mine compound last night. We drove them off, killed more than thirty. This morning we found a squad spying on us, and we killed something like eighteen of them—"

"I got your reports and the prisoners. They didn't seem to know much."

"No one does." Mykel stifled a yawn. He was tired. "We interrogated the captives, enough to learn where they were going to rejoin their captain. We set up an ambush. Pretty much wiped out one of the companies. At least, we left seventy bodies on the road. We brought back the rifles and ammunition, and some extra mounts. All the rifles are new Cadmian pieces. My scouts found at least three more companies to the west of the mine road, maybe four. They were riding west. I didn't bother with bodies when I could have been outnumbered five to one. I also thought you ought to know."

"Five to one?"

"Four and one makes five," Mykel said. "There might be more. We didn't finish up until close to dark. Oh . . . the western bluecoats burned a score of cots north of Dramuria."

"I got word on that when we got here earlier tonight. We got tied up with snipers on the smuggling road. Didn't lose many men, just three, captured a small boatload of ammunition last night. Five cases. Then we started south. It's a long ride back here. It's a long ride anywhere on this friggin' island."

"Yes, sir."

"How much of your company do you have left—that can fight?"

"A little less than fourscore. Some of my earlier wounded might be well enough in another week or so to rejoin the company." Mykel paused, then asked, "Have you heard anything from Seventeenth Company?"

"No. Have you?"

"No. That's why I asked. They were supposed to be patrolling the west road. When I found out there were five-odd companies that came down the road . . ."

"Could be Heransyr had enough sense not to engage them."

"It could be," Mykel agreed politely.

"You don't think so."

"I don't know. The other thing that really bothers me is that these bluecoats can't fight. Why are they sending them over here to get killed?"

"Maybe they didn't know they couldn't fight," Dohark said quietly.

Mykel sat there for a moment. He'd never considered that possibility.

"They can get reinforcements. We can't," Dohark pointed out. "Not for a long while, anyway. We'll have to scout the western road and protect Dramuria. I've called Sixteenth Company in from the north. They should be here tomorrow. I'll also be suggesting to Majer Herryf that he either station both Cadmian companies at the mine or pull everyone out." Dohark laughed harshly. "He won't. He might get by with it because the walls there are high and thick."

Mykel nodded.

"As for you, Mykel. You look like shit. I'll bet your men do, too, or you wouldn't have brought them back. We can't afford exhausted troopers, or captains. Get some sleep, and check in with me in the morning."

"Sir?"

"Yes?"

"The same goes for exhausted overcaptains, sir."

Dohark laughed, briefly. "You get some sleep, and I'll get some. Now . . . get out of here, so I can finish figuring out something, and we'll both get to sleep sooner."

"Yes, sir."

Mykel eased out of the study, realizing that Dohark was using it because the Myrmidon colonel was gone—and because Dohark didn't expect him back soon. He shook his head, then slipped out of the building and into the cool night air. He did not head for quarters, but to the officer's cell that he hoped still held Rachyla.

The guards looked at him. One opened his mouth.

Mykel looked back, hard. "I won't be long."

"Ah . . . yes, sir."

As always, they held their rifles ready as they unlocked the cell and let him enter.

Rachyla turned from the desk where she had been writing in the dim light of the lamp hung on the wall. She did not rise from the stool. "It's rather presumptuous of you to come so late. What if I were asleep?"

"I would have left."

She studied him before speaking. "You have blood all over your neck."

"You were right."

"What does that have to do with the blood. Have you been out slaughtering more helpless and untrained men?"

"Yes. We ambushed two companies of bluecoats after they had burned out cots and dwellings north of Dramuria."

"After? How brave of you."

"We'd fought our way out of one ambush the night before. That was where your equally noble bluecoats tried to massacre the mine prisoners." Mykel managed, somehow, to keep a dry tone to his words, rather than the anger he felt. "We'd already fought another skirmish earlier in the day. In the last fight, since we were outnumbered more than two to one, we were the ones to spring the ambush. And no, I don't feel good about it. But . . . you were right. They were all from the west."

"And they wounded you."

Mykel laughed, ironically. "No. They didn't. Someone hit a tree beside me, I was hit by a big splinter. I pulled it out. I didn't even know I was bleeding."

For a moment, she was silent.

"How many large or powerful seltyrs are there west of the mountains?" he asked.

Rachyla cocked her head, then said, "Twelve. There are only twelve of the west, as there are only . . . were only twelve of the east. Some of the growers in the west hold more land than some of the seltyrs in the east, but they are not seltyrs."

"Thank you." Mykel forced himself to breathe easily.

"Why did you say I was right?"

"You said—you hinted, rather—that the seltyrs of the west might be a problem. They are. There are at least four companies east of the mountains."

"So . . . you will kill them all, too."

Mykel wanted to break through her composure, almost to scream at her that she didn't understand, that he didn't like slaughter, didn't want to kill so many men. "Perhaps."

"If you do not, the Myrmidons will."

"The Myrmidons have left," Mykel said. "Didn't you know?"

Strangely, Rachyla laughed, softly and musically. It was anything but a happy sound. "You, too, have been betrayed."

Mykel understood exactly what she meant. Was the whole campaign really just meant to destroy Third Battalion? Were the Cadmians being scattered across Corus so that they could be destroyed piecemeal? Or was there any explanation? Would it be any better?

"You see, Captain?" She stood. "You need sleep. I have nothing more to say. Good night."

They faced each other for several moments.

Finally, Mykel said, "Good night, Lady Rachyla."

He rapped on the door and left without saying a word to the guards. Whether he was right or not, there was no way that the seltyrs could have gotten so many Cadmian weapons without some alectors supporting them. While the seltyrs saw more clearly than other landers that the world ran on force, their mistake had been that they'd thought that the alectors would respect force, rather than crush it. The rest of Corus accepted what was—mostly, anyway—and that was that there was no practical way to use force against the alectors and their Myrmidons—or even against the Cadmians. Because of its comparative isolation, or for some other reason, the seltyrs and those who controlled Dramur hadn't learned that lesson. Mykel wasn't particularly happy being the one to administer it. What was happening in Dramur should have been obvious to him much earlier, but it just wasn't the sort of thing that a Cadmian captain would expect. What else was likely to happen that he didn't expect?

Mykel walked back toward the stables. He needed to find his gear. He needed to check his own weapon. He needed to get washed up and get rid of the blood. And he needed sleep.

70

What then is the role of belief for an alector in these times and those to come?

Understanding the hold that belief lays upon the undiscerning is the first step. There are beings who discern and those who do not. Those who discern are, in the normal course of events, of the alectors, although we must admit that not all alectors are as discerning as they should be, and some discern not at all. Likewise, not all people of the lands are undiscerning, and, as will be discussed later, those of the lands who are discerning are most dangerous and must be handled with the greatest of care.

Whether alectors or peoples of the lands, those who do not discern are but the highest of the animals. Because they are like unto the cattle of the fields and the sheep in the meadows, a discerning alector's role is to care for them. They must be fed, and they must be kept happy and healthy. They must also come to understand that not all their desires can be satisfied, and therein lies the role of justice and discipline, for, as in the case of animals, one cannot appeal to the reason of an undiscerning individual, for one such has no true ability to reason. Rather, such an individual wants and feels, then uses a crude form of logic to rationalize those desires. The most dangerous are those who are skilled with the tools of logic and reason and yet have no true understanding of the universe that surrounds them, for they will use such logic to make themselves the center of their limited world, regardless of the cost to others—or to themselves.

Most important, because not all desires can be satisfied, an alector must also offer comfort to the undiscerning. One of those comforts is that of faith, the comfort of the irrational, the comfort of believing that a supreme being cares for each and every being who prays to this deity. An alector may claim, "But I care for those for whom I am responsible." That should indeed be true, but the truth as such does not offer comfort to the undiscerning, for an alector is not seen as supreme being.

It matters not that an alector ensures that murderers are caught and punished, or that food is shared equitably so that none starve. It matters not that an alector provides justice and a land where the industrious prosper. The undiscerning will not praise the alector for such; they will claim that all the benefits provided by the alectors are the "will of the deity."

For these reasons, a truly wise alector will always align himself with the perceptions of the undiscerning. He will not claim credit for what he has done, but will remain modest, and assert that he was but carrying out the will of the deity, "the One Who Is," or "the Almighty," or whatever divine appellation the undiscerning of that time and place have adopted. By so positioning himself he will reduce unrest among those over whom he is placed to care, and thus minimize the use of force and applied justice.

Views of the Highest
Illustra
W.T. 1513

71

Novdi morning dawned as gray as Octdi evening had been, but with a sheen of rain across the stones of the compound's courtyard. The rain had stopped falling even before Mykel ate, but the clouds remained. A cold raw wind blew out of the northeast as he walked from the officers' mess toward headquarters. He managed a quiet burp and hoped his guts would settle. Fried fish, day after day, was wearing, and then some; but he understood why, when the nightwasps had made large herds of cattle impossible and when no one raised many hogs, although Mykel didn't know quite why. There wasn't much fruit either, except for the apple bananas.

Dohark was in the same position as when Mykel had left the night before, looking down at a map on the desk. Mykel saw that the overcaptain had even deeper circles under his eyes.

"Close the door."

Mykel did. "What happened? Seventeenth Company?"

The overcaptain nodded. "The survivors came in late last night. All eight of them."

Mykel winced. He'd feared that, but fearing and having those fears confirmed were two different mounts.

"Somehow, Heransyr let his company get strung out on a lane running through a valley. According to the scout, it looked peaceful. Men tilling fields, repairing stone fences. Then a squad of those bluecoats rode in on the other side of the valley, and began shooting. People were falling like rain—"

"It was a trap," Mykel said. "They were pretending to fall."

Dohark frowned. "You know that now. How would you have known it then?"

"In all the time we've been here, I've never seen more than three men working together in one place. With that many men out in the fields, there should have been some women."

"Maybe you ought to be the overcaptain."

Mykel wasn't quite sure what to say. "It's easy to say that afterward, but I'm sure you would have seen the same thing if you had been there. It wouldn't have felt right. You might not have been able to say why it was wrong, but you would have known."

A brief smile flitted across Dohark's face. "You can go by feel as a captain. It's harder when you can't see what's happening." He looked at Mykel. "How many companies do you think the western seltyrs have?"

"I'd say that they had thirteen to start, and that the eastern seltyrs might have eleven."

"Where did you come up with those numbers?"

Mykel shrugged. "It's a guess. The captives we took yesterday morning said that every seltyr in the west had raised a company, except for one, and he had raised two. Seltyr Ubarjyr's daughter—she's a captive here—told me last night that there were twelve seltyrs in the east and twelve in the west. We wiped out Ubarjyr's company. So . . . twenty-three or twenty-four."

"You talked to her last night?"

"After we talked. I've been trying to find out things from her all along. Every so often she says something, and it goes with something else."

"That's one thing I like about you. Behind that agreeable face, you're like a dog looking for a bone. You just keep sniffing around, and you don't give up. What else have you learned?"

"Not much. She was the one that hinted that we might have trouble with the western seltyrs. She also intimated that there are companies here in the east."

"We haven't found any."

"Would we, sir, after the raid on Stylan Estate?"

"It'd be unlikely, that's certain," admitted Dohark.

Silence stretched out in the study.

"I have a question, sir," Mykel finally said.

"Do I want to hear it?" countered Dohark, with a flat laugh.

"Don't you find it a little disturbing that all of the rebel companies raised by the seltyrs have unmarked Cadmian weapons and that the moment that the Myrmidon colonel leaves with his pteridons we get attacked?"

"I'd thought about that." Dohark gestured around the study. "One reason why I took this over. I don't think he'll be back soon." He paused. "With or without pteridons, we still have a mission. What do you suggest?"

"Find out as much as we can about where their companies are. Pick them off, one at a time. They're no match for us if we choose where and how we fight."

"How many good scouts do you have?"

"Four."

Dohark nodded. "We'll need them. If we're going to choose where to fight and pick off these bluecoats, we'll need to know where they are and where they can go." After a moment, he looked squarely at Mykel. "Do you want to add the two squads—one full squad, really—from Thirteenth Company to Fifteenth Company?"

"I'd like the extra men, but it would cause more trouble. I'm sure they feel I set them up in Jyoha, and, in a way, I did. I didn't think Vaclyn would be that stupid."

"Most of Heransyr's survivors are all right. You take them, then."

"Thank you. We could use them."

"Go get your scouts and come back in a glass. We'll assign areas to all the scouts then."

"Yes, sir." Mykel stepped back and headed for the study door.

"She is pretty, Mykel," Dohark said conversationally, "and useful. But I wouldn't put her in a position where you have to trust her."

"Sir?"

"You know exactly who I mean." Dohark's voice carried a trace of good humor. "The seltyr's daughter. Just be careful."

"I intend to be very careful, sir."

"Good. Go round up your scouts."

Mykel slipped out of the study and down the corridor to the entrance foyer. He wished he could be as dispassionate as Dohark about the possible betrayal of the Cadmians by either the Myrmidons or other alectors. The overcaptain accepted that possibility and went on. Mykel was still trying to figure out why. And then there was Rachyla—an enigma—much like the ancient dagger in his belt, both beautiful, both able to cut deep, and perhaps . . . both deadly.

He stepped out into the courtyard, where a light rain had begun to fall once more. If the rain continued, it might keep the bluecoats from trying to fire more cots or from attacking the Cadmians in the next day or so. Fifteenth Company could use the rest, and so could the others.

72

After two long days of flying, late on Novdi, just before the sun set behind the western horizon of the seemingly endless grasslands of Illegea, Quelyt called back over his shoulder, "There it is, sir!"

Dainyl looked eastward toward the Spine of Corus and what lay at the base of the red cliffs footing those snowcapped winter giants. The late, late-afternoon light fell across the redstone spires of the Vault of the Ages, turning them a deeper and duskier shade, outlining them against the lighter stone and scattered trees of the peaks to the east. Directly below the columned entrance to the Vault were the wide stone steps that descended westward to the polished redstone plaza, empty so late in the day. In the still air just before twilight, a haze blanketed the lower areas of the hills to the east and north of the Vault.

"We'll set down on the plaza, sir," added Quelyt.

"Go ahead!" Dainyl had flown into the plaza himself, more than a few times, but he'd seen little of Lyterna, outside of the barracks tunneled into the cliffs to the south of the Vault, where he had waited as a ranker to carry dispatches to regional centers and other places without Tables. There was little visible from the air, or the ground—except for the great steps and the plaza—because the entire complex had been carved into the rock ages before.

Quelyt made a long and shallow approach across grasslands that remained tan and brown, without any traces of green, although all the winter snows had melted. Then, the long blue wings spread, and the pteridon flared and touched down gently on the plaza.

Once the pteridons had landed, and the three Myrmidons had dismounted, Dainyl took the saddlebags that held his gear and turned to Quelyt. "I doubt I'll see you for a while. You have tomorrow off, and you'll head back in the morning on Londi."

"You don't want us to wait, sir?"

"No. I'll be here for a while. There's no reason for you to wait." That was true. Dainyl would be in Lyterna for a time, and, if he were successful in learning to use the Tables, he wouldn't need a pteridon to return. If he weren't successful, he wouldn't need one, either.

"You certain, sir?"

"Very certain. Thank you." Dainyl shouldered the saddlebags and turned, crossing the fifty yards of the plaza between him and the great steps. As he climbed the steps toward the Vault, the wind picked up, whistling around him. Although Lyterna was south of Elcien, it was also higher and colder—much colder.

The Ifrit who greeted him at the top of the great steps had silver hair, yet his life-aura was clearly that of an alector, with the purple essence that was of Ifryn and always would be. "I'm Asulet, Submarshal Dainyl. High Alector Zelyert sent word to expect you." An impish smile crossed the broad face. "I tutored your mother. Briefly. You don't look at all like her."

As Dainyl smiled wryly, the older alector laughed. "She had definite opinions."

"She still does."

"I imagine you're hungry and a bit chilled."

"Somewhat," Dainyl admitted dryly.

Asulet turned and stepped through the wide-open space that matched the width of the great stairs and walked past the first columns, toward a blank stone wall that parted as he neared. The stone panels were a good nine yards high and seven wide, but they moved quickly and silently, retracting flush into the walls, so well fitted that Dainyl doubted a knife blade would fit between the stones. When open, no one could have guessed there were stone doors. Dainyl noted the deftness with which the elder alector had used his Talent to activate the portals.

Within moments after the two passed through the entrance, the stone doors closed behind them. Dainyl could feel the immediate and welcome warmth and dampness to the air within the chamber, more like summer in Lysia or Tylora.

Asulet stopped and gestured around the columned hall in which they stood. "For reasons I never quite grasped, the first lifemasters here decided to call this the Council Hall." He laughed once more, again with an ease that Dainyl envied. "We never have had a council, nor any need for such, but then, maybe they knew what they were doing. It's the smallest of the three great halls. The other two originally were used to house the first pteridons until we tunneled the barracks and squares to the south."

Dainyl glanced around the space, modestly lit with light-torches set in wall brackets exactly three yards above the polished red eternastone floor. The hall was not exactly small, not at fifty yards in length and fifteen in width, with ceilings easily ten yards high. Like the floor, the walls and ceilings were of polished red eternastone. The redstone so treated did not reflect light, for all its apparent shine and shimmer.

"Your quarters will be in the upper quadrant," Asulet went on as he resumed walking toward the square archway set in the middle of the back wall. "They're quite spacious, with a private bath and accommodations. No windows, of course, but when they were built, there wasn't anything to see, and the winter cold might well have shattered any glass."

The floors, the light-torches, the walls—everything looked so crisp, so recently formed that it was hard for Dainyl to realize just how ancient Lyterna was.

"We will have dinner in a glass. That should give you some time to refresh yourself." Just past the archway, Asulet touched a light-torch bracket on the light wall. Another stone door opened, revealing steps leading upward. "The upper level is far more comfortable."

Dainyl followed the silver-haired alector up the staircase cut from the solid stone, a distance more than twice the height of a staircase in most structures. There was no portal at the top, and they stepped out into a circular foyer nine yards across. Three wide hallways radiated from the foyer. All were four yards wide and brightly lit with light-torches set at three-yard alternating intervals along the stone walls.

"The center corridor leads to the dining and common rooms, and the library," Asulet explained. "Quarters for distinguished guests, such as you, are set along the far left corridor. Somewhat larger apartments for those of us who toil here are set along the right-hand corridor." He turned down the left corridor. "Most of these are seldom used. We get very few guests for long these days, and it's always good to see a new face."

"Once an alector gets . . . a great deal of experience . . . is this where?"

Asulet laughed again. "Very few alectors age enough for it to show, but Lyterna is always available for those with, as you put it, experience who wish a quieter life. There is much we do not know about life here on Acorus, and there have never been enough minds and hands to properly study and catalog what is here, much less to mold additional useful lifeforms."

The older alector stopped at second door and turned the flat bronze lever, letting the door swing open. He gestured for Dainyl to enter.

Dainyl took two steps inside and surveyed the sitting room. On the right wall was a large mural-like painting, showing the grasslands to the west in spring green, with wildflowers blossoming, and a herd of antelope. Beneath the lifelike depiction was a settee, with the long legs and higher back designed for alectors. On the wall directly before him was a wide and high white oak desk, with rounded edges, but clean and unornamented lines. The desk chair reminded Dainyl of the chairs in the chambers of the High Alector of Justice, without cushions or upholstery, but gently curved. On the wall above the desk was an oval painting of the High Court of Illustra, with the twin green towers that framed the palace of the Archon. On each side of each of the two paintings was a light-torch in a bronze holder.

The walls were of the redstone, but pale green hangings, like full-length drapes, ran from ceiling to floor on each side of the desk and on each side of the painting on the wall to Dainyl's right. The floor was almost entirely covered by a large oval carpet of dark green, bordered in gold, and with a gold eight-pointed star of the Duarches in the center.

Asulet gestured toward the ceiling, pointing to the corners of the room. "The ventilation louvers have levers so that you can adjust them. The lever with the blue handle is for cold air, and the one with the red handle is for warm moist air. You can't close them completely because there has to be some circulation, but you ought to be able to find a mix that's comfortable."

Dainyl glanced around the room before catching sight of the two narrow but wide air return ducts set just above the floor beyond the edges of the hangings on the wall he faced. "How do you get the warm moist air?"

"That was one reason why Lyterna was located here. There are boiling springs. We tapped them, for both hot water and heat. Be careful with the hot water for a bath or shower. It is *very* hot." With a smile, Asulet stepped back into the corridor. "I'll meet you in the foyer in a glass."

After the older alector had headed back in the direction of the foyer, Dainyl closed the door. On the inside of the heavy oak door was a simple privacy bolt, no more. He turned and walked through the sitting room to the bedchamber, dominated by a triple-width bed with a plain white oak headboard and footboard. The coverlet was dark green. A white oak armoire two yards wide stood against one wall, far more space than Dainyl would ever use. With a smile, he set the saddlebags holding his gear on the rack beside the armoire.

On the polished white oak stand beside the bed was a mechanical glass, the circular face with its single hand. There were five marks between each of the ten triangles. Dainyl nodded. Without any sight of the sun, mechanical glasses were even more necessary, and far better than sand ones, which had to be turned every glass or measured against a gauge. Light-torches were set in wall brackets on each side of the headboard.

He moved through the open archway to the bath chamber, which held both shower and a deep redstone tub, coated with a clear enamel or glaze. Beyond to the right was a much smaller chamber with the other necessary facilities. Dainyl looked at the stone-walled shower and the white bronze fixtures. A truly hot shower would be more than welcome.

Almost a glass later, feeling warmer, refreshed, and definitely hungry, Dainyl stepped out of the guest chambers, wearing a clean uniform, and walked down the corridor toward the foyer.

Ahead of him was an older alector wearing a dark gray shirt and trousers—white-haired, and slightly bent. He was carrying folded linens. As he saw Dainyl, he stepped to one side and bowed. "Terribly sorry, sir."

"That's all right," Dainyl replied, uncertain of how or why old alector was supposed to have offended him.

The man bowed quickly once more, then hurried past Dainyl.

Dainyl reached the circular foyer, but saw no one there. He debated heading down the center corridor, but decided to wait. Each of the four curved sections of stone wall between the three corridors and the staircase held a mural. The geographic locale of each mural was that of the isle and city of Elcien. The first scene was just that of an isle, rocky in the center, low and marshy near the bay on the south, with scattered stunted trees. The second showed the arching bridge from the mainland and a grid of stone streets, with the Hall of Justice, and Palace of the Duarch, and but a handful of other structures. The third depicted an Elcien similar to the one Dainyl knew, if somehow subtly different. The fourth illustrated an Elcien where a soaring palace—identical to the depictions of the Archon's Palace in Illustra—rose between two green towers far taller than those that currently flanked the Duarch's palace.

"You are most punctual," observed Asulet, entering the foyer.

"I try." Dainyl pointed to the third mural. "When was that drawn?"

"Oh . . . some five hundred years ago. They were all done then."

"That one, it's almost like Elcien today."

"It was the plan for Elcien about a hundred years ago. It's fairly close to what it is today. Matters often take longer than originally planned." Asulet's last words held an ironic dryness.

"The fourth one—that's what's planned?"

"If the master scepter is transferred here," Asulet said. "The Archon has yet to decide. Let us go eat. We will talk of that, and of other matters of which you should know." He turned.

Dainyl walked beside the older alector down the wide center corridor.

"I saw someone in gray . . ." Dainyl ventured, wondering if the rumors about old alectors were indeed true.

"Yes. The orderlies and servants. Various failures, heavily imprinted with loyalty bonds. Tragic, but it's better than execution, and someone has to do the menial work, and it's far better than letting landers or indigens know what lies behind the façade of the Vault."

What did lie behind the façade of Lyterna? The Highest had intimated that much did, and now Asulet was telling him the same thing. The engineering alone, Dainyl had to admit, for what little he had seen in the past glass and a half, had to have been stupendous.

"You are beginning to wonder, are you not, Submarshal?"

"How could I not?" Dainyl managed a laugh. "I've already seen superb engineering and remarkable crafting, and I doubt that I've seen a fraction of what is here."

"That is indeed so." Asulet raised a hand toward the open square archway just ahead of them. "The dining chamber is the most ornate space in Lyterna, and it is also among the oldest finished rooms in the complex. The thought was that we should have something of elegance and grace when outside held little but lichens, stunted trees, and winter-cold swamps." As Asulet finished speaking, he stepped through the wide square arch into a large circular chamber.

Dainyl followed—and stopped.

The space was close to fifty yards across, with a high-arched dome cut out of the very rock, soaring to nearly twenty yards overhead. Double goldenstone columns circled the chamber, set at intervals of six yards, and reaching from their pediments to a frieze ten yards above the shimmering green and gold marble floor. The green marble frieze was less than a half a yard in height. On its face had been carved a repeating design of pteridons and sandoxes. The wall space between the columns and beneath the narrow frieze had been faced with creamy white marble. Each set of double columns was flanked by lighter green hangings that dropped from the base of the frieze to just above the polished marble of the floor.

Overhead was the domed ceiling, inset with the same creamy white marble tiles, edged with green marble. The lines of green marble converged, ending at a circle of green surrounding and filling the apex of the dome. In the center of the green was the gold, eight-pointed star. The dining hall was illuminated by light-torches set in ornate bronze brackets on the goldenstone pillars.

There was a full score of tables arranged in the quarter of the chamber opposite the entry archway. So large was the space that the tables seemed well apart from each other.

"Once there were more of us living here," added Asulet. "That was when Acorus was too chill for half the year."

Four circular stands, each six yards across and a yard and a half high, were set equidistant from each other, lost in the openness of the otherwise unused space under the dome.

Dainyl glanced at the nearest stand, realizing it held the model of a city. "That's Ludar."

"Exactly, and the others are Elcien, Alustre, and Dereka."

"As they are now, or as they were planned?"

"As they were planned. The models are close to five hundred years old. There are a few differences between the plans and the final construction, but not many. Those differences are largely because of geographic peculiarities of which we were unaware at the time."

"I would never have . . ." Dainyl left his words hanging, not sure what he could have said.

"You will think better after you have eaten." With a smile, the older alector led the way to a table on the left side of the assemblage.

Dainyl noted that only eight of the tables were occupied. They seated themselves, and a server immediately appeared, a silver-haired alectress who looked to Asulet and bowed, then waited.

"What do you have tonight, Ulasya?"

"We have prairie fowl stewed and spiced in golden brandy, then finished on the grill over hot coals. We have an auroch filet, marinated in Nordan winter wine, then seared, and poached with gharo root; and we have golden noodles with fried oarfish."

"I'll have the filet." Asulet nodded to Dainyl.

"The prairie fowl."

"And a carafe of the Vyan Grande as well."

After the server slipped away, Asulet looked at the younger alector. "We may not have the best of vistas here, but we still have excellent fare."

Before either said more, the server returned with two crystal goblets, tinted slightly purple, and a crystal carafe filled with the ruby vintage. Without speaking, she departed as quickly as she had arrived.

"As a Myrmidon who began as the lowest of the low, then became a flier, then an officer, and now submarshal, you have seen most of Acorus, have you not?"

"It is clear I have seen most of what is visible, sir."

"Sir?" Asulet arched his eyebrows.

"At the least, you must be one of the senior lifemasters. I should have realized earlier."

Asulet laughed his easy laugh. "You were not told." He filled his goblet halfway, then Dainyl's.

"No, sir."

"That's one of Zelyert's little games. Sometimes, they aren't so harmless. He should have read the *Views of the Highest* more closely, but that is for another time. As a matter of fact, I am the senior lifemaster." Asulet sipped the wine. "Good vintage. They always haven't been."

"The High Alector of Lifemasters."

"That title does not exist, but something like that. I don't like being called 'sir.' It makes me feel even older than I am. You have shown more respect without the honorifics than many have with them. I'd prefer that. Try your wine."

"That won't be difficult . . ." Dainyl almost added the "sir." He did take a sip of the Vyan Grande, and as Asulet had suggested, it was good.

"You have seen most of Acorus—Corus, anyway, not that there's that much besides the frozen continent that spreads across most of the south pole and the volcanic island chains in the western ocean. That's a misnomer, too. Those in Alustre call it the eastern ocean, those in Ludar and Elcien the western ocean, but it's the same ocean. Some of the western islands are large, larger than Dramur, but the volcanoes made them unsuitable, especially for placing the scepters."

Placing the scepters? The Dual Scepters? "I understand that the scepters are necessary for the Tables to function properly . . ." Dainyl hoped the hint would be enough.

"Young Dainyl—and you are young, for all your years, at least to an ancient like me—the scepters are necessary for the Tables to function at all. They had to be placed in certain locales in order to create the stresses necessary for us to create the local translation tubes."

"But . . . if they were necessary . . . how did we even get here?"

"That is a good question, and one that I cannot answer in depth, because it is not my field. However . . ." Asulet drew out the word. ". . . a massive spear of lifeforce was used to throw a tube or a link to Acorus. Through that link poured alectors, with what crystals and tools they could carry, until enough survived to create the first Table. That solidified the link with Ifyrn. Then came the Dual Scepters, linked, of course, to the master scepter, and they were carried to different locales until the stress patterns were stabilized. Two more Tables were built at those locations, and then, within a few years, the remainder were created and linked to the grid."

"Could more be added?"

"Yes, but it wouldn't be wise. Each Table drains lifeforce from the world itself. All is a balancing act." Asulet stopped as the server set a platter before each of them, and then a smaller plate with various sliced fruits arranged in an asymmetrical pattern. "We should eat while the fare is still warm."

Dainyl waited for Asulet to take the first bite, then cut a slice of the fowl and ate it—perhaps one of the better fowl dishes he had ever had. The golden rice-grass was just firm enough without being elastic.

"Enough of Lyterna for now. I'll have your head turning in two directions by tomorrow night. Tell me about Elcien, or anything else out beyond Lyterna—but not military events. I read all the reports from the high alectors. Have you heard any new musical compositions? Read any new poems?"

Dainyl got the message, although he wondered whether those reports really reflected what was in fact happening. "I haven't heard a concert for several months. The last was a chamber concert at the palace in Elcien . . ."

The rest of the evening was pleasant, accompanied by good food, and told Dainyl little more about Lyterna or why he was there.

When, a good two glasses later, Dainyl stepped back into his temporary quarters, it was more than clear that someone had been there.

He saw the uniform he had worn on the flight to Lyterna, and his flying jacket, both spotless and hung in the armoire, its doors left open to let him know that they had been cleaned.

As he undressed and prepared for bed, he smiled sadly, thinking of the old alector in gray.

73

A pall of smoke hung over the compound on Decdi morning, pungent and acrid, as Mykel and Rhystan walked from the mess toward the headquarters building under a hazy gray sky. The sun had barely climbed out of the ocean and was trying to fight its way through the clouds, showing little more than a bright patch amid the gray.

"Still looks like winter," observed Rhystan.

"It is," replied Mykel, "the last day of winter."

"Worst mess we've been in," said the older officer. "You think they'll attack here?"

"Sometime, if we don't stop them first."

"With three companies, Mykel?"

Put that way, Mykel reflected, the situation didn't sound all that hopeful. He decided to say nothing, at least until they heard what Dohark had to tell them. When the two captains reached the study that had belonged to the local majer, Dohark was pacing back and forth. He stopped and motioned them inside. Mykel shut the door.

"I wouldn't worry about that," said Dohark. "Majer Herryf's not around. He told me he wouldn't be. Nothing happens on Decdi in Dramur." The overcaptain shook his head. "Friggin' idiot. He wouldn't listen to me. Who knows? Maybe he's right." He took a long deep breath and leaned against the desk but did not sit down.

Neither did either captain.

"The western seltyrs have moved their troopers out of the valleys to the west. They're scattering into the east here. There look to be three companies to the south of Dramuria, and four or five to the north and east. They haven't burned any more cots or houses. There's been no fighting or attacks in any of the towns outside of Dramuria."

"Did the scouts take a look at the estates of the eastern seltyrs?" asked Mykel.

"I don't have any reports on them." Dohark looked at the younger captain. "Why don't you just say what you have in mind, Mykel?"

"I'm just guessing, sir, but the only cots burned were on the outskirts of Dramuria, and they've only attacked Cadmians. Maybe the attacks aren't against the eastern seltyrs at all, but against Dramuria and us. I'd wager that the golds from the guano don't go to the seltyrs."

"Some of the eastern seltyrs get a little, I've been told," replied Dohark. "The westerners don't get any. The guilds and the crafters in Dramuria put up the golds to open the mine, and to build the road—some sort of pooled thing, and they have to pay off lenders in Elcien. What's left goes to the guilds and the council and the eastern seltyrs who put up the coins."

Mykel would have wagered that Seltyr Ubarjyr had been one of those.

"What are you getting at?" asked Dohark.

"The seltyrs who aren't getting anything from the mine are the ones we'll be fighting."

"You don't know that," pointed out Dohark.

"No, sir. I could be wrong, but why else would they be here? The western seltyrs and the easterners don't get along that well. There has to be something in it for them."

"We don't know what that is," replied Dohark.

Mykel decided not to say more. Dohark either believed him or didn't.

"What does Majer Herryf plan to do?" asked Rhystan.

"Nothing. He says that he warned the marshal and that he has but two companies, but they can hold the compound against ten times that number, if the seltyrs are foolish enough to attack." Dohark snorted. "Besides, today is Decdi, and nothing will happen on Decdi."

"Why don't we turn the tables on them?" asked Mykel.

"What do you have in mind?"

"Tracking and hitting them with ambushes and shoot-and-run. Like the Reillies did."

"After what's happened, you think that will work?"

"The only time I've lost more than a few men is when I've been forced to be in one place or another, sir."

Dohark nodded slowly. "You're volunteering Fifteenth Company to keep the seltyrs off-balance while the seriousness of the situation sinks in to Majer Herryf and the colonels?"

"It might be better said that we can only afford to send out one company at a time to do this, and Fifteenth Company was the one chosen."

Dohark laughed. "When do you want to go?"

"I don't. I just don't like the alternatives. But . . . today. No one does anything on Decdi."

Rhystan looked at Mykel. "Do you know what you're asking for?"

"Probably not," Mykel lied. He knew very well. He also knew the seltyrs would only get better with time—if they were given the chance. He didn't want to give them that chance.

"You might end up as an overcaptain," Dohark said. "Most likely, you'll end up dead."

Mykel had the feeling that he'd more likely end up dead by doing nothing. He did not say so, but just waited, a pleasant expression on his face.

"If that's what you want to do . . . go ahead. At this point, you can't make things worse."

Left unspoken was the statement that Mykel would delay, at the least, any attack on the compound and the other companies.

"What do you want me to do?" asked Rhystan.

"We need to look to the compound's defenses," replied Dohark. "I don't want to find out that there's some secret way in or that the east or west gates don't work because they haven't been used in years."

"If you don't need me . . ." offered Mykel.

"You can go." Dohark laughed, half-sardonically and half-sadly. "I'm glad I don't have to tell you not to make foolish head-on attacks."

Mykel bowed, and left, making his way to the barracks, then to the stables, when he learned that was where Bhoral had gone. The senior squad leader was standing outside the stable, talking to one of the ostlers, as Mykel crossed the courtyard.

Bhoral said a last word to the man, who hurried into the stable, and turned to Mykel. "What's the news, sir?"

"Do you want the bad news or the worse news?" countered Mykel. "We've got something like eight companies of horse troopers from the west around here. That's in addition to whatever the eastern seltyrs have. The Myrmidons have big problems elsewhere, and we don't know when they'll be back. The good news is that we're going to do something about it."

"Sir? Against eight companies?"

Mykel smiled. "The westerners have split up their companies all over the place. How many men did we lose in destroying those bluecoats on Octdi?"

"Just a few," admitted Bhoral.

"How many would we lose if they all got together and attacked?"

"More."

"We need to get to them the way we did before and whittle them down before they unite. We'll ride out in a glass," Mykel said. "I need to check the maps and reports a last time."

"Yes, sir." The senior squad leader sounded anything but happy.

After leaving Bhoral, Mykel made his way back to headquarters, where he went over the reports and maps Dohark had received. Dohark handed them to him and left with Rhystan to inspect the compound. Mykel went through the stack as carefully as he could quickly, taking notes. One thing stood out. A single company of bluecoats had ridden just north of the compound, then due east to one of the larger estates in the east on the coast—Fynhaven.

Mykel wagered that the coastal estate held another company—of greencoats. Since they were both closer than any of the others, Fifteenth Company might as well look into Fynhaven. He took some of the maps—and his notes—and headed back to the stable, stopping by his quarters for his rifle and a riding jacket, and the armory for more ammunition.

When Mykel reached the stables, Bhoral was standing beside his mount adjusting the saddlebags. The senior squad leader still looked glum. "Hazy out there. Might rain. Hate to be riding in the rain."

"If it rains, we'll change our plans," Mykel said. "Is the company ready?"

"In a few moments, sir."

Mykel walked into the stables. By the time he saddled the chestnut, with his gear in place, including extra ammunition in his saddlebags, and led his mount out into the courtyard, Fifteenth Company was forming up. Mykel listened, trying to pick up what was being said.

". . . riding out on Decdi . . ."

". . . had to be us . . ."

". . . don't fight a friggin' war on a crafter's calendar . . ."

Mykel smiled at those words and swung up into the saddle with workmanlike skill, if not grace. In less than a quarter glass, Fifteenth Company was heading out the east gates of the compound, with Mykel riding just forward of first squad with Gendsyr. Bhoral rode with Chyndylt at the head of third squad.

"Where are we headed, sir?" asked Gendsyr.

"East, to an estate called Fynhaven. We're going to take out another company of bluecoats, and maybe some greencoats as well."

"Are they expecting us?"

"I hope not." Mykel laughed. "No one does anything on Decdi."

The words brought a momentary smile to Gendsyr's face.

They had ridden slightly more than two glasses, heading first east, then north and east once more, when Gerant came riding back from his scouting to report to Mykel. The scout pulled his mount in beside the captain, but they both kept riding.

"About a half vingt ahead, there's another crossroad, and it heads southeast. Wider, too, with shoulders and stone walls," the scout reported. "Lots of tracks on the road. Not in the past few glasses, but in the last day."

"That should be the road to Fynhaven. It's another four vingts along that road. We'll take a break when we get to the road. See what you and the others can find out, but try not to be seen. We'll wait there for a while."

In less than a quarter glass, Fifteenth Company halted in good order just short of the larger southeast road.

"Make sure everyone drinks and takes whatever breaks they need," Mykel told Bhoral and the squad leaders.

While he waited for the scouts, he studied the maps again. Fynhaven was the closest estate to the Cadmian compound, and from what he could tell, one of the larger ones in the east.

A half glass later, as Mykel saw the first of the scouts returning, he ordered the squad leaders forward. He dismounted, handing the chestnut's reins to Aloryt, one of Gendsyr's rankers, and waited until the squad leaders and scouts had gathered around him on foot. Then he drew a rough map of lanes and the road with a stick. "Is this right?" He looked to the scouts.

"Pretty much, sir," said Jasakyt.

Mykel handed the stick to him. "Add what you saw."

"There's a gated entrance on the main road. Here. Maybe, five or six guards." Jasakyt used the stick to add lines in the road dirt and dust. "The estate is back almost a vingt along a lane lined with trees. Fields, or meadows, on both sides. Real open."

"Is there any area with cover?"

"All the grounds behind the villa and buildings are casaran orchards. They run to those hills to the south," said Dhozynt. "More than a vingt. Easy to ride through the trees, but not easy to see from the villa there."

"Behind the orchards?"

"There's a lane, comes off the main road, leads to a hamlet to the west." Dhozynt took the stick from the other scout and added the lane.

"How close are the orchards to the outbuildings?"

"A hundred yards. Best as I could tell, they've got the mounts here, southwest of the main buildings, some in a corral, and some on tielines. They got barrackslike sheds here, and some tents next to them. Bunch of them were playing some sort of game over here. That's why I couldn't get any closer," Dhozynt said.

"Could we come down between the trees in the orchard behind the stable sheds?"

Dhozynt cocked his head. "Might not be seen that way."

Mykel looked at the squad leaders. "Here's what we'll do. We'll take that back lane. Squads one and two will get as close as we can. If there's anyone playing that game, we'll ride up and take them down. If not, we'll take out as many mounts as we can—just until they come running. We'll stand just long enough to get in some good shots, and then we'll ride back up between the trees. Squads three, four, and five will be spread in firing lines in the trees. I'll drop off with squad three, and we'll hit anyone that's coming, then withdraw. If no one comes after us at all, we'll withdraw to the lane. If anything looks wrong, and I give the order to withdraw—that's where we'll re-form. There are two objectives. The first is to kill as many of them as we can without losing men. The second is to make them think we're everywhere."

"Shooting unarmed men . . . mounts . . . that won't go down well with some of the men."

"Squad leaders," Mykel said firmly. "You might ask some of the survivors of Seventeenth Company how they feel about that. You'd also best remind each of your rankers that these are the same men who shot shackled and unarmed prisoners. The bluecoats will get a better chance than they gave those prisoners."

"They did?" asked Vhanyr.

"Why don't you answer that, Chyndylt?" suggested Mykel.

"They shot eight prisoners, dead. We lost four men," said Chyndylt.

The other three squad leaders looked at each other.

"We're going after troopers, not helpless prisoners," Mykel said firmly. "They've already wiped out most of Seventeenth Company, and they've attacked us. Remember, they started this." That wasn't totally true, but the seltyrs had started most of the skirmishes and battles, including the one at Stylan Estate. "Get the word to your men. We'll ride out in a tenth of a glass."

After the squad leaders moved back toward their squads, Mykel turned to the scouts. "Jasakyt? Is there any way to avoid riding by the gate?"

"Yes, sir. Thought you might ask about that. Take another half vingt, but there are two lanes and a short ride across a field . . ."

Mykel committed the directions to memory, but added, "You'll lead the way."

"Yes, sir. Figured that, too."

Another glass passed, quietly, as Fifteenth Company followed the scouts down the southeast road and circled away from Fynhaven Estate, only to return to the lane bordering the casaran orchards on the south.

"Company! Halt!" Mykel ordered. "First and second squads, follow me. Stand by." He rode back along the column until he reached third squad, where Bhoral rode with Chyndylt.

"Bhoral, fifth squad will hold just short of the lane. I want you to ride back to Vhanyr, and explain that. Hold there with them. You'll need to re-form the squads as they leave the orchard, so that we can move out immediately. We'll head west on the lane."

"Yes, sir."

"Chyndylt, third squad will take position a hundred yards south of first and second squads in a double staggered firing line abreast in the trees . . ." Mykel then rode back to Dravadyl and explained what he wanted from fourth squad.

After that, he returned to first squad. "Follow me. Quiet riding." He turned the chestnut through the opening in the low stone wall, a wall low enough that a mount could jump, if necessary, and headed northward. The rows of casaran trees were well tended, and the spaces just wide enough for a rider. Occasionally, Mykel had to duck his head. Once he had to ride back to position fourth squad, but Chyndylt had no trouble with third squad.

Less than a quarter glass had passed when he reined up, close to thirty yards back from the end of the orchard. He had to duck to see through the last trees, toward the outbuildings and the villa beyond.

No one was on the field where Jasakyt had reported seeing men playing a game. Several bluecoats lounged against the corral. None even looked in the direction of the orchard. Mykel could see others walking or standing near the tannish tents short of the barracks. He turned to Gendsyr. "We'll move in fast, come to a firing line, and take out anyone who's standing there. If no one else shows up, shoot a few of the mounts."

"Sir?" asked Gendsyr, his voice low.

"We need to get them stirred up so they'll come out in a hurry. Pass the word," Mykel said, in a low voice. "When I start to fire, everyone does, and if their men and a lot of mounts don't go down, then some of our men will die. It's that simple." Mykel lifted his rifle, waiting for Gendsyr to pass the word. He didn't want to shoot the horses. It wasn't their fault, but facing possibly as many as fifteen companies in the days and weeks ahead he had to do something to cut down the odds—any way he could. Besides, the horses were wealth as well, and it wouldn't hurt to bleed the seltyrs in every way possible.

"Ready, sir?" Gendsyr finally said, easing his mount up near Mykel.

Mykel nodded. "Forward!"

He urged the chestnut through the last thirty yards of the casaran orchard, then across the open space toward the corral, the tielines, and the space between the tents and shed barracks.

As he reined up less than twenty yards from a startled bluecoat, he ordered, "Squads! Firing line on me! Fire!" His rifle came up.

The stunned bluecoat looked up. Mykel forced himself to aim and will the bullet home.

Crack!

The trooper's death stabbed at him, and he pushed it away, aiming at a second bluecoat.

Shouts and yells began to rise, but troopers still peered out of the tents, and several streamed out into the open, wearing but undertunics. After a few shots, screams came from the tethered mounts as well as those in the corral. Two or three handfuls of bluecoats finally came rushing out of the stables and sheds. Perhaps half had weapons in hand. All looked dazed.

Mykel kept firing, as coolly as he could, then reloaded. Absently, he realized that he'd seen none of the officers or squad leaders. With that thought, he looked toward the villa.

Two men in what looked to be dress uniforms—one in green and one in blue—were running toward the barracks and stables. One held a rifle.

Mykel shifted his aim to the one with the rifle, then concentrated and squeezed the trigger. The captain went down face-first. The second officer threw himself to the ground and rolled sideways.

A horn sounded, and more bluecoats appeared. A number had made it to the stable sheds. Mykel smiled.

"First, second squads!" he ordered, "Withdraw! Withdraw!" His eyes swept the area as he wheeled the chestnut. From what he could tell, twenty bodies lay sprawled across the area, perhaps more.

Now . . . if some of them followed . . .

A hundred yards into the orchard, Mykel reined up and pulled the chestnut beside a casaran tree, one adjacent to the one behind which Chyndylt remained, mounted. The remainder of first and second squads rode past, not pell-mell, but at a quick trot, under control. Dust roiled up and around the trees, and Mykel stifled a cough.

The third squad leader shot an inquiring look to the captain. Mykel nodded, then pointed.

Before that long, a thin line of riders in blue appeared, moving at a quick walk.

Mykel waited until they were less than twenty yards away before he ordered, "Open fire! Fire at will!"

More bodies fell, and the riders turned and fell back.

"Third squad, withdraw!"

Mykel rode back toward the lane, but slowed as he neared fourth squad. "Dravadyl! Fourth squad! Withdraw and re-form! Withdraw and re-form." Whatever the bluecoats did, they weren't going to ride blindly any farther into the orchard. Fifteenth Company had done what it could for the day.

Mykel rode to the lane, then stood in the stirrups. "Bhoral! Forward! I'll check the rear!"

"Fifteenth Company! Forward."

Once he was certain all his men had cleared the orchard, he rode at the rear for a good vingt and a half until it appeared likely that the bluecoats—or their hosts—were not on their tail. Then he checked with each squad leader as he rode forward toward the van.

He finally pulled his mount in beside Bhoral. "We got between thirty and forty. We lost one man, two wounded. Neither too serious."

"One dead, two wounded," Bhoral said, his voice flat.

"Let's ride ahead a bit," Mykel said quietly. "Alone."

The captain didn't say anything until they were well away from first squad. "You don't like what we're doing, Bhoral." Mykel paused. "Do you?"

"I can't say as I do, sir."

"There are somewhere between eight and fifteen companies of men armed with Cadmian rifles in the eastern part of Dramur. Right now, they're not well organized. Their men really aren't used to fighting, not with real bullets, and they haven't figured out that if they massed everyone and swept down toward the compound, we'd have real trouble."

"The Myrmidons—"

"They've been gone for a solid week, and we have no idea when they'll be back. Or if they'll be back." Mykel paused. "Bhoral . . . just how do you think the seltyrs got hold of over a thousand Cadmian rifles?"

"Sir?"

"Either the Myrmidons got betrayed by other alectors, or we got betrayed by the Myrmidons. Take your pick."

For a long moment, the senior squad leader was silent.

"Either way, we can't count on much support. It might come tomorrow. It might come next week. It might not come."

"You've known this?"

"Only since last night," Mykel temporized. He didn't know it for certain, and he'd suspected it for longer, but Bhoral had to understand, or the company wouldn't be worth a frigging lame mount over the days ahead. "I don't want the men knowing all that. If anyone asks, tell them that the Myrmidons have big problems elsewhere. That much is certainly true, and that's why we were sent, and why we don't have any pteridon support right now, and why we can't count on it."

"Put that way, sir, I don't suppose we have much choice."

"No. We don't." Not any choice that Mykel could see, at least. If the seltyrs ever got organized, Third Battalion was dead. Mykel's task was to keep them from getting organized. Any way he could.

74

Dainyl's lessons in Lyterna began right after breakfast on Decdi when he followed Asulet down the steps from the upper level and then inward from the Council Chamber through yet another square arch. They walked a hundred yards down a stone corridor until they reached a wall on which was a relief sculpture that was also a mural, the brilliant and varied colors shimmering forth from the stone itself, rather than having been painted over the marble. Yet the wall appeared to have been carved from a single block of stone, with no lines that revealed joints.

Twenty Myrmidons flew in formation, each of the enforcers of justice seated upon his blue-winged pteridon, each pteridon flying below high clouds, and each Myrmidon carrying a blue metal skylance. From each lance, a ray of blue light flared down upon the ranks of an army drawn up upon the grasslands, the yellow-blue flames created by those rays consuming the soldiers of that massive army.

"The mural is marvelous," observed Dainyl, "although I'm surprised to see it here. There were a few such battles as those upon Ifryn, but not here."

"Tradition is always valuable, and a visual representation always outlasts the stories."

"That is so." Yet Dainyl could not help but wonder what someone might read into the mural in years to come.

"Lyterna is also called the Vault of the Ages—for many reasons." Asulet turned, and a section of the wall silently swung back, revealing a passageway.

"Lead on, Submarshal."

Dainyl stepped through the oblong opening a yard and a half wide and three high, followed by the older alector. Once the two had passed, the stones closed behind them, silently, massive as they were, and the two walked in dimness lit only by intermittent light-torches mounted on the walls.

Dainyl could feel grit under his boots. "Not a great deal of maintenance here lately," he observed, still puzzling over what might lie ahead—and how it related to his dispatch to Lyterna by the Highest.

"We do what we can. This section is a museum, open only to those with a need to know. Museums, especially those that are hidden, are seldom high in the allocating of resources."

At the end of a marble-walled passage—the stones there also without seams—the two emerged in a vast hall. Dainyl glanced up at the smooth stone ceiling twenty yards above.

The older alector cleared his throat, then spoke. "Each of these recesses holds something of value, of one sort or another, frozen, in more ways than one, through time. You should study each, and take your time in doing so. The first you will recognize."

Dainyl turned his attention to the right wall, unadorned blue-tinged marble, within which were set at regular intervals a series of recesses, each roughly ten yards wide. Each recess was a yard deep and ended in a flat sheet of what appeared to be blue crystal. The crystal rose ten yards, but the space between the top of the crystal and the ceiling was empty.

Sensing the other's expectation, Dainyl moved forward until he stood before the flat crystal. The crystal had looked far darker when he had been standing back, but closer, it was almost clear, and but lightly shaded with the merest hint of blue. Farther back in the solid blue crystalline mist, embedded within it, was a shape—that of a pteridon, its blue leathery wings folded back, its long cruel blue crystal beak slightly parted, as if it had just landed. The blue crystal eyes also glittered and held that dark sentience common to all pteridons. Set just below the thick neck and above the shoulders that anchored the wings was the saddle of a Myrmidon.

"One of the first pteridons? How have you been able to preserve it? It looks so lifelike."

"It *is* one of the first. It is as alive as any of those on Acorus."

"It's alive?"

"Very much so. The crystals beneath each recess interact with the lifefields to suspend them. Very simple, but it took much work. They'll be the last things to fail if it comes to that."

Dainyl bowed his head in respect. "My deepest apologies, Most Highest."

"I'm not a Highest. Never was. Just a biologist trying to get things to work out . . . and they have." The older alector smiled. "Mostly, anyway."

"If you turned them off . . . ?"

"They would be ready to fly. It would take a few days to charge the lance."

Dainyl shook his head. He had certainly not expected this in Lyterna. "Are these set aside for an emergency? Because no more can be created?"

"Exactly. Outside of Lyterna, the only alectors who know of them are the high alectors and the Marshal and Submarshal of Myrmidons."

"Are there any more?"

"Just these twenty. That should be more than enough."

Asulet moved farther back, passing the other recesses with pteridons. "Farther along, past the pteridons, each recess holds something from the past, each from farther back in time."

When Asulet finally stopped and gestured, Dainyl stepped forward until he once more stood just short of the flat crystal. There, Dainyl studied the shambling apelike figure, caught in midstride. "Was that what the indigens looked like after the seedings?"

"That *is* one of the first indigens. I preserved him myself."

"Like the pteridons, if you turned the crystals off . . . ?"

"The poor thing would be frightened and try to run." Asulet sniffed. "Timid sorts, really. Took years to breed in more aggressiveness. We needed that to get the expansion and the ability to herd. Cattle, very important sources of methane. They came from the aurochs, the cattle did."

"If . . . you turned the crystals off, could you turn them back on?"

"Oh, yes. Several times. Once or twice we have had to replace things. The switches are Talent-hidden, on the right."

Dainyl extended his Talent and let it sweep over the hidden controls, verifying what Asulet had said.

"Now here, this is what the grasslands looked like just before we released the indigens."

Before looking at the next recess, Dainyl turned to the older alector. "How . . . how did you . . . could you . . . ?"

"In essence, we mixed together the smallest components—parts of cells, if you will—taken from ourselves, from samples of steers on Ifryn, and from one of the life-forms existing here. We kept at it until it worked. It was hard on us, and harder on the brood mothers."

"Brood mothers?"

"Ulasya was one of them. Those condemned on Ifyrn were allowed a second chance here. For her services, she has every comfort Lyterna has to offer. She is a server by choice. She says that she can meet people that way."

Dainyl turned his eyes on the next recess. The greenish grass was sparse, with open patches of dirt and sand, and he could see a grass snake, clearly stalking some rodent.

Slowly, he made his way down the line of preserved exhibits.

"This was what it looked like after the first three hundred years," explained Asulet, gesturing to a scene that showed a snowy tundra with grayish flowers protruding from an icy expanse. "That is a summer scene, by the way."

The last recess showed a pool surrounded by snow and ice, a faint hint of steam rising from it. The only vegetation seemed to be lichens on the rocks closest to the water.

"That was what it was like in full summer when we began."

Even with the crystal field, the chill seemed to reach out and sink into Dainyl's very bones. He shivered.

"That was also close to the equator," added Asulet. "This world would never have developed life, not our kind of life, without our efforts."

"I thought it did have life. What about the so-called ancients?"

"They were dying out back then. It was getting too cold for them, and there wasn't enough lifeforce. They're no different from us, really. They need lifeforces to exist, and they weren't getting enough. Their only city was Dereka . . ."

"That was theirs?"

"We had to rebuild it, but it was abandoned before we ever made full-body translations to Acorus."

"How . . . If there wasn't intelligent life to build a Table?"

Asulet laughed, harshly. "Blind translations are possible. I know. The success rate is less than five percent. It took five hundred to get the first forty of us here, carrying what little we could, and there were only twenty alive when we cobbled together the first receptor Table."

Dainyl turned and looked into Asulet's violet eyes, a violet so deep that it was almost black. He couldn't imagine attempting that kind of blind translation.

"I was brilliant—and arrogant, Submarshal. Much like you. I paid, and so will you."

"I'm scarcely brilliant," Dainyl protested. "It has taken me more years than most to become a submarshal."

Asulet laughed. "You may deceive Marshal Shastylt, because he is far more arrogant than either of us, and the arrogant too often see what they wish to see in their subordinates. You may even deceive Zelyert. You cannot deceive me. I would venture to say that your progress has been slow because you do not see things in quite the same fashion as most other alectors. It has also been slow because you have recognized that quality within yourself, and it has made you most cautious. Your shields are among the strongest I have seen, and you show no sign of Talent. That is not possible. That can only mean great Talent, and the ability to listen with both Talent and ears."

Dainyl managed to keep a pleasant smile upon his face. "You're most complimentary, but I'm afraid you do me too much honor."

Asulet laughed easily once more. "I have little interest in who becomes the Marshal of Myrmidons, or the High Alector of Justice. My interest is in seeing Acorus blossom. It will not blossom if too much intellect and Talent, and too much lifeforce, are spent in determining who rules. Already, we run close to the ragged edge. Each time we move to a new world, a little more is lost. More knowledge, more understanding, is lost because some of the brightest are lost, one way or another. Once we could fashion the very cells of our being. Here, we managed to mix together cells to create the life we needed, and that took long years. I have tried to impart my knowledge to a score of those who have come here to learn, and not one has learned all that I have to share. Always, the question is how can that knowledge be used for power. And so, with each transfer of the master scepter, there is more arrogance, more squandering of lifeforce, and fewer alectors. It cannot continue, or we will not continue. That is why I look for strong and cautious alectors. They can be far bolder when necessary and seldom waste energies." Asulet paused. "Do you know why you have seen this?" He gestured back toward the crystal recesses.

"I doubt I understand all of it, but you are suggesting that life has a much more fragile hold on Acorus than most alectors imagine, and that the effort taken to allow life is far greater than anyone can acknowledge, and has taken far longer than we are told."

"Exactly."

"How long?"

"Almost five thousand years."

"You . . . ?"

Asulet laughed. "I did not *live* all those years. Many were spent in those recesses, once we set them up. We alternated for centuries, tens of centuries."

Dainyl looked to the frozen recess, then back to the older alector. He could sense the absolute truth of the other's words, and that chilled him more than the cold of the preserved past.

75

By the second glass of the afternoon on Londi, Fifteenth Company was set up behind a stone fence, and in the trees of a woodlot a half vingt north of the main entrance to Khalmyn Estate—the home of the eastern seltyr Sheludjyr. For the first day of spring, the day was warm. The white sun cast shadows from the casaran trees to the west onto the shoulder of the road, but was high enough that Mykel did not have to squint when he looked westward.

Blocking the road was an overturned wagon with a Cadmian uniform tunic lying in the dirt beside a rifle. There were gouges and hoofprints in the road, and the wagon was missing a wheel. The site was some two hundred yards to the north of a gentle curve in the road just sharp enough that a rider could not see the wagon until he had ridden to the end of the curved section.

From the trees, Mykel surveyed the scene. Then he looked at the stone fence five yards in front of him, set several yards back from the shoulder of the road. Second squad was deployed on foot, each man crouching close behind the stones, concealed from those on the road.

Mykel glanced to the south. He could barely hear the sound of hoofs on the dry road, the occasional murmur of voices of the oncoming companies of rebels. While he was certain he and his men were well concealed, for the ambush to be most effective, the column of riders—one company of greencoats and one of bluecoats—needed to get within forty yards of the wagon. He'd debated about the diversion, but had decided to use it, because, with the center of the road blocked, the men riding into the ambush would be more likely to turn back or bunch up around the wagon. He'd also placed more of fourth and fifth squads in the trees in the middle of the curve, so that they would be in a position to fire at any troopers turning and trying to flee.

Mykel continued to wait. Sweat oozed down his back. The sound of hoofs slowly grew louder, as did the voices. Then the first outriders appeared, coming around the last section of the curve. Neither seemed to notice the wagon until they were only about a hundred yards from it.

"There's a wagon overturned!" called one.

Words were shouted back, but Mykel could not make them out.

Both riders continued toward the wagon, until they were less than thirty yards from it. Then one reined in, and the other continued northward. He reined in just short of the wagon.

"It's empty. Lost a wheel, looks like. Wait! There's a tunic here—and a rifle." The outrider straightened in the saddle. "Someone left a rifle. Good rifle, too."

By then, the first squad of the oncoming troopers was through the turn and on the straight section of the road toward the wagon.

"Empty wagon and rifle!" the second outrider called back. "Wagon's missing a wheel!"

Mykel waited, hoping that the column would keep moving forward.

The leading riders of the first squad had just passed Mykel when the captain riding in the front ordered, "Column! Halt!" He rode forward toward the wagon.

As Mykel had planned, the front of the column slowed, then stopped, while the later riders failed to hear the orders—or did not react as quickly. The spacing between the squads of greencoats narrowed, then vanished. Mykel couldn't tell what was happening farther back to the south, but the seltyr's troopers were about as close as they were likely to get.

"Fire!" ordered Mykel, aiming at the captain in green near the front of the column.

Crack! Crack! Crack! . . . The initial shots came from out of the trees, where the other squads were arrayed, because they did not have to reveal themselves to fire.

The green captain pitched forward in the saddle.

The next volley came from the stone fence and second squad.

"Return fire!" came a command from somewhere, but few of the riders on the road heard it or heeded it immediately.

One squad leader repeated the order, and had his own rifle out. Mykel aimed and fired, willing his shot home. The squad leader dropped. Mykel kept firing, deliberately, dropping a man with almost every shot. Then he leaned back behind the short-needled pine to reload.

Some of the greencoats bolted northward, but they had to slow to get around the wagon. More were hit, some wounded in arms or legs, others slumping in their saddles or toppling onto the road.

Mykel winced as one second squad trooper slumped over the wall. He turned and fired on a group of greencoats that had formed into a rough line and were firing at second squad. Three went down before the other three wheeled their mounts and withdrew.

Within moments, the road was empty of mounted bluecoats and greencoats, with only the wounded and dead and at least a half score of mounts milling around.

"Cease fire! Cease fire!" Mykel ordered.

He mounted the chestnut and moved out through one of the openings in the stone wall. "Second squad, mount up! First squad, round up the loose mounts!" Then he rode back southward toward the curve in the road. He had to pick his way around the bodies. At a rough count, there were probably close to sixty, all told.

"Fourth and fifth squads! Mount up and re-form! Gather the rifles and ammunition. Leave their wounded."

He turned the chestnut back northward.

When he neared the wagon, he could see that Gendsyr's men had managed to get control of more than a half score of the rebel mounts. Several of the second squad rankers were strapping and tying the rifles they had covered to the captured horses. Others had dragged the wagon clear of the road. Mykel looked back, and saw that Bhoral and fourth and fifth squads were formed up and riding northward toward Mykel.

"Squads one, two, and three, mount up! We need to get riding." While Mykel doubted that the routed rebels would immediately return, he wanted to get moving before they had a chance to regroup and return. If he had had a full battalion at his command, he might well have pursued and captured or eliminated the two rebel companies entirely.

Once Fifteenth Company was riding in good order northward, with both scouts and outriders ahead, and after Mykel had gotten the casualty reports from the squad leaders, he turned the chestnut and rode back to find Bhoral.

"Sir," acknowledged the senior squad leader, as Mykel eased his mount beside him.

"We didn't do too badly," Mykel said. "Two dead, and two wounded."

Bhoral looked at Mykel. "Captain . . . they didn't even know what happened."

"No." Mykel felt disturbed about that, but he didn't see that he had that much choice.

"It won't be too long before they catch on."

"Probably not, but if we can take on two or three more companies this way, we won't have to worry about being outnumbered." Equally important, from Mykel's point of view, was his hope that the rebel squad leaders and rankers would come to fear the Cadmians.

76

Dainyl stood in a stone-walled chamber. Two sets of double light-torches set five yards apart in bronze brackets on each side wall provided all the illumination. The only furnishing in the chamber was a black oak chest slightly over a yard in height and set against the north wall, equidistant between the light-torches. Nothing was rested on the chest's shimmering black surface. The sole apparent entry and exit to the Table chamber was through a square arch at the west end of the chamber. There was no door attached to the archway, and a set of stone steps led upward from the chamber. In the center of the chamber was a square stone pedestal that extended a yard above the stone floor. The stone appeared black but did not reflect any illumination from the light-torches. Each side of the tablelike pedestal was three yards in length. The walls and ceiling were all of polished redstone, and outside of the light-torches, the stone pedestal, and the single chest, the chamber contained no other furnishings or decorations.

Asulet gestured to the stone pedestal. "That is a Table. It does not look terribly prepossessing, but used properly, it is a tool of immeasurable value. Look at it closely, not only with your eyes but with your Talent."

Dainyl studied the stone pedestal, slowly, carefully. After a moment, he realized that there was a purple glow suffusing the Table and emanating from it.

"The Table is actually closer to a cube," Asulet added. "It extends well below the floor."

"It's not solid, is it?"

The older alector smiled. "It is, and it isn't. The outer layers are a form of stone. The interior contains certain crystals in a matrix. Once placed and linked to the grid, the matrix is extremely stable—unless one attempts to move the Table. It could last for thousands of years, if not longer."

"And if someone tries to move it?"

"You wouldn't want to be anywhere near. The Table stores energy from every use. This Table has been in use for a long time, although it doesn't get as much use now as do the Tables in Elcien and Ludar."

"Would it explode?"

"With force enough to collapse the chamber." Asulet stepped toward the Table, resting a hand on one edge. "Traveling on Acorus is just a local translation, taking the tubes to go from one Table to another. Using the Tables or any translation tube is all mental. It requires the use of Talent and mental vision and positioning to go through the barriers and to find a locator marking another Table, then to break out. Each Table has its own location vector, and every alector sees the shape of the locators slightly differently. Some see the locators as arrows, others as mathematical vector symbols, and still others as triangles."

"What do I do?" asked Dainyl.

"You step onto the Table, and think about the blackness beneath. You should feel yourself falling into darkness, as cold as anything you have ever felt. Around you, your Talent should show you the various locator arrows. They should seem nearer or farther away by their size, although that is not always a good guide. That is why you should know the color of the locator. Each Table has a different color. The Table here in Lyterna is pink. The one in Elcien is white."

"Is there a map?"

"Somewhere, but it's better just to learn the colors."

"Could I go to Ifryn as well through the Table? By mistake?"

"You'd have to make that mistake on purpose. The long translation tunnels are large purplish tubes, and they feel far away. You can't sense the locators on Ifryn from here, just as alectors using the Tables on Ifryn cannot sense ours." Asulet looked sternly at Dainyl. "No matter how experienced you may become with the Tables here, there is always a risk to a long translation. It is a risk not worth taking if you're already here on Acorus."

Dainyl understood the unspoken message. Ifryn was dying as too many alectors and too many uses bled the world's lifeforce away, and what was the use of risking his life to travel to a dying world?

"There is some risk the first time you use a Table," the older alector admitted. "Once you master the technique, then there's virtually no risk to travel to any of the other thirteen Tables on Acorus."

Dainyl wasn't certain he wanted to try the Table just yet. "What about using the Table to see things?"

"That's a different technique, and you shouldn't try that until you've mastered traveling."

"I've heard that a Table can't show anything created through Talent or anyone who can use Talent. Is that true?"

"Generally speaking, yes. An experienced recorder can still often determine what an alector with Talent is doing by watching the surroundings."

"What about seeing what has already happened?"

"Events fade. Insignificant events, those which do not impact the lifemass, are impossible to recall with a Table within glasses, certainly within a day. Others . . . it depends on who is involved, where, when, and the ability of the recorder or whoever is using the Table. Never more than a week, I understand."

From what Dainyl could sense, Asulet was telling the truth as he knew it.

"Enough of that for now," said the older alector. "You need to try the Table."

Dainyl looked at the Table, and the purple glow, visible only through his Talent, seemed almost ominous. "Is there anything else I should know? Where should I go?" Asulet's instructions seemed sketchy at best.

"I can't tell you more, because a Table has to be experienced. Even if I stepped onto the Table with you, the moment we dropped into the dark and cold, you'd be on your own. It is a total solitary experience, and you either master it on your own . . . or you don't. You'll have to decide your own destination. The easiest Table to translate to seems to be Tempre. Its locator is a bright blue." Asulet smiled. "Just step onto the Table and concentrate. When you get to Tempre, wait a while to warm up before you come back."

The submarshal stepped up to the Table and brushed it with his fingers. The surface was cool to the touch, but not cold. Looked at from the side, there was a mirrorlike finish to the surface. He bent over the Table, seeing his own reflection.

Then he took a half step back, studying the Table once more before he half stepped, half jumped, onto it. The surface felt as hard as stone, and there was a chill that seeped through his boots, even though the Table had not been cold to his touch.

Concentrate on the blackness. Asulet had said. Dainyl reached out with his Talent to the Table, and below it, where he sensed a well of darkness. He could feel it rising around him . . .

Dainyl found himself in turbulent river of purplish blackness, a darkness that buffeted and battered him. Yet he was carried nowhere, much as he felt as though he were caught in an underground river. Bitter chill penetrated every span of his body, sweeping through his garments as if he wore nothing. Instantly, he felt colder than he had in winter at Eastice. He could see nothing. He tried to lift his arms, but they would not move.

Sluggishly, as if his thinking had been slowed by the chill, he remembered to reach out with his Talent, to try to find the locators. After what felt like glasses, he began to discern several narrow wedges, colored wedges. One hovered above him, a bright pink-purple. Another wedge of bright blue seemed closer than all the others except for the pink. Beyond, somewhere in the blackness and chill, he could sense wedges of color—crimson-gold, amber, brilliant yellow, green, gray . . . Beyond, in a sense he could not have explained, stretched a deep and distant purple-black wedge. The sense of distance was so overpowering that Dainyl felt almost nauseated.

What was he supposed to do? To concentrate on using his Talent to move himself toward one of the wedges—the bright blue wedge.

He concentrated . . . trying to focus on the blue, so near, and yet not so close as it seemed, seeking to bring himself to it, before the chill of wherever he was slowed his thinking so much that he could no longer use his Talent.

He sensed no movement, nothing.

He had to do something before he ceased to exist, or turned into a brainless wild translation—but what?

Could he link himself to that blue wedge that was Tempre? He attempted to cast out a Talent-line, and a thin line of purple flowed from him, a line of Talent-energy that connected with the blue wedge. Abruptly, with a swift pulsation, he felt himself flowing through the chill darkness, hurtling toward the blue, a blue that turned silver and shattered around him.

Dainyl had to take two quick steps to get his balance before he caught himself. Once more, he stood on a Table, this time in another windowless chamber. His entire body shivered, much as he would have willed it otherwise, and even his legs quivered, feeling weak. Frost appeared on his uniform then vanished, melting as quickly as it had appeared.

Dainyl eased himself off the Table. Unlike the Table chamber in Lyterna, the chamber was empty. The single entrance was a narrow square arch, in which a solid oak door was set—closed. There was not a single hanging on the walls, formed of fitted stone, rather than carved out of the rock itself, nor a single furnishing in the chamber.

Dainyl opened the door. Outside, stationed on each side of the arch, were two alectors, both wearing the blue-and-gray Myrmidon uniforms. The Myrmidon ranker on the right had his hand on the hilt of a lightning-edged short sword, the weapon used for guard duty inside buildings. As his eyes took in the uniform and the stars on Dainyl's collar, the Myrmidon relaxed. "Submarshal, sir?"

"Just looking around," Dainyl replied. "This is Tempre, isn't it?"

"Yes, sir." Puzzlement appeared in the other's eyes.

"Good. Thank you." Dainyl closed the door behind him and walked into the corridor, turning right, since he saw some sort of light in that direction. Behind him, he could pick up the murmurs between the two.

". . . said only the ones with stars, submarshal and marshal, and the high alectors . . ."

". . . what's behind the door . . ."

". . . don't know, and Furtryl said I'd better never ask, and never look . . ."

Dainyl kept walking. After fifty yards, he came to a circular stone staircase. Did he want to go up? He decided against it—Asulet was waiting—and walked back to the Table chamber.

Neither guard said a word as he opened the door to the Table chamber and closed it behind him.

He looked at the Table, took a deep breath, and stepped onto the black stone surface, concentrating on the blackness below. As he dropped through the Table, this time, he was aware of silverness spraying away from him.

Again, the chill purple blackness enfolded him, but this time, he was already focusing on finding a pink-purple wedge. He fumbled for a moment before Talent-linking to the pinkish wedge. Silver sprayed away from him . . .

He stood on the Table at Lyterna.

Asulet smiled. "Congratulations, Submarshal. You are now qualified to be considered as a High Alector."

Dainyl stepped off the Table. That made sense in a way. "At least, the Highest and Marshal Shastylt won't have to look for another submarshal."

"Not until you become marshal; then it will be your problem."

That was likely to be many, many years away—if ever. Dainyl still recalled all too vividly what had happened to Tyanylt—and how no one had ever mentioned his name again, even to Lystrana, once he had crossed the marshal and the Highest.

77

On Duadi, Mykel had sent out the scouts but given the rest of Fifteenth Company a day of badly needed and well-deserved rest. Then he had headed off to see Dohark.

The overcaptain was standing in the study that wasn't his, rather than pacing, and he still had dark circles under his eyes. "You might as well come in, Mykel."

Mykel closed the study door behind him.

Dohark sat behind the desk and waited for Mykel to seat himself. He did not speak.

"What have you heard?" asked the captain.

"I've heard that I have a captain who's managed to slaughter between one and three entire companies of rebels, and who has probably shot half of them himself."

While Mykel felt he'd shot and killed all too many rebels, the number couldn't have been that high. "I've shot a few. Most rankers in Fifteenth Company have."

"How long can you keep it up?" From his tone of voice, Dohark might have been asking about what was being served in the officers' mess.

"For as long as they don't know how to use scouts and don't trust each other." Mykel paused. "Is there any word on when the colonel will return back? Or on reinforcements?"

Dohark shook his head.

"Do you think that we've been left here to rot on the vine, sir?"

"I don't think so. I don't have any delusions about the warmth of the

Myrmidons and the alectors, but I can't see any benefit to them in abandoning us." A wry smile appeared. "Waiting until we're in great difficulty before pulling us out . . . I can see that as a way of reminding everyone of our dependence on the power of the alectors."

Mykel could see that as well. He just didn't like the implications for Third Battalion—especially for Fifteenth Company.

"What new idea do you have for keeping us less dependent on them?" asked Dohark.

"Can you get me several barrels of gunpowder?" asked Mykel. "And a length of good fuse, and two or three kegs of nails? Big nails."

Dohark looked across the desk at the captain. "How are you going to manage that, without blowing up your own company? What happens when the locals decide to reciprocate? Or the Myrmidons show up again? They're not exactly fond of large explosive devices."

"I've heard words about that, but I've never seen anything."

"You won't. It's not written anywhere. I was a ranker for longer than most officers," Dohark said. "I'd been with Ninth Company a year, maybe two, when we were sent east to deal with a bunch of Squawts in the hills around Dekhron. They'd built a redoubt on a hilltop, walls a good three yards thick, and at least four high. Had a well or a spring there, and enough food for years. Stone roof as well. Firelances didn't do any good."

Mykel nodded. Solid stone would stop a skylance.

"We had a captain. Bright man. You remind me of him. He didn't like us getting picked off one at a time. He suggested that maybe we ought to leave the Squawts alone. Majer Bryten said no—we had orders to take the place, even if it meant killing half the battalion. He was like Majer Vaclyn. The captain did pretty much what you were thinking about. Did it himself. Sneaked up the hill on the darkest night and climbed up the stones where the Squawts couldn't see him. He lowered the barrel of powder somewhere, lit the fuse, and made off. Blew a big hole in the redoubt. We attacked, and the Squawts surrendered."

"What he did worked," Mykel said. "Then what happened?"

"He was recalled to Elcien. Told to ride there immediately the next morning. He never made it. One of the Myrmidons thought he was a Squawt—fried him to a cinder. Terrible mistake." Dohark paused. "The word is that anytime someone starts using gunpowder for anything besides rifles, there's a terrible mistake."

Mykel could not only sense the truth of Dohark's words, but the concern behind them. He also realized he'd never heard or seen gunpowder used for anything except rifles or work in the mines. "I'd better think of something else."

"I worry about you, Mykel. All you've been doing is thinking of ways to kill people."

"Isn't that what we were sent here to do?" Mykel heard the tiredness in his own voice.

"You seem to like it."

Mykel could feel his face stiffen. "Sir, I don't like it. I never have. I'm getting good at it, but that's only because the choices don't seem to be very great. If Fifteenth Company can't strike first and harder, then Third Battalion loses more men."

"Frigging tough problem, isn't it?" Dohark laughed, a sound both harsh and soft. "Do you have any other ideas?"

"I'll have to think about them, after the scouts get back."

"Maybe the lady seltyr can give you some ideas. She seems to talk to you. She won't say a word to me, or Majer Herryf. She wouldn't even say anything to Colonel Dainyl. Do you know why she talks to you?"

"No," admitted Mykel. "She doesn't say much. I'm fortunate if I can get her to say more than a few sentences."

"That's more than she'll say to anyone else." Dohark stood. "Do you still think you can operate effectively against the seltyrs?"

"For now." Mykel rose as well.

"Don't push it. There'll be a time when you can't. Just ride away when that happens."

"I will." Mykel had no desire for a so-called glorious death in the face of impossible odds. He'd tried not to roll the bones except when the odds favored him. That wouldn't change.

"See that you do. We need you."

Mykel inclined his head, then left the study. He appreciated Dohark's warning about the gunpowder, and the fact that the overcaptain had explained, rather than just dismissing the idea, as Majer Vaclyn would most likely have done.

Once outside the headquarters building, Mykel had to squint for a moment while his eyes adjusted to the bright morning sunlight. A light wind blew out of the south as he walked across the courtyard toward the structure holding the officer's cell—and Rachyla. The air was far warmer than it had been, giving the compound the feel of early summer in Elcien. Mykel had no desire to remain in Dramur for the long hot summer that was sure to come.

Even before he reached the cell, one of the guards was watching him. Mykel stopped in the shade cast by the overhanging balcony and blotted the dampness off his forehead.

"Sir?" asked the guard.

"Overcaptain Dohark sent me. If you want to check—"

"No, sir. He already told us that you were in charge of questioning the woman."

Mykel suppressed a smile. He owed Dohark for that. He wasn't sure what he owed the overcaptain—a thank-you or a practical joke, or both.

Rachyla did not even look at Mykel until the guards closed and locked the door. She said nothing. In turn, for several moments, he just looked at her.

"Your splinter wound has healed," she finally said.

"Yes." He waited, still standing a good two yards from her.

After a moment, she asked, "Why are you here? Again?"

"Because I want to be, because the overcaptain asked me, because . . ." He shrugged.

"You are losing?"

Mykel shook his head. "Not so far. It might be easier if Fifteenth Company were."

"Do not ask me for sympathy, Captain."

"I'm not." He paused. "More than a week ago—it seems longer—we were attacked by bluecoats at the mine. Some prisoners tried to escape. The bluecoats stopped shooting at us long enough to shoot down all the prisoners. Why?"

"A slave or a prisoner can never be allowed to be free again. That is the law of the seltyrs."

"What about you?"

"I will not be freed. When my usefulness is over, I will be killed."

"That's why you talk to me?"

"I must talk to someone, or I will have no usefulness. You are honest. You are as sharp and as direct as a dagger of the ancients, and with that edge you will likely cut your own throat."

"As sharp and as direct as a dagger of the ancients? What does that mean?"

Rachyla looked hard at him. "You are a dagger of the ancients, Captain. That is a curse and a prophecy, but the daggers are real. I have only seen one. It was my grandfather's. He gave it to his worst enemy. Where it is now, who can say?"

Mykel couldn't help but wonder if the dagger concealed in his belt was the same one. He doubted it, because he couldn't imagine a seltyr stooping to have a chandler as his worst enemy, but one never knew. "Don't you think the seltyrs are cutting their own throats?"

Rachyla shrugged. "Do they have any choice? Do you? Do I? Only the stupid talk of choices. Wisdom is when you see that there are no true choices."

"You don't believe that we have choices?"

A laugh filled the cell, that same ironic and melodic laugh that he tried to recall once he had left her—and never could. Mykel waited, hoping she would say more.

"We have choices, Captain. We have one true choice at any one time. The rest are but illusions."

"The illusion of choice," he said softly.

"You understand. You wish you did not, but you do."

"So I am fated to kill hundreds of men whose only fault is that they follow an unwise seltyr, and that seltyr is fated to fail because he sees no other choice?"

"Not if he would remain a seltyr," Rachyla replied.

"You're saying that the Myrmidons are using the Cadmians to destroy the seltyrs."

"Are you not? My father is dead. How long before the others are dead—or wish that they were?"

Mykel didn't have an answer for that, not an honest one. "What of you?"

"I told you. Unless someone makes a foolish choice, I will die."

"Then why don't you just give up?" Mykel managed not to snap the words out.

A sardonic smile crossed her lips. "Because, Captain, there are enough men who make foolish choices that I see no point in seeking death. Death comes to all, sooner or later, but I would rather not hasten it. Besides, it is amusing to see you try to avoid your fate."

"What *is* my fate?"

For the first time, her face showed just a touch of indecision, but that indecision vanished even as he read it in her green eyes. "You will be tormented by the One Who Is until you no longer know what you believe or whom to trust—and that is but the beginning." Abruptly, she turned away.

"So . . . what do you suggest, Lady Rachyla?"

She did not turn or respond.

She would not. That he could tell, and he bowed, even though she could not see the gesture. "Good day, Lady. Until the next time."

He rapped on the door, and waited until it opened.

Once he was outside, the guards looked at him.

Mykel shook his head.

"Seems to go that way, sir."

"Still . . . each time, I learn a little more." Mykel wasn't about to reveal all that he learned, and some of what he learned didn't seem applicable. Not yet.

As he crossed the courtyard, he hoped that the reports from the scouts would offer some ideas on what he could do with Fifteenth Company. Rachyla hadn't been helpful there, except to reinforce his feeling that the seltyrs weren't about to surrender or submit—just as she would not.

78

Dainyl had felt exhausted after his two Table trips on Duadi, brief as they had seemed, and had gone back to his guest quarters in Lyterna to rest.

At the evening meal, Asulet had reassured him, "The first trips are tiring. With each translation, it gets easier. You'll hardly notice it when you go back to Elcien tomorrow."

"No more secrets?" Dainyl had asked, with a smile.

"There are always more secrets," Asulet had replied with a laugh, "but those you don't know won't help you until you master what you've just learned."

That had been the end of the information, as Asulet had asked about the latest music from Ifryn, and about the weather in various places where Dainyl had recently been. He politely refused to answer any questions that dealt with substance.

Early on Tridi morning, wearing his flying jacket and gloves, Dainyl had stepped onto the Table in the chamber in Lyterna, his saddlebags over one shoulder. He concentrated . . . and felt himself dropping through the silver barrier . . .

. . . into the chill blackness. He extended his Talent, seeking out the brilliant white wedge at Elcien. With his Talent-link, he rushed through the darkness, yet without a real sense of motion, toward another silver barrier, one limned in white. White silver sprayed from him . . .

He stood on another Table. For a moment, he shivered. The jacket and gloves had not helped against the cold blackness between Tables. The Table was identical to the others he had used, or so it seemed. The walls of the Table chamber walls were of white marble, and the floor of green. He stepped off the Table and walked to the heavy white oak door. He opened it and stepped into a small foyer, with a second door. The second door had a Talent-lock, and it took a moment for Dainyl to release it.

After he stepped into the familiar lower-level corridor in the Hall of Justice, he replaced the Talent-lock and walked toward the Highest's study. Even before he reached it, he could tell it was empty. He made his way to one of the other smaller chambers, one where the door was ajar.

An assistant who vaguely resembled Kylana, Dainyl thought, looked up. "Submarshal? Can I help you?"

"The Highest?"

"Sir . . . he and Marshal Shastylt are in Ludar today. He hoped to return this evening."

"Oh. I've been traveling. If you would tell the Highest that I've returned."

"Yes, sir. I'll make certain he knows."

"Thank you." With a nod, Dainyl turned and made his way to and up the hidden staircase, out through the Talent-concealed stone doorway, and through the Hall of Justice. Outside, the fat and chill flakes of a spring snowstorm pelted him.

It took almost a quarter glass before a hacker and carriage drove by the Hall. It took less time than he had waited to get him back to Myrmidon headquarters, since there was no reason to go to his house, not when Lystrana would not be there for glasses. The interior of headquarters was welcomingly warm as Dainyl stepped inside, still carrying his gear.

"Welcome back, sir," offered Undercaptain Chelysta, standing by the duty desk.

"Thank you." Dainyl smiled, gesturing toward the window from where the duty officer could see the flight stage. "Fourth squad has the duty? Is anyone flying?"

"Viosyna lifted off on the dispatch run to Ludar before the snow came in. I told her to hold there until she was sure the storm had blown through."

"Good. What else has gone wrong while I've been away?"

"You mean outside of the mess in Iron Stem, the missing skylances in Dereka, the wild Talent in Hyalt, the rebellion in Dramur, the furor in Coren, the floods in Catyr, or the missing pteridon and Cadmians on the North Road?"

Dainyl managed to offer an ironic smile. "Let's start with the missing pteridon and Cadmians. Does this have anything to do with the Cadmian relocation from Scien to Norda?"

"Yes, sir. An entire company of Cadmians vanished riding south to Norda. An unseasonal blizzard hit, and there's no sign of them anywhere. Third Company in Alustre sent two pteridons to Pystra to see if they could find the Cadmians. One pteridon is missing."

"Missing? How could a pteridon be missing?" Sometimes a rider had a mishap, and the pteridon returned without the flier, but there was no record of a pteridon and rider vanishing. Not in recent years, at least. "Could they have landed somewhere to wait out a storm?"

"We don't know," replied Chelysta. "It's never happened before. We heard on Londi, and they had been missing for a week. The report's on your desk."

"What about Iron Stem?"

"The mines are open, but third squad has been patrolling there . . ."

"What about the skylances? Are more of them missing?"

"One more. No one knows how it happened."

Considering then-Majer Dhenyr hadn't known how the first disappearances had occurred, that there was nothing new on the second wasn't exactly surprising. "Hyalt?"

"Yuasult lost Synetra to the Talent-wielder, but they flamed him down, finally. Everything's under control there."

"Coren?"

"The marshal's been handling that, and he hasn't said anything, sir."

"What about the floods?"

"Catyr. That was another case where the locals logged a section of the lower mountains, in a place where we don't usually overfly. They had warm rains, and some of the hillside slid across the river. Then there was more rain, and a big lake built up behind the mud—"

"The mud gave way, and all that water washed downstream and flooded the town?"

"Yes, sir."

Dainyl almost wished he hadn't asked. "Are Quelyt and Falyna around?"

"Quelyt has the day off. He did a long message run to Salcer and back yesterday. Falyna was out in the squares a while ago."

"I'd appreciate it if they weren't sent on any more runs without first checking with me."

"Yes, sir."

Dainyl headed to his study. As he had feared, there were reports stacked on his desk, but as he read through them, it was clear that they added only a few details to what he had already known or to what Undercaptain Chelysta had told him. There were no reports from Dramur, but then, there was no way for there to be any. There were no Myrmidons there. Dainyl had no doubts that the situation had gotten worse. It couldn't have developed any other way.

He sat back in his chair. Over the winter and the first days of spring, *everything* had gotten worse. He couldn't recall as many problems hitting at once. He also didn't believe in coincidence, but he couldn't see a common cause—except in the cases of Dramur, Catyr, and Coren, where one consistent factor was lander greed, tied to a lack of understanding about the fragility of the world's lifemass.

It wasn't that the schools didn't teach about natural balance; it wasn't that the landers and indigens hadn't been told that mature forests were better for the world. It was that lifeforce couldn't be measured except through Talent, and steers didn't have any. So, without a way to see the truth with their own eyes or senses, when golds were involved, steers just let those teachings fall away—unless the alectors stepped in with skylances or sent in a Cadmian battalion.

Yet, there was more at work than golds. He still had no idea why he was being kept, so indirectly and yet so obviously, from heading back to Dramur. It seemed clear enough that the marshal and the Highest wanted things to go wrong there, but Dainyl still couldn't figure out why. Was it to weaken the Cadmians? Or because they disliked the culture being built up by the seltyrs and needed an excuse to destroy it, in a way that would be seen as justifiable by landers outside of Dramur? The latter was certainly possible. From what he'd seen, he didn't care much for the way the seltyrs controlled the island. That possibility was something he could broach, at least in a veiled way, with the marshal.

He went back to studying the reports, then reviewing the accounts, a task he would be more than happy to turn over to his successor, whenever Dhenyr reached headquarters.

The marshal arrived in the duty coach right after the fourth glass of the afternoon, presumably after having used the Table at the Hall of Justice to return to Elcien. He stopped at Dainyl's door. "If you have a moment, Submarshal?"

Dainyl stood immediately. He not only had the moments, but wanted to hear what Shastylt had to say. He'd hoped the marshal wouldn't be too long in returning, because he was looking forward to seeing Lystrana, and not late in the evening.

Dainyl followed the marshal, closing the door to the marshal's study. He waited for the senior alector to seat himself before settling into one of the straight-backed chairs.

Shastylt looked tired, one of the few times that Dainyl had seen him that way, with redness around the edges of his eyes and a sense of lagging lifeforce. His left eye twitched several times. "How was Lyterna, Dainyl?"

"Most interesting. Asulet clarified a number of things."

"He has that habit." Shastylt's tone was dry. "I assume you've read all the reports?"

"Yes, sir. I also talked to the duty officer to see if anything new had happened."

"Is there? I would hope not. Enough has gone awry in the past few weeks without something else."

"I didn't see a report on the floods in Catyr. Everything else was covered."

"Catyr is another example of lander stupidity and greed. It just came at a bad time, but it's manageable."

"I don't like the report that we lost a pteridon," Dainyl said bluntly. "We've never lost one, to my knowledge."

"In the early days, we lost a few to the ancients."

"Is that possible? Now?"

Shastylt took a long and slow breath. "The North Road is the northernmost high road in Corus, and the coldest. The ancients have always preferred cold and the north. There are occasional sightings, still. It *is* possible."

"What else could it be?"

"The Highest does not know of anything else, but one way or another, it is worrisome. I sent a message to Asulet asking for his thoughts. He said that was the most likely possibility." Shastylt looked across the wide desk, a desk that held neither reports nor papers, and steepled his long fingers together. His eyes looked at Dainyl without really seeing the submarshal. "I'd like you to brief Colonel Dhenyr when he arrives the day after tomorrow. I'm going to be tied up with the Highest, and with the Duarches' Council. They're asking questions about the problems in Iron Stem and Hyalt, and now the High Alector of Trade is claiming that the way we handled Coren has created trade problems that will affect lifeforce adversely."

"From what I have read in the reports," Dainyl replied, "what was happening there before the Myrmidons got involved was having an even larger negative impact on lifeforce. You don't let people chop down older-growth forests without some significant impact."

"Exactly. Unhappily, the High Alector of Trade seems to feel that we should be overflying every old-growth forest in Corus."

Even without calculating, Dainyl knew that sort of overflying would have taken every moment of the year for the hundred-and-eighty-odd pteridons of the Myrmidons, not to mention what the drain on the world lifeforce would have been.

"What about the situation in Dramur?" asked Dainyl. "It will have been several weeks by the time I return, even if I leave first thing on Sexdi. With all that is happening here, it might be best if I returned there to see if I could wind matters up there. That way, I could return here, and help deal with some of the other problems. Several of them look to be even longer-running than Dramur . . . and more serious."

Shastylt nodded. "The Highest and I talked that over earlier today. That might be best."

"What do you think about the seltyrs and the growers on Dramur?" Dainyl asked.

The marshal shrugged, then gave a half smile. "Like most landers, their concern is for golds and comfort. They are more ruthless than most in power, but that is because Dramur is an island, and other landers cannot easily challenge them." He raised his eyebrows. "You think that they should be replaced?"

"I had not made plans in such a direction, but I have thought about what might happen if they had taken matters into their own hands in my absence."

"You should follow what you think, Dainyl. Dramur needs to be settled quickly, now. Since there is an ancient tunnel there, also, you might take care to avoid it . . . in view of what may have happened at Scien."

Dainyl caught the word "now" and kept his face pleasantly interested, as well as maintaining a tight Talent-hold over his feelings. "I will be most careful. I'll leave first thing on Sexdi . . . after I've briefed the colonel on Quinti. In the meantime, is there anything else you'd like me to handle?"

Shastylt tilted his head before speaking. It was a pose. "Not at the moment. You may have to brief the Highest and the Duarches on the situation in Dramur once you have resolved it."

"Then, by your leave? You are doubtless rather pressed . . ."

The marshal laughed once, a sound not quite humorous, and forced. "Pressed is a very good way of saying it. If I'm not summoned again, we'll talk tomorrow about what I'd like you to emphasize when you brief Dhenyr. You might give that some thought."

Dainyl closed the study door firmly but quietly on his way out.

He'd definitely gotten the impression that whatever the marshal and the Highest had planned in Dramur had not gone at all the way that they had anticipated. Now he'd be stuck cleaning it up, and it was likely to be messy and bloody, because they'd practically forced it to get out of hand. He just wished he knew why.

79

Lystrana was waiting in the foyer of their dwelling when Dainyl stepped through the doorway and out of the snow flurries that had come and gone all day. The warmth of her smile erased—for those moments—the concerns that had preoccupied him most of the day. He moved toward her, but she was faster, and had her arms around him before he could set down his gear.

"I'm so glad you're back safely," she murmured in his ear, still holding him tightly.

"Did you ever doubt it?"

"Not from you . . . but there are stories about those who never leave Lyterna," Lystrana admitted, easing back.

"I met some of them." Dainyl shook his head sadly. "They do the menial work there. They're prisoners in all but name. They have to be the ones who can't use the Table, though."

"That means they were born here."

"Or thrown through the long translation tubes blind. That was also done."

Lystrana's face froze for an instant. "It was?"

Dainyl nodded. "I learned a great deal while I was there."

"You can tell me later." Her head inclined toward the kitchen. "Sentya will have supper ready before long. We can settle at the table and talk about other things."

"I'll take my gear upstairs and be right back." He gave her another hug, brushing her smooth alabaster cheek with his lips, then stepped back and hurried up the stairs.

It took him but a few moments to hang up his clothing and set his spare boots on their rack. Everything he brought back was clean, thanks to the very industrious menials of Lyterna.

A glass of amber wine stood at his place at the table, with one before Lystrana as well. Once he had seated himself across from her, she lifted the purple-tinged crystal. He lifted his as well. There was the faintest ringing *cling* as the goblets touched.

"To your safe return." Her smiling face glowed.

"To all safe returns." He was smiling as broadly as she was. He took a sip of the wine, savoring it. "What is this?"

"It's something from Syan. Zestafyn recommended it, and I had Zistele buy some for us. How was the flight out?"

"The weather was clear and cold, but we didn't run into any storms. I'd forgotten just how wide the grasslands are. It's almost six hundred vingts from the west side of the Lower Spine Mountains to Lyterna . . ." Dainyl went on to describe what he had seen on the flight, and the view of the Vault in the late afternoon.

"Alector . . . alectress . . ." murmured Sentya, standing by the table with two bowls of steaming oarfish chowder.

"Oh . . . I'm sorry, Sentya," Dainyl said. "I didn't see you there."

"Sir, I liked hearing what you saw."

Dainyl caught a touch of wistfulness in her voice. It reminded him how fortunate he was to be able to fly and to see so much of the world. "That may be," he replied with a laugh, "but I wouldn't want your arms to fall asleep while I kept talking."

The older serving girl slipped a bowl before Lystrana, then the other before Dainyl.

"Thank you, Sentya," said Lystrana.

After the day's chill, the chowder was more than welcome, and neither spoke for a time.

"What's happened at the palace?" Dainyl finally asked.

"Very little in our area. We've had to transfer additional funds to Alustre and to some of the regional centers with problems."

"Things like the floods in Catyr?"

Lystrana nodded. "We can't pay for the reconstruction costs. The locals will have to do that, but we'll have to send in a supervisor to make sure that they don't cut corners, and that they do the necessary reforestation. Even so, that puts us farther behind in growing lifeforce mass."

"The locals won't like bearing the costs."

"They never do." Lystrana took a sip of the wine. "They cause the problem because they want golds, and they never think of what other difficulties they're causing. Then they complain when we insist that they remedy things. They think that you can keep abusing the world, as if there were no costs at all."

Zistele appeared and removed the empty bowls, and Sentya reappeared with two platters. One held cheriaf, pasta tubes filled with a mixture of minced beef, cheese, spices, particularly mint, and covered with a golden white sauce. The second platter held deep-poached onions.

Dainyl nodded to his wife, then served himself after she had. "It's good to be home."

"How long can you stay?"

"I have to leave on Sexdi morning. The situation in Dramuria is probably worse. We don't have any reports, but I don't see how it could have improved." He took a bite of the cheriaf, savoring it. He supposed he should eat the onions, but he couldn't say that he looked forward to them with as much relish as he had the cheriaf.

"That seems to be the case all over Corus."

"You don't think it's coincidence?"

"I admit to some doubt," replied Lystrana.

"That makes two of us."

They shared a smile.

"Do you think that the snow will affect the apple tree in back?" asked Lystrana.

"It hasn't flowered yet . . ."

After that, they said little beyond pleasantries while they ate.

After they finished, Lystrana stood. "Let's go to the sitting room. It's more comfortable." She walked to the sideboard, where she poured two small snifters of the golden brandy. She handed one to Dainyl and seated herself in one of the corner chairs, holding her snifter so level that the brandy barely moved.

Dainyl doubted he could do that, and set his brandy on the side table before sitting. "You think the weather will turn springlike before long?"

"About the time you leave." A mischievous smile appeared on her face.

Once the girls had finished clearing the dinner and retired to their quarters for the evening, Lystrana looked at her husband. "I'd like to hear about Lyterna."

"I'm not certain where to begin." Dainyl took a sip of the golden brandy. "Asulet met me. I never really talked to anyone else, except in passing or in trivialities. He is the High Alector of Life-form Creation, in practical terms, even if he doesn't have the title . . ." Dainyl went on to explain all that had happened, and all that Asulet had conveyed to him. ". . . he as much as warned me not to trust High Alector Zelyert."

"You've known that all along."

"Zelyert and the marshal have an agenda, and Dramur is tied into it. I'd thought it was mostly Dramur, but I'm getting the feeling that is only a portion of it."

"Do you think the Highest wants to be Duarch?"

"No. I think he wants to control the Duarches, but it's not just about power. At least, I don't think so, but that could be because I'd like to ascribe higher motives to them."

"You're the number two officer in the Myrmidons, and you still have ideals."

At her sardonic tone, Dainyl laughed, but his laugh faded as he thought about Asulet.

"You have that look, the thoughtful one."

"I was thinking about Asulet. There was a sadness behind his words. One thing he said truly disturbed me, after I had a chance to think about it. He said that we had lost so much, that once his predecessors could mold the very cells of the body, but that he and the others working to build lifemass here on Acorus had been forced into combining and modifying cells."

Lystrana nodded.

"You don't seem surprised," Dainyl said.

"I hadn't thought of it that way, but it makes sense. The archives reference the numbers of alectors on Aciafra—"

"The world before Ifryn?"

"Two before Ifryn. There was Aciafra, then Inefra, then Ifryn," Lystrana explained. "When I first saw it, I thought someone had made an error in transcription. The reference was to more than twenty thousand alectors who would need to be translated."

"Twenty thousand?"

"Slightly less than ten thousand made the translation to Inefra, and somewhere around seven thousand made the translation to Ifryn."

"If we've lost that many alectors to translation . . ." mused Dainyl.

"More likely both through translations and between translation. We have to have lost knowledge. Only a few volumes can be carried by each alector who makes the translation."

"There's something very wrong here," protested Dainyl. "If we're losing so many alectors, and so much knowledge, why are we restricting the number of children we have?"

"Did you know that there aren't any illustrations or descriptions of Aciafra? Or even of Inefra? Not one. I've always wanted to ask why, but there's never been anyone I trusted to ask."

Dainyl caught the amused and intellectual expression in her eyes. "What else?"

"There was a reference to a mortality table. Just one. I couldn't find the table or the data, or any other references to it."

"Mortality table? But that suggests that alectors died, that many died . . ."

"Exactly. We don't die often now, but that takes more lifeforce . . ."

Dainyl took another sip of the golden brandy, thinking. "We're each taking far more lifeforce. Is that just to extend our lives or because we're more and more removed from wherever we started?"

"I don't know. It could be, but I don't think so. I think it's also about power and comfort. Do we really *need* all the things that drain lifeforce? The eternastone highways and buildings? The pteridons? The personal shields used by those with Talent?"

"They all help increase lifeforce," he pointed out. "I saw what Acorus was once like, and Asulet wasn't lying about that. Without what he and the early life-formers did, Acorus would be cold and dying, if not dead."

"We could talk about this until it rains on the Dry Coast, or until indigens obtain Talent. Is there anything we can do about it tonight?"

Dainyl took another sip of the brandy. Finally, he shook his head. "I don't even know what I could do tomorrow or next week, except to straighten out the mess in Dramur—if I even can. There's certainly no one I can talk to about it, except you."

"Then," said Lystrana as she set down her brandy. "We'll have to think about it. Later. Much later."

Dainyl left his brandy on the table and stood, extending his hands to his wife.

80

The Fifteenth Company scouts Mykel had sent out on Duadi had discovered a disturbing pattern. Most of the western seltyrs had withdrawn from the area around Dramuria and appeared to be consolidating their forces to the north. One of the few still-isolated forces was the one bluecoat company at Weslyn Estate to the southwest of Dramuria.

Mykel would have liked to pursue that company on Tridi, before it could rejoin the others, but Bhoral had advised against it, suggesting both men and mounts needed another day of rest. So Mykel had persuaded Dohark to send Fourteenth Company scouts out on Tridi. Those scouts had ridden back late in the afternoon, reporting that the bluecoats had set up a more or less permanent camp at the estate. Mykel decided Fifteenth Company could ride to the area the next day and find some way to ambush or otherwise catch the bluecoats unaware.

Fifteenth Company rode out through the west gates at dawn on Quattri morning. Mykel had drawn field rations for his men, rather than wait for the mess cooks and the later meal. Although there was a brisk wind out of the northeast at his back, he could see no clouds and no other sign of rain to come.

Should he really be trying to pick off another seltyr company? Yet, what else could he do? Sit with the other companies in the compound and wait for an attack? Or wait and do nothing as the seltyrs took over all of Dramur? The other four companies could certainly defend the walled compound against anything the seltyrs could mount—and it was unlikely that an attack would come soon, in any event since many of the bluecoats were more than a day's ride away.

Still . . . as he led Fifteenth Company south through Dramuria, Mykel worried.

As early as they passed through the town, there were folk out and about, but not many, and the streets were mostly empty and quiet. Of those who were on the streets, all seemed to avoid looking at the Cadmians. That was another aspect of Dramur Mykel didn't understand. Even after only a season or so, it was clear to him that only the Cadmian presence had kept the seltyrs from taking over Dramuria. The guano mine and trade kept Dramuria alive and independent of the seltyrs, and the Cadmians kept the trade and the mine from being controlled by the seltyrs. Yet the people of Dramuria didn't seem to care much for the Cadmians.

On the southwest side of Dramuria, there were more people out, many of them working on the shallow irrigation ditches that ran through both the few fields and the many casaran orchards. Others were hoeing up various weeds from both the orchards and the fields.

A glass and a half after riding out, the company stopped for a ration and water break, in an area shaded by one of the ever-present casaran orchards. By a glass past noon, Fifteenth Company was less than three vingts from Weslyn Estate, beside a woodlot with a small stream, and Mykel had called a halt for another ration and water break, then sent out the scouts to see what, if anything, had changed at the seltyr's estate.

Mykel had dismounted and watered the chestnut and stood beside his mount in the shade. Even in early spring the sun in Dramur was warm. All he could do, for the moment, was wait for the scouts, try to think up alternate tactics . . . and worry.

"You think the bluecoats'll still be there?" asked Bhoral.

"I don't know. They should have moved out days ago, but they were there yesterday."

"What do you have in mind, sir?"

"There are hills to the northwest, and the orchards run up and over the hills. The trees are planted in rows up the hillside. We'll ride down those rows. We can get within a third of a vingt of where the bluecoats are set up without being seen."

"Like that other estate?"

"Mostly." That bothered Mykel as well. If Bhoral could tell what he was going to do, so could the seltyr's officers.

Dhozynt was the first scout to return, less than half a glass later. His report was brief. "Nothing to the east of the place, sir. No tracks on the road."

"Nothing at all headed toward us?"

"No, sir."

"What about the estate?"

"There's a gate with two guards in green. From where I was, I couldn't tell much more. That whole side is those nut trees. Can't see the buildings from there, and the road's so open that I couldn't cross it without them seeing me."

The second scout back was Gerant, and his report was similar. "No sign of anything on the south lanes, sir. Not a track."

Sendyl followed Gerant. "They've been doing maneuvers and training on the fields to the north of the villa and grounds. Not today. No dust in the air. Not a bit, and I couldn't see anyone out on the grounds, except a few retainers. Some of the tents are gone, too."

Had they moved out? There were no tracks to the east, south, or north. Mykel decided to wait for Jasakyt.

The third squad scout was the last to return, nearly a glass later. He rode right up to Mykel. "Sir! They've pulled out. They've headed west."

"How do you know?"

"From the tracks in the northwest lane, sir. Not all that long ago, no more than two glasses, I'd wager. They weren't riding that hard, though. The whole place looks deserted, except maybe for some retainers here and there."

Mykel's guts tightened. He mounted the chestnut and stood in the stirrups. "Squad leaders to the front!"

He waited uneasily for the five to gather. As soon as they rode up, he looked over the five men for a long moment before speaking. "The bluecoats have pulled out, heading west. We're headed back to the compound."

"You don't want to follow them, sir?" asked Vhanyr.

"Like Seventeenth Company did? I think not." It was all too likely someone among the seltyrs wanted to ambush Fifteenth Company, and he didn't want to pursue, as outnumbered as Third Battalion was. "There's a time to fight, and this isn't it. We'll head out immediately."

He needed to check the maps, but he wasn't about to travel back the same way they had ridden in. That was one precaution he intended to take, even if it meant riding over some seltyr's fields to get to another road or lane.

"Company! Forward!"

Mykel wanted Fifteenth Company off the road they were on as soon as practicable. Even so, he did not breathe that much easier. The less direct route only meant crossing the corners of two fields and riding down the center of one unkempt casaran orchard.

Between the not-quite-so-direct route and Mykel's caution in not getting the mounts overtired on the return, the sun had already dropped behind the Murian Mountains as Fifteenth Company rode eastward toward the compound. A light breeze carried the faintest hint of a most unpleasant odor to Mykel as he led Fifteenth Company toward the closed gates of the compound.

"It's Fifteenth Company! They're back!" That came from the guards on the gate towers, and Mykel caught a tone of relief. He didn't like that at all.

The gates opened, just halfway, and closed quickly behind the last riders of fifth squad.

Once inside, as he rode toward the stables, Mykel studied the compound courtyard. The few troopers he saw moved slowly, and carts—filled with canvas-covered shapes—seemed to be everywhere. The sickening odor was stronger within the walls. What had happened in less than a full day? An attack of some sort? He didn't see any wounded. Disease didn't strike in a matter of glasses, not to create that many bodies in so short a time.

A ranker hurried on foot toward Mykel, staggering slightly as he did. "Captain Mykel! The overcaptain needs to see you soonest, sir! Right now!"

Mykel reined up and dismounted. He handed the chestnut's reins to Bhoral. "Have the squad leaders stand by after they've settled the men. I'll be there as soon as I can."

"Yes, sir."

Mykel followed the ranker to the headquarters building and the study that Dohark had taken over, at least while the colonel was gone.

The overcaptain sat behind the desk. In the light of the single light-torch, his face looked faintly green, or perhaps yellow-green, and his eyes were red-rimmed. "Good to see you back."

"What happened?"

"We've been poisoned. Had to be in the morning meal. A good third of the men are dead. That includes both Mersyt's and half of Benjyr's company. How are your men?"

"They're fine. I drew field rations this morning."

"Lucky you."

"We just didn't want any more fish for breakfast." Mykel refrained from pointing out that luck hadn't always been with Fifteenth Company. "Do you know how it happened?"

"One of the cooks is missing. He was the one in charge of breakfast. None of the others know anything."

"What about the officers?"

"Everyone's been sick, but not so badly. I don't know about Majer Herryf. He didn't come in this morning."

"He hasn't been staying at the compound?"

"No. He says that he's from Dramuria, and that if he stays here, it will cause too much fear in the town."

"You think he's in trouble?"

"He is, or we are, or both."

"What was poisoned? The fish?" That seemed most likely to Mykel, since it tasted bad, even under the best of conditions.

"Who knows?" Dohark's face twisted momentarily. "Fifteenth Company needs to take charge of the guards tonight."

"I'll take care of it. What about food?"

"We're using field rations. I've got those guarded. The water comes direct from springs . . ."

When he and the overcaptain had finished a quick outline of what Fifteenth Company needed to do, Mykel left the study, and headquarters, crossing the courtyard quickly and hurrying toward the stables.

All five squad leaders were waiting, with Bhoral. The questions began before Mykel even reached the six Cadmians.

"How come . . . dead troopers everywhere . . ."

"What happened? They got bodies everywhere. Some sort of plague . . ."

Mykel held up his hand, and there was quiet. "One of the cooks poisoned breakfast. He's vanished. The overcaptain thinks a third of the Cadmians are dead. We'll be eating off the field rations. They're under guard. No one feels worth sowshit. So we have to take over compound guard duty."

"We just rode all day . . ." began Gendsyr.

"Most of the Cadmians who survived can't hold a rifle yet," Mykel said firmly. "Do you want to trust them to guard you against ten companies of bluecoats?" His eyes knifed through each squad leader in turn.

No one spoke.

"Now . . . we'll rotate squads. First watch—first squad takes the gates and walls. Second watch—second squad. Third squad will take the morning watch. After that, I'll let you know."

After arranging the sudden duty rosters, Mykel walked over to the officer's cell. There was but one ranker there, and he sat slumped on a stool.

"Sir?"

"How's the prisoner?"

"Don't know, sir. Only me here, and no way to check."

"I'll check. You watch."

"Yes, sir." The Cadmian trooper sounded too tired to argue.

There was no sound from inside the cell as the guard unlocked and opened the door, or as Mykel stepped inside. Rachyla was stretched out on the cot. She did not move when the door closed behind Mykel, but even in the dim light, he could see she was breathing.

"Lady Rachyla?"

She turned her head, slowly. "It . . . would . . . be . . . you."

Her face was greenish, or yellowish. It was hard to tell in the dim light, but it certainly wasn't her normal color. He could almost sense the miasma of sickness—or poison—that shrouded her form—a greenish pink, it seemed. He blinked. Had he really seen that?

". . . so thirsty . . ."

There was water in the pitcher on the desk, and he poured it into the cup, then bent and held it while she drank.

After drinking, she lay on her side, looking at him. "Do . . . you poison all your . . . prisoners, Captain?" Each word was labored.

"No. Someone poisoned everyone who ate breakfast. There are bodies all over the compound."

"You . . . look . . . fine."

"We left before breakfast this morning."

Her lips curved into a parody of a smile. ". . . fortune of cursed one . . . dagger of the ancients . . ."

That made little sense to Mykel, but he didn't pursue it. "How are you feeling? I mean . . . I know you feel terrible . . . but better or worse lately?"

"Better . . . worse fortune . . . no sense . . . dying twice."

"You won't die here." Mykel spoke without thinking.

"Your . . . promise?"

Mykel had been caught off guard by her condition, but he wasn't that green or stupid. "I can't promise anything. You know that."

"You . . . said . . ."

"That's a prediction, not a promise." He held the cup. "You need to drink more."

Her face twisted, the way Dohark's had, but she said nothing. Several moments later, she drank. Mykel finally took back the cup, nearly empty.

"What is . . . happening?"

"A third of the Cadmians are dead. Eight companies of bluecoats are here in the east. The Myrmidons haven't returned, and neither has the majer in charge of the compound."

"Majer Herryf. None of the seltyrs . . . care for him. He will not be back."

"How do you know that?"

"I know . . . people." Her eyes flickered, as if she were having trouble keeping them open.

"Are you . . . is something the matter?"

"I am tired. Good night, Captain." She closed her eyes.

Mykel watched for a time, but her breathing seemed stronger. Finally, he rapped on the cell door. She did not stir as he left.

81

From Dainyl's point of view, Quattri had been both productive in getting caught up with the piles of paper and unhelpful in discovering what he really wanted to know. He'd gotten to headquarters before the morning muster, but the marshal had already left to meet the High Alector of Justice at the Duarch's Palace. Since Dainyl had been able to work uninterrupted all day, he'd finished reviewing the reports from all eight Myrmidon companies on Acorus.

The marshal had returned to headquarters late in the afternoon and immediately summoned Dainyl to make sure he would be at headquarters on Quinti to welcome and brief Colonel Dhenyr. Then the marshal had departed for a formal dinner at the Duarch's Palace.

Dainyl had gone home to Lystrana—most gratefully—for a more than pleasant evening.

Although the spring snow had all melted, the streets had still been damp and the air raw. The rawness had persisted into Quinti, when Dainyl had arrived early at headquarters to prepare to meet Colonel Dhenyr, although it was likely that the new colonel would not be flying in until midday. The marshal was not in, and, perhaps would not be. Before he began his own projects for Quinti, Dainyl stopped to talk to Undercaptain Ghanyr at the duty desk.

"Submarshal, sir, what can we do for you?"

"Is first squad up to strength?"

"Yes, sir. Weather's clear, and we've got a dispatch run to Ludar. Nothing else, yet."

"How did things go in Iron Stem?"

Ghanyr shook his head "Wouldn't have been a problem if anyone talked to anyone. The local trade director claimed he'd sent three messages about cutting the timber, because he'd been turned down on his requisition for stone and bricks. The regional alector never saw any of the messages or the requisitions, and the trade director produced a dispatch that gave him authority to cut. It was forged, but not by him. Cadmian majer claimed he'd been ordered to do what was necessary. Some hothead blew the shaft because he was tired of living in a tent with all the wind. They were all trading dispatches, and half of them were false—"

"How did that happen? Do you know?"

"Marshal didn't say." Ghanyr looked down the corridor toward the submarshal's study.

"That's interesting," mused Dainyl. "I didn't even know about Iron Stem until after the miners blew the shaft."

"No, sir. Most didn't. Just the marshal and the submarshal, that's what I heard Marshal Shastylt was telling the regional alector." Ghanyr was telling the truth, and still doing his best to convey that the blame would fall on the dead Tyanylt. It was also a warning.

"I'm glad everyone's back safe." Dainyl smiled warmly.

"Yes, sir. Yuasylt didn't have it so easy out in Hyalt."

"I heard. That's why it's important to watch for wild Talents before they get established."

Ghanyr nodded. "Heard you found one of those places of the ancients down in Dramur."

"We did. We circled and watched, but neither Falyna nor Quelyt ever saw anything there. Some indigen rebels took a shot at us, though."

"Strange times, sir."

"The strange happenings come in groups. They always have, and now is no different. Then they settle down." Dainyl paused, but briefly. "Anything else I should know about?"

"No, sir. There's nothing new, no special dispatches." Ghanyr did not quite look at Dainyl as he asked, "Are there going to be any more deployment orders, sir?"

"Quelyt and Falyna will heading back to Dramur with me tomorrow, as things stand now. That's the only deployment, if you can call it that."

"Lucky them. It's warm there."

"It's getting warmer here." Dainyl offered a parting smile before heading for his study, thinking about the false dispatches. Why had Shastylt fomented the problems at Iron Stem . . . and in Dramur? What possible reason could the marshal have had? Yet, when Shastylt had talked to Dainyl on Tridi, the marshal had been most clear on wanting Dainyl to resolve the problems in Dramur. That had not been the case before. What had changed? And why?

Dainyl settled behind his desk, thinking.

After a quarter glass, he shook his head. There was doubtless some simple reason, but he couldn't figure it out. Shastylt was loyal to the High Alector of Justice, and to the Duarchy. Dainyl had been able to sense that, and so far, he'd never been mistaken. Could he be now? Was Shastylt that much stronger with his shields, strong enough not only to hide lies but to actively project untruths? Dainyl didn't think so, but he no longer knew, not for certain.

He lined up all the reports, and all the background files, that Dhenyr would need to read and review and carried them to the study that had once been his, placing them on the corner of the desk. Gathering and arranging all that material took less than half a glass.

After that, he turned to the side table in his own study, and the ledgers stacked there—the consolidated supply accounts for all the Myrmidon companies. He started looking for something to prove or disprove his suspicions. Midday came and went, and Dainyl only took a short break to eat before returning to his review of the ledgers.

Four months back, he found the only irregularity—if he could call it that. A page in the ledger had been replaced, and there were two fewer lines of entries on the page than on any other page. That was all. Nothing much, except that in scores of pages, all were the same length and the pages had not been touched. The figures all balanced. Dainyl put the ledgers aside. He suspected that someone had made a mistake, and it had been covered up, but what had been covered up he wasn't about to find in the official records, and it couldn't have been just a bookkeeping error. That could safely have been corrected.

He stood and stretched, then took a walk down the corridor toward the duty desk, only to find Ghanyr walking toward him.

"Viosyna just reported two pteridons inbound from the east, sir," the undercaptain said. "It must be the new colonel."

"I'll go out and meet him." Dainyl did not put on his flying jacket, but as he stood, looking to the south and east, he began to wish he had. The wind was light, out of the north, but still raw. He stood well back and to the east of the landing stage, watching as the two pteridons circled to the south, then made their final approaches into the wind. The first pteridon settled, then the second. Colonel Dhenyr was in the second saddle of the trailing pteridon. Within moments, he had vaulted off the flight stage and walked toward Dainyl.

Dhenyr was the image of the perfect Myrmidon—two and two-thirds yards in height, black hair so dark and straight that it seemed to reflect light while absorbing it, deep purple eyes, a well-formed oval face with black eyebrows neither too thin nor too bushy, and an alabaster skin whiter than the whitest marble or limestone. Even after two days of flight, he scarcely seemed to have anything out of place in either his bearing or his uniform.

"Colonel Dhenyr . . . Submarshal Dainyl." Dainyl offered a pleasant smile.

Dhenyr inclined his head slightly before replying. "A pleasure to meet you, sir. Marshal Shastylt has told me a great deal about you. You're the first Myrmidon born on Acorus to become submarshal. That's quite something."

"It had to happen sometime," Dainyl replied, smiling politely and keeping his shields locked and impermeable. Dhenyr's warm and deep voice should have been reassuring. For some reason, it was not. "Let's go inside. They can bring your gear to your study. Your personal furnishings are being sent overland?"

"They left before I did." Dhenyr laughed. "With my wife. She was fortunate that there was an opening for an assistant to the High Alector of Transport."

"You both were fortunate. There aren't that many good positions." Without saying more, Dainyl turned and led the way into headquarters and to his own study, where he gestured for Dhenyr to seat himself, then settled behind his own desk. "How were the flights?"

"Long. There aren't many that aren't, anymore. We came straight, and that was cold, just below the Aerlal Plateau." Dhenyr waited, politely attentive.

"I'll be relatively brief with you . . . although there is a large stack of reports waiting for you to review. As operations and maintenance director of the Myrmidons, you'll see, read, and review more reports than you knew existed . . ." Dainyl went on for close to a glass, outlining everything from the duty and dispatch system and structures to the general locations of what Dhenyr would need to know immediately. ". . . and that's probably more than you want to hear."

"I hope I can explain it that clearly before long," replied the newly promoted colonel.

"I'm sure you'll manage." Dainyl leaned back in his chair. "Now . . . I do have a few questions."

"If I can answer them, sir . . ."

"First, I was hoping that you might be able to explain how three—or is it four—skylances vanished from Fifth Company in less than two seasons. I read your reports with interest, but I'm afraid I never did get a good picture of what happened."

Dhenyr smiled, ruefully. "None of us did, either. The skylances were racked with the saddles, each in the square for that pteridon. The pteridons never left the squares, and no one could have gotten to the skylances without coming within a yard or two of the pteridons. I requested that the regional alector interview each ranker and officer. The interviews revealed nothing. Both the regional alector and the marshal were less than happy with the results."

"Do you have any ideas who took them—or how they managed?"

"Well, sir, it is Dereka, and some of the locals said that it could have been the ancients, but there was no Talent-trace of anything—not alectors, not ancients, not anything else. The recorder used the Table, but it revealed nothing untoward, either. The last time, he used the Table within a glass of the disappearance, but there was no sign of anything. The regional alector sensed no Talent-use, either."

Paradoxically, that meant that Talent *had* to have been involved, Dainyl knew, but how had it been managed with no Talent-traces? "What do you think happened?"

"I'm truly at a loss, sir. Dereka is an old city. Maybe it *was* the ancients." Dhenyr shrugged.

The colonel didn't really believe that, Dainyl could tell, but seemed mystified by what had happened, and not all that upset. His reactions told Dainyl more than just what Dhenyr didn't know, and that suggested Dainyl would learn little more from Dhenyr, about anything.

All Dainyl really wanted to do was to go home to Lystrana.

82

All alectors who deal with steers each and every day must keep in mind that there are significant differences in outlook between alectors and steers. Some of these differences, while fundamental, are anything but obvious to casual observation. One of the most critical differences is that steers instinctively believe that there is an intrinsic worth to each and every person, no matter how useless or even destructive an individual may be. This is often expressed in terms such as, "every life is sacred" or "we are all worthy in the eyes of [whatever deity is fashionable]."

As alectors, we understand the feelings behind such quaint phrases. All beings who can think, even those who do so on a rudimentary level, seek meaning in their lives. They wish to be appreciated, to be recognized, to be granted a place and position of some value. At the same time, the universe does not place any value on any life. Life is. It is the result of physical and chemical processes, and it arises in some places and not in others as a result of the interactions between the components of a world.

What value an individual may have to the world or society is determined solely by his or her abilities and contributions. To say that a mature individual has an intrinsic worth, independent of acts, is mere wishful thought. Thus, a newborn child has no worth—only potential worth. That potential may be great indeed, but it is only potential until the child matures and demonstrates through abilities and acts what that value may be. History has shown that the worth of individuals is not the same, and yet the delusion persists that because individuals are created by the same process, they are equal. Anyone who has observed individuals knows they are not equal, and that their worth is anything but equal. While the laws of a society must assure that no one is treated inequitably, no society that has forced equality of worth upon its members has lasted long.

Yet the delusion about intrinsic worth is necessary in steer societies because, without it, too many individuals would become excessively self-centered and spend their lives seeking only to gratify the most basic and base of instinctual drives, using all their resources against those with less strength or wealth. This reduces creativity, such as it is, and productivity, and is not acceptable, either in terms of maximizing higher lifeforce or in assuring fairness to others.

As alectors, we understand that what value we may represent or attain comes solely from what we can create or produce of higher worth. Great art, soaring architecture, inspiring music, well-organized and functioning cities—all these and other like achievements are the manifestations of individual worth.

We must recall, however, that such worth is as we deem it. The universe makes no judgments and bestows no awards for worth or merit. Because the universe does not, we must make such judgments. One of the most critical requirements of any society is to define "worth" fairly, accurately, and in a way that inspires all thinking members toward achievements that create such worth.

This understanding, which is taught to and accepted by all discerning alectors, is seldom accepted by steers. Therefore, any alector who deals with them must always recall that it is the fashion and custom to act as though all individuals have worth, even the most worthless, and that, when a steer must be disciplined or terminated because the individual in question is truly a destructive and negative force on others and the world, such discipline must be administered with a show of regret that the worth of such a life has been wasted . . .

Views of the Highest
Illustra
W.T. 1513

83

Mykel woke up on Quinti just before dawn, still worrying about Rachyla. He sat up on the hard and narrow bed. Why was he so concerned about her? It wasn't as though there happened to be any romantic attraction between them. He had to admit she was beautiful—not just pretty—and he admired her intelligence and poise, but she was hardly likely to be interested in a Cadmian officer, and he couldn't afford to get close to the daughter of a rebel leader, even a dead one. Besides, in her own way, she was as deadly as the dagger of the ancients he still carried.

Still . . . he did worry.

He forced himself out of bed and into washing up, then dressing. Even before he went to find the field rations that would be breakfast, he gathered Bhoral and the squad leaders outside the barracks under a slightly hazy sky.

Mykel looked at the five squad leaders. "We'll need to expect an attack here. Fifteenth Company is the only company at anywhere close to full strength, and we'll bear the brunt of any attack until the others recover. I'd like you to have your men stand down, except for two on watch on each wall. Have them keep their weapons nearby. Bhoral will work out the watch arrangements, while I meet with the overcaptain." He nodded to the senior squad leader.

Bhoral stepped forward, and Mykel slipped away.

Dohark was not in the study in headquarters, but at a table in the mess. Before joining him, Mykel served himself from the ration cases set on the table and tapped his own ale from the keg. A Cadmian ranker guarded both food and drink.

As Mykel settled across the table from the overcaptain, Dohark looked up from the stale flat biscuits, hard yellow cheese, and dried apple slices before him. "Not much to choose from. Better than being poisoned." Dohark took a bite of the biscuit. "Not much, though."

Mykel took a bite of the dry and crumbly biscuit, then a small sip of the ale. He didn't care much for either. Both officers ate quietly for a time.

"The men are getting better, those that survived," Dohark finally said. "You think it had to do with the seltyr's daughter?"

"Whatever it was poisoned her as well," replied Mykel. "She couldn't even sit up last night. She was greener-looking than you were."

"What do you think they'll do next?"

"They'll have to attack. We won't be fortunate enough to see a siege."

"No. We've got enough supplies for months, and they'd have to know that. They also can't count on the Myrmidons staying away forever."

"No, but it could be a while," Mykel pointed out. "Is there anything that burns well?"

Dohark raised his eyebrows.

"Well . . . sir . . . if they have siege ladders or ramps, maybe we could throw oil on them. Or is that something that the Myrmidons frown on, too?"

"No. I've never heard anything about that, but there's nothing like that in the armory."

"What about in the kitchens? Some cooking oils burn well."

"I hadn't thought about that."

"If you don't mind, sir, I'll see what they have."

Dohark nodded. "Your men are still guarding the walls?"

"I have some on watch. The others are standing down until there's an attack."

"You're optimistic. Not *if* there's an attack, but when there is one."

"I'm hope I'm wrong, sir."

"You get very formal and very proper, Mykel, just before you predict something unpleasant, and then think up something even worse than the enemy has. If we get through this, I'd suggest you change that mannerism." Dohark offered an off-center smile.

"I'll . . . see to it, sir. By your leave, sir?"

"Go and do what you have to, Captain."

"Yes, sir. Thank you, sir." Mykel stood.

After leaving the mess, he returned to the barracks and gathered up Chyndylt and half of third squad, waiting until the squad leader and the nine rankers stood before him in the southeast wind that warmed the courtyard.

"We have a few tasks to attend to here in the compound. Just come with me." That was the only explanation he offered.

"Yes, sir." Chyndylt smiled faintly.

The first stop was the mess kitchen, which was cool because there had been no cooking. In the storeroom, Mykel found seven full casks of cooking oil, and one half cask. He tested some of the oil with a splinter of wood. It burned brightly. He turned to the head cook. "We'll be borrowing these for a time."

"Borrowing, sir?"

"If we're fortunate, borrowing. If we're not, then tell Majer Herryf."

"Yes, sir." The cook's voice was less than enthusiastic.

"Chyndylt, have the men roll these out to the west gate—carefully. Just the full ones. Put one barrel at the top of each guard tower—inside—and leave the others beside the steps on each side. I don't want a drop spilled."

Chyndylt gestured. "Rykyt . . . you four . . . you heard the captain."

Once he saw that Rykyt and the four rankers with him had that task in hand, Mykel led Chyndylt and the remaining four rankers to the armory.

The senior squad leader who served as armorer was not there, his place taken by a local Cadmian squad leader Mykel did not know.

"I need to inspect the armory and draw ammunition."

"But . . . sir . . . you need a requisition."

"I tell you what, squad leader. If . . . if we all survive the bluecoats' attacks later today, I'll be happy to provide that requisition. In the meantime, we'll need the ammunition."

The dark-haired squad leader looked from Mykel to Chyndylt and to the four rankers behind the captain. "Ah . . . I suppose . . . you will put a requisition in, sir?"

"If it's necessary, and when we have time, I'd be more than happy to. Now . . . if you'd care to show us what we have?"

"Yes, sir." The armory squad leader kept looking back as he unlocked both doors.

"Jonasyr," Mykel ordered. "You guard the entrance here."

"Yes, sir."

The storage areas of the armory were down a long ramp, within solid stone walls set into the ground on which the compound was built. The ceiling consisted of solid stone beams, each a good third of a yard thick. Mykel had no idea how thick the side walls were, but the combination of stone and earth behind it was strong enough to keep any inadvertent explosions confined.

"Here is the main section, sir."

In the dim illumination of but two light-torches, one on the east wall and one on the west, both set almost up to the ceiling, Mykel slowly inspected the armory. On the west wall were four locked racks filled with rifles. Across from the rack, stacked out from the east wall, were cases of ammunition—almost floor to ceiling in a space three yards high and ten yards long. Mykel walked to the north end looking for what else might be there.

In the northwest corner were four kegs. All looked old, but they were sealed, and "gunpowder" was stenciled across the staves in white. Mykel hid a smile. "Chyndylt . . . we'll need at least three cases on each wall of the compound. We won't have the time or the men to lug up ammunition if they rush the compound."

"Sir? That much?" asked the armory squad leader.

"There are at least ten companies of bluecoats. How many cases would you suggest?"

The squad leader did not reply.

"Do you have dollies or something for carting the cases?"

"Just that flat truck there, sir."

"That will do. Why don't you station yourself at the top of the ramp there. You can count the cases as we bring them up." Mykel turned to Chyndylt. "We'll start at that end." He gestured toward the north end.

The armory squad leader looked at Mykel uneasily before retreating up the ramp, not quite to the top.

"The truck can handle four cases easily," Chyndylt suggested.

"I want those four kegs there, as well." Mykel kept his voice low and pointed. Stack them between the cases."

"Sir?"

"I need to make sure that the oil will ignite. They're old. Don't drop them, but they should help with the task."

Chyndylt nodded.

Mykel could tell the senior squad leader didn't quite believe him, but he knew Chyndylt wasn't about to say anything. That was one of the reasons Mykel had picked third squad.

"If you'd handle this . . . I need to organize a few other items for our defense."

"Yes, sir."

Mykel walked back up the ramp. He stopped beside Jonasyr. "See anyone, or hear any alerts?"

"No, sir."

"Good. Thank you."

Mykel's next stop was the carpentry shop, set in the southwest corner of the compound, beyond the last of the stables.

"What might you be looking for, sir?" asked the gray-haired man in a leather apron even before Mykel had a chance to announce himself.

"An old barrel of some sort, one that will roll downhill on its side."

The carpenter frowned. "I'm not a cooper . . ."

Mykel waited.

"There might be one in the back, sir."

Mykel kept looking at the carpenter.

"One moment, sir." The carpenter moved slowly through the open door into the storeroom behind the workroom.

Mykel studied the supplies stacked in various places, and without much regard for order, from what he could tell. Some time passed before the carpenter returned.

"There is one, sir."

"Thank you. What about big nails, or spikes? Do you have any of those?"

The carpenter looked at Mykel. "Maybe half a keg here . . . Might I ask why, sir?"

"We don't have any caltrops here. Large nails or spikes would be better than nothing."

The crafter's dubious expression turned to puzzlement.

"Caltrops are special four-pointed spikes that disable horses. We're very likely to have a thousand or more bluecoats charging the compound. I'm looking for something that can act like caltrops."

"They're just heavy nails, sir."

"They'll do. I'll be sending some men for the nails and the barrel. If we don't need them, I'll return them." Mykel smiled. "You do understand that the bluecoats slaughtered Seventeenth Company almost to the last man?"

"They did, sir?"

"The rebels did the same to Thirteenth Company. We do need those nails and spikes."

"Yes, sir."

"Thank you." Mykel nodded and walked back across the courtyard.

He was passing the headquarters building when Dohark appeared.

"Mykel—I'd like a word with you." He motioned for Mykel to join him outside the south entrance to headquarters.

"Yes, sir?" Mykel inclined his head.

"There's dust on the roads to the north. Three vingts or so north."

"I've gotten the oil, and I have my men setting cases of ammunition on the walls."

Dohark looked steadily at Mykel for a moment. "There are enough able men left from Fourteenth and Sixteenth Companies to man one wall and part of another. The locals are down to half a company. What do you suggest?"

"The south wall for the others in Third Battalion, the east wall on each side of the gates for the locals. Fifteenth Company will handle the rest. I'll be keeping a squad back until we see where they attack. If there's enough for a reserve squad from the others, that would be good."

Dohark nodded. "There should be. I'll be at the west gate's north tower. That offers the best vantage point."

"How is Rhystan doing?" Mykel asked.

"He's too weak to stand, but he seems to be getting better. Sixteenth Company took the worst of the poison."

"Good that the survivors will be all right."

Dohark raised his eyebrows.

Mykel grinned. "After this attack, we'll need everyone to clean up the mess."

Dohark shook his head. "And maybe the colonel will promote you to majer, too."

Mykel offered an exaggerated shrug. "I can always hope."

"Best you get on with your preparations, Captain Mykel."

"Yes, sir."

Before he returned to his special preparations, Mykel gathered the squad leaders again, with Bhoral, making sure that all the mounts would be saddled and ready to ride out, if necessary. Then he went back to doing what could get him into great difficulties—if he survived.

By the time another glass had passed, the ammunition and casks of oil were in place, and Mykel had the older barrel, the half keg of heavy nails, and the gunpowder kegs in a shaded place just behind and north of the west gate. He also had a number of other items, including lengths of old, near-rotten canvas and a small bucket of glue.

One cask of oil would fit inside the larger carpenter's barrel, as would a cask of the gunpowder. Mykel set to work with the glue, canvas and nails, until the inside of the barrel was lined with two layers of canvas with the nails glued inside. The glue wouldn't harden before Mykel would probably have to use the device, but all he cared about was something to keep the nails from clumping together too much.

By the time he had finished and replaced the head of the barrel, he was soaked with sweat, and another glass had passed. With a sardonic smile that he quickly erased, Mykel noted that he had not seen Dohark. The overcaptain had most conspicuously avoided him while he had been working, and that was probably for the best—for both of them.

Another glass and a half passed. The men had eaten noon rations. The breeze had died off, and the sun beat down on the compound.

Vhanyr came sprinting across the courtyard. "Captain Mykel! Bluecoats are coming! Some greencoats, too. Hundreds of 'em!"

"Fifteenth Company! Squad leaders! Forward!"

Mykel barely waited before he began issuing his orders, orders that the squad leaders already knew. "Fifteenth Company to the walls! Squad one to the main gate, two to the rest of the west wall, three to the north wall, and four to east gate. Squad five, stand by."

"Fifteenth Company to the walls!" snapped Bhoral, "Squad one . . ." He echoed Mykel's orders.

Once he was satisfied that all his men were in place, Mykel climbed the steps beside the west gate, where he stood on the walls below the south tower. He looked westward under the noon sun. The seltyrs' forces had halted a good half vingt to the west, and were stretched out in front of the end of the casaran orchards, forming a line of riders a good five hundred yards across and at least three ranks deep. Most of the riders had dismounted.

That bothered Mykel, although it was what he would have done.

He turned and walked along the top of the wall to the southwest corner, then most of the way toward the east wall of the compound. A half vingt to the east was another formation, considerably smaller, with more clad in green than in blue.

After studying the second formation and confirming that they were also dismounted, Mykel returned to his former position on the wall beneath the south guard tower.

"Sir?" Bhoral appeared.

"Have the men stand down in position. There won't be an attack for a little while at least. But check on the mounts. We still might need them—one way or another."

The squad leader nodded and slipped away.

"You don't think we'll see an attack right now?" asked Dohark, who had appeared at the top of the steps.

"Not for a while. Do you?"

"No. They're not mounted. They're resting their horses."

"They've got something else in mind, I'd wager," suggested Mykel.

"Siege ladders?"

"Could be."

"They wouldn't try blasting powder," said Dohark.

"They probably would if they could get any." As Mykel said that, he wondered if that happened to be the reason why whichever alectors had provided the rifles had done so—so that the seltyrs wouldn't develop something worse?

"You're cheerful."

"I expect the strongest aspects of human nature to surface—greed, destructiveness, shortsightedness—all the good things." Mykel's tone was more sardonic than he'd meant it to be.

"I'm headed over to the north tower to see if I can get a better view," Dohark finally said.

"Yes, sir." There was little that Mykel could do but wait.

Another half glass went by before Mykel heard a dull rumbling sound. He looked northward, thinking it might be a storm, but the sky remained clear. His eyes went to the west. Six wagons with angled timber barricades five yards wide reaching from knee height to almost two yards lumbered down the road toward the west gate, slowly, but seemingly by themselves. It took Mykel but a moment to realize that troopers behind the timbers were pushing the heavy wagons. He had no doubts that behind or in the wagons were long siege ladders that would be swung up to the walls, that or something else to allow them over the walls.

Very shortly, he had to wonder, because the wagons swung wide of the road and stopped short of the walls, a good sixty yards back, three on each side, lined up barricade to barricade.

A long single note on a horn sounded.

Crack! Crack!

Mykel ducked as he heard the first shots. Staying low behind the stone parapets, he studied the barricades, realizing that the regularly placed narrow slits in the heavy timbers were for rifles.

A long wagon moved slowly down the road toward the rebels' movable barricades, drawn by eight riders, four on each side of what looked to be an enormous wagon shaft. As it neared the barricades, Mykel looked more closely. A tree trunk almost a yard across had been fastened to an eight-wheeled wagon, and the forward end of the trunk had been covered in iron. As Mykel watched and waited for the riders to get closer to the walls, they began to urge the horses into a fast trot, then even faster.

The firing from behind the timbered wagons intensified.

"First squad! Aim for the riders!" He raised his rifle and began to aim.

Just as he squeezed the trigger, with the wagon-ram less than thirty yards from the west gate, the riders swerved away and let the wagon rumble toward the heavy oak gates alone.

Thuddd! The impact of the heavy tree-trunk ram, with its iron cap, shook the walls, but the gate held.

"Gates held!" called a ranker from somewhere.

Peering from beside one of the merlons, Mykel watched as the wagon began to roll backward. How could that be? Then he saw the long cable attached to the rear of the wagon-ram. While the road from Dramuria rose most of the way from the town to the compound, the last eighty yards before the gates were flat, and the smooth and level stone road leading across that stretch to the west gate made the scheme possible—and all too likely to succeed. The riders didn't have to get that close, and they could try until the ram failed or the gates collapsed.

Almost half a glass passed before the wagon-ram had been drawn back past the barricade wagons. The riders—or another group—re-formed on each side of the front part of the wagon-ram. Several moments passed before the device began to move along the road toward the west gate.

"Aim for the riders on the north—just on the north!" Mykel ordered.

"Aim for the riders! North side!" echoed Gendsyr.

Mykel sighted on the lead rider, squeezing the trigger, and willing his shot home.

The rider crumpled in the saddle, but dropped the lead or whatever linked him to the ram, and his mount carried him off the road. The ram continued to rumble toward the gates.

Mykel shifted his aim to the second rider, aiming and firing.

Just as he squeezed the trigger, the riders broke away from the ram, earlier than they had before, and the heavy contraption rumbled inexorably toward the gates.

Thuddd! Once more, the gates and walls shook.

Mykel looked down. The gates were definitely bowed, and at least one of the heavy timbers was splintered in one place.

"Aim for the horses!" ordered Dohark from the north tower. "Drop the horses!"

The Cadmians waited, and Mykel wondered if they would not have done better if all the Third Battalion companies had followed his example and tried to whittle away the seltyrs' forces in the field. Then, Heransyr had tried that, and Seventeenth Company had been wiped out.

Once more the wagon-ram began to move forward, but this time, the horses only started it, well behind the barricades, and moved away, while a good score of bluecoats used leads attached to the rear of the ram and others just pushed it from behind.

"Fire!" ordered Mykel and Dohark near-simultaneously.

Mykel brought down three of those pushing the ram, and another half score fell to other fire, but other bluecoats took their places and the ram rumbled toward the west gate.

The *thudding* impact was accompanied not only by the shaking of the walls, but by the sound of splintering timbers.

Mykel looked down to see the north side of the gate ripped open wide enough for a man to enter. Outside the walls, the rebels were dragging back their ram once more.

"One more time, sir, and the gates'll go," Gendsyr said. "Two at most, and we're not stopping 'em with rifles."

Mykel could see that. So far there were perhaps twoscore bodies strewn on the flat east of the gates—if that. There were a good thousand bluecoats waiting back out of easy rifle range.

After a quick glance back outside, Mykel scurried down the steps to where one of the kegs of gunpowder had been placed at the base of the stone wall. There were also several casks of oil. The gate was bowed enough that he could squeeze both through—he thought.

Overhead he could hear Dohark barking out orders about timbers and wagons, but Mykel would leave that to the overcaptain. If the ram weren't stopped before it did more damage, Dohark's timbers would do little good.

"Fifth squad! To me!" Mykel ordered.

Vhanyr appeared instantly. "Sir."

"We need to get that keg and two of those casks out through that gap. I need someone to go out there with me."

Vhanyr turned. "Lortyr! Fonyt!"

Mykel looked up. "Gendsyr! We're headed out in front of the gates! Open fire at those barricades and anyone who even looks up!

"Yes, sir. First squad! Stand by to fire!"

Mykel waited until the two rankers stood beside him. "You're going to set those casks of oil out in front of the gates—a good five yards. Put them so close together that they touch—right in the middle of the road. I'll be right behind you with this keg of powder."

The two rankers looked at Mykel and the keg of gunpowder.

"You don't mind if we hurry, sir?" asked Lortyr.

Mykel grinned. "The faster, the better." Behind him, he could see rankers pushing two wagons toward the gate, probably to overturn and block the entry as well as they could.

Lortyr rolled one cask to the gate, right up to the opening, then turned it sideways. He had to lift it—with the help of two others—almost chest high to get it through the bowed part. Then he slipped under the cask and helped lower it to the stone pavement. Keeping low, he turned the cask and rolled it out five yards or so. He kept the cask between him and the bluecoats, even while he levered it upright.

Behind him, Fonyt followed the same example.

Once Fonyt was through the gate, Mykel lifted the smaller keg of powder, standing by the gate, waiting for both rankers to dash back.

Mykel scuttled out, quickly setting the powder directly behind the two barrels of oil, then returning, almost diving through the narrow opening in the gates. He'd sensed shots, but all had seemed high, perhaps because the angle of the slits in the rebel barricades had been designed more to allow shots at the positions on the top of the wall.

The two rankers grinned at the captain. "That all, sir?"

"For now." Mykel grinned back, but only for a moment.

"Clear the gate space!" Dohark bellowed from above.

Mykel hurried back up to the top of the wall on the south side.

Out to the west, the rebels were readying the wagon-ram for another run at the gates. Below, behind the gates, rankers were wedging timbers and the wagon beds into place, as well as they could be, to reinforce the battered and bowed west gates.

More slowly, the wagon-ram began to move eastward.

"First squad! Fire!"

More of the bluecoats pushing the ram dropped than on earlier runs, and the ram did not seem to have quite the same speed. Mykel also thought that it was wobbling somewhat, but it still stayed on the road.

He watched, his rifle ready, sighting on the gunpowder keg. He needed that keg to explode in flame. He truly *needed* it. As the shadow of the ram neared the oil casks, he fired—once, twice, and a third time, *willing* the explosion.

Crumpt! The walls shook, and a wave of flame spewed upward across the wagon and the ram. The front two wheels on the right shattered, and the weight of the ram dropped the corner of the wagon. Then the iron-tipped ram skidded sideways, coming to rest against the stone gate supports. The wall shook again.

The flames from the oil and from the burning powder and wagon created a heat so intense that the Cadmians on each side of the gate were forced to duck completely behind the merlons and walls.

Mykel studied the gate below. His explosion had twisted the north side of the gate open farther, despite the wagon beds and timbers, leaving an opening wide enough for one rider, perhaps two, once the flames and fire died away—and if the riders could force back the timbers and wagon bed behind the opening.

The firing from the timber barricades died away, not that there had ever been that much.

Mykel frowned as he realized that. Why hadn't they fired more?

He wanted to shake his head. Because they were worried about ammunition. They had to be concerned.

He climbed down the steps and crossed behind the gate, then climbed up to the tower where Dohark surveyed the road and the still-massed bluecoats.

"You didn't do much for the gates, Captain." Dohark's tone was half-humorous, half-rueful.

"No, sir, but another hit from that ram would have done much worse." He paused. "Did you notice that they're not firing that much."

"Wouldn't do that much good."

"No. I don't think that's the reason."

"Neither do I. They can't have smuggled in that many cartridges. That's why the timber barricades and the ram. They'll probably move up the barricades to shelter their foot, or what passes for it, and rush the gates. They have to take us now, or they won't ever."

Mykel wasn't certain of that, but Dohark had a point.

"Besides, the western seltyrs don't care that much about how many men get killed so long as they get control."

The overcaptain had more of a point there, Mykel reflected.

"You were working on something else earlier," Dohark said quietly, still looking westward through the blackish smoke rising from the burning wagon-ram. The sun, faintly orange from the smoke, was well past mid-afternoon. "Would it work against a mass attack?"

"It should."

"You'll probably have to use it." Dohark paused. "I only saw cooking oil, you know?"

"That's all you saw, sir. I need to see what I can do."

Dohark nodded, but said nothing as Mykel left the small north guard tower.

Almost a glass passed before the flames died down to embers. The bluecoats remained gathered back in the casaran groves, well out of range.

In the meantime, Mykel had moved his unwieldy device to a point just behind the gap in the north gate. First, he'd had to persuade one of the local squad leaders to move two timber braces and slide back a wagon bed. Then, it had taken three rankers to lift and carry the big barrel over the bracings to get it into position.

The second keg of gunpowder stood behind it.

"Cadmians—to the west wall!" ordered Dohark.

Carefully, Mykel climbed up the bracing behind him. He could see a line of riders outlined against the late-afternoon sun. He made his way down, then wrestled the barrel out the gate and onto its side. Carefully, he rolled it around the embers and charred wood of the wagon-ram and back onto the road.

He could hear hoofs, even feel them through the stones, by the time he had the barrel in place a good twenty yards out from the wall. He would have liked to have moved it out farther, but didn't know that he'd be able to get everything to work if he did.

Then he ran back to the gate and grabbed the keg of power, lugging it back to the adapted barrel. Once he was behind the big barrel, he poured almost half the ancient powder into a pile and set the keg in the middle of the powder. Then he sprinted for the gate and squeezed through. As soon as he did, the rankers pushed the wagon bed back into place and began to rewedge braces into position.

Mykel stood there for a moment, panting, before he scrambled back up the steps to the wall. He was sweating, both from the heat, the exertion, and from thinking about what could have happened to him had anything gone wrong with his device.

The rebel bluecoats were pouring toward the compound. Even some of the greencoats from the east had circled around to join the attack.

"Open fire!" ordered Dohark.

Mykel picked out one of the riders in the fore and fired. The bluecoat went down, slowing those behind him. Mykel fired again, and again. By then the bluecoats were within a hundred yards of the barrel, but as a result of the heavy fire from the compound, they had condensed into a more compact mass.

Mykel reloaded quickly, waiting until the bluecoats were almost upon the ancient barrel, sitting in the middle of the approach causeway to the compound.

Finally, he aimed at the powder around the base of the keg—and fired. The barrel and the keg sat, there, with the rebels almost upon them. He fired again. Still nothing. The third time he fired, he willed the bullet home, *willed* it with power and heat.

After that shot, Mykel ducked, not even knowing whether it hit, but knowing something was about to happen.

CRUMMPTTT! Before his head was fully behind the merlon, the entire west wall of the compound shook, and fragments flew above and against the wall. Then, pattering sounds like rain followed as bits of things dropped onto the stones.

Mykel slowly peered around the stone edge. A circle almost fifty yards across had been carved out of the rebels, bodies and sections of bodies lay strewn everywhere. Beyond that, mounts were rearing, many riderless.

Mykel swallowed, hard, then ordered, "Full fire! Cadmians! Full fire."

More rebels dropped.

The bluecoats and greencoats began to turn, riding in almost every direction.

"Fifteenth Company! To mounts! To mounts!" Mykel scrambled

down the steps and raced toward the area north of the south wall, where the mounts were supposed to be lined up and waiting.

They were.

Then he had to wait for his men.

When he finally rode toward the east gate—a good fifth of a glass later—he only had about two-thirds of Fifteenth Company, but he didn't want to wait any longer.

The east gates did open, but they shut quickly.

Mykel led Fifteenth Company across the flat north of the compound, flanking the timber barricades, until he saw that they had been abandoned.

A squad of bluecoats turned, as if to form up, but when they saw that they faced a larger force, several riders on the ends turned their mounts.

Mykel rode straight for the squad leader, his sabre out and ready.

The squad leader tried to lift his rifle.

Mykel dropped almost flat against the chestnut's neck for a moment, then swept in from the right. His sabre cut was awkward—but effective enough that blood welled across the other's arm, and his rifle dropped onto the ground. Mykel kept riding, turning toward the bluecoat in the second rank, who half raised his sabre. Mykel's momentum slammed his weapon aside.

In moments, there was a melee, but within a fraction of a glass, half the rebels were down, and the others were scattering. Fifteenth Company had gone through them like a newly sharpened sabre through rotten cheese, leaving a half score dead.

Ahead, Mykel saw another formation in one of the few small meadows on the south side of the road. He sheathed the sabre, more slowly than he would have liked, and called back, "Fifteenth Company! Ready for firing line!"

The rebels had grouped into a tight formation and drawn blades, clearly awaiting a sabre charge.

"Fifteenth Company! Firing line and halt!"

Mykel almost couldn't believe what he saw, with the rebels standing flat, but he wasn't in the mood to be forgiving or charitable, not after poisonings, battering rams, and ambushes.

He reined up and slipped out his rifle, aiming at the squad leader. "Open fire!"

By the time Fifteenth Company had emptied its magazines at a distance of less than fifty yards, at least a third of the rebels were down.

"Sabres ready! Forward!"

Several of the rebels tried to fight—not well. The others tried to flee, and a number were cut down from behind.

Less than a glass later, short of the river bridge, Mykel turned Fifteenth Company back. His sabre was bloody, as was his uniform.

As they rode slowly back to the compound through the growing twilight, Mykel saw bodies everywhere. He could smell blood and burned flesh, and already the flies and nightwasps were circling in on the ground around the compound.

He wouldn't have been surprised if a third of the rebels had died. With those wounded, and those deserting, the seltyrs could have lost half their forces.

The east gates opened just long enough to readmit Fifteenth Company, then closed with a dull thud.

Dohark was waiting at the stables.

"Wasn't that taking a risk?" he asked after Mykel dismounted.

"The whole day was a risk," Mykel replied, adding, after a moment, "sir." He took a deep breath. "I thought they'd be disorganized. They were. We probably killed off another company or so."

"Do you think they'll be back?"

"Not soon. It'll take them a few days, maybe even several weeks, to regroup. After the men rest, I'd suggest harassing them more, picking off stragglers and anyone else we can."

"You've got the only force that can do that."

"Is that an approval?"

"We'll talk about it tomorrow."

"Yes, sir."

"The colonel might want to know why you helped the rebels blow apart the gate," said Dohark. "When he returns."

"He might." Mykel shrugged. "I was trying to use some powder to spread the burning oil to burn up their ram. Things got out of hand."

"You could put it that way," Dohark said. "I'm reporting that the kitchen oil that you used to set the ram afire exploded."

"That's also true, sir."

"That's the way it is. That powder . . . it must have been misplaced when the rebel sympathizers took the rifles last year."

"Yes, sir."

"There's one other thing, Mykel."

"Yes?"

"How in the Anvils of Hel did you get that stuff to explode? It's frigging near impossible to get powder to burn by shooting it with a bullet."

Mykel managed to keep from looking blankly at Dohark. "I guess I was just lucky. I don't have any other explanation."

"Too much luck is as bad as too little, at times."

"I suppose so."

"After you get your men settled, get some rations and rest." Dohark nodded and walked into the dusk.

Why wasn't Dohark all that pleased with a battle that had turned a sure disaster into something better, with a chance to wipe out the rebels in the weeks ahead? What was it about command that turned officers into men more concerned about what methods were used than about winning with the fewest losses? He stifled a yawn. He'd worry about that later.

"Bhoral? Make sure that they groom their mounts and clean their weapons. Tonight."

"Yes, sir."

Mykel led the chestnut toward his stall. He had to take care of those chores himself, or before long, men would ask why he issued orders he didn't follow. He couldn't have that. Not the way things were going.

84

Marshal Shastylt never did return to headquarters on Quinti, and Dainyl finally left, much later than he would have liked, after confirming arrangements with Quelyt and Falyna for an early flight on Sexdi.

He and Lystrana ate quietly, and did not say much of great import throughout the meal. Once the girls had finished with the cleanup and had settled themselves for the evening, Dainyl and Lystrana retired to their bedchamber. Each brought a goblet of the golden brandy.

Dainyl sat on a tall padded stool, sipping his brandy and watching as Lystrana, wearing a pale gold dressing gown, brushed her shimmering black hair. Each stroke was smooth, efficient, yet subtly sensual. Nevertheless, he could not totally concentrate on her, beautiful as she was, close as she was.

"Something's bothering you. I can feel it."

"You always can." He laughed softly.

"Tell me." Her voice was gentle.

"I don't understand," he said quietly.

"Understand what?"

"I'm convinced the marshal and the Highest fomented this revolt in Dramur, and, now, they want me to put it down quickly. There wasn't any urgency before, and now there is."

"Too many things have gotten out of hand," she suggested.

"Why now? Because we're approaching the time when a decision has to be made on the master scepter?" He shook his head. "The landers and indigens know nothing about that. There are few of them who even have a trace of Talent. How could they know?"

"My Highest mentioned that there had been a wild Talent in Hyalt, but I've never sensed that in any lander. Do you think any of them really does? Or was that another situation that got out of hand, and the marshal claimed that it was caused by a wild Talent?"

"Either is possible," mused Dainyl.

"Do you really think so?" She laid down the brush and turned.

Dainyl just took in her perfectly shaped oval face, her form, and the deep violet eyes he could look into endlessly.

"You're not thinking about my question." She laughed softly.

"I wasn't," he admitted. "I was thinking that this was our last night for a while, perhaps a long while."

"If you think about it, more quickly, it might settle your thoughts, and then we might have more time to get on with what else you have in mind." Her lips curled into a playful smile. Then, she took a sip from her goblet.

"There are landers with Talent—at least potential Talent. I've run across a Cadmian captain who has the potential. He doesn't know, and I hope he never learns. He's one of the better junior officers. I'd hate to lose him."

"Competent landers in positions of responsibility are hard to find, but . . . the way they breed, we can't afford to have all that wild Talent loose. You know that. You know what a toll that would take on Acorus."

"He doesn't even have a consort, and he's not the type to spend himself on other women, or not much."

"That's not all that's worrying you, dearest."

"No. There's Colonel Dhenyr." Dainyl shook his head.

"He's polite. He's well-mannered. He has a long, but not terribly distinguished record in the Myrmidons. His Talent is limited, and he has no real grasp of what is happening," suggested Lystrana.

"Exactly. You've met him?"

"I've never even seen a report on him," she replied. "That's the way you would have appeared when they made you colonel."

Dainyl winced.

"Why do you think they made you colonel? Why do you think we worked so hard at concealing the full extent of your Talent?"

"They don't want someone looking into what they're doing." He laughed ruefully. "I don't see that it matters. Who could I tell who could do anything?"

"You could tell the Duarches."

"I could, indeed. And then what? Do you think that the High Alector of Justice would exactly allow himself to be disciplined? Or the marshal, after what he did to Tyanylt? We'd have a revolt among alectors. That's if I'm right. If I'm wrong . . ."

"You're not wrong," she affirmed.

"I can't chance destroying everything. I have to find a better way."

"You will."

"How?" Dainyl shrugged, conveying frustration and helplessness with the position in which he found himself.

"Resolve the problems in Dramur. Then, once you're back here in Elcien, there will be an opportunity."

He took another sip of the brandy. "I suppose you're right."

"Then . . . is there anything you can do about it tonight?"

"No . . ." He laughed. "I suppose not."

Lystrana set aside the goblet and stood, letting the dressing gown slide away.

85

On Sexdi, Mykel reported to Overcaptain Dohark right after his breakfast of field rations.

Sitting behind the study desk, Dohark no longer looked at all greenish, just exhausted, with deeper circles under his eyes.

"They killed Majer Herryf," Dohark said, without preamble.

"When?"

"The night before last. There was a squad of bluecoats waiting for him. They had tied up his wife and children. They shot him as he came in the door, then rode off."

Mykel wasn't totally surprised. From what he had seen, Herryf had never understood fully what was happening in Dramur, and because he had identified with the people of Dramur, he had thought they would believe him one of them rather than an outland Cadmian. To most people, even his own family, he suspected, a Cadmian was a Cadmian, and Cadmians were tools of the alectors and Myrmidons. "Does that leave you in command?"

"Not really. He reported directly to Colonel Herolt in Elcien."

"For the time being, Meryst and Benjyr might accept your command."

"Meryst might. No one's seen Benjyr."

"You think he's with the rebels?"

"He might be. He might be up at the mine compound. Or he might be dead."

"What about the mine?"

"I sent a squad up there a glass ago. It'll be a while before we hear. What have your scouts found?"

"Dead bodies, more than four hundred, from the looks of it," replied Mykel. "That doesn't count the wounded who won't make it, and the deserters."

"You still want to go after the rest of them?"

"Tomorrow. I'll need today to put together the supply wagons and ammunition."

"You're not going to operate out of the compound, I take it," said Dohark.

"They'll stay away from here for a while. We need to go where they are, while they're still not organized."

"You'll do anything to get away from the dirty work." A faint smile creased the corners of Dohark's mouth.

"Dirty work?"

"Those four hundred bodies have to be buried, in addition to the ones of ours that still aren't in the ground. There's also a gate that got rammed and exploded that needs repair." Dohark paused. "Oh, and the armorer said that you never got a requisition for all the ammunition." His smile broadened. "I told him you'd have it to him today."

Mykel inclined his head. "I'll take care of that immediately."

"I'd suggest one for the cooking oil as well."

Mykel understood the reasons for that, even though the cooks probably could have cared less about a requisition for cooking oil, so long as they got replacement casks.

Dohark looked hard at Mykel. "Thc scltyrs arc pcoplc, Mykel."

"I know, sir. So are we, and they're trying to kill us. They're also willing to kill anyone who doesn't meet their standards. They shot prisoners who wanted to escape. They wiped out almost all of Seventeenth Company. They sent more than a thousand troopers across the mountains and against the compound—and we never did anything against the western seltyrs. All that suggests that it's them or us. I'm doing my best to make sure we're the ones still standing—or riding—when the smoke clears."

Dohark said nothing. He merely nodded.

"Are you suggesting that I remain here, sir?" Mykel finally asked.

"No. The Cadmians need you to do what you've proposed. I wish there happened to be another way. I don't see it."

Neither did Mykel, at least not a way that would result in any chance of survival for what was left of the Third Battalion.

"Is that all?" asked Dohark.

"That's all, sir. By your leave?"

The overcaptain nodded.

Mykel left the headquarters building at a quick walk. He still had one other problem for which he had no answer, and that was Rachyla. Should he see her first—or later? He decided on sooner. She might offer some insight. Then again, he reflected, she just might not.

He walked toward her cell. There was still only one guard on duty, although a different Cadmian.

"Sir? You need to talk to the prisoner."

"If she'll talk," Mykel replied.

The guard unlocked and opened the cell.

In the dimness within, Rachyla sat at the desk, one forearm resting on the edge. She did not turn until after the door had *clunked* shut.

"How are you feeling?" Mykel asked.

"Better. The food isn't helping. If you can call it food."

"Those are field rations. No one wanted to trust the cooking after a third of the Cadmians died from poisoning."

"A third?"

"Something like that—around a hundred and fifty."

"It is too bad it wasn't more."

"It was enough."

"All the firing yesterday—what was that all about?"

"The eastern and western seltyrs attacked the compound. We killed almost half of them. They've scattered everywhere."

"They won't give up."

"No," Mykel agreed. "Not until they're all dead."

"And you, brave captain, will see to that?"

"If I have to. They seem determined to kill all of us. The only way to stop that is to kill them—or their men."

"You must be very good at killing." Rachyla looked at Mykel evenly.

"It would be better if I didn't have to be."

"So noble . . ."

Mykel forced himself not to take a deep breath in exasperation. "You might explain why the seltyrs are so determined to attack us."

"If they do not attack, they lose everything they have built. They lose it without honor. Without honor a seltyr is nothing more than a fat grower."

"I don't understand. What are they losing? The only thing they're being asked to do is not to create personal armies with contraband weapons."

"An unarmed seltyr is without honor."

"You said that before, but the weapons they want are banned by the Duarches. If the Cadmians are not the ones to disarm and defeat them, then the Myrmidons will turn their estates into ashes and dust."

Rachyla shrugged. "You asked. I have told you before. The Duarches will not be here forever. We will be. They do not belong. Those who do not belong will vanish as if they had never been."

"Who told you that?" Mykel should have asked that before, but he wasn't used to questioning people like Rachyla.

"All in Dramur know that. We have since the times of the ancients. It will not be long before they vanish. If not in my life, then in the life of my children, or their children."

Were most of the Dramurans secret followers of the Ancienteers? Or of something similar? "The alectors have been here as long as we have."

"It matters not. We belong. They do not."

What Rachyla said made no sense. She was an intelligent woman, but she was uttering sheer nonsense. Even a fully trained Cadmian battalion could not stand against a squad of Myrmidons—or even a pair with their flaming skylances.

"They may not belong, but it takes more than honor and belief to stop pteridons and skylances . . . or even Cadmians and rifles. What do they have to stand up to those?"

"What will be . . . will be."

"Could you explain a bit more, give me an example?"

"You will see when the time comes, Captain. That is all I know and all I can tell you."

Mykel could sense that she fully believed what she said and truly did not know more.

"Good day, Captain."

He inclined his head. "Good day, Rachyla."

He walked to the door and rapped on it for the guard to let him out.

He still had to write up two requisitions and work with Bhoral and the squad leaders to organize the supplies for the coming campaign of attack and harassment.

But . . . he wished he knew what Rachyla had really meant and why an intelligent woman could believe something so impossible.

86

As on every flight from Elcien to Dramur, both Sexdi and Septi were long, and Dainyl's legs and back were already aching as he rode behind Falyna across the channel from Corus to the northern tip of Dramur. A glass later, after descending carefully through breaks in the clouds, the two pteridons reached clear air at less than five hundred yards above the ocean. Dainyl could see the northeastern shore of Dramur less than five vingts away.

Three glasses later, the fliers were on approach to the Cadmian compound at Dramuria. Falyna swept in toward the compound just before twilight, swinging to the west north of Dramuria and making a final descent toward the courtyard from the west.

In the last few moments aloft, just before landing, Dainyl studied the ground around the compound. The rebels had clearly attacked, but several days earlier. That was obvious from the state of the ground, the lack of bodies near the compound and those remaining farther west and short of the casaran orchards, and the ongoing repairs to the west gate. There were also two large circular and overlapping patches of scorched ground, one immediately in front of the west gate, and one perhaps fifty yards farther west.

The pteridon crossed the walls and flared to a stop just to the right of the closest pteridon square. Dainyl waited only until Falyna had dismounted before he eased himself out of the harness. His legs almost buckled when he first stood on the stones of the courtyard, but he stretched one leg, then the other before turning to Falyna.

"Thank you," he told Falyna. "That was a very smooth flight. If you'll excuse me, there's been some heavy fighting here, and I need to find out what happened."

"Yes, sir." She smiled. "We'll be ready first thing in the morning if you need us."

"I just might." With that, he turned and hurried toward the headquarters building, hoping that either Majer Herryf or Overcaptain Dohark—or both—were still there.

Overcaptain Dohark was waiting outside the study that Dainyl had been using. He'd obviously been alerted to the Myrmidons' return.

The submarshal motioned for Dohark to follow him inside. Dohark shut the door.

"I thought we might have Majer Herryf join us," Dainyl said.

"He was killed on Quattri night, Colonel . . . I mean, Submarshal. Congratulations, sir."

Although the desk was clear, as Dainyl had left it, his Talent indicated that the overcaptain had been using it, but there was little point in saying anything about that. Because the last thing Dainyl wanted to do was sit, he leaned against the side of the desk, his eyes on the overcaptain. "You'd best tell me what happened."

"What was bound to happen with an understrength battalion, Submarshal, and no Myrmidon support. The bluecoats and greencoats attacked on Quinti—"

"Bluecoats? Greencoats? Remember, Overcaptain, I have been out of touch."

"Yes, sir. All the troopers of the western seltyrs wear blue. The troops of the eastern seltyrs wear green. The bluecoats moved more than ten companies across the mountains . . ."

As the overcaptain explained, Dainyl listened, intently. The poisoning confirmed his beliefs that the local seltyrs had decided to use any weapon at hand before the marshal's—or the High Alector's—support was withdrawn. It also confirmed Lystrana's view that the marshal had never intended the revolt to be successful, and that the marshal—or some high alector—had to be behind the revolt, because the majority of seltyrs had cooperated in sharing, at least to some degree, the contraband weapons. Without some hint of alector power, the majority of weapons would have gone to the handful of stronger and wealthier seltyrs. Dainyl would have to avoid that aspect in his final report, as well as emphasize the more barbaric aspects of the seltyr tactics.

". . . the wagon-ram was about to splinter the gates, but we poured cooking oil on it and set it afire. A cask of oil was dropped on the fire, and it exploded. That scattered some of the rebels and disorganized them. The Cadmians managed to shoot a number because they were packed in. Then, and because they were taking heavy fire, the rest of the rebels began to fall back. Captain Mykel pursued them with Fifteenth Company and killed a number of the stragglers and sent the others off."

"How many seltyr casualties?"

"We've buried over four hundred. How many died away from here or deserted, that's something we can't tell."

"I noted what seemed to be explosions . . ."

"As I mentioned, we used cooking oil to burn the ram. Some of it exploded."

"Whose idea was that?" Dainyl added quickly, "Please don't tell me it was yours."

"No, sir, but it was my responsibility. I authorized the use of the cooking oil."

Dainyl paused, thinking. The overcaptain might not have come up with the idea, but he was trying to protect his officers. Dainyl suspected he already knew whose idea it had been.

"How did Captain Mykel come up with that idea, Overcaptain?"

"Sir?"

Despite Dohark's evasions, it was more than clear that it had to have been Captain Mykel. None of the other officers had enough creativity and initiative to carry out anything involving cooking oil and whatever else the captain had used. "Where is Captain Mykel?"

"He took Fifteenth Company out early this morning. He's pursuing some of the seltyr forces. He's the only one with enough able men to do that."

"You thought it was necessary?"

"Mykel pointed out that they were disorganized, but that they wouldn't stay that way. He also said that we didn't know when you and the other Myrmidons might return."

What Dohark said rang true, and it also suggested that Captain Mykel either knew or suspected far more than was wise for a junior officer. The captain's abilities were likely to create as much of a problem for Dainyl as the lack of ability of his former superior had.

"Do you know his plans?"

"Not in detail, sir. One or two companies had headed northeast, and Captain Mykel had thought he would attack them before they could rejoin the main body of rebels."

"You allowed the only fully functioning company to leave the compound?"

"Sir, with all deference, I believe Captain Mykel was correct. The best strategy was to attack before they could regroup and attack again. While the massed forces of the rebels could not stand against the skylances of your Myrmidons, we had no word as to when you would be able to return. It seemed imprudent to assume that you would return so soon. We could have been badly outnumbered in a second attack, and we would not have been able to mount as successful a defense as we did the first time."

Dainyl nodded slowly. "I would have done the same under the circumstances." He smiled. "At the very least, we may be able to use the pteridons to make the captain's tasks much easier." Because he could sense Dohark's combined sense of relief and apprehension, he smiled. "We cannot begin that until tomorrow, and not with full support until Novdi, but I have complete authority to use the Myrmidons in any way necessary to put a stop to this rebel foolishness and to return the mine to normal operations."

"Yes, sir."

"We'll talk in the morning after muster, Overcaptain." Dainyl stepped away from the desk, but let the captain leave the study first.

As Dainyl walked to the officer's mess—where he was scarcely looking forward to dining on Cadmian rations—he just hoped that he could end the revolt without too many complications, including those posed by the potentially Talented and enterprising Captain Mykel.

87

For Fifteenth Company, following the trail of the withdrawing rebels had not been that difficult, either on Septi or Octdi. They had made no effort to conceal their tracks, and while, after the first few vingts, they had carried their dead with them, they had left clear signs of their passage, from discarded garments, bloody bandages, empty cartridge belts, and one mount that had broken its leg and been shot on the side of the road.

Mykel and his men had followed at a measured pace, not pressing, but not slacking. While they had ridden through a few showers, those had been brief and light.

At twilight, they had made an encampment on a grower's lands south and east of Enstyla. Mykel had simply ridden in with the company and taken over the outbuildings and the stables. He also slaughtered enough of the livestock to feed his men. After all that he had seen in Dramur and more than a week of stale field rations, Mykel was feeling far less charitable. The family had remained in the main dwelling, and had been left to themselves. The handful of retainers had vanished.

On Octdi morning, they had ridden out, carrying some additional food. Only a thin high haze remained of the previous day's clouds, and by midmorning, Mykel was uncomfortably warm. He had to remind himself that while it was early in spring, he was in Dramur, not Elcien.

Less than a glass before noon, Jasakyt came riding back down the road toward Mykel.

"Fifteenth Company! Halt!" Mykel rode ahead to meet the scout. Bhoral followed his captain.

Jasakyt reined up a yard away from Mykel. "Sir . . . there's almost two companies up ahead. Don't know whether it's a seltyr's place or just a big grower's. Not many sentries, just by the main entrance. They're sort of scattered. They look pretty beat."

"How far?"

"No more 'n vingt and a half. Sort of sits on a long gentle ridge. Doesn't hardly drop off at all, but the highest point is between the big house and the casaran orchard."

"Did they see you?"

"No, sir. Pretty sure they didn't. Dhozynt went around back, circled the woodlot, and an orchard."

"What sort of encampment?"

"Doesn't look like much. They just stopped and sat down, almost . . ."

Mykel continued to ask questions until he saw another scout returning.

Within moments, Dhozynt had joined them.

"You circled to the back side?" asked Mykel.

"Yes, sir. They don't have any sentries there, not a one, and there's a back cart path off the side lane. We could ride the whole way without anyone seeing us—till we got to the last part of the casaran trees, anyway."

Mykel went over what Dhozynt had seen as carefully as he could. Then he turned to Bhoral. "If you'd have the squad leaders join us?"

"Yes, sir."

While he waited for the squad leaders to gather, Mykel strapped an extra cartridge belt across his chest, considering how he wanted to attack the bluecoats, although there didn't seem to be a need for much strategy—just a quiet hidden approach, a wide field of fire, and a restraint of any pursuit, until and unless it was clear that Fifteenth Company had total control. He had the feeling that if matters went as he planned, he wouldn't care for the results. But if they didn't, he'd like it even less.

Gendsyr and Alendyr were the first to rein up on the road next to Mykel, but only moments later Bhoral and the other three joined them.

Mykel looked at the squad leaders. "There are two companies up ahead. They don't expect us. We'll be taking the back road to this estate where they've set up camp. There aren't any guards, and few sentries. We'll ride in the last quarter vingt hard and set up by squad into firing lines across the front of their encampment—at less than twenty yards. I'll set first squad on the north end, and you'll take intervals on us. We'll shoot everything that moves. No pursuit unless and until I give the order—or Bhoral does. Is that clear?"

Nods and muttered replies of "Yes, sir" came back.

"Now . . . this isn't going to be easy on the men." Mykel went on. "Some of the rebels will fight hard. Others will have trouble fighting back. Some are killers, and some are tired and discouraged. It doesn't matter who your men are facing. They need to shoot and shoot well. I don't want this attack ruined by pity. Make it simple. Tell your men these were the same rebels who gunned down almost all of Seventeenth Company in an ambush. They're the same people who poisoned Third Battalion. If we don't take out as many as we can now, they'll do the same things to us again in half a season or less. They still outnumber us overall, and we've got to change that while we can. Tell them one other thing. The seltyrs like to shoot prisoners who escape. They'd rather do that than fight an armed foe." He paused. "These aren't the poor folk of Jyoha. These are the men who will be trained as killers for the seltyrs if we don't stop them now." After another pause, he added. "I'm counting on you to get the message to your men."

"Yes, sir."

"Dismissed to your squads. We'll ride once you pass the word."

Once the squad leaders had left, and the scouts had moved back forward to lead the way, Bhoral looked at Mykel. "You think this will be a slaughter, sir?"

"Like I said, Bhoral, there will be some who fight and some who will look at us as they're shot down. We have to kill either kind, because if we don't, they'll be trying to kill us next week or the week after . . . and I'm getting frigging tired of losing men who shouldn't be here in the first place." As he finished the last phrase, Mykel wished he hadn't gone quite so far.

"Yes, sir. You don't think the Myrmidons will be back soon, then?"

"I don't know what to think about that," Mykel admitted. "I only know that these people don't think the same way anyone else I've ever met does. The only thing they respect are either golds or force, preferably both."

"Seems that way, sir."

Mykel could tell that Bhoral had his doubts, but he didn't care to discuss it further. The seltyrs, as Rachyla had told him, believed it was their right to rule as they saw fit, and that the alectors and their Myrmidons—even the Cadmians—would vanish. A Cadmian captain couldn't reason against that attitude, and Mykel wasn't particularly happy being in a position where the only practical solution was greater firepower. He looked at the empty road ahead, then shook his head.

In less than a quarter glass, Fifteenth Company was again moving northward, with orders to ride silently. Within another quarter glass, Mykel had dropped the wagons behind, close enough to be reached quickly, if necessary, with a four-man guard, two of whom had been stung by nightwasps the evening before.

Finally, Fifteenth Company reached the back of the casaran orchards to the east of the bluecoat encampment. Ahead, there was the slightest slope up through the orchards.

Mykel blinked. For a moment, he thought he'd sensed something like a road beneath the dirt, a faint black trail running along the barely perceptible high point of the gentle rise that split the orchard. He looked again, but saw nothing.

"Now," he ordered quietly. "Forward." He urged the chestnut into a fast trot down the lane between the nut trees.

As he rode past the last of the casaran trees and turned right, toward the north end of the bluecoat encampment, Mykel took in the bluecoats he saw. Several had started to run. Only one had a rifle immediately at hand, and he seemed frozen.

After a moment, a single cry rang out. "Cadmians! Cadmians!"

Mykel and first squad reined up in a firing line at the north end of the encampment, taking the highest ground, even if it was but a yard or so higher than that to the east.

"First squad! Rifles ready! Fire!"

Five or six of the closest bluecoats were down within the first two volleys.

"Second squad! Fire!"

Bluecoats began to scramble toward the sheds, toward any form of shelter.

Abruptly, two older-looking bluecoats appeared, and one took dead aim at the Cadmian captain. The other turned as well.

Mykel had one shot left. With all his thought, desire, everything, he *willed* the bullet home.

The first bluecoat dropped, but the second brought his rifle to bear, taking his time, as if to indicate that he might die, but that Mykel would as well.

All Mykel could do was duck, urge the chestnut forward, and *will* that the bullets not strike him. Time around him seemed to slow, and he could sense the bullets moving toward him. Somehow, some way, he twisted his body out of the line of fire as the chestnut carried him forward.

Still in that slow movement, he watched the bluecoat's mouth open. For a moment, the man froze, and then Mykel and the chestnut were upon him. Mykel *knew* that he could not have covered that distance so quickly, but he had. Without cartridges in the magazine, he did the only thing that he could, reversing the rifle and slamming the butt across the bluecoat's temple. The man dropped. Mykel felt a sudden emptiness, a feeling that he had come to recognize as death.

He wheeled the chestnut back to the firing line, but the return seemed far slower. The area closest to him was empty of able rebels. He reloaded quickly, then slipped the rifle into its saddle case. "First squad! Sabres! On me!" He stood in the stirrups. "Second squad! Hold!"

Very few of the rebels had lifted rifles in the face of the attack. Even so, Mykel thought he had lost some of his men, or that some had been wounded. He urged the chestnut toward the handful of fleeing men. "First squad, forward!"

The next glass was a confused mixture of pursuit, slashing sabres, moments of silence, intermittent rifle shots . . . and slaughter.

Mykel finally led first squad back to the villa, where they re-formed.

Led by Bhoral, the other squads rejoined them.

"Fifteenth Company stands ready, sir."

"Thank you. What were our casualties?" Mykel asked the senior squad leader.

"One dead, three wounded, not badly."

It could have been much worse, Mykel thought, glancing back toward the ruined tents, then toward the apparently silent villa.

"What now, sir?" asked Bhoral.

"We'll take a half score of the best mounts, and whatever good supplies will fit in the wagons." Mykel gestured toward the villa. "Burn it. Not the outbuildings or the stables. Just the villa."

"Sending a message to the seltyrs, sir?"

"And to their retainers and the others. I hope they'll get it." Mykel had his doubts, but it was worth a try.

As Bhoral conveyed his orders to four rankers in first squad, Mykel surveyed the devastation around the villa. It had been a slaughter. Over a hundred bluecoats lay dead, left where they had fallen, in the fields, in ditches, beside the stables, on the dirt lanes of the estate.

Slowly, he took a rag from his saddlebags and cleaned his sabre and sheathed it. Then he checked his rifle, making sure that the magazine was full.

They hadn't taken prisoners. That bothered him, because the rebel troopers weren't really to blame, but he didn't have any choices. If he let the troopers escape, he'd have to fight them again later. Every prisoner taken meant Cadmians who had to guard them, and Fifteenth Company was already understrength and needed every man. Finally, there was no reciprocity—the seltyrs didn't take prisoners . . . and wouldn't, and they seemed to regard such mercy as weakness.

He took a deep breath. There were other bluecoats left to find—and deal with as best he could.

88

Despite his tiredness and the effects of flying two long days, Dainyl did not sleep well. Images swirled through his dreaming thoughts, images of pteridons and their fliers vanishing into dark tubes, of hundreds of landers and indigens cutting each other down with bright shimmering rifles, of an ancient soarer in midair above a peak pointing a tiny finger at him and telling him, "Change or perish."

He woke covered in sweat on Octdi morning, for all that the officer's chamber was more than pleasantly cool. It was a relief to get up. He washed and dressed, and made his way to the mess, where he ate hurriedly, washing the rations down with ale, as a single sleepy-eyed Cadmian watched.

Then he began a thorough walking inspection of the compound, starting at the east gate, and going through each building. Several were locked. Most of the locks he could open with his Talent. One, which had a heavy hasp lock, he severed with the light-cutter sidearm. He could find nothing amiss, nothing that should not have been there.

In the armory, he noted—through his Talent—that there were traces of where barrels of ancient gunpowder had been recently removed, but he did not mention that to the senior squad leader who was bemoaning just how much ammunition had been used in the past weeks. When he finished, it was past the morning muster, and he made his way to the headquarters building.

Overcaptain Dohark had taken over the smaller study, the one to which Majer Herryf had retreated after Dainyl had assumed command in Dramuria. He looked up as Dainyl appeared, then stood, quickly but smoothly. "Sir?"

"I was just checking."

"Battalion rosters, sir. It's really the first time I've had a chance to go over them in detail to assess what we have. We've got a little less than half a battalion left. Fifteenth Company is closest to full strength, with eighty-four men, but that includes nine from Seventeenth Company."

"Have you heard anything from Captain Mykel?"

"No, sir. I doubt that I will until he returns."

"If he returns."

The overcaptain gave a harsh short laugh, more of a bark. "He'll return, Submarshal, sir. Worst he'd do would be if he only brought back half his men. If he did that, there wouldn't be a seltyr left alive in a hundred vingts."

"You have a high opinion of the captain." Dainyl pressed a hint of Talent toward the overcaptain, a suggestion that Dohark needed to say more.

The overcaptain frowned, then nodded, as if to himself, before speaking. "Fifteenth Company has accounted for something like nine out of ten rebel casualties. He seems to sense where the enemy will be. He gets people to talk to him, too. He's found out more from that seltyr's daughter than I'd ever thought possible. The local captains, they didn't want to talk to us much. They were polite, but not much more. Mykel—I don't know how he did it—got them to talk. On top of that, he's the best marksman in any of the battalions. Anything he can see, he can bring down, and some that he can't." Dohark stopped abruptly.

With each revelation by Dohark, Dainyl became more concerned. All of the skills that the overcaptain mentioned were potentially Talent-driven or Talent-enhanced. "Majer Vaclyn didn't know this?"

"He didn't want to know it, sir. He was the kind who was afraid that good captains would show that he wasn't a good commander."

"And the Cadmian colonel, what did he think about Captain Mykel?"

"He didn't know that much, except that Fifteenth Company stopped taking heavy losses once Mykel became captain."

"You praise the captain, yet you sound concerned," Dainyl pressed.

"Yes, sir. Mykel's realized that there's only one way to win here in Dramur, and that's to kill off most of the seltyrs' bluecoats and greencoats quick-like, before they can replace them, and take as many of the seltyrs as possible. He's getting real good at using Fifteenth Company to wipe out scores—more like hundreds—of rebels. I'm not sure that's a good attitude for the rankers to develop. Leaves some of 'em real cold, killers."

"Isn't that what they have to do?"

"It is here, sir, and that's the problem. Other places in Corus, we killed rebels and folk, but the idea was to show force and control. Folks understood. Here, they don't. Mykel sees that, and he'll do what he has to bring his company through with the fewest casualties. Ambush, shooting down men as they rest or eat, night attacks, if he thinks they can work . . ."

In short, thought Dainyl, *Captain Mykel is becoming as ruthless as any alector, and far more efficient than his peers—and it is clearly disturbing the overcaptain.*

". . . thing is, sir, Captain Mykel's not like that, not inside, and someday, he's going to have to live with what he's done here."

"Don't we all, Overcaptain?"

"Yes, sir." Dohark's voice turned flat and polite.

Dainyl regretted his choice of words, but he'd never had to deal that much with Cadmian officers, and he'd forgotten the emotional overtones and issues differed. The *Views of the Highest* had a section on that, but it had been some time since he'd reviewed that wisdom. He wished he had, or that he could have talked to Lystrana. After a moment, he offered a rueful smile. "I think that sounded harsh. What I meant was that all officers end up having to do unpleasant duties. It's the nature of what we do, and Captain Mykel has had the misfortune to be in a position where, to get the job done, he must undertake particularly distasteful acts. I'm sure that he will regret the necessity, as I am sure you have at times, Overcaptain. Regret . . . and a wish that matters could have been otherwise . . . those we all face."

Dohark seemed to relent, at least slightly. "That'd be true for most of us. I worry more about Mykel because he seemed to care more, and worried about the folks here—or when we dealt with the Reillies. I think it tears at him, where he won't even let himself see it, when other folks' cruelty requires the same, or worse, from him."

Dainyl nodded. "There are some who simply don't care about the impact of their acts. If all people did, then we wouldn't need as many Cadmians and Myrmidons as we do."

"I suppose not, sir, but it's a sad world at times."

"That it is." Dainyl offered a smile he hoped was understanding. "I'll be in the study if you need me."

"Yes, sir."

Dainyl spent the morning reading through all the reports that the overcaptain had left him. A number appeared to have been written most recently, and he had to wonder if Dohark had composed them hastily after Dainyl's return.

From the reports and from what Dohark had told him, Dainyl had to admit that the situation had not only gotten too far out of hand, but that Captain Mykel seemed to be the only one who understood—or the only one willing to face what had to be done.

Dainyl also needed to check on the local Cadmians and how and whether they were getting the mine back into production, but he'd wanted to get a better feel for the military situation before he talked to Benjyr and Meryst.

Just after midday, when he was considering trying to go to the mess to choke down more ale and rations, Dainyl stiffened. From somewhere to the north had come a flash of Talent, not ifrit-Talent, with its pinkish purple feel, but something like that of the soarer, green, but overlaid with black, rather than with the gold he had felt from the ancient.

Without a word, he left the study and walked out into the courtyard, turning to the north.

The greenish black Talent had already begun to fade from his senses. Yet, in its place, to the northwest, he could sense, if but faintly, that of the ancient—as if whatever he had felt had also summoned her. He didn't need the ancients around, not when they were apparently the only creatures who could summon forces to bring down a pteridon.

Had that other flash of Talent been Captain Mykel? Had he begun to understand and use his Talent? Or was another Talent-wielder loose on Dramur?

89

Mykel looked out into the darkness from where he sat on an old bench in front of an outbuilding that had seen better days. After the slaughter southeast of Enstyla, Mykel had led Fifteenth Company a good fifteen vingts westward until he had found another grower's place to commandeer for the evening. Fifteenth Company had taken all the buildings, except for the main dwelling. There, behind barred doors, the wife and children of the absent grower huddled, Mykel was certain, dreading what might happen.

So long as no one attacked, he would let the dwelling stand. He realized that he would be seen as arbitrary in what he destroyed, but those who openly supported the rebellion would pay. In a way, though, that just encouraged hypocrisy. There were no good answers, not that he saw.

As he considered the day just past, and the day yet to come, Mykel felt both drained and, in a strange way, somewhat more alive. The fighting and the killing discouraged and depressed him, necessary as he felt it was. Yet in some fashion, he felt more alert than he had in years.

The skies were clear, and Selena had not yet risen. Asterta was but a pinpoint just above the mountains to the west. There were no lamps or light-torches anywhere, yet it did not seem that dark. Mykel could see the sentry on the inner line, standing in front of a fence just in front of a short-needled pine tree, slowly chewing on something, then turning away.

"Banayt!" he called out. "If you're going to eat on watch, at least keep looking!"

The sentry jumped. "Yes, sir."

"Sir?" Alendyr's voice was tentative.

Mykel hadn't realized that the squad leader was so close, but he had not been paying that much attention, lost as he had been in his own thoughts. "Yes?"

"You can see what Banayt's doing from here?"

"He's only some fifty yards out," Mykel said.

"It's dark as pitch out there, sir. I can barely make out the tree."

Mykel offered a shrug.

"Sir? About today . . ."

"I wish we didn't have to do things like that, but there's no help for it," Mykel said, tiredly. "These people only respect force." He felt like those words were becoming an excuse for everything.

"No, sir. We all know that. This was something different. I was just wondering how you managed to get across that field so fast this afternoon. Those bluecoats who were aiming at you, you dropped one, and then, all sudden-like, you were almost on top of the other one."

"It just seemed that way," Mykel replied. "When you're fighting, strange things seem to happen. Things speed up and slow down. It seems that way to me, at least."

"I don't know, sir. Never seen anything like that . . . like you were in one place one moment, and another the next."

While that was how it had felt, Mykel was reluctant to admit it. "Sometimes, it feels that way. You're fighting. Then, suddenly, it's all over. Haven't you felt that way at times?"

"Yes, sir." The squad leader paused. "You think there are that many other rebel companies out there?"

"I'd guess there are still four or five. We need to take down a couple more, at least, before they'll even think about surrendering." That was being optimistic, but Mykel saw no point in saying so.

"Seems like a shame . . . they haven't been trained that well . . . If we had two battalions here, we could just roll them all up and get it over."

"It'd be quicker and easier on everyone, but . . . we don't. No one calls us in until there's a real mess."

"Myrmidons would help."

"They would, but there are so many rebels that they'd have to burn the whole island. There aren't that many of them, either." Mykel offered a rueful laugh. "That's why we're here."

"Yes, sir . . . just thought you'd like to know."

"I appreciate it, Alendyr. I just hope we can finish this up before long."

"Yes, sir. It'd be good to get back to Elcien. Had some more nightwasp stings. Say they'll get worse as it gets hotter."

"We can always hope we can finish before it gets too hot." Was that another aspect of the rebel strategy? Drag things out so that the nightwasps and other summer pests made things worse, until the Cadmians just wanted to leave?

"Hope so, sir."

After Alendyr slipped away, Mykel looked into the darkness. He knew what had to be done, just as he could see Banayt walking his post. Why did so few others? Or was he trying to justify what he had done and would do?

90

Fifteenth Company moved out early on Novdi morning, heading along one of the larger farm roads that meandered northward and was one of the few that descended into and crossed the stream valley that held the smuggling trail. The scouts had reported some hoofprints in the road, no more than one or two days old, possibly messengers between two rebel forces.

As he rode through an early morning that was already too warm, he considered how long and to what degree he should pursue the disorganized rebels. The bluecoats had not brought supply wagons eastward through the Murian Mountains, perhaps one reason why the rebel companies had not remained in one unified force. They needed to forage or buy supplies—or obtain them from those eastern seltyrs with whom they were allied. Contrary to what Rachyla had said, Mykel was convinced that some of the eastern and western seltyrs were acting together. Admittedly, the decision to work together could have come after her imprisonment.

Mykel frowned. He couldn't see that her imprisonment was doing much for either her or the Cadmians. He also worried that she was right about her fate, but what could he do? If he appealed to Dohark or Colonel Dainyl, they'd assume it was because he was attracted to her—and dismiss his suggestion. In a way, he was, but certainly not in a lustful or romantic fashion, and she definitely had no interest in him.

He glanced at the road ahead, catching sight of the dust that heralded a rider, one of the scouts. In less than a tenth of a glass, Sendyl had pulled his mount alongside Mykel.

"A company of bluecoats, sir, maybe two vingts north, but they're heading south. Looks like they're going to head west on that farm road on the south side of that valley. Right now, they've stopped down in the valley. Maybe for rations or water."

"Squad leaders! Forward!"

As he waited for them to gather, Mykel got out the maps he had. There was a lane that angled to the northwest. The road heading west passed through an area where the descent into the stream valley was so rugged that it was almost impassable and where the land to the south was marshy, even in drier weather. If Fifteenth Company set an ambush to the west of that and then followed with a charge, the ability of the bluecoats to retreat or withdraw quickly would be hampered. Yet, if they mounted a strong defense, Fifteenth Company could withdraw quickly.

Once the squad leaders arrived and pulled up in a semicircle facing him, Mykel began to speak. "We've got another bluecoat company headed our way. It looks like they'll be turning westward north of here. We're going to set up a surprise . . ." He went on to outline the plan as quickly as he could, finishing up with a summary. ". . . I'll be with first squad, up front. If they don't notice us until they're fully in range, the whole company will fire from cover as long as we can. Then I'll order either a charge or a withdrawal. If they react sooner, first squad will make a quick sabre charge. This will allow the other four squads to set up in the oblique firing lines to rake the road. We'll be riding back as quickly as possible." Mykel offered a rueful laugh, looking at Bhoral. "Just make sure first squad is clear on the way back before you open fire."

Bhoral even smiled in return. "We can manage that, sir."

Chyndylt chuckled.

"That's it. We'll be heading northwest at the next cart path. Back to your squads and pass the word."

The cart path that Mykel had noted and recalled was more like an overgrown trail, and he heard the creaking of the supply wagons at the rear—even as far ahead as he was riding. After half a vingt, the path emerged from between two woodlots and became a dike between two marshy areas. As soon as the chestnut set foot on the dike section of the path, clouds of gnatlike insects swarmed up around the riders. While not as bad as nightwasps, the gnats found their way into eyes, ears, and even noses. Swatting them released an odor much like rotting meat.

At the far end of the raised path, where a casaran orchard that had seen far better days replaced the marshy ground, the gnats vanished—but not the lingering odor. Mykel didn't recall the insects, but the last time they had ridden the area had been winter. Based on what he was seeing, feeling, and smelling, he wasn't looking forward to the summer ahead in Dramur.

He could hear the mutters behind him.

". . . longer we're here . . . worse it stinks . . ."

". . . better to let 'em fight among themselves . . ."

Mykel had some sympathy for that view, although he wasn't about to voice it.

Another quarter glass passed before they neared the junction with the south valley road. Jasakyt, whom Mykel had sent ahead, was waiting, just off the road, in a shaded spot. He rode forward to meet Mykel.

"Nothing on the road, sir. No tracks. Way's clear to a stand of trees a half vingt east."

"Thank you. Fall in with your squad."

"Yes, sir."

"Supply wagons! Hold here! Pass it back!" Mykel stood in the stirrups and looked back to make sure that the wagons had halted before turning his attention to the east–west road. "Fifteenth Company, to the right!"

After covering another two hundred yards, Mykel turned to Bhoral, on his left. "Up there, where the woodlot south of the road thickens, that's where I want the rest of the company."

"You want them set up so that they can take the road if necessary—in a firing line?"

"Right. That won't give as much concealment, but I want them able to ride at a moment's notice."

"You're thinking that this group might be better prepared, sir?"

"Something like that." Most of the rebels couldn't have been less prepared. Was that because the more disciplined companies had stayed away, or had their own scouts and information allowed them to avoid the Cadmians?

"Be a good thing to be ready to ride."

That was about as far as Bhoral was likely to go in saying that he approved.

As they drew abreast of the trees, seemingly less tended than most woodlots, with more than a few bushes between and under the trees, Mykel turned in the saddle. "Company, halt!" He looked to Bhoral. "They're yours."

"Yes, sir."

"First squad, forward!"

Gendsyr rode forward and took the position beside Mykel. They rode toward a copse of trees, standing alone on the right, large enough to conceal a squad, but certainly not a company.

"Squad, halt!" Mykel reined up well short of the trees and turned the chestnut so that he faced the squad. "Find cover, but stay mounted, and make sure you have a clear line of fire at the road. Don't ride any farther east on the road itself. And don't open fire until I order it."

Within moments, first squad was off the road and settling into the trees.

Waiting was one aspect of being a Cadmian that Mykel had the most trouble with, especially on hot days where flies and other insects buzzed around looking for exposed flesh. It seemed like a glass or more had passed, but he doubted that it was much more than half a glass. Then, another quarter glass went by before Mykel could see two riders on the road, with a larger group behind them. "Quiet! Rifles ready!" he hissed. "They're coming."

The few murmurs that had competed with the insects and birds died away.

Mykel kept waiting, his rifle in hand.

The rebel outriders were no more than seventy-five yards in front of the main body. They continued to ride toward the Cadmians concealed in the trees south of the road. Neither outrider gave the trees more than a passing glance—until they were within a few yards of Mykel, when one of them abruptly lifted a rifle and wheeled his mount, firing toward the trees.

"First squad, open fire!" As he yelled out the orders, Mykel brought his own weapon up and fired, concentrating hard.

The rebel outrider dropped, knocked back in the saddle. The second outrider fell a moment later, but not from any shot Mykel had fired.

"First squad! Forward!" Mykel guided the chestnut out from cover and turned eastward, not riding full out, so that Gendsyr and first squad could catch up.

He tried another shot, but wasn't certain he hit any of the approaching bluecoats, still a good fifty yards away. He sheathed the rifle and brought out the sabre. "Forward!"

The bluecoats in the lead were slow to react, and first squad was on them before most ever had their rifles out or aimed. Only half even had sabres ready.

Mykel aimed himself and the chestnut at the squad leader—he hadn't seen anyone resembling an officer. The rebel parried Mykel's sabre, but Mykel slipped it, ducked slightly, and countered with a slash to the back of the other's neck and shoulder as he passed.

He was slightly off-balance, and barely managed to get his blade back into position for his own parry of a blow from a rebel ranker, but the less experienced ranker had put too much effort into his slash, and Mykel caught him across the throat before he recovered.

Behind them, in the following companies, Mykel could hear orders, so clearly that they must have been bellowed at full throat.

"Lead squad! Break and withdraw! Second squad, rifles ready! Four abreast! Measured advance! Fire at will!"

Mykel pulled to the side of the road, knocking back a weak blow from a retreating bluecoat, and issued his own orders. "Fifteenth Company! First squad! Withdraw!"

Studying the confusion of the retreating squad of bluecoats and the order behind them, Mykel watched as first squad rode past him, heading back toward the rest of Fifteenth Company. Then he urged the chestnut along, bringing up the rear.

Several quick glances over his shoulder told him that the bluecoats were pursuing, if at the measured pace ordered by their commander. When first squad was out of easy rifle range, he called out, "First squad! Re-form! Now!"

The squad slowed and re-formed, still headed westward. Mykel checked the advance of the bluecoats against the position of the still-concealed main body of Fifteenth Company.

"First squad. To the rear, turn! Staggered firing line!"

"That's a long way, sir," Gendsyr pointed out, from his mount beside Mykel.

"I don't care if we hit them. I want them to keep coming after us." Mykel had cleaned and sheathed his sabre and taken out his own rifle, reloading it as well. After a moment, he ordered, "Fire!"

He concentrated on one of the lead bluecoats, once more fully concentrating and *willing* the shot to hit.

The bluecoat sagged in the saddle.

"Cease firing! To the rear, quick trot!"

After another hundred yards, Mykel repeated the firing line. He took down another bluecoat, and the rebels began to pick up the pace.

As they drew near the woodlot where the remainder of Fifteenth Company waited, Mykel called out, "Bhoral! Fifteenth Company! Stay under cover! Stay under cover!"

First squad rode past the first section of the woodlot before Mykel called a halt and had the squad turn and form a full firing line.

"First squad! Stand by for two shots, then reload and hold! Commence firing!"

The bluecoats were closer, little more than sixty yards to the east, when they broke into a full charge, riding five abreast, and filling the road.

Shots flew past Mykel, mostly overhead, and he forced himself to wait . . . longer than he felt comfortable before ordering. "Fifteenth Company! Open fire! Fire at will!"

The rifles of a full company sounded like thunder, and the first two ranks of the bluecoats went down. That slowed the charge, but the rebels struggled forward past riderless mounts and downed horses and men and kept coming. Mykel could sense the combination of hatred, frustration, and desperation. He kept firing, until the bluecoats were within twenty yards. "Rifles away! To sabres! Charge!"

Since Mykel couldn't see an officer, he charged the nearest ranker, a young dark-haired man who flung up his sabre wildly. Mykel beat it down, but could only deliver a second slash to the other's sword arm as he passed.

When Mykel finally broke free of the melee, a handful of bluecoats were riding westward. Mykel glanced west, then east. To the east, a body of rebels, equal to perhaps two squads, was withdrawing, riding hard. They were already too far away for Fifteenth Company to pursue.

An enormous shadow fell across Mykel, then passed on. He looked up to see a single pteridon diving toward the retreating bluecoats.

A line of blue flame jetted from the skylance, moving across the riders. Then . . . the flame was gone. So were the riders. A wave of *something* passed over Mykel—a feeling of mass death? He wasn't sure, except that he had felt something. Even from almost a vingt away, he could see the blackened spot on the road and the heat rising from where there had been twoscore rebels.

"Make it look easy, they do," said Dravadyl, reining up beside Mykel. "That's after we've done all the hard work."

"They can't do much unless the enemy forces are away from us," Mykel pointed out. "Otherwise, we'd be cinders, too."

"Ah . . . sir?"

Mykel looked at the fourth squad leader. "Yes?"

"Might want to bind that wound."

Abruptly, Mykel looked down, suddenly conscious of the slash across his left arm. "It's not that deep, but you're right." He glanced back at the pteridon, which had banked and turned back toward the Cadmians.

Within moments, the flying creature had swept back overhead and was overtaking the handful of rebels riding westward.

The skylance flamed once more, and once more Mykel sensed death, and it felt like something had been severed. He doubted that any of those killed had even seen the pteridon.

The pteridon circled back and began to descend toward the road junction. Mykel could see that it was coming in to land. "I'd better go meet them."

"Here, sir," offered Dravadyl. "Just take a moment. Let me bind that."

Mykel waited until the white bandage was around his arm, not too tightly, but enough to staunch the blood oozing out, he hoped.

"Bhoral! Re-form the company and get a casualty report. I'm going to meet the colonel."

"Yes, sir."

Mykel urged the chestnut forward, but only at a walk. He'd asked too much of his mount already. Ahead of him the pteridon had spread its wide wings and settled in the wide space where the two roads joined.

As he neared the flying beast, which had folded its long blue wings, he saw that there were two saddles on the pteridon. The forward saddle held a Myrmidon ranker. The second saddle was empty, because Colonel Dainyl had dismounted and stood waiting for Mykel.

91

With no messages from Captain Mykel on Octdi, nor by two glasses after morning muster on Novdi, Dainyl was concerned. The Cadmian scouts had reported more of the remaining forces of the various seltyrs had joined and were withdrawing into the rugged country to the north of the guano mine. None of the scouts had gathered any information to indicate where Fifteenth Company was or where it might be headed.

The mine was back in operation, and guano was being carted down to the port, but that would last only so long as the seltyrs' forces remained to the north and east of the mine—or if they were destroyed.

Dainyl stood in the study that had belonged to the late Majer Herryf, considering his options. He had to agree with Captain Mykel's feelings that delay in dealing with the rebels was unwise—that was how the overcaptain had presented it—but Dainyl would have appreciated some message as to how the captain was proceeding. Then . . . could Dohark—and the captain himself—have overestimated Mykel's abilities and underestimated those of the rebels? That had already occurred with two other Cadmian captains—and landers did have a tendency to think they were more able than they in fact were.

There was a knock at the study door.

Dainyl turned to see Captain Meryst standing there.

"Submarshal, sir?"

Dainyl motioned for him to enter. Meryst did, his eyes reluctantly meeting those of the Myrmidon. Dainyl could sense the apprehension there.

"You have something to tell me, Captain?" Dainyl remained standing, looking down at the junior officer.

"Yes, sir." Meryst squared his shoulders slightly. "We got some information from one of the squad leaders. His younger brother brought it this morning."

Dainyl waited.

"A company of Cadmians rode into the grounds of the grower Fhezart yesterday afternoon. There were some men in blue there. The Cadmians pulled up into a line and began shooting. Then they rode after those who hadn't been shot and cut them down with sabres. After that, they burned the place."

"All the buildings?" asked Dainyl.

Ah . . . no, sir. Just the villa. They left the other buildings. They took all the weapons and ammunition and some supplies and put them in their wagons. Then they rode off. They left the bodies where they fell."

"Captain Mykel, I would say. Where is this grower located?"

"East-southeast of Enstyla, forty vingts from here."

Dainyl nodded.

"Sir?"

"Yes?"

"People are going to be upset at that. You just don't ride in and shoot people."

The submarshal tilted his head slightly. He said nothing.

Meryst shifted his weight from one boot to the other and back again. He did not speak.

After the silence had drawn out, Dainyl cleared his throat. "Let me see if I understand the reasoning behind this. The locals revolt against the Code and against the Duarches. They obtain contraband weapons, and they ambush and destroy two companies of Cadmians. They use some sort of subterfuge to poison and kill a third of the Cadmians in the compound. Then they assault the compound. Captain Mykel follows some of them, catches them off guard, and shoots them. He rides down others and kills them, too. He does not burn the entire estate, but only the villa belonging to those who sheltered the rebels. What the rebels did was acceptable, but what he did is not? Can you explain that to me, Captain?"

"They feel that they are defending their land, sir." Meryst stiffened.

"Convenient rationale," Dainyl replied dryly. "Buy or take the land from those who once had it. Because you now hold it, that entitles you to revolt against those who made having the land possible, and to use any method at all. Those who are upholding the Code, of course, can only attack the armed men who are revolting under certain 'honorable' conditions." He looked hard at Meryst. "Dramur would not exist were it not for the Duarches. The seltyrs would have nothing. The Code makes that quite clear. They have broken the Code. They are not entitled to even the consideration that Captain Mykel has offered. I strongly suggest that you recall that, Captain." Dainyl forced himself to relax and to smile understandingly. "I appreciate the information, and I very much appreciate your conveying it to me. I realize that, as someone raised here in Dramur, this entire revolt places you in a most difficult situation. It puts us all in that situation, in different ways, and I trust you understand that. You do not wish to be involved in this. Neither do I, Captain. I ask you to remember one thing. All the seltyrs had to do . . . was nothing. No one was taking anything from them. No one raised their tariffs. The only real problem was that prisoners were escaping from the mine."

"Yes, sir."

"Now"—Dainyl shrugged—"we have to do the best we can, and the best course is to crush resistance as quickly and absolutely as possible. Unless the seltyrs surrender unconditionally and immediately, I intend to do so."

"They will not do that, sir."

"That is unfortunate." Dainyl nodded. "Thank you, again."

"Yes, sir. By your leave, sir."

"You may go."

Dainyl watched the captain leave. He could sense the anger and the frustration, but nothing Dainyl could have said would have eliminated either. What bothered Dainyl most was the fact that he'd had to mislead the captain. Either the Highest or the marshal had appealed to the greed and fear of the seltyrs and arranged for them to receive contraband weapons, suggesting that they would need them. With the arrival of Majer Vaclyn and his heavy-handed ways, the seltyrs began to prepare, and the Cadmians had reacted to that. In turn, the seltyrs had reacted to the Cadmians, and now Dainyl had no options but to finish what Captain Mykel had begun—because he certainly couldn't reveal the duplicity and schemes of the marshal and the Highest. Not and survive. There was also no point in revealing those schemes until he was in a position to do something about them, because, until he had some power over the marshal and the Highest, or some hard proof to submit to the Duarches, all he would accomplish would be his own demise.

His lips tightened. After a moment, he shook his head. He walked to the peg on the wall, took down his flying jacket, and donned it, walking quickly from the study and the headquarters building out into the courtyard.

Quelyt was waiting beside his pteridon, the one wearing the second saddle for the day, since he had the duty. "Submarshal?"

"Are you ready to fly?"

"Yes, sir. Where to?" After a pause, the Myrmidon asked, "Do you need us both?"

"Not today. We'll see if we can find our missing Cadmian company. Yesterday, they were some forty vingts to the northeast. They'll be moving to the northwest."

"Anything we're looking for?"

"When we get to the northeast, a burned-out villa. There won't be much smoke. It was burned yesterday."

"Could be some," Quelyt suggested. "It's clear enough we might be able to see it." He finished checking the saddles and harnesses, then slipped into the forward saddle.

Dainyl mounted behind him and adjusted the straps.

With a burst of Talent-energy, the pteridon leapt into the light wind, wings spread, and began to climb, barely clearing the eastern wall of the compound. Quelyt continued eastward directly into the wind for another vingt before turning northward.

As the pteridon carried the two Myrmidons northward, Dainyl studied the narrow roads. There were no large groups of riders on the roads, no lines of wagons, no large pillars of smoke climbing skyward, and no Talent-sense of the ancients—or of anything else except the pteridon. He couldn't help but worry about the ancient soarers. With only an understrength Cadmian battalion and two pteridons, if he were to put down the revolt quickly, he didn't need any interference from the soarers.

After slightly more than a glass, Dainyl caught side of a black patch in an open area, farther to the east than the course on which he had directed Quelyt.

"To the right!" he called forward. "To that black spot."

The pteridon made a gentle, banked turn eastward. The crystal beak pointed directly at the black spot. As they drew nearer, Dainyl could see faint lines of thin smoke still rising from the blackened mass. He could also see that only one building had been burned.

"Follow the road to the east of the burned villa—the one that heads north."

Again, Quelyt turned the pteridon.

They had traced the course of the road, at an altitude of around two hundred yards, for less than a half glass when Dainyl sensed Talent, the same sort of greenish force that he associated with the ancients—yet it was not the same, not exactly. The Talent-trace vanished before he could pinpoint it, although it was generally to the northwest.

"Turn more to the northwest."

"Coming northwest, sir."

Another quarter glass passed before Quelyt turned in his saddle. "Fighting up ahead, sir. South side of that long valley."

"Drop a little and get your lance ready."

"Yes, sir."

The pteridon lost another hundred yards and continued westward almost down the center of the valley that the Cadmians had patrolled for the arms smugglers. Below to the left was the road that ran along the top of the bluff forming the south side of the valley.

Dainyl sensed another flash of greenish Talent, far closer, and he leaned to the left, studying the road, making out two mounted forces. Even from two hundred yards above, Dainyl could make out the difference in uniforms between the maroon and gray of the Cadmians and the bright blue and green of the rebels.

"A little lower!"

As Quelyt swept down, Dainyl could see that whatever the Cadmians had done, the rebels were getting the worst of it and were breaking off the fight.

"Circle back and flame the riders in blue, the ones riding eastward and trying to escape!"

"Yes, sir!" A grim satisfaction filled Quelyt's voice.

Dainyl could also see a handful of rebels riding westward, but those would have to wait.

The pteridon banked steeply and dropped into a dive, centering itself on the road and coming down to less than fifty yards above the road as Quelyt aimed the skylance.

A long burst of blue flame flared over the more than two squads of riders, and then the pteridon was past the section of road that held only soot and ashes.

"There were a some rebels headed west," Dainyl said.

"We can get them, too."

This time Quelyt climbed slightly before bringing the pteridon into another tightly banked turn that brought the pteridon onto a westward heading. They swept over the Cadmians and in moments were closing on the fleeing rebels. A quick burst from the skylance was enough.

"Now what, sir?"

"Can you set us down somewhere west of the Cadmians?"

"Need a wider place, sir. Let's see."

Yet another tight turn followed.

"Right at the road junction," Quelyt finally said. "Plenty of room there."

The pteridon flared and landed on the road. A brief cloud of dust rose, then began to settle.

"You stay mounted. Keep the skylance ready," Dainyl ordered. "I need to talk to the captain."

"We can do that, Submarshal."

Dainyl unfastened the harnesses and dropped to the road. His legs buckled slightly for a moment. He supposed he'd never again get as used to flying as he had been as a full-time flying Myrmidon. After stepping well away from Quelyt and the pteridon, Dainyl waited for the captain. He kept a pleasant smile on his face as Captain Mykel rode toward him, hard as it was. The bare hint of a greenish aura surrounded the captain, the unmistakable sign of emerging Talent. Stronger Talent would have blared forth or been hidden behind shields. He should deal with the captain immediately, or soon, at least.

Yet . . . Mykel was the only captain in the battalion who seemed to know what he was doing and who was able to do it. Dainyl had been ordered to end the revolt quickly, and ending it would take longer, perhaps far longer, without the captain.

Mykel reined up a good three yards back from the submarshal. He inclined his head in respect. His uniform was bloody, and one arm was roughly bound.

"Captain Mykel."

"Colonel . . ." The captain paused. "I'm sorry, sir . . . have you . . . do the stars mean you're a marshal?"

"Submarshal."

"Yes, sir. Submarshal."

"You seem to have been most effective in dealing with the rebels," Dainyl offered.

"You and the pteridon were more effective, sir."

"It's going to take both Myrmidons and Cadmians. I heard that you attacked a company yesterday while they were in bivouac on an estate. Was that report accurate?"

"There were two companies. We killed more than a company. The rest scattered. I had the villa burned. Not the outbuildings. That would have hurt the retainers more than anyone else."

"Was pursuing the rebels your idea or Overcaptain Dohark's?"

Mykel smiled uneasily. "I requested permission to undertake the pursuit after they had attacked the compound. Overcaptain Dohark granted my request."

"With some trepidation, I would wager." Dainyl laughed.

"Sir . . . you'd have to ask the overcaptain about that."

"I did. He was worried about losing Fifteenth Company. Did you think about that?"

"Yes, sir. Every time we've lost badly has been when we fought on their terms. Sitting and waiting would have been fighting on their terms."

"What would you suggest now, Captain?"

For the first time, Mykel looked uncertain. He did not answer immediately.

Dainyl waited.

"If . . . if Third Battalion were up to full strength, I'd keep pursuing until we wiped them out or until they made a stand."

"So would I," Dainyl said. "That's exactly what we're going to do. Two Myrmidons with skylances will help." He studied the captain. His Talent was still intermittent and unfocused, and he might not even be aware of what he was doing. Dealing with the captain could wait. The rebels could not.

92

Late on Novdi evening, Mykel sat on a sagging and backless pine bench outside yet another grower's stable—where, this time, Mykel had taken the tack room with its single narrow bunk for his own. This grower had been on his lands, and he had explained that he had not backed the rebels and wanted no trouble. He had been telling the truth, and Mykel had told the man that he wanted no trouble either, just fodder and some food and shelter, and that Fifteenth Company would be leaving in the morning.

Mykel looked from the dark main house, its shutters fastened tight despite the warmth of the evening, toward Bhoral, who sat on a sawed-off log set on end across from his captain.

"Colonel—the submarshal—talked to you for a long time," observed the senior squad leader.

"He did. We'll be getting messengers regularly now. He might even drop messages by the pteridons."

"Glad to see that they finally decided to use the Myrmidons," Bhoral said.

"I have the feeling that the submarshal wanted to all along," Mykel replied. "He said he was recalled, and that there had been some changes made."

"Made him submarshal for one." Bhoral shifted his weight on the log. The planks underneath creaked slightly. "You think his plan will work?"

"We don't have to do anything but what we've been doing."

"Not until we get them all bunched up. If they gather their forces. You think they will?"

"That part seems likely," mused Mykel. "We've already proved that they can't stand against us if they're separated. Once they're together, the Myrmidons can fly in."

"They have to know that—after this afternoon."

"They might, but who will tell them? I didn't see any survivors," Mykel pointed out. "We could have burned the bodies."

Bhoral pulled at his chin. "Don't know as I'd count on it."

"What else can they do?"

"They could hide and wait."

Mykel laughed, a sound ironic and rueful. "You and I could hide and wait. The seltyrs have based everything on their power. They can't wait, not if they want to remain seltyrs." He couldn't help but think of the legacy he had left in Jyoha. There, the people had learned exactly what could be done against arrogant and unprepared power. Mykel hadn't meant to teach them that, but he had, however inadvertently, and that was something else that might change the future of Dramur—one way or another.

"They could still dig in someplace, where there are caves, holes, rocks, and make us come get them," Bhoral said.

"The submarshal expects that. He thinks that, if we push them in the right way, they'll move into the rocky ground some twenty vingts north of the mine. There's a forest in front, with big pine trees, the kind that the Myrmidons can't use those flame lances through, but the trees are far enough apart for mounts underneath. They can retreat upslope to a cliff with caves."

"We're going to do that, with one company?"

"He's going to put Rhystan in charge of an oversized company, what's left of Fourteenth and Sixteen Companies. They'll push from the south."

"We'll still have to lose men digging them out."

"The submarshal says that he and the Myrmidons can take care of that part. Our job is to whittle them down and get them into the open or into the caves."

"Coldhearted bastard, isn't he?"

"You could say that." Mykel didn't see that Submarshal Dainyl was any more coldhearted than Mykel himself had been recently—or than the seltyrs had been more than a few times. "Better coldhearted than hotheaded."

"Suppose so. I still don't like it."

"Neither do I, but it's better than what we faced without the Myrmidons." Mykel stood and stretched.

"We going to push tomorrow?"

"No. It'll take Rhystan another day to get far enough north. We're supposed to move west and north some, and make sure that we're seen—and not get ambushed or lose any men. If there's a small group or company, and I think we have a solid edge, we can attack." Mykel snorted. "That's not likely."

"No, sir. Everyone knows we're here. Either find five companies on our doorstep, or none in a half score of vingts." Bhoral yawned and rose from his log stool. "Going to check the sentries. See you in the morning, sir."

"In the morning." Mykel continued to look out into the darkness, taking in the corral fence and the sentries beyond. While Selena had risen earlier, it had vanished behind the clouds to the east, providing only a faint glow behind them. Asterta hung, a miniature circle of green, above the Murian Mountains, reminding Mykel of the ancient soarer—who had also hovered above the mountainside and told him to find a talent that allowed him to look beyond, as if he even knew where to start. And when had he had time for that? The only talents he seemed to have time to find and use were being able to shoot a rifle with lethal effect under almost any conditions and finding more effective ways to kill rebels.

Somehow, he didn't think that was what she had meant.

Was there a link between her and the ancient dagger? Alone in the darkness, he slipped it out from the slot in his belt. The blade shimmered greenish in the darkness, yet in a way that shed no light, cast no shadow. Why was he still carrying it?

Because not to would be worse. That he knew, even if he didn't know why. He slipped the miniature dagger back into its slot.

Then he turned and headed for the door to the tack room.

93

Decdi morning was pleasantly warm, if drier than Dainyl preferred, when he left the officers' mess after breakfast, now back to cooking normally, and walked to the stables. There he watched as Captain Rhystan mustered the bulked-up Sixteenth Company and headed them out. Four supply wagons brought up the rear as the Cadmians rode out the west gate.

Once Sixteenth Company was well down the road, and the rebuilt gates had closed, Dainyl strode across the courtyard to the headquarters building. Early as it was, the building was empty, except for the squad leader on duty, who sprang to his feet as Dainyl passed.

"Carry on." The submarshal smiled and kept moving.

Once in his study, Dainyl walked to the window and looked out into the courtyard, far emptier than on previous days. How long would it take for the two Cadmian companies to herd and prod the seltyrs into gathering their forces? What if they remained separate?

A cold smile appeared. If they remained separate, between the pteridons and Captain Mykel and Captain Rhystan, soon there would be no sizable rebel forces left.

Dainyl still pondered over why the marshal and the Highest had armed the seltyrs and fomented such disorder in Dramur. The unrest clearly reduced lifeforce, both through the actual deaths of higher lifeforms and through the disruption of guano deliveries to the mainland. Why would they want that, particularly at this time?

Still having no answer, he turned to the rack set against the inside wall and picked up the map of the area north of the mine. He needed to study it before he had Falyna fly him over that terrain later in the day. It wasn't the best of maps, but it was what he had, and he systematically committed the major terrain features to memory.

Sometime later, there was a quiet rap on the door. Dainyl looked up.

"Sir?" Meryst stood in the study doorway.

"Yes?"

The captain held up an envelope. "A messenger delivered this to the guards on gate duty a little while ago. It's addressed to you."

Dainyl took the envelope. The outside bore the inscription "Colonel Dainyl." He broke the blue wax seal, unfolded the parchment, and began to read the flowing script.

> Colonel Dainyl,
>
> Dramur and its people are not and will not be mere counters or tokens in a game played by a handful of alectors who appear only when they wish to take something. On behalf of those who have entrusted their futures to our leadership, we urge that you leave Dramur to its people and their traditional leaders, for we cannot and will not submit to the rule of outsiders who have neither understanding nor appreciation for our ways.
>
> If you do not choose to leave, and to take your Myrmidons and Cadmians with you, you and they will suffer. We will not surrender, and

alectors will never rule Dramur, for you can never be a part of the land and the world upon which it rests.

At the last words of the message, Dainyl barely managed to keep from frowning, recalling what Lystrana had pointed out earlier. How had the seltyrs known that? Were they guessing? Or had they just used flowery words and come up with that phrase? There was no signature, only a seal, set in the same blue wax.

"Sir?" asked Meryst.

"We have been told that we will suffer, and that they will never surrender. I didn't expect something in writing, but I understood the message without a formal declaration." He extended the missive so that Meryst could see the seal. "Do you recognize this seal?"

"No, sir."

About that, the captain was telling the truth, and his puzzlement seemed genuine.

"Why do they think they can defy the Myrmidons? Do you have any idea, Captain?"

"Sir . . . the seltyrs have always felt they are the true and rightful rulers of Dramur. So long as no one interfered in what happened on their lands, they paid token allegiance to the Duarches."

Was that the reason for the marshal's plot? But . . . if that were so, why would the seltyrs have trusted any emissary who was an alector? Or had they just pretended to trust to obtain the weapons? Or had someone else acted as an intermediary? "That speaks poorly for everyone." Dainyl's words were dry.

"Yes, sir, but that is the way they have felt."

"Thank you, Captain."

Meryst nodded, then turned and left.

After a moment, Dainyl walked across the corridor to the smaller study, where Overcaptain Dohark stood at the window.

The overcaptain turned. "Sir?"

"The seltyrs have declared war to the death, or some such," Dainyl announced, holding up the missive. "They actually sent a message. Almost touching, their belief in their power and the rightness of their ways."

"Yes, sir."

"You sound doubtful, Overcaptain."

"Not doubtful, sir. A Cadmian finds out soon enough that every man feels his ways are the right ways. Otherwise, he couldn't face the next day. Most wouldn't declare that they'd fight to the death. Fewer would."

"You don't think the seltyrs will?"

"They will. Some of their men will."

"And the rest? What will they do?"

"They'll go home and do what they must."

"Even if that means following the next seltyr?"

"If that's the only choice, and it will be for many."

"I fear you're right about that." Dainyl nodded. "I'll be out flying for most of the morning. It could be longer."

The submarshal returned to his study, where he reclaimed his flying jacket from the study and made his way out of headquarters and into the courtyard, striding toward the square that held the duty pteridon.

Falyna was waiting. "Just recon today, sir?"

"Just recon—unless we happen to see a massed force of rebels in the open."

Dainyl thought that most unlikely, and, from her expression, so did Falyna.

94

Under the midmorning sun of a warm Duadi, Mykel blotted his forehead, then leaned forward slightly in the saddle to look at the half score of houses that lay five hundred yards ahead down a barely perceptible incline.

Over the past few days, following the submarshal's orders, Mykel had slowly moved Fifteenth Company westward and northward. While they had occasionally seen the hoofprints of the rebels' mounts, the prints had been at least a day old, and all were headed in a westerly and more northerly direction.

Gerant cleared his throat. "Sir, roads and lanes look clear."

Mykel shifted his eyes from the small hamlet back to the scout reined up beside him. "There's no one out in the hamlet?"

"No, sir," replied the scout. "Saw me coming, and every door and every shutter slammed shut, quick as a lightning bolt. A couple ran and shut up their stables."

"We're not exactly popular," Mykel said.

"No, sir. Not as though we shoot women or children."

"Or poison people," Mykel added dryly. "We'll ride through, but with rifles ready." He doubted that they would need the rifles, since he couldn't sense any real danger, but there was always the chance that his senses wouldn't pick up all dangers.

He straightened in the saddle. "Fifteenth Company! Rifles ready! Forward!"

"First squad, forward!" repeated Gendsyr.

Mykel studied the hamlet as they rode closer. The fields on each side of the road alternated between sunbeans and pastures where grass alternated with bare soil. The grasses that had been green throughout Dramur a few weeks earlier were showing signs of tan and gold as the days continued to warm.

Small orchards grew behind most of the small cots, but Mykel had no idea what the fruit might be. He'd thought the people who lived in the north Westerhills had been poor, but they were well-off compared to the peasants in small hamlets in Dramur. Yet the seltyrs lived like rulers—they were rulers of small domains in all but name—and people accepted it. They not only accepted their poverty, but they seemed to be against anything that would make the seltyrs more accountable. From what he could see, the young men willingly joined the ranks of the rebels, even while the seltyrs were bleeding their families and parents.

"Quiet." Bhoral pulled his mount alongside Mykel's. "Every hamlet has been like this. You think they fear us that much?"

"I don't know whether they fear us, or they fear what we might do, or they fear not showing fear because of what the seltyrs and growers will do once we've left."

"You think things will be that bad?"

"Oh, there will be new seltyrs, and some growers will become seltyrs, but these people will stay poor. For them, nothing will change."

"I suppose not. My folks still live in the same house in the same village outside of Hafin as my grandparents and their parents did."

Mykel's parents lived in the same house where his grandparents had. Was it like that for most people? Was that why so little changed? Mykel's lips tightened as he considered the thought.

95

Dainyl leaned against the study desk that was too low and small for him to sit behind for any length of time. He supposed he could have ordered a larger one built, but he'd never expected to be in Dramuria so long, and he wouldn't have felt right about wasting the resources for something used so infrequently or for such a short time.

For a moment, his eyes flicked to the window. Outside headquarters, the Tridi morning sun was beating down on the stones of the courtyard. A faint heat haze was forming, although noon was a good two glasses away. His eyes turned back to the overcaptain who stood before him. "The rebels are slowly being pressed back north of the mine and well west of Enstyla. Within another day or so, they should be in a position where we can attack."

"I'll head north this afternoon, then," said Dohark.

"That wouldn't be a good idea. I'll have to be there." Dainyl handed a folded sheet to the overcaptain. "That is my commission designating you as officer in charge of all Cadmian forces in Dramuria, under my supervision, as well as the officer in charge in my absence, injury, or death."

Dohark's eyebrows lifted. "Sir?" He did not unfold the sheet he had accepted.

"While I don't plan on anything happening in my absence, if you join this assault on the rebels, there will be no one I can trust here in the compound—or in Dramuria. In my boots, would you wish to leave command in the hands of Captain Meryst or Captain Benjyr?" Dainyl didn't mention that Benjyr had spent the last weeks avoiding even getting anywhere near him, although Dainyl had not pressed the issue.

"No, sir." Dohark's words were grudging.

"I know you're a fighting officer, and a good one, but my choices are simple. I can either relieve Captain Mykel and give you Fifteenth Company, and put him in charge here, or leave you here. You have more rank and stature, and you are not perceived in quite the same . . . light . . . as Captain Mykel. Didn't you tell me he was being called the Knife of the Ancients, or something like that?"

"Yes, sir. That's a blade that cuts so sharply that it wounds both the user and the victim. Supposedly, such blades actually exist. They're very rare, though, and no one admits to ever having seen one."

"Does the captain know this?" The idea of Captain Mykel being termed a tool of the ancients disturbed Dainyl, but then, the captain and his emerging Talent already worried at the submarshal.

"He knows what that means, sir, but I don't think he's aware of being called that."

As he stood in the study, Dainyl sensed, for the third day running, the use of Talent to the north. It was clearly the Talent of an ancient—the soarer—and not the unfocused and shorter spurts of Talent that he associated with the Cadmian captain. Unlike earlier manifestations of the soarer, the more recent appearances had lasted far longer. So much use of Talent by an ancient, or ancients, at a time when his plans were coming to fruition, troubled Dainyl. It suggested that the ancients were aware and interested, if not involved.

"The name fits, in a way," added Dohark.

"That the captain is far sharper than most realize?" Dainyl kept his tone dry.

"Yes, sir. Right now, he could be a good majer. In time, he could be a good colonel."

"As I recall, you were worried that he could be too ruthless."

Dohark flushed. "Ah . . . that was not quite what I said. I said he was as ruthless as necessary, and effective, but I worried that it would take a toll on him."

Dainyl, distracted by the continuing sense of the ancient to the north, perhaps near the old tunnel that held what had to be the equivalent of a Table, nodded. "I apologize for overstating, Overcaptain." He paused. "I trust you understand why I must insist you remain here."

"I understand, sir. It might be helpful . . . at the appropriate time . . ."

"If it is necessary, I will inform Colonel Herolt."

"Thank you, sir."

"There are a few other pressing matters. Until later, Overcaptain." Dainyl waited for several moments until Dohark had left, trying not to look hurried. Then he pulled on his flying jacket and strode out and down the corridor, nodding at the duty squad leader before leaving headquarters. He crossed the courtyard rapidly to the pteridon square, where Quelyt waited.

The Myrmidon ranker had seen Dainyl coming and stood by the pteridon in his own flying jacket. "Where to this morning, Submarshal? North again, sir?"

"Yes. We'll swing west, head north past the mine, then do a recon of the area where the seltyrs seem to be gathering."

Quelyt vaulted into the first seat and began fastening himself in.

Dainyl waited a moment and did the same in the rear seat. After a moment, he called forward, "Anytime, Quelyt."

The pteridon sprang into the air above the courtyard, blue wings spread wide, into the wind out of the north. In moments, they cleared the northern wall of the compound. Once they were a good hundred yards above the ground, Quelyt swung more to the northwest, until they reached the mine road and paralleled it.

Dainyl leaned slightly to the left, studying the ground below, but he saw no one on the mine road, nor on the winding lanes farther east. He still sensed the soarer to the north. It had been half a glass since he had noted her presence—a far longer time than ever before—except over the last three days.

They flew northward for more than half a glass before Dainyl saw plumes of dust on an older and narrower road heading north. "Up ahead, on the road. See how close you can get!"

"Heading down, sir!" The pteridon half folded its wings for a moment, starting a shallow dive, then extended them again, so that the dive became an extended downward glide.

By the time the pteridon had descended to a hundred yards above the road, a point where Dainyl could have determined who was riding, the rider or riders had vanished—hiding in casaran orchards, woodlots, under single large trees, whatever cover was available. Such disappearances alone suggested that the riders were rebels and that their officers had scouts detailed to watch the skies for pteridons.

While Dainyl knew that some of the orchards below held rebels, he couldn't very well have Quelyt flame every tree under which rebels *might* be hiding. That was one reason he needed the Cadmians to herd the rebels into a more circumscribed area. He kept scanning the area on both sides of the road, but the riders remained concealed.

"What now, sir?" called back Quelyt.

"Head north, toward that mountain where we found the ancient tunnel."

"North it is." The pteridon began to climb, turning slightly to the northwest.

Dainyl looked back over his shoulder, but the rebel riders remained hidden and doubtless would stay so until they were certain the pteridon was well out of sight. He turned his eyes and Talent northward, seeking out the soarer's peak, with its odd-angled shape.

Another half glass passed before the pteridon neared the site, and with each vingt that the Myrmidons drew closer, Dainyl could sense the soarer more clearly.

Below the peak, in the charred grove that the Myrmidons had flamed a season before, Dainyl could see greenery where there should have been none—not so soon after the destruction wrought by a skylance. The presence of the soarer remained strong, with a hint of something implacable behind the green Talent.

"There's something there, sir. Can't tell what it is, but it's like a fog in front of that cave," Quelyt called back.

For Dainyl, there was no fog—just a circle of green iridescence with the soarer hovering in the center two or three yards out from the front of the cave. "Don't get any closer. Just sweep by, then circle back again at the same distance."

"Yes, sir."

As the pteridon flew by, Dainyl could sense a Talent-probe of some sort, but one so light, so delicate, that he might not even have noticed it had he not been fully concentrating with his Talent and all his senses. He tried to block it, but his own Talent skittered off and through the fine line of green, as if it were smoke or mist, or not present at all. Yet there was a sense of strength there.

With a suddenness that took Dainyl's breath away, the pteridon dropped a good fifty yards, almost instantly. The wide wings beat faster to regain altitude. Dainyl had felt the Talent drain, but not any link to the soarer.

Quelyt banked to the right, gently, so as not to lose more altitude, swinging the pteridon out away from the peak and the higher ridges to gain separation from them.

"Sir . . . there's a downdraft or something there."

"Just head back to the compound," Dainyl replied. "We've seen enough for now."

The pteridon kept turning until Quelyt straightened on a southerly heading, pointed toward Dramuria and the Cadmian compound.

Was the soarer able to divert lifeforce from the pteridons at will? That was what the last few moments had strongly indicated, reinforcing what the marshal had suggested about the ancients being able to destroy pteridons. In using the pteridons, Dainyl would have to watch for the ancient soarers, avoiding them completely if at all possible and giving them a wide berth if not.

After all these years, why had the soarers reappeared now?

Dainyl couldn't help but feel that it was neither accident nor coincidence, and to avoid disaster he would have to be most careful, most careful indeed.

He looked southward, out over Dramur, recalling and wondering exactly what the ancient had meant when she had told him that he would change or perish. How could an ifrit and an alector change? An alector's very nature was unchanging. What had she meant? Or had she merely meant to confuse him?

96

Mykel looked down from the ridge at the swale below, mostly reddish sandy soil, covered in parts by wild grasses. Absently, he blotted his forehead. Even in the late afternoon of Sexdi, past the heat of the day, spring in Dramur was hotter than most full summer days in Elcien.

On the far side of the swale, which was close to two hundred yards wide, the older-growth pine forest began. Each of the giant trees had a trunk close to a yard across. The rebels had retreated to the old forest to the north of the mine, a wedge of giant pines with a front only half a vingt across. The warren of tall pines extended more than two vingts back, on a gradual slope. The top of the slope was a barren and sandy flat plateau covered with pteridon-sized boulders, and ringed by an irregular semicircle of cliffs. Those on the northern end were three hundred yards above the forest, while those to the west were half that, and those in the south were more like reddish bluffs only fifty yards high.

Within the forest itself were somewhere between four and six companies of rebels and several seltyrs. Thin trails of smoke from the rebel cookfires rose into the silver-green sky. Mykel frowned for a moment. Cookfires meant men gathering. Did he dare try the approach the scouts had found? Did he dare not to, given the alternatives?

He glanced to his left, where Rhystan had reined up beside him. Beyond the older captain, a half vingt to the south, Sixteenth Company was drawn up on the more southern ridge facing the forest, a vingt to the south, just far enough back that the rebels could not fire from the trees and hit the Cadmians.

"We've got them in the forest, like the submarshal wanted," Rhystan said. "Now what? We've been here for nearly three days. We just can't keep sitting here and patrolling. We go down that slope, and we'll lose half the men we have."

Mykel had to agree. While they could cross the open swale under heavy fire, they would not be able to make much headway in moving through the trees, not without losing too many men. Even with Sixteenth Company joining Fifteenth, they were heavily outnumbered, with no chance of obtaining replacements anytime soon. Under those circumstances, he wasn't about to sacrifice men for position. "It will be worse in the trees."

"You have that look, Mykel. What do you have in mind?"

"To the northwest, there's that jumble of rock beneath the cliffs. It fills in the space between this ridge and the northwest corner of the forest."

"You said that they had men stationed there."

"They do, but most of them are facing the lower ground. My scouts think there might be a narrow passage right under the cliffs. If I could bring Fifteenth Company up behind them . . . and if most of their men are near the cookfires . . . and if I wait until they're eating . . ."

"That's three 'ifs,' and two are too many for a good operation," Rhystan pointed out.

"Only two," Mykel countered, with a laugh. "We bring the company in early in the morning, before it's light, and we just wait until they're eating."

"That's two dubious propositions."

"Only one. That's whether I get the company past their sentries. If I can, then there's either a way or there's not. If there's not, we come back, and we're no worse off. If there is, then we wait and attack. All you have to do is be ready to deal with anyone who leaves the forest."

"Or charge in and rescue you," replied Rhystan dryly.

"One way or another . . . it's best if you don't attempt a rescue. Just slaughter them, if it comes to that."

"You're going to try it, aren't you?"

"I'm going to see if it can be done. If we don't finish this quickly, then the other growers and seltyrs will raise more men, and we'll be in an even worse position."

"That's what I like about you, Mykel. You're such a cheerful fellow." Rhystan shook his head. "You're certain you want to do it?"

Mykel nodded.

"Then I suppose we can attempt a few diversions, to keep their interest focused on us."

"Nothing that loses men. We don't have any to lose on diversions."

"Just on problematical operations?"

Mykel laughed. "Look who's being cheerful."

"Realistic," countered Rhystan. "Go see what you can do. We'll divert them."

"If it doesn't work, we'll let you know. Otherwise, I'll need you to start the diversions at a glass past dawn tomorrow. Would you send a message to the submarshal that it's likely we'll be attacking early tomorrow?"

"I'll tell him Fifteenth Company will attempt certain unspecified actions in the morning."

"That's better. Thank you." With a smile, Mykel turned the chestnut and rode back two hundred yards to the northwest, where Bhoral waited, mounted in front of Fifteenth Company.

Bhoral looked at his captain, but did not speak, waiting.

"We're heading farther northwest—opposite that rock pile below the cliffs. We'll stay well back below the top of the ridge. I don't want the rebels to see us."

"Yes, sir. Are you planning an attack on that section of the forest?"

"Not until tomorrow before dawn. The scouts had suggested there might be a path between the rock pile and the cliffs. If I can find a way to take out the sentries, then we'll try it."

"If you don't?"

"Then, we'll have to think of something else—or wait." The thought of waiting beyond Septi chilled Mykel, because every day the seltyrs would get stronger and find more men. "Fifteenth Company! To the right, and forward!"

He rode at the head of a column of rankers that had gotten gradually but steadily shorter with each week, leading them across the back side of the ridge. A slight breeze gusted across them, but died away, and the silver-green sky remained clear of clouds, but hazy from the heat.

A half vingt later, Mykel reined up the chestnut short of the crest of the ridge and dismounted, handing the reins to Sendyl and taking out his rifle. He also extracted a spare cartridge belt from his saddlebags and fastened it across his chest and shoulders.

While he could sense Bhoral's disapproval, even without looking, he ignored it, instead turning to the senior squad leader. "Just hold the company here. After I see what the situation is, we'll stand down and make sure that the men and their mounts are rested for tomorrow."

He turned and, rifle in hand, motioned to Jesakyt. The two Cadmians walked up toward the crest of the ridge, angling toward one of the scrub oaks near the top. Keeping low, they slipped behind the bushy oak.

Mykel peered through the leaves. The swale directly below was a slight depression barely five yards below the ridge crest, rising to the northwest until it reached the base of the cliff another hundred yards to Mykel's right. There, it merged with the ridge top in a flat and open expanse—except that half of that open expanse was covered with a jumble of sandy red boulders that appeared to have been piled haphazardly just out from the base of the cliff.

"You see, sir," Jasakyt said in a low voice. "The rocks look like they fell away from the cliff. I could see light all the way through. I could have ridden to cover behind the rocks, but coming back, they would have been waiting, and I thought you should know."

"I appreciate that." Mykel studied the rock pile, then the forest to its left and behind it. The rocks rose close to thirty yards above the base, not quite so high as the tallest of the giant pines, but higher than most. Between the top of the ridge and the forest were a few of the scrub oaks, spaced irregularly. There were none on higher ground short of the rock pile and the cliff, and nothing else that would offer cover.

Mykel studied the ground for a while, then nodded. He turned and started back down the back of the ridge. Jesakyt followed.

97

In the darkness close to three glasses before dawn, Mykel stood on the back side of the ridge, looking at Bhoral. "You can let the men sleep or rest for another glass. We're aiming at riding through the defile at the base of the cliffs at a glass before dawn, while it's still dark. I don't want it to be dark that long, though, because they'll need the light once we're in the forest and clear of the rocks. When you get word from Jasakyt or one of the scouts, you'll have to bring the men through in single file and quickly."

"Yes, sir." Bhoral nodded stiffly.

Mykel understood the older squad leader's feelings—that the only dangerous thing officers were supposed to do was to lead charges against enemy fire, and that was something Mykel had always preferred not to do until he'd found a way to change the odds. One simple way of changing the odds was sneaking through the darkness in which he could see better than could most people, then shooting sentries with his gift—was it a talent?

"Every so often," Mykel went on, "have someone near the crest of the ridge fire a rifle. Not at the forest, either." He didn't want to get hit by his own men, even by accident. The occasional shots were another cover. Mykel hoped his own use of the rifle, with shots from outside the forest, would be heard as an intermittent exchange of fire between scouts and sentries.

"Yes, sir. Jasakyt and Dhozynyt will be watching the defile for your signal. They'll bring your mount."

"Good." Mykel lifted his rifle and walked up the hill toward the first of the scrub oak bushes, keeping low so that he would not be outlined against the sky. He wore crossed ammunition belts over his chest, heavier than he would have liked, but he was afraid he might need every cartridge.

Behind the first scrub oak, he paused, looking across the flat section of the ridge and planning his route from oak to oak toward the dark and looming mass of the pine forest. Keeping low, he slipped from behind the first scrub oak and moved at a quick, but measured pace, still staying low. He crossed a space of thirty yards before he reached the second, where he stopped and caught his breath, peering through the leaves toward the forest.

He didn't sense any of the tension he felt when people were watching him, but he also didn't want to feel that instants before a bullet blasted into him.

After several moments, he slipped downhill toward the next scrub oak, a distance of less than ten yards. His boots skidded as he stopped, and a small stone skittered down the steeper section of the slope, clicking several times before it came to rest. Cool as it was in the darkness, Mykel had to blot his forehead with the back of his sleeve to keep the sudden sweat from running into the corners of his eyes.

He looked through an opening in the leaves, focusing his eyes on the darkness of the forest, but while he could make out tree trunks, and some undergrowth, he could see no sentries. He knew they were there and could sense their presence in that clear but undefined feeling he had always had, but which had become more and more certain since he had been in Dramur. Absently, he wondered why, then pushed away the question.

The next scrub oak was back to the right, more than twenty yards away. Mykel was halfway there when he could feel someone, something looking at him.

He flattened himself on the ground, just before the *crack* of a rifle. Then he scrambled forward over the last ten yards, zigzagging erratically before dropping flat behind the base of the small bush, just before two more shots sounded.

Mykel did not move, waiting to see what would happen. His head and chest were shielded, but a really good shot might hit his legs—if the shooter were far enough to one side. From what Mykel could tell, the shooter seemed to be directly south of him.

Slowly, he eased the rifle into position, still waiting, and looking out the right side of the base of the tree. Nothing happened.

He eased himself sideways, just a fraction and aimed at where he thought the shooter was, and fired once. The return shots were high, but Mykel marked the slight flare of the muzzle flash and took aim and fired, once more *willing* his shot to its target.

He could sense that he had hit the other, with a flare of emptiness.

Not waiting, he scrambled forward, dodging forward and behind several scrub oaks in a row, but without the sense of anyone looking for him until he was within a few yards of the edge of the forest. Once more he half flattened, and half scramble-dived toward the roots of a huge tree. His chest slammed into a root that felt as hard as iron.

Crack! Crack! Crack! At least one bullet struck the trunk above him at enough of a glancing angle to drop fragments of bark across the back of his all-too-damp neck.

He squirmed around the base of the tree so that it was between him and the direction of the shots. For a time, he remained silent, letting his straining lungs take in air until he was no longer breathing hard, while listening intently.

The rock pile lay to his right, but there was at least one sentry in the trees to his left. The sentry he thought he had killed lay somewhere more immediately to his right. For a moment, he froze. *How* did he know the man was dead? He'd been acting on those kinds of feelings more and more, the longer he'd been on Dramur. He'd always had some sense of where people were, but not to the degree he did now, and the sense of knowing death was far more recent. Was that part of the talent the ancient soarer had been saying he had to find?

In the darkness of the forest, he shook his head. Now wasn't the time for that.

A shot from up on the ridge, from the area of Fifteenth Company, echoed through the darkness. Mykel nodded, then eased, as quietly as he could, from the trunk of the one pine to the next, trying to keep trunks between him and where he thought/felt the nearest sentry was.

As he moved, he picked up sounds that became more clear as he moved eastward.

". . . shots . . . swear one came from out there . . . like the last one . . . you heard it."

". . . Dhurcan's always shooting at shadows . . . wastes ammunition . . ."

". . . saw something . . . sure I did . . ."

". . . could have been a forest cat . . . seen some here . . ."

Mykel stopped, then stepped sideways behind a slender pine trunk. There, less than ten yards away, three yards back from the northern edge of the forest, were two rebels, kneeling behind a crude log barrier, looking out into the darkness.

Slowly, he raised his rifle, aiming, and firing.

The sentry on the right dropped. The other dropped behind the logs, his head below the topmost, but clearly still visible from where Mykel stood.

Mykel fired again. He did not move for several moments, but heard nothing. He quickly but quietly reloaded, then began to move back through the forest to the northwest. He kept his senses alert, knowing that at least one more sentry was stationed somewhere between where he was and where the rock pile was. He had to keep moving, because he had less than two glasses before it started to get light. Should he have started earlier? That had risks as well, such as running into changes in the watches.

The last sentry in the forest was in the same kind of revetment as the pair had been. Like them, he never seemed to have considered someone approaching from behind. Mykel dropped him with one shot.

That left the men in the rock pile, and Mykel had to remove them all, if he possibly could.

He circled to the south in the darkness, still remaining in the darker shadows of the trees. As he moved southward, a slight clearing appeared between the forest and the rocks. He stopped and moved back northwest, halting behind the trunk of one of the last giant pines. Then he peered around the ancient trunk, studying the jumbled mass of scrub pine and rock at the far side of the clearing, directly west. At one time in the past, part of the cliff farther to the southwest had peeled off and fallen, leaving the jumble of rock and trees from which the rebel sentries could rake the approach to the defile between the cliff and the rock pile, barely wide enough for a single mounted Cadmian at a time. If any sentries remained, the Cadmians would be better targets than tethered chickens, even in the darkness, standing out against the face of the cliff.

He eased around the tree, moving as quietly as he could toward a large boulder at the base of the rock pile. From what he could sense, there were only a handful of rebels in the rocks, perhaps as few as four or five. While he would approach them from the side, almost the rear, coming up from the southeast, he would have to be careful, because the southern part of the rock jumble overlooked the rear of the forest, the area where the rebels had set up camps.

Mykel would have placed more men to guard the flank, but even the rebels only had so many men, and the rocks looked impassable, especially to men on horseback. He moved up the back of the rocks, a boulder at a time.

The first sentry heard something, and turned. "That you, Buirstyn?"

Mykel put the single shot through his forehead.

"Stop the target practice!" came a call from Mykel's left.

Mykel coughed, loudly.

"What's the matter there, Visort?"

Mykel made choking sounds, even as his eyes, ears, and senses tracked the oncoming squad leader. He assumed that the man was something like that.

Scraping sounds, and the clicking of small displaced rocks suggested that the squad leader was descending from a position slightly higher and to the west.

Mykel just waited.

As he did, another shot rang out from the ridge, followed by one from the far side of the rock pile.

"Stop it! They're firing to see if you'll fire back so they can figure out where we are." The man's voice carried across the rocks, as though he were within yards, but Mykel still couldn't see him.

Another rock bounced past Mykel's foot. A large figure appeared three yards or so upslope, sliding down the flat smooth surface toward Mykel. The Cadmian barely had to aim.

The shock of the other's death slammed through him, and he took a half step backward, before catching himself. He'd sensed death before, at least recently, but he'd not felt a physical impact. He shook his head, trying to clear it.

"What was that?"

"Don't know, squad leader went down to see Visort."

Mykel noted the general direction of the second voice and started to make his way up through the rocks. He was getting tired, and the actual operation hadn't even begun.

The last two sentries were less than ten yards apart, one at each end of a boulder that had split. The rear section had dropped, leaving the forward part as a near-perfect stone revetment.

Despite his care, his boot scraped on the rock as he moved into position behind and above the two.

"That you, squad leader?" The nearer sentry turned his head, but not his rifle or his body.

Mykel hated to shoot. He did. Then he hurried his shot at the second man, who whirled, looking around blindly.

Mykel forced himself to concentrate on the last shot. Then he just stood there for several moments. There were no sounds, no voices, and no sense of any other rebels nearby.

He reloaded, his fingers seeming stiff, but he managed, before he began to climb down the northwest side of the rock pile. When he reached the corner, where the defile started, he whistled, once.

Two low whistles responded.

He returned a triplet, and waited.

After what seemed a good quarter of a glass, but was probably less, Jasakyt appeared, riding slowly, peering into the darkness, his face tight with apprehension. Mykel wanted to laugh, seeing the scout with a look that mirrored a belief he was about to be shot.

"Jasakyt . . ." he hissed. "Just ahead on your left."

"Captain?"

"Right here. Get the others. We don't have as much time as I'd hoped."

"Yes, sir."

The sky was beginning to show signs of silver-gray to the east by the time all of Fifteenth Company had ridden through the narrow defile and formed up behind a copse of trees below the southwest corner of the rock pile.

"We'll ride by squads around the back of the rocks. If no one challenges us, we'll move into the edge of the trees and keeping moving south toward the cookfires. We'll walk the mounts as close as we can. If they give an alarm, or when I order a charge, we'll ride to a firing line on the north side of the cookfires, then fire until they start to regroup. That's when we'll switch to sabres and use the trees." Mykel looked across the squad leaders. "Is that understood?"

"Yes, sir."

"Let's head out. Silent riding." According to any tactics manual or training Mykel had received, what he was doing was unsupported and dangerously foolish, but there was a time to follow standard tactics and a time not to. He hoped he was right in choosing the time not to.

He and first squad rode close to half a vingt, around the rock pile, and another three hundred yards just inside the trees at the back edge of the forest, on the flat short of where the ground rose toward the rocky and sandy plateau above and to the west. The sky had lightened into the silvery gray that immediately preceded dawn.

Then, from the trees, came a shout. "Cadmians! They're here! Cadmians!"

"Forward!" Mykel urged the chestnut into a fast trot, as much as he dared while dodging trees and branches, angling out of the forest and pushing his mount into greater speed toward the northernmost of the cookfires.

A good three hundred rankers were gathered, either in lines at the cookfires or standing or sitting. Others were still lying on their bedrolls and blankets. At the sight of the mounted Cadmians, rebels in blue scrambled for weapons and for cover.

"Fifteenth Company! Firing line!"

Mykel reined up and took aim at a man dressed in blue and silver, wearing something similar to what Seltyr Ubarjyr had worn. He fired, and the seltyr dropped. He turned his rifle on a captain and fired again.

He had dropped more than five bluecoats and reloaded once before the rebels began to return fire with more than scattered shots—and those faded away quickly. He surveyed the space around the cookfires, taking in the bodies lying at so many odd angles, and swallowed. Now what? The rebels had melted into the trees.

Only a fraction of a glass had passed, or so it seemed, but the angled rays of the early-morning sun sifted through the tops of the giant pines.

Mykel caught sight of mounted rebels to the southeast. "Sabres! Fifteenth Company! Forward!"

Pressing the attack seemed less dangerous than trying to withdraw through a forest he did not know, and going back through the defile would take too long and allow the rebels to regroup and fire at Fifteenth Company when the Cadmians would be in a position where they could not return fire effectively.

While he did not know how much of Fifteenth Company followed his lead, he could hear the hoofbeats and sense riders behind him, and several moving up abreast of him, if separated by the pines.

Mykel had his sabre at the ready as the chestnut carried him toward the middle of a single squad of rebels. Several had rifles up. Mykel ducked as shots whispered past him.

Then he was among the rebels, slashing the shoulder of a too-young ranker, then parrying a thrust from an older rebel.

"South! To the cliffs! South!"

"To the cliffs . . . to the cliffs!"

The surviving bluecoats spurred their mounts up the gradual slope to the southwest and away from Fifteenth Company, now spread in the trees. Mykel didn't like that, and realized he'd pushed too much.

"Fifteenth Company! Re-form! Re-form!"

The company hadn't been that scattered, because he had his men back in squads in less than a quarter glass, and they were following the fleeing rebels. When they came out of the trees at the top of the gradual slope, there were other bluecoats riding slowly southward, less than a hundred yards away.

"Full firing line!" Mykel ordered.

He waited only until his men were in a rough semblance of a firing line. "Fire at will!"

After the first shots, the rebel laggards began to spur their mounts. Even so, another ten or fifteen rebels went down before those fleeing vanished into the welter of boulders, although Mykel could see dust and sand rising in various places.

"Cease fire!"

At the top of the slope, as he reloaded, Mykel studied the area before him more closely, a sandy plateau, with boulders and long and short rocky ridges rearing up everywhere. The ridges were as short as ten yards, but in length some seemed to stretch for a hundred. A few of the boulders were as small as his foot. Most standing alone were larger than a peasant's cot, and one to his right was as large as a seltyr's villa.

Should he follow the rebels?

A shadow flashed over him, and he glanced up. Two pteridons circled overhead. One bore two riders, the other but a single Myrmidon.

A skylance flared down, then another.

"By squads!" Mykel ordered. "Toward the cliffs! Measured pace! No quarter! Third squad on me!"

"First squad! Toward the cliffs . . ."

"Second squad . . ."

"Third squad! On the captain!"

"Fourth squad . . ."

Mykel followed the tracks of the rebels rather than trying to navigate a new path. That way, he hoped, he could avoid pitfalls in the sandy soil.

For the first several hundred yards, that also meant riding around fallen mounts and men.

He glanced to the southwest, where another line of blue fire lashed down from one of the pteridons. Mykel could sense a wave of deaths.

From the sand and dust, he could see that the remaining rebels—those that had fled the forest—were gathering under a rocky point jutting out from the cliffs, as if to make a stand.

Mykel couldn't help but feel sorry for them. Gathering was the worst possible tactic against Myrmidons and their skylances. They had to know that. So why were they doing it?

He glanced upward, looking for the pteridons, but they had circled back around.

Maybe the tactic wasn't so stupid. Could it be that there was some angle to the rock or a protected area there?

Mykel certainly didn't want to assault a natural stone fortress, but he couldn't see more than a hundred yards ahead. He didn't sense anyone that close, but he slowed the chestnut to a walk. "Measured walk! Measured walk!"

They weren't going to catch the rebels immediately, and the base of the cliff where the rebels were looked to be less than a vingt away, although it was hard to tell with the fine sandy dust raised and the long shadows cast by the early-morning light.

Mykel had ridden less than a hundred yards farther when the profusion of low rocky ridges and boulders ended, and a flat expanse of low sandy hills replaced the rocks. Half a vingt away, the rebels were re-forming with their backs directly to the low cliffs.

"Fifteenth Company! Halt! All squads! Halt!"

Something was happening on the rocky point above where the rebels gathered. There was a greenish cast to the air just above the point. The green intensified, growing into a glowing greenish sphere. Side by side in the center of the sphere were two of the winged soarers.

The lead pteridon ignored the sphere, and Mykel took an indrawn breath, sensing power still rising in or from the sphere until it began to glow more brightly, almost as if Asterta had appeared over the plateau in all her green glory. Yet Mykel could feel no heat.

"Fifteenth Company! Stand fast!" He didn't want anyone getting any closer to the soarers, especially with the Myrmidons closing on them.

"Stand fast!" repeated Bhoral.

A line of blue flame flared from the skylance of the first Myrmidon, angling down toward the gathered rebels.

Mykel winced, waiting for the eruption of flame and the hundreds of deaths. Instead, the blue flame flared and then *curved* backward, turning and twisting back toward the Myrmidon's lance. A line of green flashed and joined the blue flame, and the lance of blue and green tore through the Myrmidon and into the pteridon.

"Oh . . ."

The pteridon's wings folded inward, and like a duck shot in midair, it seemed to cartwheel downward in an arc toward the massed rebels.

A squad of bluecoats bolted from the right side of those gathered beneath the red-walled cliff. They rode hard, galloping to the northwest, sandy dust rising from the hoofs of their mounts. None of the other bluecoats moved, seemingly frozen in place.

The injured pteridon struck the cliff twenty yards above the remaining mass of rebels. Blue flame exploded out from the impact, spraying across the rebels below. The few screams of mounts and men were brief, and most came from the stragglers of those galloping northward. Those closer never had a chance to react.

The heat from the impact blast washed over Fifteenth Company like that of a forge fire in a gale, but subsided almost instantly.

Mykel's eyes flicked back to the soarer's green sphere. It had paled and remained so for several moments before beginning to regain its intensity. Only a single soarer remained within the sphere, although Mykel could not have said when the other had vanished.

The second pteridon turned toward the sphere and the soarer within. A line of blue flame flashed toward the single soarer.

Once more the flame did not reach its intended target, but twisted back, turning into a mixture of green and blue before striking, then knifing through the forward Myrmidon and into the chest of the second pteridon. The pteridon's wings bent upward and back as the pteridon nosed down and began to drop, more swiftly, toward the southwest of Fifteenth Company.

The remaining soarer and the green sphere had vanished.

One of the Myrmidons separated from the falling creature, and Mykel watched—fascinated—because he could sense something happening. Was it the submarshal? Whoever it was, whatever it was, he fell far more slowly, in an arc that carried him toward the rocks to Mykel's right.

"Third squad! On me!" Mykel turned the chestnut and urged him into a fast walk.

Barely had he done so when another explosion of blue flame flared from the cliffs to the southwest, the heat washing once more over the Cadmians, then dissipating.

Mykel glanced up once more. The Myrmidon was tumbling, end over end, but falling far more slowly than he should have been. Even so, he was falling, and disappeared behind a long ridge of rock a good hundred yards ahead of Mykel and third squad.

Mykel had covered another twenty yards when he could sense someone ahead. "Rifles ready!" He had his own weapon up even before he finished speaking.

Crack! The shot was close.

Catching sight of a figure in blue behind a low boulder, he fired. The man dropped.

More shots came from behind the rock ridge.

"Third squad! Drop back and take cover!" Mykel couldn't see losing a squad—or even several men—at a time when the majority of the rebels had been destroyed. He guided the chestnut back behind one of the larger boulders, finding Chyndylt and his mount coming around the other side.

"Fancy seeing you here, sir," offered the squad leader.

"You, too." As he flashed a grin to Chyndylt, Mykel could sense a faint purpleness farther to the west, to the right of where the rebels seemed to be. Was that purpleness the Myrmidon? Could it be the submarshal?

Crack! Another bullet smashed into the boulder behind which he had taken cover.

"Chyndylt, keep the men under cover, but keep them firing at those rebels. I think the Myrmidon colonel's still alive, but he's out to the north of where they are."

"Must be hurt, or we'd know it. He'd use that weapon of his."

Mykel dismounted. "I'm going to circle around." He reached up and handed the chestnut's reins to the squad leader.

"Yes, sir." Chyndylt sounded doubtful.

"If he survives, would you want to be a captain who left him out there?"

"No, sir. I see what you mean."

"Just keep the squad firing enough to occupy the bluecoats."

"We can do that, sir."

Mykel moved to the right side of the boulder, then crouched before he peered around it. The rock ridge that sheltered the rebels was high enough that they would have more trouble aiming at a man on foot.

He dashed across the five-yard space to the next rock, one less than a yard and a half high, but enough shelter for a man. More shots peppered the area, most of them high and ricocheting off the taller ridges behind him.

The next dash was a shade longer, but the cover was higher, and longer.

As he moved to the northwest, more and more outcroppings blocked the rebels from getting a clear view of him. He could sense the purplish pinkness that had to be the colonel, and felt that he was getting closer, but he was also getting a sense that there were others nearby.

Ahead, behind another series of more jumbled boulders, he heard voices.

"Just shoot him. Too big to move him."

"If he'd wake up . . . we could use him to get out of here. Won't do us much good dead."

"Won't do us any good alive . . ."

Mykel inched forward, peering around the base of an eroded chunk of reddish sandstone, trying to move more into a better position without being seen. Three rebels stood over the prone figure of the Myrmidon submarshal, who had apparently dragged himself into a half sitting, half-lying position against the rocks before losing consciousness. Mykel could see that the submarshal's right arm and left leg were bent at angles suggesting they were broken. If they were not, then alectors' bones were very different from landers', and Mykel doubted that. He was amazed that the alector had been able to move at all.

"Need to get the others over here," said one of the rebels.

That was the last thing Mykel needed.

He raised the rifle, aiming—and firing.

The speaker dropped, and both the other rebels whirled.

Mykel fired twice more. The others fell where they stood.

He listened, and tried to sense whether there were other rebels nearby.

He didn't hear anything, except rifles exchanging fire to the south and sensed no one. After several moments, he eased around the boulder and moved toward the submarshal.

Crack!

The impact on his left shoulder spun Mykel around and to the ground.

Several more shots went overhead.

Mykel's left side was a mass of fire. He still held the rifle in his right hand, but doubted he could aim it that well. He *might* be able to prop it to get a shot in the general direction of someone. Why hadn't he sensed the other rebel? Had he been too worried about the submarshal?

He had to scrabble, slowly easing himself into a position propped against the rocks. He could see the blood welling across his tunic.

". . . certain dangers . . . to commanding from the front, Captain . . ." The submarshal's voice was labored.

Mykel glanced toward the alector. He could hear the crunch of boots on the sandy ground, and he doubted those boots belonged to a Cadmian. He levered the rifle up, across his knees in at least the right direction—he hoped.

"Well . . . look what we got here . . ." A bluecoat stepped around the boulder directly across from the submarshal, his rifle held at the ready, swinging from Submarshal Dainyl to Mykel and back again. "Like to take you for a ride, but looks like neither of you is going anywhere."

Mykel couldn't sense anything about the rebel, unlike the others, even as he stood there and fired.

The bullet bounced off the Myrmidon's tunic.

In that moment of surprise, Mykel squeezed the trigger of his rifle, *willing* with all the concentration he could muster the bullet to strike the bluecoat. A single hole appeared in the bluecoat's forehead, and he toppled forward.

Mykel *knew* the rifle had not been aimed that well.

He could feel his vision narrowing, then widening.

". . . if you want us to get through this, Captain . . . you need to get my sidearm into my good hand . . . can't reach it . . . otherwise . . ."

Mykel scrabbled forward, leaving the rifle, crawling, then resting, crawling, until he was beside the Myrmidon.

His right hand fumbled with the catches on the holster, but he managed to loosen them and ease the weapon onto the submarshal's chest.

"We might . . . have a chance now . . ."

Mykel slumped back. He could barely see . . . and then . . . he could not.

98

With the pale orange-white of a sun that had just crept above the eastern horizon out to his right, Dainyl shifted his weight in the harness and second seat of the pteridon he rode behind Falyna. Ahead, and to his left, were Quelyt and the other pteridon, as the two flew across the old-growth forest. As the dispatch from Captain Rhystan had indicated, Captain Mykel had indeed attacked the rebels at dawn. Whatever he had done had scattered them away from the forest, and Cadmians were pursuing, in a measured fashion.

Both pteridons had circled to the northwest to make a long pass across the rebels heading southeast, in order to avoid the higher cliffs. At that moment, Dainyl Talent-sensed the appearance of one of the ancients. He leaned to one side, trying to pinpoint the source of the amber green force. There was a distortion in the sky, just above a rocky point where the rebels had begun to re-form. The distortion resolved itself into a greenish sphere.

Suddenly, the pteridon began to lose altitude as the ancients drew on lifeforce as well, leaving less for the pteridon. Dainyl dropped his shields, except around his head, and let the energies flow to the pteridon.

"Falyna! Avoid that point, and fire from as far away as you can!" Dainyl leaned sideways to see past Falyna. Her pteridon's blue crystal beak shimmered in the bright white light of the morning sun. Farther to the south, Quelyt had clearly not seen or sensed the soarer, and he had dropped his pteridon into a dive toward the remaining rebels beneath the rocky point; his skylance flared toward the rebels, a line of blue flame.

The blue flame that had been aimed at the rebels at the base of the red bluff curved and reversed itself, retracing its path back skyward to the lance and turning green. The shaft of green exploded through the lance, then drove through the impenetrable skin of the pteridon.

Dainyl blinked. Quelyt slumped in his harness, the upper part of his body a blackened mess. More impossibly, the pteridon's wings froze, then folded against its body. The pteridon nosed downward toward the rebel force and slammed into the stone above the rebels. The bluish explosion cascaded off the stone and across the rebels below.

Falyna raised her lance and triggered it.

"Get away from there! Turn east!" snapped Dainyl. He'd sensed that the soarer was dangerous, almost from the beginning, but he hadn't thought that she'd get involved in something like a minor revolt.

A second line of green extended from the green sphere and met the blue flame from Falyna's skylance. Dainyl saw and sensed the energies flaring back at them and drew all the lifeforce he could, throwing up shields.

The green lance struck, and Dainyl found himself swatted clear of the pteridon, his harness straps snapped, tumbling in midair. Time seemed to slow, and he reached out with all his Talent, thrusting out force to the ground below, trying to slow himself, to break his fall. The wind past his face seemed less fierce, but was that enough?

He could see rocks and sand below, and he cast out more Talent-force, could feel himself slow . . . but not enough. From somewhere came another infusion of Talent—green?—tinged with black, and his speed slowed yet more. Then he had no more strength left, and he dropped out of the sky, slamming into a line of rock with one leg. Instinctively, he put out an arm—and wished he hadn't as he heard and felt it snap as he crashed into another boulder.

Pain washed over him from too many places for him to count—but he was alive, at least for the moment. In addition to the broken arm and leg, Dainyl's chest was badly bruised. With his good hand, he tried to straighten himself, to push himself into a sitting position against the rocks beside him. He moved a bit, and then a pinkish blackness washed over him.

He couldn't have been unconscious too long, before, in between waves of pain, he could hear voices, but the words were indistinct. Dainyl could vaguely sense three rebels, standing less than two yards away. If he could reach his sidearm . . . but it was on his right hip, and that was the arm that was broken so badly he couldn't move it, even blocking the pain with Talent.

"Need to get the others over here," said one.

A single shot rang out, and the rebel who had spoken pitched forward. Two more shots followed, and the other two rebels dropped.

Dainyl wasn't surprised when Captain Mykel slipped out from behind the rocks.

Crack!

The captain was twisted by the force of the bullet that had slammed into his shoulder, and he went down hard. For several moments, the Cadmian officer lay on the sand stunned, then slowly twisted himself onto his back and used his legs to lever himself into a position against the rocks. Blood was staining his tunic, slowly.

"There are certain dangers . . . to commanding from the front, Captain." Dainyl forced the words out. He could sense someone else coming, but not who it might be.

The captain laboriously moved the rifle up, but Dainyl couldn't see how the captain would be able to aim it one-handed and one-armed—and wounded. Yet there was little Dainyl could do. He was anything but mobile.

"Well . . . look what we got here . . ." Another rebel stepped out from behind the boulder directly across from Dainyl.

Dainyl could sense that the man had a natural Talent-shield, but seemed unaware of it, another indication of how much the captain relied unconsciously on his Talent.

"I'd like to take you for a ride, but looks like neither of you is going anywhere." The rebel smirked, then fired directly at Dainyl.

The bullet blasted into Dainyl's tunic. For a moment, he could sense nothing, except pinkish blackness, and, as he came back to quick consciousness, the pain radiating through his already bruised chest.

A second rifle went off—the captain's—and Dainyl felt the focused Talent that twisted a horribly misaimed bullet right through the forehead of the rebel. The man toppled forward, dropping his rifle and landing facedown in the sand just short of Dainyl's less injured leg.

Talent—potentially strong Talent. Dainyl had known many alectors who did not have a fraction of the Talent the captain might have—if he were allowed to live to develop it.

For the moment, Dainyl could do nothing about that. Even if he could persuade the captain to reach his sidearm, the weapon was best saved for any more rebels who might appear before the Cadmians did.

"If you want us to get through this, Captain," Dainyl said slowly, with more effort than before, because every breath hurt, "you need to get my sidearm into my good hand. I can't use it otherwise."

The captain eased sideways, then stopped, then moved some more. Dainyl could sense the pain, pain that the captain could have controlled better if he knew how to use his Talent. Finally, Mykel was almost beside the Myrmidon. His good hand fumbled at the catches, but he finally loosened them enough to ease the sidearm clear and ease it onto Dainyl's chest.

Dainyl had to force his left hand up to take the weapon, but he had it. "We might have a chance now."

The captain slumped back, unconscious.

Dainyl looked at him. The captain was still bleeding, enough that all Dainyl had to do was nothing, and a Talented lander would die, and no one would know.

Dainyl looked at the captain who had risked his life to save him. He was so young, and he would die young in any case. He might never develop his Talent more, either, Dainyl told himself. With the tiniest point of Talent, he reached out and fused the point where the bleeding was the worst, then in a second place.

His eyes closed, and he tried to listen, since he could not see. For a time, he did neither.

When he could open his eyes again, he heard voices.

"Captain! Captain Mykel!"

"He's over here!" Dainyl rasped out. He smiled, raggedly, waiting.

99

Alectors who govern should avoid explaining their actions, if at all possible. Life is complex and filled with conflicts, and few of even the most intelligent know the background information. Fewer still can calculate the implications and ramifications of a decision. For these reasons, the facts and conditions that underlie a ruler's decisions, or the decisions of an alector who administers for the Archon, can seldom be presented fully in a manner that will accurately describe the rationale for such action.

Even if all such information could be presented, doing so would be useless, if not dangerous. Both steers and less discerning alectors demand certainty in their life, yet the only certainty is uncertainty.

Equally important is the fact that they do not want to study the world around them and all that lies behind it. Nor do they wish to spend the time necessary to master understanding. They wish simple explanations to support their baser desires and a sense of certainty in their lives. To this end, they delude themselves that they understand their world. In point of fact, they will perform all manner of contortions in thought to retain that illusion of understanding. That illusion is the fundamental basis for their acceptance of their society and their world.

In the vast majority of instances, the simple and appealing answer or explanation is inaccurate or misleading, if not both. Therefore, the wisest course for an alector is never to explain. If an explanation is necessary, however, the one given should be simple and straightforward, couched in a manner that appeals to the simplistic beliefs of those for whom it is intended. There should be no lies and no inaccuracies, for those can often be easily determined, merely the use of what is factually correct in a manner supporting the decision at hand.

Views of the Highest
Illustra
W.T. 1513

100

Mykel did not remember much after shooting the last bluecoat. There were images of the submarshal looking at him strangely, and warm pressure across his chest, and being carried somewhere on a stretcher, then rolling in agony in a wagon.

After that, there had been blackness, and heat and chill. He remembered liquids down his throat, and voices, but not whose voices or what he had tasted. He could recall talking to someone, more than one person, but his words had made no sense, not even to himself. Through it all, his left side and his head had been splitting, or throbbing dully.

Slowly, he opened his eyes. He lay in a large bed that looked out through two open doors to a balcony. Beyond the balcony railing were trees, deep green, not because of summer, but because of the late-afternoon sunlight. The chamber walls were all of white plaster, wide golden wooden shutters folded back from the windows, and fabric hangings, showing trees and flowers. He was propped up in a half-sitting position with pillows. His left shoulder was heavily bound, and dull aches throbbed everywhere.

A Cadmian ranker stood inside the closed oak door.

Mykel coughed.

The ranker turned, and Mykel recognized Wejasyr. "Sir? Are you awake?"

On the surface, it was a stupid question, but Mykel understood what he meant. "If you're asking whether I'm in my right mind, Wejasyr, I think so."

"Yes, sir!" The ranker rapped on the door. "Captain's awake."

Within moments, an older woman came through the guarded doorway first, carrying a tray, on which were a beaker and a pitcher. She filled the breaker and tendered it to Mykel. "The more you drink, Captain, the faster you'll heal."

"Thank you." He accepted the beaker and took a swallow. The ale tasted good, very good, Mykel had to admit, and took another long swallow.

By then Rhystan stood by the foot of the large bed. "I'm glad to see you're back with us."

"How is Fifteenth Company?"

"Bhoral has them in line. You only lost five men, and seven wounded. Amazing, really, given all that mess."

"What about Sixteenth Company?"

"We had three wounded. That was all. A few rebels tried to leave the forest, but when we shot at them they didn't want to try. Later, we let them surrender, those that were left."

Mykel moistened his lips, glad that things had held together after he'd been stupid enough to get shot—and after the battle had been largely won, at that. "When is it? What day?"

"Londi afternoon." Rhystan smiled.

"That long?" Mykel knew he hadn't been himself, but . . . he hated to think of what he might have said, because he recalled saying things, but not what they had been. He hoped he hadn't said anything about his shooting or about Rachyla. It would be best if he hadn't said what he had seen when the pteridons had been destroyed. "I must have been raving for days."

"You weren't raving. You mumbled a lot, and some of it didn't make sense. The only thing that did was that you couldn't let them shoot the submarshal. You kept saying something about soaring, several times—must have felt like you were flying."

"I didn't feel that way. Maybe I wished that I had been." Mykel offered a soft laugh.

"You lost a lot of blood, almost too much, but they said you should be all right. They were more worried about your head. You whacked it against the stone pretty hard after you were shot, the submarshal said."

"The submarshal? How is he?"

"He's tougher than . . . he's tough."

"You were right," Mykel replied slowly. "It was problematical—and foolhardy."

"I'm glad it was you, but it worked. There aren't any rebels left, and the handful of seltyrs who survived pledged full allegiance to the Duarches."

"No rebels?"

"A few. We rounded up maybe thirty, and there were others who ran and don't want anyone to know that they were part of the bluecoat force."

Mykel nodded slowly.

The door opened again, and another figure entered the chamber. More properly, the submarshal was rolled through the doorway in a chair with wheels that creaked as it moved. The ranker who pushed it must have been from Sixteenth Company, because Mykel didn't recognize him.

The submarshal's left leg and right arm were both splinted, and the leg was supported by a plank fastened at an angle to the rolling chair. A large bruise covered the left side of his forehead and his cheek. Mykel could sense a purplish pink aura around the alector. Was it his eyes? He glanced at Rhystan and the older woman, who had stepped back, but he saw nothing out of the ordinary with them.

"Captain, I'm glad to see you're recovering," offered the submarshal. "Without your courage and abilities I would not be here."

Mykel smiled crookedly. "I'm afraid I didn't handle things as well as I could have."

"You did far better than any had a right to expect. Far better."

Rhystan nodded emphatically.

Mykel took another swallow of ale. It eased the dryness in his throat, as well as the headache he hadn't been totally aware that he had.

"There's one thing I'd like to know . . ." Rhystan said slowly, looking from Mykel to the submarshal and back to the Mykel.

"What's that?"

"How did the rebels manage to shoot down the pteridons?"

Mykel would have shrugged, but that would have hurt far too much. "I don't know. I saw them go down. The first one was flying too low, I think, but the submarshal would know."

Both captains turned to look at the submarshal.

Dainyl smiled ruefully. "You may recall that one of the reasons why the Cadmians were sent here was because of the nature of the Murian Mountains. Some mountains are more dangerous than others. There are downdrafts and other problems. We had known about those just north of the mine, but not about those above the plateau behind the forest. We should have guessed from the nature of the ground, but when you are pursuing a foe, you don't always see things so clearly. Because of the problems that caused the first pteridon to crash into the cliff, my flier was distracted, then was hit—I would guess—by a lucky shot from below. The lack of guidance and the terrain combined to cause the second impact. I was fortunate—mostly fortunate—to have been thrown clear."

Mykel could sense a combination of truth and misleading statements, although not quite lies, in the submarshal's words. He also understood that the submarshal would say nothing else except along the same lines.

"I saw you flung clear," Mykel said. "I wasn't sure you would survive, but we thought you might."

"For that, Captain, I am most thankful."

There were no conditions or evasions in those words, for which Mykel was most grateful.

"We will be here for several more days, at least," the submarshal said, "until we have healed further. Overcaptain Dohark reports that all is calm and quiet in Dramuria, and that there is no need for haste in our return."

Mykel stifled a yawn.

"I think we have tired Captain Mykel enough," said the submarshal.

After they had left, Mykel took another swallow of the ale. Rachyla had hinted that the alectors were different, and from what Mykel had seen, they definitely were. How the submarshal had survived a fall of over a hundred yards onto rock and sand—and was in better shape with a broken arm and leg and bruises across his entire body than Mykel was with a single gunshot wound to his shoulder—that was amazing.

Mykel looked down at the binding across his left shoulder. Then he swallowed. He could tell that the bullet had been far lower than he had thought. Men didn't survive long where he'd been shot . . . but he had. Had the submarshal done something? Or had he just been extraordinarily fortunate?

101

Dainyl examined his leg, then his arm, with his Talent, and nodded. They were healing well. Within another two weeks he would be able to walk, if with a brace of some sort. By then, his next set of troubles would begin.

While he had been healing at the estate of the former Seltyr Veluasyr—who had been one of those shot by the intrepid Captain Mykel—Dainyl had had time to think, too much time, in some ways.

He felt guilty about the deaths of both Quelyt and Falyna. They had followed his orders, and died. Both had been faithful Myrmidons, and a pleasure to command and work with—and he had failed them by not recognizing how great a danger the soarers had represented. He had been warned, but, deep inside, he had not believed those warnings. Even though it had been his failure, he had been the one to survive, and he did not understand how—or why.

The drop from such a height should have killed him outright. While Talent could cushion or slow falls from lesser heights, he was not aware of any alector's surviving such a fall. He had a vague recollection of a brief flow of Talent-energy, but it had been green. Had he been imagining that? He had to have been. The soarers would not have spent all that force bringing down two pteridons—then helped him save himself. However it had all happened, a great deal of luck had to have been involved.

Then, too, he knew that both the Highest and Marshal Shastylt would have been horrified that he had used Talent to heal Captain Mykel enough so that he would recover, rather than die. They would have been horrified more if they knew that the captain had Talent. Yet the captain had done more than anyone could have asked, and he had saved Dainyl when no one else could have. Without the captain, Dainyl would not be eventually going back to Elcien and Lystrana—perhaps even to a child. He had not been certain when he left, but . . . they had been hopeful.

To let the captain die, after he had failed Quelyt and Falyna, that would have been intolerable, a decision he could not have made. He had chosen to save the captain, and that was a choice he would have to live with. He could but hope it would not come back to torment him.

For all the fighting, and all of what he had learned in Lyterna, he still had no understanding of why the Highest and the marshal had set up the revolt in Dramur. It could not have been just a test of his abilities, nor could it have been to weaken the Cadmians. Part of the reason might have been to teach the seltyrs a lesson of sorts, but that could have been far more easily accomplished with greater forces over a shorter period of time.

He also considered Asulet's words, especially those about how much the alectors of Ifryn had lost in transfers from world to world. Those words were part of the answer, but what part?

When he and the Cadmians returned to Elcien depended in large degree on whether the recorders of deeds at one of the Tables had been able to determine—indirectly, since the Tables displayed nothing of Talent or created by Talent—that the two pteridons had been lost. But return he must, and fairly quickly, to report on how the two ancients had destroyed the pteridons. He knew of nothing that could stand up to a skylance, but the soarers had, and he was perhaps the only one still alive who had witnessed that. But . . . how much should he say? And to whom?

102

The Submarshal of Myrmidons looked from the too-small desk, behind which he was seated sideways and awkwardly, toward the open window. Dainyl would have preferred to have flown back to Dramuria, but without pteridons and with a leg that had not healed enough for him to ride, he had been forced to take a carriage, and it had been a long trip. A welcome breeze blew into the study, warming him after a cool and restless Decdi night, during which he had slept badly, and a long Londi, dealing with more administrative details than he would have wished.

During all that time, his thoughts had swirled between the loss of Quelyt and Falyna, the two irreplaceable pteridons, half of the Third Cadmian Battalion, and more than a thousand rebels. For what?

As soon as he had been able, Dainyl had written up a detailed dispatch outlining the events in Dramur. He had not sent it, because there had been no ships of the Duarches porting in Dramuria, nor any pteridons arriving. Writing the dispatch had not been difficult. He had reported what had occurred and that Dramur and Dramuria were now calm, partly in a state of shock and partly through a numb acceptance by the remaining seltyrs and growers that the Duarchy would do whatever was necessary to maintain control.

In Dainyl's absence, Overcaptain Dohark had taken a firm control over the compound, as well as over the local Cadmian companies. Captain Benjyr was in full evidence, and no longer made an effort to avoid Dainyl, even if he did not go out of his way to speak to the submarshal, and the compound gates remained open once more. The daily wagon loads of guano had resumed, rumbling down to the storage buildings off the piers at the port, and the dwellings burned by the rebels were being rebuilt.

Dainyl looked to the window, noting that the sun had dropped behind the mountains. Where, exactly, had the day gone?

At the knock on the study door, Dainyl turned his head. "Yes?"

One of the local Cadmian rankers stood there. "Submarshal, sir?

There are two pteridons on their way inbound. The overcaptain thought you would like to know."

"I'll be right there. Make sure two of the rooms in the officers' quarters are ready."

"Yes, sir."

Dainyl stood and took the heavy polished cane from where it rested against the wall. He hated using it, but there were times that his legs still did not respond, and it would be far worse to fall and injure himself again than to appear incapacitated. What was in his favor was that enough of the Cadmian rankers had seen him fall that they regarded his remaining alive—let alone walking with only a bound arm, a splint, and a limp—as a testimony to the indestructibility of alectors.

Although he had hurried, both pteridons were on the stones of the courtyard beside the squares by the time he reached the two Myrmidons.

"Submarshal, sir!" Ghenevra—the senior ranker in third squad—stiffened.

"Sir!" added Rhenyt.

"The marshal sent us to serve at your pleasure, sir." Ghenevra extended a thin envelope. "He sent this for you."

Dainyl took the envelope. "Thank you."

Rhenyt's eyes looked past Dainyl, speculatively.

"You won't find them, Rhenyt," Dainyl said quietly. How much should he tell them? "What I'm about to tell you is to be kept to yourselves. If I ever hear a word about this anywhere else, you'll be out of the Myrmidons. If you're fortunate, you'll be a servant in Lyterna for the rest of your life. That's if you're fortunate." Dainyl couldn't count on complete secrecy, but all he wanted to make sure was that word didn't pass to the landers and indigens. He waited.

"Yes, sir," replied both Myrmidons.

"The pteridons ran into a pair of ancients. Both the pteridons and the ancients were destroyed." Strictly speaking, Dainyl knew, that was not true. He was certain that at least one ancient had survived, but both pteridons had been destroyed, and the ancients had vanished.

"Ancients?" murmured Rhenyt. "There are still . . ."

"There are a few left, and they're quite dangerous, because it takes a great deal of Talent to sense where they are. If you leave them alone, they have always left us alone."

"But . . ."

"That's why you're not to fly along the crest of the Murian Mountains unless I'm with you. Is that understood?"

"Yes, sir." They both nodded emphatically.

Dainyl could sense that he'd explained enough, both why they should not say anything, and why the Cadmians should not know the true cause of the loss of the pteridons. "Welcome to Dramuria. We'll need to get you settled. It's always a long flight from Elcien."

"Yes, sir."

Once he had the two in the hands of the duty squad leader, Dainyl took the dispatch and returned to his study, closing the door behind him. He could sense the overcaptain's curiosity, but Dohark would have to wait until Dainyl had read what the marshal had sent. After reseating himself, awkwardly, Dainyl opened the dispatch and read through it quickly.

> Submarshal Dainyl—
>
> We trust that this dispatch finds you in health. The recorders of deeds under the High Alector of Justice have surmised from what the Table reveals that the revolt in Dramur has been successfully put down and that you have been restoring order. We have also received word from Lyterna that there appear to have been certain uses of energies that have far-reaching implications for the Duarchy.
>
> In view of these circumstances, we would request that you immediately restructure Cadmian operations in Dramur to preclude a repetition of the events just past. Once this is complete, and once you feel the situation in Dramur is fully stable and will remain so without your presence, you are to return to Elcien at your earliest possible convenience to brief us on events in Dramur and their resolution. We request that you convey any written reports only upon your person. If your departure will be more than two weeks from the time of receiving this, send a brief report indicating when we may expect you.

The document was signed and sealed by both the High Alector of Justice and the marshal.

After a time, he read it again, but nothing changed. They were definitely concerned, and the half surprise shown by the two Myrmidons indicated that neither the Highest nor the marshal had been that certain whether they would find Dainyl, and in what condition.

Dainyl was not looking forward to returning to Elcien to explain matters. His eyes drifted to his leg. He would have to wait another few days, perhaps a week, before his leg would be strong enough, even with Talent-assisted healing, for him to make such a long flight. By then, he might have a better idea how to present what had happened. He also had to determine what to do about Dramur. Neither the Cadmians nor the Myrmidons could afford another commander such as Majer Herryf.

Dainyl looked out into the twilight, thinking.

103

More than a week passed, and it was Tridi of the following week before Mykel mounted the chestnut and began a slow three-day ride back south to the Cadmian compound north of Dramuria. The submarshal had left by carriage on the previous Octdi, insisting that Mykel not leave before Tridi at the earliest.

In midafternoon on Sexdi, Mykel rode through the open gates of the Cadmian compound, accompanied by six rankers from Fifteenth Company who provided his escort. His shoulder and chest throbbed, and his head ached as he dismounted—one-armed and carefully.

After arranging for Estylt to carry his gear to his quarters, Mykel walked toward the headquarters building to report his return. In the center of the courtyard, two pteridons sunned themselves on the top of their squares. They had to be another pair. He'd seen—and sensed—the total destruction of the two in the battle that had destroyed the seltyrs' mounted forces.

Mykel stepped into the comparative cool of headquarters and turned toward the study that Dohark had to be using, then stopped by the duty desk, manned by a local Cadmian squad leader.

"Is the overcaptain in?"

"Yes, sir. He was a moment ago."

"Thank you." Mykel smiled and headed toward Dohark's study, only to see Captain Benjyr walking toward him.

"Good day," Mykel offered cheerfully.

"Good day, Captain," replied Benjyr, his voice very polite, but not cold. "If you'll excuse me."

"Of course." Mykel smiled. Benjyr had radiated fear of Mykel. But why? Had Dohark or the submarshal said anything?

Behind him, Benjyr murmured something under his breath, words that sounded like "dagger of the ancients."

Mykel's hand went to his belt. The ancient dagger was still there. With a half smile, he continued to Dohark's open door.

"Mykel! I thought you might be back today. Come on in." The overcaptain motioned for Mykel to enter the study.

Mykel stepped inside, leaving the door ajar, not quite fully closed. He settled carefully into the straight-backed chair across from Dohark.

"How are you feeling?"

"Sore, but better."

"Most people don't recover from bullets that close to the lungs and heart. You're fortunate." Dohark smiled. "I'm glad you're back."

"So am I. Have you heard anything?"

"Not yet. The submarshal is working on something, though. He's been asking questions about everything, studying ledgers and accounts. I'd wager that it won't be long."

"I wanted to talk to you about something." Mykel had no idea if Dohark would support him. If necessary, Mykel would go to the submarshal, but he should ask Dohark first.

Dohark raised his eyebrows.

"Rachyla. Everyone else who survived has been allowed to keep their lands, so long as they pledged to the Duarch. She should be freed as well . . ." Mykel saw the amusement on Dohark's face. "Have you already let her go?"

"I had thought it might be best for you to be the one to release her," said Dohark, "since you captured her. Besides, she won't talk to any of us." He handed a folded sheet of paper to Mykel. "I already drafted her release order, and I've told the guards that she'll be released soon."

For some reason, Mykel had been expecting an argument. He just sat there for a moment.

"Sirs?"

Both Mykel and Dohark looked to the door of the study.

"The submarshal has asked that you both join him."

"We'll be right there." Dohark stood.

So did Mykel.

They crossed the hallway to the larger study. This time, Dohark closed the study door. The submarshal was seated behind the desk, one of the few times Mykel had seen that. He waited until Dohark and Mykel had settled into chairs.

"I have been summoned back to Elcien. I'll leave within a few days, and I will not be returning here. I've been ordered to make sure that the situation that occurred here does not happen again. For that reason, I have developed a plan for Dramur." The submarshal looked at Dohark. "First, over the next year, the number of Cadmian companies here will be increased to five—a full battalion. Second, those companies will *not* be commanded by a Cadmian from Dramur, ever. Third . . ." Dainyl paused.

Mykel caught a hint of amusement in the eyes of the submarshal, and he could feel that the submarshal was enjoying himself.

". . . third, they will be commanded by Majer Dohark here—assuming you are willing, Majer."

"Majer . . . I . . . ah . . . Yes, sir. I'd be pleased to, sir."

"You are to institute full Cadmian training, and we will work out the details to ensure that you receive some junior captains not from Dramur." The submarshal extended a pair of insignia. "Your new rank is effective now."

"Yes, sir." Dohark took the insignia. "Thank you, sir."

The submarshal turned his eyes upon Mykel. "Captain . . ."

"Yes, sir."

"You demonstrated a solid grasp of both strategy and tactics in your campaigns here in Dramur. Your sole weakness is the occasional individual foray, but I trust that the results of your last effort have impressed upon you that such . . . exploits . . . can have a high price." Again, the submarshal smiled. "Admittedly, I am most grateful for that last exploit, although it was not in your best personal interest." He paused before continuing. "I will be sending an overriding recommendation to Colonel Herolt for your immediate promotion to majer and for command of Third Battalion. It is technically only a recommendation, because, until I confer with the Marshal of Myrmidons, I do not have the authority to order it, unlike here in Dramur, where I do. But . . . I seriously doubt that Colonel Herolt would wish to dispute such a recommendation, not when my letter points out that you and your company routed and destroyed fifteen armed companies over the course of two seasons and that your actions kept Third Battalion from being totally destroyed by the late Majer Vaclyn."

"Yes, sir." That was all that Mykel could say. Majer? Skipping the entire rank of overcaptain?

"You may not be familiar with all the administrative details of command, Captain Mykel, but since it will take at least several seasons to rebuild and retrain Third Battalion, I am certain you will have time to learn those. One can never learn the instinctive grasp of tactics and motion which you have already demonstrated."

"Thank you, sir."

"You may not always thank me." The submarshal smiled. "That is all for now. You'll pardon me if I don't escort you out."

"No, sir." Both Cadmians smiled and stood, nodding as they left.

Back in Dohark's study, Mykel looked at the new majer. "Do you *want* to stay here?"

"Why not? It's a good position, if you just listen and don't let the seltyrs get out of hand. Besides, you think an old former squad leader like me would make majer any other way? I don't think like you, Mykel. I don't know as I'd want to." Dohark grinned. "Besides, any of the seltyrs get out of hand, and I can call for the 'dagger of the ancients.' I'll also tell them that you're a majer, with a whole battalion that you've trained."

"That's what they're calling me?" Mykel had overheard the expression used by Benjyr, but hadn't connected it to himself.

"It fits, doesn't it?" Dohark pointed to Mykel's bound arm and shoulder. "I don't envy you, Mykel. The submarshal's right. Old Herolt can't very well ignore the Marshal of Myrmidon's recommendation, especially when you've managed to do what you have. You'll be a majer. You know what else, though?"

"Third battalion will get the dirtiest and nastiest tasks, and they'll be looking for me to do the impossible—or fail, and it won't matter much which it is. Is that what you mean?"

"You've got it." Dohark shook his head.

"You wouldn't mind if I escorted Rachyla back to her estate?"

"Might be the best thing if you did."

Mykel wasn't sure about that. It might protect her, and then, it might have every other seltyr looking to remove her. He just sat there for several moments, considering.

"Go free your lady friend," Dohark finally said.

"Not until tomorrow morning. I can't ride tonight, and she'll be gone in moments if I'm not ready to escort her."

"You've thought that one out, too."

He had. How well was another question.

104

Almost at dawn on Sexdi, Mykel rode up to the sentries outside the officer's cell where Rachyla was held. He was followed by Chyndylt and Fifteenth Company's third squad—and one mount saddled and riderless. Mykel had not mentioned his possible promotion to any of them. No matter what the submarshal had said, it hadn't happened, and there was no point in saying anything until it did. If it did. He dismounted carefully.

"Overcaptain said to expect you, sir," offered the older guard.

Mykel held out the release document. The sentry barely looked at it. "You taking her back?"

"It seemed best that way."

"Be a long ride for you, sir." The Cadmian turned and unlocked the door.

Mykel stepped inside, letting his eyes adjust. As always, Rachyla was dressed and sat at the stool before the desk. She stood immediately, as if she wanted to step back.

"You're up." He looked at her, taking in the still-clear skin, the raven hair, and the deep green eyes, eyes that recalled something to him, something he could not place.

"I could not sleep. I felt something was about to happen." She squared her shoulders. "Tell me, Captain, and don't lie to me. You have not lied to me yet. Do not lie now. Are you here to take me to my death?"

"No. The rebellion has been crushed. I'm to escort you back to Stylan Estate."

For a long moment, Rachyla just stood there, studying him. Then she nodded. "That may be to my death as well."

"I have an armed squad to accompany us." He laughed ironically. "I thought it might help if you were escorted by the dagger of the ancients."

"Do not joke about that."

His lips curled. "Why not? That's what everyone on Dramur seems to call me."

Only then did her eyes drop to his shoulder, rebound under his tunic. He no longer wore the sling, but there was one in his saddlebags, in case he needed it. "There's a dressing under your tunic. How badly were you wounded?"

"Badly enough," Mykel replied.

"How long ago?"

"Two weeks."

"You almost died, did you not?"

Mykel flushed, not certain how he could answer that. The honorable answer was to lie, and the truthful one was almost boastful.

"I see. You did almost die. Others would have."

"I don't know that." He offered an embarrassed smile. "I couldn't move for a while."

"What about the evil one?"

"In the last battle, both pteridons crashed in flames." That was true. "Two of the Myrmidons died. He was badly injured. Any man would have died. He's walking around now."

"I said that they did not belong here."

"Yes, you did." Mykel kept his voice even.

"Why am I being allowed to go back to Stylan?"

"The seltyrs who submitted were allowed to keep their lands. You never revolted. Your father did. Since you did not, you deserve the same treatment as those others who did not or who submitted."

"You know how I feel." She did not move.

"Yes, I do. That was not the question. You cannot be judged on what you would have done, only on what you did do."

"What will keep another revolt from happening?"

"It will take a few years to replace those lost. Over a thousand Dramurans died. There will also be a full Cadmian battalion here at the compound. It will be commanded by a majer not from Dramur."

"You?"

Mykel laughed. "I'm to be sent back to Elcien. If I'm fortunate, I might get promoted. Overcaptain Dohark has been promoted to majer. He's in command here."

Another nod from Rachyla preceded her words. "I would like to leave, if I may."

"You may." Mykel inclined his head to the clothes on the wall pegs. "Do you . . . ?"

"No. I will burn what I wear when I reach Stylan."

Mykel stepped out of the cell.

When Rachyla stepped into the silvery light of the moments before dawn, Mykel gestured to the horse he had brought, then mounted himself.

Rachyla mounted, wordlessly.

105

All decisions worthy of being called such result in change. Changes never occur without cost, and the greater the decision, the greater the cost. For this reason, all decisions cause pain and discomfort. An alector who does not understand such should never be placed in a position where he or she must make decisions. When an administrator declares that a decision is good because no one is affected adversely, that alector is either duplicitous or self-deceptive, if not both. A good administrator determines both the benefits and the costs, both the pleasure and the pain, that his actions will cause. He will not shy away from determining what that pain may be, either in loss of life, of lifemass, or of food or golds for those steers under his care.

With such an understanding, an alector should also never boast of either the pain or the gain of his acts or of those required by his decisions. He should not state either, only that his decision has balanced all factors and is as just as possible.

Those alectors and steers who suffer will resent the results of such a decision, while those who gain will not be able to refrain from telling others of their good fortune. Such telling will invariably be linked more strongly to the alector's decisions if the alector has been the one to announce either gain or loss, and the resentment of those who suffer will be far greater. In consequence, the authority and respect for the Archon and his administrators will be thus diminished.

In this, as in all matters, those entrusted with the powers of the Archon must weigh fully all aspects of what decisions they make and how those decisions are declared to those affected . . .

Views of the Highest
Illustra
W.T. 1513

106

As Mykel had feared, the ride north was long, and painful. Not until the sun was low in the sky, on the second day, just above the Murian Mountains, did Rachyla offer more than a few words at any one time, although she had ridden beside him the entire journey.

"We should be at the estate before too long." Mykel tried not to think about how uncomfortable he was. His fingers brushed his belt above the concealed miniature dagger. For some reason, letting the hand of his injured side rest near the ancient weapon helped relieve the worst of the nagging pain, if but for a time.

"Not only are you the dagger of the ancients, but you carry one, do you not?"

"You knew?"

"Yes. There is a feel to one. I always knew when my grandfather carried his. How did you obtain it? Steal it?"

"No. A chandler in Jyoha gave it to me. He said I was an honorable man who was his worst enemy. I paid him good silvers to feed the children in return."

For a moment, Rachyla looked at the road ahead, rather than at Mykel. "They say that those who are the daggers are also like the ancients, that they can feed upon the spirit within a person, and that they are without mercy."

"Was your grandsire without mercy?"

"Many said that he was. I never saw that. Would you say you lacked mercy, Captain?" The seltyr's green-eyed daughter looked at Mykel, intently.

"Recently, many could have said I offered little mercy. That was because they had offered less." Mykel laughed softly. "If people acted better, less mercy would be necessary."

"Then they would not be people," replied Rachyla.

"You think highly of people." Mykel kept his voice light.

"People are what they are. So are the alectors. One can change neither. People cannot be changed because there are so many. Alectors could be killed or removed, for they are few, if one had the power, but they cannot be changed."

"From what I have seen, Lady, alectors are most difficult to kill."

"Not for a dagger of the ancients who could become as the ancients were. If the alectors learn what you are, Captain, they will destroy you far more quickly—and more painfully—than any you have dispatched. And with less regret."

Mykel did not know how to reply to her words. Him? He knew he had some abilities, such as that of directing bullets he fired, and sensing where people were—but those were nothing compared to what he had seen from the submarshal alone.

"You doubt me, Captain. Do not. I know what I know. You told me that two of the Myrmidons and their pteridons perished. The evil one did not, but was gravely injured. Do those events not prove that they can be destroyed? Those who are few in number and hold great power have little choice but to destroy any who have the ability to bring them down. Did you not see that with the seltyrs of the west? Can you imagine your mighty alectors as being any different?"

Mykel had not thought of the parallel, but once Rachyla had pointed it out, he could not deny it. For a time, he rode without speaking, considering her words.

Ahead, he saw the gates to Stylan Estate. "There is your estate."

"It is not mine. It was my father's." Rachyla's words were clipped, and she looked away. "We will not speak of that."

With the coldness of her words, Mykel decided against saying more.

The road gates were open, without guards, and they proceeded up the long drive without challenge or welcome. Not until they had passed through the villa gates and were nearing the rotunda of the villa did anyone appear, and that was a single older woman who ran down the steps, then halted as he saw the Cadmians.

"I have returned, Velenda," Rachyla said firmly.

"It's really you, Mistress? You're back?"

"I am." Disdaining the mounting block, Rachyla vaulted from the saddle and stepped away from the horse. "Thank you, Captain." She did not incline her head to him.

Velenda stepped closer to her mistress and spoke, her voice almost a whisper, although Mykel heard the words as if he were standing beside them. "Mistress Rachyla, there is a message for you. From your cousin Alarynt. He said that he will arrive next Duadi." Velenda's eyes were bright. "He said that—"

"I am most certain I know what he said. We will have time." Rachyla turned back to Mykel. "Will you and your men stay upon the estate grounds tonight? There is a separate lodge to the south. You must stay somewhere."

Mykel was exhausted, but he could not inflict more upon Rachyla. "I would not wish to cause you more difficulties, Lady Rachyla."

"Your presence, and that of a Cadmian squad, would inflict less, Captain. No one would dare enter the grounds with you here."

"You are the daughter of a seltyr."

"Exactly. I was his daughter. My brothers would have held the estate, save that neither lived to do so."

Had Mykel killed either of them?

"That was something that had nothing to do with you, Captain."

"Can we do anything, Lady Rachyla?" After her last words, Mykel feared he knew what the message from her cousin had meant.

"For an enemy, Captain, you are most gallant. No . . . there is nothing you can do. Nor would I have you do anything. Will you stay or not?"

"We will."

He hoped that his decision was the right one, but he sensed no treachery in her words. Something else, perhaps concern, desperation? He wasn't certain.

"You may leave as you wish. I trust you will not expect to see me again."

Mykel would have liked to have seen her one more time, but it was not something he expected, not at all. "I would not impose further, Lady Rachyla."

"If you would wait a moment, someone will guide you to the lodge."

Mykel watched as she disappeared through the columns.

"You think that's a good idea, sir?" asked Chyndylt.

"We'll look over the lodge. If it's not, we can leave." Mykel could hear the tiredness in his voice. Why had he been so determined to escort the woman home? It had been necessary—that he felt in his every bone—but he did not know why, except that it was neither love nor lust. His lips curled into a wry smile. He was a man, and Rachyla was attractive to him. Not lust alone, he reflected.

107

Dainyl and the two Myrmidons landed in the headquarters compound in Elcien a glass before twilight on Decdi. Because it was end day, and late, no one was there, except for Undercaptain Ghanyr and his squad, since they had the duty. Dainyl was glad for the duty coach because it would have been difficult to find a hacker near headquarters late on Decdi afternoon, and his leg was definitely not up to walking more than a vingt, especially with personal gear.

The sun was barely above the Bay of Ludel, or rather the rooftops of the dwellings that blocked his view of the bay, when Dainyl stepped through the front door.

"Lystrana!" he called, setting his gear beside the door he had just closed.

"You're back!" She rushed from the sitting room toward him, as if to wrap her arms around him, then stopped. "You're hurt."

"I'm better. It's much better seeing you." He was the one to step forward and put his arms around her.

Her arms tightened around him, but gently. After a time, she eased back slightly, studying his face with her eyes, and the rest of him with her Talent. "You were hurt that badly, and you didn't send word?"

"I got here as fast as word would have come."

"You need to sit down in something comfortable. I'll get you some of the good red wine, and I'll see what we have to eat. The girls won't be back until late. It is end day." She looked at him once more, then kissed him again, before slipping from his embrace and leading him through the foyer.

"You sit down in the comfortable chair . . . right there."

Dainyl was tired enough that he didn't even offer a token protest as he eased himself down into the chair.

"You'll need a hot bath, too."

"After a bit," he replied.

Lystrana hurried to the kitchen, returning quickly with a goblet half-filled with the dark red wine.

Dainyl looked at his wife with both eyes and Talent. Then he smiled. "I had hoped . . ."

Lystrana bent down and set the wine on the table beside him. "A daughter."

Dainyl couldn't help but smile even more broadly than before. "She'll be like you."

"More like you, I suspect, but who can tell?" She rose. "I'll be right back."

Dainyl lifted the goblet and sipped the wine, enjoying it, just taking in the comfort of home and the presence of Lystrana. He had several swallows of the Vyan Grande before she reentered the sitting room with a small tray, filled with sliced early peaches, cheeses, and dark bread. The tray went on the side table she pulled over so that it was between their chairs, and she sat down.

"You said you couldn't send word . . ." she said softly.

"Not any faster than I could come," he replied. "We lost both pteridons in the last fight against the rebels . . ." He went on to explain, as briefly as he could, in between bites of the fruit and cheeses, what had happened in Dramur, including the power of the ancients and what had happened after that. "Captain Mykel came out and found me. He shot four rebels who would have killed me. The fourth one he took down after he'd been shot. He almost didn't live. After that, his squad found us, and we recovered, but there was no way to let anyone know until the marshal sent two more pteridons. I left Dramur within a few days of the time they arrived." Dainyl offered an embarrassed smile. "I could have sent a message three days earlier, but . . . I was asked not to send messages until I returned."

"You returned late on Decdi." Lystrana's left eyebrow lifted. "I suppose that was coincidence?"

"Novdi was as soon as I could leave. I did make sure that we would arrive late enough that the marshal would not expect me. I did want to see you first, and . . . our daughter. I had hoped."

"I had no doubts." Lystrana beamed. "I did tell your mother. I couldn't resist, and I suppose that means everyone knows."

"I'm glad she's a daughter."

"Because of your mother?"

"That's one reason." Dainyl took another sip of the Vyan Grande, enjoying it in the growing dimness of the sitting room.

"It seems so sad, in a way," mused Lystrana. "The landers and the indigens can have as many children as they want . . . and so many of them don't seem to care."

"The Highest claims that they rut like animals."

"Some doubtless do. So do some alectors," noted Lystrana dryly.

"We pay a price for being Ifryns. We bring beauty and culture to a world, and music and soaring song, but what sustains us means there can never be too many of us."

"Like on Ifryn now," she said somberly. "Have you read the latest dispatches?"

"When would I have seen . . ." He laughed. "You're teasing me."

"Just a little." She cleared her throat, then sipped her wine. "The dissipation point is somewhere between five and eleven years from now at the current alector population levels."

"How many now?"

"Eight thousand."

"What is the surplus lifeforce carrying ability here and on Efra at present?"

"Eleven hundred here, and twenty-one hundred there."

Dainyl fingered his chin. "Thirty percent survival rate for a world translation is normal, and both worlds will have greater lifeforce within another year or so. Some will choose not to try the translation."

"Most will put it off, and that will reduce the margins," she pointed out.

"When will they begin mass translations?"

"The Archon has . . . indicated that key alectors will have to begin translations in six months—if they want a guarantee of a position here or on Efra."

"You don't look happy, dearest."

"The Marshal of Myrmidons on Ifryn attempted a coup, along with several colonels. Almost fifty alectors died."

"That won't help much," said Dainyl. "Just a week or so."

"Dainyl!"

"What do they expect?" He snorted. "Our forebears took the risk of the translation here when the success rate was more like fifteen percent. Five percent for the very first, according to Asulet. Their chances are at least four times that, and for someone with the ability and lifeforce of a senior alector, it's more like forty-five percent."

"Dainyl . . ." she said softly.

"Yes?"

"We can talk about all that later. You're back, and I missed you."

"I missed you." Dainyl set aside the wine goblet.

108

On Londi, Dainyl did not hurry unduly, but neither was he late in reporting to Myrmidon headquarters. He had no sooner settled into his study, not even with a chance to look at the reports neatly stacked there, than Colonel Dhenyr knocked on the door.

"Come in, Colonel." Dainyl offered the words with a smile and gestured to the chair across from him. "How are matters with the other Myrmidon companies going?"

Dhenyr shifted his weight in the chair. "I'm most glad you're back, Submarshal. Most glad. Might I ask about Dramur first?"

"The revolt is over, and the mine production is back to normal. We did lose two pteridons to unusual circumstances. I'll have to brief the marshal before I can say more. Most of the rebels and rebel leaders were killed, well over a thousand rebel casualties. The Third Cadmian Battalion had a particularly effective captain. When I have a moment, I'll be recommending him for promotion to majer and command of the battalion. You may have to follow through on that. Now . . . what have you to report?"

"You knew about the pteridon lost near Scien?"

"Didn't that happen before I returned to Dramur?" Dainyl frowned. "Or did we lose another one?"

"Yes, sir. In that same area. The marshal has ordered all flyers to avoid it until further notice."

"Have we lost any more pteridons anywhere else besides Dramur?" asked Dainyl dryly.

"Ah . . . yes, sir. One flying out of Dereka over the Barrier Range on a message run to Indyor, and one near Aelta. Fifth Company found the burned rock in the Barrier Range, but no one has found any sign of the pteridon that was flying north of Aelta."

"What were they doing up there?"

"I've put in an inquiry to Captain Fhentyl, sir, but we don't have a response."

Dainyl managed to take a long and slow deep breath. In less than a season, six pteridons had been lost—six out of slightly less than two hundred, and none could be replaced. According to the records, not one pteridon had been lost in the past three hundred years. Why had the ancients decided to attack pteridons now, after so many years of being invisible? It had to be their work. "What else? What about Coren, Catyr, and Hyalt."

"Hyalt's calm, and all of First Company's second squad has returned—except the one Myrmidon lost, of course. We've been able to stop overflights of Coren, and the marshal ordered the return of the squad covering Catyr yesterday. They haven't returned yet."

"Any more skylances missing in Dereka?"

"No, sir."

"What else should I know?"

"I understand that the Duarch is not pleased with events, sir. That's what the marshal said on Octdi, anyway."

"Thank you."

"Yes, sir."

Dainyl nodded, and the colonel slipped away. From what he could tell, Lystrana's analysis of Dhenyr was accurate. He tried hard, and he was conscientious, and he had even less Talent than people had thought that Dainyl had—and far less insight. Dainyl wasn't sure whether to be more worried about Dhenyr or about the lost pteridons. Clearly, the marshal and the Highest did not want any higher-ranking officers in headquarters with both insight and Talent. Dhenyr had neither. They'd accepted Dainyl—for the moment—because, while he had insight, they did not know that he had more Talent than was obvious.

"Submarshal! Welcome back!" Shastylt stood in the doorway.

Dainyl rose, not quite so easily as he had before and would again.

"You were injured, I see."

"Broken arm and broken leg. They're mostly healed. It happened when we lost Quelyt and Falyna and their pteridons."

Shastylt nodded slowly. "I feared something like that."

"I have a report here, sir. Would you like me to tell you, or would you prefer to read it, then discuss what happened?"

"Why don't I read it? It won't be long. That's the first thing we need to deal with. I assume that you resolved everything in Dramur?"

"Yes, sir."

"Good." A twisted smile appeared on the marshal's face. "The Duarches would like some good news. If you have that report . . ."

Dainyl lifted the thick envelope off the desk and handed it across to Shastylt. "It may be longer than you need. As you requested, that is the only copy."

"Good. I'll be back to you shortly."

After Shastylt departed, Dainyl settled down with the reports. He'd only made his way though five when the marshal reappeared, stepping inside the study, and closing the door.

The marshal settled into the chair across from Dainyl, looking solidly at the submarshal. While Dainyl was well aware of the Talent-probing of the marshal, he left his shields in place, with the same apparent unaware stolidity that Lystrana had helped him develop years before.

"I've read your report, Dainyl. It's most remarkable. Or rather, I should say that your actions were most remarkable. You seem to have prevented a runaway rebellion with a minimum of casualties, that is, given the feelings of all those involved."

Dainyl had his doubts about the "minimum" of casualties. To him, nearly half of the Third Cadmian Battalion, more than a thousand dead rebels, and two Myrmidons and their pteridons were far greater than minimum casualties. He'd managed to salvage the situation, but his actions were anything but remarkable. The only thing remarkable was the fact that he hadn't seen what was happening earlier. In hindsight, it had all been so obvious. There hadn't been a rebellion, until the combination of Majer Herryf's arrogance and stubbornness and Majer Vaclyn's stupidity had collided and created one. But then, that was clearly what the marshal and the Highest had intended. Things would have been worse if it hadn't been for Captain Mykel.

"There was one aspect of all this that troubles me, Marshal," Dainyl said, trying to inject puzzlement into his voice. "As we discussed much earlier, there could not have been a rebellion without large numbers of Cadmian rifles present in Dramur. Has anyone been able to determine how such unmarked weapons got there?"

Shastylt laughed. "Coins. Golds. All the steers of Acorus are obsessed with accumulating what they perceive as wealth. The landowners on Dramur tend to be fearful of both the prisoners and each other. They have more wealth than many. The smugglers knew that, and they bribed one of the assistant weapons engineers in Faitel to produce extra rifles. Over time, he reported a number of production runs as spoiled, requiring extra production. The runs were not spoiled, but were slipped out of the manufactory as scrap to be reused, then were diverted. The engineer in question has been discovered and punished. Before he died, he revealed what happened." The marshal smiled coldly.

"I see. Thank you." Dainyl returned the smile, hoping he could keep to himself, behind his shields, the knowledge that the marshal was not telling the entire truth.

"The more important aspect of your efforts in Dramur was the discovery that the ancients are still alive and active, if in a reduced capacity. Things could have been much worse," reflected the marshal, "but, in many ways, matters turned out better than they might have."

"Better, sir?"

"We are aware of the problem before the ancients have been able to act against us on a larger scale."

"Colonel Dhenyr reported that we have lost four other pteridons in the past season."

"That is true, but only in Dramur do we know what happened. In all other cases, the pteridons either disappeared or mysteriously crashed. We would be guessing, or acting with less than complete knowledge . . ." Shastylt was clearly more concerned about the ancients. He had seemed almost amused about the abortive rebellion. ". . . the Highest and I have decided that it would be best if you were the one to brief the Duarch on the events in Dramur. You have the greatest personal acquaintance with the situation, and you were the one to bring everything back under control."

Dainyl understood that as well. The marshal and the High Alector of Justice were tired of being called to task.

As abruptly as he had entered, the marshal stood. "The Highest requested that you attend him immediately upon your return. I took the liberty of summoning the duty coach. It will be here shortly, after taking a message to the Hall of Justice."

"Right now?"

"That is the meaning of immediate," Shastylt replied wryly.

Dainyl laughed and stood. "I'll be on my way."

He did have to wait a quarter glass for the coach to take him to the Hall of Justice.

Once he arrived there, what surprised Dainyl even more than the immediate summons was that the High Alector of Justice ushered Dainyl into his private chambers instantly, and with a broad, almost relieved, smile.

"I had feared you had been even more seriously injured than you were, Dainyl."

"I was fortunate, Highest."

"We have not talked since you returned from Lyterna, Dainyl. We've been somewhat preoccupied. What did you think of what you learned there?" asked the High Alector of Justice.

"Some of it, sir, I knew," replied Dainyl carefully. "There was much I did not know."

"Asulet knows more about life-forming and lifeforce than perhaps any alector in our history here on Acorus. We are most fortunate to have had him guiding us."

"He is most knowledgeable, and he was most instructive."

"You have seen much of Acorus over the years, Dainyl. What do you think about our progress in building lifeforce mass?"

Dainyl kept his expression pleasant and a tight rein on his emotions and shields, even as he wondered why the Highest was more interested in Lyterna than Dramur. "I would not be the one who could best judge, but I would say matters are progressing more slowly than might have been hoped."

Zelyert laughed, a hearty booming expression. "You are so tactful! 'More slowly than might have been hoped!' So delightfully droll." His voice dropped into a lower tone, one almost sad. "And so unfortunately true. Life here on Acorus is still most fragile, despite outward appearances. We must be most careful. That was one reason why we did not wish to send a full Myrmidon company or even a full squad to Dramur."

"I had wondered," Dainyl said politely.

"As you have doubtless seen, over the past year, the lifeforce mass here is slow to respond, and that is something that we have had some difficulty conveying to the high alectors who serve the Archon in Ifryn. Using the Tables for messages is most difficult, because recorders at each Table must hold the link open simultaneously, then read and write down what appears."

That was something Dainyl did not know.

"The only alternative is to send a courier, and that tends to be hard on the couriers." After a moment, Zelyert went on. "We have tried to point out the fragility of the life structure on Acorus, and how we are caught between two difficult alternatives. Because of the rapidly deteriorating conditions on Ifryn, the Archon and the Duarchs have directed the high alectors here on Acorus to manage the lifeforce growth for maximum gain. This requires strict controls on the landers and indigens. They resent it, and there are uprisings and disobedience. The ensuing violence and the greater use of pteridons and skylances reduces growth as well. You saw this in Dramur. The recent events in Catyr and Coren are other examples. If we are less strict, then we do not face so many uprisings, but lifeforce growth is slower, and that is not acceptable to the Archon and the Duarchs." Zelyert offered a sigh. "This problem is also why we have permitted so few alector births. Oh, I understand that you and the most honorable Lystrana will be expecting a child?"

"Yes, we are," replied Dainyl. "We are most grateful."

"As you should be, but I can think of no couple who more deserves a child." Another smile crossed the face of the Highest. "In addition, Marshal Shastylt and I have decided that you are worthy of being not only submarshal, but designated, unofficially, of course, as the next Marshal of Myrmidons."

"That is quite an honor and responsibility," Dainyl replied.

"After you brief the Duarch of Elcien—and that may be a good week or so, if not longer, for he has a crowded schedule, I also have a small task for you. I would like you to travel to Alustre—by Table, of course—and consult with Submarshal Alcyna. I would like you to find out if she knows more about the disappearances of the pteridons near Scien than we have heard. You are, I believe, far better suited to such a task than anyone else."

Dainyl nodded. "By then, I will be more conversant with what occurred in my absence."

"I am most certain you will." Zelyert stood. "I congratulate you on your handling of a most delicate situation, and, of course, upon your child. I am confident that we can continue to rely upon your judgment and discretion, and that you will provide an instructive briefing to the Duarch on the events that transpired in Dramur."

Dainyl stood, more slowly, and inclined his head. "I hope that I will prove adept in conveying to the Duarch not only our successes in Dramur, but also the difficulties of relying upon landers and indigens to build lifeforce when resources for supervision are as limited as they have been."

"You do that, Submarshal," replied Zelyert, "and you will have our gratitude. I fear he has heard that too often from us. He needs to hear it from one who has just returned from the field. As for the matter of the pteridons and the ancients . . . I would suggest that you also note that we are working to develop a contingency plan, should it appear necessary, but that the details have not all been worked out."

Dainyl nodded again. "I can see the wisdom in that."

"I thought you would. Give my best to Lystrana, and do not strain yourself too much until you are more recovered."

Dainyl maintained a pleasant smile on his face until he was well away from the Hall of Justice.

109

Mykel had barely finished stabling the chestnut and hauling his gear to his room in the officers' quarters in the Cadmian headquarters compound in Elcien when he turned to find a senior squad leader standing at the door.

"Captain Mykel, sir?"

"Yes?"

"Colonel Herolt would like to see you, sir. At your earliest convenience."

Mykel set down his gear. He might as well see what the colonel wanted. It had been a long day, already, after five days at sea, and a tedious unloading of all the mounts and men remaining from Third Battalion, although far shorter, unfortunately, than the loading out had been when they had left Elcien more than two seasons before.

"If you'd follow me, sir."

Mykel followed the senior squad leader across the courtyard and into the headquarters building, then to the door of the colonel's study, which had been left open.

"Captain Mykel, reporting as requested, sir."

Colonel Herolt, with his iron gray hair and black eyes, looked up. "Come in and close the door, Captain." He motioned for Mykel to seat himself.

"Captain—or should I say, Majer?—I have a report here from the Submarshal of Myrmidons, with an endorsement from the High Alector of Justice."

"Yes, sir?" Mykel allowed himself to look puzzled.

"Do you know the Submarshal of Myrmidons?"

"Submarshal Dainyl, sir? Yes, sir. He took command of all operations in Dramur, sir."

"How well do you know him?"

"Not well at all, sir. I saw him preside over a court-martial, and I briefed him on Fifteenth Company operations—it couldn't have been more than three or four times. I could check on that, but that's what I recall. He was injured in the last battle in Dramur, and Fifteenth Company recovered him and provided cover."

"You and Majer Dohark most clearly impressed him." The colonel stared at Mykel.

Mykel met the colonel's eyes. After dealing with the submarshal, the colonel seemed far less intimidating.

"I don't like promoting junior officers too soon. I like being ordered to do so even less. On the other hand, both Majer Dohark's reports and the submarshal's indicate that your conduct and your accomplishments were all that stood between a successful revolt and the destruction of the entire battalion."

Mykel waited, sensing that it was best to say nothing.

"I can see a certain calmness and responsibility that was not there a half year ago. It might even be enough to get you through." Herolt sighed. "You understand that, once Third Battalion is back to full strength and retraining is finished, you will be ordered to handle the most challenging and unpleasant assignments?"

"Yes, sir."

"Do you understand why?"

"Yes, sir. To prove that Third Battalion will receive no special favors or easy assignments, and that any officer who receives early promotion not only earned that promotion, but will have to continue to prove that it was earned."

"Majer . . . what do you intend to do with your senior squad leader?"

"Make him the battalion senior squad leader, with particular emphasis on training and retraining."

"You would not recommend him as an undercaptain?"

"No, sir."

"Are there others who might be considered in the future?"

"Chyndylt, the third squad leader, would make a solid senior squad leader for Fifteenth Company. He might make a good undercaptain, but I'd want to see him with greater responsibility first."

A faint smile appeared on the colonel's face. He extended a small cloth pouch. "Here are your insignia, Majer. For all of our sakes, I wish you well. You will have to continue in command of Fifteenth Company, as well, for several weeks, until we determine your captains or undercaptains."

"Yes, sir." Mykel took the pouch.

"Majer . . . I am curious about one thing."

"Sir?"

"Does a guano mine smell as bad as everyone says?"

Mykel laughed.

After a moment, so did the colonel.

110

For all the towering halls of the Duarch's palace in Elcien, Dainyl was escorted into a comparatively small library, six yards wide and twelve in length. Oak shelves filled with volumes lined all the inside walls, while the outside wall held smaller sections of shelves set between the narrow floor-to-ceiling windows overlooking the southern sunken garden.

The Duarch sat behind a desk piled high with books. Even seated, he was a towering presence, with shimmering black hair and deep violet eyes. Talent radiated from him. As he caught sight of Dainyl, he smiled, but did not stand. When Dainyl bowed, he could feel a warmth issue from the older alector.

"Submarshal, I am pleased that you could come to brief me on what has happened in Dramur. Please sit down. Both the High Alector of Justice and Marshal Shastylt have spoken in glowing terms about your success there."

"We did what was necessary, Most High." Dainyl took the chair toward which the Duarch had gestured.

"I trust that there was not too great a loss of lifeforce?"

"More than I would have liked," Dainyl admitted. "Over a thousand rebels, and half of the Third Cadmian Battalion."

"That is not good." The Duarch frowned. "Not good at all. We must be making all possible efforts to expand lifeforce so that we will be ready to host the Master Scepter. The Archon must choose Acorus. We have accomplished so very much under the most adverse of conditions, and for that, he must find us the worthy ones, as we are." A broad smile appeared, then vanished. "All is judged on lifeforce mass, yet today's measurement does not always reflect what it will be tomorrow or next year. Nor what a world will be or could be."

Mykel kept his own expression pleasant and waited.

"The marshal tried to explain why there was a revolt, but I must confess that his explanation lacked a certain . . . cohesiveness. There is enough food; there is enough shelter; and there seemed to be enough golds to satisfy the greedier of the landers. We had neither increased levies on the seltyrs nor imposed greater controls on them. Ingratitude, while universal, does not provoke rebellion." Another warm smile followed his words. "Could you make it clearer?"

"I will try." Sensing the more pointed feelings concealed by the smile, and the danger of being caught between the Duarch and the High Alector of Justice, Dainyl composed himself. "The landers and indigens are split into two areas, those east of the mountains and those to the west. The guano mine is on the east side of the mountains, and the golds that come from it go to those in the town and some of the eastern seltyrs. For reasons that remain unclear, all the seltyrs decided that they needed weapons—"

"Unclear to whom?"

"To me, Most High. I talked to a number of those close to the seltyrs, and all suggested that they believed that an unarmed seltyr is without honor. This is a belief that has existed for some time, but has never been reported. Why, I have not been able to discover."

"Go on."

The seltyrs used golds to persuade smugglers to bring them Cadmian rifles . . ."

"Who permitted that?" The Duarch's voice turned cold, and a perceptible chill filled the library.

Dainyl could sense a strong Talent force, as strong as that of the High Alector of Justice, if not stronger. "No one, as I understand it. They paid the smugglers to bribe an assistant engineer to divert weapons reported as flawed and scrapped. He was punished and executed, but not before the rifles and ammunition had been shipped to the seltyrs."

"Always the golds. The landers and indigens, they think of nothing but golds, nothing at all. The steers are worse than spoiled children. Acorus would have long since died without us, and they cannot see that. Pardon me, Submarshal. Please continue." The sense of chill dispersed, although the Duarch did not smile.

Dainyl went on to describe what had happened, in plain terms, with the first attack by Seltyr Ubarjyr, then the sniping at the Cadmians and the uprising by the Jyohans.

"You did not impose discipline?"

"I was ordered to observe only, unless the Cadmians failed . . ." Dainyl went on to explain the increasingly erratic behavior of Majer Vaclyn as well as the lack of understanding by Majer Herryf. ". . . Once I assumed command, under the conditions laid down by the marshal, immediate discipline had to wait until the military situation was resolved, because the Cadmians were under attack by more than twenty companies of the seltyrs. Despite being vastly outnumbered, and with only two pteridons, we crushed the revolt. Once that was accomplished, we restructured the Cadmian command in Dramur so that the local commander will be able to control matters in a fashion that will not destroy any more lifeforce."

"That is right." The Duarch nodded, then looked at Dainyl. "Do you think that they truly believed that they could prevail? Against the Myrmidons?" An expression of calculation dominated the Duarch's face, especially the violet eyes that darkened. "You did not mention the lost pteridons."

"Both pteridons were lost. That is true. Two of the ancients appeared just as the pteridons attacked the last of the rebels."

"You did not wish to mention that?" The Duarch's pleasant smile dropped away, and Dainyl could sense a chill coldness.

"I admit that I did not," Dainyl admitted. "I had not realized that the ancients were present so far south, or that they were so powerful, and that was my oversight and failure." At the word "failure," Dainyl could sense the coldness projected by the Duarch vanish, and that mystified him.

The Duarch laughed, once, a sound that mixed rue and humor. "You are the first submarshal—or marshal—ever to enter this study and admit that he failed at something." After a moment of silence, he asked, "Are there other failures you might admit?"

"I am certain that there are aspects of what happened in Dramur that I could have handled better, Most High. Unfortunately, I don't have the range of knowledge that you and the High Alector of Justice have. So I doubt I could identify what those might be."

"You're sounding like Shastylt. Please don't. As for the failure to tell you about the ancients and pteridons, that is something that I will take up with the marshal directly."

Dainyl didn't like that at all.

"Oh . . . I won't mention you. We've lost too many suddenly, and you couldn't have had anything to do with that. Please continue."

Dainyl decided to risk more directness. "I still don't really know what sparked this revolt. We stopped it, and we've taken steps that I think will preclude it from happening again, but I could be mistaken."

"We all could. For all that, you have not told me everything, Submarshal."

"No, Most High. We would be here for days were I to do that. I will be happy to answer any questions you may have, now or in the future, or to provide more details about anything."

"At least you are more honest than many. What else should I know?"

"I would say that the revolt shows that we face a delicate balance between the need to keep from spending lifeforce and in maintaining order among the landers and indigens. They will easily squander lifeforce as though it meant nothing, because to them it means nothing. They think only of either amassing golds or controlling other landers and indigens. If we do not step in, as we did in Dramur, they could easily destroy more lifeforce than we did. Yet to keep them from doing worse, we also spend more lifeforce than we would prefer, especially with the transfer of the master scepter not that many years away. Yet we cannot explain the importance of lifeforce in a fashion that would mean anything to the landers and indigens, not without revealing our own needs and vulnerabilities."

The Duarch's face twisted, and Dainyl could sense . . . something . . . a conflict . . . but that vanished within a fraction of an instant.

"Yes, that has always been a difficulty, and yet, we must prepare for the transfer, whatever the cost, because if we do not receive the Master Scepter, our future will be in the hands of those on Efra, and they calculate even more than those who claim to serve me. You have told me what I need to know." There was a sense of sadness, followed by another smile and more warmth. "I understand that you and Lystrana are expecting a child."

"Yes, Most High." Dainyl wondered exactly what the Duarch had needed to know, but he wasn't about to ask. He was relieved to have gotten through the briefing.

"A wonderful thing. Wonderful. She will be old enough to behold the transfer of the Master Scepter." The sense of chill returned. "Do be careful in what you believe of Shastylt and Zelyert, Dainyl. They do not see everything, although they think they do. Be most careful." Another smile appeared, with the same warmth as earlier. "You may go. Thank you."

Dainyl stood and bowed. "I am at your command, Most High."

"So you are."

Dainyl stepped toward the library door, and it opened. Two alector guards appeared, walking beside him, escorting him back to the entry foyer, with its high-arched dome, as they had escorted him from it. He felt like running, but he kept walking, flanked by the silent guards. The palace, for the first time in all the years he had been in it, felt confining, as though the walls would fall in upon him.

111

Mykel stood at the edge of the warm-weather dining porch, in the light breeze that reminded him that spring in Faitel was far cooler than winter in Dramur. For a time, he looked at the still-fragile grape leaves, barely unfolded. The lower trunk and the outer canes had yet to leaf out. He let his eyes take in the ancient vine, not really seeing it, just feeling that it was alive, in a way that he had not felt before, not exactly. He was so motionless that a redbird alighted on the far end of the arbor, cocking its head in a perky fashion.

A faint halo of *something* surrounded the redbird, golden brown. Mykel blinked, and the halo vanished. Yet it had been there, and too real to have been his imagination.

"The grapes aren't out yet," said Olent, crossing the porch toward his son. "It was a wet and cold winter. That usually means they're late leafing out, but, if the summer's warm, we'll have a good crop come harvest."

Mykel turned, studying his father, trying to recapture what he had felt when he had looked at the redbird. After a moment, he could sense a warm brownish gold around Olent.

"Supper's almost ready." Olent paused. "You've been more quiet since you got back. Are you all right?"

Mykel stopped to consider his father's words and lost the sense of the aura he had felt, but he knew, now, that he could recall it. What exactly it meant or signified, other than life itself, that he would have to discover. "I'm fine. I've just been thinking."

Was he fine? He'd killed scores of rebels, and that didn't include the poor and hapless debtors of Jyoha. Many of the so-called battles had been little more than massacres, and he'd succeeded by being more ruthless than the seltyrs. He'd been placed in a situation where he'd had little choice if he wanted to survive—and if the men under him were to have had any chance. And he still didn't really understand why, other than the seltyrs and the alectors both wanted power. Was that life? The struggle for power? Did it have to be that way? Could he change things as a majer? Or would he be pressed to create more destruction?

"You've been thinking a lot."

"I suppose that's true. Dramur changed things." He offered a smile. "I'm probably hungry, too. It's been a long day." He turned and walked back across the empty dining porch and into the cramped inside dining room.

Following him, Olent closed the door to the porch behind them. "Let's eat before it all gets cold," he announced, taking the chair at the head of the table.

Mykel settled into the place at his father's right, across from his sister. As he sat down, Sesalia offered a smile. Olent looked to the other end of the table at Aelya, and his wife nodded back at him.

"I think that means I'm saying the blessing," commented Olent. "I don't know why I even asked. With everyone here, it's always the same."

He cleared his throat. "In the name of the One Who Was, Is, and Will Be, may our food be blessed, and our lives as well, in the times of prosperity and peace, and those which are neither. Blessed be the lives of both the deserving and the undeserving that both may strive to do good in the world and beyond, and may we always recall that we do not judge our worthiness, but leave that judgment to the One Who Is." After a moment of silence, he looked up. "Everyone take whatever's closest."

Mykel lifted the basket of hard dark bread to Sesalia first, who served herself, then Bortal, before handing it back to Mykel. The main course was a mutton pie, heavy on early carrots and onions, that Olent passed to Sesalia.

Aelya glanced at her daughter, "I still miss the children, dear."

Olent guffawed. "Every time she doesn't bring them, you remind her. You'll make her feel guilty for being able to eat a meal in peace."

"I don't see them that often now," replied Aelya.

"You see them more often than Sesalia and Bortal get to see Mykel. Now that he's a majer, we'll all probably see him even less."

While the others talked, Mykel took several bites of the mutton pie, enjoying it and the sweet and heavy black bread, so much better fare than he had eaten in seasons.

"Mykel . . . you're a majer, now? A real majer?" asked Viencet.

"Where have you been, Viencet?" asked Bortal. "Hiding in the cellar?"

"Ah . . . studying . . ."

"With that young Dalya?" probed Sesalia.

Viencet flushed. "She's smart . . ." His words trailed off.

"Well, he is a majer," announced Olent. "My son, the commander of a battalion, and only twenty-seven years old."

"They're saying that the Myrmidons lost some pteridons out east," offered Viencet quickly. "Did you hear about that?"

"People are always saying, things," replied Mykel with a smile. "Who's been telling you those stories?"

"It was Trebyl, and he got it from his uncle. What he says has always been right before."

"It doesn't mean it is now."

"He claims that it proves the ancients are still around, some of 'em, anyway, because the ancients are the only thing that can kill pteridons."

"It's a good story," Mykel said. "Maybe you should become an Ancienteer."

"Nah . . ." Viencet shook his head. "They'll believe anything. We know the ancients existed, but soaring through the sky without a pteridon . . . I can't swallow that."

Mykel just nodded.

"Some people," added Aelya. "They'll say anything."

Mykel took a swallow of the wine, then another bite of the mutton pie.

"You haven't said much about Dramur, and how come you got promoted to majer," Viencet pressed.

"I suppose I haven't," demurred Mykel. "There's not much to say. I managed to survive and keep most of my company alive."

"I'd wager you were a hero," said Viencet.

"No. I wasn't a hero. I was a moderately effective company commander when most others weren't. I looked good by comparison."

"Did you kill lots and lots of rebels?"

Mykel lifted the heavy goblet, only brought out for special dinners, and took another sip of the red wine. "People always get killed when they shoot at each other long enough."

"I can't believe—"

"Viencet," said Olent quietly, but forcefully, "I don't think your brother really wants to talk about it. Maybe later, when he comes home another time."

Mykel silently thanked his father. He didn't want to talk about it, but didn't want to announce that publicly, either.

"And none of the Dramuran women took a liking to you?" teased Sesalia, after a moment of silence.

"I saw very few, almost none," Mykel said with a laugh, "except from a distance. Most of those were trying to stay out of our sight." He wasn't about to mention Rachyla, especially since he would never see her again, and since she'd hardly been the friendliest toward him. But then, had their situations been reversed, he doubted that he would have been all that friendly, either.

"You must have been busy," offered Bortal. "Corylt says that his captain never has a free moment."

"We're always busy." Nodding absently in agreement, Mykel looked at Sesalia, heavy with the child to come, seeing not one aura, but two, the second almost a ghost of hers, but growing stronger, he knew. That had to be a part of his talent, the talent that had started with his being able to aim and fire a rifle more accurately than almost anyone, and now seemed to be growing. What else could he expect? Was that the talent that the ancient soarer had told him to find? Or was there something else?

"Mykel? Mykel?"

At Sesalia's voice, he almost jumped, but managed a smile. "Yes?"

"You were looking at me so strangely."

"Oh . . . I'm sorry. I guess I'm still more tired than I thought." That wasn't it at all, but better to say so than what he thought. Where would that talent lead him?

He forced a smile. "Are there any sweets?"

112

Dainyl and Lystrana lay side by side in the darkness of their bedchamber, warm covers over them. Dainyl's fingers twined around hers.

"When do you go to Alustre?" she asked, her voice soft, but not sleepy.

"On Duadi."

"Do you know what the Highest truly wants?"

"He hasn't said. Not exactly. He wants my impressions about Submarshal Alcyna. He has something else in mind."

"As he did with your briefing the Duarch. You're still upset about your meeting with him, aren't you?"

Dainyl thought about dismissing her concerns, but Lystrana would see through him. She always had. "Yes. There's tremendous Talent there, but . . ."

"But what?"

"It's as though he wears a blindfold about some things. I tried to point out the problems with lifeforce, and how the landers and indigens just don't understand the way the world works, and he kept talking about how we needed to increase the lifeforce and how fortunate we were to have a child, and how Kytrana would see the transfer of the Master Scepter here to Acorus. One moment he was smiling, and the next it was as though he were ready to turn his Talent on me, especially when he talked about Zelyert and Shastylt."

"He told you not to trust them. Was that unwise?"

"No. We know that." Dainyl took a deep breath. "But . . . I don't trust the Duarch, either I feel that his heart is better than theirs, but that—I said this before—he is blinded. He will do anything to bring the master scepter here."

"The loyalty imprint," suggested Lystrana. "That is why those who seek power do not wish to be Duarch."

"I feel as though I'm trapped between two sets of masters. The Highest and the marshal see the world as it is, but I don't trust what they have in mind, even if I don't know what it is. The Duarch—he would do the best he could, so long as it does not conflict with what the Archon requires. He has great Talent, but how he might use that Talent is hampered because the imprint does not allow him to see all that is before his eyes. Both would destroy those who disagree with their visions." Dainyl turned and reached out with his free hand, letting his fingers touch the cheek and jawline of his wife.

"So you must not show any disagreement. That has always been so for a prudent alector. What you have seen changes nothing."

Dainyl laughed, once. "I had hoped that seeing more would provide greater hope, not less. Matters need to change. Even the ancient soarer said something like that."

"Was she talking about you, or about all alectors?"

"I had thought she was speaking to me, as I told you the other night, but now . . . I don't know."

"You are submarshal, and someday you will be marshal. That will give you the opportunity to change matters."

"Nothing changes quickly."

Lystrana turned toward him and brushed his cheek with her lips. "We can only do what we can."

"I didn't tell you everything about the Cadmian captain," Dainyl said slowly.

"I had thought you held something back."

"He has Talent. He used it to save me. The Highest told me that landers with Talent had to be destroyed."

"That has always been the policy," Lystrana said softly.

"I couldn't do it. I kept thinking about how he nearly died to save me, so that I could come back to you and Kytrana. He's so young, not for a lander, I suppose, but . . ."

"You think that the marshal will discover your failure?"

"No. Talent can emerge at any time."

"Then why do you worry? He serves the Duarchy. It's not as though he happens to be a wild Talent, like that one in Hyalt."

"I still worry. He did more than I did to stop the revolt in Dramur."

"You succeeded in the end."

"But . . . without the captain I would not have. Are we too frightened of Talent in landers? Or am I too frightened to make the hard choices?"

Lystrana's fingers squeezed his. "You made the choice, and we will live with what comes of it."

Dainyl looked up into the darkness. He had made the choice, an alector's choice.